Liquor has never been so disturbingly saucy

DAIQUIRI DREAMS
MALT ME ~ TEQUILA HEALING
WINE NOT ~ THE FINAL SHOT

All five books in the liquor cabinet series are together in one suspensefully sexy boxset.

DAIQUIRI DREAMS
It was the trip of a lifetime in so many ways, proving dreams really do come true… or do they?

MALT ME
College. It's supposed to be both exciting and daunting. For me, it turns into a nightmare.

I'm given a second chance at happiness, and I won't allow the horrifying memories to take that away from me.

But turns out he wants more.

He wants another chance to own me, possess me, and then ruin me if he wants to. But there's no way I'll let him.

I am Mackenzie Merlot. I am strong. I am a survivor.

And this time…he'll lose.

TEQUILA HEALING
I had been fooled once. Misled and lied to. There was no going back from that, and it was causing me to self-destruct.

Sav is there whenever I decide to wallow in regret. She somehow worms her way into my life without even trying.

When the devil from her past comes knocking, I realise how much danger she's really in.

If it means I have to walk through hell twice, then that's what I'll do.

WINE NOT
My life was filled with rainbows and unicorns…until it wasn't.

After accepting an offer I couldn't refuse my life went from bad to worse—except the part where I met Logan.

Too many secrets lurk in the shadows waiting for the right moment to strike.

When it does…it will ruin us both.

THE FINAL SHOT
Finding a happily ever after is the easy part.

Keeping the ever after happy…now that's the tricky part.

Liquor has never been so disturbingly saucy

The Liquor Cabinet series box set

Edited by Karen Hrdlicka, Barren Acres Editing

Cover by Tash Drake, Outlined with Love Designs

Interior design by DL Gallie

AUTHOR NOTE

The legal drinking age is Australia is 18.

This book contains Australian slang as it is set in Australia and uses Australian spelling.

Here is a glossary to help you out:

Missus – Wife / Girlfriend / Partner
Arvo – Afternoon
Headjob – Blowjob
Undies – Panties
Franga – Condom
Singlet – Tank
Trackies – Track pants
Thongs – Flip Flops
Hinterland – Mountains
Esky – Cool Box / Cooler
Ambo – Ambulance Officer
Up the duff – pregnant
Obs – vitals – blood pressure, temp etc.
Maccas – McDonald's

Bottle-O – Liquor store
Mines – that is mine
Brewski's – alcoholic beverages

THE
Liquor Cabinet
SERIES

Daiquiri
DREAMS

A Liquor Cabinet short story prequal

DL GALLIE

Dreams can come true.

It was the trip of a lifetime in so many ways, proving dreams really do come true... or do they?

1

THE SUN IS BRIGHTLY SHINING AND TODAY, SARAH AND I ARE COMMENCING our schoolies trip to the Whitsundays. We've just checked in at reception and are heading towards our bungalow. Spinning around, I take in the scenery and shake my head. "Babe, I cannot believe our parents sent us here, just for graduating high school. Imagine what we'll get after graduating college?" And by sent us here, I mean paying for a seven night island hopping adventure around the Whitsunday's; well staying at three different islands—Hamilton, Daydream and Haymen Islands.

"I know, right," she excitedly says as I continue to take in the majestic scenery of Hamilton Island. White sandy beaches, crystal clear waters, palms trees, smoking hot men. "Maybe after college they'll send us to Europe."

"We can only dream."

"Dreams are free, Mac." It's now her turn to spin. She eyes a few guys walking to the pool and smiles at them, after offering a flirty wave. "This place is gorgeous."

"The scenery or guys?"

"Both," she says, as she raises her eyebrows cheekily at me.

"What about your boyfriend, Josh?"

"Josh and I are just fine. Besides, I'm just looking out for my best friend," she says, draping her arm around my shoulder. "A holiday fling is just what you need."

"Mmmhmpf," I say, but she's right. The scenery is stunning, both the resort and males. Maybe I do deserve a holiday fling. I guess time will tell.

"I cannot wait to work on my tan and drink my weight in daiquiris," she says as we arrive at our bungalow.

"You had me at daiquiri." I wink at her as we walk up the stairs to our beachfront bungalow and unlock the door.

Stepping inside, we drop our bags and quickly change into our togs. Unpacking can wait, its daiquiri and pool time.

Sarah's one piece is black with side cut-outs—its totally hot,—and I'm wearing an orange bikini with black accents; especially bought for this trip. We each have our floppy sunhats and sunnies; sun safety is key when you live in Queensland. We slip on our cover-ups and thongs before we grab and fill our beach bags. I slip in a book, sunscreen, and towel into mine. Sarah does the same and adds a bag of lollies for a sugar hit later on.

"Let's do this," Sarah says, linking her arm with mine. We step outside and head over to the pool.

Grabbing a lounger, we place our things down. Sarah immediately strips off her cover-up and smothers her body in a coconut scented lotion. "Sarah, that smells delish."

"I know, right? I just hope that it has the SPF it says." She lies down, pulls her hat over her eyes and relaxes, while working on her tan...with the delicious smelling lotion.

"I'm going for a swim," I say, as I look at the ginormous pool in front of us.

"Mmmhmpf," she replies with a wave, not lifting her head—she's already in chillax mode.

Lifting my cover-up over my head, I grab my sunscreen—my non-lovely smelling cream—and lather up before walking over to the pool edge. Dipping a toe in, I grin. "Perfect temperature," I whisper to myself as I walk to the stairs. Gripping the railing, I carefully wade into the water, moaning as the cool waters hits my heated skin. Making my way over to the edge, I take off my hat and sunnies before dipping my head under the water and sinking to the bottom. It's peaceful under the water; that is until someone dives into the pool and bumps into me, causing me to inhale a mouthful of water. Breaking the surface, I'm coughing and spluttering.

"Ohh shit, I'm so sorry, are you okay?" a deep husky voice says from behind me.

Spinning towards the voice, I freeze. The guy before me is smoking hot. Blond hair, emerald green eyes, and a chest that looks like it was carved by the Gods. Lifting my gaze back to his face, I nod and smile. "Nah, yeah, I'm okay."

"Are you sure? I hit you pretty hard."

"No, I'm fine." I pause and notice him still intently staring at me. "Really."

"I didn't see you under the water. I would have dived in the other way had I known you were there."

"It's fine, really," I say, as walk to the edge, grabbing my hat and placing it on my head before slipping my sunnies back on. I face him again and this time, I stretch out my hand. "I'm Kenzie." I shock myself with that name, my name is Mackenzie, or Mac, I never tell people it's Kenzie.

"It was nice to smash into you, Kenzie. I'm Jordan." He places his hand in mine and when our palms touch, an electrical current zaps through my body. My eyes open wide, as do his. We stare at one another. I've never felt a connection like this before. I know I'm only eighteen but I've read Nicholas Sparks, connections like this only happen in books and romance movies...and on schoolies, it seems.

Our book/movie moment is interrupted when a guy splashes Jordan. "Dude, hurry up."

He drops my hand and looks over his shoulder at an equally good looking guy. "Give me a sec." He turns back to me and we smile at each other.

"It was nice to meet you, Jordan," I shyly say and, with a wave, I turn away from him and walk over to where Sarah is now sitting on the pool edge with her legs dangling in the water.

"Ummm, what was that?" she questions.

I turn around, leaning against the edge of the pool. Raking my fingers absentmindedly across the pool's surface as I replay my encounter with Jordan.

Sarah poking my arm snaps me back to the present.

"What was what?" I nonchalantly reply as I lift myself out of the water and sit next to her. Readjusting my hat and sunnies, I look everywhere but at her, because I know what she's going to imply and I don't know what to tell her.

"That." She points to the pool and a retreating Jordan.

My eyes lock on him as he exits the pool . His back is just as fine as his front...I know, how is a back sexy? But if you saw his, you'd know exactly what I was referring to.

"You two, just now, were steaming it up," she adds.

"Were not," I scoff. "We were just chatting."

"Mmmhmpf, I call bullshit."

"Call it what you want. It was nothing. Now, do you want a cocktail?"

"Umm, is the Pope Catholic?"

Laughing at her reply, I shake my head and stand up. "Back in a jiffy."

As I'm walking to the bar, I feel someone watching me. Glancing over my shoulder, I see Jordan staring at me while chatting to his friend. His gaze heats my skin from across the pool area. Maybe a little schoolies fling is just what I need...but first, daiquiris.

2

It's late afternoon and Sarah and I are still lazing by the pool. We alternate between taking a dip and sipping on strawberry daiquiris. It's the perfect start to our schoolies. Unfortunately, I don't see Jordan again, but we still have another two days here before we jet over to Daydream Island, the next stop on our schoolies getaway. I hope to see him again before we leave. I'd really like spend more time with him...not that I'll admit that to Sarah; the teasing would be relentless.

As if he knows I was thinking about him, Jordan and his friend walk back into the pool area. My eyes follow him and when he walks past the lounger I'm on, he winks at me. He doesn't say anything but that wink speaks volumes—he's been thinking about me too.

Picking up my daiquiri, I smile as I take a sip.

"What's got you grinning?" Sarah asks, as she places another daiquiri next to me before sitting back on her lounger.

"Nothing in particular," I reply. "Just super chillaxed and happy to be here with my sister from another mister."

"I'll drink to that."

We raise our cocktails in a salute and each take a sip.

I moan, "These are the best daiquiris I've ever had."

Placing my drink down, I lie back and close my eyes. I'm just about to drift off to sleep when a splash from the pool drenches me. A squeal

breaks free and I sit bolt upright. Looking to the pool I see a grinning
Jordan staring at me. He shrugs his shoulders in a sorry-not-sorry way
and turns away from me. I don't think so, buddy. Standing up, I walk
to the pool's edge, and dive into the water. From below the surface, I
wrap my arms around his legs and pull, dunking him under the water.

I surface first and wait for him to come up when someone taps me
on the shoulder. Turning my head, I see Jordan smiling and laughing.
My eyes bug wide open, ohh shit, I dunked a stranger. Looking back to
where someone has just surfaced, I sigh in relief when I see it's
Jordan's friend.

He looks at me and I shyly say, "Sorry."

"Ohh it's on," he growls, as he lunges for me and takes me under
with him.

A water fight erupts, two against one. The three of us splashing
each other and laughing like loons.

When the water fight winds down I turn to his friend. "I'm really
sorry about that…"

"Mike, Mike Mustange." He offers me his hand and we shake.

"Pleasure to dunk you, Mike. I'm Kenzie."

"I know," he says. "And on that note, I think we need drinks."

Mike swims to the edge and climbs out, leaving me in the pool with
Jordan.

I look to him. "Sooo, what exactly have you told Mike about me?"

He steps closer to me. "Kenzie," he purrs, "If I tell you, then I'll
have to kill you."

He steps around me and climbs out. My eyes rake over his body
and I swallow deeply as I take him in. I watch as water trickles down
his toned and tanned skin. He turns around and totally catches me
checking him out; he winks and walks towards, Mike.

Taking a deep breath, I slip below the water and let out the air in
my lungs. The bubbles releasing all the tension—hormones—building
within… I'm totally screwed. I really like this guy, and I love when he
calls me Kenzie, something I've always hated. As I break the surface, I
grin to myself. I'm pretty sure he likes me too…but I don't know what
to do. Guess all I can do is make good use of the three, well now two
days, we have left here on Hamilton and see what happens.

If it's meant to be, it will be.

3

SARAH, MIKE, JORDAN, AND I LAZE BY THE POOL UNTIL WELL AFTER sunset, drinking, laughing and generally talking shit; it's the perfect afternoon. The four of us get along like a house on fire. They close up the poolside bar so we all agree to go shower, change, and meet back up for dinner and more drinks at Bomme, the main bar restaurant on the island.

The door to our bungalow hasn't even shut and Sarah pounces. "Okay, spill!"

"Spill what?" I try to play dumb, but I know exactly what she's referring to.

She eyes me.

"Fine," I huff. "I really like this guy. I've never felt a connection to someone like this before. We haven't even kissed but when he's around, my skin buzzes."

"And the air crackles," Sarah adds.

"Yeah, that too." Flopping back onto my bed, I stare at the ceiling. "What am I going to do?"

"Have a shower, dress sexy, and have the night of your life with that sexy as sin man."

Looking over to her, my lips lift in a smile. "Do you really think that I, Mackenzie Merlot, can do that?"

"I think you can do anything you set your mind too and, babe, that boy is hot, hot, hot for you."

And I'm hot, hot, hot for him.

Staring at the ceiling, my mind drifts to Jordan, and I realise she's right. He also feels what I feel, but I don't know how to take it further, and just how far do I want to go with him?

Next thing I know, Sarah's tapping my arm. "Babe, your turn in the shower."

Shaking my head, I blink my eyes repeatedly to wake myself up. "Guess I drifted off to dreamland for a bit," I sleepily say as I sit up.

"It's exhausting relaxing," Sarah jokes, as she sits on her bed and rubs moisturiser into her legs. Legs that are a lovely tanned shade already; I cannot wait to see how tanned she'll be at the end.

Looking down at my legs, I sigh dejectedly. They're red-ish and knowing what my skin is like, tomorrow they'll be white once again.

Sarah looks over at me. "What up, Buttercup?"

"As usual, you're rocking a lovely tan. Me? I'm red, and I guarantee tomorrow, I'll be pearly white."

She stands up, grabs her beach bag and digs inside. She pulls out an orange bottle. "Two words, Bondi Sands Protect and Tan oil."

"That was six words."

"Potato. Partato. Use this tomorrow and I guarantee you a sexy tan will be in the works."

Taking the bottle, I flip open the cap and inhale. "Oh my God, that smells like heaven."

"It feels like heaven on your skin too. Trust me. We'll use this tomorrow and start 'Operation Tan Mac' and you'll be a sexy tanned gal in a few days' time."

"I like that." Standing up, I walk to the shower. "Pick something for me to wear," I call over my shoulder as I close the door behind me.

Ten minutes later, I emerge freshly showered and I stop mid-step when I see Mike and Jordan are out on the front deck with Sarah. Jordan looks up and grins when he sees I'm wrapped in only a towel. He raises his eyebrows at me and I spin on my heel, racing back to the bathroom, and slam the door. Holy embarrassment, Batman.

Leaning against the door, I rest my head against the timber. My heart's racing. My palms are sweaty, but most of all, I wish Sarah and Mike weren't here. If they weren't, I'd go back out there, drop my towel, beckon Jordan to me, and then I'd ravage him. Oh My God, where did that thought come from?

A knock on the door startles me. "Mac, it's me. Open up."

Stepping back from the door, I open it a smidge and stare at Sarah through the gap. "Yes."

"Let me in," she says, as she pushes on the door.

I take a step back and she slips into the bathroom, closing the door behind her. "Sorry, I was taking them outside, and then I was coming back here to tell you they were here, but you came out and beat me to it." She says all of that without taking a breath.

"It's fine," I say but really, I'm not fine. I'm a freakin' horny bundle of nerves.

"Are you sure?" she questions me. "You look like you're about to tip over the edge."

I nod my head and sigh.

Sarah takes my hand and squeezes. "What up, Buttercup?" She looks at me intently, studying my face. "I know that face and sigh, something's eating at you?"

Of course she'd know, she's my sister from another mister. She knows me better than I know myself sometimes. "What's with the 'what up, Buttercup?'"

"I read it in a book and it's bloody awesome to say." She steps to me and squeezes my shoulders. "Now stop avoiding, what's up? And are you okay?"

"I don't know, Sar. This guy is doing things to me and I don't know how I feel about it."

"Good things?"

"Very good things."

"Then what's the problem?"

"I don't know how to act around him."

"Just keep doing what you're doing. That guy is gaga for you."

"You think?" I'm excited to hear that he might feel what I feel.

"Yeah, I do. Now, slip on this dress and let's go have a fantabulous night with two sexy as sin guys."

And a fantabulous time is exactly what we have.

4

AFTER DINNER, SARAH AND MIKE HEAD OFF TO THE NIGHTCLUB ON THE island to dance the night away, and Jordan and I stroll to the beach for some quiet time... alone time. He laces his fingers with mine and we walk along the shoreline. Apart from the rapidly loud beating of my heart, the only other sounds are the waves crashing onto the shore and the dull thud from the booming music at the nightclub.

We stop and stare out at the ocean; the moonlight is shimmering on the dark water and waves, causing a ripple effect.

"It's beautiful," I say, breaking the silence.

"You sure are," he says in reply.

Turning to face him, I see he's intently staring at me. He steps towards me and in the dark of night, Jordan and I share a kiss; our first kiss and it couldn't have been more perfect. He threaded his fingers into my hair, pulled me towards him, and pressed his lips to mine. Everything around me faded away. It was just us on the beach.

He pulls back and rests his forehead on mine. "I've wanted to do that all day long."

"I've wanted you to do that to me all day long." I bite my bottom lip and stare into his eyes. "And I want you to do it again."

"With pleasure," he growls.

He grips my cheeks and presses his lips to mine again. This kiss is just as amazing as the first one, and I could happily die right now; I'd have no regrets. I wrap my arms around his waist, pulling him into me. Squeezing his ass and crushing my breasts into his chest, I deepen the kiss and our connection.

We end up lying in the sand at the shoreline kissing. The waves continue to crash into the sand, lapping at our feet, but we don't notice. All we notice is each other.

A while later, when our hormones aren't in overdrive, we're snapped back to the present by the sound of laughter in the distance. It startles us and we pull apart, panting and breathing heavily. Gazing at each other, neither of us speak, but our eyes tell us everything.

Jordan sits up and I shimmy myself between his thighs. He wraps his arms around me from behind and we cuddle, staring out at the ocean and talking about anything and everything. We fall back to the sand, staring up at the night sky and eventually, we drift off to sleep.

Only to be rudely awoken when the sun peeks over the horizon, shining in our eyes. Sitting up, I notice the tide's coming in and we're in its path, precariously close to getting wet. Standing, I brush off the sand and we begin walking towards the bungalow. Lacing our fingers together again, Jordan escorts me back to my room and, with a quick kiss on the cheek, he leaves me to head inside and grab a few more hours sleep.

Quietly, I sneak into mine and Sarah's room. Slipping on my nightie, I climb into bed when Sarah sleepily says, "Have a great night?"

I jump in fright, her voice startling me in the dark. With a smile on my face, I whisper, "It was perfect."

"I'm glad. I'll be grilling you later for details but now, I'm going back to sleep."

"Night, babe."

"Night, ho."

I laugh at her reply, and with a goofy grin on my face, I blissfully drift off to dreamland, thinking of Jordan and our perfect night.

5

SARAH AND I SURFACE JUST BEFORE LUNCH. WE BUMP INTO MIKE AND Jordan as we're exiting the restaurant, where we've just eaten our weight in pancakes and coffee.

Jordan steps over to me and places a kiss on my cheek. "Morning, gorgeous."

My skin tingles where his lips just were. "Morning," I squeak out.

"We've just booked out a cat, would you ladies like to join us?" Jordan asks.

"We'd love to," Sarah says, just as I say, "Thank you, but no."

The three of them turn to me and a chorus of "What?" "Huh?" and "Why?" are thrown at me.

"Ummm, I get sea sick."

"Pffft, you'll be fine," Sarah says and she links her arm with mine. "Lead the way, boys."

Reluctantly, I follow. Thirty minutes later we are sailing through the crystal blue waters of the Coral Sea. Everyone is having fun. Me? I'm trying not to vomit. The three of them think it's hilarious, and after I do actually throw up, they decide to be nice and we head back to shore. I get of the catamaran and tell them to go have fun without me; I don't want to ruin it for them.

After a little argument, they relent and agree to head back out, with an agreement to collect me from our room when they return and we'll head to the bar for happy hour. I wave them off and they sail away for the adventure they had in mind. I head back to our bungalow to lie down and recover from the horrid experience.

I'm woken a few hours later by knocking at the room door. Presuming it's Sarah, forgetting her key—again—I swing it open, but when I do, it's not her. "Can I help you?"

"You sure can, Sweetcheeks." A drunk, creepy guy says from the bungalow patio. "I saw you earlier, you want me. I know you do." He thrusts his hips towards me. "All chicks want me."

A feeling of unease washes over me with each second that passes as this drunk asshole lingers at the door. The hairs on the back of my neck stand on end when recognition hits, I vaguely remember seeing him hitting on some poor chick at the bar yesterday. I shuddered then too. "Yeah, I don't think so."

I try to slam the door closed but he's stronger than me. He pushes on the timber, not allowing me to close it.

Through clenched teeth, I snarl. "I think you have the wrong room."

His eyes rake over my body and I shudder at the lewdness in his gaze. "Sweetcheeks, I'm pretty sure I don't," he growls. "You are and I going to have fun." He licks his lips, raises his eyebrows and thrusts his groin at me.

His words and actions shake me to my core. "I'm pretty sure you do," I snap back at him, fear simmering in my veins as I stare at the unwanted guest before me.

"Pretty sure I'm in the right fucking place," he snarls, hitting the doorframe to intimidate me. "Now, let me in, Sweetcheeks."

"I said no!" I shout through clenched teeth, my heart beating erratically in my chest.

"And I say yes." He steps forward but is suddenly pulled back and is slammed into the deck railing.

My rescuer presses their arm across the guys chest. "The lady said no." I recognise that voice immediately. It's Jordan.

I stand and stare in shock as Jordan and this guy have words. It's about to turn physical when Mike and Sarah come racing along. Mike assists Jordan and Sarah steps to me. She wraps her arm around me, and that's when the tears start. I fall apart and sob in her arms. Relief hits me that I'm no longer alone with this guy which only causes me to sob harder.

"I was so scared," I blubber.

A warm hand begins rubbing circles on my back; Jordan. Spinning to face him, I wrap my arms around his waist and cry into his chest. His embrace is soothing and just what I need right now. He hugs me tightly to him and whispers over and over, "Shh, you're okay."

When I look up again, I'm in my room, perched across Jordan's lap. I was so consumed with fear and relief I didn't notice we'd walked inside. Sarah and Mike are looking on, worry marring their faces.

"I'm fine, guys, just a little shaken," I tell them.

"Are you sure?" Sarah asks.

Nodding my head, I plaster on a fake smile. "Positive. How about we head to the beach for an afternoon of lazing in the sun, drinking cocktails, and chillaxing. Let's not allow this ruin what has been a perfect start to schoolies." I'm looking at Jordan as I say this, just being in his presence is calming and I know it will all be fine.

"Sounds good to me," Mike says as he jumps up, slapping Jordan on the back. "Let's go, dude. Let the ladies freshen up and we'll meet them shortly."

Standing up from Jordan's lap, I turn to face him and smile. He reaches out and grabs my hand, squeezing it. My gaze drops to our entwined fingers, but when I look back at him, I don't like the expression on this face. He's still worried.

Leaning down, I place my lips on his and whisper, "Jor, I'm fine."

He looks to me and smiles. "You're so strong, Kenz. You really amaze me."

My cheeks darken at his compliment.

"Hell yeah she is," Sarah adds. "She clearly takes after her best friend."

I roll my eyes at her comment but in truth, it doesn't surprise me at all. Sarah is truly my sister from another mister. My ride or die. She's the Thelma to my Louise. I love her to pieces, and cannot ever imagine keeping a secret from her, and vice versa.

"Let's do this, assholes," Mike declares.

After a quick discussion, we agree to meet the guys at the beach bar in fifteen minutes for an afternoon and evening I'll never forget.

6

SARAH AND I ARRIVE THIRTY MINUTES LATER AND FIND MIKE AND JORDAN. They've snagged four sun loungers and on the table is a bucket of beers, a jug with a red concoction inside—strawberry daiquiri—a plate of what I hope are arancini balls, and a platter of deep fried goodness: buffalo wings, spring rolls, wedges, and prawn twists. Sarah squeals in delight when she sees the spread.

"You guys are the best," she shouts as she bites into a prawn twist and moans.

Jordan walks towards me and my eyes roam over his body. I'm thankful for my sunnies hiding my blatant ogling of him, but the expression on my face must give me away.

Jordan slides his arm around my waist and whispers, "Like what you see? 'Cause I sure like what I see." He places a kiss on my temple and gazes down at me.

I'm wearing my army green one-piece, with a super sexy plunging neckline and strappy sides, as well as my Daisy Duke denim shorts. It's the most revealing swimsuit I've ever worn, but I feel a million bucks in it.

"Meh," I playfully reply. "I've seen better." Leaning over, I place a kiss his cheek and whisper, "I'd rather see you in nothing."

Pulling away from him, I spin and walk backwards as I stare at him. Lowering my sunnies down, I wink at him before I take the lounger next to Sarah. She hands me a drink and we toast one another. Bringing the cocktail glass to my lips, I take a sip and a slight moan slips from my lips when the strawberry and rum flavours hit my taste buds.

Jordan is suddenly next to me. He leans down and whispers, "I love hearing you moan like that." Kissing my temple, he takes the beer from Mike that he's just uncapped and sits on the end of my sun lounger. "I propose a toast." We all look to Jordan. "To fun in the sun and new friendships."

We all raise our drinks to the middle and tap them together. "Cheers to that," we all say in unison. We spend the afternoon drinking by the pool, swimming, and having a great time.

The sky is a vivid orange and the sun is about to set when Jordan looks to me and smiles, "Kenz, babe, would you like to have dinner with me tonight?"

"I'd love to."

My tummy immediately fills with butterflies. Jordan and I have spent time alone before but this feels different, it's an official date. A 'date' date. I'm nervous, excited, and everything in between. Before I have time to think about it further, Sarah's grabbing my arm and telling Jordan I'll be ready in an hours' time.

And true to her word, fifty-five minutes later I'm ready for my date. Sarah straightened my hair and then lent me her LBD—which I'm totally keeping by the way. I slip on my blingy thongs and apply some lippy. Looking at my reflection in the full-length mirror on the back of the bathroom door, I smile. I look great and I'm rocking an amazing tan—thank you Sarah and Bondi Sands.

Stepping into the bedroom, Sarah wolf whistles. "Dude, if I batted for the same team, I'd totally do you."

"Thanks...I think," I say, as I pick up my clutch and drop in my lip gloss, phone, wallet, and room key. "What are your plans for tonight?"

"Mike and I are getting a couple's massage."

Looking to her, I raise my eyebrows.

"No, not happening." She shakes her head side-to-side as she says this. "I'm blissfully in love with Josh, you know, my boyfriend?" And just a she says his name, her phone rings. "Speak of the sexy devil." She answers her phone, just as there's a knock at the door. She mouths 'have fun' and suggestively wriggles her eyebrows at me.

With a wave, I shake my head and walk towards the door. Opening it, my mouth drops open when I see Jordan. He's styled his hair in that sexy 'I-crawled-out-of-bed-like-this' way and he's wearing denim jeans and a black button-down shirt rolled to the elbows. Holy hotness, Batman.

"My God, Kenz, you are stunning."

My cheeks heat at his compliment. "You scrub up pretty well yourself, Mr. McRoberts."

Stepping outside, he links his arm with mine and we walk down the stairs and head along the path towards the beach.

"So, where are we dining this evening?" I ask.

"It's a surprise." He winks at me and we continue to the beach.

Stepping onto the sand, my mouth drops open. Before us is a table set for two. Tiki-torch lanterns are lit in a circle around the table.

"Surprise," he says, lacing his fingers with mine, as we walk towards the table.

He pulls out my seat and I sit down. He places a kiss on my cheek before taking the chair across from me, pouring me a glass of bubbly and uncapping a beer for himself.

I grin at him from across the table. I don't think I've ever been this happy or content. My grin widens when I hear Jordan, "A toast, to a night we'll never forget."

"I'll drink to that." I click my champagne flute against his beer bottle and take a sip.

Staring at Jordan over the top of my champagne, I notice his eyes shimmering in the moonlight, the flicker of the tiki-torch flame dancing in the orbs of his irises. I've never seen anything more beautiful.

A waiter arrives with a chicken pasta dish that is amazeballs and dessert is a platter of chocolate dipped strawberries, which we take over to the blankets and cushions set up near a beach fire. We snuggle together on the blanket and watch the world go by. After chatting throughout dinner, the quiet is perfect.

Finishing my drink, I look to Jordan. Cupping his cheek, I rise up onto my knees and I press my lips to his. My eyes drop closed and I give myself over to the kiss and Jordan. This is the sexiest kiss of my life and one I'll remember forever. Without breaking our connection, I straddle his thighs and wrap my arms around his neck, continuing to kiss him.

Jordan lowers me back, laying me down on the blanket. He covers my body with his, cocooning me underneath him. In the dark of the night, we make out on the beach before making love under the stars.

7

THE MORNING IS A SOMBER AFFAIR. LAST NIGHT WAS THE BEST NIGHT OF MY life, and as much as I'm excited to be heading to the next stop on our schoolies island hop, it also means not seeing Jordan again. We said our goodbyes earlier this morning when he walked me back to our bungalow, after our magical night together. He gave me the sweetest goodbye kiss before he turned around and went back to his room.

As soon as I step inside, I slide down the door, and with a smile on my face, I cry. My sniffles wake Sarah. She flips on the bedside light and when she sees me on the floor, she immediately hops up and wraps me in her arms. "Why are you smiling and crying?"

"I'm smiling because it was perfect, a night I'll remember forever and I'm crying cause I'll never see him again." I wail the last six words.

"Ohh babe." She sooths, wrapping her arms around me tighter as I sob harder. Eventually, she tugs me up and walks us over to her bed and we climb in. She hugs me as I cry over never seeing Jordan again.

We're all packed and walking down the jetty, heading towards the boat that will transfer us over to Daydream, when I hear someone yelling my name, "Kenz, Kenzie, wait up." Turning around, I smile when I see Jordan racing towards me. He stops in front of me panting, but he has the most gorgeous smile on his face. "Kenz, I need to do this one last time before you go." He grips my cheeks and slams his lips to mine. Just like every other kiss, my eyes drop closed and fireworks explode throughout my body.

Jordan breaks the connection with my lips and rests his forehead against mine. "I'll never forget you, Mackenzie Merlot."

"I'll never forget you either, Jordan McRoberts."

With a quick kiss to my nose, he turns and walks away. Leaving me standing on the jetty, tears in my eyes and my heart full. He was my first amazing toe-curling perfect kiss. My first holiday fling. He will forever be etched in my heart and soul.

I sit upright in bed, my lips tingling and my heart full of joy. Tapping Jordan furiously on the arm, I whisper shout, "Jordan, babe, wake up." He groans. I keep hitting him until he wakes up and answers me.

"What?" he groggily says.

"I just had a dream," I excitedly tell him.

"That's nice, babe," he mumbles. "Can we talk about it in the morning?"

"Nope, I need to tell you about it now, while it's fresh." I don't give him a chance to reply. I flip the bedside light on and cross my legs. "You and I met at schoolies and fell in love there. I never met assface douche hole. It was wonderful and perfect."

"Sounds great, babe, I wish that had of happened too," he leans over, kisses my cheek, "but we are living our wonderful and perfect life. And it will be even more wonderful and perfect if you let me get some more sleep." He closes his eyes and falls straight back to sleep.

"Fine," I huff. "Nite nite." Leaning over, I kiss his temple and turn the light off, before lying down and stare at the ceiling. A smile graces my face as I think about my dream. If only that really was how we fell in love.

THE END!

Malt
ME

I'M GIVEN A *second chance* AT *happiness*...
THERE'S NO WAY I'LL LET HIM TAKE THAT FROM ME

DL GALLIE

I'm given a second chance at happiness…there's no way I'll let him take that from me.

College. It's supposed to be both exciting and daunting. For me, it turns into a nightmare.

Now everyone looks at me with pity, treating me like I'm glass. I don't blame them. Not a lot of people can survive what I have. But I refuse to let the darkness swallow me whole, to let the monster win.

I'm given a second chance at happiness, and I won't allow the horrifying memories to take that away from me. He's already taken too much.

But turns out he wants more. The devil won't stop until he's consumed every part of me.

He wants another chance to own me, possess me, and then ruin me if he wants to. But there's no way I'll let him.

I am Mackenzie Merlot. I am strong. I am a survivor.

And this time…he'll lose.

To my husband, Troy,

For giving me the confidence to take this leap
and for always loving me, especially when I am being irrational

PROLOGUE

STANDING ON THE MEZZANINE LEVEL LEANING ON THE TIMBER RAILING, MY foot resting on the wire cable I look down and realize that we did it; we bloody did it. Our dream of opening a brewpub has actually come true. I never imagined the path to get to this point would have been as rocky as it was, but despite it all, here we are.

Malt Me is officially open and it's currently full, yes it's at maximum capacity on opening day. The beer is flowing, the kitchen is pumping out orders, and it seems like everyone is having a blast. You cannot wipe the smile off my face; I'm glowing with pride and achievement.

Looking towards Jordan my heart flutters, just like it did all those years ago when we first met. I see that he is just as happy as I am, if not happier. He looks up at me and smiles. After all these years, his smile still makes me weak at the knees. He takes the checker plate stairs that wind along the side of the room, two at a time. He saunters over and wraps his tanned muscular arms around me, lifting me up into a hug, spinning us around, "We did it, Kenz, we really did it." Lowering me down, he places a soft kiss on my lips that quickly turns heated.

I step back, gently pushing him in the chest, "STOP! We have to be professional." He pouts, so I place a quick kiss on his lips and whisper into his ear, "Later, I promise to make all your dreams come true." I wink as I pull back.

"Kenz, all my dreams have come true. I have the girl of my dreams in my arms and we are standing in OUR brewpub."

He bends down for another kiss and from below I hear Mike yell, "Get a room, you two!"

"Fu…whatever, Mike, if I wanna kiss my missus, I'll kiss my missus." Turning his attention back to me, Jordan says, "Come on, baby, lets go play boss and mingle"

"I'll be down in a sec, I just wanna stay here for a moment and take it all in. I still can't believe we did it, Jor. There was so much in our way and at times, I wasn't sure I wanted to do this and then Clint happened." He goes to interrupt me, but I put my finger on his lips to stop him. "I'm not dwelling on that, Jor, but it happened. It's a part of who we are and a major part of this journey. I just want to enjoy this moment, cause I'm still amazed that we did it. Now, go and have a beer to celebrate and tell Mike to behave. I'll be down in a sec to celebrate with you, promise."

Jordan leans down, giving me a quick peck on the cheek, "Don't be too long, Kenz." He winks at me and walks away. His wink still sends shockwaves to my girly parts.

When he gets to the top of the stairs, he looks over his shoulder and says, "I love you, Kenz, and I promise to look after you and our beers forever." I laugh as he jumps down the stairs, and when he gets to the bottom, he yells, "Beer me baby" and throws his arms wide. I cannot help but laugh, like really laugh.

"Wait for it!" Mike yells, and then I snort. Yes, I snort laugh for everyone to hear and laughter erupts from down below.

I take a bow and since everyone is looking at me, I clear my throat, "While I have your attention, Jordan and I want to thank you all for being here today, at the grand opening of our baby, Malt Me. The journey here hasn't been smooth, but we got here, thanks to the support of many of you. We both thank you all so very muchly. BUT I want to give a special shout out to my partner in crime…"

Mike interrupts and yells, "Naw shucks, Kenz, you don't have to thank me!"

"As if, Mike. As I was saying before I was rudely interrupted, I want to thank Jordan. We would not be here today if it wasn't for his love of beer and his passion for everything beer; specifically one awesome drunken decision that was made at the Oktoberfest all those years ago. Jordan, I love you so very much and I'm so so proud of you.

Together we are going to make beautiful beers and live hoppily ever after." Everyone below laughs at my beer joke but to Jordan and I, it's our mantra. "So, if everyone can raise their drinks and toast Jordan. Congrats on making your dream come true baby."

"You mean our dream!" he yells.

Below everyone says, "Cheers, to Jordan and Kenzie." They all start congratulating Jordan and waving for me to come down. I walk towards the stairs with a huge happy smile on my face. I look down at everything and freeze, something by the front doors catches my eye and I stumble. Before I know it, I'm tumbling down the stairs.

Vaguely I hear someone yelling "Kenzie!" Then it all goes dark...again.

1

KENZIE

...Seven years earlier

THIS PAST SUMMER HAS BEEN AMAZING. I FINISHED HIGH SCHOOL BEFORE Christmas and had a fantabolous week long holiday with my bestie, Sarah Bryant, for schoolies; we went island hopping in the Whitsunday's. I finally turned eighteen and to top it all off, I was accepted into the college course that I had my heart set on.

Today I'm moving into my first apartment and this time tomorrow I will officially be a college student. I was accepted into Stratton's School of Business and I will be completing my diploma of Tourism Management, which is twelve months in length. If I enjoy it, I can transfer my credits to university and complete a Bachelor of Tourism.

I found a cute apartment, a short ten-minute bus ride from the city center and college. Thankfully I have my inheritance from Dad to help with expenses. There are six apartments in total and mine is number two; they are in a two story red brick with the apartment being on one level and the garage and laundry underneath. As it's my first apartment, the majority of my furniture I had to buy. It's being delivered later today, so apart from my clothes and personal items, all the heavy lifting is taken care of.

Hoping I'd get an uber hottie to deliver my stuff; luck wasn't on my side and I ended up with a balding beer bellied rough nut, who stinks, just my luck. Thankfully, he gets everything unloaded pretty quickly and placed into the rooms I want, now all I have to do is put it all together. I love to hate *IKEA* flat packs. I love that they are cheap, but hate having to put them together.

I quickly change into my grey trackies and fluro pink Wine Time Finally singlet, grab a bottle of wine, and I decide to start with the bedroom stuff first. After all, I'll need to get a good night sleep in order to be fresh and ready for college tomorrow. Pouring a glass of wine, I try and decipher the bed instructions when my phone starts to play *Love Shack* by The B-52's. I glance at the screen and see Mum's smiling face looking at me. "Heya, Mum"

"Hi, Mac, how's the unpacking going?"

"I'm drinking wine."

"That good, huh?"

"I'm starting to wish I had paid extra and gotten them to put it all together for me. Why am I such a tightass?"

"Language, honey, but if I can put a BBQ together, I am sure you will be fine with a bed and a few shelves"

"I know, I know, I'm just not in the mood for it tonight." We both laugh "I've decided that I'll put my bed together tonight and then work my way through each room. Enough about my flat pack hell. How are you?"

"I'm good, missing my baby girl."

"I'm eighteen, Mum, not really a baby anymore, but I miss you too. You know you can always move here. There is nothing really keeping you guys there, and Skye can always go to school here, in the city!"

"I don't want to disrupt your sister's schooling, she was doing really well at the end of last year. She has decided she wants to be a nurse."

"For this week?"

"Mac, that's not fair. You were just as indecisive as her. If I remember correctly, you were going to be a chef, remind me again what you are studying?"

"Fair enough, Mum, I was just teasing. Look, I'd love to chat, but I really need to get this done and get a good night's sleep. My first class is at 9:00 a.m. tomorrow. Tell Skye I love her, I'll give you guys a call tomorrow night and let you know how my first day went."

"Sounds good, baby girl. Good luck with the furniture and I'll chat to you tomorrow. I love you, Mac. Your dad would be so proud."

"I love you too, Mum and I hope he would be. I still miss him." Tears rise to my eyes when I say that.

"I miss him too, honey, and I know he would be because I'm very proud of you. I'll chat to you tomorrow."

"Thanks, Mum, I love you."

"Love you too, baby girl."

After hanging up, I grab my family photo out of a box and I sit and stare at it, a lone tear cascades down my cheek. I still miss Dad, even though he died five years ago. One minute he was mowing the front lawn, and the next, we are organising his funeral. He had a bleed on the brain, also known as an aneurysm and the ambos were unable to revive him. There's not a day that goes by that I don't think of him. I stare at the photo. "Love you, Dad," I whisper, as I kiss my finger and place it on his head. I put the frame on my chest of drawers, the only non-flat pack item. Grabbing my wine, I take a sip, turn up the tunes and dive in.

It only takes me three hours to put together my bed and shelf. I'm putting away the last shirt and *Baby One More Time* by Brittany Spears comes on, I grab my brush and sing at the top of my lungs, shaking my booty around my new bedroom. This has been a great day. I quickly grab a shower and put on my new, silk, Peter Alexander PJ's before jumping into my newly built and made bed. I'm pretty proud, as I managed to get the draws and the intricate headboard shelf thingy put together with only one tantrum, and I didn't damage the chocolate brown timber either.

I snuggle under my sunflower comforter that my Mum and sister bought me for my high school graduation present. I still can't believe Mum and Skye got me this; I pointed it out months ago when we had a girls' shopping day. When I went back into Talking Pillow to get it, they'd just sold the last one; little did I know it was Mum and Skye who purchased it. It's the softest Egyptian cotton, and it's covered in sunflowers with a bluish green background. The thousand thread sheets are a buttery yellow, with blue accents that match the comforter. My mum always says you need to sleep like the dead and to do so you need comfort. She's a total sheet snob, and I have now inherited this trait too. I snuggle down, looking forward to the new adventure that starts tomorrow.

My alarm goes off at 6.30 a.m. and I'm so excited. Jumping up, I race to the kitchen, and turn on my coffee machine; while the coffee is brewing I grab a quick shower. For my first day of college, I settle on my Wrangler jeans that hug my curves and make my ass look amazing. A wine coloured sleeveless shirt with black lace at the top, which I pair with my black Diana Ferrari ballerina flats. I look in the mirror and I'm pleased. I look sophisticated, yet sexy. Perfect for my first day of college.

Pouring my coffee into my travel mug, I grab my bag, lock up and I walk to the bus stop. I catch the 115 express into the city, and depending on traffic, I should arrive with plenty of time to spare. Traffic is light for a Monday morning so I don't have to rush. The bus arrives early enough that I head to the Java Lava Cafe, which is next door to the college and grab another coffee, I'm totally addicted to coffee…and wine.

After my coffee, I head to college. Walking up the front steps, I admire the building. I've never seen so many windows before; they're that reflective stuff, which has always fascinated me for some weird reason. Gazing towards the building, I bump into someone while my neck is craned and I fall flat on my ass.

Looking up, I see the hottest guy I have ever seen, he has an electric smile, likable lips, bulging biceps and the most mesmerizing blue eyes. His sandy blond hair is short on the side with a waved fringe, and I imagine myself running my fingers through it, while biting those luscious lips.

"Um, sorry. I wasn't watching where I was going," I say, as a slight blush creeps onto my cheeks, due to my inappropriate thoughts.

He puts out his hand to help me up, and I wrap my fingers around his. I feel an electric current sparks between us when our hands touch and he helps to pull me up. I feel sad when he drops my hand. "No worries, I probably should not have stopped in the middle of the walkway. I'm Jordan McRoberts." He lifts his hand to shake.

Reaching my hand out, I grip his hand and shake. "Nice to smash into you, Jordan, I'm Mackenzie Merlot." I feel the same spark that I felt moments ago. Letting go of his hand, I push my golden blonde hair over my shoulder and smile.

"Pretty name for a pretty girl."

I snort laugh at his comment and can't help but smile. "That's the cheesiest line ever, dude, but thank you for the compliment. I'm really sorry about bumping into you, I was mesmerised by the building and all the windows."

"It's partly my fault too, I should have been paying attention and not playing on my phone."

Stepping around him, I look over my shoulder. "I hope to see you around." I shamelessly wink at him as I walk up the stairs into the building.

Heading to reception, I fill out more paperwork, finalise my registration, get my amended timetable, and head to my first class. I walk into the classroom and I take a seat in the middle. My gaze moves towards the seat next to me. There's this guy sitting there, staring at me. He has wavy, dark brown hair that hangs just below his ears, and his eyes match the darkness of his hair. *Great, I'm sitting next to a weirdo.* I consider getting up and moving seats but he looks over and smiles. His smile lights up his face and he looks less creepy now. His smile makes his dark eyes pop and sparkle, making him less of a weirdo and spunky, a Patrick Bateman from *American Psycho* kind of spunky.

"Hey, I'm Clint MacNicholson," he says in a deep rough voice.

"Hi, Clint, I'm Mackenzie Merlot." Putting out my hand to shake his.

He takes my outstretched hand and returns the shake. "Nice to meet you Mackenzie."

The lecturer, Michele, walks in and gets straight into it. No pussy-footing around. "Welcome, everyone. I'm Michele. When you enter this classroom you are on Michele time. All phones are to be switched off. If I see or hear one, it's mine and I have lots of friends in China, so be prepared for an excessive bill." Everyone laughs, but by the stern look on her face, I don't think she's joking.

This teacher is hardcore and kind of badass. We're given our first assignment; we have to write a travel magazine and we are partnered with the person sitting next to us. Looks like I'm working with Clint. I later find out that Michele owns the college and is a total ball-buster, but the best lecturer around.

My first day flies by, and by time I get home, I'm exhausted.

Welcome to college life, I think. Before having my shower, I call Mum and Skye to give them a run down of my day. After my shower, I climb into bed and fall straight to sleep. I'm so shattered that I don't even read. Usually, I need to read to make me sleepy.

2

JORDAN

TODAY IS THE FIRST DAY OF COLLEGE AND I'M SUPER EXCITED. My childhood friend and best buddy, Mike Mustange, and I are attending the same college. I'm studying business and marketing, as I'd like to run a bar one day. I love all things beer related and I hope to turn that into a career.

As I'm walking up the college steps, I vaguely hear someone calling out to me, I look over to see Mike waving. "Earth to Jordan. Hello ... anyone home?" I was totally lost in thought, thinking about my encounter with Mackenzie. Everything else faded away, and I was consumed with thoughts of her, even though I only spoke with her for about a minute.

She is the most gorgeous girl I have been near; dazzling green eyes, long golden blonde hair and the most kissable lips I have ever seen. When she placed her silky smooth hand in mine for me to help her up, I felt a spark. My cock twitched, sparking to life just from her touch. It was like a scene from the movies where fireworks explode and every-thing around you fades away, leaving just the two of us staring at each other. My heart rate accelerated, just from her touch. I didn't want to let go of her hand and break our contact, but if I didn't, she'd think I'm a creeper. So I reluctantly let go of her hand.

We did our introductions, and her name was just as beautiful as her face. I could feel my cock starting to harden, and from the discomfort I said the dumbest line ever. *Seriously, what was my cock making my brain do?* I've turned into a complete pussy, so glad Mike wasn't here to witness my pussiness. She snort laughed at my cheesiness; it was refreshing to see her not hide it, and I hoped she didn't think I'm too cheesy or a douche.

As she walked off, she winked at me. Her wink went straight to my dick and my pants became really uncomfortable and tight as my cock pressed against my fly. I subtly adjusted myself as I watched her walk off. Being male, I had to check out her ass and its one mighty fine ass. Her jeans hugged and accentuated her curves. I imagine holding onto her ass as she wrapped her legs around me, and I sank my teeth into her shoulder before kissing the life out of her.

I shake my head to clear those dirty thoughts, but her ass will stick in my mind for a longtime to come. Shaking my head, I reply, "Sorry, dude, I was just thinking."

"Ouch, did it hurt?" he says.

Reaching out, I punch Mike in the arm. "Whatever, douche, let's get to our first class. I hear the lecturer is super strict and I want to make a good first impression." I slap Mike on the back and we head into our first day of college.

3

CLINT

I CAN'T BELIEVE MY LUCK WHEN I LOOK UP AND SEE WHO WALKS INTO MY first class...the hottie I saw when I was walking out of registration. She has the most amazing green eyes and her ass is incredible. Thoughts of gripping her ass as I plow into her enter my mind. I smile at that thought, and it's also when I decide that she is mines. Wriggling in my seat, I adjust my dick, which, seems to have a mind of its own where this hottie is concerned. I can't take my eyes off her as she makes her way across the classroom. As luck would have it, she sits next to me. After she sits, she turns her head in my direction. I smile.

After I introduce myself, she smiles and it lights up her face. I feel my cock twitching again. I'm thankful for the table blocking it.

When she takes my hand to shake it, I feel all giddy. Her hand is ever so soft, and I imagine what it would feel like wrapped around my cock, gripping it tightly, stroking up and down. Wriggling in my seat again, I discretely adjust my growing cock.

I want to know more about her, she is so mesmerising. I haven't felt like this with anyone since high school, not since Laura. Just as I'm about to ask her another question, the lecturer walks in. *Damn it.*

Turns out this class isn't going to be as easy-going as I was hoping, as the college owner is the lecturer. Just my luck, so much for an easy semester.

Mackenzie and I get paired up for our first assignment, and I thank the heavens that I'm partnered with her; everyone else in this class is a bore.

Is it fate that Mackenzie and I are paired up?

Are we destined to be together?

All signs are pointing to yes, Mackenzie Merlot will be mines.

4

KENZIE

OVER THE NEXT FEW WEEKS, CLINT AND I MEET UP AFTER CLASS AT THE Java Lava and on weekends, at my apartment to get this magazine assignment completed. We smash out an amazing magazine and I'm really proud of the final product. All the work we put into it really paid off. We manage to get a ninety-three out of a hundred, which is pretty good for our first assignment. To celebrate, Clint and I agree to head to the, Dirty Duck, after class. The Duck has become the local for the Stratton college students.

I finish at 2:00 p.m. and wait for Clint outside the building. Looking up, I see Clint walking towards me and I can't help but smile. I tell him I'm just ducking to the bathroom and then I'll be ready to go.

"Tik tok, hurry up," he says, as I race to the bathroom.

It's quiet for a Thursday, or it could just be that it's 2:00 p.m. and most people are either at work or still in class. Clint and I grab a booth in the back. The Dirty Duck is your typical college bar, wooden high-top tables in the middle. Red cracked and peeling vinyl booths along the back wall. There are pool tables to the left as you walk in and the bar runs the length of the room with bathrooms off the right. The lighting is dim, but enough that you can see. The neon signs along the walls and the backlights from the bar provide extra lighting.

Heading to the bar, I order us a jug of beer and some nibblies. The Buffalo wings here are the best, not too spicy just perfect. Once I'm seated back at the booth, I pour us each a beer and raise my glass. "To us, for acing our first major assignment. Cheers!"

Clint raises his glass and shouts, "Cheers," before we clink glasses.

After taking a sip, I look towards Clint. Pointing at him I say, "You know what? You and I make a pretty good team. Here's hoping we get another assignment together before the year is out."

Clint raises his glass again "To us, the kick ass combo that is M and C."

"Cheers to that," I say holding my glass in the air.

The afternoon flies by and before I know it, I'm kind of wasted. I haven't been this drunk in a long time, it feels good to let loose and feel kind of numb. The past few weeks at college have been pretty full on. I know I'm wasted, as I can't stop giggling, which results in me snort laughing. Everyone in turn laughs at me, which only makes me snort again; it's a vicious laugh/snort cycle. Some of the other students join us when their classes are over. We consume way too many jugs of beer, eat a gazillion wings and dance the night away.

Clint and I return from the dance floor after dancing for a few songs. Just as we sit down, he leans over, tilts my chin up, and kisses me. His lips are soft and it's not bad for a first kiss. I wouldn't mind doing that again, so I lean over and I kiss him again. This time, when he pulls away, my lips are tingling. I smile and lean into him again. I whisper in his ear, "You know, I've thought you were kind of hot since our first day in class." I nibble his ear lobe and kiss along his jawline, pressing my lips to his once again. Running my fingers through his silky soft hair, I gently tug on the ends, as I slip my tongue into his mouth. Our tongues gently caress one another, as our hands explore each other.

Clint groans into my mouth before pulling back, gazing into my eyes he whispers, "You know what, Mackenzie? I thought you were pretty hot too. From the moment you walked into that classroom, I was secretly hoping you'd sit next to me."

I think it's all the beer, or the high from getting such a good mark on our assignment but I kiss Clint passionately, again. Grabbing Clint's hand, I entwine our fingers and softly whisper, "Let's get out of here."

Leaving the bar, we manage to grab a cab straight away, which never happens...especially on a Thursday night. We're back at my place before we know it. We go up the back stairs, enter through the kitchen, and head into the lounge room.

I place my bag and keys on the breakfast bar, and Clint wraps his arms around me from behind, holding me close to him. I feel his cock hardening against my ass, as he nibbles on my neck and earlobe. I moan and start grinding myself against him, his cock getting harder. Spinning around in his arms, I kiss him intensely, devouring his mouth, our teeth crushing together. He deepens the kiss as he turns us, pushing me up against the hallway wall.

Grabbing the hem of my shirt, I lift it over my head and drop it on the floor. I unzip my navy blue skorts and am left standing there in my satin purple bra and matching undies; internally high fiving myself for dressing sexy this morning. Clint eyes me up and down. "Fuck me, your gorgeous," he says, before he kisses me deeply. I run my hands up under his shirt and around to his back. Moving my hands down, I grip his ass, pulling him closer. I grab the bottom of his shirt and lift it over his head. Raking my eyes down his chiseled chest, I moan and dart my tongue out to moisten my lips. Reaching for his hand, I tug and walk down the hall to my bedroom.

We reach the end of my bed and I make quick work, removing his jeans and boxer briefs. I push him back and begin to crawl my way up his body. Grabbing my arms, he pulls me up so I am straddling him. I rest my arms either side of his head, my hair creating a curtain around us, leaning forward I kiss him passionately, our tongues meshing together. He sits up, snaking his arms around my waist, quickly removing my bra. The straps fall down my arms and he takes my nipple into his mouth. He bites down before sucking the tip between his lips, gently raking his teeth over my hard peak; the pain is quickly replaced with the most delicious pleasure. Moaning, I throw my head back. Not wanting to be selfish, he takes the other nipple into his mouth and repeats the same process, which has me once again throwing my head back in ecstasy as I shamelessly grind my pussy into him.

He literally rips my undies off me and flips us over, so he is now on top of me. He grabs a condom and sheaths his rock hard cock before stroking it a few times, not once removing his eyes from me. In one stroke he thrusts deep into me and I moan. I draw him down towards me and rub my tongue over his lips before I slip into his mouth. Our kiss becomes more passionate and I embrace him tighter. Grabbing my left leg, he places it over his shoulder and begins to thrust in and out. I've never felt pleasure like this before.

"Ohh, Clint!" I moan.

He continues to move in an out and his pace quickens. Before I know it, I feel my whole body tense as my orgasm rips through me like a tsunami; tingles wash over me from head to toe as the most amazing feeling ripples through me. I see fireworks behind my closed eyes… this is the most intense orgasm that I have ever had. It's not long before I feel Clint spasm inside of me.

Lowering my leg, he falls on top of me. "That was fuckin' amazing Mackenzie."

All I can manage in response is, "mmhmm."

He lies on top of me for a while; I can still feel his heart frantically beating and his hot breath on my shoulder. I wrap my arms around him, and slowly rub my hands up and down his back while we both catch our breath. Easing off me, Clint removes the condom and chucks it into the bin next to my bed. He lies back next to me and I snuggle into him, running my fingers back and forth across his chest, gently tugging on the smattering of light brown hair. We both drift off to sleep in the early hours of the morning.

I wake alone the next morning and I feel a little sad until I see a note on his pillow with a sunflower. I can't help but smile that he remembered sunflowers are my favourite flower.

MACKENZIE,
YOU LOOKED SO BEAUTIFUL SLEEPING. I DIDN'T WANT TO WAKE YOU.
I WILL CALL YOU THIS AFTERNOON. I'D LOVE TO SPEND THE EVENING WITH YOU.
CLINT

Rolling over onto my back, there's a huge smile on my face and I get excited thinking about seeing Clint again tonight. My girly bits tingle just thinking about a repeat performance from last night. I roll onto my side, smiling and fall back to sleep.

A few hours later, I wake when I hear a noise outside my bedroom window. I peek through the timber blinds but I can't see anything. I climb out of bed, head to the bathroom, and run myself a bath. While the tub is filling, I grab a bottle of wine out of the fridge. *It's 5:00 p.m. somewhere.* I soak in the tub to ease my muscles; sore from last night's extracurricular activities, I ache all over.

Reaching for my Kindle, I lose myself in my book, *Break Open* by A.M. Gillham. It's an Aussie version of Sons of Anarchy and these guys are hot and the story is addictive. I eventually realise the water is cold and I'm pruned. This soak was just what I needed; I feel so relaxed right now. Grabbing my fluffy purple bath sheet, I dry off. I'm in a lazy mood so after I hang my towel up I grab another glass of wine and jump back into bed with my Kindle. I must have fallen asleep again because when I wake up, Clint is sitting on the black and grey chair in the corner of my room. I shit myself, as I wasn't expecting anyone to be here.

"Damn, Clint, you scared the shit out of me," I scold, holding my hands to my chest to calm the erratic beating of my heart.

"Sorry, Sweetcheeks." He smiles. "You looked so beautiful sleeping, I didn't want to disturb you."

"It's all good. I just wasn't expecting anyone to be in here when I woke up. Wanna come join me?" I pull the covers back, raising my eyebrows seductively as I reveal that I am still naked from my bath.

His eyes light up. "Shit, had I know you were naked, I would've joined you as soon as I got here. " He quickly strips off his green cargo shorts and charcoal grey T-shirt before jumping onto the bed. He grabs my face and kisses me; I can feel this kiss all the way down to the bottom of my toes. We don't make it to dinner, or breakfast, or lunch the next day. Man, does Clint have some stamina. Thankfully, I have Sunday to recover before college on Monday.

Over the next few weeks, Clint and I become inseparable, spending all our free time together. He and I get along really well together, I just wish he and Sarah got on. He's always putting her down, and then he snaps at me when I defend her; not sure what the issue there is.

One Friday after class, Clint and I stopped in at the Duck for an end of week drink. While I grab a booth, Clint heads to the bar to get us a jug of beer. I've just sat down when I get a text.

SARAH – *Yo bitch, girls nite 2nite. I'll be at yours at 7*

ME – *Bestest idea you have ever had. See you then XO*

SARAH – *Whatevs. See you soon XO*

Putting my phone back in my bag, I look up to see Clint walking across the bar and I can't help but smile. He really is good looking and he only has eyes for me. I feel special when I'm with him. He places the mugs and jug down before pouring us each a beer. While he is pouring, I tell him about tonight, "Sarah just texted me and we are having a girls' night tonight, so I'll have to get going after this jug."

Clint stares at me. "What about me? You just going to leave me high and dry?" He takes a sip of beer before adding, "You are such a fucking selfish bitch at times Mackenzie." He finishes his beer, before slamming it down on the table, making everything rattle. He grabs the jug and refills his mug.

I'm dumbfounded by his actions, one minute I'm checking him out and feeling good, the next I start to question everything. I finish my beer and tell Clint I'll see him over the weekend.

Sarah and I have a great night together, as we always do. We dance for hours, laugh and drink way too many cocktails; it's never a dull night when Sarah and I get together.

Late Saturday arvo, still feeling worse for wear, Clint comes over. He walks in and I smile. "Hey, baby, how was your day?"

"You look like shit."

"Well hello to you too. Sarah and I had a great night, thanks for asking."

"Don't be smart with me."

"Looks like someone got out on the wrong side of the bed this morning. What's crawled up your ass?" I walk over to him and wrap my arms around his waist for a cuddle. He shoves me aside and sits on my couch. Shaking my head, I snarikily say, "Please sit down." I walk into the kitchen and I grab us a beer each, I pass Clint his as I sit down on the opposite end of the couch. Taking a sip, I look over at him, "Are you okay? You seem off."

"Just leave it Mackenzie, I'm fine," he snarls. He finishes his beer and slams the empty on the coffee table before abruptly standing up. "I can't be around you when you're like this, Sarah is such a bad influence on you. I knew I shouldn't have let you go out with her. I'm out of here." He stands up. "Later, bitch." Slamming the front door on his way out.

Open-mouthed and shocked, I sit staring at the front door. *What the hell was that all about?* This is the second time he has acted like this, I'm not sure I like this version of Clint.

5

CLINT

Oh My God, sex with Mackenzie is out of this world. Who knew she was such a devil in the sack? I really picked a wild one this time. I can't help but smile when I think back over this past weekend. I snuck out early Friday but not before leaving a note and flower for my girl. I wanted to give her some time alone, I'm nice like that.

I couldn't stay away, right now, I'm peeking in her window, watching her sleep. I slip, knocking over the crate I'm standing on. The noise startles her awake. I manage to duck out of sight, just as she lifts up the timber blinds to have a look around. I stay hidden until I hear the water start to run in the bathroom. I take this chance to head home and freshen up before I come back over.

Later that afternoon, I let myself into Mackenzie's apartment with the key I took when I left this morning. She is back in bed sleeping, so I sit on the chair in the corner and again, I watch her sleep. She is so beautiful, I smile to myself and I think how happy we are going to be together. My cock is starting to get hard staring at her. She starts to stir and when she opens her eyes, I frighten her.

God she's beautiful when she sleeps.

She pulls the covers back and she's naked.

Fuck Me!

My eyes rake over her beautiful body, pausing at her amazing tits before I look to her face; she is winking at me seductively.

I quickly strip off my clothes and jump onto the bed. I grab her face and passionately kiss her, pulling back to stare into her beautiful green eyes. I quickly roll on a condom and pin her to the bed. I fuck her hard and fast. We spend the next twenty-four hours in bed and they are the best hours of my life so far.

The next few weeks are amazing. Mackenzie was meant for me and I for her. I'm so glad I found her. I thought Laura was the one when I met her in high school, but her leaving me was the best thing to happen.

She is *nothing* compared to Mackenzie…My Sweetcheeks.

I spend as much time as possible with her, only letting her spend time with her best friend, Sarah, when she begs me. I really don't like that bitch, but I always get what I want, so I guess letting her out now and again will be okay.

Later in the term, we are paired together for another assignment in Michele's class. This time, we have to create an all-inclusive tour and come up with the marketing plan; again we kick ass. Mackenzie and I are a great team, in and out of the bedroom.

6

KENZIE

THE JUNE LONG WEEKEND FOR THE QUEENS'S BIRTHDAY IS FAST approaching and it's time for Sarah and my annual, long weekend, girls' getaway. We take turns arranging the weekend away; this year it's her turn to plan it. I always get scared when it's her year as she can be pretty wild at times; which is one of the many reasons I love her so much.

We started this tradition when we were thirteen; somehow we managed to convince our parents to do this for us. This year's will be amazeballs; as for the first time there will be no parents. We really were lucky to have parents who were happy to do this for us. I have no idea what she has planned this year and that scares me. Sarah can be crazy when left unsupervised. Even though I'm scared, I'm also super excited to see what craziness she comes up with.

Grabbing my phone, I text her to discuss the finer details, like what to pack and maybe get a hint on where we are going but she is currently locked up tighter than Fort Knox, and the not knowing is really frustrating me. I'm such a pushover; I always cave and tell her what we are doing and where we are going.

ME – *Yo bitch, what do I pack for the weekend? And where are we going?*

SARAH – *Togs and winter woolies*
SARAH – *PS. Not telling*

ME – *WFT woman? That gives me no clue whatsoever*

SARAH – *I know :P I'll pick you up Thursday afternoon after class. I'm really looking forward to this weekend. It feels like forever since I have seen you. You are all loved up with Clint. You know, if you two get super serious, he is going to have to learn to share*

Sarah's text gets me thinking. Have I been neglecting everyone? I reread it to make sure I read it right. Am I so wrapped up in Clint that I have become one of those girls?

ME – *I have not been that bad. I can't wait for this weekend.*

SARAH – *Me neither. Love you XoXoX*

ME - *Love you too XoXoX*

I throw my phone on the couch and Clint waltzes in, he looks pissed off. Walking into the kitchen, I give him a kiss on the cheek. "Hey, baby."

He storms past me, shoving me out of the way; I bang my hip on the corner of the breakfast bar and wince in pain. He plonks himself down on my charcoal grey, suede, L-shaped couch; he grabs my phone as it was digging into his leg. He looks down and glances at the screen. "Who the fuck are you saying, 'love you' to?" He air quotes love you.

"It's just Sarah. We are finalizing our girls' weekend."

"What girls' weekend?" he spits.

"I told you, Sarah and I go away every June long weekend."

"Well, where are you going?" he shouts at me,

"No idea, it's her year to plan. All I know is I need to pack togs and winter woolies."

"Well, I don't want you going!" he shouts. "You never asked me if you could go." He slams his fist down on the coffee table.

"Excuse me?" I turn to face him with a shocked expression on my face "You are not the boss of me, and if I want to go away with my friend, I will." I state matter-of-factly, with my hands on my hips.

"Like hell you are, you belong with me." He slams his fist down on the timber coffee table again and throws my phone. It slides across the monochrome rug onto the floor in front of the TV cabinet.

"I what?" I stare at him dumbfounded.

"You heard me, bitch, you're mines and mines only." He spits through his teeth, in a tone I have never heard him use before. My body tenses, I start to get a horrible feeling, as fear courses through my veins.

"I am no ones, and with an attitude like that, I think you can leave." I bend down, pick up my phone, slide it into my pocket, and walk back to the kitchen to grab a glass of wine for myself.

Clint jumps off the couch, grabbing me by my upper arms, gripping tightly, slamming me up against the wall. The very wall that we first made out against, all those months ago, making the pictures rattles. He grabs my face roughly, squeezing my chin tightly, he glares into my eyes, and through clenched teeth spits, "You are mines, Sweetcheeks, and I say you are not going away with that slut." Raising his right hand, he backhands me, his hand colliding with my left cheek. My head slams back into the wall with a thud. He let's go of me and I slide down the wall. I start to cry.

My head is throbbing, I rub the spot that hit the wall, with such force that I was sure the pictures were going to fall down this time. I'm scared out of my wits; I look up towards Clint, who is hovering above me. "I…I think you should go."

"Whatever, Mackenzie." He storms out slamming the kitchen door as he goes. I hear him yell, "And there's no way you are going away next weekend!"

Sitting on the floor, I hug my knees and begin to sob. After I don't know how long, I stand up, shaking like a leaf. I lock all the doors and slowly make my way to the bathroom. I run a hot shower to try and wash away everything. I slide down the cold tiles, the hot water cascading over my body. Wrapping my arms around my knees, I sit there and cry, resting my forehead on my knees. When the water runs cold, I climb out, dry myself off and climb into bed.

Lying in bed, I stare at the ceiling; my mind starts thinking about everything.

Have I changed since dating Clint?

Have I neglected everyone?

Why has Clint changed?

I don't understand this change in him. I'm so confused. I start to doubt everything that I know about Clint, about myself, about everything. I start to cry again, and eventually, I cry myself to sleep.

Before I know it, my alarm goes off. My alarm song of choice at the moment is *Barbie Girl* by Aqua. That song puts a smile one my face, and for a moment, I forget about all of my worries. Jumping out of bed, I head to the bathroom to get ready for college. Looking in the mirror, I notice a huge purple bruise on my left cheek where Clint hit me last night. Gently I run my finger along my cheek, and then I notice marks on my arms from when he grabbed me. I gasp in shock, I cannot go out in public like this. Grabbing my phone I ring in sick and leave a voicemail for Sarah, cancelling our lunch date; we were going to meet up in between classes today.

Feeling pretty shitty, and not up for doing anything, I change into my comfy grey Bonds trackies and LA Kings jersey. Heading to the kitchen, I make myself a coffee and plonk myself on the couch. I go over everything that has happened in the last twenty-four hours to try and make sense out of it.

I'm so confused right now.

Making myself another coffee, I grab my Kindle and try to lose myself in my book but I can't concentrate. I keep reading the same line over and over. Eventually, I give up reading and turn the TV on. I end up watching watch some random cooking show.

A few hours later, I wake up to banging on my front door; my heart freezes thinking that Clint is here. I realise that I'm not sure I want to see him. Cautiously, I walk over to the window and peek through the timber blinds, seeing Sarah standing there with two coffees and a brown paper bag. She must have left work to come see me. She is in her black slacks and a white sleeveless silk top with a big flowey bow at the front. I unlock the door an open it. "Bitch, there better be an orange poppy seed muffin in there to go with my caramel latte."

Sarah is smiling but her face immediately drops, "Kenz, what the fuck happened to you face?"

Subconsciously, I reach up and rub my finger across my cheek; I completely forgot about the bruise. "I, ah, bumped into the kitchen door."

"Nice try, want try and improve that lie?" She pushes past me and comes inside. I wince when she bumps my upper arms, thankfully she doesn't notice. Sarah sits on the couch, tucks her legs under her, and she places the coffees and muffins on the coffee table. I feel her staring at me. Watching me like a hawk as I walk over and sit next to her. Finally, I look over at her and I can't hold back the tears. She pulls me into a hug and gently rubs my back in circles, just like she used to when we were younger. She whispers, "Shhhh."

Leaning into her hug, I cry in her arms for a while. I sit back, sniffle, and wipe my nose on my sleeve as I tug away from her; earning myself a look of disgust from Sarah; she hates when I wipe my nose like that. She's staring at me with raised eyebrows, waiting for my explanation. Sitting back on the couch, I snuggle into the corner with my purple nana blankie. "It's nothing, Sarah, just leave it."

"Kenz, that is not nothing." She points to my face. "Did Clint do this?"

Staring into my lap, the tears start to fall again, "Sar, he's changing. He's not the guy I started dating at the beginning of term. He's always so angry, he appears everywhere I go, he's always waiting for me here. Apparently I'm his, and the latest is, he doesn't want me going away with you this weekend for some reason. I told him I'm going whether he likes it or not. That's when he shoved me against the wall and hit me."

"That fucker." She jumps up and startles me. "Shit, sorry, chicky." She sits down next to me and wraps me into a hug, "Listen to me, Mackenzie." She pulls back to stare directly at me.

"Wow, you called me Mackenzie. You only do that when I am in trouble."

"Mackenzie Merlot, you listen to me and you listen goodly. You need to think long and hard as to whether you want to be with Clint. You have changed. We never see you anymore and he is always with you, like always. I was actually surprised he wasn't here now, but after seeing this." She spins her finger around my face. "I know why."

"But…"

"No buts, lady, you need to look out for you. I seriously think this weekend away is just what you need." Sarah jumps up excitedly and squeals in excitement, "I have an idea, let's blow off the rest of the week and take off now. You need to get away to clear your head and me being the uber, awesome bestie will happily accompany you earlier. Plus work is slow and I'm totally bored out of my brain."

I sniff and wipe my nose on my sleeve, again, earning another scowl from Sarah. "Okay, that actually sounds really great. I think extra time away is just what I need."

"Squee, I'm so excited," she squeals.

"Hang on, we will have to wait till tomorrow, as I have a presentation due..."

"Well that sucks donkey balls," Sarah interrupts me but I put my hand up to silence her.

"If you let me finish, my presentation is due first thing but I should be done by eleven. You can then pick me up from college, like we planned, and we can leave straight from there."

"Woo-freakin-hoo. Okay, I'm going to head home make a few changes to our weekend plans and pack. You finish your assignment and I will see you out outside the college tomorrow at eleven. No later, or I'm stalking in there and dragging your ass out."

"Thanks, Sar, I can always count on you to make me feel better."

"Happy to help, Kenz. That's what best friends are for. Make sure you text me if you finish earlier."

Sarah and I chat for a while and it's just like old times. Before she leaves, she gives me a crash make-up course to cover the bruise on my face. I suck when it comes to make-up, so I really appreciate this help. It reminds me of our makeovers we used to do when we were twelve.

A few hours later, we walk arm in arm out to her car, it feels good to be with her again. She gives me a big hug and tells me to call her if I need anything. I wave as she drives off; I check the letterbox on my way back inside and get excited when there is nothing. *No bills*, I think to myself.

Feeling a lot more relaxed after my visit with Sarah; I head back inside. After locking the front door I turn around I see Clint standing in the kitchen. I freeze and stumble back into the door.

"Hey, Sweetcheeks."

Hesitating a little, I reply, "Hey, C." I race over to the couch, sit down with my purple blankie that Nan knitted for me, cover my legs, and I curl up into myself. I feel really uncomfortable having him here. "What are you doing here?"

"I missed you in class and I was worried, Sweetcheeks."

"I'm fine, I just wasn't feeling very well this morning. Sarah stopped by with a coffee and a muffin. I'm feeling a little better now." I take a deep breath a quickly add, "She and I have actually decided to extend our weekend away, we are now leaving tomorrow after my presentation."

"I thought I told you that you are not going," he snarls through clenched teeth. I notice his hands, fisting by his side.

"And I told you that I was, this isn't up for discussion. If you have a problem with it, then I think you need to leave."

Clint grabs the dish rack throwing it against the wall; cutlery, glass and plate fragments fly everywhere. I sit there open-mouthed and frozen; my heart racing with terror. I'm unable to move for fear that he will pound on me next. Fortunately for me, he turns punches the wall near the kitchen door and storms out. Before he's out the door he yells over his shoulder, "Fuck you, bitch!" and storms off.

I sit there on the couch in shock. After a few minutes, I get up and lock all the doors; I also put the deadlock on. I lean against the front door, close my eyes, and take a deep breath. I look to the kitchen and see the enormous mess that Clint has caused. Shaking my head, I walk to the kitchen and begin to clean up the devastation after his outburst.

Walking past the stereo, I turn it on and crank the music to drown out all the white noise and any thoughts that keep appearing in my head right now. Grabbing the dustpan and brush, clean up the mess and add new cups and plates to my shopping list.

Girls Just Wanna Have Fun by Cindy Lauper comes on. Normally I would sing at the top of my lungs and shake my booty around the room, but I'm too frazzled right now. If that song doesn't excite me, then I really am in a funk.

With the weight of the world on my shoulders, I head to my room to start to packing for my trip away with Sarah. While packing, I forget about all my Clint worries. As soon as I'm finished, I lie on my bed and pull up the covers. I start to think about what I'm going to do and I start to cry again. I don't have a friggin clue on how to handle this. On one hand, I think I'm falling in love with Clint, but on the other, I'm scared to be alone with him.

I let out a frustrated sigh and shout, "Fuuuuck!"

Kicking off the comforter, I head into the bathroom to clean my teeth. Looking up into the mirror I don't recognise the girl reflecting back and it's not because of the huge, now almost blackish purple bruise. I feel lost. Alone. Scared. I finish cleaning my teeth, and before heading back to bed I recheck all the doors are locked.

Once everything is secured I climb back into bed. Grabbing my Kindle from the nightstand, I read for a bit to lose myself. However I can't concentrate, I keep thinking about what I'm going to do.

Eventually, I drift off to sleep.

Around 2:00 a.m., I startle awake and feel like someone is watching me. I turn on the bedside lamp but my room is empty. I shake my head and tell myself I'm going crazy. I lie back down and fall asleep again but I still feel like someone is watching.

7

CLINT

AFTER A LONG DAY, I HEAD OVER TO MACKENZIE'S AND WHEN I GET there, I'm in a pissy mood. Waltzing into her apartment, I storm past her, shoving her into the bench. She smiles, but I'm too pissed for niceties, so I sink down onto her couch to finally relax. *A head job would be great right now.* Her phone is digging into my leg so I grab it, glancing down to see a text ending with, 'love you.'

Now I'm really pissed. My mood darkening by the minute. Why is my Sweetcheeks saying "love you" to someone when she hasn't even told me yet? I bet the bitch is cheating on me.

Thank fuck it's only that slut Sarah messaging her about a girls' weekend, but I don't fucking think so. She is not going away with that tramp; she is such a bad influence AND to not know where they are going, that's just crazy.

What if I need to reach her?

Why is she not thinking about me in all of this?

She goes on and on and on about this fucking weekend, I've told her several times that she isn't going, why isn't she listening to me? Why is she being like this? I can't believe she is talking back to me; she's never done this before, I'm seriously going to loose my shit in a minute.

"Like hell you are, you belong with me." She has really pissed me off now. She's still back chatting so I slam my fist down on the coffee table.

The final straw is when she shakes her head at me and tells me that she isn't mine. Think again, bitch; you are mines...forever. I snap and slam the bitch against the wall. I roughly grab her face and stare directly into her eyes and spit, "You are mines, and I say you are not going away with that slut."

With the rage simmering, I slap her across the cheek and her head slams back into the wall. I let go of her and she slides down the wall, crying. I fucking hate when bitches cry. She rubs her head and looks up at me with sad, puppy dog eyes and asks me to leave, as if I want to fucking stay here anyway.

I throw my hands up in the air. "Whatever, Mackenzie."

I storm through her kitchen, slamming the door on my way out. I'm halfway down the stairs when I bellow, "And there's no way you are going away next weekend!"

Jumping into my car, I throw it into gear, and drive home.

The next day Mackenzie isn't in class, this is the first class this year she has missed. I start to worry about my Sweetcheeks. I decide after this class, I'll head to her place to see if she's okay; after all, I'm a caring and nice boyfriend. I think I'll get her some sunflowers on my way over too, flowers always cheer chicks up...and open their legs.

Pulling up at her apartment complex, I realise I forgot to get the flowers but they are soon forgotten when I see that slut Sarah's car out front. I head down the driveway when I hear her and Sarah walking out. I quickly race up the back stairs, the door is unlocked so I let myself in and wait. A few minutes later my Sweetcheeks comes in the front door, I inwardly sigh when I realise that she is okay and nothing terrible is wrong.

She's blabbering on about going away and I start to fume. Looking at her dumbfounded, does she not remember our conversation last night? She continues to back chat me, I'm a little turned on by her feistiness. I unclench my fists, which I didn't realise I had clenched. I turn and grab the dish rack, and with all the anger coursing through my veins, I throw it against the wall. That stops the bitch in her tracks, she sits there frozen as I punch the wall in anger. It hurts like a bitch but I am too pissed off to care right now. I roar, "Fuck you bitch!" and I storm out.

I get in my car, and like most times when I am pissed off, I drive. I drive around for hours. It's the middle of the night and I find myself back at Mackenzie's place. I try and unlock the door but she has it deadlocked and I can't get in; Goddamn *it*.

Walking around to her bedroom window, I peek in; my beautiful Mackenzie is sound asleep, the moonlight glistening on her silky soft skin, illuminating her gorgeous face.

Seeing her sleeping, looking so alluring, makes my cock harden. I walk over to her front steps, stroking myself through my cargos. I lean against the railing and yank my cock out as I continue to tug and pull on my shaft.

Closing my eyes, I imagine it's my beautiful girl's hand wrapped around my engorged throbbing cock. After a few more strokes, I explode all over her steps, with a contented sigh, marking my territory. Slipping my now limp cock back in my cargos, I blow a kiss to my girl and whisper, "Sweet dreams, Sweetcheeks," before quietly walking back to my car and driving home.

8

KENZIE

SETTING MY ALARM EARLIER THAN USUAL, I HOP UP AND USE THE techniques Sarah showed me yesterday to cover the bruise on my cheek. I also wear a long-sleeved silk shirt to cover my arms. I get to town early so I grab a coffee from Java Lava and go over my presentation one more time.

My presentation goes extremely well and I get 97.5 out of 100, the highest in the class so far, YAY ME. Seriously, I am digging this course and my lecturer Michele is amazing. She really knows her stuff, hence why she probably started the college and has turned it into a world-renowned institution.

She's become a great mentor to me also, not only with school stuff but personal stuff too. I thank her and mention that I'll be away for the rest of the week as I'm heading away with my bestie for the long week-end. She tells that's a good idea and to have a great time and I quote, "Don't do anything that will get you kidnapped, killed or arrested, you're too pretty for jail." She is seriously the coolest person I have ever met. We both laugh as I turn and leave.

Skipping out of the building, I literally, skip into Jordan, again. He's just as hot; if not hotter than the first time I bumped into him. I'd know, with all the times that I've bumped into him since college started. "Shit, dude, I'm so sorry. You must think I'm such a klutz. This is like the fifth time I have run into you this year,"

"Actually, it's about the tenth but who's counting?"

"Obviously you are, Jordan," I laugh, pushing my hair behind my ear.

He starts to laugh too but looks concerned, he reaches out to touch my cheek. "Mackenzie, what happened to your face?"

"Shit," I mumble, I thought I managed to hide the bruise with my make-up this morning, but I guess up this close it's hard to hide. "I, ah, ran into a door." Just as I say that, I see Sarah pull up and I thank her for being on time. "That's my ride, I'll catch ya later. " I run towards Sarah's green Toyota Corolla and jump in, "Hey, bitch, ready to ride?"

"Umm, who's that Hottie McHottie you were just chatting to?"

"That's Jordan, I think he goes here or works nearby. I keep running into him. Like literally running into him, he must think I'm such a klutz."

"Please, the way he watched your ass as you ran to the car, I bet he's thinking about how he can get you on your back and be buried balls deep inside of you, while you scream his name as you have the best orgasm of your life."

"Sarah!" I shout and whack her arm, "You are so crude and FYI, Jordan does not think of me like that." I look out the window and see him staring at us; I smile at him and wave goodbye. "Besides, I'm with Clint."

Sarah doesn't acknowledge that comment, she indicates and we take off but her comment about Jordan liking me sets my mind racing, giving me butterflies; I can't help but smile as I think about Jordan... great, now there's another item to add to my ever-growing list of concerns.

9

JORDAN

I'M SO GLAD THAT I HAVE A LATE START TODAY; I'M REALLY NOT IN THE mood for adulting today. Stopping at the corner store, I pick up a packet of Chicken Twisties and a Diet Coke. *The breakfast of champions.*

Just as I am about to open the glass doors, my arm is grabbed, and I'm flung around. "Back off, asshole, she is my girlfriend." I look up into the wild eyes of the dickwad himself, Clint.

"Excuse me?" I growl.

"I said, back off, she is my girlfriend and I don't appreciate you ogling her like a piece of meat. She is mines."

"Okay, dude, whatever." I shrug free and walk inside to see Mike waiting for me. As I'm walking up the stairs, I start thinking about Mackenzie, again. Whenever I think about her, I can't help but smile. She is the most beautiful girl I have ever laid eyes upon. Today her long blonde hair is down, framing her gorgeous face, her lips are a cherry red colour. What I wouldn't give to kiss those lips, but I can't as she is dating that dickwad, Clint; lucky bastard.

When she crashed into me, again, I inwardly smiled, like I do each time she bumps into me. She says something about being a klutz but I'm lost in her green eyes, sparkling in the sunlight. *God, she is beautiful.*

I can't believe I turn into a blabbering tool when I'm around her. Did I really just confess to counting the number of times she's bumped into me? Why do I become pathetic around her? Thankfully, she just laughs at me. She has the most amazing laugh, and if you get her going, she snorts; it's really cute.

Glancing over at her, I see a bruise on her cheek. Without thinking, I lift my hand to brush the bruise, gently caressing her cheek. When I ask her what happened, her face changes from her happy smile to sadness and hesitation. I quickly pull my hand back and wonder who did this to her? I bet it was that douche she is dating.

She lies to me but before I can reply or ask her any more questions, a car pulls up out front and she says, "That's my ride, I'll catch ya later."

I stare at her ass as she skips off, her denim jeans clinging to her perfect tight butt. As usual, my cock starts to twitch when I watch her ass as she walks away.

Walking over to Mike I slap him on the back. "Hey, asswipe, how's it hanging?"

Mike grabs his crotch and replies, "A little to the left." We both burst out laughing. "What did 'I'm a dickwad' grab you for?"

"He told me to stay away from his girlfriend, she bumped into me, again, on her way out."

"If she was my girl, I'd tell you to stay away too. She is mighty fine if I do say so myself."

"As if you'd stand a chance with her. Besides, I ran into her first therefore as part of our aforementioned bro-code, which was established when we were ten, I get first dibs," I smugly reply before quickly adding, "Not that I'm interested or anything."

"Right, dude, not interested. Come on or we will be late, and Mr. Denon will be pissed."

Is it that obvious that I'm interested in Kenzie? I think to myself as we head into the lecture hall. I've been interested in her since the first time she bumped into me...but I missed my chance. Now she's with that asshat.

10

KENZIE

SARAH AND I ARE DRIVING BACK INTO TOWN AFTER SIX GLORIOUS DAYS AT *Peppers Ruffles Lodge & Spa* in the Gold Coast Hinterland. We wine, we dined, we drank, we pampered and most of all, we chillaxed; it was just what the doctor called for. Looking over to Sarah, I smile, "Sar, thanks for extending our weekend. It was just what I needed."

"I'm happy to help, besides this has been the best six days. I think we need to extend our long weekend, into a weeklong getaway from now on. I haven't felt this relaxed in forever, and I must also add, you look much more relaxed too."

"I am, and if I'm honest, I haven't thought of Clint once. I'm such a bad girlfriend,"

"You are not a bad girlfriend." She, hesitates, and then adds, "Can I be honest with you?"

"When have you not been honest with me?"

"True." Reaching over she squeezes my hand, takes a deep breath, "There's something about Clint that irks me. I can't put my finger on it. Are you sure he's the one you want to be with? What about that other hottie?"

I know she is referring to Jordan but I can't let on about my feelings towards him, she would never let it go. "Which hottie?"

"The one you keep bumping into, Justin?"

"You mean Jordan?" My cheeks flush when I say his name and think about him. "What about him?"

"Well, for starters, you just turned fifty shades of pink when I mentioned his name just now, and this past week, you have spoken about him and not Clint, who IS your boyfriend."

"I did not," Pausing, I add, "Did I?"

"Ya ha, you did. Look, if you want to be with Clint, I'll support you. And if you want to be with Jordan, I'll also support you. Just promise me you'll think about this, I want you to be happy. I want me bestie back. You haven't been you lately, except for the past six days. I finally saw my, Kenzie, this past week."

"I promise to think about it. But truthfully, I'm totally confused right now." Lifting my feet up, I rest them on the dashboard, lean forward, and sigh, "Why can't we live at the spa forever. Be pampered everyday, drink margaritas, and chillax?"

"Well, for one, we aren't billionaires…"

"You just about are. You're lucky your dad is uber rich. I know I have my inheritance, but you literally have no worries in the world."

"No, that's Daddy, not me, and I refuse to mooch off him, but I know what you mean. I work just as hard as anyone else, but if Daddy wants to spoil me, and you by default, I'm not going to say no."

"And that right there is why I love you. You have such a generous heart. I'm so glad you guys moved in all those years ago. Sarah, you are my sister from another mister and I'm so honoured to call you my best friend."

"Naw, I love you too, Kenz. Even though people always mistake us for lovers when we go away together."

In unison, we both shout. "Bitch sistas for life!" Before, we both burst out laughing.

"Seriously, Sar, thanks for this week away. I have to say the high-light for me was our sunset horse ride. That was the most spectacular sunset, I have ever seen." Remembering the sky, I can't help but smile; it was filled with magnificent oranges and pinks; very romantic, especially with the hamper of bubbly and antipasto that Sarah arranged for us.

"I'm happy to assist. I think the highlight for me was the dinner and drinks that first night. I've never eaten such an amazing meal. That creamy garlic mushroom sauce was to die for and the chocolate lava cake was the bomb". *My mouth waters as I remember how amazing that meal was, the word foodgasm comes to mind.*

"Sarah, you really out did yourself with this retreat. Pretty sure that my credit card will hate me this month and I'm positive that my liver needs a holiday, but my body feels amazing. I also have pretty nails; and pretty nails make everything perfect." *I silently add, my mind is relaxed; albeit confused as to what I am going to do but I am relaxed.*

It's almost 8:00 p.m. when Sarah drops me off. I flick on the lights and dump my bags on the floor, deciding that I'll deal with them later. Grabbing a bottle of water, I sit on the couch and smile, as I think about the last six days; they were totally amazing. Sarah really out did herself this year. Undecided on what I am going to do, I change into my PJ's and climb into bed. Even though it was a relaxing week, I'm shattered.

Before I know it, my alarm is blaring and its time to get up and head to college. My alarm song choice at the moment is *Israel's Sun* by Silverchair, the base get me up and going each morning. Jumping out of bed, I head to the bathroom and take a long hot shower. After putting my hair up into a ponytail, I forgo make-up, as the bruises have faded but I do add a touch of lip gloss. I decide to wear the new sundress I bought while away, from this cute little boutique up in the hinterland. Looking in the mirror, I decide to add a jacket, since the bruises on my arms haven't yet completely faded. The dress is black and white with spaghetti straps and comes to mid-calf. I pair it with my Nine West black wedge sandals. Looking at the time, I realise I'm running late, so I make a mad dash to the bus and get there just in time. As I take my seat on the bus, I sigh, no coffee for me this morning, ugh.

As I'm racing into the building, I see Jordan across the street. I smile, wave, and wait for him. He crosses the street, saying "Hey, Mackenzie, did you and your friend have a nice trip?"

"Oh My God! It was seriously amazing. We tried every treatment on the spa menu. I don't think there is one spot on my body that hasn't been pampered. The cocktails were amazeballs and the food was to die for. I think I gained 10kg."

I notice his eyes rake over my body, I feel those damn butterflies appear and I can't help but smile. "You still look amazing to me, and you also look a lot more relaxed then the last time I saw you."

I blush at his comment, but it also causes the butterflies in my tummy to intensify and flutter. He looks at me with compassion and kindness, it makes my smile grow.

"That door must have hit you pretty hard," he snidely adds.

I look up at him, and I'm pretty sure he knows the door story is fake. "Yeah, it did. I'm such a klutz, as you know, with all the times I'm falling for you."

"Falling for me, hey?"

"Umm, I meant into you." I feel my cheeks heat and turn a shade of pink, I look towards the ground in embarrassment.

We walk into the building together, and I'm laughing when I look up, I see Clint. He looks over and smiles but as soon as he sees me with Jordan, his expression instantly changes to rage. He stalks over to us and shoves Jordan in the chest, "Dude, I told you last week, she's mines. Now get the fuck away from my girl." He pauses, before looking directly at me and snarling. "She. Is. Mines."

I look to Jordan and he is staring at Clint. Jordan then gazes towards me and I shake my head, subliminally telling him to let it go. "I'll catch you later, Mackenzie, glad you had a great time away."

Sighing in relief, he walks around Clint, up the stairs, and I see him walk into the lecture room on the right. *Huh, I guess he is a student here.*

Clint grabs my arm roughly and drags me towards the street, and then down the alley near the college. "Ouch, you're hurting me, Clint."

Managing to yank my arm free, I step back, rubbing where he was squeezing. He shouts, "What the fuck is going on with you and that asshole?"

"W..w..wwwhat?" I stammer, looking at him dumbfounded.

"Don't play dumb with me, Sweetcheeks, you were fucking him this weekend, weren't you?"

"What the hell?" I yell, "You know I went away with Sarah, why would you even say that?"

"Don't lie to me, you little bitch. You chicks are all the same. Get what you want and then leave. Everyone always leaves me."

"Clint, I don't have to put up with this." Spinning, I turn to leave, but he grabs my arm, nearly ripping it out of its socket when he turns me around to face him.

"You are mines and mines alone. "

"NO, I am not yours!" I pull my arm free and stalk away. After a few steps, I turn back and point directly at him; I stare into his soulless brown eyes. "You know what Clint? I'm done. I can't do this anymore. I don't like the person you've become, and most of all, I don't like the person I've become. I wish you the best." I turn around and I walk back into the college.

Of course, being Monday morning, Clint and I have our first class together but he doesn't show, I sigh in relief. I find it really hard to concentrate in class, and normally, it's my favourite.

After class, I head to the Java Lava Café for a much-needed coffee. Having just placed my order, I'm digging in my monstrous Guess handbag for my wallet, when the person behind me says, "And add a hazelnut latte, full cream milk, and a double chocolate brownie to that order too, please." They hand over a twenty to pay. I spin around ready to seethe and see Jordan standing there, smiling. His smile stops me in my tracks and then he winks at me. Pretty sure my ovaries went boom.

After staring at him for a few seconds, I smile. "You didn't have to do that."

"It's my pleasure, Mackenzie, but there is an ulterior motive to me buying you a coffee."

"Here we go, what's your condition?"

"You have to have it with me." He winks at me again before smiling smugly at me.

Ovaries: boom…again.

Cheekily, I reply, "I guess I can lower myself to have a coffee with you," winking as I walk past him to the end counter to wait for our coffees.

We grab our food and drinks, and head to a table by the window. Grabbing my coffee, I lift the lid take a deep breath of the caffeine goodness that I am about to enjoy and take a sip. My eyes close and I savour the flavour, letting out a little pleasurable moan. When I open my eyes again, Jordan is staring at me; the look in his eyes is intense but electric. "Who knew drinking coffee could be so erotic?"

My neck and cheeks immediately heat, I lower my head in embarrassment. He reaches over and lifts my chin; I feel a spark as soon as his fingers touch my skin, leaving my chin tingling and warm. He looks directly into my eyes. "Don't be embarrassed, that was the hottest thing I've ever seen, Kenz."

"Umm, that doesn't make me feel any better." Jordan lets go of my chin, and I feel naked and alone, missing his touch. He grabs his coffee, and copies what I just did. I burst out laughing. He opens his eyes and looks at me, trying to contain his laugh, but he can't hold back. We are both laughing and before I know it I'm snorting. He is laughing at me for snorting and it becomes one vicious laugh/snort cycle, as it usually does the first time I snort around someone.

We eventually compose ourselves and manage to have a normal conversation, with no awkward silences. It turns my shitty morning around. He tells me about his course and how he hopes it will lead to a job managing a bar. Jordan is so passionate about beer. It's a total turn on, seeing him so enthusiastic about it. At one point, I zone out and imagine him pinning me to the couch, kissing the life out of me. Yep, I'm going to need a change of undies, as that mental make out session was hot.

As we are finishing up, I look out the window and see Clint glaring at me from the corner. If looks could kill, I'd be dead right now, as would Jordan and everyone in a five-kilometer radius. Jordan notices the change in me and he looks to where I'm staring, and then looks back to me, "Is everything okay with you two?"

I look at him, then I look back to where Clint was standing but he's gone. Looking back at Jordan, I feel my eyes start to water. "Ummm, I broke up with him this morning."

"I'm sorry to hear that." He reaches across the table and gently gives my hand a reassuring squeeze.

"He's not the person I thought he was, the way he spoke to you this morning was one of the final straws. I was so embarrassed."

"You have nothing to be embarrassed about, Kenz. He's a douche, plain and simple."

"Don't be like that, you sound just like him. This week away with my friend Sarah, made me realise that I didn't like the person I'd become while I was with him. I didn't like the person he was becoming either. It's for the best," pausing, I add, "I think."

"Well, he's a fool for pushing you away. If you were mine, I'd do everything in my power to keep you happy and smiling." I can't help but smile at that statement. "Much like you are now," he adds.

Again, I blush at his words. "I bet you say that to all the girls."

"Nope, only the pretty ones."

Looking up, I see he is intently staring at me. I smile back at him and think to myself, *he is the kind of guy I need to be dating.* My phone pings with a text, bringing me back to reality. Reaching into my bag, I slide the screen and see it's a text from Sarah.

SARAH – *Morning bitch. Thanks for a great time away. I think our annual weekend needs to become an annual week...but no fucking horses*

I laugh as I read her text. I quickly reply,

ME – *Sounds like a plan...the horses stay*
ME – *I broke up with Clint this morning*

SARAH – *I'll bring wine and choc chip cookie dough, be at yours in an hour. Love you XoXoX*

ME – *it's a date, see you then. Love you too XoXoX*

I look up to see Jordan staring at me. "Sorry, that was Sarah. I just told her Clint and I broke up, and we now have a date with wine and Jerry."
"Jerry?"
"Ben and Jerry's Jerry."
"Righto," he laughs.
"I have to go meet her now, but thanks for the coffee and chat. Next time it's on me," I say as I stand up and clean away our plates and cups.
"On you, hey?"
"Oh My God, not on me on me, but on me, you know my treat"
Jordan laughs, "You are too funny, Kenz, I can't wait to have coffee on you." He winks at me as he says this. My cheeks heat and I giggle like a schoolgirl. Jordan and I walk out of the coffee shop; I head to the bus stop to go home and he goes back to college.

Sitting on the bus, I think about my coffee with Jordan; my heart rate increases when I think of his smile. I had a really nice time with him and was so relaxed. Smiling to myself, I remember him calling me

Kenz, the way he wraps his tongue around the Z is kind of hot. I'm now imagining other things he can do to me with his tongue and his hands. Clenching my thighs together, I blush when I realise I'm having dirty thoughts on a public bus. My cheeks turn a deeper shade of red and I become hot under the collar.

Deciding to get off the bus a stop early, I duck into the local bottle-o. I'm winning as they have my wine on sale, two for one, so I grab four bottles and race home to chillax and unwind with Sarah. I want to forget all about this morning, well not the coffee with Jordan part.

Placing the wine bottles on the front steps, I notice a stain on them. "I'll clean that off on the weekend," I mumble to myself. I'm digging in my bag for my house keys, when I feel someone behind me. I recognise Clint's cologne, but before I can turn and acknowledge him, he whacks me across the back of the head and I black out.

11

CLINT

THIS PAST WEEK WITHOUT SWEETCHEEKS HAS BEEN TOUGH, I MISS HER SO much. Doesn't she realise that she and I are meant to be together? I can't and will not let her go.

I'm looking forward to today, Mackenzie and I have a class together first thing on Mondays. After class, I'm going to take her to the Dirty Duck, where we are going to get super drunk. Then, I'll take her back to her apartment and fuck her silly. I get hard just thinking about her sweet, sweet pussy.

Looking up, I see her walking in with that asshole that hangs around her like a bad smell, and they are laughing. My blood starts to simmer as I stalk over to them. With all my might, I shove the asshole in the chest, I should pound him into the pavement for laughing with *my* Sweetcheeks.

The pussy has no balls.

He doesn't say anything.

He doesn't fight back.

Pussy.

My blood boils when he looks at my Sweetcheeks and smiles.

Who does this fucker think he is?

I so badly want to beat the shit out of that asshole right at this minute, instead I grab Mackenzie's arm, dragging her towards the street, and down the alley near college. I'm going to find out what the fuck is going on between her and that douche hole, once and for all.

It occurs to me that this weekend she was away with him and not Sarah. Deceitful fucking bitch!

She keeps denying it but the bitch is lying to me, I just know it.

Why do they always lie?

Do I look stupid or something?

Why do they always do this to me?

Reaching out, I roughly grab her, spinning her towards me. I growl between clenched teeth. My blood boiling with fury.

"You are mines and mines alone." I angrily shout.

She pulls away and when she turns back around, our eyes lock; it's magical. My cock hardens seeing the anger in her emerald green eyes boring into me. I'm lost in her beautiful eyes when she shocks me by breaking up with me. I don't think so, she is mines.

She storms off, leaving me standing here in shock. There is no fucking way I'm letting that bitch break up with me. I turn and punch the wall in frustration, I'm too pissed off for the lecture. I decide to skip class and head to the pier to think. I always go there when I need to think, or I drive around but I'm not in the mood for driving today.

Why does this always happen to me?

Why do they always leave me?

I'm a nice guy.

I'm fantabolous in the sack, and my cock is quite impressive, if I do say so myself.

Why do they always leave me?

As I sit at the pier, I think about Mackenzie when it hits me. I know what I have to do. I race back to the college to talk to her, but I see her and that douche in the Java Lave Café together. I fucking knew it! I knew she was with him this weekend and not Sarah.

She looks over at me and her beautiful face lights up when she sees me, but I'm so pissed that she is with him. I can't be near him, or her, right now, I need to calm down. I decide to go to her place and wait for my Sweetcheeks.

On the way to her apartment, the perfect plan comes to mind; I'm going to take her away, it will be just the two of us, together forever.

Sitting in my car I wait for my Sweetcheeks to arrive home. When she gets here she doesn't see me, so I decide to surprise her.

She places her bags on the steps, so she can dig in her ginormous handbag for her keys. *I will never understand why chicks need such a big handbag.* I sneak up behind her and whack her across the back of the head. She collapses into my arms and I catch her before she hits the ground. I'm caring and nice like that.

She groans and screams when she opens her eyes, why is she wailing? Something inside of me snaps when she starts to scream. Pulling my fist back, I punch her over and over, I can't stop.

I tell keep telling her, "You are mines."

I keep punching and kicking her, repeatedly, hoping that it will click in her mind that we are meant to be together. I wish she would stop screaming, fucking bitch.

Sarah and her nosey neighbour arrive, and they are shouting at me to stop but I can't. I need Sweetcheeks to know how much I lover her, to remind her that she is mines. That we belong together…forever.

She groans and I swear I hear her say, "Baby, I love you." I pause, mid-swing and smile. Turning around, I smile and want to show these assholes that she does love me, but there is nothing but anger radiating off them.

Old mate from next door pulls me off her and I stumble down her stairs. Sarah races over to Mackenzie. I sit there frozen until I hear them call 000. I decide to leave Sweetcheeks with her friends, I'll come back later to see her.

Blowing her a kiss, I turn and run off.

12

KENZIE

WHEN I WAKE UP, I'M IN A HOSPITAL BED, WITH A DRIP IN MY ARM, A throbbing head and my body aches from the top of my head, to the tip of my toes. Everything is foggy; I blink a few times for my eyes to adjust to the light when all of a sudden I remember. Everything comes rushing back to. I start to scream as I remember Clint hitting and kicking me at the apartment.

The door to my room flies open and in rushes a nurse and a doctor. Their words are all muffled as the fear I felt earlier courses through my body. They pump something into my drip, causing my body to immediately relax. My eyes become heavy, and I drift back to sleep.

A few hours later I wake up and I see Mum and Skye huddled together on the green pleather sofa. Mum looks over at me and smiles; she shifts Skye off her and comes over to my bed. She sits on the edge and grabs my hand, squeezing it.

"W…where am I?" I stutter, "W…what happened?"

"Honey, you're in the hospital. You were attacked. Do you remember?"

I'm stunned at what Mum tells me, but after a moment of silence, I nod my head and start to cry. Mum stands up and wraps her arms around me. I wince from the discomfort, but I really need a Mum hug right now, so I push through the pain.

Pulling back, I look at Mum and sadly whisper, "I remember

Mum," The tears start to fall again. "I remember it all. Clint attacked me at the apartment. Sarah and Mr. Neil saved me."

Panic sets in again when I start to think about Clint, "Wh...where's Clint?"

"He took off when Sarah and Gavin arrived but the police picked him up earlier this evening and he's currently in jail. The police want to speak to you but the doctor said not today. They'll be coming by tomorrow to get your statement." I just nod my head, too shocked to speak. You read about this happening, but you never think it will happen to you.

I'm starting to get sleepy again when the door to my room opens and in walks a nurse. Smiling, she says, "Hi, Mackenzie. I'm Paula and I'll be looking after you."

"Hi, Paula!"

"On a scale of one to ten, how would you rate your pain right now?"

"I'd say an eleven." Laughing at myself, I lift my hand and rub the back of my head gently before adding. "My heading is killing me, my face hurts, my ribs are aching. Everything hurts."

"I'm not surprised honey, the doctor has prescribed endone for the pain. I'll go and get them for you and I'll be right back." Paula returns a few moments later and hands me the pills and a cup of water. Swallowing the tablets, Paula leaves and I lay back down.

Skye comes over and sits on the end of my bed, rubbing my leg gently. "So glad you're okay, Mac. When Mum got the call, it felt like Dad all over again. We jumped in the car and got here in record time."

"I'm sorry that I made you worry."

"Don't be sorry, I'm just glad he didn't do more damage. Who knows what would have happened had Sarah and Mr. Neil not intervened? Besides, us Merlot's are tough, it takes more than one asshole to bring us down."

"Language, Skye," Mum scolds.

Skye and I both laugh.

Paula comes back about half an hour later. "Sorry, ladies, but visiting hours are over. You can come back tomorrow morning and see Mackenzie."

Mum and Skye both give me a hug and tell me they will be back in the morning.

Sleep eludes me, each time I close my eyes, I relive the attack. It's about

1:00 a.m. when the night nurse gives me something to help me sleep. I drift off quickly but wake up an hour later in a cold sweat, my heart racing. Tears pouring down my cheek, I see his evil face every time I close my eyes. Staring at the ceiling, I wonder, if I'm strong enough to deal with this?

Early, the next morning Mum and Skye are back to visit me. The doctor does his rounds and I am to be discharged later in the day. They decide to go to my place and pick up a change of clothes for me.

Not long after they leave, there's a knock at my door; Sarah pops her head in. As soon as she see's me, she bursts into tears and races over to my bed. She sits in the chair next to the bed, grabs my hand and sobs, I lean forward and rest my head on hers and together we cry. A movement by the door frightens me, I look up to see Jordan standing there. He has one hand in his jeans pocket and the other is holding a tray of coffee. He smiles at me. "Hi," is all he manages to say and for the first time in twenty-four hours, I genuinely smile.

"Hi yourself." I manage to squeak out.

He walks towards the bed and places the coffees on the tray table. He is staring at me and I feel really self-conscious. I let go of Sarah's hand, discretely smoothing down my hair, I look towards the bed as I must look like a mess. My heart rate increases, and I feel my cheeks flush. When I look up into his eyes, a sense of calm washes over me and for the first time since the attack, I relax.

Sarah blows her nose and it sounds like a foghorn. She throws the tissue towards to bin in the corner and misses. She then turns to me. "You scared the freakin shit out of me woman. I got to your place, heard a scream, and raced down the path. Clint was on top of you and he was kicking and punching, mumbling to himself, "You are mines." She pauses to make sure I'm okay, I nod and she continues, "Mr. Neil came out, grabbed him and shouted at Clint to stop. He ran off and Mr. Neil called triple zero while I went to you. The police and an ambulance arrived pretty quickly, you were whisked off here and we gave our statement to the police, and…"

I sniff, "I'm so sorry, Sar."

"Don't apologise but if you ever do that again, I will punch you in the vagina." I cringe at her choice of words, but oddly enough, it also causes me to smile. Man I love this woman, even when she is being totally inappropriate. "Shit, sorry, babe, but please don't ever do that again."

"Not planning on ever doing that again. Trust me."

Turning my head I look out the window, I notice it's a dreary, dark and overcast day outside. *Much like I'm feeling now*, I think to myself, as I look back over at Jordan. With a smile, I say, "Not that I'm not glad to see you, but what are you doing here?" Looking between Sarah and Jordan, I'm confused as to how they got in contact, and also a tad jealous that Sarah has been spending time with him. "How do you two know each other?"

He smiles and takes a seat on the windowsill, and goes to answer but Sarah butts in, "After I had finished with the police at your place, I had to do something. So I headed to the college, hoping that Clint was there so I could kick his ass. I did a Kenz move and smashed into Jordan. He could see the distress on my face and asked what was up. I remember he was the guy checking your ass out before we went away." Jordan and I both blush at this comment, but I'm secretly thrilled that he's embarrassed about it. "I told him what happened when I got to your place, he and I then searched around the city for Clint, but we had no luck. I felt to stupid and helpless."

"Sar, you are not stupid. If anyone is stupid, it's me. You warned me about Clint, several times, but I didn't listen. This is entirely my fault."

In unison they both shout, "NO!"

Before Sarah can reply, Jordan says, "This is not your fault, Kenz, this is that asshat, Clint's, fault. Don't you ever say this was your fault."

Smiling at them both, I nod in agreement, but deep down I know this is my fault.

Reaching out, I grab one of the coffees, take a sip, and moan.

"What is it with you, coffee, and moaning, Kenz?" Jordan says with a grin.

I giggle, shrugging my shoulders, I smile and take another sip of this amazing brew. As I savour that sip of coffee, I think to myself, *I really like him calling me Kenz*. I glance over at him as he is taking a drink, I check him out and smile. Hiding my grin behind my coffee cup, I continue to smile but Sarah sees. She grins back at me and winks. That butterfly feeling from when we had coffee the other week is back, with a vengeance.

I'm lost in thought when the door opens, Mum and Skye walk in with my bag and another tray of coffee. Skye nudges Mum. "Told you Sarah would have bought coffee, she is just as much of an addict as Mac is, if not more." Sarah and I look at each other and shrug our shoulders in agreement and laugh.

It's true, we are. If I could drink coffee intravenously, I totally would.

Mum eyes Jordan sitting on the windowsill, then looks at me and smiles. "Mum, Skye, this is Jordan, a friend from college. Jordan, this is my mum, Margaret, and sister, Skye."

Standing up he puts his hand out to shake Mum's hand. "It's a pleasure to meet you Mrs. Merlot and Skye."

"Please, call me Margaret. Mrs. Merlot is my mother-in-law and I'm nothing like her."

The conversation is flowing and its comfortable, not awkward like it was with Clint. Jordan gets along really well with Mum and Skye, which makes me happy. No one, except for me seemed to get along with Clint.

There is a knock at the door, it opens and in walks two police officers. "I'm Officer Ferguson, and this is my partner, Officer Jones. Are you up for a chat Ms. Merlot?"

"Please, call me Kenzie and yeah, that's fine."

"Do you want everyone to stay?" Officer Ferguson asks me.

Nodding my head, "Yes, if that's okay, I'd like them to stay."

"That's fine. I'd like you to know that Clint MacNicholson has officially been charged with assault causing grievous bodily harm. He made bail earlier this morning but there is a domestic violence order (DVO) in place. He cannot come within fifty meters of you, except for the court appearance. Someone from the department of prosecutions will be in touch and they will inform you of dates and anything else that they need."

I sigh in relief that he has been charged, but I'm also scared that I will have to face him again in court.

"We will need your recount of what happened yesterday."

Mum sits on the bed next to me, squeezes my hand and whispers, "You can do this Mackenzie. I'm right here."

Mum's words of encouragement give me the strength that I need to give my statement. Officer Jones sets up a recorder, I take a deep breath, close my eyes and begin.

"I had just gotten home and I was digging in my handbag for my house keys. I felt someone behind me and I knew it was Clint, I smelled his cologne. He whacked me on the back of the head and I fell into his arms, I blacked out. Then I remember screaming in agony. He was punching and kicking me, each impact harder than the last." The tears are pouring down my face by this point. Sarah hands me a glass of water, I take a sip. Taking a deep breath, I try and slow my rapidly beating heart. The fear I felt yesterday is bubbling to the surface. I'm not sure that I'll be able to finish. Taking another deep breath, I manage to continue. "I remember screaming for him to stop but he didn't. He kept repeating, 'You are mines' over and over and over. Eventually, I blacked out from the pain and when I woke up I was here."

Reaching over, Officer Jones turns off the recorder. "That timeline of events matches up with the other witness statements." He digs into his pocket and hands me a card. "Here's my card, if you think of anything else or have any other questions, please do not hesitate to contact me."

"Thanks Officer."

Mum escorts them out of the room and after closing the door, she comes back to the bed. Wrapping her arms around me, she whispers. "I'm so proud of you, baby girl."

"Thanks Mum." I sniff.

I excuse myself to have a shower. Even though I'm in a crappy hospital shower, with zero pressure, this is the best shower that I have ever had. Digging in the bag, I pull on the denim shorts and sunflower shirt that Mum packed and make my way back into the room. I bump the bed trolley as I'm getting back into bed and wince in pain, "Shit... fuck...shit." I grab my side. Jordan is there to push the table away and help me back into bed.

Mum looks at me. "Mackenzie, language."

"Sorry, Mum, but that really freakin' hurt." She glares at me again over my language.

The doctor walks in and asks everyone to leave, so he can check me over once more before discharging me. Everyone slowly shuffles out, and he proceeds to poke and prod me like I'm a piece of meat. He's happy and I'm allowed to go home. He recommends that I follow up with my local doctor in a week's time. He also gave me details for a therapist to talk to.

Everyone shuffles back in when the doctor leaves, and I say, "Let's get me out of here." Jordan carries my bag and we all make our way to the car park. We say our goodbyes, gentle hugs all round and Sarah and Jordan agree to pop over tomorrow. They head to the left, while Mum, Skye, and I head up a level and make our way back to my apartment.

Mum and Skye stay with me for the next week until I can do most things myself. You don't realized how much you use your ribs until they hurt like a bitch when you try to do anything. Sarah is over for breakfast the morning they leave and as they pull out of the driveway, I start to cry. She carefully pulls me into a hug, and ushers me back inside. She demands I lay on the couch as she heads into the kitchen. She returns with a bottle of wine and a tub of ice cream. I look at her and smile; she knows just what I need, when I need it. I don't even care that's its 10:00 a.m. and I'm drinking wine. After what I've been through, I deserve it.

We spend the rest of the day on the couch drinking wine, eating ice cream, and watching *One Tree Hill*. This is just what the doctor ordered.

13

CLINT

SOMETHING SNAPS WHEN I GET TO SWEETCHEEKS' HOUSE, I DON'T MEAN TO hurt her. After Sarah and nosey Mr. Neil intervened, I take off. I drive around and around until I calm down.

Before heading home, I stop by my Sweetcheeks apartment but she isn't there. I wonder where she could be?

Stopping at Maccas, I get a feed and head back to my place. When I get home the police are here. Oh no, something must have happened to Mackenzie and that's why she wasn't home.

The Officer walks over to me, "Are you Clint MacNicholson?"

"Yeah. What's it to you?"

"You are under arrest in relation to the assault of Mackenzie Merlot. You're not obliged to say or do anything, unless you wish to do so, but whatever you say or do may be used in evidence. Do you understand?"

"I understand." I mumble as I'm handcuffed and escorted to the squad car.

We arrive at the station and a few hours later, I am formally charged with assaulting Mackenzie. I'm not allowed to see or be near my Sweetcheeks; that's going to kill me.

A few weeks later at my court hearing, I manage to get a glimpse of her, she looks so beautiful, my cock comes to life. It breaks my heart that I can't touch her. When I see that she was with that slut and asshole, my blood starts to boil.

"She. Is. Mines." I growl under my breath.

My lawyer persuades me to plead guilty. Luck is on my side and I'm only to serve two years. Sweetcheeks bursts into tears when I'm sentenced. Her reaction proves to me that deep down, she still cares for me. As they lead me out of the courtroom, I look over at her and smile.

One day, we will be together again, Sweetcheeks, one day.

14

KENZIE

...6 weeks later

For the last six weeks I have only seen three people: my therapist Jeannie, Sarah, and Jordan. I've only left the house for my doctor appointments or therapy. I started to buy my groceries online and get them delivered, so I don't have to leave home. I feel protected this way, locked in my little cocoon, safe and sound. A plus, I'm saving heaps without the impulse buys, so it's win/win. My local bottle shop, *Dan Murphy's*, also delivers so I don't even have to go out and get my wine and beer either; hashtag winning.

The only time I was truly frightened at home, was when I got a locksmith in to change all the locks, add window locks and another deadlock to the front and back doors. He was running late, neither Sarah nor Jordan could be here, so I had to do it by myself. The hour he was here was pretty rough but I survived; just. I sat on the couch and didn't move a muscle. My eyes followed him every time he came into the lounge room; I'd hold my breath until he left the room. As the minutes ticked by I slowly started to crumble and freak out, my heart pounding with every second he was in my apartment. Sweat was beading on my brow. When he said he was finished, I nearly passed out with relief.

As soon as he left, I completely lost it. Racing around, I deadlocked all the doors and windows before heading to my bedroom. Hiding and rocking in the corner, I knew I had to call Jeannie. When I dialed her number, I could barely breathe. My chest tightening as the panic attack set in.

After a few moments, she had calmed me down: my breathing returning to normal and the tightness in my chest disappearing. She told me that it was a massive step that I allowed a man alone into my house, and I should be proud of myself. After hanging up, I sat for a little longer going over what she said. She was right, I *am* strong. I can go on with my life, without fear.

A few days later, I'm chatting with Jeannie, and we decide it is time I get back to my everyday life and routine, which includes college and seeing my friends, in public and not at my apartment. I admit to her that without the support of Jordan, I don't think I would be as strong and confident as I am. I finally tell her about the time, a few weeks ago when Jordan popped over between classes. He found me in a heap in the corner in my bedroom. I'd been to the letterbox and a delivery guy tapped me on the shoulder. I completely freaked out. Jordan sat with me for the whole afternoon. He even let me watch *The Hills*, and he hates that crap. He has seen me at my weakest moment and not once has he made me feel afraid or inferior.

He's become my person...my rock.

I'm not one hundred percent sure I'm ready to go back to real life just yet, but I can't keep sitting at home, dwelling on what happened. If I do, I'd be letting him win, and Clint does not get to win.

I refuse to let him win.

I'm stronger than that.

I am a survivor.

After I returned from my appointment with Jeannie, I decide there is no time like the present. Pulling on my big girl undies, I call Michele. While I'm waiting for the call to connect, I smile. *Today I take back my life; Mackenzie Merlot is back!*

After the call connects, I take a deep breath and explain that I'm ready to come back to college and asked if it's okay. She says I'm more than welcome to come back, she also reiterates that Clint has been expelled from the college, and there are rumors circulating around about what happened.

Due to the circumstances of my absence, Michele has given me an extension on the two assignments I missed, and she is confident that I will be finished in time to graduate in October, with the rest of the class. If not, I will have to wait until March.

Sarah and Jordan are at my apartment, and we are having Indian take-away and a few beers. Taking a deep breath I say, "So, I'm going back to college tomorrow."

They both look at me and don't say anything. I'm starting to think that they don't agree, when Sarah turns to Jordan. "Cough up, buddy, told you she'd be back before the two month mark."

Shaking his head, he grabs his wallet and hands over fifty dollars. Looking at me, he says, "Even though you just cost me fifty bucks, I'm glad you're getting back out there"

"You guys bet on me? Seriously?"

They both reply, "Yep."

Sarah comes over, hugs me, and whispers so Jordan can hear, "Thanks for winning me fifty bucks, but even if I didn't win, I'm happy you are getting on with your life. I would hate to see assface douche hole win."

"Assface douche hole, I like that. Has a good ring to it. Jeannie and I were talking yesterday and I think it's time. As you said, we don't want assface douche hole to win."

Jordan smiles at me. "I'm so proud of you, Kenz. Do you want me to pick you up in the morning?"

"Thanks, Jordan, but I'm going to catch the bus. To get back to the old me, I need to keep to my original routine and the bus is it. I will take a coffee break, if you are free? After all, I still owe you one."

"Coffee it is then," he says, with a big smile on his face, causing those butterflies to once again take flight.

After dinner, we decide to watch *Prison Break*. It's about 10:00 p.m. when they both leave. Grabbing the rubbish, I walk them out. After saying our goodbyes, I race back inside, lock all the doors, and jump into a steaming hot shower. I put on my navy blue satin pajama shorts and Wine Time Finally singlet, and I snuggle in bed with my Kindle, reading the next book in the Break series.

Today is my first day back at college: my emotions are all over the place. I'm excited and scared but most of all, I'm confident. The first face I see when I'm walking into the building is Jordan's. He sees me, waves, and rushes up to me. He envelopes me in a bear hug and I smile into his chest. "It's so good to see you here at college, with you hair done and wearing actual clothes, Kenz." He is trying to hold back a laugh. I look up at him in shock and then I laugh too because he's right. For the last six weeks, I've lived in trackies and a singlet, with my hair piled up in a topknot. If I were having a good day; I'd also put a bra on.

Still laughing, I reply, "Hardy har har, Jordan." I can always count on him to make me laugh; he really has been my rock over the last six weeks.

He smiles and I swear my ovaries explode, just like they did on the first day of college. I smile at that memory. Draping his arm over my shoulder, we turn and head in for our first class of the day.

The first week back at college was tough but I survived. It was the pity looks and the whispers that got to me, but Jordan and, his best mate Mike Mustange, were always there to assist me. I've gotten to know Mike much better since my attack and I love to hate him. He's my 6-foot-1, bald-headed teddy bear with a goatee, and a heart of gold. He comes across all tough and macho, but he's a big softie underneath his grough exterior. Pretty sure they each have a secret, 'Kenzie is in distress' beacon because they were always there when I needed help.

Jordan and I are hanging out more and more and for the first time since the incident, I'm genuinely happy and content. Every Friday we end up at the Joker; the Dirty Duck holds too many memories and I'm not ready to deal with those yet. Sarah and her new boyfriend, Josh, always join us. We become the four amigos, or five if Mike tags along.

Jordan and I officially started dating a few weeks before I graduated. I managed to catch up and get everything finalised so I can graduate with my class on schedule.

It took me a long time to decide that I wanted to date Jordan, in the back of my mind I kept thinking, what if it happens again? Deep down, I know he's not Clint, but it's still there, niggling at me. It wasn't until Jeannie made me realise, that my fear won't immediately disappear, there will be set backs, like the deliveryman incident, but it was all part of the healing process.

At a session with Jeannie one afternoon, that was when I realised I can't keep living in fear. By living in fear I let Clint win and I am stronger than that. See I can even use his name now, even though assface douche hole has a great ring to it. I remember her words from that day clearly, "You are the owner of your emotions. You control everything. You are the only one holding you back." Those words really stuck with me.

Once I finally admitted my feelings for Jordan, I fell for him and I fell hard. For the first time in a longtime, I feel free, happy, and safe, and I knew I would survive.

My new motto is "I am Mackenzie Merlot and I'm a survivor."

15

JORDAN

It is so nice to see Kenz smiling again, like really smiling. Even though we have only been hanging out for a few weeks, I can already tell the difference between her fake and her real smile. When it's her real smile, her eyes sparkle and her face lights up.

It feels like I've known her forever, we click on every level. We have the same taste in music, *Empire Records* is our favourite movie, we both love beer; especially craft beers. Oddly, we like white wine in summer, and red wine in winter; I've never met anyone who drinks and likes wine like this. But most of all, we agree wholeheartedly that the best way to spend a Sunday afternoon, is down at the local pub having a few brewski's with friends.

Even though what Clint did was horrible and horrific, it bought us closer together. The last six weeks have been tough, not only for her but for me too. I'll never forget how I felt when I ran into Sarah at the college the day she was attacked. If hearts could break, I swear mine broke into a million tiny pieces that day.

When I walked into her hospital room the day after, and I saw her beautiful face, bruised and swollen, my heart skipped a beat and started to race erratically. I swear it was going to beat out of my chest. It was in that moment that I realised, I was falling for Mackenzie Merlot.

After visiting her at the hospital, I broke down and cried when I got home. Relief flooded through my body that she was safe and okay, but all the emotion I was holding in came rushing out.

Keeping my feelings for Kenz hidden was tough. I didn't want to scare her; she'd been through enough as it was. Kenz had just been to hell and back, she didn't need me to make it harder, even though she made my cock hard, constantly. I'd get hard seeing her smile, seeing her laughing. Actually, I get hard whenever I think about her. And when she sips her coffee, that is the ultimate hard on.

Kenz has no idea how sexy she is, and that only increases her sexiness.

Selfishly, I bought her coffee all the time, just so I could hear her moan. Hearing that was enough to make me smile, plus it gave me an excuse to see her. Hearing her moan was stored in my spank bank for use later…when I was alone. Don't judge me, you'd totally do it too if you heard her.

One Saturday, when I was at the coffee shop near Kenz's place, I bumped into Sarah, who had the same idea. Adding another coffee for Sarah to the order, we waited together. She turned to face me, staring me in the eyes she leant forward, pointed directly at me and warned, "You better not hurt her, buddy," She poked me in the chest. "She is not only my best friend, but she's also like a sister to me. If you hurt her, I will hunt you down, and you will feel pain like you have never felt before."

Looking back at her, right in her eyes, I replied. "Sarah, I would never do anything to intentionally hurt Kenz. She is the most amazingly beautiful person, inside and out, that I have ever met. If I get a chance with her, I assure you that I will never do anything to jeopardize that or her. It will be my life's mission, to give her the happily ever after that she deserves."

Sarah looked at me dumbfounded. "Um, wow, that totally was not what I was expecting you to say, but I'm very glad that we are on the same page, and that you will look after my friend when you get your chance."

Our order is called, Sarah collected it and walked out. I stood there, staring at her retreating form in shock. Her reply was totally out of left field and it knocked me off kilter. I was sure she was going to warn me off, tell me to stay in the friend zone. Walking out to my car, I smiled to myself when I realised that she said when and not if. My heart did a little flutter at that tidbit of information.

Kenz and I see each other just about every day, and most weekends we hang out, either at her place or mine. This weekend she suggested we go out for lunch. Reaching for my phone, I tell her I'll call Sarah to meet us and she hesitantly says, "No, just us. If that's okay?"

Smiling at her, I reply, "Yeah sure. That's fine." Inside I'm mentally high fiving myself, yelling fuck yeah and doing my happy dance; yes I have a happy dance. I try to act all cool, but my heart is bursting with happiness right now. I'm pretty sure she knows that I'm falling for her, just like I'm pretty sure she's falling for me too.

Kenz and I have our first date, unofficially of course, and it could not have been more perfect. We go to Just Catch and get fish-n-chips, then head to the pier and watch the sunset.

We sit down at the pier for hours, chatting and laughing. It isn't until we realise it's dark out that we pack up and head back to her apartment. I pull up at her place, and after seeing her inside safely, I drive home. The drive home is a blur, but I do know that I've never felt so happy to be on a non-date before.

Two weeks before Kenzie's graduation, I finally grow a pair and I officially ask her to be my girlfriend. It's a Saturday afternoon and we are sitting on her couch, watching some chick crap, when I ask. My heart is pounding, my palms sweaty. I look over at her and I decide that it is now or never. It isn't very romantic, I'm too nervous for romance, I just blurt it out. "Kenzie, will you be my girlfriend?" The silence after I ask is deafening, I feel like I'm going to throw up, but when I see her face is lit up like the Rockefeller Center Christmas tree, I know she is going to say yes.

Smiling, she immediately says, "Jordan, I'd love to be your girlfriend".

Best seven words ever to have been spoken.

Before my brain has a chance to register that she actually said yes, she leans over and kisses me. I'm telling you, this kiss is the kiss of all kisses. It feels like fireworks are exploding within my body, and when she runs her fingers through my hair and pulls me closer to deepen the kiss; I nearly come in my pants like a horny fifteen-year-old.

Pulling back from the best kiss ever, she looks deep into my soul and whispers, "Hi, boyfriend."

Smiling, I lean forward, placing a gentle kiss on her nose before drawing back, I run my finger slowly down her now healed cheek and whisper, "Hi, girlfriend."

She gives me a megawatt smile, before kissing me again. My cock begins to twitch. She climbs over and straddles my lap, my cock is now pressing painfully against my fly but I wouldn't change a thing. We make out on her couch, like horny teenagers on a Saturday night at the drive-in. We are interrupted by the sound of the kitchen door slamming shut, and Sarah yelling, "I've come to clean ze pool!" Sarah and Josh walk into the lounge room, Josh laughing at her cheesiness.

Kenz and I freeze, we turn our heads to see both Sarah and Josh standing there open-mouthed. In unison we both say, "Hey, guys," We both burst out laughing; we constantly do the speaking in unison thing.

Sarah smiles, turns to Josh, slaps him on the chest, and says, "Cough up, buddy, told you they'd be together before Kenz graduated." Josh shakes his head, reaches into his wallet and hands over one hundred bucks.

He looks to us both and says, "Seriously, guys, you couldn't have held off a little longer?"

With that statement we all burst our laughing.

Kenz climbs off my lap and steps into the kitchen and grabs four beers out of the fridge. She leans in to Sarah and says, "Did you seriously bet on me again?"

"Yep, and at the rate I'm going I'll soon be able to buy my very own vineyard."

"I think I should get a cut of these winnings, after all it's due to me you keep winning."

"Keep dreaming Kenz. I won fair and square."

Sarah grabs a beer from Kenz and then Kenz passes one to Josh and me. The girl's head down the hall into Kenzie's room to get ready to go out to dinner. Josh sits down and we catch the last of the footy game on TV while we wait.

Half an hour later, they both emerge and my heart stops. Kenzie is wearing a sexy as hell purple dress that accentuates her curves and these killer heels that make her already sexy legs look even sexier. Managing to stand up, I walk over to her. "Wow, you look stunning."

Sarah squeals, "Fuck, yes, she does. My girl is smokin hawt!"

She turns towards Josh, clears her throat while doing a spin. Josh rolls his eyes. "Sarah, you also look hot." He wraps his arms around her and dips her upside down. She squeals, and when he places her back on her feet, he kisses her senseless.

While they are making out, I gently grab Kenz around her waist, hugging her closer to me. Lowering my head, I gently place my mouth against her soft luscious lips. Her tongue slipping inside my mouth, our tongues twisting together passionately before resting our foreheads together, gazing into each other's eyes.

Breaking our moment, Josh slaps me on the back. "Come on, you two, lovebirds, I'm starving."

Kenz pulls away and grabs her purse off the breakfast bar, I grab my keys and wallet, and we all head to Dragon Garden; for the first of many official double date nights.

———

Sarah and Josh drop us back at Kenzie's place after dinner. We offer for them to come in for a nightcap, but they decline, thankfully. I want some alone time with my girlfriend. *Man, I love saying that Kenzie is my girlfriend.* As they drive off, I grab Kenzie's hand and entwine our fingers together as we head inside. Kenzie is taking her shoes off, so I grab a couple of beers from the fridge and we sit on the couch chatting, just like we used to.

A few hours later, I get up to leave, and Kenzie reaches out grabbing my wrist. She looks up at me and hesitantly says, "Please stay."

"Are you sure?"

She stands up and lifts her purple dress over her head; she is standing there like a goddess in a black lacy strapless bra and matching lacy boyleg undies.

"I guess you are sure then."

She steps towards me giggling, before wrapping her arms around my neck, nuzzling her way to my ear and whispers, "I've never been more sure of anything in my life, Jordan."

Placing my hands under her ass, I lift her up and she wraps her legs around my waist and kisses me. I carry her down the hall into her bedroom, gently setting her down next to the bed. Reaching out, she slowly untucks my navy dress shirt. One by one, she carefully undoes the buttons, the anticipation is killing me. Once the buttons are all undone, she rakes her fingers up my stomach and pushes the shirt off my shoulders and down my arms. She then turns her attention to the button and fly of my jeans, but her fingers are shaking. Her breathing is labored. Placing my hand over hers, I undo the button and fly; she places her hands inside the waistband and pushes them down along with my boxer briefs. Stepping out of them, I stand there in front of her fully naked. My dick is rock hard and standing to attention.

Stepping towards her, I wrap my arms around her silky soft shoulders and I pull her into me, our lips colliding. She slightly opens her mouth, and I take the chance to slip my tongue in. I gently nip her lip as I pull back. Looking into her eyes, I see they are ablaze with lust and desire, and it makes me harder knowing she wants this as much as I do. Kissing down her neck and along her collarbone, I unclasp her bra and it falls to the floor.

When I see her breasts for the first time, I near come right there. She has the most amazing tits I've ever seen; they are the perfect size for my palm. Her pert pink nipples are erect and hard, I can't wait to suck them. Gently massaging them, I softly tug her nipples, rolling them between my thumb and finger, before bending down and taking one into my mouth, gently suckling and nibbling the taut peaks.

She pushes away; I panic, thinking that she doesn't want this anymore but she bends down and quickly removes her undies. We are both now fully naked, the air between us thick with erotic lust. Glancing down her beautiful body, I see her bare smooth pussy is glistening already. Stepping forward, I gently place my hands on her cheeks, "Are you sure about this Kenz?"

She looks deep into my eyes. "Yes, Jordan, I'm sure. You make me feel safe and I've never felt that before. I want you to make love to me." That's all the reassurance I need, I lean forward and kiss her, pulling her closer to me; I escalate our kiss. Reaching down I rub my finger around her clit, she is soaking wet. We both moan into our kiss, as I continue to circle her clit with my finger, she begins to grind her pussy on my hand.

Easing her back gently, I lay her on the bed. Once we are both lying down, I kiss my way down her chest. Licking from her belly button to the top of her mound; when I reach her clit I take it into my mouth and suck. Her back arches off the bed and she moans, shoving her pussy further into my face. Inserting a finger, I suck on her clit harder. She moans as I lick down her slit, flicking my tongue into her tight hole, before licking back up to her clit. I gently bite her swollen nub as I insert another finger. Arching her back as I hook my finger around to find her G-spot, her movement, effectively shoving her pussy further onto my face.

She reaches out and tugs on my hair, while I continue to suck and nip on her clit, I feel her walls clenching around my fingers. I hear her whimper, "I'm coming." She tugs harder on my hair as I thrust my tongue deeper into her pussy, my tongue and fingers pumping in and out, faster and faster until I feel her explode all over my fingers and tongue. I suck all of her glorious juices, as she comes down from her orgasmic high.

When I feel her relax, I work my way back up her amazing body. Looking into her glorious green eyes, I say, "Hi, girlfriend."

She giggles and tugs me in for another kiss. I swear each kiss is more electric than the last. Breathlessly, she pulls back, "Hi, boyfriend."

Before I register what she's doing, she wraps her hand around my dick and pushes me onto my back. Stroking my cock as she works her way down my chest. When she reaches my cock, she licks the tip while continuing to pump up and down my shaft with her hand. She hollows her cheeks and takes my cock deep into her mouth and sucks. "Fuck me, Kenz, ohm yeah, suck me harder." She keeps pumping and sucking. I feel myself about to come when I lift her up. "Kenz, as much as that is fuckin' amazing, when I come with you for the first time, I want to be buried balls deep inside of you."

Giggling, she slowly kisses her way back up to my mouth. I grab her face and slam my lips against hers. She reaches into her nightstand, grabs a condom, and straddles me, ripping it open with her teeth before slowly rolling it over my thick, throbbing cock. Getting up on her knees, she slowly lowers herself onto me, her eyes rolling back in delight, as she seats herself completely on my cock.

Watching her ride my cock is the hottest thing I have ever seen. We move into a sensual and evocative rhythm, our bodies aligning together. Closing my eyes to savour the moment, I groan with desire, opening my eyes, I see Kenz squeezing her tits and tugging on her nipples. She moans and I feel her muscles tighten on my cock. She explodes around me and screams my name as she rides out her orgasm, letting out one final moan as she grinds her hips on my cock.

With a guttural grunt, I release my seed deep inside of her and we ride the final waves of our orgasm together.

Kenz collapses onto my chest, we are both breathless, our hearts frantically beating. After a few minutes, she lifts off me; I remove the condom and place it in the bin in the corner. Lying back down, she snuggles into my side and throws her leg over me. We lay there in each other's arms, subconsciously, I rub my hand up and down her arm; I'm so content right now. *The world could end, and I'd die a very happy man,* I laugh at that thought.

Kenz lifts her head to look at me. "What's so funny?"

"I was just thinking that I could die right now and I'd be okay with that. Kenz, that was the most intense sex that I've ever had. You are amazing Mackenzie Merlot. I'm so glad that you came crashing into my life."

Her smile grows and her cheeks turn a deeper shade of pink, enhancing her post orgasmic glow. "Jordan, you're amazing and I'm ever so glad I bumped into you, too."

Leaning over, I kiss her. Pulling back, I stare into her eyes, I'm lost in a sea of green and I smile. She returns my smile and my heart skips a beat. "Kenz, you are the most beautiful person I have ever met and your after orgasm glow is sexy as."

She reaches up, grabs my face and kisses me. I roll us over, so I'm between her legs; my cock is already hard when she starts to rub her pussy against me. Grabbing another condom, we make love again before falling asleep, in each other's arms.

16

KENZIE

GRADUATION COMES AROUND QUICKLY, AND AFTER STRUGGLING TO CATCH up, I pull some long nights and big weekends and I manage to complete all that I missed. Officially, I graduate with the rest of my class in October, minus one person of course.

Clint is still safely locked away, not able to hurt me or anyone again. I used to check in weekly with the Department of Corrections to ensure he is still locked away, but I haven't checked in with them or thought about him in a long time. I'm ever so grateful that he's locked away, it allows me to get on with my life but most of all, I'm not letting him win.

Graduation day is hectic but amazing at the same time. Mum and Skye travel down for it and stay with me for the weekend. I finally tell them that Jordan and I are dating. "Finally," they both say in unison. I'm glad they approve and are happy for me; looking back, I wish I had listened to everyone's concerns regarding Clint. Maybe then he wouldn't have assaulted me.

Before the ceremony I'm super nervous, I'm scared that I'll trip on my gown and fall flat on my face. To be on the safe side, I decide to wear black ballerina flats, with my Nine West black three-quarter pants and a fuchsia silk sleeveless top. After several different hairstyle trials, I decide on a simple and chic, low bun. Looking at myself in the mirror, I look and feel sophisticated, I feel like a graduate.

The ceremony goes off without a hitch and I don't trip when I walk up onto the stage to collect my diploma. When my name is called, Mum, Skye, and Jordan are all shouting with glee; it's quite embarrassing but I can't help but smile. I've not felt this happy, or relaxed in forever, it's very refreshing. Kenzie is finally back.

Once the ceremony is over Mum and Skye take me out for a celebration dinner, just the three of us. It is nice to be just us girls again, I realise how much I miss them. They bought me a beautiful gold and white gold watch as a graduation present; I cry happy tears when they give it to me.

After dinner Jordan meets up with us for drinks. We head to the casino, and as Skye is under eighteen, she heads back to my apartment. Jordan, Mum and I end up doing karaoke and drinking margaritas until three in the morning. Man, do we all have horrible hangovers the next morning.

Waking up early the following day, I decide to do some laundry while I wait for the coffee to brew. Mum and Skye are still sleeping, so I quietly grab the basket and head down to the laundry, which is located in the garage. Walking through the kitchen, I open the back door and there is a package sitting on the top step, addressed to me.

It's a beautiful eggplant purple box with a shimmery silver bow. I immediately smile and think it's from someone close, as it's my favourite colour. When I open it up its full of sunflowers, I smile and think they are from Jordan…unbeknownst to me, they're not from him.

The weekend with Mum and Skye flies by. I wish they could stay longer but they have to get back in time for Skye to be at school on Monday, as she has her end of year finals. It's hard to believe my baby sister will be in her last year of high school next year. Just before lunch on Sunday, I wave Mum and Skye off, and this time I cry happy tears when they leave.

Jordan wraps his arms around my waist, and we stand there, enjoying being in each other's arms. It isn't until Sarah and Josh pull up that our trance is broken. Sarah knew I'd be a little upset with them leaving, so they decided to pop over and whisk us away for a relaxing beach day.

This impromptu beach trip is just what I need, Sarah knows me too well. We all have a great afternoon and it definitely takes my mind off missing Mum and Skye. As usual, I proceed to get extremely sunburnt and my face looks like a Goddamn ninja turtle from my sunglass tan.

Who knew that expired sunscreen did not work? I didn't, but I do now, ouch.

After everything that happened and working super hard to graduate on time, I decided I wasn't going to get a job until the new year. A little 'me' time was called for. However, the universe had other ideas, and two weeks after graduation I was offered an amazing job at the local tourism board. Turns out Michele knew someone there, and when she heard they were looking for someone she suggested me. I felt pretty honoured to have her recommend me.

As fate would have it, this job didn't start until January so I still got to have a few months off before entering the workforce. Early in the new year, I start working at the tourism board. It was an amazing position and I loved going into work each day. It really was my dream job.

Just before Easter, Jordan and I officially move in together, we are pretty much living together anyway. When we made it official we decided to get a new place, somewhere that was ours and had no memories. My apartment has memories of Clint and I don't want those memories tarnishing the relationship that Jordan and I have. Some nights, those memories haunt me but a fresh start with Jordan is what we both need. He agreed when I told him why I wanted us to get a new place and the house hunting began. Even though moving in together is a big step, I have no qualms about it at all.

I'm excited for this next adventure and I'm so glad to be taking that step with Jordan.

We found an amazing cottage with everything that we wanted and it was pretty much in the middle of my work and Jordan's university. After graduating college, Jordan decided to continue his studies. He now wants to own his own bar, not just manage one for someone else. Luckily, his diploma from Stratton College managed to cut eighteen months off his bachelor course.

I cannot wait to move into our cottage, I fell in love with the kitchen as soon as I saw it, it's amazeballs, I don't care about anything else. I wanted this cottage for the kitchen alone. It has chocolate granite bench tops, honey coloured timber cabinets, a built in coffee machine, thirty-two bottle wine fridge and a stainless dishwasher. It also has the most gorgeous verandah that leads onto a massive entertainment area. Our little cottage is perfect and exactly what I had in mind.

The first thing I bought, just for us was a kwila timber Jack and Jill setting with green cushions for the front verandah. It will be the perfect place to sit and have my morning coffee or a quiet wine/beer with Jordan, at the end of the day.

Jordan's only stipulation was the house had to have a shed, or beer cave, as I like to tease him, so he can start brewing his beers on a bigger scale. He has become fanatical about brewing beer recently. I've never met someone so passionate about beer, or life in general.. His passion and heart are two of the many many things I love about him.

It's finally moving day and the last box has been unpacked. We are sitting on the verandah enjoying a beer, and organising a house warming party, Mike's idea of course. Even though I sometimes want to gaffe tape his mouth shut and throw him off the pier, with a ball and chain wrapped around his ankles to keep him there, Mike is harmless and I love him to pieces. He is always there for Jordan and me, and we really appreciate it.

Jordan told Mike he needs three weeks to get the beers brewed and ready for the party, to which Mike agreed as he is Jordan's number one beer fan. It's really nice to see him passionate about something other than my safety.

17

CLINT

No... no ... no ... no! Why is she moving in with twat boy? When my cousin came to visit me today and told me the devastating news, I lost it.

How can she do this to me? To us?

She is mines; her and I are meant to be together.

Why is it all going wrong?

I've left her flowers; doesn't she know that I love her? That we are meant to be together?

I need to up my game.

Soon, Sweetcheeks, soon you will be mines.

18

KENZIE

IT'S THE DAY OF OUR HOUSEWARMING, AND I'M IN THE KITCHEN MAKING sausage rolls, Thai chicken balls that I can never get to actually look like balls, home made dips including, mum's super yummy cheese log, and my famous brownies. Jordan walks in, and he wraps his arms around my waist, nuzzling my ear as he pulls me in tighter. "Do you know how sexy you look, right now?"

Turning around, I wrap my arms around him and he bursts out laughing. I look at him confused. "What's so funny?"

"You have brownie mixture smeared all over your face, it kinda looks like shit."

Without even thinking, I dip my finger into the mixture and I smear it down the side of his face whispering, "Now you have shit on your face, too."

"Oh it's on like Donkey Kong, woman." Jordan chases after me, with the brownie bowl in his arms; I manage to sidestep him, running around the bench, so that I am now standing across from him. He places the bowl back on the bench, I lean over and dip my finger in. Slowly I lift my finger to my mouth and suck the mixture off, while letting out an exaggerated moan. Jordan stops and stares at me, his eyes immediately heat with desire.

We both step around the bench towards each other, our lips colliding in a passionate kiss. He pulls back and dips his finger into the bowl. As he lifts it up towards his mouth, I lean forward and suck the mixture off his finger and moan. Angling towards him, I slowly lick the mixture off his face that I smeared there earlier and look into his eyes. "Mmhmm, that tastes amazeballs," I huskily whisper.

I suck his cheek and lick along his jawline, groaning as I go, slowly kissing my way up to his lips. Coaxing his lips open with my tongue, I slip mine in and out of his mouth. Leaning up onto my tippy toes, I wrap my arms around his neck and pull him closer, deepening our kiss. Sighing into his mouth, my pussy tightens when I feel his cock pressing into my stomach.

Taking a step back I slip the straps of my sundress down so I am standing there only in my blue silk undies. Looking deep into Jordan's eyes, I dip my finger into the mixture again and smear it across my breasts. "Oops," I seductively say.

Jordan steps towards me, lowering his head, he licks across my collarbone and down my breastbone. Sucking the mixture off my skin before taking my nipple into his mouth. It immediately pebbles and with his other hand he massages the other breast. He alternates between the two, my body tingling all over. I cry out in pleasure as he gently bites my nipple; the pain quickly replaced with ecstasy as he sucks my nipple harder.

Dunking my finger into the mixture again, I smear it down his neck. Bending forward, while he keeps massaging my breasts, I lick and suck the batter off him. I work my way down his abs and lower onto my knees; I undo his button and make quick work of his zipper. His cock springs free when I lower his boxer briefs, moving forward I lick the pre-cum glistening on the tip of his erect penis. I push his shorts and boxer briefs down to his ankles and he steps out, kicking them to the side. I begin to massage his balls while, I suck him further into my mouth, hollowing my cheeks I take him deeper down my throat, just like I did the first time we made love.

"Fuck, Kenz, your mouth is amazing."

That's the added encouragement I need, I start bobbing my head faster, working up and down his thick shaft. Feeling his balls tighten in my hand, I know he's close. Seconds later, I feel the first creamy spurt of his cum hit the back of my throat. I suck every last drop from him and I lick any that spilt. Wiping the side of my mouth with my finger I look up into Jordan's eyes and then suck my finger. "Mmhmm."

Standing up, I draw him closer and kiss him deeply. Jordan lifts me up and I wrap my legs around his waist. He pushes aside the mixing bowl and lowers me onto the edge of the island bench and quickly removes my undies. Leaning over, he dips his finger into the mixture, smearing it over my stomach and the top of my mound.

Jordan proceeds to suck it off me, while massaging my breasts. Rolling my nipples between his forefinger and thumb. I lean back on my elbows, closing my eyes and I lose myself in the pleasure overtaking my body.

He licks down my stomach to the top of my mound, his tongue darting out, flicking my clit. When his tongue hits my clit a second time, it sends a bolt of electricity to my pussy and I feel myself instantly get wetter. I moan and lie down on the bench, as he takes my clit into his mouth and sucks harder. His tongue laps my slit, sliding in and out, before sucking and nibbling on my clit once again. Clenching his head between my thighs, I never want this feeling to end, I let out a loud moan and run my fingers through Jordan's hair. With one final flick of his tongue on my clit, I'm coming. My body buzzing from head to toe, as wave after wave of pleasure rushes over my entire being. He sucks every last drop of my orgasm from my body.

Once my orgasm has finished, he pulls me closer to the edge of the bench and guides his throbbing cock into my pussy. Wrapping my legs around his waist, grasping him closer to me; he slowly pulls out and slams back into me, again and again. We pick up a frenzied sensual rhythm, our mouths hungrily devouring each other as he continues to pound into me. Without warning he stops, lowers my legs, and tells me to turn around. Quickly, I spin around and grab the edge of the bench. He enters me from behind with such force that my orgasm immediately starts to build.

Arching my back, I reach my hand up to cup his cheek, turning my head to kiss him. Jordan reaches around and starts to rub my clit. I can feel my climax intensifying. Reaching down with my other hand, I help Jordan massage my clit; our fingers working together, rubbing my swollen nub in circles, skimming our fingernails across my sensitive core. Before long, I'm exploding around his cock, my whole body shuddering due to the force of the climax. While I'm riding out my release, I feel Jordan still before he detonates inside of me.

We stand there, with our arms wrapped around each other, panting, gazing into each other's eyes over my shoulder. Jordan is the first to speak, "Fuck, I love your brownies," and we both laugh.

He spins me around and kisses me, this is the kiss of all kisses. I can feel it deep in my soul. In this exact moment I know that I love Jordan with all my heart. Mid-kiss he pulls away, "Fuck, we didn't use a franga."

Without hesitating, I reply. "I'm due next week, we should be fine, and if not, we will deal with it. I love you, Jordan." Realising that this is the first time that I have said it to him, I don't panic. I'm happy that I said it and I don't regret those three words. Grabbing his face with both of my hands and I look deep into his eyes. "Jordan, you and I can overcome and do anything, as long as we are together." I say it again, "I love you."

"I love you too, Kenz."

We stare into each other's eyes, Jordan leans down and kisses me again, but this kiss feels different somehow. I think because it's a kiss of love and not just lust. Pushing back, I smile. "Ummm, we better go have a shower and get cleaned up, and then I need to finish cooking. Our guests will be here soon."

"Yeah, I guess we got a little sidetracked. Come on; let's have a shower. To be earth conscious, and all that shit, I think we should have a shower together."

"Yes, cause we are so earth conscious," I sarcastically reply with a laugh.

Grabbing my hand, he leads us into the bathroom, but us saying the 'L' word has unleashed something inside of us. We make love on the bathroom floor … and again in the shower together, being all earth conscious about the amount of water we use.

An hour later, I'm putting the last brownie batch in the oven, and have just set the timer when Sarah and Josh arrive. Josh pokes his head in to say hey and then heads to the backyard where Jordan and Mike are setting up the tables.

Sarah stays and helps me get the rest of the food organised. Once everything is ready, we take the food, rest of the drinks, and cutlery outside. We have just finished setting up when everyone starts to arrive.

Jordan's beer is flowing and it tastes amazing. I haven't seen him this happy in a long time. Actually, I haven't been this happy in a long time. Everyone has a fantabolous night, and Jordan's beers are a hit, as are my brownies.

It's just after midnight, and only Mike, Sarah, Josh, Jordan and I are left. We are lounging in the living room when Mike pulls out a bottle of tequila…that's when things start to get really messy. Jordan hides as he and tequila don't mix very well, kind of like oil and water. I remember one messy night in first term after exams; all the Stratton College students were at the Dirty Duck celebrating. Someone decided to start a game of higher or lower with tequila as the prize; I use the term prize loosely. Poor Jordan sucked at that game. I have never seen someone so sick before. Thinking about that night, I start to snort laugh and everyone looks at me. "Jordan, remember that evening in college at the Dirty Duck, after first term exams and we were playing higher or lower?"

He shudders. "How can I forget, worst night of my life." Everyone laughs. "And I have not touched tequila since and it's not gonna happen tonight either." He gives me a kiss goodnight. "Night every-one, thanks for coming and all your help." He then walks down the hall to our bedroom.

"You're such a pussy," Mike teases and slaps Jordan on the back as he walks past. He grabs the bottle, turns to us with the biggest smile on his face, "Let's play, assholes."

We start playing higher or lower, the card game from hell. You pray for the card to be higher than the previous one and nine times out of ten, luck is not on your side.

The next morning when, my mouth feels like the bottom of a dirty ashtray, and I feel like I have been hit by a bus and then reversed over, twice, I wish I had hidden like Jordan. Ugh! Why do I do this to myself?

Worst. Hangover. Ever.

19

KENZIE

JORDAN HAS BEEN MY ROCK, MY HERO, THE ONE I TURN TOO WHEN IT FEELS like everything is crashing down on me. He is my savior and I want to do something for him, something to show how much I appreciate all that he has done for me. I've arranged for us to go to Europe and attend the opening weekend of the Oktoberfest. The idea came about when I won a $2000 travel voucher.

Originally I had planned for Mike and Jordan to go, but Mike had just gotten a new job and was unable to attend, so I stepped in, such a shame that was. Plus, when I think about it, Mike would have totally gotten them both arrested, so it was probably better that Jordan and I went. I didn't tell Jordan what we were doing, or where we were going. All I told him is that were flying to Europe for a tour, and everything is arranged. As soon as Jordan realises we are flying into Munich, he puts two and two together and figures out we are off to the Oktoberfest.

We arrive at the hostel and I immediately question my decision. "Oh My God, Jordan. What have I done?"

He looks at me confused. "What's up, Kenz?"

"Dude, this place looks like the one from that creepy *Hostel* movie, I don't think I can stay here."

Laughing, he replies. "You are too funny, Kenz, this place will be fine BUT if we get inside and you're still creeped out, I'll find us some-where else to stay."

"Jordan, it's the opening weekend of the Oktoberfest, nothing will be available." Taking a deep breath, I add, "Guess I just have to put on my big girl undies and go with it."

"Personally, I prefer you with no undies but if it means we can stay then by all mean, grandma undie it up."

Punching him in the arm as I walk past, I lug my suitcase up the stairs and head inside. Thankfully when we get inside it loses it's creepy vibe and any fear I have vanishes. "Oh, thank God!" I whisper to Jordan.

He laughs, "Man I love you and your over active imagination. Let's get checked in and enjoy ourselves."

While Jordan checks us in, I look around. It's a pretty retro hostel; black and white checked flooring, neutral walls, which are covered in pictures, musical instruments and artwork, ranging from historic photos from around Munich, to old school record covers, and a few classic black and white film posters. The ceiling is littered with thou-sands of tiny fairy lights, I'd love to just lie back and stare at them. It would be like lying under the stars.

We meet the tour group in the basement of the hostel at 5:00 p.m. as per our itinerary, where we get our shirts and all the information that we need to know for the weekend. We all then head to this awesome outdoor beer garden, which is about a ten minute walk from the hostel.

This beer garden is magical. There are long rows of picnic tables with red and white checked tablecloths, little wooden crates filled with cutlery and condiments sit in the center. At one end of the garden there is a L-shaped timber bar with wooden barstools along one side of the L, the other side is a standing only service area. Through the rafters there are thousands of fairy lights hanging down.

We spend the afternoon, and well into the evening, drinking steins of beer and getting to know the rest of the group. After drinking five too many steins, Jordan and I stumble back to the hostel and pass out.

Today is the opening day of the Oktoberfest. The sun is shining and there's excitement in the air; Munich is buzzing. Bright and early Jordan and I are up, surprisingly not hung-over; *I love German beer*. After getting a coffee, we make our way to the Oktoberfest grounds, which is a short fifteen-minute walk from the hostel. Even though it doesn't officially open till 12:00 p.m., we need to be there at 9:00 a.m. in order to get into the Hofbrau Haus beer hall that the tour guides say is the best.

When we arrive, we get the typical touristy photo under the Oktoberfest rainbow entry, similar to the one in the hostel, and we make our way to the Hofbrau house and line up. The gates to the beer hall open at 10:00 a.m. and when they open, it's a free-for-all. Luckily we are with a tour group and get unofficial priority once inside. While we wait for the first keg to be tapped at noon, we eat German pretzels and drink Coke in steins.

The band keeps playing *Ruby Ruby Ruby* by Kaiser Chiefs, and when they do, everyone goes mental and sings at the top of their lungs. If it's this much fun when no alcohol is being consumed, I can only imagine what it will be like when the beer is flowing.

The first beers arrive just after 12:00 p.m., our waitress, Helga, can carry twelve steins at once; she's a rock star. I struggle to lift my stein, let alone carry twelve and dodge drunken fest goers at the same time. The day progresses and Jordan and I get extremely drunk and have a beertabolous time.

I'm so glad that I decided to surprise Jordan with this trip, and I'm really happy that Mike couldn't come; sorry not sorry, Mike. By 9:00 p.m., we are all beer'd out and we head back to the hostel. We shower and fall into bed, ready to do it all again tomorrow.

The next morning is a bit of a struggle, but apart from a queasy tummy, I feel fine. After a greasy brekky and a big ass coffee, Jordan and I walk back to the fest with the others. We start day two, or three if you count the day we arrived, in an outdoor beer garden. Once again the sun is shining and there is not a cloud in the sky. This beer garden is similar to the one from the first night, timber tables and bench seats, adorned with red and white checkered tablecloths and mini timber kegs filled with cutlery, serviettes and condiments. Hanging along the fence are wooden planter boxes with amazing red, white and pink peonies.

Sitting in the sun, drinking beer with the man of my dreams, I'm deliriously happy. This is what dreams are made of. Hours later, it's pretty hot and perfect outdoor drinking weather. Jordan looks to me and slurs, "Kenz, I'm gonna make beer just as good as this, and we are going to open a brewery. Yep, you and me are gonna open a brewery, and we is going to become the beer king and queen of Queensland, move over XXXX there's a new Queensland beer coming for you."

I look over and laugh, "Whatever you say, dude, have another beer."

He places his hands on my shoulders, squeezes and looks directly into my eyes, "No, Kenz, I'm serious. We *are* going to open a brewery and we're going to make amazing beers and live hoppily ever after."

Along with the rest of the group, I laugh at him. "Did you seriously just say hoppily ever after?"

"I sure did, Kenz, and I'm serious. Babe, we are going to open a brewery, I can feel it in my bones."

I look over at him and smile; I know that if Jordan wants to open a brewery that it will definitely happen … one day.

20

JORDAN

Seriously, I can't believe that Kenz surprised me with a trip to Europe and the opening of the Oktoberfest. Boy, am I glad that she bumped into me on the first day of college. If I had my time over, I would have asked her out sooner. That way she would have never hooked up with Clint and maybe I could have prevented her from getting assaulted and hurt by that asshole.

The Oktoberfest was so much more amazing than I ever thought it would be. I know Kenz thinks I'm joking about opening a brewery, but after saying that on the second day; I can't stop thinking about it. I decide that I'll chat to Kenz on the plane ride home and see if she'd like to embark on this venture with me.

After a rough cab ride from the hostel to the airport, we check in and decided to get some brekky while we wait for our flight. Kenz can only stomach a coffee, but I get the works: bacon, eggs, sausage, mushrooms, tomatoes, toast, and a big ass coffee. Her face turns a little green when my food arrives, and she takes off running to the bathrooms. *Poor baby,* I think to myself, before diving in and devouring my brekky.

She comes back ten minutes later and has a terrified look on her face. "Kenz, babe, what's wrong?"

"So, umm, yeah. I was sick and when I flushed, the toilet backed up and it overflowed, and I kinda vomited some more." Spitting my coffee out, I can't help it and I burst out laughing. Kenz doesn't look too impressed with my laughter. "I'm sorry, babe, but that is so friggin funny, I can't wait to tell Mike."

When Kenz sees me laughing, she starts to laugh as well. One minute she is mortified and the next, she's pissing herself laughing and snorting, in the middle of the Munich airport.

Man, I love this woman.

Our flight is called and we make out way to the gate. We get seated and the flight takes off, I turn in my seat and look at Kenz. "Hey, babe, you know how I said I want to open a brewery?"

"Yeah." She looks at me curiously.

"Well, I really want to do it, I can't stop thinking about it. In my mind I can see it now, all my brewing equipment behind glass walls so you can see everything that goes into making your beer, an awesome bar along one side. Tables and booths around the place, I seriously can't wait to start this. I've got it all worked out and I've only been thinking about it for thirty-six hours. I know which building in town I want. I have an idea for the layout, including a kitchen that serves kick ass food, and in honor of the Oktoberfest, and the creation of this dream, an outdoor beer garden, complete with timber bench seats, planter boxes, and flowers. Maybe I'll plant a sunflower garden in honor of you. "

Pausing, I add, "I want you and I to do this together. I know you enjoy helping me brew and you have a keen eye for everything. I can make the beers and you can manage the rest."

"Ooh my God, you seriously are serious about this."

"Deadly serious, Kenz. I think between the two of us we could make this happen and it will be amazing. Together, we can make beautiful beers and live hoppily ever after."

"Actually, if I'm honest, I haven't been able to stop thinking about it either. I'd love nothing more than to do this with you, Jor."

"Are you shitting me?"

"I'm serious, Jordan, I think this will be incredible. You and I can make beers and live hoppily ever after, as you would say. Besides, we will be adding a wine bar once the brewery is up and running and I can stock all my fav wines. Its win/win in my eyes."

"You seriously are awesome, Kenzie Merlot. I'm so glad you smashed into me eighteen months ago."

"Naw, you are too kind, Jordan McRoberts."

Kenz puts on her headphones and watches a movie. I, on the other hand, have a million and one ideas running through my mind. Before I can do this, I need to finish my course, so I can dedicate all my time to this venture.

21

KENZIE

After we return from the Oktoberfest, Jordan and I are stronger than ever. This is the happiest I've been in my entire life. Jordan concentrates on finishing his degree, perfecting his already amazeballs beers, and setting up our brewery. He's so determined; I have never seen him like this before, and it's a total turn on watching him.

Sometimes I feel like I hardly see him during the week. He has increased the number of subjects he's doing each term, so he can finish his course quicker. However on the weekends, we both spend time together in the shed perfecting the beers. Much to my surprise, I'm really enjoying the behind the scene beer creation process. I mean, I like drinking beer but I never thought I would enjoy making it. My only wish is be that it smelled better while its fermenting—the hops and mash are disgusting, and when I comes to cleaning, ugh, I gag and dry retch every time.

Jordan finishes his course in record time and graduates in the top two percent of his class. I was so proud to see him walk across that stage and collect his degree. His graduation present from his parents is a two-week holiday in Mexico. They booked us into this amazing, all-inclusive adult-only resort in Cabo San Lucas. It has its own 2.5km private beach, five restaurants and bars, a spa, and a golf course. We treat ourselves and upgrade to an oceanfront suite with a butler, yes, our own personal butler. The room has a private balcony with unobstructed ocean views, and when we head to the beach we have our own dedicated cabana, also with our very own butler—this place seriously is heaven.

For the first three days, we laze by the pool or swim in the ocean; it's pure bliss. The sea is an amazing blue colour and the sand is so fine and white; I've never seen anything like it. Jordan teases me as I love sitting on the shoreline, digging my feet into the sand, and then I lie back and stare up at the sky. Whether it's sunrise, sunset, or the middle of the day its perfect and ohh so peaceful.

On day five, I send Jordan off on a deep sea fishing trip, and I spend the day in our cabana reading and drinking margaritas. At one point, I doze off because I wake up with Jesus, our cabana butler, tapping my leg. He's holding a silver box with a purple bow; reminding me of the one I received at graduation. He places the package on the end of the cabana and walks away.

Smiling, I think Jordan has sent me something special since I sent him off fishing for the day. I quickly sit up, untie the bow, and quickly lift the lid off. Looking inside I see that it is full of yellow daisies. It's similar to the one I received after graduation, again there is no note but something doesn't feel right this time around.

I keep an eye out for when Jesus returns with my margarita, I want to ask him about the package. I see him approach the cabana, and after he has placed my margarita down, I ask, "Jesus, who delivered my package?"

"I'm not sure *Señorita*. Someone from reception asked where you were and I offered to bring it to you. Is everything all right?"

"Yeah, I was just curious, that's all."

I pass the box to him and ask if he can deliver it to our room. With a smile he takes the package from me. Picking up my margarita I take a huge sip and moan. Jesus sure knows how to make a killer margarita.

After I finish my cocktail, I signal to Jesus for another, and I also order two shots of tequila. That eerie feeling I had earlier is back, I need to settle my imagination and tequila will fix that…I hope.

Jesus delivers my drinks and after sinking my shots, one after the other, I start to feel relaxed. Looking to my left between the flapping cabana materials, I see Jordan walking towards me. My heart flutters, he's wearing his favourite Billabong boardies and no shirt. I clench my thighs to ease the tingly feeling developing in my girly bits.

His aviator Ray-Ban's cover his eyes and he has the most amazing smile on his face, I'm guessing fishing went well. Our eyes lock, I jump up and race over to him. Wrapping my arms around him, I hug him tight. Him being here is just what I need. Closing my eyes I savor this moment. I rest my head on his chest, the beating of his heart calming me further.

"Well hello to you, Kenz." Pulling back he notices my uneasiness. "What's wrong?"

"I'm probably being silly, but I got a package while you were fishing. I thought it was from you but I'm not so sure anymore."

"What was in the package?"

"It was a box of daises, similar to the sunflower package you sent me after graduation."

Shaking his head, he replies, "Kenz, I didn't send you a package after graduation."

"What?" I shriek, garnering the attention of a few other guests.

"Kenz, I didn't send you flowers after graduation. The only present from me was the dinner I took you to."

"Then if you didn't send them, who did?"

"I don't know baby, maybe we need to check in with corrections and make sure that Clint is still locked away."

"That's a good idea, I'll text Mum and ask her to call. Actually, I'll text Sarah, I don't want to worry Mum. She's been through enough."

I have just finished texting Sarah when Jesus arrives with a Modelo for Jordan, and another margarita for me; seriously he is the best bar guy ever.

Jordan leads me back to our cabana and we snuggle, enjoying our drinks and watching the sunset over the ocean. The sunset tonight is remarkable; each day's sunset is more beautiful than the previous one. The colours are so vivid; oranges, pinks, purples, and yellows all meshing together.

The sun has just set and we are still snuggling in our cabana. I look over and see Jesus and another guy walking towards us with dinner. Jordan sits up and says, "So, I had a great fishing day, and the chef has prepared a feast for us with my catch."

We dine in our cabana on fresh Mahi Mahi, Bonita, prawns, salad, and chips. It is one of the best meals I've ever had. Jesus comes and clears our plates, returning with churros for dessert.

He returns a few moments later with two tumblers of tequila, which apparently goes amazingly well with churros. I snort laugh as he places the tumblers down, Jordan thanks him and he heads off. Being the ever so nice girlfriend that I am, I grab Jordan's tumbler and have a sip. It is seriously the best tasting tequila ever and I moan. Jordan looks at me and I say, "We should grab a bottle to take home for Mike, and by Mike, I mean me."

Jordan laughs and I manage to convince him to try the tequila. He hesitantly takes a sip, after swallowing, he looks to me and says, "After drinking that, I think I might like tequila." With his seal of approval, we ask Jesus to bring us a bottle. I see him smile in approval because Jordan has refused every tequila he has bought over to us to try so far. I, on the other hand, have knocked back every single one offered, and I have loved every one of them.

After dessert, Sarah texts me back to say that Clint is still locked up, and that he has not had any visitors except his cousin and lawyer; however she did say that he will soon be up for parole due to good behavior. I feel relieved to know he is still locked up, scared that he is up for parole and anxious about the flowers. I try and relax with Jordan, but the flowers weigh heavily on my mind. Jordan and I spend the rest of the night in our cabana drinking tequila and relaxing.

Jordan puts me at ease, telling me it was probably delivered to me by mistake; after all there was no card so it could have been for anyone. That makes me feel a little better, so I relax and enjoy the rest of the evening.

With the amount of tequila I consume, I soon forget about my anonymous gift and enjoy my time unwinding, with the man of my dreams.

The next two days we spend at the resort lazing about. Jordan and I even manage a round of golf. Well, I would not call what I did golf but we had a blast together.

I convinced Jordan to go to a local tequileria that Jesus recommended to us. This place had over three hundred different tequilas on offer, I had died and gone to tequila heaven. We tried a few, but between us we didn't even come close to trying them all. We both tasted one that was velvety smooth on your tongue, and easily slide down your throat, leaving you warm and fuzzy on the inside. We bought a bottle to take back home, but this will be one that we hide from Mike. We did however find one that would be perfect for him.

A week after we arrived, Jordan arranged a spa afternoon for me; while I was being pampered, he was going to play a round of golf. He was acting strange as I was leaving, but I was too excited for the bliss that I was about to enjoy to really take notice. Leaning down, I gave him a kiss and headed off to the spa.

I'm booked in for a Spa Indulgence Package, which includes a body wrap, facial, massage, and a glass of bubbles. I also added on a spa manicure and a glam pedicure.

Three hours later, I emerge feeling chillaxed and amazing. My skin is as soft as a baby's bum, and I have pretty toe and fingernails to go with it. Bright fuchsia pink for my toes and fairy floss pink for my fingers. *The ladies back home need to come here for training,* I think to myself on the way back to our room. As I pass the sports bar, I look at the time and decide to stop in and enjoy a glass of bubbly before heading back.

After two glasses of bubbly, and a chat with Miguel, the bar tender, I look at my watch and guess that Jordan should be finished by now. Waving goodbye to Miguel, I head back to the room. I start thinking about what we will do tonight. Since I'm super relaxed from my spa afternoon, I'm thinking room service on the balcony and more bubbly sounds perfect.

On my way back to the room, I see a private table being set up in the Oceanfront Bar, and I make a mental note to ask Jordan if we can do that one night before we leave; it looks so romantic.

Arriving at our room, I open the door and my mouth drops open in shock. There are tea light candles everywhere and a rose petal path leading into the bedroom. On the bed, there is an amazing pink chiffon strapless dress and silver wedge strappy sandals in a box next to it. On top of the box is a note in Jordan's handwriting. As I read the note from Jordan, tears well in my eyes, and my face breaks out in the biggest smile. This is the most romantic thing anyone has done for me.

MY GORGEOUS KENZ,
I HAVE ARRANGED A SECRET SURPRISE FOR YOU THIS
EVENING, COMPLETE WITH CLOTHES AND SHOES. YOUR
MAKE-UP ARTIST WILL ARRIVE AT 5.30PM AND I WILL PICK
YOU UP AT 6.15PM FOR A NIGHT TO REMEMBER.
THERE IS A BOTTLE OF BUBBLY IN THE BATHROOM WAITING
FOR YOU, ENJOY AND I WILL SEE YOU SOON GORGEOUS.

ALL MY LOVE,
JORDAN XOXOX

There is a knock on the door and I rush over; it's Rosa-Maria from the spa, she did my nails. Smiling at her, I step aside so she and her trolley can come in.

She works her magic, and twenty minutes later I look stunning, if I do say so myself. I have smoky eyes, rosy but subtle cheeks, and my lips look amazing. My hair is in a low bun that looks awesome. She then helps me slip on my dress and I put my shoes on, while she packs up her stuff.

I stand up just as she walks out of the bathroom and she looks over at me, with a smile she says, *"Te ves Hermosa."* She laughs at my confused look, I don't speak Spanish, so I have no idea what she said but it sounded beautiful. Walking over to me, she places her hand lovingly on my cheek. "You look beautiful."

As I am not one for compliments I blush. She nods at me before grabbing her things and leaving. Looking at the clock I see I still have ten minutes until Jordan arrives, so I pour myself another glass of bubbly. With my glass full, I head out onto the patio and watch the sun start to set while I wait. The sky is already filled with amazing colours, I can't wait to see the sunset tonight.

22

JORDAN

Kenz just left for the spa, she thinks I'm playing golf but I'm not. Secretly I'm setting up the most epic proposal in the history of proposals, I hope. Before she left, I was so nervous; I felt like I was going to vomit, but I don't think she picked up on it. Heading to the Oceanfront Bar, I meet up with Alejandro; he and I have been covertly speaking since we arrived to get this all arranged. Kenz and I don't keep secrets from each other, and I hate keeping this one, but I know that it will all be worth it in the long run.

Arriving at the Oceanfront Bar, I see that all the couches and lounges have been moved to the side, and there is a lone table in the middle, set for two. Smiling, I think to myself, *it looks amazing already; I can only imagine how it's going to look at sunset with all of the fire pits lit.*

I walk over to Alejandro, "Dude, this looks amazing, thank you for everything."

"Your welcome, *Senior*. The flowers will be delivered just before you arrive, as it's still quite hot, and I would hate for them to wilt. Everything we have arranged for your soon-to be-fiancée is happening as we speak. I must tell you, you are a lucky man, *Senior*."

Slapping him on the back, I smile. "Tell me about it, Alejandro. I pinch myself everyday that I get to wake up beside Kenz. I want to make this a night she will remember fondly, forever. I'll let you get back to it." Turning, I head towards the bar to grab a beer to calm my nerves. My heart is erratically beating and I'm sweating like a bitch right now.

Miguel looks up from the bar as I walk in, smiling he says, "Here's the man of the hour, you nervous?"

"Not at all, dude, not at all…okay, maybe just a little." We both laugh, "I've been waiting for this day my whole life. I can't wait to see the look on her face. She deserves all the happiness in the world, and I'm the lucky son of a bitch, who will get to wake up next to her every-day, for the rest of my life" I hope. *Shit what if she says no?*

Miguel places a Modelo in front of me. "Thanks dude, I need this to calm my nerves." Taking a sip, I groan in pleasure, "Fuck this is good beer, one day I will make beer, just as good, if not better."

After throwing back two more beers, I feel a sense of calm wash over me. My nerves have changed, from scared to excited. On my way to get change, I spy Kenz, and hide behind a column and watch her. She looks extremely relaxed and so, so, beautiful; my cock twitches at her beauty in the afternoon sunlight.

I'm unbelievably lucky that she fell into my life. She heads towards the Oceanfront Bar and I start to panic. Then I see her detour towards the sports bar where I just was. *Lucky I left when I did.*

After changing into beige linen slacks and a charcoal grey button-up shirt, I head back to the sports bar for another calming beer, my nerves have reappeared with a vengeance. It's amazing how beer can calm me. I finish my beer and look at my watch. "It's show time, Miguel, wish me luck."

He puts down the cocktail shaker he was wiping, and shakes my hand, saying, "*Buena suerte,* Jordan." Looking at him confused, he laughs and says, "Good luck, Jordan".

I nod my head, "Thanks," I nervously reply, before rushing off to meet my girl.

23

CLINT

THE PAROLE HEARING GOES IN MY FAVOUR, AND I'M LET OUT EARLY FOR good behavior. It was so easy to trick those fuckers. Luckily my cousin has taken me in, without her I would be screwed. You can always count on family to help you in a time of need, just like I was there when she needed me. We have each other's back when it counts.

My cousin managed to get the address of where she moved, I've been watching Sweetcheeks from a distance. It has been so hard staying away but I need to wait, we will together again soon. I'm currently outside her house, I can't stay away. It's been too long since I have seen her, so I pop over for a visit. Standing on her back patio, I'm looking into her and asshats house. It doesn't look like anyone is home, and it doesn't look like anyone has been here for a while. Being ever so nice, I wanted to drop off a package for Mackenzie, but I decide that I'll deliver the package when I know she is home.

I really hope my Sweetcheeks is okay.

Starting to worry, I look through the French doors and see a photo of her on the fridge. She is smiling at me, I forgot how beautiful she really is, my cock hardens when I think about her. Unzipping my cargo shorts, I walk over to the green timber lounger, where I have photos of her sunbaking topless; I sit down and take my throbbing cock out. Thinking about her beautiful tits, my cock hardens, it's now rock hard, it could slice through steel. Licking my palm, I rub it over the head, closing my eyes. I grip it tight and imagine that it's Mackenzie's hand and not mine. Clenching my shaft, I pump faster and faster, squeezing tighter with each stroke. With my eyes still closed, I visualize her beautiful green eyes staring up at me as she pumps my cock faster and faster, flicking her tongue out before taking me deep into her throat.

Rolling to my side, I lean over and can just see her picture on the fridge. Her beautiful face is smiling back at me. Increasing my strokes, they become quicker and more aggressive, before I know it, I'm coming all over my hand and the lounger.

As I put my cock back inside my cargos, I smile and picture her, lying here topless again. My cock twitches as I think about my Sweetcheeks naked, lying here in the future. Now that I have marked my territory, we will be that much closer until we can be together again.

After I leave her place, I meet up with my cousin and we head to a bar for a few drinks. There is a blonde checking me out. It's been a while since I have sunk myself balls deep in pussy and I think she will do. I stalk over to her and its too easy, she's heading out back with me before I've even bought her a drink.

Grabbing her roughly, I slam her against the brick wall near the industrial bins and shove my tongue deep into her mouth. She kisses me back before she bites my lip, drawing blood. The metallic taste turns me on, and I plunge my tongue back into her mouth, roughly kissing her before spinning her around so she's facing the building. Lifting her non-existent skirt over her hips, I rip her red g-banger off and slam myself balls deep into her tight hole. She grinds her ass further into me, so I continue to pound into her. I wrap my hands around her throat, squeezing it, shutting off her air way. The panic radiates off her body and it's such a turn on. I keep slamming into her, squeezing tighter and tighter with each thrust. She starts scratching at my hands and it makes me squeeze tighter. "Ohh, Sweetcheeks, I've missed this," I growl as I continue to plow into her. I feel her body start to slacken just as I pull out and release my load all over her ass.

Letting go of her, she stumbles away, turns around and slaps me hard across the cheek, "You fucking prick, you were choking me."

"Yeah, and?"

"You are one messed up asshole." She pushes her skirt back down, tears flowing down her cheeks. "Stay the fuck away from me, asshole."

"With pleasure, you were a lousy lay anyway."

She storms off and I head back into the bar where I have another drink with my cousin before we head home.

24

KENZIE

SWALLOWING THE LAST OF MY BUBBLY, THERE'S A KNOCK AT THE DOOR. MY heart rate increases and nerves settle in; I'd recognise that knock anywhere, its Jordan. Placing my empty glass on the wooden TV cabinet, I make my way to the door; with each step my nervousness increases but I'm sure that this will be a night to remember.

Opening the door, I see Jordan standing there in a charcoal grey shirt and beige linen pants; the muscles between my thighs immediately tighten when I see him. Raking my eyes up and down his svelte body, I smile. Looking up I see he has a smug smile on his face. "You like something you see?" he cockily says, raising his eyebrows seductively before winking.

Staring into his eyes, I shrug my shoulders and innocently reply, "Meh, I've seen better." We both burst out laughing.

It's Jordan's turn to look me up and down, and I can't help but notice some movement in his pants. I can't help but cheekily say, "Like what you see?"

He stares into my eyes and I can feel his gaze deep within my soul. "Fuck yes. My God, Kenz, you are stunning."

Wrapping his arms around my waist, he leans down and kisses me, his tongue grazing across my lips, before pushing in. Our tongues do the tango, fighting for dominance. I moan into his mouth as he deepens our kiss and draws me in closer. He pulls back and rests his forehead against mine, panting, "We better get going, otherwise I won't be held accountable for what I do to you. I knew this dress would look stunning on you, Kenz, but fuck me dead, you are gorgeous."

The smile on my increases at his comment. "Thanks, you don't look to bad either, handsome. So, what have you got planned for tonight?"

He pats the side of his nose. "It's all a surprise, baby, now come with me. Tonight will be a night you will never forget." He winks at me, grabs my hand, interlaces our fingers and we head towards to beach. My nerves kick up a notch as we head off and happiness courses through my veins with each step we take.

Jordan leads me towards the Oceanfront Bar where they were setting up earlier. In the middle is a single table set for two, beside the table is a bucket of bubbly and an amazing bouquet of sunflowers.

When I see the sunflowers, I realise that this is for me. I stop midstep and take it all in. There are several fire pits lit and the flames flicker, their shadows dancing on the sandstone paving, creating a romantic atmosphere. The serenity is enhanced by the sound of the waves crashing onto the beach below. A cool breeze is blowing, wafting the scent of the ocean and kitchen towards us. I'm in awe of the scene set out in front of me.

As we walk towards the table, our waiter, Alejandro, approaches with two flutes of bubbly. He hands the glasses to us with a smile and slight nod of his head, "*Senior, Señorita,*" before turning and walking away.

Jordan grabs hold of my hand and we head to the edge of the bar area and gaze out at the sunset over the ocean. The sky is burnt orange, filled with many shades of red. The fiery orb of the sun is slowly sinking into the horizon; leaving in its wake a midnight blue sky filled with millions of tiny shimmering stars; it's spectacular.

"Jordan, that was the most magnificent sunset I've ever seen. I don't think I've ever seen such vivid colours or so many stars." I say in amazement, looking up into the night sky. "It was stunning, Jordan."

Looking over I see Jordan staring at me. "Yes, you are stunning."

My cheeks heat and I feel my neck breaking out in my nervous rash. I lower my head in embarrassment, my heart is beating so loud within my ears. Jordan takes my bubbly and places it on the stonewall next to us. Turning back, he grabs both of my hands in his, his thumb rubbing back and forth, I can feel him shaking. I gaze into his eyes and the moonlight shining from behind me makes them sparkle. Any and all thoughts disappear, I'm lost in Jordan.

Jordan clears his throat and takes a deep breath. "Kenz, you came crashing into my life, literally, and I was mesmerized by your emerald green eyes and the red wine coloured top that you were wearing. You were, and still are, the sexiest person I have ever met, you constantly take my breath away and you are just as beautiful on the inside. From that day on, I went out of my way to see you whenever I could. I know it was a dick move considering you were with him, but I just had to be near you. When I got my chance, I was over the moon. I do wish I got my chance without all the shit that went with it, but it led us to this point right here. You have brought such joy into my life, Kenz. I can't imagine my life without you in it."

Excitement builds when I realise what's about to happen. My heart rate increases, my palms become sweaty, I feel sick with nerves and excitement and I'm pretty sure, I stop breathing.

Letting go of one of my hands, Jordan reveals a handcrafted timber box with two love hearts engraved on the top. Still holding my right hand, he lowers down on one knee. "Kenzie Louise Merlot, will you do me the honour of becoming my wife?"

Through tears I look down at Jordan, I look around and it's just the two of us under the moonlit sky. I'm so nervous and floored; I ask the stupidest question ever. "Is that for me?"

Jordan laughs, "It sure is, baby. There is no one else I want to spend the rest of my life with. Kenz, baby, will you marry me?"

Pulling my hand free, I cover my mouth, and with a smile I yell, "Yes, yes, Jordan McRoberts, I will marry you!" Jordan opens the box to reveal a stunning gold and white gold engagement ring. It has one central diamond and on either side encased in white gold are six tiny diamonds, three on each side. He slips the ring onto my finger and stands up. Wrapping his arm around my waist, I wrap mine around his neck and we have our first kiss, as a newly engaged couple.

Lifting me up, he spins us around, our lips meshing together in one of the most romantic kisses of my life. He places me back down and stares into my eyes. "You have made me the happiest man alive."

He turns around and shouts into the night sky, "Kenzie Merlot just agreed to marry me, I am the happiest man on Earth!!! WooHoo!!"

He turns back to me and places his hands on either side of my face, pulling me in for another kiss. This one is full of passion; I place my arms tightly around his neck and deepen our kiss, just as fireworks go off in the distance. Out to sea, we can see a boat on the horizon and the fireworks are coming from there. Jordan spins me around, and we watch the fireworks show, with our arms wrapped around each.

When the fireworks finish, Jordan leads me over to the set table and signals Alejandro to bring the meals. We sit down and enjoy an amazing three-course feast.

After Alejandro clears away our dessert plates, he brings another bottle of bubbly, places it in the ice bucket, and then moves it next to one of the wicker lounge chairs by a fire pit.

Jordan stands up and puts his hand out to help me up. I place my left hand in his and my engagement ring flickers in the moonlight; I smile and wiggle my finger in the moon's radiance. We make our way over to the lounge, where we snuggle together by the fire, not saying a word, just enjoying each other's company, the bubbly, and the serenity. Blissfully dozing off to sleep in Jordan's arms, I wake up when he lifts me and is carrying me back to our suite.

We arrive at our room and Jordan tenderly places me on the bed, removes each of my shoes, stands up and stares down at me; his eyes are full of desire and I'd say mine are the same. Positioning myself up onto my knees, I smile as I wrap my arms around his neck. Kissing and nipping along his jaw line and up to his mouth, I gently tug at his bottom lip before crushing my mouth to his. Our tongues do the tango but this time Jordan wraps his arms around my waist, crushing me flush against his chest, intensifying our kiss. He kneels onto the bed, and gently eases me back so he is lying on top of me. Not once do we break our kiss, our lips sealed together. I run my fingers up the back of his head and back down his shoulder blades, gripping onto his tight perfect ass, pulling him closer to me.

Our kiss builds up, as the muscles between my legs clench, I drag him closer to me, moaning into his mouth, loosing myself in this perfect moment. Jordan gazes down at me, his eyes ablaze with lust, I whisper, "Make love to me, fiancé."

Jordan smiles. "As you wish, fiancée."

He quickly removes his shirt, stands up, and removes his pants and boxer briefs, in one swift motion. I lay there, staring at my sexy fiancé, wondering how I got so lucky to be engaged to this fine specimen standing naked in front of me. My eyes, roam over his body before landing on his impressive erection. I lick my lips in anticipation; he reaches his hand out for me and pulls me until I'm sitting up.

Grabbing the hem of my dress, he gently and ever so slowly slides it over my head, discarding it to the pile with the rest of his clothes; leaving me in my bra and undies. He gently pushes me back onto the bed and crawls his way back up my body. Placing kisses gingerly up my legs and across my stomach, sadly bypassing my pussy. He arrives at my breasts and begins to rub me through my purple strapless bra. My nipples peak immediately, reaching behind I unclasp my bra. Jordan flicks it to the side and takes my erect nipple into his mouth and begins to massage the other.

Pleasure cascades through my body, as I start to grind myself against his leg, my wetness seeps thru my undies, coating his leg. Jordan alternates between my breasts, and I can feel myself getting wetter and wetter. Tugging on his hair to get his attention, he kisses his way up my neck towards my ear, nibbling on my earlobe, I giggle. He kisses along my jawline much like I did earlier and then up to my mouth. Opening up, I let him in and he kisses me deeply.

We kiss like this for a few moments before I spread my legs, inviting him in. Smiling as I feel his hard throbbing cock at my entrance, he gently rubs my sex from top to bottom, the friction from the satin intensifying. He shreds my undies and gradually slips the tip of his rock hard cock into my wet folds, before withdrawing all the way back out. I cry out in frustration as he continues to tease me.

Finally he enters me.

"Ohh, Jordan."

He gently thrusts in and out of me, I wrap my legs around him as we fall into a passionate rhythm. Reaching down, I grab Jordan's ass, digging my fingers in, our rhythm quickening. I start to feel that magical tingling sensation develop deep in my belly. Before I know it, I'm tumbling into my orgasm, fireworks exploding, my whole body quaking; the hairs on my head prickling as my orgasm continues to erupt through my body. As I'm coming back to earth, I feel Jordan exploding inside of me, his body trembling with ecstasy as he releases his seed.

He pulls out and collapses next to me. We are both breathless from the most intense sex we have ever had. We roll onto our sides, and stare into each other's eyes. No words are said but the air is electrified. Love radiates uncontrollably between us. Reaching out, I grab Jordan's hand and I entwine our fingers together, leaning forward I gently kiss his knuckles. Pulling our clasped hands towards me, I tuck our hands between my breasts. We fall asleep gazing at one another with our hands held close to my heart.

The sun is shining through the shutters the next morning, and I wake up to Jordan lifting my leg over his shoulder and his head between my legs. Nipping and sucking at my clit. Smiling, I arch my back, pushing my pussy closer to him. He sucks harder and licks down my slit, inserting his tongue into my wet passage, darting his tongue in and out and occasionally sucking on his way out. He inserts one finger and then another, all while rubbing my clit with his thumb. It doesn't take long for the tingly feeling to appear in my belly. I come with such force; I grip the sheets tightly, turning my knuckles white, as pleasure courses through me. I scream out his name as my orgasm reaches its peak.

Lifting his head, he wipes the side of his lips. "Mmhmm, breakfast of champions." He lays back down next me and I take the opportunity to straddle his hips. I grind my drenched pussy onto Jordan's growing cock. Leaning over, I drag my breasts up his chest and kiss him. Tasting myself on him, makes me wetter.

Lifting up onto my knees, I gently lower myself onto his pulsating cock. Arching my back I take him deeper, as thrust and I ride him. Reaching down, I start rubbing my clit with one hand as I massage my tits with the other, pulling and tugging on my nipples. Closing my eyes, I feel my orgasm building. My head falls back and Jordan nudges my hand out of the way. He uses his thumb on my already swollen clit. I whimper in delight as my orgasm continues to build. Jordan reaches up with this other hand and grabs my nipple between his thumb and forefinger, squeezing tight before massaging my breast with his palm. The pain is quickly replaced with pleasure, and I begin to ride him faster and faster.

Feeling Jordan's cock harden within me, I clench my pussy tighter riding him quicker and quicker. Within moments, together we tumble over into the orgasmic abyss.

Climbing off of him, we lie next to each other, breathless, our chests rapidly rising and falling as we try and catch our breath. Smiling, I look over at Jordan. "Morning, fiancé, you can wake me up like that anytime."

He rolls onto his side to look at me, "Morning, fiancée, I will happily wake you like that everyday for the rest of your life." He leans over and kisses my cheek.

"Don't make promises you can't keep, fiancé"

A few hours later, I wake up alone and see Jordan sitting on our verandah in a robe sipping coffee; grabbing the other robe, I head out and join him. When I open the slider, I'm hit with the amazing smell that is coffee and fresh salty ocean air. Leaning over, I kiss Jordan's shoulder, and then his cheek before I walk around and sit on the other timber lounger.

Smiling at me, he leans over and pours me a coffee. As I take my coffee from his outstretched hand, I smile. Taking a sip, I groan.

Jordan grins. "Fuck, I will never tire from hearing you moan like that. I remember the first time we had coffee at Java Lava, I near came in my pants I hearing you moan like that."

Laughing at the memory, I also smile, it's one memory of Jordan that stands out in my mind too. That day I was so upset and in an instant Jordan made me feel safe and relaxed. Even though it all went to shit later that day. But again, Jordan was there for me when I was recovering, I don't think I would be sitting here if it weren't for him.

Looking up, I see Jordan staring at me. "Thank you for making me the happiest girl in the world, Jordan. Yesterday was just perfect, like beyond my wildest dreams perfect. I love you, almost as much as I love coffee."

"Your welcome, Kenz, and I love you almost as much as I love beer." He winks at me, "You saying yes has made me the happiest man in the universe." He stands up and sits on the end of my lounger, before kissing me fervently, pulling back to rest his forehead against mine. He then kisses the tip of my nose. "So, fiancée, what should we do today?"

I love hearing him say fiancée and it's only been twelve hours; what am I going to be like then he calls me wife? "Well, fiancé, how about we head to our cabana and have a lazy pool day? Actually, lets sit at the swim up bar and get super rotten drunk. Then we can come back here and have super drunk fiancée sex in the bathtub, I've been dying to do that since we got here. We can ask the bar dude to get our butler dude to fill up the tub, just before we are ready to come back.

What do you say fiancé?" *I love saying fiancé just as much as hearing Jordan say it.*

Jordan rests his chin on his fingers and taps his lip as if deeply thinking about what I just suggested. "Well, fiancée, I think that is the second best idea you've ever had."

Looking inquisitively at him. "Second best?" I question.

"The first was when you agreed to marry me last night," he says matter-of-factly.

"Dude, that was a no brainier. You could have taken me to Maccas and I still would have said yes, but I do absolutely love the way you proposed to me. I can't wait to tell Sarah all about it." As I get up to get changed, I wonder when Josh is going to propose her?

Half an hour later we are both changed and ready to go. Jordan is wearing teal Billabong boardies, and I have a patterned orange and beige tankini that shows off my girls nicely, with a solid orange bikini bottom with ties of the same pattern as the top.

After placing our stuff in our cabana, we dive into the pool and the water is amazing, so refreshing. We swim over to the Aqua Bar and it's none other than our favourite bartender, Miguel, on duty today. He looks at us and smiles. "It's the newly engaged love birds, congrats, *Señor y Señorita.*" He shakes Jordan's hand and leans over to kiss my cheek, as I flash my hand towards him to show off my ring.

"What can I get you, *Señorita?*"

Looking at the cocktail menu I say, "Miguel, can I please get one of your amazeball margaritas." Looking up I add, "And Jordan will have a Mo..." Before I finish, Miguel is placing a Modelo in front of Jordan; I shake my head.

"What?" Jordan asks as I raise my eyebrows at him. "What can I say? Miguel is awesome at his job and knows what I like."

Five minutes later, Miguel places the biggest margarita I have ever seen in front of me, and I cannot help but smile. Taking a sip I close my eyes, savour the taste and moan. It is seriously the best margarita I have ever had. I look over towards Miguel and shout, "Thank you, Miguel, this is freakin' amazeballs!" He nods and smiles before he starts serving another couple.

Jordan and I spend the rest of the day swimming and drinking beer and margaritas. It's so relaxing and the most chilled-out holiday I have ever had. I cannot ever remember being this happy and relaxed. *Thank you Mr. and Mrs. McRoberts for this amazing trip.*

We spend the next few days how we started our holiday, either lazing by the pool or swimming in the ocean. Before we leave, we finally manage to christen the tub and I have one of the most intense, electrifying, mind-blowing orgasms of my life in there. I even have the bruises to show for it.

This has been one amazing trip. Not just because I got engaged, but it was spent with my soul mate Jordan. Never have I been this happy before, I am literally on cloud nine right now and nothing could change that...or so I thought.

25

KENZIE

...7 months later

OUR WEDDING IS ONLY SEVEN WEEKS AWAY AND I'M OVER THE MOON excited. Everything is organised for a small intimate wedding with just our immediate family and close friends. The ceremony will be at the rotunda on top of Mount Coo-tha, with the reception hosted at the Summit Restaurant. We have about twenty-five guests in total, I think, and so far everything is going to plan. There may have been one or two bridezilla moments, so I think I am doing extremely well.

Clint was released seven months ago from prison; surprisingly it doesn't bother me. Even with him free, I feel safe and happy. Thankfully, I haven't seen or heard from him. I can finally put the nightmare that is Clint MacNicholson behind me and keep moving forward with my life.

Currently I'm on cloud nine and could not be happier. In seven weeks I'm marrying the man of my dreams and today, at work, I was promoted to team leader. When we returned from Cabo I thought I was happy but at the moment, I am ecstatically happy and nothing can bring me down.

Hopping off the bus, I walk down the street to our house, as usual, and in my peripheral vision I see a yellow car pull up beside me. All of a sudden, the hairs on the back of my neck stand on end, fear building inside me. Before I have a chance to look around, a cloth is placed over my face and everything goes black.

26

CLINT

Fuck! I left it too long. Sweetcheeks is engaged to that wanker.

I can't fucking believe it.

She is mines not his!

I need to make my move but she's always with him or with that skank ho slut, Sarah. I'll get my chance and then Sweetcheeks and I will be together forever.

Finally, she is alone.

I'd just left another flower package on her doorstep, and as I was driving down the street I look up and see her. Her golden hair blowing in the breeze as she steps off the bus and I know that it's finally time to put my plan in motion.

This is my chance.

Thank you fate.

Driving past her, I pull over and park. I open the boot and soak a rag to make my move. I'm ever so thankful that I had all of this ready and waiting in my car.

Sneaking up behind her, I wrap my arms around her waist and shove the cloth in her face. She goes limp quickly and I catch her as she falls, cradling her in my arms. *My beautiful Sweetcheeks.*

Taking a deep breath, I breathe her in; her scent is remarkable. Having her in my arms again is wonderful, and my cock agrees. He hardens in my jeans, it hasn't been this hard in a long time.

My beautiful Sweetcheeks is back in my arms...I cannot wait to sink myself inside her.

Quickly, I throw her in the boot before climbing into the driver's seat, and I race away to our cabin. We arrive a short time later and it's just as I left it when I came here a few weeks ago. Looking around, I smile; our love nest is perfect.

I cannot wait to be with Sweetcheeks forever.

27

KENZIE

WHEN I COME TO, ITS DARK AND THEN I REALISE THAT I'M IN THE BOOT OF a car. Fear takes hold and I kick and scream. We drive for what feels like hours, but in reality it was only about thirty minutes. We eventually screech to a halt. I hold my breath and anxiously wait for the boot to open. When it does, the sunlight is blinding. It takes a few moments for my sight to come into focus and I see Clint's evil face staring back at me. "Your awake Sweetcheeks, welcome back to our happily ever after."

Grabbing me by my upper arms, he roughly wrenches me out of the boot of a canary yellow SUV of some sort, dropping me on the ground before he slams it shut. I scream at the top of my lungs. He slaps me hard across the face, I see stars from the force. He pulls me up by my hair and drags me towards the cabin, again I scream. When he hits me again, I black out.

This time when I wake, I find myself handcuffed to a rusty metal single bed, which was once white with pink little flowers, similar to Sarah's when we were growing up. The mattress is ratty and torn in spots; springs poke through, digging into my back. There's a white wooden dresser by a door, with a full-length mirror that has seen better days, it has a jagged crack down the center. I presume there's either a wardrobe or ensuite bathroom behind the door. There's also a small side table next to the bed, similar in design to the dresser.

The window has been painted black, casting the room into darkness. The only light is from a dim bulb hanging down from the ceiling. I've no idea what colour the walls are since they are covered in a light sheen of dust. I'd guess they are a buttery yellow. The room is absolutely disgusting, the musty smell nauseating, and I'm scared shitless.

My chest tightens; I struggle to breathe, my body shaking, and sweating, as the attack sets in. I close my eyes, trying to calm myself down. Telling myself, "breathe in, breathe out." Taking a final deep breath, I calm myself down, keeping the attack at bay…for now.

Opening my eyes again, I take another look around the room and notice that one wall is covered in photographs; photos of me. There are pictures of me at work, me lying topless in the backyard, Sarah and I at the gym, Jordan and I at the beach; any photo with Jordan in it has his face scratched out. There are even photo's from my graduation; it seems that while he was locked up, he had someone watching me.

From the corner of my eye, I notice Clint sitting in the corner in a wicker chair. Staring at me. He doesn't say a word, he just silently stares at me. I can feel the anger radiating off him. I start to panic and wrench on the cuffs, but as I thrash about they get tighter and tighter. As the panic escalates, I start to cry.

He looks at me and smiles, it's the creepiest smile you can image, I cringe as his eyes roam over my body. "Mackenzie, baby, now we can be together forever. No one will come between us. I have everything we need here. We will never have to leave again. It will be you and I, forever."

I stare at him in shock, I cannot possibly be hearing him correctly. Finding my voice I manage to squeak out, "Wh…what d…do you m… mean fff…forever?"

"Mackenzie, Sweetcheeks, baby, we are meant to be together and you and I now will be. We are the modern day Romeo and Juliet."

Before I have a chance to reply, he jumps on top of me. Gyrating his hips into me, grunting and groaning; his cock hardening against me. He continues to dry hump me, each thrust becoming rougher, and rougher.

"Mackenzie, feel how hard you make me?" He licks up my cheek, "No other girl has ever made me this hard. Your sweet pussy was made for me. I am never leaving you."

He kneels up, unzips his fly, and his pulsating hard cock springs free. He begins stroking himself and then he lifts up my work skirt, rips off my undies, and forces himself inside me. I scream in pain, it burns. I scream and he punches me in the face. He continues to thrusts in and out of me. Harder and harder, deeper and deeper. He continues to thrust over and over. The burn is unbearable, I feel like I'm being split in half.

Just when I think that I can't take anymore, he pulls out and sprays his cum all over me. With a sickening smile, he stares down at me. He reaches out to wipe my tears away, I shake my head to avoid his touch. He grips my chin, leans down and tries to kiss me. I thrash not wanting him to touch me. This pisses him off again and he slaps me hard, right near where he punched me. I can feel my face start to swell. With the crack of his palm against my cheek again, my head flies to the side. I keep it there staring at the yellowing wall…into nothingness.

With a grunt, he stands up, puts his cock away, zips up his pants, and walks out of the room, slamming the door behind him. Leaving me alone with my own thoughts. I begin to cry again. I pray that someone will find me, and soon. This is so much worse than when he attacked me at my apartment, I have never been this scared in my entire life.

Returning moments later, I notice a sharp knife in his hand. My eyes widen in fear as he begins to cut my black pencil skirt down the middle, pulling it from beneath me, he tosses it onto the timber floor. Placing the knife on the side table, he rips open my worktop; buttons fly everywhere. Picking up the knife, he cuts my teal green bra between my breasts, nicking my skin. I scream out in pain when he digs the knife in.

He slaps my left cheek. "Shut it, bitch," he growls.

He picks up my undies he tore off of me, scrunches them up in his fist and sniffs them. Breathing in deeply. "Beautiful," he whispers, licking his lips while he looks down at me with an evil grin, I notice the bulge in his jeans starting to grow. Shutting my eyes, I hope that when I open them again that this will all be a horrible life-like dream. Opening them, I deflate when I see him standing above me.

He's staring down at me, his hand stroking his cock through his jeans. He unzips his black denim jeans, works them down his legs, exposing his purple throbbing cock. He slams him cock inside of me before I have a chance to comprehend what's about to happen.

Screaming out in pain, I start to cry. Once again, it feels like I'm being split in two. He repeatedly pounds into me, the tears flowing down my cheeks, I whimper and scream louder as the pain becomes intolerable. Drawing his fist back, he punches me in the face, as he continues to thrust into me.

"Shut the fuck up, bitch." He growls as I lay there and let him violate my body.

Over the next few days he rapes me over and over, but he never comes inside of me. He always pulls out at the last minute, spraying his cum on my body. I lose count at how many times he rapes me. I begin to wish for death; I'm don't know how much more of this I can survive.

My body aches. My face is throbbing, and between my legs is torn to pieces. There is dried cum on my body and blood between my thighs. Bite marks adorns my body. He told me he was marking me as his. "You are mines." He repeated over and over and he bit and marked my skin.

I've given up screaming, I realise we must be somewhere pretty remote.

No one has come to rescue me yet.

I don't know how much longer I can go on.

I'm ready to give up.

I feel like I have been here forever, but it's only been seven days, I think. Time is ticking by so slowly. Everything is starting to blur together. I continue to wish for death but fate is a cruel bitch. I'm still alive, broken, but alive.

I'm shocked awake when I feel something roughly being shoved into my ass, followed by a long thin silver dildo into my pussy. When he turns the one in my pussy on, I groan, but when he turns the one in my ass on, I scream out in pain. My ass has never been touched before and the pain is horrendous. It feels like I'm being ripped open from the inside. I start to sob again. He plucks the one in my pussy out and quickly shoves his cock back into me with such force that my teeth pierce my tongue. I can feel the metallic taste from the blood in my mouth and I start to cry, my sobs wrack through my body.

He slaps me across the face and between clenched teeth he spits, "Stop crying, bitch, you had this coming." He keeps thrusting harder, faster and deeper; just before he comes he pulls out and squirts his load all over my chest and chin. He bends down licking the cum off me, roughly rubbing what's left into my skin. Once he's finished licking and rubbing me clean, he starts slapping my face, over and over; eventually I pass out from the pain.

The next morning, Clint comes back into the room with a contented look on his face; immediately I'm fearful for my life. He places a tray with orange juice and a sandwich onto the bed. That's when I notice the carving knife. I start to panic; why does he need a carving knife for a sandwich? My heart starts to race and my breathing becomes shallow.

It's in this moment that something deep inside of me clicks; I decide I want to live and that today I will escape; even if it's the last thing I ever do. If I want to get out of here alive I need to pretend to be the Juliet to his Romeo.

God, I hope I can do this.

Looking towards him I smile and whisper, "Clint, baby."

"Don't call me baby, you lying whore. I saw you having coffee with that twat, right after you ripped my heart out. How long have you been screwing him, huh?" He is yelling now, seething with rage, "Where do I fit into this scenario, huh?" Between clenched teeth he hisses "You. Are. Mines."

I'm dumbfounded by what he is saying. "Clint," I plead, "I'm not screwing him, or anyone else for that matter, Jordan and I are just friends."

He clenches his jaw and glares at me. "Don't say that fucker's name." He looks towards the window before looking back at me. "I know you two are friends who fuck. What's that called? Yeah, fuck buddies."

"No!" I scream. "Clint, I swear." As the panic sets in, I start to cry again. I sniffle, "You are the only one I want to be with."

"Bullshit, you little slut. You're just using me to bide your time. Bitches like you always do."

At this point I have no idea what's going to happen but I need to do something quickly; otherwise I will be here forever. Clint sits on the side of the bed and looks down at me. He almost looks sad and I think this is my chance. I try and lift my hand to reach him, to sooth him but my hands are still bound. I take a deep breath and in my sweetest voice possible I whisper, "Do you think you can unlatch or loosen the cuff, please?" I look at him pleading, I try and lift my hand, but it barely moves. "Please, Clint, I need to make this up to you. I…I need to fix us." I whisper before quickly adding, "I made a mistake breaking up with you, please, please forgive me? Let me fix this, baby, let me fix us."

He looks away before turning back to me and rubbing his hand down the side of my face. I try really hard not to flinch. "Do you really mean that?"

I tilt my head into his palm. "Of course I do baby." Inside I'm saying to myself, *You wish you fucking freak."*

Again I plead with him, "Can you please uncuff my hands, so we can be together again?" Glancing up at him I bat my eyelids, hoping like hell that I don't look like I'm having a fit.

Dropping his hand from my cheek, he stands up. My heart sinks, but he pulls out a little brass key. He reaches across me and uncuffs both of my hands. I slowly sit up, rubbing my wrists. He bends down and cuts off the cable ties, holding my ankles together. I sit there staring at the floor, he sits down next to me and rubs my leg. Shivering from his touch, he assumes I'm cold. He takes off his shirt and slips it over my head; at least I'm not naked anymore.

Looking towards him, I take a deep breath and quietly murmur, "Thank you!" Leaning over, I pretend that I'm about to kiss him, but instead, I lunge for the knife on the tray. Grabbing the knife, I swing with everything that I have left. I manage to slash his face, and with all my might, I shove him off the bed. I swing back my leg, kick him in the stomach, turn and run.

I make it out the front door and down the rickety wooden stairs. I run like I've never run before. Huffing and puffing, I don't stop. I just keep running. My body is aching, but the adrenalin coursing through my veins keeps me going. I have no idea where I get the energy or the confidence from, but somehow I make it to the main road.

After what feels like an eternity, I finally see a car. I turn around, waving my arms, yelling and screaming for them to stop. My waving becomes erratic, my arms flinging around above my head like a mad person. The SUV stops and a middle-aged gentleman gets out. He walks over to me and I collapse into his arms with relief and begin to sob. He calls triple zero and hold me tight, rubbing my arms reassuringly.

"My name's Trevor darling." He sooths after hanging up, "Help is on the way." I thank the powers above, Trevor is definitely my guardian angel.

The police and ambulance arrive at the same time. Trevor lifts me onto the stretcher and the ambo looks me over. He can't see any major injuries, but he is concerned that my cheekbone might be fractured. Due to the amount of swelling he cannot tell for sure. Again he tells me that I'm very lucky as none of my injuries are life threatening.

Before we leave, the police ask me questions regarding what happened. I tell them what I remember and after I give my statement. Just as they are closing the ambulance doors, the officer returns and tells me that that a missing person's report was filed, and they have someone contacting my family now. As the doors slam shut, I start crying at the thought of seeing everyone again. I never thought I'd see them again, the emotions overtake me and the ambo gives me something to calm down and I drift off into a peaceful abyss thinking of Jordan and my family.

28

JORDAN

KENZ JUST CALLED TO TELL ME SHE WAS PROMOTED TODAY, I'M SO PROUD of her. I'm also glad that my trip to Melbourne has been cancelled. I really don't feel like going to meet these investors; my head just isn't in it at the moment. All I can think about is our wedding and making Kenz, Mrs. Jordan McRoberts.

Stopping atthe bottle-o around the corner, I pick up a bottle of GH Mumm to surprise Kenz and celebrate her promotion; another reason I'm glad that my trip is postponed. As I'm driving up our street, I see Kenzie's monstrosity of a purse and her jacket on the footpath. Pulling over, I stop and pick them up; immediately that sick feeling from earlier is back, with a vengeance.

Quickly racing back to my car, I haul ass to our house but no one is home. There is a bunch of sunflowers sitting at the front door, but this time there is a card, its signed 'Love, C,' my heart immediately drops.

I know that Clint has taken her.

I've failed my beautiful Kenz when I promised to protect her.

Grabbing my phone I call the police immediately. They send someone over, but it takes the officers an hour to get to our place. They tell me that Clint didn't check in with his parole officer yesterday and with the flowers signed 'Love, C' they also think that he has taken Kenz. The assholes also ask if it could be a case of cold feet as we are getting married soon. I lose it with the officer, "My ass she has cold feet. She's just as excited as I am for us to get married." He apologises and says he had to ask; they need to cover all bases. They leave and tell me they'll be in touch when they have news.

Standing in the kitchen, I yell, "Fuuuuck!" I stare at the pic of Kenz and I on the fridge, I say, "Fuck this, I know Clint has you baby, I will save you."

Snatching up my phone, I call Margaret and let her know what has happened. She tells me that she and Skye are on their way. I tell them to drive safely and I'll see them soon.

Next, I call Mike and tell him what's happened, and he tells me he will be over as soon as possible. Mike gets here ten minutes later, racing in the front door. "Dude, what the fuck is going on?" He takes a seat on the chaise, staring at me.

Taking a deep breath, I fill him in on everything. "I've failed her again, Mike. What if I lose her? I can't live without her."

"Kenz is one tough chick, if anyone can beat this, it's our girl."

Mike quickly stand ups and says, "Let's go for a drive and see if we can find her. I don't know where to look but we can't just sit around and do nothing."

"Sounds like a plan, Mike." Standing up, I grab my keys but Mike stops me.

"Okay, let's go but asshat, I'm driving. You're too worked up and we need to get there safely, for our girl."

I knew I could count on Mike.

Mike and I drive around for hours but we don't find her; I wasn't holding out any hope that we would. By time we get back to our place, Margaret and Skye are waiting on the front steps. I wrap my arms around Margaret as she cries. I feel broken and lost right now, I can only imagine how Margaret must feel.

The next seven days are pure torture.

I can't eat.

I can't sleep.

I just keep thinking about Kenz, hoping and praying she is safe.

When we get the call to say she's been found and alive, we are all so relieved. We race to the hospital to wait for Kenzie to arrive. When I see her, my heart breaks into a million tiny shards.

The girl lying in front of me is broken, physically and mentally.

She's fragile.

She's lost.

And there's nothing I can do to help ease her burdens.

29

KENZIE

I'VE JUST GOTTEN SETTLED IN MY ROOM WHEN THERE IS A KNOCK AT THE door, the officer from today is here. He informs me that the police searched the area, and they found the cabin but Clint was nowhere to be found. They will keep searching and looking for him but at this stage there is no trace of him. It's like he vanished into thin air, if it weren't for my injuries you'd think I made this up.

A warrant for Clint's arrest has been issued, and his parole terminated. They assure me that they are doing everything they can to find him and that an officer will be stations outside my room until Clint has been apprehended.

The next morning, Clint is arrested when he tried to visit me at the hospital. As soon as I heard he was here, I lost it. I was crying and screaming, fear coursing through my body. They had to sedate me to calm me down.

Later that day, the officer returned by to let me know that Clint was formally charged with parole violation, assault causing grievously bodily harm, criminal sexual conduct, violating a restraining order and kidnapping. He is to be remanded in custody as he is delusional and they fear he will be a menace to society; and me. I sigh in relief knowing he is locked up again.

I'm kept in hospital for ten days due to the extent of my injuries and mental state. My left cheekbone is fractured, I also have two broken ribs, four cracked ribs, five stitches to the laceration between my breasts and my lower intestine is torn from the anal penetration. Due to the savageness of the rape, there is also a high probability that I will never conceive a child.

I've hardly spoken a word to anyone. I pretend to sleep most of the time, and when I'm alone, I sob. I'm numb, broken beyond repair and even though someone is always around, I feel alone.

When I'm released, I crawl into myself, and stay locked in our bedroom, only venturing out when I need the toilet. I only shower, eat, or drink when Mum, Jordan or Sarah make me. The rest of the time, I just lie in bed and stare at the ceiling.

I'm not sleeping. Every time I close my eyes, I see his face. When I do fall asleep, I wake up screaming from horrible nightmares. Every time I close my eyes, I relive it all over again. Someone always races in to soothe me, but I cannot stand to be touched at the moment, so it takes a while to calm me down.

It's been two weeks since I was released from hospital, and I haven't left the house. Whenever I get near the front door, I start to panic and run back to our room. My fear is heightened when corrections called to let me know that due to Clint's mental state, the doctors feel he is unfit for trial. He is to be remanded in custody indefinitely at a psychiatric hospital.

As soon as I hang up, I have a complete break down. I scream. I cry. I let out all my frustrations. Mum and Jordan, just stand there and watch, helpless to help me. Once I'm finished, I race back to our bedroom and I'm so exhausted, I cry myself to sleep.

I see his face when I close my eyes.

I see his face when my eyes are open.

I see him everywhere, I can't go out in public.

I'm broken.

I'm scared.

I'm lost.

I decide to take an indefinite leave of absence from work; it's not fair to my coworkers. My boss, Karl, is awesome about it, and he tells me that my job will be waiting for me when I'm ready again. *I'm not sure I will ever be ready again.*

Two weeks later, and four weeks after the incident, I move out of Jordan's and my bedroom and I lock myself in our spare room. It isn't fair for him to be on eggshells in his own room. Each and every time I look at him, I feel guilty. I try to explain how I feel but he doesn't understand, no one understands. Every Tom, Dick, and Harry tells me that I'm not to blame and that they love me, but *I am* to blame for this and love won't fix this…nothing will.

I wish they would just treat me like they did before all of this happened. They all look at me with pity and that makes me feel inferior. Internally I keep screaming at myself for letting this happen again.

Again?

How could this happen to me again?

I've let down Jordan, I can no longer give him a child.

I've let down Mum, I can no longer give her grandchildren.

I've let down myself.

I've let everyone down.

I'm worthless.

I'm nothing but a waste of space.

This time it's much harder to deal with it. This time the attack was much more brutal. How stupid I am to get attacked again? And by the same person? Being attacked once is bad enough, but to be attacked twice by the same monster makes me weak and unworthy.

I just want to be me again.

Thankfully, Jordan gives me the space I need, but I can see it's taking a toll on him. The only good thing to come from this mess is Jordan spends all his time in his beer/man cave, perfecting his recipes. I guess that's the silver lining to all of this.

A few weeks later, I'm in the toilet when Mike arrives, I overhear him and Jordan talking in the kitchen. Jordan says, "I don't think she is getting any better Mike, if anything she is pulling away even further."

"Give her time, dude. I can't fucking imagine what she is going through right now. To be attacked once is terrible, but twice and the second time being so much more brutal; I know if it were me, I wouldn't be the same. She just needs time, Jordan." Pausing, he looks at me and adds, "Just remember, Kenz is strong. She will get through this."

"I know she is strong, and I know she will get though this but I'm not sure how much more I can take." I gasp at hearing this, and they both turn and look at me standing in the hall with tears streaming down my face. Turning, I run back to my room and lock the door.

Jordan races down the hall, he tries the handle but thankfully I locked it. I can't look at him right now. He keeps rattling the doorknob and when it doesn't budge, he starts knocking and banging on the door. "Kenz, I didn't mean it like that. It's not what you think, please let me in."

Ripping open the door with tears pouring down my face, I stare at him. The floodgates have opened and there's no stopping them now. "How am I meant to take not sure how much more I can take? Huh? Tell me? Tell me?" I yell, beating my fists against his chest; my tears are uncontrollable by this point. "It's killing me, Jordan, I feel so weak, so useless, so...so..." But I can't talk anymore; the tears have taken over. My whole body is shaking as I collapse into Jordan's arms. He wraps them tightly around me and for the first time since the attack, I feel safe in his arms.

We sink down to the floor in the hallway and we sit there in each other's arms while I cry into his chest. He doesn't say anything, he just keeps whispering. "Shhhh, let it out, baby." Occasionally, he kisses my head, reassuring me that he is still here for me.

After crying for what feels like days, I look up at Jordan. "Why can't people see that I'm strong? I survived this once before, I can survive this again, I just need time Jor." Pulling away, I stare at him, and add, "I refuse to let him ruin my life, because if I do, then he wins and I will not let him win."

Jordan doesn't say anything, he leans forward, kisses my forehead and whispers, "You are the strongest person I know, Kenz. You will survive this and I'll be right there with you, every step of the way."

We snuggle into each other further and Jordan starts to rub my back in circles, just like Sarah does when I'm upset. When I realise what he is doing for the first time in weeks, I laugh. Jordan pulls back and looks at me, "What's so funny, Kenz?"

"You're rubbing my back exactly how Sarah does to soothe me when I'm upset. It's not really funny, but it is, if that makes sense."

Jordan lets out a throaty laugh, leans down and kisses my forehead just like he used to. *It's starting to feel like old times*. We sit in the hall together, not saying a thing, both sitting there quietly supporting each other. Glancing up I notice that it's now dark outside, and that Mike is no longer here.

Jordan is still rubbing my back and he hasn't stopped since we ended up sitting here. "This is nice," I whisper. I push away and look up at him. I gaze into his eyes. All I see is love; no pity, no remorse, just love. Smiling at him I say, "I think I need to make an appointment to see Jeannie. I can't do this to you or me anymore. I want to be me again."

"I'll call her in the morning for you, Kenz, but for now I want to take my fiancée to bed." Tensing in his arms, I start to panic. He draws back and looks lovingly into my eyes. "To sleep, but first you need a shower."

Reaching up, I wrap my arms around his neck for a cuddle. "I like that plan," I whisper, as I hold him tighter. Feeling better after my meltdown, I smile against Jordan's chest.

I AM strong and I WILL survive this.

We stand up and Jordan leads me into the bathroom. Jordan takes his shirt off and starts to unbutton his jeans. I freeze. "Umm, Jor, I'm not ready to shower with anyone yet, baby steps." A look of hurt flashes across his beautiful face but he quickly smiles. "No worries Kenz, I'll go lock up the shed and be right back." He grabs his shirt from the hamper and walks out.

As I climb into the shower, I start to cry again. I stand under the steaming hot water and let it all out. Wishing I could just wash away all my fears. *If only it was that easy.*

After my shower, I put on my grey trackies and Kings jersey and head to the kitchen. Jordan is on the phone, he looks up at me when he hears me coming into the kitchen, and his face lights up just like it used to. He quickly finishes his conversation and hangs up. "Hey, baby, feel better after your shower?"

Jumping up onto the island bench I look over at him. "Yeah, I do, actually. I um, um, I want to apologise for everything."

He leans on the bench opposite me. "Kenz, you don't need to apologise for anything, if anything I should be apologizing to you." I look over and see sadness in Jordan's eyes, "Once again I didn't protect you. I promised your mum that I would always protect you when I asked her permission to propose." Looking up at me, he smiles sadly, before adding, "But most of all I failed you, I promised to do so, when you agreed to marry me, and I didn't live up to that promise. I've failed you both."

I look at him inquisitively, "You asked Mum's permission?"

"Yeah, it's the right thing to do," he replies, as if I asked him to pass the chips.

Again I find myself smiling, a genuine smile not the fake plastered on one I have been wearing recently. Looking over at him with such love in my heart I say, "You are amazing, Jordan McRoberts, how did I get so lucky?"

"Well your clumsy ass kept bumping into me, so I thought for my safety I should ask you out." He looks up at me with a sneaky grin.

"Hardy har har, asshat."

As I sit here with Jordan, I realise that for the first time in weeks I'm not scared and I can't help but smile at that revelation.

Jumping off the bench, I walk over to where him and I wrap my arms around his waist, resting my head on his shoulder just like I used to. I breathe him in and sigh, "I'm sorry for pushing you away, Jordan. I'm sorry for letting you down."

He tilts my head up and looks me in the eyes. "How did you let me down, Kenz?"

"By letting him take me, I'm a failure." Lowering my head again, that happy euphoric feeling is quickly disappearing. The fear and weakness sneaking back in.

"Kenz, look at me."

Lifting my head, I look up and I see nothing but love in his eyes. "I'm only going to say this once, you are not a failure. It's not your fault that some psycho asshole douchcanoe fuckwit did unspeakable things. You are not to blame, you hear me?" I nod, and I snuggle back into the comfort of his arms, but deep down; I know I'm to blame.

Pulling away I say, "Can we snuggle on the couch and watch *That 70's Show*?"

"We can watch whatever you want, Kenz, but I refuse to watch that Kardashian crap." Laughing I grab his hand and we head to the lounge room. We snuggle together on the couch and watch *That 70's Show* for a few hours, just like old times.

Later that night, for the first time in weeks, I fall asleep, peacefully in Jordan's arms. I sleep the night through and no bad dreams plague me.

The next day, Jordan and I call Jeannie, and she makes room for me on her schedule. We meet with her, and just like last time; she makes me see that I did nothing wrong, and that I am strong. I am a survivor and I will get through this; again.

After we get home Jordan heads to his beer cave and I take a relaxing bubble bath. While soaking, I shake my head in frustration at myself, I really I wish I had been back to see her earlier. She helped me the first time, and after just one session I feel so much better already. I really am lucky to have such amazing people on my team.

For the first time in weeks, I feel free, liberated, and not scared. Yesterday's meltdown was exactly what I needed.

30

JORDAN

LAST NIGHT SNUGGLING AND WATCHING *THAT 70'S SHOW* WITH KENZ WAS amazing. I was starting to feel like I was losing her, but after her hallway breakdown, I think we are back on track.

When I realised she had heard my conversation with Mike, I felt like a piece of shit. While I meant what I said, I never wanted her to hear it. I was just venting. There's no way in hell I would ever abandon her. Kenz is my everything. I would do anything for her, anything.

Today though, I can see that it was the jolt Kenz needed. As much as it pained me to see her breakdown like that, it was the push she needed to start her recovery. I'd been pestering her to go and see Jeannie, but no one tells Kenz what to do; she's quite stubborn. I'm glad she decided to go back and see her therapist. She worked wonders the first time around, and after just one session, I can see that this time will be just the same.

After her appointment, I suggest that we stop at the Java Lava for a coffee, but I see the hesitation in Kenzie's eyes, so I don't even wait for her answer and we head straight home.

We get home and she heads upstairs to have a bath and read one of her dirty books. Leaving her alone, I head to the beer shed and start working on a new pale ale. The last one wasn't quite right, so this time, I use a different hops. I hope and pray to the beer God's that it works.

Once all the new ingredients are in the wort tun, I turn off the lights, lock up, and head back upstairs. Just as I get upstairs, Kenz is coming down the hall, still rubbing cream into her arms. She looks up at me. "Hey, baby, how'd you go?"

Smiling back at her, I say, "All good, got the new pale down, and I hope to God it tastes better than the last one. Do you wanna watch *That 70's Show* before bed?"

"Actually, I think I'd like to watch *The Walking Dead*, if that's okay? I'm also going to open a bottle of wine, would you like a glass?"

"I'd love one and *Walking Dead* sounds great."

Kenz opens a bottle of white and I grab the wine bucket and two glasses. Then we snuggle on the couch, drinking wine and watching *Walking Dead*.

Smiling, I realise, that things are starting to feel normal again and that we will be okay and we will get through this.

31

KENZIE

...6 months later

OUR WEDDING DAY IS THE BEST DAY OF MY LIFE, AND THE WEDDING NIGHT is one I will not forget anytime soon. Jordan and I are married on Hayman Island with our closest friends in attendance. It's just Jordan and I, Sarah and Josh, and Mike and his latest floozy, De-Niece.

The day is absolutely perfect.

Our parents were upset not to be included, but as I explained, I don't want a big fuss anymore. We each had our special one-on-one time with them for specific wedding related things.

Mum and I had a lovely girls' day out the day I found my wedding dress, complete with pampering at the local day spa.

Jordan and his dad went golfing together one day, where his dad passed on the secret to a happy marriage. Apparently, Jordan just needs to remember two very important phrases, "Yes dear," and "You're right."

The morning of our wedding, Sarah and I get ready in her suite. Jordan and I had to give up our room, as Mike and Sarah have a surprise for us; if Sarah wasn't involved I would be scared. Who knows what Mike would get up to on his own? Actually, leaving those two to their own devices IS super scary.

I'm in the bathroom and yell out to Sarah to give me a hand with my dress. My dress is a Collette Dinnigan original; it's made from beautiful French lace with cap sleeves, a low V-back with scalloped lace edging and three layers of silk lining. It comes with a gorgeous detachable belt that has small pearl and bead detail. Leaving my hair down, I curl it and wear the tiara that Mum wore when she married Dad.

It's ten to three, so Sarah and I make our way down to the beach. When I reach to the archway, *Pachelbel: Canon in D Major* starts to play, that's my cue. Taking a deep breath, I start walking towards Jordan. I even manage to stumble when my foot gets caught on my dress. I look up and everyone is laughing, tripping on my wedding day is so me.

Glancing up, I look towards Jordan and get lost in his emerald green eyes. It's in this moment that I know that this is it for me; there are no butterflies in my tummy; this is where I'm meant to be. I've never been happier, and I'm pretty sure the smile that is currently on Jordan's face, is a mirror image of mine.

It's a quick ceremony, and before I know it the celebrant is pronouncing us husband and wife. Jordan dips me and we have our first kiss as Mr. and Mrs. McRoberts; it's sensual, erotic, and it left me breathless. It's the second best kiss of my life. The best being my first kiss with Jordan after our first official date.

As we sign the registry, *Nothing Else Matters* by Metallica starts to play. Mike yells, "Fuck Yeah!" We all laugh, trust Mike to swear at a pivotal moment on our special day.

After the ceremony, we pose for a few photos and then we head to the restaurant for a relaxed reception. They place us at a table in the back of the restaurant. The table is laced with sunflowers and tea light candles; it's absolutely breathtaking.

The bubbles are flowing and the food is to die for. After dinner Mike asks everyone to follow him; we are walking down a pathway that is lined with tea light candles. As we get closer to the beach, *Lanterns* by Birds of Tokyo starts playing. When we step onto the beach, we look up and there are hundreds of paper lanterns floating in the sky. On the sand is a big love heart, lined with candles, with J and K etched in the center.

Looking over to Mike, I see him smiling. I'm pretty sure that the smile I have on my face is just as big as his. Letting go of Jordan's hand, I walk over to Mike and give him a hug. No words are said but none are needed in this moment. After the incident, Mike and I have a newfound relationship. It's one I will treasure forever, and this gift has left me speechless. It's so enchanting, something right out of a fairytale.

The next song to play is, *Everything I Do (I Do It For You)* by Bryan Adams. Jordan asks me to dance, placing my hand in his we walk to our heart. We stand in the middle and lose ourselves to the music. I look over and see that Sarah and Josh, and Mike and De-Niece, are also dancing. We dance for several songs, drink the bubbly, and enjoy the night together.

Leaving the beach, we head to out room. When we arrive, Jordan lifts me up and carries me over the threshold; I can't help but giggle. He places me down just inside the door, and I place a quick kiss on my husband's lips. *I love saying husband.* We turn around and there are, what feels like, thousands of tea light candles flickering and sunflower petals strewn on the floor, making a pathway to the bed.

Turning to Jordan, I see he is staring at me. "Mackenzie McRoberts nee Merlot, you are the most beautiful bride I have ever seen. This dress is absolutely stunning, and I cannot wait to see it on the floor."

Blushing at what he says, I look up into my husband's eyes and in a low sultry voice I whisper, "Well, what are you waiting for, husband?"

"Absolutely nothing, wife."

He pushes me up against the back of the door and kisses me senseless. This kiss is now the most romantic kiss of my life; it leaves me lightheaded and my lips are tingling when Jordan pulls away. I wrap my arms around his neck and I drag him in closer. I lift one leg up and wrap it around his thighs, his hands roams up my leg and over my garter. I shiver in delight as his hands inch higher up my thigh. He groans into my mouth when his fingers reach my undies and feels how wet they are.

He rubs my slit through the silk of my undies; I moan and rub myself on his hand. Lowering my leg, I spin around, lifting my hair, and without prompting, he carefully undoes the clip at the top. He places feather light kisses across my shoulder blade as he lowers the zip. Carefully, I lower the straps down my arms, wriggling my ass, my dress falls down, the lace and silk pillowing out at my feet. Turning around, I face my husband in nothing but my tiara, silk undies, silver heels, and a beaming smile. Jordan's eyes roam over my body; I have never felt sexier in my entire life. "Fuck me, Mrs. McRoberts, you are fucking beautiful."

Carefully stepping out of my dress, I step towards my husband, "You, my husband, have far too many clothes on for me to really appreciate you." As I reach him, I rip open his dress shirt. Pearl buttons fly everywhere, and I make quick work of removing his shirt. Reaching forward, I undo his belt and lower his fly. Slipping my hand inside for a quick squeeze before I push down his pants and boxer briefs in one swift motion.

Kneeling down, I take his thick throbbing cock in my mouth. Licking from tip to base and back up again, while squeezing the base of his cock; I hollow my cheeks and take him deeper into my mouth. With my other hand, I massage his balls while I bob my head up and down, sucking and licking his pulsating cock. His balls tighten in my hand and I feel his cock tense. Just before he comes, he lifts me up by my shoulders and kisses me deeply. He pulls back and cradles my face is his palm. "Kenz, the first time I come with you as husband and wife will not be in your mouth, it will be together as one."

Leaning forward I kiss him again; I drape my arms around his neck and raise my leg, wrapping it around his waist. He grabs my ass and lifts me up. I wrap both legs around his waist, digging my heels into his ass. Our kisses becoming frenzied as he walks us over to the bed. He gently lays me down on the mattress and hooks his fingers into the sides of my undies and slowly works them down my legs.

Grabbing my ankle, and ever so slowly, he kisses his way along my calf, up my thigh and across the top of my mound. I think he's going to suck on my clit, but he pulls back and spreads my legs wider. He bends down and finally licks my slit. Starting at the bottom, taking his sweet time, he slides his tongue to the top, before sucking on my swollen nub. My back arches off the bed as he twirls his tongue around and around, sucking, licking and gently nibbling my clit. Gripping the sheets, I throw my head back in ecstasy as my orgasm starts to build. Arching my back further, I thrust and grind my pussy onto his face. He licks down, spreading me open wider as he slips in a finger. Pulling out his fingers, he smears my wetness all over my pulsating pussy.

His tongue darting in and out of my pussy is mind-blowing. He inserts two fingers and finds that magical spot deep inside. As I run my hands over his head, I gently massage his scalp, tugging on his hair; the tingling in my pussy intensifies. I'm writhing in ecstasy when he inserts a third finger and sucks on my clit. Gently blowing on my sensitive nub, as his fingers scissor in and out of me. I scream Jordan's name when he sucks on my clit, as my orgasm detonates, it's like fireworks going off on Australia Day. My body vibrates from head to toe, as my orgasm takes over my soul; it's the most amazing feeling, ever.

As I am coming back down to earth Jordan kisses and licks his way up my stomach, over my nipples, up my neck, and along my jawbone. Gently nipping my earlobe before he eases back to look at me; I see nothing but lust and hunger in his eyes. Closing his eyes, he leans forward to kiss me, and that kiss takes my breath away. I can taste myself on his lips and it ignites a fire deep in my belly once again.

Wrapping arms around his neck, I bring him closer to me and I guide his cock between my legs. He gently eases into me, before pulling out and slamming back in. I lift my hips to give him better access and spread my legs further apart. I have never felt Jordan so deep inside of me; I moan into his mouth and kiss him deeper. Meeting him thrust for thrust, Jordan reaches between us and rubs my clit as I tighten my legs around his waist. My pussy muscles clench his cock tighter, as we tumble over the edge, and orgasm together, for the first time as husband and wife.

Jordan rolls off me and I snuggle into his side. We lie together, both catching our breath. I run my fingers over his chest and nipples, back and forth until I feel his nipples harden. Rolling onto my side, I rest my head on my palm and I look into his beautiful green eyes. "Wow, Mr. McRoberts, that was just…wow."

"You're not wrong there, Mrs. McRoberts."

He reaches out to brush a tendril of hair behind my ear and whispers, "I love you, wife," before kissing the tip of my nose.

"I love you too, husband." Leaning over, I kiss him. Shuffling towards him, I deepen the kiss, pushing up so I'm straddling him. Rocking my hips, I feel his cock growing beneath me as I continue to grind my pelvis onto him.

He sits us up, wrapping his arms around me as I wind my legs around his waist. He bends down to take my breast into his mouth, alternating between sucking my nipple and massaging my breast, while twisting and tugging my other nipple between his thumb and forefinger; which he knows I love.

Pulling up I gently lower myself onto his hardening cock; I push him back so he is lying down and I ride him. Throwing my head back as that tingling sensation starts to creep all over my body, I keep riding him, rocking my hips faster and faster. Arching my back, I reach down to rub my clit while playing with my own nipples. "Kenz, that is so hot." Rubbing and circling my finger faster; the sensation on my clit becomes overwhelming and my orgasm quickly ruptures through my body. At the same time, I feel Jordan's balls tighten, and he releases himself inside of me for the second time tonight.

Collapsing onto Jordan, I lie there for a few moments before I roll off onto my back. Jordan leans over and kisses my cheek and whispers, "Good night, Mackenzie McRoberts," but I'm already fast asleep.

The next morning, I wake up to Jordan's cock pushing between my ass crack and him nibbling my neck. Grinding my ass into his cock, I throw my leg over his hip and guide his cock into my pussy. His hand snakes around and he starts to tweak my nipples. Letting out a contented sigh, I turn my head to kiss him. He starts thrusting into me quicker, and I reach down and rub my clit, sending myself over the edge. I keep thrusting and Jordan soon releases inside of me.

Rolling over to face my new husband, I give him a kiss on the cheek. "Good morning, husband, that was a wonderful way to wake up."

"Good morning, wife, I'm happy to wake you up that way for the rest of your life."

"Mmhmm, I won't say not to that." I snuggle into him and soon we both fall asleep wrapped in each other's arms.

After a horrible start to the year, Jordan has managed to turn it around and into one that I will never forget.

I am Mrs. Jordan McRoberts. I'm blissfully happy and safe...for now.

32

KENZIE

...18 months later

TODAY IS THE DAY THAT WE FINALLY MOVE IN TO THE OLD QUEENSLANDER we renovated and I'm sooo excited. We stripped the house back to bare frame, removed a wall, added internal stairs, and started from scratch. Repainting the outside a deep brown with reddy-brown surrounds, we added beautiful French doors that lead out to an extended verandah, which runs the length of the house. There are timber stairs that lead directly to the beer shed and a paved undercover entertaining area which leads out to the grassed backyard and inside to the family room, laundry and internal stairs.

Jordan insisted on putting a shed in straight away and I'm glad we did. Having an ice-cold beer at the end of the day after renovating, especially in the summer when it was hotter than hell, was beertabolous. I'm pretty sure this is why the renovation took so long as he'd tinker with his beers rather than renovate but Jordan really knows how to make a great beer, so I'll allow it.

Now that the reno is complete, Jordan and I can concentrate on our next dream, opening our brewery, Malt Me. If it had not been for my attack, Malt Me would be up and running by now.

With the last piece of furniture coming through the door, we are officially moved in; thank firetruck for that. I've come a long way in the last two years. For a while there I was lost, but I have the support of my family and friends; but most of all I have Jordan. He is my rock. I honestly don't think I would have survived this the second time, if it were not for him.

The only major DIY injury I sustained was severe blisters on my hands from removing the glued lino-on-lino that was in the old kitchen; ohh and a broken ankle when I was taking empty paint tins to the bin. That was twelve weeks that I never want to go through again. The only good thing about my broken ankle was all the reading I could do.

Jordan and Mike have just hooked up the stereo system, and I head down to the shed and pour three beers. Coming up the back stairs, I walk in as Mike and Jordan are laughing their asses off. I can't help but smile, it's nice to see him relaxed, for a change.

Handing them their beers, I raise my mug and say, "A toast, to finally moving in."

Jordan adds, "Cheers to that. I guarantee you, we are never doing that again, tell me again why I let you convince us to do this?"

"Well, it looked easy on The Block, ohh, and you love me."

Mike clears his throat and says, "As long as you keep brewing stuff like this, asshat, I'll hang around. This is the bomb dude."

Quickly I jump up and yell, "Jordan, never make this one again if it means we get rid of Mike!" I wink at him as I walk into the kitchen to grab us some snacks. It feels good to finally relax and enjoy our house.

I'm bending down in the pantry, to get out the platter, when Jordan walks over and places his arms around me, "I love you, Kenzie McRoberts. I can't wait to christen every room in this house."

Mike interrupts, "Hello, I'm still here."

"There's the door, don't let it hit you on the way out!" I shout as I wriggle out of Jordan's arms and step to the fridge to get the cheese, olives, and salami's. After placing it all on the platter, we head to the side verandah and sit at the high-top table with timber-backed chairs and super comfy chocolate brown cushions, which match the window surrounds.

Jordan heads down to the shed to top up our beers. We hang out for a few hours, relaxing and just being us.

"I'll catch you later guys, and Kenzie, it's good to see you still smiling."

Jumping off my chair, I give Mike a big bear hug, and whisper,

"Thanks for everything, Mike, you have not only helped me but you've been there for Jor when I couldn't be. I'll never be able to repay you for that."

"You can pay me in beer," he whispers, I can't help but laugh.

Mike heads inside to get his phone and keys, and on the way out, he yells, "Later, assholes!" before slamming the front door. Just as Jordan and I both yell in unison, "Don't slam the door!"

Jordan takes the pizza boxes out to the bins after dinner, and I relax on my uber comfy, charcoal grey suede corner lounge with chaise at one end, and recliner at the other. I look around at all that we've done to this place, and I smile. We, well Jordan, has done a brilliant job.

Jordan walks back in and his smile is just as big as mine. "It's so great to see you smile, I love seeing you smile." He leans over the back of the couch and pecks on the forehead. "We finally finished this place and I couldn't be happier."

Looking up at him I say, "It's all thanks to you, baby."

He jumps over the back of the couch and pushes me down. He lies on top of me before crashing his mouth to mine. Our tongues fighting it out as my girly bits begin to tingle. Jordan pulls back and looks deep into my eyes. "Now, about christening this place." He leans down, I close my eyes and he places a kiss, just under my ear. "I" **kiss** "think" **kiss** "we" **kiss** "should" **kiss** "start" **kiss** "right" **kiss** "here" **kiss**.

Opening my eyes, I look into his mesmerising green ones; before I can reply, his mouth is on mine again. Any coherent thoughts I have evaporate, and I lose myself in Jordan. Wrapping my legs around him, I intensify our kiss when I feel his hands slide under my magenta singlet and cup my breasts. My nipples immediately pebble, and he pushes my shirt up further and sucks on my nipples through my lacy bra. *This man knows exactly how to pleasure my tits.* I moan at the sensation escalating between my thighs. With his other hand, he wriggles my shirt over my head and slides my shorts down.

Lying on the couch in just my bra and undies, his eyes wander over my body and darken with lust. He quickly removes his shirt and then crushes his lips against mine once again. I start to wriggle under him and rub my hands up and down his back, eventually cupping his ass, squeezing and guiding him closer to me. Sliding my hands around, I work his button free. In one go, I get his boxer briefs and cargos down far enough that I use my feet to push them down the rest of the way and nudge them off completely. Reaching down, I cup his balls and grip his shaft, stroking him from base to tip, while rubbing myself on his leg.

He manages to undo my bra, while I shimming out of it, he pulls my undies down my legs. He slowly crawls back up my body and in one swift motion, he fills me completely. Pulling back out before slamming back in. I bend my knee, allowing him to get deeper. We move into a steady rhythm and before I know it, I'm plummeting over the edge as my orgasm bursts through me. I feel Jordan's body tense and I know he isn't too far away. A few thrusts later, Jordan shatters as his orgasm takes hold.

We lie there in each other's arms before I say, "Jor, you're squishing me. Let's take this to the bathroom to clean up, and if you're up for it, old man, maybe round two."

He lifts up and looks into my eyes. "Old man? Really?"

We both giggle; he helps me up and wraps me in a bear hug, before throwing me over his shoulder like a caveman, slapping my ass, and carrying me into the bathroom. We christen the bathroom twice, before falling into our newly built bed, courtesy of my man. We christen our bed and bedroom before we fall asleep, wrapped in each other's arms, blissfully happy.

It was a perfect evening for the first night in our house.

33

TRAITOR

LOOK AT HOW HAPPY THAT BITCH IS? SHE SO DOES NOT DESERVE TO BE happy; her breaking her ankle was karma of the best kind. Clint lost his shit when I told him that she broke her ankle, but not as much as when I told him that she was married.

To this day, I don't know what Clint sees in her. She must have a magical, hypnotic pussy or something. I just don't see it. For Clint's sake, I hope that when this is all said and done that he's happy with this bitch.

After what this bitch has done, my cousin deserves happiness. If being with her makes him happy, then I'll help him anyway I can, that's what family does for each other. He was there for me when I needed him and now it's my turn to return the favour. That's what family does for each other.

The local florist is going to love me with all the sunflowers that I'll be delivering on Clint's behalf. It's time to put his final plan in motion

34

JORDAN

THANK GOD, WE HAVE FINALLY FINISHED RENOVATING AND ARE NOW completely moved in. It's great to see Kenz happy and relaxed, it's been a while since I've seen her this content. Finally, I have my girl back and I couldn't be happier. If I had known renovating, looking after Kenz, and getting Malt Me off the ground would have been so tough, I wouldn't have let her convince me to do this.

I must admit, it is pretty awesome to see all our hard work and effort pay off; we have a magnificent and unique house. Kenz did an amazing job picking colours and coordinating everything, that woman continues to amaze me.

Looking at the shiny polished floors, I'm glad she convinced me to sand and polish the floorboards; they look gorgeous and really add character to the house. Her squeal when we lifted the old carpet up to find the blackbutt boards underneath, in amazing condition was priceless; she was like a kid in a candy store. Only a few had to be repaired, but as Kenz reminds me, it's a forty-year-old house and they give it charm and charisma; as does the half V-Jay walls with feature belt rail, Colonial skirting and cornice, and plantation shutters. I'm so glad I managed to convince Kenz to put them in, they really are amazing.

I'm relieved today is over, because I hate moving. I cannot thank Mike enough for helping us move today. It was also nice to have a few chillaxed beers with him before chilling with Kenz.

We decided on pizza for dinner, as neither of us could be assed cooking. After a day of moving furniture, beer and pizza was definitely called for.

After having my way with her on the couch, and again in the shower we fall into bed absolutely exhausted. She falls asleep immediately and I lie there staring at her. Kenz is amazing; she has been though so much yet she's so strong.

I will never get my fill of this woman. She is my life. I will do anything to protect her and give her the happily ever after that she deserves.

35

KENZIE

THE NEXT MORNING, JORDAN COOKS ME HIS FAMOUS BACON AND CREAMY scrambled eggs on my new stove. Yes, he christened my stove before I did. However, Jordan's eggs are to die for; like *Masterchef* winning good, so I was happy to allow him to christen my stove.

After breakfast, we both head down to the shed to set up the new kegging and bottling system. We only set up the brewers and filtering system while renovating, as we needed the space for renovating materials.

Ducking back upstairs I grab my surprise for Jordan. He has worked his ass off to get this house finished, and he has been my rock. Now that it's completed, it's time for Jordan to be in the spotlight, for a change.

Skipping back into the shed, Jordan has his back to me as he places a canister on the top shelf. I wrap my arms around his waist and say, "Babe, don't get mad but I did something."

Jordan turns around, wraps his arms around my waist and eyes me questioningly. "I know that you said when the house was done we'd concentrate on getting this all up and running but..." He tries to interrupt me, as usual, I place my finger over his lips to shush him. "And that's why I did this..." I hand him the package and watch him as he registers what it is

"Is that what I think it is?"

"It sure is, baby, it's our registration for the four day Black Gold Premium brewing course at the Coleuses Brewing Company in Melbourne, including flights and accommodation. I also got us two House of Red Bull tickets for the F1 on Saturday and Sunday. If we are lucky, we will be able to meet Colton Daniels."

"Seriously?"

"Seriously, we fly out Sunday lunchtime."

"Oh My God, Kenz, this is the best surprise ever, even better than the Oktoberfest surprise. As much as I was looking forward to having some downtime, this is seriously...I'm speechless, this is amazing. I love you so very muchly, woman."

"I know. I am pretty awesome." I wink at him. "So...wanna christen your beer cave?" I look seductively at him.

"Are you trying to be sexy again? You look like your having a fit," he laughs.

"Screw you, asshole." Walking past him I look back over my shoulder and seductively murmur, "Well, I guess you don't wanna see what I got online from Victoria's Secret then."

Before I can make my getaway, Jordan picks me up, and I'm on my back on the black pleather couch. He is nipping and nuzzling my shoulder, while his hands are rubbing me ever so seductively in all the right spots. "You mentioned something about Victoria's Secret?"

I look up and his eyes are full of heat, and a pulsing begins between my thighs. My breathing is short and fast, my heart racing. "Maybe, why don't we swap positions and I might show you...if you're lucky."

Before I know it, I'm on my feet, and Jordan is sitting down, staring intently at me; his eyes filled with desire and lust. Taking a step back, I lift up the hem of my emerald green, halter sundress, but I drop it back down. Hearing Jordan exhale in frustration, I reach behind and undo the tie at my neck. My dress falls to the floor, and I am standing before him in a pale pink strapless bra with black trimming and matching boy legs.

Jordan rakes his eyes over my entire body; I have never felt so sexy in my life. "Fuck me, you're gorgeous. Come here, woman, so I can worship your body."

Swinging my hips from side to side, I walk back over to the couch and straddle him. My mouth is on his before he has a chance to reply. Pulling him closer; I escalate our kiss as I wrap my arms around his neck. Rubbing myself on his growing cock, I feel it hardening by the minute. His hands graze up my sides, cupping my breasts and squeezing, before moving around my back. He swiftly works my bra free, exposing my tits to the air, my nipples immediately pebble. I let it fall away without breaking contact, our tongues melding together to become one.

Jordan lets out a moan, "Kenz, if you don't stop, I'm gonna blow my load." Standing up, I slide my undies down, while Jordan quickly strips out of his cargos and boxer briefs.

Straddling him again, I rub myself over the end of his thick pulsating shaft, "Please, Kenz, fuck me now," he whispers, so I lower myself over him, rubbing the end of his cock on my drenched pussy. Slowly I slide down his length, taking his hard cock deep inside me.

Jordan pinches my left nipple and takes the right into his mouth and sucks. I throw my head back as the pleasure courses through my body. My pace quickens and I lean forward to kiss him. Our kisses become aggressive and frenzied. "Jor, I'm gonna come are you with me?" I don't wait for his reply as my orgasm flows through me, my entire body tingling. I feel Jordan's body tense and together, we ride out our orgasms.

We sit with our foreheads touching, our breaths slowly returning to normal. "Seriously, Kenz, are you trying to kill me? Four times last night and just now. If I'd known finishing the house would have unleashed this side of you, I'd have finished it a year ago."

Laughing, I give him a passionate kiss before standing on shaky legs and getting dressed. "Jordan, you just bring out my inner devil... remember when we first started dating? Well, I think that your lil' sex kitten is back."

Jordan shakes his head and says, "Well, yeay for me." We both laugh. He stands up and we finish getting dressed. Once clothed, he kisses my forehead and we continue to unpack and set up the remaining brew gear.

A few hours later, I look over and Jordan is leaning against the stainless steel bench that houses all the brew ingredients and he is smiling. He must feel me looking at him as he looks towards me, and smiles. "Kenzie, thank you for everything. You seriously are awesome. Thank you so very muchly for smashing into me on the first day of college."

Winking at him, I reply, "That smash was my pleasure."

36

JORDAN

OKAY, SO I THOUGHT I KNEW A FAIR BIT ABOUT BEER AND BREWING, BUT I actually know jack shit. This course has opened my eyes up, I am now confident about moving forward with our brewpub. I seriously cannot thank Kenz enough for this. After this course, I am certain that between the two of us, we now know everything that we need in order to open and successfully run Malt Me.

The F1's are phenomenal, they are best two days ever and it's the greatest way to end the week. Hearing the roar of the engines, as they as they buzz past you in excess of two hundred kilometers an hour, is indescribable. It's deafening. It's thrilling. It's Goddamn awesome. These driver's really are talented; to drive at the speeds that they do and on such a tight course, wow, just amazing. Watching them on TV does not do them justice; up close and personal is so much better. We even manage to meet Colton Daniels, getting photos and an autograph, which is a super highlight for Kenz and me.

On the plane home, I tell Kenz that I'd love to get my hands on the co-op just out of town, but the old fart who owns it has already turned me down once, maybe this time will be different. *Please, beer God's, help a guy out.*

I'm on such a high right now; I can't wait to get back into my cave.

37

KENZIE

WE ARE HAVING A TASTING AT OUR PLACE THIS WEEKEND; IT WILL BE amongst our closest friends. We will be asking them to rate the names and see what they think of the beers. Jordan has just ducked out to pick up the food from the caterer, and I'm doing a final tidy up, getting everything ready for tonight. I'm nervous and excited for Jordan.

I've just stepped out of the shower, and I'm standing in the kitchen, wrapped in a bath sheet, having a glass of water when all of a sudden all the hairs on the back of my neck stand on end, like someone is watching me. Looking around I can't see anyone, I tell myself I'm being paranoid, I'm the only one here.

As quickly as the feeling appears, it disappears just as quick, so I head back into our bedroom to finish getting ready. I put on my favourite ass-hugging jeans and an emerald V-neck singlet, slipping on my sparkly thongs to complete my outfit. After applying my lipstick and one final check in the mirror, I head down to the shed to make sure everything is set.

As I'm walking down the stairs, a navy blue car slows down as it passes our place and the creepy feeling from earlier is back. A car horn beeps and they quickly take off. Jordan then comes zooming into the driveway. Getting out of the car, he looks up at me, standing on the stairs and smiles. "Hey, sexy lady."

Smiling back, I race down the stairs, run up to him, jumping into his arms, wrapping my legs around his waist; I envelope him in a hug, just having him near makes me feel safe. Placing me back on the ground, he lifts my chin and quietly asks, "What's up, Kenz?"

Taking a deep breath, I tell him about the feeling inside and the blue car just now. He doesn't have an answer for the chills but he says, "Most people slow down to have a look at the house. For so long, we've been 'the house that will never finish.' Naturally, people are intrigued now that it's complete. I'm sure it was nothing and they were just sticky-beaking. You called and checked with the hospital last week and Clint is still safely locked away."

I'm sure he's right. "Yeah, you're right babe. Thanks for reassuring me." Helping unload, I grab a few bags from the boot and head down to where the fun tonight will happen.

As soon as I've finished arranging the cheese platter, Mike rocks up with De-Niece. There is something about her that irks me. The way she looks at me all the time is really off putting. Plastering on a fake smile, I say, "Hey guys." I quickly rush back upstairs, pretending that I have forgotten something. I secretly hope that Sarah and Josh get here soon. No sooner do I finish that thought and reach the top of the stairs, they pull up. Looking to the skies, I say a silent thank you.

Walking out, I greet Sarah, " Heya. Let me help you there, bitch."

She envelops me in a hug, "Thanks, ho, how've you been? It's been ages since I have seen you."

"I'm doing okay. Had a little freak out earlier, like I did that day you and I went to the movies but Jordan and I came to the conclusion it was someone just looking at the house and my mind overreacting."

"Kenz, you're allowed to freak out. It was a lot to deal with. I can only imagine how you feel but I'm glad you are talking about it and not bottling it up like you usually do." She pauses, "Kenz, you are the strongest person I know."

Wanting to change the subject I say, "To tell you the truth, Sarah, I'm nervous about tonight. I know you guys have played guinea pig before, but tonight it's different. This is the final test run for our Malt Me beers, there is a lot at stake."

"Kenzie, it will be fine. Jordan would not be doing tonight if he weren't one hundred and ten percent sure with the recipes. Hell, you wouldn't even give me a taste test and I'm your sister from another mister. Now, let's get these chairs set up and drink some amazeballs beers."

Just as we have set up the chairs, Jordan comes out with six beers. *What perfect timing.* Passing them out, he toasts, "Cheers everyone, here's to a beertabolous evening"

We all salute and clink mugs. "Cheers!"

Mike takes a sip. "Ahhhh, one of the best brews around. Here's to a beertabolous evening."

All our guinea pigs are seated and Jordan dives right in. He goes into professional beer man mode, explaining each beer. We try six different beers. Jordan describes the different flavours and how mellow and crisp they each are. It's a total turn on seeing him all professional.

We proceed to have a great night, and we score six out of six with the beers. By the end of the night, everyone is absolutely shitfaced. Mike and De-Niece, and Sarah and Josh, decide to crash at our place, as they are in no state to drive, and getting a taxi this time of night is a total bitch.

As usual, everyone else has crashed out and I'm left cleaning up. Finally, the last of the dishes have been loaded and I have just turned the dishwasher on. Not ready for bed just yet, I head downstairs and pour myself a beer. With my beer in hand, I head back upstairs and I sit on the Jack and Jill on the front verandah.

As soon as I sit down, my hairs stand on end again, just like they did earlier in the day. Looking towards the road, I see there is someone standing on the other side of the street, staring at me. I'm absolutely frozen, I can't move. They start to walk across the road, towards the house when Jordan opens the front door. Startling them, they turn and run off.

Jordan looks at me, and he immediately knows something is up. Striding towards me, he squats in front of me, "Kenz, what's wrong?"

Holding my arms, he lovingly rubbing up and down to bring me back to the present. I'm still frozen and all I can manage to say is, "Clint." He immediately turns around, runs to the street, and looks up and down but no one in the there.

A few moments later, he returns and sits next to me on the Jack and Jill. Standing up, I climb onto his lap and he rubs my back just like I like. Eventually I look into his eyes and the tears begin to flow down my cheeks. "How is he here?" **SOB,** "He should be in hospital." **SOB**

"Kenz, I checked, there's no one out there. You've had a lot to drink and tonight was a big night for us. You're on a high, your exhausted and your seeing things. Trust me, no one out here, except you and I.

We'll call the hospital tomorrow to make sure he's still there. Besides, they'd have called us if anything happened. "

I'm too tired to argue. "Okay," I sniff, but I know what I saw and deep down, I know that he's back.

"Kenz, even if he is out there, I will not let him hurt you again. Look at me, Kenz."

Looking up into his eyes, which are currently sparkling in the moonlight, he reassures me, "I love you to the moon and back, and I'll do everything in my power to protect you, but you have to remember you're strong." He leans over and kisses my forehead, "You are the strongest person that I know. You need to tell yourself, 'I'm Mackenzie "Kenzie" McRoberts nee Merlot. I'm strong and hot, and I'm not afraid.' Now, say it, Kenz."

Again I sniff and wipe my nose on Jor's shoulder. "Sorry," I giggle.

"Kenz, say it."

Taking a deep breath I say, "I'm Mackenzie "Kenzie" McRoberts nee Merlot. I'm strong and hot, and I'm not afraid."

"That's my girl, now let's get you into bed. It's been a long day and I want to fall asleep with my wife in my arms."

"Sounds perfect to me." Jordan slings his arm around my shoulder, pulling me closer. I wrap my arm around his waist and snuggle in.

After locking the doors, we climb into bed together. Jordan pulls me close and whispers, "I love you, Mrs. McRoberts nee Merlot" He then places a kiss on my lips.

"And, I love you too, Mr. McRoberts."

The next morning after everyone has left, Jordan and I call the hospital. They confirm that Clint is still safely locked.

Jordan is relieved but I still have an uneasy feeling.

Jordan and I are both a bundle of nerves at the moment. On Thursday, we have a meeting lined up with the cranky ass who owns the co-op. Fingers crossed the stick up his ass has been removed and this time he will sell it to us for a great price.

The meeting with old Mr. Cranky Ass went better than either of us could have hoped for; he passed away, unfortunately, yeay, and left it to his son. Luckily for us, the son has no interest in the co-op and was happy to sell it to us, for a bargain price and with a quick settlement.

In ninety days time, subject to us finalising our finance, we will have a building for Malt Me.

Fortunately, I had already started the finance ball rolling and the bank were happy to lend us the money. In ninety days time, we will officially have our premises.

That's when the fun will begin: gutting, designing, rebuilding, and setting everything up on a larger scale for the opening of our dream; Malt Me brewery.

Holy shit, we bought the building for our brewery.

Holy shit, we are starting a brewery.

Holy shit, our dream is coming true.

Holy shit, I'm a real adult now.

The next ninety days fly by and as of 2:00 p.m. today, Jordan and I are now the proud owners of the co-op, future home of the Malt Me brewery.

Just as the agent leaves, Mike and De-Niece pull up; I'm glad to see Mike but De-Niece, not so much. It's confusing as to why she is still around. Normally, Mike would have moved on by now, but he seems to be hypnotized by her. *She must have a magical voodoo pussy.*

Mike jumps out of his truck, meets her at the back. They then emerge with a huge balloon bouquet saying CONGRATS, an esky full of beer and wine, another one full of food, and a huge bunch of sunflowers, which I presume are for me.

Running over to Mike, I wrap my arms around him. "Oh My God, Mike, you are awesome." He hands me the flowers and I hug him again.

"Don't thank me, this was De-Niece's idea."

Looking over his shoulder at De-Niece, I'm slightly confused, she has always being such a bitch to me. Why is she being nice now? She's standing there with her creepy smile; I walk towards her, "Thanks De-Niece. This is totally awesome." I pull her in for a hug, her body is stiff at first, but she eventually relaxes and hugs me back.

Releasing her from the hug she says with a smug smile, "Your welcome, Mackenzie." Emphasising, Mackenzie.

"Please, call me Kenzie. I hate being called Mackenzie."

"I know." She smugly smiles at me.

Shaking my head, I see Sarah's Corolla pull up and grin. She jumps out of her car, yelling "Surprise!" Running over to me, she envelopes me in a huge hug. "Congrats, bitch, I'm so happy for you guys."

With drinks in hand, the five of us stand the in car park of our brewery. Mike makes a toast "Cheers to Malt Me," and we all salute, cheer and celebrate our new venture.

The co-op building is just perfect for Malt Me. I'm so happy that we were able to get it. Everything is falling into place.

The following three weeks are freaking crazy and full on. It took two solid weeks of working, sun up till sun down, to gut the inside. Once we had cleared everything out, that's when the fun—and I use that term loosely, very loosely—began.

Now that the building has been gutted, and we finally decided on the inside plans, it's over to our builder. He will work his magic and turn this empty space into something amazing.

Four long exhausting months later, our builder is finished with the construction. It's now up to us to paint, fit out and get everything ready to start production. Once that is complete, we can then open to the public.

We arrived early in the morning to get more painting done. Between the two of us, we are plowing through our to-do list, ticking off items left, right, and center. It's all going smoothly, until late in the afternoon, when Jordan has to go meet with the bottle people, there is an issue with the custom bottle caps. As he's walking out the front doors, he shouts, "Back soon, Kenz, I'll stop and get dinner on my way back!"

"Give me a buzz, and I'll let you know what I feel like. You know how hungry I get when I paint, and this place is a gazillion times larger than our Queenslander. Thankfully, here there are no V-Jay walls or belt rail's to paint. I hate V-Jay, it looks amazing, but it's a total bitch to paint. If I can get a good run this arvo, I should get the toilets, bathrooms, and our office done, and maybe even start on the kitchen while your gone."

He laughs, "You are a painting machine, but don't push it. I'll call and see what Picasso wants for dinner when I'm done. Love you, wifey."

I laugh at his Picasso comment, "Love you too hubster."

I've got the iPod plugged in and cranked; I totally love the emotional rollercoaster that is iPod random. I love when it switches from *Take Me To Church* by Hozier to *Shut Your Mouth* by Garbage, before switching to *Never Tear Us Apart* by INXS.

When Sinatra's, *Come Fly With Me* comes on, I put the paintbrush down and start dancing around the office, until I hear a noise in the main room. Heading out, I think it might be Sarah, as she said she might pop out. Walking into the main room, I see a box by the front door.

Smiling, I skip over as I think that Jordan has left something for me; he's always hiding things here and there or I'm getting special deliveries. Crouching down to open the box, I start to get a strange feeling.

Opening the box, I discover a bunch of sunflowers have been shredded and there's a note sitting on top of them.

Tik Tok
Hurry Up

My heart drops.

I'd recognise that message anywhere.

Clint is back.

I race into the office and lock myself inside. With shaking hands, I call Jordan. I'm a sobbing mess when he answers, I can't get the words out. He tells me to wait inside and he'll be here soon.

Twenty minutes later, I hear him call out, "Kenz, baby, where are you?"

I immediately jump up, unlock the door and race out to him. I wrap my arms tightly around him and start to cry again. He holds me while I sob in his arms.

There is a knock at the door, we turn around to see two uniformed officers standing there. "Good afternoon, I'm Officer Hamilton and this is my partner, Officer Kincaid."

Jordan walks over to meet them. "Thanks for coming so quickly. Kenz was pretty shaken when she called me so I immediately called you guys. I called the hospital but they wouldn't tell me anything."

"You did the right thing calling us. After I spoke with you Mr.

McRoberts, I called the hospital too. Clint was taken to The Royal with suspected appendicitis. That's why they couldn't tell you anything."

I stammer, "Hhhh…he's out?"

"No, he is safely back at the facility now. It was just a case of food poisoning, but it does look like he managed to get access to a phone and arrange your package. All his privileges have been revoked."

I go into shock, their words not registering. I feel like all the progress I have made is crumbling around me. Closing my eyes, I take a deep breath and say Jordan's mantra for me, "I'm Mackenzie "Kenzie" McRoberts nee Merlot. I'm strong and hot, and I'm not afraid."

Jordan finishes up with the officers, locks up and drives us home. He runs me a bath and leaves me alone to process it all.

After my bath, I find him in the lounge room, on the couch watching *Top Gear*. He mutes the TV, grabs my hand, and pulls me down onto his lap. "How you doing, baby?"

"I'm not sure to tell you the truth. When I saw that package, my heart dropped. When the officers said he was out, I nearly lost it. I'm glad he's locked back up but all my fears are coming flooding back. What if next time he escapes?"

"I can't answer that, Kenz, but after chatting with the officers today, I have faith that he will stay locked away and that you'll be safe. I'm not going to let anything happen to you."

"I love you, Jordan. Thank you for being my rock."

"No need to thank me, Kenz. I love you too. Do you want to watch this or go to bed?"

"I'm going to go to bed. You stay and watch, I'll be fine."

Standing up, I kiss him on the cheek and head to bed.

The next week is tough emotionally. I make an appointment to see Jeannie. Talking with her helps, as does my daily call to the facility to make sure Clint is indeed still locked away.

The following weekend, I'm back at Malt Me painting and Jordan is still dealing with the bottle cap drama from the previous week. I'm finishing up the office window architrave when my phone starts to play Jordan's tone, *Nothing Else Matters* by Metallica. "Hey, husband."

"Kenz, I'm so glad to hear your voice. These bottle caps have been a nightmare. I'm going to look for another supplier. I don't want to work with this asshole anymore. Enough of my issues, how'd you get on, Picasso?"

"Hardy har har. I've done the toilets, bathrooms, and our office is just about finished. I've just got to do the kitchen and then that's the painting done."

"You're a rock star, babe. What did you want for dinner?"

"I'd kill for a burrito and Modelo from Guzman. Since I'm nearly done here, why don't I call it a day? We can meet at home and head there together, have a night out, just you and I?"

"You read my mind, Kenz. I'll see you at home soon."

"It's a date, I just need to finish the frame and clean these brushes, and then I'll head home. See you soon for date night...you might even get lucky, if you play your beers right."

"I see your beer jokes are still just as lame, and by the way there's no might about it. Love you."

"Whatevs, I'm hilarious. Love you too, Jor, see you soon."

Once the frame is finished, I quickly wash the brushes and pack them away. Before leaving, I make sure all the windows and doors are locked, I jump into my car and text Jordan to let him know I'm leaving.

ME – *Just leaving Malt Me now XO*
Before I'm out of the car park, my phone beeps.

JORDAN – *I just got out of the shower, looking forward to date nite. Drive safely, I love you XO*

ME – *I always drive safely I'm not you Love you more*

Walking in the front door, I yell in my best Lucy voice, "Honey, I'm home!" From the back of the house I hear Jordan laughing. After taking off my shoes, I head down the hall to our bedroom. Pushing the door open, I see there are thousands, well maybe not thousands, but a crap load of candles lit and a huge bunch of sunflowers on the dresser. I gasp, Jordan thinks it's because of the surprise, but I see the sunflowers, and kind of freeze.

Jordan walks over to me, wraps his arm around my waist, and places a sensual kiss on my lips. Before long, the kiss turns heated and

I have all but forgotten about the sunflowers. Pulling back, I look into his eyes, which look amazing with the flicker of the candles reflecting in them. "Hi," I manage to say.

"Hey, yourself, have I told you how sexy you look? Especially when you have paint sloshes all over you."

"Not recently, but I'm not opposed to hearing it."

"You, my dear, are the sexiest." He kisses my neck. "Most amazing." He nibbles my ear. "Hottest woman on this earth, and I am going to worship every inch of your body. Now strip and get on the bed."

Grabbing the hem of my shirt, I slowly raise it over my head, and then I shimmy out of my shorts. I'm left standing in my plain white bra and undies. Jordan is sitting on the end of our bed, in just his dress pants. If the look in his eyes is anything to go by, I'm going to be panting his name very soon.

"Fuck me, Kenz, you are beautiful."

"You're just saying that in hopes of getting lucky." Walking over to him, I push him back onto the bed and straddle his hips. Leaning down, I place feather light kisses over his pecs, up his neck, and I take his earlobe into my mouth and gently bite down. While rubbing myself on his leg, I feel his cock growing beneath me. I pepper kisses along his jaw and make my way to his mouth, I gently coax his lips apart and slip my tongue inside. Before I know it, he's kissing me back; I don't know where his mouth begins and my mouth ends.

Lifting up onto my knees, I pull back, spin around, and I slowly make my way down his abs; while I arch my back and straddle his face. He reaches up and gently caresses my ass before pulling my pussy to his face. He pushes my undies to the side and his tongue attacks my slit, licking and sucking like it's a melting ice cream on a hot summer day. Moaning, I lower his zipper and grab his shaft with my hand, freeing it from the confines of his boxer briefs. Gently stroking him up and down, a bead of precum quickly builds on the tip. I lick and suck the head before taking his cock into my mouth. He slides a finger into my soaking wet pussy as I suck him deeper into my mouth. I lick down his shaft to his balls before sucking one into my warm welcoming mouth. As I pull back, I reach my hand down to gently massage his scrotum.

Hearing Jordan moan turns me on, so I pucker my cheeks and take him deeper down my throat. His balls tighten, just as I feel my orgasm starting to build, sucking him harder as my climax reaches boiling point. The first spurt of hot salty cum hits the back of my throat just as my orgasm bursts forth. Writhing in pure bliss, my climax continues to surge through me; I continue to suck him until I've milked him dry.

Rolling off Jordan, we lie next to each other, hearts racing, breathing labored, blissfully happy. Once our heart rates have returned to normal, and our breathing settles, I stand up, pull my undies down, unhook my bra and flick it at him. Turning around I say, "I'm gonna get a shower and then we can go."

Before I take a step, Jordan grabs me around my waist, throws me onto the bed and straddles me. "I don't think so, wifey, I want to be buried balls deep inside of you and have you screaming my name at the top of your lungs before we go anywhere." His mouth is on mine before I get a chance to reply.

With our tongues melding together; I start rubbing my already throbbing pussy on his leg. The friction hitting that magical spot, so I shamelessly rub faster. I start to feel my orgasm building when Jordan pulls away. He licks down my neck, across my shoulder blade and down to my breasts. He takes my nipple in his mouth and sucks, while pinching and rolling the other between his thumb and forefinger before swapping to the other breast. He licks and kisses his way down to my pussy. He caresses my clit with his thumb and my hips start to buck, then he rubs a finger up and down my slit before slipping it inside. Still massaging my clit with his thumb, he whispers, "You're so wet, baby."

"Mmhmm" is all I can manage, as I'm lost to the euphoria building inside. Reaching out, I massage and twist my nipples as Jordan adds another finger. Then I feel his mouth sucking my clit. "Fuuuuck, I love your mouth." I feel the fireworks explode. I tumble over the edge screaming his name, as I climax for the second time this evening.

I'm lying here sated, when Jordan begins to kiss, lick, and nibble his way back up my body. Tugging on his hair, I urge him to move quicker. I pull him towards me and kiss him deeply. Our tongues gently caress each other's. Both our juices mix together, creating an intoxicating blend, which turns me on even more. Before I have time to register, he enters me in one swift motion. We both start rocking back and forth, our hips meeting thrust for thrust, our pace gradually quickening. Lifting my leg over Jordan's shoulder, his cock hits that magical spot. I whisper, "I'm close."

He reaches down to rub circles on my clit. "Come for me baby."

After a few more thrusts we both topple over the brink, each murmuring the other's name, as we ride out our orgasm.

I'm still shaking when he lowers my leg and collapses on top of me; we lay here together until our breathing evens out. Lifting my head, I look into his eyes and get lost in a sea of green. All of a sudden I register that Jordan is talking to me. "What?"

With a laugh he replies, "Wow, where did that come from?"

"When I came home and saw all this, I just lost control, sorry."

"Don't ever be sorry for that, feel free to do that anytime, Kenz. Fuck, that sixty-nine was awesome, it's one for the vault on the nights I'm all alone."

"You weren't so bad yourself," I giggle. "I guess we better get showered. I'm kinda starving now, and I'd kill for a beer."

"How did I get so lucky to get a hottest girl in the world, who also just happens to love beer as much as me?"

"Luck and my clumsiness come to mind."

"And you couldn't resist my ass."

"And all these years later, I still can't resist that perfect tight ass of yours..." Leaning over, I kiss him deeply, losing myself as I kiss the man of my dreams. Before things get too heated, I draw back suddenly. "....and on that note, we better get a move on, cause I don't think Guzman would allow us in dressed, or not dressed, like this, and this lady needs a beer and a burrito."

"You had me at beer, baby."

Climbing off the bed, I put my hand out to help him up. Once we are both standing, I wrap my arm around his neck and kiss him again. "I love you."

"I love you too, Kenz."

We both head into the shower and quickly get washed. I'm adding the finishing touches, when there's a knock at the front door. Mike and De-Niece are here, seeing if we want to head out for a few drinks. I'm just finishing my hair, secretly hoping that Jordan says no, as I'm not in the mood to spend a night with De-Niece; seriously who spells their name like that anyway? When I hear Jordan, "Awesome, Kenz and I were just about to head to Guzman, wanna join us?"

Fuck, I silently scream.

"Sounds great, man." *Fuck,* I silently scream again, so much for a night just us.

I've finished putting my lipstick on and I walk into the lounge. Plastering on a fake smile, I say, "Hey guys."

Mike looks up and whistles, much to De-Niece's disgust. "Looking hawt, Kenz."

Jordan whacks Mike across the back of the head. "Stop ogling my wife, asshat."

De-Niece chimes in, "Mike, you can't say that about Mac...Kenzie."

"Why not? It's true. She looks smokin' hot tonight." Walking over, I kiss Mike on the cheek, while looking directly at De-Niece, and snarkily say, "And you're mighty spunky too tonight, Mike." I wink at him. He envelops me in a hug and swings me around, and I squeal like a giddy schoolgirl.

The taxi arrives a few minutes later and we all hop in. On the way to dinner, I discreetly send an SOS text to Sarah.

ME – *SOS!!! Heading to Guzman with Jor, Mike and you know who, please come*

Just as we are taking our seats, my phone beeps; I grab it thinking it will be Sarah and don't even look at the ID.

UNKNOWN – *You look pretty tonight XO*

Saying to the guys, I'll be right back, I run off the to the toilets. I lock myself in a stall and sit on the lid. My heart is pounding and my breathing is labored. I need to calm down or I'll have a panic attack.

"Breathe in, breathe out." I keep repeating to myself. After a few moments, I calm down. I unlock the cubical and I look at myself in the mirror. I say out loud, "I'm Mackenzie "Kenzie" McRoberts nee Merlot. I'm strong and hot, and I'm not afraid."

My phone beeps again and I freeze, but this time it's Sarah. I sigh in relief, as I slide the screen to read her text.

SARAH – *Just cause I love you Josh and I will come save your sorry ass. I'll have a margarita and it better be waiting for me when I get there*

Before heading back out, I call the hospital and once again, they confirm the Clint is still there. Maybe it was a wrong number. *Yeah it was a wrong number,* I tell myself.

Pulling myself together, I head back out. Jordan has a beer waiting for me and he tells me he's ordered. I tell them Sarah and Josh are on their way. I then head to the bar to order her a double strength margarita and another Modelo bucket for the table.

By time I get back, Sarah and Josh have arrived. Placing the bucket on the table, I give Sarah her drink and a quick peck on the cheek.

Whistling as I sit down, Sarah says, "Your lookin hot tonight, Kenz."

De-Niece rolls her eyes, and in 4.2 seconds flat, Sarah has managed to make me smile, piss De-Niece off and make me forget about the text.

It's about 2:00 a.m. when we leave; Jordan and I manage to get a cab quickly, which never happens in this town. Leaning over, I start rubbing his crotch in the cab; when we get home as soon as the front door is closed, I jump him.

We start ripping each other's clothes off and we make it as far as the couch. Jordan sits down and I straddle him, this is fast becoming one of my favourite positions; I love our new couch. Rubbing my pussy up and down his shaft as he tweaks, pulls, and sucks my nipples; I throw my head back in delight as I lift up and impale myself on Jordan's hard throbbing cock. Gripping his shoulders, I ride him up and down until we both find our release.

Jordan lifts us up and carries me to bed. He climbs in next to me, and we spoon wrapped up in each other's arms.

We are blissfully unaware that we are being watched.

38

CLINT

I'M SO GLAD THAT MY COUSIN HELPED ME GET OUT OF THAT PLACE, IT TOOK a few weeks to arrange but we finally managed it. The plan she came up with was brilliant. I'm so glad to be seeing my Sweetcheeks in person again.

It has been far too long since I've seen her. Seeing the pictures of her face every time she gets my gifts has been priceless. It's becoming harder and harder watching her from a distance but I need to make my reappearance perfect; she deserves nothing but the best. As much as I wish I could tell her that I'm back, I have to play this carefully. Getting put away again would be pure torture.

I'm watching her hang the washing out and I'm hard as stone. Reaching down, I unzip my fly and wrap my fingers around my cock. I grip and stroke until I blow my load all over the front seat of the car.

Smiling, I can't wait until it's my Sweetcheeks hand doing this and not me.

"Soon, Sweetcheeks, soon, you and I will finally get our forever."

39

KENZIE

THE PAST SIX WEEKS HAVE BEEN A MAD HOUSE, I DON'T KNOW WHETHER I'm coming or going most days. But it has all been worth it because today is the grand opening of Malt Me. The last eight months since signing the papers for the building have been hectic. But it's all paid of I can't wait to celebrate.

Waking up early, I roll over and no surprise Jordan's side of the bed is stone cold. He must not have been able to sleep, I know exactly where he will be.

While I'm having my morning coffee, there's a knock at the front door. Placing my cup down, I walk over and open the door, but no one is there. Looking down, I freeze when I see a single sunflower with a note attached to it with barbed wire. Shuddering, I bend down and pick it up. A creepy feeling washing over me as I turn the not over and read.

TIK TOK
HURRY UP

Dropping the note and flower on the verandah, my heart rate accelerates and I break out in a cold sweat. I glance up and down the street, but I can't see anyone.

This is really starting to freak me out, I know I need to talk to

Jordan about it but today is not the day; I'll tell him tomorrow. I don't want anything ruining today for him.

Heading back inside, I change into my charcoal Cue dress pants and white, sleeveless silk button up shirt, adding a silver bracelet and my Diana Ferrari black ankle boots. Once I'm ready, I head over to Malt Me. On the way, I stop at Java Lava and get us some coffee and muffins.

When I arrive, I find Jordan in the brew house tinkering. It's what he does when he's nervous. "Hey, babe, what time did you get here?" I ask, handing him one of the coffees and giving him a quick kiss.

"The sun was just coming up. I couldn't sleep and I didn't want to wake you. I wanted to check and make sure everything is set for today. I just want this to be perfect, Kenz. I never thought this would happen; yet here we are, the grand opening of our brewpub. It all feels surreal."

"I know what you mean, babe. In less than five hours the doors will open and we will sell our first beer to our first paying customer. Today is going to be amazeballs."

If only we knew…

40

KENZIE

IT'S 11:00 A.M. AND THE DOORS TO MALT ME ARE NOW OFFICIALLY OPEN. You cannot wipe the smile off Jordan's face, or mine for that matter. All our nearest and dearest are here to help us celebrate, as well as the locals, who have been a pillar of support since we lodged the redevelopment application with the council.

We thought there might be some hurdles, but touchwood, everything has been smooth sailing. Jordan and I couldn't be happier.

The kitchen are pushing out the orders and the consensus is that the food is amazing. The beers are flowing and reviews, so far, are all positive. After some convincing, I persuaded Jordan to stock wine too, because not everyone likes beer; shock horror, I know.

I sneak up to the mezzanine level to get a few minutes to myself. I don't think I've stopped smiling since the doors opened; it reminds me of all the smiling on our wedding day. That was the last time I was this excited, nervous, and happy. I'm seriously on cloud nine right now.

I'm looking down at everyone enjoying themselves, and I feel proud, we played a part in their happiness. My eyes gravitate to Jordan, like they always do. He looks just as happy as me. He locks eyes with mine and he heads towards the stairs, racing up them to meet.

He strides across the mezzanine level, lifting me into a hug, spinning us around. When he lowers me down, he places the softest of kisses on my lips, which quickly turns heated. I spin away before it goes any further; after all, as the owners we have to be professional and shit. Jordan heads back downstairs and I stay a little longer; he can sense I need a time-out.

After a few minutes of taking it all in, I do a quick speech, since I have everyone's attention. Managing to thank everyone for coming today and all their support, as usual Jordan pipes in, but I don't mind at all as I could not be happier.

After everyone toasts us, I decide to head back down. I see Jordan smiling and waving for me to come down. Heading towards the stairs I take another look at all that we have achieved, when something by the front doors catches my eye.

I look again and I see Clint standing there, smiling directly at me. He lifts his hand and blows me a kiss. I stumble and before I know it, I'm stumbling down the stairs. I vaguely hear someone yelling, "Kenzie!"

Then it all goes dark....again.

———

When I come around, I'm lying on a stretcher being lifted into an ambulance; my whole body is aching and everything feels foggy. Lifting my hand to my head, I take a deep breath, I hear Jordan but I can't see him; I start to panic. "Jordan, Jordan!" I shout.

"I'm here, baby." Hearing him but still not being able to see him, my panic starts to increase. He pops into my line of vision and the floodgates that I'd been suppressing open. "I'm so sorry, I didn't tell you." I'm sobbing by now and cannot catch my breath. "I'm so sorry, I...I...I didn't want to worry you or ruin today." By now tears and snot running down my face.

Jordan is holding my hand. "Shhhh, don't cry. It's okay, you're okay. Look, they are taking you to the hospital to check you over. You just tumbled down a flight of stairs and bumped your head a few times."

"Don't leave me. I can't do this again."

"Do what?"

"Clint's back." I start sobbing again.

"What?" he bellows.

The ambo interrupts us, "Sorry, guys, we need to get you to the hospital."

"Hang on a sec." He turns to Mike. "Can you wrap up here and meet us at the hospital, please?"

"Sure, man, whatever you need. You look after our girl, I'll get here sorted and meet you there."

Looking at Jordan, I can see all the questions running through his head. Reaching up, I cup his cheek. "I'm so sorry, Jordan, I ruined your special day by keeping this from you."

Jordan takes my hand and squeezes. He hesitantly asks, "Kenz, what else has happened?"

"You know about the flowers. This morning I got a Tik Tok note with another flower. I was going to tell you tomorrow, I didn't want to ruin today."

"Kenz, you should have told me. We need to go to the police; you could have died today. I won't let him hurt you again. I made you that promise, all those years ago, and I still mean it now."

Once again the tears flow down my cheeks, I'm so sick of crying, I've become such a girl lately, crying at the drop of a hat. Clint really has rattled me.

The ambo interrupts us again, "Okay, you need to rest now, your blood pressure is still elevated, which is a concern. We're almost there, but for what it's worth, your husband is right. You could have really hurt yourself today. It sounds like this guy is crazy."

"See, even the ambo agrees with me." Jordan looks at me with raised eyebrows in an 'I told you so' way.

"Fine, I'll go to the police when I am finished here." Jordan smiles and I see him mouth, 'Thanks,' to the ambo.

We pull up at the hospital and I am taken into an exam room. A few moments later, the doctor walks in. He asks me what happened and I tell him. He then checks me over and wants to send me for an MRI scan to make sure everything is okay. I'm still feeling nauseous and keep getting black spots when I try to sit up, but on a good note my blood pressure is back to normal. They wheel me off for the scan and Jordan waits in the room they have moved me into. I tell him to call everyone and let them know I'm okay.

When I get back the police officers from the other week are in my room talking with Jordan. Once I'm settled in bed and comfy, well as comfy as you can be in a hospital bed, all attention is turned to me.

"Your husband is telling us that you think you saw Clint MacNicholson today, and you've received another package?"

"Yep," I let the p pop when I reply but I don't expand, as I don't want to relive this again.

The officer looks sternly at me. "Can I ask why you didn't tell anyone?"

Taking a deep breath, I quickly spit out without breathing, "I didn't want to ruin today's opening. I was going to tell him tomorrow. I haven't had any more packages since we last saw you and I've only received the one text."

Jordan jumps up from the chair. "Are you fucking kidding me Kenz? He almost killed you last time, there is no way this fucker is going to decide to just let it go." I roll my eyes and shake my head at his outburst. "Don't you dare roll your eyes at me, Kenz. I almost lost you twice to this asshole, I'm not going to let him succeed this time."

Officer Kincaid leaves the room to take a call, Officer Hamilton interjects, "Mackenzie?"

Interrupting her, I say, "Its Kenzie, I hate being called Mackenzie... Unless I'm in trouble, which it's starting to feel like I am."

"Okay, Kenzie, Jordan is right. His behavior is escalating,"

Officer Kincaid reenters the room, and clears his throat, "That was the facility where Clint was being held. I'm sorry to tell you but Clint escaped two days ago."

"What? How? This can't be happening." Jordan wraps me in his arms and I begin to cry.

"We need you come down to the station so we can discuss your options. I also recommend a restraining order."

Jordan scoffs, "Like a piece of paper will stop him." He turns to me and grabs my hand. "Kenz, please. Take this seriously, I can't lose you. I won't lose you to him again."

"Fine," I huff, "I'll go to the station as soon as I'm out of here."

As soon as I say that, the hot Canadian doctor walks back in. He turns to the officers, "Can I please ask you to step out, I'd like to talk to my patient in private? You are more them welcome to come back in as soon as we are finished."

"Sure, no problem, we were just finishing up. Kenzie and Jordan, here's my card." She hands her card to Jordan, "If there are any issues before you get in to see us, please call me. My after hours number is on there as well. I'll see you both when you come down to the station."

Jordan shakes each officer's hand and both of them exit the room. I really don't like Officer Kincaid; he's an asshat.

The doctor picks up the chart that he placed on the bed trolley and looks up. "So, the scans all came back fine, but we did discover..." I gasp, thinking the worst "...you're pregnant, congratulations."

"Wh...what, pregnant? I can't be," I shake my head in shock. "I was told that the chances of me conceiving were slim to none." Looking over at Jordan, he is just as stunned as I am. After the incident with Clint, the doctors said it was going to be nearly impossible for me to fall pregnant due to the internal damage sustained.

After a few moments of stunned silence, Jordan turns towards me and wraps his arms around my shoulders and envelopes me in the biggest hug.

Releasing me, he bends down near my belly. "Hey, baby, I'm your daddy and this here is your mummy." He winks at me, "She's stubborn as a mule, but she's gonna be the bestest mummy in the whole entire world. You are one lucky lil' dude." He places a kiss on my stomach before looking at me, his face beaming with excitement.

I'd resigned myself to the fact that I was never going to have a baby. I start to cry and for once, I'm crying happy tears. Over the moon, excited, thrilled tears.

The doctor interrupts us, "Sorry to disturb you guys, but due to the fall that you had today, I've asked one of the attending OB's to come down and do an ultrasound to make sure everything is all right with you and the baby. With the history you just gave me, I definitely think it's a good idea. I'll go and see how far away the OB is." Dr. Canadian-McHottie leaves the room.

Jordan grabs my face and his lips crash with mine, the kiss is full of emotion and love. When he pulls away, he rests his forehead on mine. "Kenz, as much as I'm mad at your for keeping this all to yourself, I am over the fucking moon happy right now. I'm so incredibly in love with you." He pauses, "Kenz, we're gonna be parents."

I'm too shocked to speak, I just don't believe it. I wrap my arms around Jordan and hug the life out of him; that's all I can manage at the moment.

I'm speechless.

I'm stunned.

I'm pregnant.

Holy shit, I'm pregnant.

41

CLINT

Waiting for dickwad to leave so I could drop off another flower for my beautiful Sweetcheeks was torture. I missed seeing her in person but most of all I want today to be special for her. For us, and our reunion.

I'm sitting in my car and I watch her open the front door and receive my gift. Seeing her in her nightie gets me hard, I lower my fly, lick my palm, and start stroking myself. Closing my eyes, I imagine it's her hand yanking and tugging my cock. It doesn't take long for my balls to tighten, and I explode all over a pair undies that I stole from my beautiful angel.

About half an hour later, I see my Sweetcheeks walk out to her car and drive off; she looks absolutely stunning today. Not wanting to be seen yet, I duck down in my seat as she drives past. I follow her to see where she is going. She stops off for coffee at our coffee shop and then she heads to Malt Me.

There are balloons and a big banner out front, stating that today is the grand opening. Parking my car around the corner, I settle in and wait. *Today is a great day for a party*, I think to myself.

ME – *Hey cuz, I'm here. Let's make this a party to never forget. Let me know when shes alone*

TRAITOR – *You got it*

Just after lunch, its go time.

TRAITOR – *She is up on the mezzanine all alone, I will keep asshat busy*

ME – *Thanks cuz*

My cousin is the best.

This task would be so much harder without her help. Walking around the back of the building, I peak through the side window, and feel my cock hardening at the sight of her standing up on the mezzanine level, looking like the angel that she is. She gives a speech, her voice is beautiful. My cock stirs at the sweet sound of her words. She seems happy and that makes me smile, but I think how much happier she will be later; when its just the two of us again.

She starts walking towards the stairs, so I pop into the doorway. She looks right at me. Our eyes connect. Everything but her fades away. I smile and blow her a kiss. Her eyes light up, the look on her face is pure delight. And then it all goes wrong, she trips and falls down the stairs.

My heart stops at seeing her fall. She was so excited to see me she tripped. *See, it's fate that we are meant to be together.*

Looking over, I see my cousin standing near at bar. She's staring at me, while everyone else runs to see if my Sweetcheeks is okay. She tells me to go with a nod of her head. As much as it kills me to leave, I know I have to. Being this close, I cannot let asshat see me.

Sitting in my car, I stare at the entrance and wait to see my Sweetcheeks. They wheel her out and that fuck-stick is beside her. He reaches for her hand, and in anger I dig my nails into my palm, drawing blood. "Don't touch her you asshat," I growl.

As I drive down the street, I say. "Happy opening day fuck-stick."

42

KENZIE

There's a knock on the door and it opens, Jordan and I jump apart, as a petite doctor enters my room. "Sorry to interrupt, I'm Dr. Greene the on-call OB. I understand congratulations are in order."

"Thanks." I manage to squeeze out, nodding my head, still in shock that I'm pregnant.

"Well, let's have a look and you can meet your lil' one." Dr. Greene wheels the ultrasound machine closer. She pushes a few buttons and the machine starts up. Picking up the wand and some gel, she says, "Now this might be a little cold." She squeezes the gel onto my belly, placing the wand against my skin, and the screen flickers. All of a sudden we hear a sound that I never thought I'd hear coming from inside me—*badunk badunk badunk*—it's magical. My eyes immediately fill with tears and I squeeze Jordan's hand. Looking up at him, we are both beaming at what we are hearing.

The doctor points to the screen, and says, "That right there is your baby, and hiding behind is bub number two."

Both our mouths drop open in shock; with a smirk she says, "Congratulations, you're having twins. I'd say you are about six weeks along and everything looks perfect."

Looking up at Jordan, I smile. My mind is counting back; our babies were conceived on our impromptu Guzman date night. I whisper, "Guzman."

Jordan mumbles, "Guzman, right, so that night was doubly fun."
We both laugh.

"Mackenzie..."

I cringe when she calls me Mackenzie "Please, call me Kenzie."

"Okay, Kenzie. I'll give you my card. Since you're having twins, if
you have private health insurance, I would recommend that I see you
privately." I look at her in shock. "There's nothing to worry about, but
carrying twins and with your history, I want to be doubly careful.
Don't get me wrong, the public system is just as good." She hands her
card to Jordan. "But I think in your case, private will be best."

"Okay, we'll call your office to schedule an appointment. Thank
you so much, we really appreciate it."

"Its my pleasure, Kenzie. Now you rest up, and I'll see you in two
weeks for your first appointment." Dr. Greene leaves, quietly closing
the door behind her. It's now just Jordan, me and the two lil' beans
growing inside me.

Dr. Greene returns a few moments later and hands us a print out of
our lil munchkins.

It all so surreal, I never thought I would be able to fall pregnant, let
alone with twins. I hold the picture tightly to my chest, grabbing
Jordan's hand, I pull him in for a kiss and whisper. "Congrats Daddy."

"Congrats Mummy."

Jordan bends down and kisses my belly again.

Holy shit! We're having twins.

43

JORDAN

I'VE NEVER BEEN SO SCARED, SEEING KENZ TUMBLE DOWN THE STAIRS; I swear my heart stopped beating. Racing over to her, I see that she's out cold. I shout. "Someone call an ambulance!" As I drop to my knees next to her.

Behind me, I hear someone reply, but I don't register anything that they say. Holding Kenz in my arms, I try to wake her but she won't come to. "Please, wake up, baby. Please, don't leave me."

The ambulance arrives and the paramedic asks me to step back, I don't want to but I know I have to. Stepping back, they immediately start working on Kenz. They put on a blood pressure cuff and are concerned, her pressure is dangerously high. The second paramedic rushes outside and returns with the stretcher, they lift Kenz onto it and are wheeling her out. As they roll past me, I see her eyes flutter and I breath a sigh of relief.

I follow them outside when I hear Kenz calling out, "Jordan, Jordan!"

I rush to her side. "I'm here, baby."

As soon as she sees me, she starts to cry and my heart breaks for her. I'm confused by what she's saying, the tears pouring down her face. I keep holding her handing, grazing my thumb along the back to sooth her. "Shhhh, don't cry. It's okay, you're okay. Look, they are taking you to the hospital to check you over you. You just tumbled down a flight of stairs and bumped your head a few times."

There is a complete look of fright on her beautiful tear-stained face. She grips my hand tighter, not wanting me to leave. This tumble has really shaken her, she seems confused and then she tells me that Clint's back. I'm taken aback by what I hear and I bellow, "What?"

Kenzie then explains what occurred this morning. I'm angry that she didn't tell me, but I also understand why she didn't. The ambo interrupts us to say it's time to go.

Turning, I ask Mike to lock up for me and to meet us at the hospital. He doesn't hesitate and he runs back inside. He's a trooper; I don't know what I'd do without him.

On the ride to the hospital, Kenz fills me in on the flowers and the text messages. I'm beyond pissed but seeing her strapped to a stretcher and scared; I reign in my fury…for now, I'll let her have it later.

The paramedic tells Kenz that I'm right and I silently thank him.

We see the doctor as soon as we arrive. He admits her immediately and requests a scan due to her fall. We are moved into a private room and just after we're settled, an orderly comes and takes Kenz off for her scan, and I wait in the room.

While I'm waiting, two police officers arrive. I fill them in on what happened today and the bits that Kenz told me. She returns from her scan, and they ask her a few more questions. I start to get angry at what she's telling them.

Why didn't she tell me?

My wife is so stubborn at times.

When they tell us the Clint has escaped, I'm fuming. We have just agreed to come down to the station to make a statement, when the doctor returns and asks them to leave. Once the officers leave, the doctor picks up Kenz's chart. He tells us the one thing that I never thought we would hear. "We did discover your pregnant, congratu-lations."

Kenzie's grip on my hand tightens, and I stare at him in shock. I can hear Kenz talking to him but nothing is registering. I just keep repeating in my head, *"We're pregnant, we're pregnant."*

Holy fuck, I'm going to be a Dad.

Leaning over, I hug Kenz but I quickly lower myself to her belly, gently placing my hands on her tummy. "Hey, baby, I'm your daddy and this here is your mummy. She's stubborn as a mule, but she is gonna be the bestest mummy in the whole entire world. You are one lucky lil' dude." I softly place a kiss on her stomach before looking up at Kenz.

Her beautiful green eyes are filled with tears, and she has the biggest smile on her face. I rest my forehead on hers, staring into her eyes, still in shock that we are going to be parents.

A few moments later, the baby doctor walks in. Kenz and the doctor chat but I'm in shock, nothing they say registers. Then we hear her say, "Well, let's have a look and you can meet your lil' one."

She picks up this stick, squirts this clear blue gel onto Kenz's belly, pushes a few more buttons and then I hear the most amazing sound I've ever heard—*badunk badunk badunk*—it's a sound I will never forget.

My eyes immediately fill with tears, and I squeeze Kenz's hand. I'm already in love with the lil blob on the screen, even though all I see is black and white static. The doctor points to the screen and says, "That right there is your baby, and hiding behind is bub number two."

I whisper, "Fuck me dead."

Staring at the screen, I'm dumfounded; both our mouths drop open. The doctor looks at us and with a smirk, *cheeky bitch*, "Congratulations, you're having twins."

Holy fuck, we are having twins.

Here we were thinking that we'd never conceive naturally, or even at all and now we're having twins. *I have super sperm*, I can't help but smile.

The doctor and Kenz discuss follow up appointments, and the next thing I know she's leaving the room. She returns a few moments later with the first picture of our munchkins. Kenz grips it tightly to her chest. My heart is bursting with pride at seeing her so happy.

There are so many emotions coursing through my veins right at this moment: excitement, fear, unconditional love, apprehension, joy but most of all happiness. I'm beyond excited to become a dad.

Kenz and I are staring at each other. I notice her hand gently rubbing her tummy, when we are pulled from our blissfulness by a commotion in the hall, and hear, "Kenz, Jordan where are you?" I jump up and run out.

"Mike, what the hell, dude?" I quietly shout.

"These asshats wouldn't let me through as I'm not family." He air quotes family. "But that's bullshit, dude, I'm your brother from another mother, and that means I'm family."

"Dude, we're in a hospital. You could have just texted me, and I would have come and got you." I look towards the nurse and security guard, who is coming up behind her. "I apologise for my brother, he's a little emotional about Kenz."

The nurse eyes Mike and says, "One wrong move and you're out, I don't care that your family." She air quotes family and storms away.

Mike and I walk back into Kenz's room. He leans over and hugs Kenz. "Hey, baby girl, how you feeling?"

"Like I fell down a set of stairs and bumped my head."

"I see your sense of humor wasn't bumped out."

I slap Mike on the back, ready to spill the news when Kenz interrupts, "Mike, can you be a gem and get me a Diet Coke please?"

"Sure can, baby girl, you want anything, dickwad?

"I'm good but, dude, keep it down we are in a hospital, and that nurse out there wants your balls on a silver platter."

"Yeah, right, okay. I'll be back with your Diet Coke in a jiffy."

Walking over, I sit on the edge of the bed as soon as Mike leaves, "Why did you interrupt me when I was going to tell Mike the good news?"

"Jor, I don't want to tell anyone, just yet. It's early days, and as it is, I shouldn't have fallen pregnant. I don't want to risk telling people to then have to tell them we're not." A lone tear falls down her face; I reach over and wipe it away. Leaning over, I kiss her forehead.

"We can wait, but I'm just so excited," I say as Mike waltzes back in.

"Oh dude, your excited I'm back, shucks." He hands Kenz her Diet Coke and sits on the end of her bed.

"Thanks, Mike, not just for the Diet Coke but for handling everything back there. We really appreciate it."

"Anything, for you guys, you know that. As I said to Nazi Nurse out there, we are family and family sticks together. We go together like peas and carrots, Cheech and Chong, ham and cheese, lube and..." Kenz puts her hand up to stop him, and I punch him in the arm and shake my head.

"We get it, Mike, trust me we get it. And yes, we are family and we stick together. But anyways, thank you."

44

KENZIE

Dr. Canadian McHottie walks back into my room. "Okay, Kenzie, after conferring with Dr. Greene we've agreed that you no longer need to stay tonight as your blood pressure has returned to normal and all scans came back clear. Here are your discharge papers; you're good to go. Make sure you follow up with Dr. Greene, she really is the best." Mike looks at us apprehensively. We just assured him I'm fine, this will be fun to explain away.

"That's great, thanks, Doc. We will."

He leaves my discharge papers on the bed trolley and walks out. Leaning down, I grab my shoes and put them on and we all head out.

When we get in the car, before we even have our seatbelts on, Mike turns towards me. "Why to you need a follow up with Dr. Purple?"

Laughing, I reply, "It's Dr. Greene and it's just a precaution, Mike. I did just fall down a set of stairs. I'm fine, really." Reaching forward, I squeeze his shoulder in reassurance. He reaches up and squeezes my hand back.

Jordan turns around. "Do you want to go to the police station on the way home or do it tomorrow?"

"Police station?" Mike shakes his head confused, "What's going on? I thought everything was fine?"

With a sigh, I take a deep breath and again in one breath I say,

"Clint escaped. I saw him at the opening today, and that's when I tripped and fell down the stairs."

Mike whacks the steering wheel and shouts, "Mother-fucker!" Then he turns towards Jordan and punches him in the arm. "What the fuck, dude, why did you not tell me this?"

Jordan rubs his arm where Mike just hit him. "OUCH, fucker. I didn't know. Miss I Can Handle Anything, in the back there didn't tell anyone. She got a package this morning but didn't want to ruin the opening."

"Look, guys, I'm fine. I'll go see the officers tomorrow, get the restraining order and any other information they have. We can then get back to running the brewpub, whose opening I kind of ruined today." Then I lean back into my seat and close my eyes, I'm shattered.

"You didn't ruin anything and don't think you will be going in anytime soon. You, my wifey, are on bed rest for a few days, you just took a tumble down two flights of stairs and you're..." I raise my eye at him and scowl. "You're, not going in."

"I agree with Jordan, Kenz, you need to rest up."

"Fine, I'll take one day and one day only. Just take me home, Mike."

He looks at me in the rearview mirror and winks. "Do you know how long I've waited to hear you say that, Kenz? You just made my life complete."

This time Jordan punches him in the arm.

"OUCH!"

"Stop flirting with my wife, asshat." Mike pokes his tongue at Jordan and winks at me. "Just take us home."

Mike turns towards Jordan. "Do you know how long I've wait to hear you say that, Jor?" And bat his eyelids at Jordan.

We all burst out laughing. *Man I love Mike.*

Twenty minutes later, Mike drops Jordan and me off, and I climb straight into bed. I fall asleep immediately, subconsciously rubbing my belly.

45

TRAITOR

HOLY FUCK, WE COULD NOT HAVE PLANNED THAT BETTER IF WE TRIED. IT was so hard not to laugh because the bitch is getting exactly what she deserves.

Clint will be eager to hear how the rest of today goes. Maybe this is what we need to finish this, not sure how much longer I can keep this charade up.

For the life of me, I don't know what he sees her but I owe him my life. If I didn't owe him, there's no way I'd be leading this double life.

A few hours later, I'm hiding out at the hospital and I hear the doctor tell her she's fine, *drama queen,* and wouldn't you know it, she's up the duff. This is gonna be interesting now.

ME – *She's fine but guess what?*

CLINT – *Do tell cuz*

ME – *Your little princess is pregnant, with twins. They released her just a few moments ago*

CLINT – *Great work cuz*

46

KENZIE

THE NEXT MORNING JORDAN DRIVES ME DOWN TO THE STATION. THE TRIP IN his Jeep is eerily quiet. Reaching over, I rub his leg. "I'm sorry I didn't say anything Jordan."

I see him glance across at me, it's a mixture of sadness and anger, before returning his eyes to the road, "I'm so angry that you didn't tell me, we don't keep secrets, Kenz. But mostly I'm pissed that he escaped. "

"Me too," I scrunch my face up, "Jor, I'm so sorry I didn't say anything this morning. I didn't want to ruin our special day, guess I ended up ruining it anyway." A lone tear falls down my cheek.

"Please don't cry baby. It's not your fault, it's his. The sooner he's caught, the sooner we can get on with our lives"

"Jordan, you are the one thing that gives me strength," I rub my tummy, "And now I have these lil' ones looking after me as well."

We pull up at the station; Jordan turns towards me and grabs my hands. "Kenz, I love you more than anything, even beer." We both laugh. "I would do anything to protect you, and now I would do absolutely anything to protect you and our munchkins."

Leaning over, I wrap my arms around his neck and hug him. "I love you Jordan. I promise not to keep anything from you again."

"I love you too, Kenz. Just keep that promise to me, and don't do anything stupid."

"I promise, Jordan. Now let's go in and get this over with."

We walk inside, and Jordan tells the officer at the front desk that we are here to see Officer Hamilton or Officer Kincaid. Kincaid seems like a grumpy asshole, who needs the stick up his ass removed, but Hamilton is pretty kick ass; I'd love to be friends with her.

Of course, it's Kincaid that comes out to meet us. He greets us and we head further into the station, he stops outside an interview room and asks us to wait inside. The room is small, cold and void of any ambiance whatsoever. The walls are grey; there's a table in the middle with a single chair on one side and two chairs on the other.

Shivering, I had hoped I would never end up back here, but I was wrong, as usual. The door opens and both Kincaid and Hamilton come in.

Kincaid sits down and Hamilton stands in the corner, leaning against the wall; she crosses her ankles and leans back. She looks over at me and smiles. "How are you doing today, Mackenzie?"

"I'm doing okay, but please, call me Kenzie."

"Right, sorry, Kenzie."

Kincaid looks back at his notes. "Kenzie, you mentioned last night that you thought you were being watched, when did this start?"

"I felt like I was being followed when we moved into our house after we renovated. I knew it wasn't Clint as I kept in contact with the facility to make sure he was still there."

Officer Hamilton asks, "What else has happened?"

"Apart from a few text messages, the sunflowers with a note left at Malt Me and at home yesterday. I hadn't seen him in person, until yesterday."

Officer Kincaid asks, "What did the notes say?"

"Umm, they all said 'tik tok hurry up'. He used to say that to me when we were dating, he was always in a rush to be wherever we were going."

"Okay Mac.. sorry, Kenzie, I think we have everything for now. We'll keep in touch, if you feel threatened or think of anything else please let us know. In the meantime, we have filed another DVO against him." He hands me his card. "Please call me anytime if you have any questions or concerns."

"Thanks, Officers."

Jordan and I stand up and they escort us out.

Not long after we get home Mike walks in, sans De-Niece. *Thank you God.* "Hey guys, how you doing, Kenz?"

Walking over, I give him a hug. "I'm good, Mike, sorry to scare you yesterday. Thanks for everything, I mean it."

"So it's really true, Mr. Douche-Canoe-Fuckface is back? I was hoping you were pulling my leg." I sheepishly look up and nod. "What the fuck are we going to do?"

"And that there is why I didn't say anything!" I yell, "I don't want you two getting hurt cause of my douche canoe ex. Please let the police handle it."

"Kenz, you're my wife. There is nothing and I mean nothing that I wouldn't do for you. Serious—" Jordan is mid-sentence when I collapse.

He and Mike rush me back to the hospital. They page Dr. Greene, she recommends I stay overnight for observations so they admit me.

Mike and Jordan stay with me all afternoon, the air is thick with animosity and worry. Later that evening, the nurse walks in and sternly says, "Okay boys, visiting hours are over and our patient here needs to rest up. Say your goodbyes, and you can come back tomorrow when visiting hours start again."

Jordan asks, "Can't I stay, please?"

"I'm afraid not, honey. New regulations don't allow it, and as much as you are a sweet, doting husband, I want to keep my job. I'll give you ten more minutes."

Mike leans over and kisses me on the forehead. "Rest up, Kenz, I'll see you when you get home tomorrow."

"Thanks, Mike, I'll see you tomorrow and thanks for everything. Again." He nods his head at me. He looks at Jordan. "I'll wait in the lobby for you, asshat." And with that, he walks out, gently closing the door behind him.

Jordan walks over to the bed, takes my hands, and gently squeezes them. He looks me in the eye before kissing my forehead. "I really don't want to leave you, Kenz, but rest up, its not just you anymore. Try and get a good night's sleep. We will deal with this tomorrow when we have a clear head. I'm so mad at you right now, but I also love you so very muchly," He leans over and places a soft kiss on my lips, wrapping his arms around me and giving me a tight, warm-hearted cuddle. He whispers, "I love you to the moon and back."

He stands up to leave, as he gets to the door, he turns, smiles and blows me a kiss. After he closes the door, I break down and cry. The tears keep coming and they won't stop. The nurse walks in. "Oh honey." She gives me a hug, which is just what I need. Pretty sure this is above and beyond the call of duty for a nurse, but I'll take it.

Finally, I stop crying and look up. I see her name badge and I say, "Thanks, Tara, that's just what I needed, and thanks for kicking the dynamic duo out. I know they mean well, but..." Then I start to cry again.

"Happy to help, hon. Now I can't give you any of the good stuff due to the babies but do you want anything, or are you okay?"

"I'm fine for now, but I'll buzz you if I need anything."

"No worries. I'll be back to check on you later."

I smile. "Thanks."

As she walks out, she dims the lights and I lie back. I start rubbing my tummy, still stunned that there are two little ones in there. Quietly I whisper, "Mummy loves you guys." I drift off to sleep.

I wake few hours later when Tara is back doing my obs. "Sorry to wake you hon. I'm just bout finished, you go back to sleep." I'm pretty tired so I nod my head and fall straight back to sleep.

A noise startles me, I open my eyes, and my heart stops beating when I see whose standing above me, Clint. I can't move, I'm frozen with fear. Leaning down, he whispers, "Morning, Sweetcheeks."

Before I have a chance to scream, he places a cloth over my face. I struggle, but everything goes black and for the third time in forty-eight hours darkness engulfs me.

47

TRAITOR

My phone rings as I'm leaving work. They inform me that Kenz collapsed and they are on their way to the hospital. I make up some excuse about being held up at work but I'll try get there later; *not gonna happen.*

There's a huge smile on my face as I text Clint

ME – *You're precious collapsed and shes back in hospital*

CLINT – *Thanks cuz, looks like I have the perfect opportunity now to finish this once and for all*

ME – *Let me know if you need anything else cuz*

I'm excited as everything is coming together perfectly, I can't wait to see what happens from here. Looks like I'll be out of here sooner rather than later.

48

CLINT

CAN THIS WEEKEND GET ANY BETTER? FIRST, I HAND DELIVERED A beautiful sunflower to my girl and had the best wank outside her place. Then I managed to ruin the opening of asshats brewery, and to top it off, I find out that my beautiful Sweetcheeks is pregnant.

Now sadly she is in hospital again, but this will allow me access to whisk her away, and we can finally live happily ever after; as a family.

I've been hiding out for a few hours when finally asshat one and asshat two leave. The cute nurse, who I've been flirting with all afternoon, kicks them out. If I have everything understood from my chat with Tara, she'll be finishing at 11:00 p.m. and there will be a shift change. I'll bide my time till then and then I can sneak my Sweetcheeks out, and we can finally all be together.

After what feels like forever, it's time to go get my Sweetcheeks and babies. Sneaking into her room with the wheelchair I stole from some old dude's room, I walk over to her bed and she's stirring. She looks up at me with her beautiful green eyes, and before she can do anything I place a cloth over her face and she drifts back to sleep.

Carefully, I lift her out of bed and place her in the wheelchair, whisking her and our babies away, to start our happily ever after together.

As we enter the car park. I laugh; I so wish I could see asshats face when he realises she's gone. Today is the start of the rest of my life; finally everything I have been through will be worth it.

49

JORDAN

WHEN THE NURSE TELLS ME I HAVE TO LEAVE, I'M GUTTED. I WANT TO BE here to be here with Kenz and the munchkins. As I say goodbye to Kenz, my heart is breaking. She looks so sad, I place a soft kiss on her lips and whisper, "I love you to the moon and back." Then I turn and leave.

As soon as I close the door, I hear her start to cry, it breaks my heart to leave. However, I know Kenz and she needs time to herself. I'll give her this moment, as much as it kills me.

Putting one foot in front of the other, I walk outside and meet up with Mike in the foyer. We both walk to his car in silence, I'm waiting for him to let loose. We get to his car and I smile when I realise he bought the Corvette, this car is sweet. Looking towards him I say, "Thanks, Mike, this is just what I needed to see. Now can I drive?"

"I know, man, and fuck no, you're not driving my baby. Now get in, start from the beginning and tell me what's going on."

I fill Mike in on the recent events as we head back to our place.

"Fuck," he seethes.

"That's not all, dude." Kenz is going to kill me for telling Mike this. "Ummm don't tell Kenz I told you, but we also found out that she's pregnant…with twins."

He snaps his head towards me, mouth gaping wide open in shock.

He shakes his head. "Fuck me dead, said foreskin Fred. That's fuckin' amazing, dude. Who knew your lil' swimmers were so awesome?"

I laugh; I can always count on Mike to make me laugh. "You never cease to amaze me with the shit that comes out of your mouth."

"Dude, I amaze myself sometimes, too. Keeps life interesting."

Shaking my head I laugh again, "And that right there is why you are my best mate. Now drive me home, it's been a long ass day. The quicker I get home to bed and sleep, the quicker I can get back to my girl and squids."

Before I know it, we are back at our place. Mike offers to hang around but I say I'm fine and tell him to go and see De-Niece. He gives me a funny look when I mention her name but I shrug it off.

Once Mike leaves, I have a quick shower and jump into bed. Lying on my side, staring out the window I think about Kenz, the babies and Clint; God I hope we can get through this.

Before I know it *Dream On* by Aerosmith is blaring through the alarm clock. Reaching over, I turn it off. I lie there staring at the ceiling thinking about everything once again. Drifting back to sleep, I'm woken later by the sound of my phone ringing. Reaching out, I sleepily answer it, "Hello?"

A stern male voice says, " Is this Jordan McRoberts?"

"Yeah, who's this?"

"It's Officer Kincaid. Can you get to the hospital quickly?"

Instantly I sit up. "Is Kenz okay? The babies?"

"Please come to the hospital and we will tell you."

Gripping my phone tighter I yell, "NO, tell me now!"

"Mrs. McRoberts is missing. It looks like she was taken during the night."

50

KENZIE

WHEN I OPEN MY EYES AGAIN, EVERYTHING IS FUZZY. I BLINK REPEATEDLY and eventually everything comes back into focus. Looking around my heart rate increases, fear courses through my veins when I realise that I'm naked and no longer in hospital. I try to lift my hand but again, I'm tied to a bed, rope wrapped tightly around my wrists and ankles.

Movement at the end of the bed catches my eye. I see Clint is sitting there, also naked. The anger is radiating off him; his eyes are filled with rage, shoulders tight, jaw clenched, and a scowl on his face. He moves and I flinch in terror. This only infuriates him more and my fear reaches fever pitch.

Looking down at me, he smirks. "Good morning, Sweetcheeks." He stands up and tugs on the ropes to make sure my hands, and feet are tightly secured. Darting my eyes around, I want to get an idea of where I am. I start to feel sick when I notice his cock is rock hard.

He looks down at me again and starts to laugh, it's creepy and grates through me. Reaching down he starts to stroke his cock, looking me directly in the eye, his strokes becoming more rapid. He calmly says, "This here is for you, but not until you have safely delivered our babies."

Groaning, his knuckles turn white as he grips his cock tighter, stroking faster and faster. "I've missed seeing your pretty face up close when I come."

Laughing, he climbs onto the bed next to me, leans over and starts to roughly massage my breasts, violently pulling and twisting my nipples. I scream out in pain, "Please stop, please!"

"There's my feisty little whore, you love it when I do this." He twists my nipple viciously, I'm sure he's going to rip it off. Releasing my nipple, he bends down and sucks on it, biting so viciously that he punctures my skin. I feel the blood dripping down my side. My eyes well with tears, squeezing them tightly shut, I will the tears away.

Against my will my nipples pucker; I hate that my nipples are so sensitive. He grabs his cock and starts rubbing it in between my breasts. Pushing my breasts together, he starts to fuck them, thrusting back and forth while painfully squeezing and pushing them together.

I can't stand to see his face, so I scrunch my eyes closed tighter and imagine I'm anywhere but here.

It's not long until I feel the first spray of cum hit my chin. Shaking my head from side to side, I try to move but I can't. He has me pinned to the bed; he keeps pounding between my breasts until he completely empties his load.

Once he's finished, he leans forward and licks me clean. He laps every last drop of cum, and then licks up my neck; I groan and shudder in disgust. He mistakes this as a pleasurable sound. "Does my, lil' Sweetcheeks like that?"

"Not fucking likely," I spit though clenched teeth.

He licks across my chin and I turn my face away. He roughly grasps my chin so I am looking into his eyes; I scrunch my eyes shut tight and he growls, "Open those baby blues, bitch, I want to see the look in them when I fuck your sweet pussy, over and over again."

Opening my eyes, I hiss, "My eyes are green, asshole."

He slaps my face and I cry. Something snaps inside of me and I completely lose it: thrashing and screaming, kicking my tied legs, as more and more tears pour down my face. "Let me go, argh. You fucking asshole, let me go. I hate your fucking guts!"

Clint stands up, glares down at me, and laughs like a maniac before turning around and walking out.

Leaving me alone.

Naked.

Strapped to the bed…again.

My tears have subsided, and I'm lying here staring at the off white ceiling. I notice a spider scamper along. *I wish I could scurry away like him.* Closing my eyes, I pray that they will find me soon, because I don't know if I can survive this again. This time I have the little squids to think about, and then I start to panic; the squids.

The door handle rattling jolts me and I freeze, Clint pushes the door open and has a sick smile on his face, "Hey, my beautiful Sweetcheeks."

Turning my head, I look to the wall, I refuse to look at him. I pray for death, again. I'm not strong enough to handle anymore. I pray with all that I have that someone will find me soon.

"Cat got your tongue?"

Staring at the wall, I continue to ignore him. I feel the bed dip, he forcefully grips my face and turns my head so I'm looking at him. I close my eyes and he slaps me hard across the face **WHACK**. My cheek stings. He jumps on top of me. I try to move my head so I don't have to look at him, but he digs his fingers in deeper, holding me still. Bending down he licks along my jawbone and bites my lip. Then he shoves his tongue in my mouth and I start to gag. I can feel the bile rising and I can't hold it in. I vomit while his tongue is still in my mouth.

Clint pulls back quickly; he spits at me and backhands me across the face. **WHACK** "You fucking sick bitch." **WHACK**, "How dare you vomit at me!" **WHACK**

When he's finished hitting me, he proceeds to lick the vomit off my face. I feel his cock hardening against my leg as he's licking me clean, and I start to cry.

Turning my head towards the wall, I cry: uncontrollable sobs overtake my body. Staring at a brown smudge on the wall, I start thinking about the precious cargo that I am carrying, my lil' squids. It's in this moment that I realise I will survive this. Jordan's mantra pops into my head and I keep repeating it; "I'm Mackenzie "Kenzie" McRoberts nee Merlot. I'm strong and hot, and I'm not afraid."

With that thought, something snaps inside of me and I tell myself to stop crying, pull up my big girl undies, if I was wearing any, and figure this out. Taking a deep breath, I decide that I need to come up with a plan to get out of here. I need to do it quickly, but I'm so exhausted, I doze off to sleep.

I wake up with a fright when I feel someone touching me. Hoping that it's Jordan here to rescue me, my eyes flicker open and unfortunately I see Clint. He reaches forward, brushing a few strands of hair off my face. "Sorry to scare you, Sweetcheeks." Pausing, he smiles. "You are so beautiful when you sleep."

Taking a deep breath, I think to myself, *this is it*. Plastering on a fake smile, I put on an Oscar winning performance, and I act like I'm in love with him. Smiling up at him I say with a giggle, "Thanks, I think, but watching me sleep is kinda creepy."

"It's not creepy when it's the person that loves you the most in this world staring at you."

I think to myself, *it's now or never*. "You love me? Still?" I whisper.

"Yes, Sweetcheeks. I've never stopped loving you, and now that you are carrying our babies, I love you even more."

My eyes go wide, how does he know that I'm pregnant? Apart from the doctors and Jordan, no one else knows. Starting to panic, I take a deep breath. Fear isn't good for the babies. *I really need to get out of here, and now.*

He gently caresses my face. "Sweetcheeks, the whole time I was locked away, I imagined this moment right here. Well, without the restraints, and that's why I had to get out of there. My cousin helped smuggle me out, and I've been hiding with her, watching you, and waiting for my chance."

Interrupting him I hesitantly ask, "So why don't you take them off? How can I show you how much you mean to me, if I can't touch you?" I choke this out and am proud of myself, I actually sound convincing.

"You're just saying that." He jumps off the bed and starts pacing.

"No, why would I lie to you? I've had time to think about it and... and I don't want to be anywhere else." I struggle to get the next part out, "The babies and I need you, Clint." Inwardly, I say, *sorry squids, I promise, Mummy will protect you.*

He snaps his head back to me, staring into my eyes, "You mean it?"

"Yyyy...yessss" I stutter.

"First I need to get rid of loverboy to make sure he doesn't ruin it for us again, and then there'll be nothing in our way."

I stare up at him, shocked at his words. "Www...what?"

"You heard me, I'm going to take out loverboy, so we can live happily ever after together in this cabin with our babies."

My mind starts racing and over and over in my head, I repeat, *no...*

no...no... I need to think of something and quickly. I didn't anticipate how fucked up Clint now is, he seems to be more cuckoo than last time.

My mind is racing as I try and think of what I used to call him when we were together. "Clint!" I shout. He turns and looks at me, like a lightning strike out of nowhere I remember. "Baby, let's not think of him. He means nothing to me now that I'm here with you. Let's just me and you start over, forget about everyone else."

He reaches down and strokes my face; I lean into his hand and turn my head to place a soft kiss on his palm. Willing myself to cry, "Clint, baby I'm sorry." Miraculously a tear falls. "I'm so, so sorry for everything I put you through." I pretend to sob.

He lays down and squishes me, stroking my hair and whispers, "Shhhh, it's alright, Sweetcheeks. You're here now and that's all that matters."

"Clint, baby, can you please untie me, so you can hold me properly? I need to be in your arms." He lifts himself up and looks down at me. I smile at him and pray to God that he's falling for this. He leans over and loosens the rope. Sighing in relief, I quickly sit up, rubbing my wrists before I wrap my arms around him. I sigh, "It feels so good to be in your arms again, baby, please forgive me for everything."

"Sweetcheeks, I could never stay mad at you." He kisses me, I hold my eyes closed tightly and kiss him back. Pushing back, I rest my forehead against his, closing my eyes, I whisper. "Thank you, Clint." I pull away and look deeply into his eyes; I take a deep breath and kiss him, again. Coaxing his mouth open, I slip my tongue in, sliding it around; I moan in disgust, but he takes it as a pleasurable moan and increases the kiss, crushing me tighter to his body. I feel his heart rate increase. It's in this moment that I know I have him; *my freedom is not far away.*

I pull back and graze my teeth over his bottom lip and sucking. Tenderly, I place my hand on his cheek and with my thumb I rub along has jaw line, "Clint, do you think I could take a shower? I want to make myself beautiful for you." Lowering my head, I look down my body before shyly looking back up at him. "I look like a mess right now."

He lifts my chin and sweetly replies, "Sure, Sweetcheeks, anything for you, but I still think you are the most beautiful woman in the world. I even have new clothes for you," he proudly declares while smiling at me.

"You're so thoughtful, baby." I put my arms around his waist and snuggle into him. I shudder, which makes him hold me in closer to him.

Clint pulls away and bends towards my feet to loosen and remove the ropes. He sees the red marks around my ankles and he gasps in shock. "Sweetcheeks, I'm so sorry that I did this to you. I promise to make it up to you."

Reaching out for him, I gently rub his arm. "You can make it up to me by letting me have a shower."

"Okay, Sweetcheeks. I'll go and get the water hot for you, and I'll come back when it's ready."

Smiling sweetly at him. "Thanks, baby, you're awesome."

He turns around and heads to the bathroom. Taking a deep breath I keep repeating to myself, "I can do this."

This shower is the best shower I've ever had. I stand under the shower-head until the water runs cold, not just because it feels great but because I don't want to be near Clint. Just before I get out, I start to doubt that I can do this. Do I have the stomach to do what I need to get out of here? Subconsciously, I rub my stomach and by doing that, it's the reminder I need. I do have the strength I need to survive and I'll do whatever it takes.

As I'm drying my stomach, lost in thought, I don't notice Clint walk into the bathroom. "You are so beautiful, I can't wait to make more babies with you."

I try to hold back the shock on my face, but I obviously do a terrible job, because in that moment Clint looks inquisitively at me, "Are you okay, Mackenzie?"

Sighing, I reply, "Just tired, baby, growing babies is hard work. Do you think we could get something to eat, once I'm dressed?"

Looking to the counter I see a bra, undies, and a purple maxi dress; he remembers that purple is my favourite colour. Smiling as I slide the dress over my head, I walk towards Clint and grab his hand, entwining our fingers together. "Thank you for my beautiful dress, and it's purple, my favourite. You're so thoughtful."

He takes my hand and leads us towards the kitchen. When we

reach it, I turn towards Clint and say, "Let me cook you dinner tonight, it's the least I can do for my man." I smile sweetly at him.

He looks sad and whispers, "I don't have anything here, Sweetcheeks."

Eagerly I reply, "Well, let's go into town. I can collect the things the make your favourite, Risotto Napolitana and chocolate self-saucing pudding for dessert. We could even stop and have a coffee while we are out, just like we used to." I smile and anxiously await his reply.

"Okay, Sweetcheeks. Let me grab a shower and then we can go." He kisses me on the cheek before leaving me alone in the kitchen. Holding my breath until I hear the water running and I let out a huge sigh in relief, *I can't believe he is falling for this.*

While he's in the shower, I look around for anything that might help me. Sitting, on the corner of the kitchen counter is his mobile phone; I quickly grab it. Scooting round the edge of the bench, I check to make sure he is still in the shower. Unlocking the screen, I check to make sure the location tracker is turned on and I quickly type a text to Jordan.

CLINT– *help me*

Once it sends, I quickly delete it and hope to hell that Jordan understands what I mean.

Just as I'm sliding his phone back onto the bench, he steps into the room. I quickly turn to face him and with a super fake smile, I say, "Hey, handsome, ready to go shopping?"

"I guess so, I hate shopping."

"Well, why don't you wait in the car while I duck in and get what we need?" I smile, and hope he says yes.

"I'm not letting you out of my sight, Sweetcheeks," he growls.

I guess he still doesn't completely trust me yet, but to keep up the rouse I say, "Okay then, lets go." Clutching his hand, I lead us towards the front door…and my possible freedom.

51

JORDAN

AFTER GETTING THE PHONE CALL FROM OFFICER KINCAID, I THROW ON MY jeans and a t-shirt and race to the hospital. When I arrive at the hospital, I notice there are four police cars here. Swiftly I park my Jeep and race inside.

Officer Hamilton is standing by the nurses' station and when she sees me running down the hall, she starts walking towards me. I know it's a hospital and I shouldn't be running but I don't give a shit right at this moment, Kenz is gone, again.

I failed to protect her, again.

Slowing down, as I get closer to her, I breathlessly pant, "Any news? Have you found her?" Struggling to breathe I think, *man, I'm unfit.*

"There's no news yet, Jordan, but Kincaid is current looking at the surveillance footage. The nurses last checked on Mackenzie at 11.25 p.m., according to her chart. They went in to do the 5:00 a.m. obs before shift change, and that's when they realised she was missing. Security did a quick sweep, and when they could not find her, they immediately called us. Once we got here and were brought up to speed, Kincaid called you, while I called in extra help."

Shaking my head, I stare at Officer Hamilton in shock, "How the fuck did this happen?" Leaning against the wall closest to me, I slide down; resting my elbows on my knees, shaking my head mumbling to myself, "Not again, poor Kenz."

A lone tear falls down my face, as soon as I start to think about Kenz and the babies, it sparks something inside of me. I wipe my face and immediately jump up, "Right, what do we do? I need to find my wife and know that her and our squids are okay."

Officer Hamilton firmly says, "You don't do anything. I'm sorry, Jordan, but you cannot be involved in this. We need to do it by the book, so we can get him locked away for a very long time."

"Fuck that!" I shout, "There is no way I'm going to sit around, while some psycho asshole has my wife."

"Jordan, I want to find Kenzie safe as well. Listen to me when I tell you this; you need to go home. Let me do my job. I can't be worrying about you too, Kenzie needs all my focus right now."

Taking a deep breath, I calm myself down. I know she's right but I can't sit around and not do anything. Throwing my hands in the air, I concede, "Okay, fine. I'll go home and wait but you keep me updated on what's happening."

"Jordan, I'll keep you updated, as best as I can. Right at the moment, I need to concentrate on finding Kenzie, that is my top priority."

Standing up, I say, "Thank you." Turning to walk away, I see Officer Kincaid coming towards us.

"I've viewed the footage, and it looks like Clint took her around 3:00 a.m. He wheeled her outside and loaded her into a yellow car, at this stage we can't make out the model. I've called the station and I'm getting them to check cameras around here to gauge which direction he went. We should have an idea within the next thirty minutes."

I'm holding my breath, as I listen to Kincaid speak; all I register is that Clint who took her. He was dressed as a doctor, has a yellow car and drove off. As it sinks in that he has her again, I slump down the wall once again, shaking my head in frustration.

Officer Hamilton tells me that they will do everything to get her back safely. I growl, "Don't make promises you can't keep, this guy is deranged. I don't believe for a second that he won't hurt her. Please just find her." With that, I stand up and walk away, before either of them has a chance to reply.

As I wait for the elevator, I repeatedly punch the button to make it get here quicker; eventually it arrives and I jump in. Grabbing my phone from my pocket, I dial Mike, he picks up on the second ring. "What's up, asshat?"

"Kenz is gone. That fucker took her from her hospital bed earlier this morning. The police won't let me help, but I'm not sitting around. That's my wife and babies."

Before I can finish Mike interrupts, "Whatever you need, I'm there, dude. Kenz is family and you know I'd do anything for family." The lift doors open and I race to my car.

"I'm just leaving the hospital, I'll be at your place in ten."

Getting into my car, I throw it into gear and haul ass to Mike's place in record time. When I get there, De-Niece is there too. She jumps up and gives me a hug, but it doesn't feel genuine. "I'm so sorry Jor."

I think it's weird that she calls me Jor, the only person to do that is Kenz, but I shrug it off. "Thanks, D."

Mike walks down the hall. "Okay, asshat, what's the plan?"

Shaking my head, I sigh, I don't know where to begin. I'm lost without Kenz. "To tell you the truth, I have no fucking idea; some husband I am." Standing up, I take a few steps before turning to face Mike. "It's probably a long shot but I'm going to head to where he had her last time. He's unhinged enough that he would do that, fucking sick bastard that he is."

De-Niece yells, "He's not unhinged!"

Turning my head to look towards her, my blood boiling at her reply. "What? Are you fucking kidding me?" I spit. "He has just kidnapped Kenz, for the second fucking time. How is that not unhinged?"

With a confused look on her face, she stammers, "What I mean is he…he…he's in love. If he loves her as much as he seems to, then I don't think he's going to hurt her."

Shaking my head, I reply, "I hope you're right." I look towards Mike. "Okay, let's go."

De-Niece says, "Sorry, I can't go, I have work." Truthfully I don't give a shit about her, but Mike walks over to her and places a gentle kiss on her forehead.

"It's okay, baby, I don't want you anywhere near that fucker anyway. At least if you're at work, I know you'll be safe."

She looks up at him with an odd look on her face. "Okay."

Mike gives her a quick kiss on the lips, and we race towards my car.

"Dude, are you okay to drive?" Mike cautiously asks.

"Yeah, I'm good." Climbing in, I look to Mike and say, "Buckle up asshat, let's go."

We back out of Mike's driveway, and head to the cabin.

Forty minutes later, we arrive at the cabin, but it's deserted. Opening the front door, it doesn't look like anyone has been here in years, a thick layer of dust covers every surface and the police tape from last time it still stuck to the verandah bearers.

My heart sinks, I don't know what else to do. I slide down the side of my car and put my head in my hands. Mike walks over to me, crouches down, and places his hand on my shoulders. I look up into his concerned eyes. He clears his throat, "Look, dude, Kenz is strong. She will be fine. Let's head home, we need to be close by when we hear that Kenz and the munchkins are found and safe."

I'm too shaken to drive, so Mike guides me to the passenger side and I climb in. He drives us back to my place and just as we pull up, I get a text. I open up the message and stare at it in disbelief. It's from a number I don't recognise. It has two words,

UNKNOWN – *help me*

As soon as I finishing reading it, I drop my phone in shock. I know it's Kenz, but I don't know what to do. Snatching my phone back up, I immediately call Officer Hamilton. She picks up on the first ring. "Hamilton."

"Hey, it's Jordan. I just got a text from a number that I don't know saying, 'help me'. I'm pretty sure it's a cry for help from Kenz."

"Okay, that's great. Tell me the number and I'll see if tech can trace it."

"Sure." I give her the number.

"Thanks Jordan…"

Interrupting her, I ask, "So, what do we do now?"

"Leave it with me and I'll be in touch. Jordan, this is a great lead. Kenzie is strong, just keep remembering that."

"Yeah, thanks. I'll speak to you soon." Sighing, I hang up and slide my phone back into my pocket.

I look over, and Mike is staring at me and says, "See, it's going to be fine." He walks over to the fridge and grabs two Diet Cokes.

We head outside and sit at the Jack and Jill. After sitting in silence for about ten minutes, I jump up. "Fuuuuuuuuck!" I yell in frustration towards the clear blue sky.

Sitting back down, I look towards Mike, "Dude, I feel so helpless. Kenz and my babies are out there, and I am sitting here doing nothing. I'm having a Goddamn freakin' Coke with my best mate. It's just not right."

Standing up, I lean over the railing and again I shout, "Fuuuuck!" I'm so frustrated that I can't do anything.

"Look, dude, I get it. You're annoyed, you feel useless and your fucking pissed off, but there is nothing we can do right now. I know it sucks donkey balls, but you need to remain calm and strong for Kenz. Why don't you go to Malt Me and tinker or brew some shit? It will take your mind off things and keep you busy. I can't be worrying about you, too."

I look towards Mike. "Shit, dude, when did you become the wise one?"

Mike fakes being hurt. "Listen here, asshat, I've always been wise and all that other shit. You are now just finally seeing me for all that I am."

"And there's the cocky Mike I know. Thanks dude, I appreciate the pep talk."

Mike says he's got to go and since we took my car, I offer to drive him home. We get to his place, just as De-Niece is pulling up. She races over and wraps her arms around Mike. "Any news?"

Mike shakes my head. "The cabin was a bust but asshat got a text."

De-Niece looks over at me confused. "From who?"

"No idea, I didn't recognise the number, but I'm sure it was Kenz reaching out for help. I called the police and they are trying to trace the number now. That was a few hours ago, so hopefully I'll hear something soon."

De-Niece looks really pissed. I guess she is just as worried as we are. Turning I slap Mike on the back. "Thanks for today, dude, I'm going to head home, I'll keep you posted."

"Anytime, man, anytime. You keep me updated and just remember our girl is strong. She is one of the strongest peeps I know, she'll be fine, Jordan. I feel it in my bones."

"Thanks, Mike, I appreciate it and I fucking hope you're right. I'll keep you posted." Turning, I jump into my car and head home.

As soon as I get home, I collapse in a heap on sofa, and I let it all out. I crumble and cry.

I cry for Kenz.

I cry for our babies

Most of all, I cry because I've failed her...again.

52

KENZIE

THE DRIVE INTO TOWN TAKES US ABOUT TEN MINUTES. IT'S MID-AFTERNOON on a Saturday and most of the shops are closed or starting to close; *I hope can pull this off*. The scenery is absolutely stunning, on one side of the road is a river and the other is a beautiful rainforest. It's secluded and peaceful, no wonder he chose to keep me here.

"Clint, it's absolutely beautiful here."

He glances towards me and smiles. Reaching over, he places his hand on my thigh and gives it a little squeeze. Inwardly I shudder at his touch, but to keep up my ruse, I look over at him and sweetly smile, before looking out the window again.

This is my chance to make my escape or at the very least get help.

We park the car outside the local supermarket and head in. To keep up the loving girlfriend ploy and make him think that I want to be with him, I grab his hand and put it over my shoulders, so I can put my arm around his waist. Slipping my hand into his back jeans pocket, I give his ass a squeeze, just like old times. Looking up at him I whisper, "I missed this," as I snuggle into him.

He sniffs my hair and I cringe, he hugs me closer and I start to tremble. Closing my eyes I take a deep breath, telling myself I can do this and to keep walking. Just put one foot in front of the other. My heart rate accelerates, as we get closer to the shop door. My mind goes into overdrive trying to figure out how I'm going to get out of here.

We race around the shop getting everything we need for the risotto, and not once do I see someone; just my luck. We get to the checkout and I place the groceries on the conveyor. I'm discretely trying to get the chick's attention but she won't look up. *Goddam teenagers.* I guess that plan won't work, so I hope and pray that Jordan got my text.

Clint pays for our groceries, and I go to grab the bags but he places his hand on my arm. "I got it, Sweetcheeks." I secretly high five myself, I didn't shudder when he touched me.

"Thanks, baby, do you want to get a coffee before we head back? I'd kill for a latte and muffin right now. Maybe we could also take a walk through the park over there, when we are finished. It's so pretty here and it's a lovely day." If he agrees, I might be able to get away if I slip to the bathroom.

"Sounds good, Sweetcheeks, let's drop the bags off first." Turning around, I smile and walk out of the store with a little spring in my step. This is my chance, I just know it.

Clint receives a text on the way to the car, but as he has the bags he can't read it. We get to the car; I open the boot so he can put the bags in. After closing it, I grab his hand, entwine my fingers with his, and we head towards the coffee shop.

As we are walking through the car park Clint pulls his phone out of his jeans pocket and checks the text.

TRAITOR – *he knows you have her*

Clint stops, lets go my hand, and I see his fist clenching by his side. He glares at me, and I know that whatever was in that text has pissed him off. "Is everything okay, baby?"

He looks back at his phone and then snaps his head up, glaring at me. In a split second, he lunges towards me but I jump back. "You bitch, you fucking lying whore bag bitch. You texted loverboy, and here I was going to let him live, but now you and he are both going to suffer, painfully."

I'm rooted on the spot.

I stare at him my mouth wide open.

I don't know how he knows but I'm screwed now.

My mind is racing, but I don't have the energy to come up with an excuse so I do that only thing that I can. I race towards him, swing my leg back, and with all my might, I stomp on his foot. Then I shove my knee into his balls and push him; he doubles over in pain.

This is my chance.

I take the opportunity and I run. I run through car park into the back street, and I don't stop; I run as fast as I can, turning down streets, doubling back. I just keep moving.

I don't stop.

I keep running.

Ducking and weaving down streets.

I don't look back.

After running for what feels like forever, I have to stop, I'm shattered and out of breath. It's becoming harder and harder to breathe. I'm lost. I have no idea where I am, or even which Goddamn town I'm in.

Ducking down an alleyway, I hide behind an old, beautiful brick building, which I think would be perfect building for a brewpub. Giggling, I shake my head, how on earth can I be thinking of beer at a time like this? Hiding behind the industrial bins out the back, bending over, I put my hands on my knees and take deep breaths.

Sliding down the wall, I rest my head on my knees and start to cry. I have no idea where I am. I have no money, and I have no fucking clue what to do next. What does one do when you have a fucking psycho looking for you?

When I look up again it's dark, I have no idea how long I've been sitting here. Taking a deep breath, I think it's now or never, so I sneak out from where I am.

Heading towards the road, sticking close to the building for cover, I peek around the corner. I find I'm back at the main street that we drove in on. There's a streetlight on the other side of the road but the street is empty. This place is deserted. *Doesn't anyone live is the fucking town?* Looking up and down the street, I decide to head back towards the shopping precinct, surely someone will be around to help me.

Taking another deep breath, I pick up my pace and keep going. It takes me about five minutes to reach the supermarket. In that time, I have not seen one person, or even a single car; the lights in the shop are off and it's closed. "Damn smalls towns," I mumble to myself.

Taking another look around, I see headlights coming from the direction I was heading. I race onto the road to flag them down, but as the car gets closer I see that it's Clint's. "Fuck," I say to myself as I quickly turn and run across the road into the park.

Clint screeches to a stop, jumps out, leaving the engine running, and runs into the park after me. "I know you're here, bitch, you'll be leaving with me!" he shouts into the dark night sky. Before he adds, "Come out, come out, wherever you are." in a sinister voice.

I'm hiding under the slide when I hear him coming towards me, I hold my breath, and he stops right near my hiding place. My heart is beating erratically and I'm sure he can hear it. I think he's found me, and I start to give up, when I see that he's turning in circles. He's frustrated and looking around. He stops and shouts again, "I know you're here, bitch, and I'll find you. I've got all night bitch!"

Holding ever so still, not breathing for fear he will find me, I flinch when he kicks the slide in frustration, narrowly missing me. Turning, he runs further into the park. I sigh in relief.

I wait until I can't hear his footsteps and I sneak out. Taking a quick look around, I see a light on in the distance. I take off in that direction, trying to be as quiet as possible. As I get closer to the light, I can feel my heart beating; it feels like its going a million miles a minute. I'm about fifty meters from the house when, from behind a tree, Clint steps out. Stopping me, dead in my tracks, I quickly turn around to run away.

He lunges forward, grabbing me by my hair. "Got you now, you little bitch. " I squeal from the pain, my hair follicles tearing out. He yanks me roughly into him. Wrapping his arms tightly around me, as I kick and lunge my legs. Without thinking, I scream at the top of my lungs, hoping someone will hear me. Viciously, he spins me around and punches me in the face. Seeing stars, I drop to the ground like a sack of potatoes. I hold my cheek, the pain is excruciating; I start to cry. Blood begins to drip down my face. I sob harder.

Clint slaps me again. "Shut the fuck up, bitch." I'm lying on the ground; I immediately draw my legs up to protect the babies and myself. He grabs me by my hair and drags me back towards the car.

Kicking and screaming I keep pleading, "Please let me go, Clint. Please don't hurt me." Clint is mumbling to himself, but I can't make sense of what he's saying, he has completely spaced out and is babbling incoherently. As we pass under a light near the playground, he looks down at me. His face is void of any emotion and his eyes are dark with rage. I've never seen him like this. I have to get away; otherwise I will not survive.

Once again, I try to dig my heels into the ground, but it's no use, he's too strong. The anger coursing through his veins, gives him super human strength. He keeps dragging me towards the car. I'm so scared, I don't know what else to do.

We get to the car and he opens the boot to shove me in. As he is shoving me in, the light from behind him illuminates the tyre iron sitting there, in plain sight. I reach over and grab it. With all my might, I turn and swing. It connects with the side of Clint's head, and he loses his balance. With the hand that is holding the tyre iron, I shove him in the chest with everything that I have. He falls backwards, and I tumble back with him. I hear a crack as we both land on the bitumen with a thud.

Lifting my head, I look towards Clint; he's not moving and vacant eyes stare back at me, not blinking, he's dead. I start to scream as realisation sets in: he's dead. I continue to scream, as I see blue and red light coming towards us. Those lights are last thing I see, as everything goes black.

53

JORDAN

I'm at home, but I can't sit still, I can't concentrate on anything. I've never felt so lost or helpless in my entire life. I've failed to protect her again and this time there's the twins to think about.

"Shit! Fuck! Shit!" I yell.

I'd accepted that Kenz and I probably would never have kids. Now that she is pregnant, I'm over the moon. However, I'm now scared shitless that I'm going to lose them all.

Sitting on the couch, I stare at our wedding picture on the TV cabinet and I start to cry. I doze off, absolutely exhausted. I'm woken up by the sound of my phone ringing, I slide to answer and sleepily say, "Yeah?" Not caring that it sounds rude.

"Jordan, this is Officer Hamilton."

I immediately sit up, instantly, I'm wide-awake. "Did you find her?" I shout into the phone.

"Yes, we have her. She's currently on her way to hospital to be assessed. I'm on my way there now, I'll meet you at the hospital."

"Okay, thanks, Officer Hamilton."

Hanging up I immediately call Mike. He answers on the first ring, "Any news, asshat?"

"They found her, she's on her way to hospital."

I hear him sigh in relief, "Swing by and get me, I want to see our girl."

"Okay, I'll be at yours in ten."

54

KENZIE

WHEN I WAKE, I'M IN A STRANGE BED, AGAIN AND I START TO PANIC. BUT when I look around, I realise I'm in a hospital room. Jordan is beside me, with my hand resting under his head; he's sound asleep. A smile appears on my swollen, bruised face. I never thought I'd see him again.

With my free hand, I lift it up, and run it over his cheek. He stirs, so I continue to run my hand back and forth across his face. He opens his beautiful green eyes and stares up at me. His face immediately lights up when he registers I'm awake and grinning back at him.

"Hi, husband." I manage to squeak out before the tears begin to fall; the flood gates have opened and my face currently rivals Niagara Falls.

Jordan stands up and slides onto the bed next to me. I lean forward and he wraps his arms around me. Still crying, I snuggle into him and continue to cry. He rubs my arm soothingly, whispering, "Shhhh. You're safe now." He keeps placing gentle kisses to my forehead, while squeezing me tighter.

We are interrupted when Mike clears this throat. "Welcome back, Kenz!"

Looking towards Jordan, I hesitantly ask, "Did the police get him this time?"

Jordan looks at me confused, before looking towards Mike, who also has a perplexed look on his face. I look back and forth between the two of them. "Guys, am I missing something?"

Jordan sits up and takes my hands between his. "Kenz, what do you remember?"

Struggling to remember, I bite my fingernails as I think. "Umm, I remember running through the park, Clint dragging me and then him trying to put me in the boot. I managed to swing at him with something, and then seeing flashing lights. Then I woke up here."

My eyes pop wide open as it all comes flashing back to me.

Running.

Clint grabbing me.

Dragging me to the car.

Shoving me towards the boot.

Swinging the tyre iron.

Colliding with Clint's head.

Shoving him.

Falling.

Crunch.

His lifeless eyes.

Flashing lights.

My whole body starts shaking, and I scream. It becomes hard to breath and I start to hyperventilate. I took someone's life.

Tears are pouring down my cheeks, I'm gasping for breath, unable to breathe as the reality of what I did sinks in. Jordan is trying to console me but I'm beyond reasoning with.

I'm shaking, screaming and crying.

Shaking my head back and forth.

Screaming, "No! No! No!"

A nurse and doctor come rushing into the room. I hear them, but nothing registers.

I feel a prick in my arm.

Finally I feel calm and at peace.

I can't keep my eyes open.

Black.

I wake up a few hours later, Jordan is still by my bed, but this time Mike is gone. I see Mum and a Skye huddled together on the recliner.

Mum and I lock eyes and we both start to cry. She jumps up, comes over to the bed, wrapping me in a Mum hug, and we cry together. This hug is exactly what I need.

Skye comes over, climbs onto the bed and joins our hug. The three of us sit here, crying, locked in each other's arms for a traditional Merlot family hug. Jordan steps back, but I grab his hand and he joins in on our hug too. We all sit there with our arms wrapped around each other.

My stomach growls, and I realise I haven't eaten in what feels like forever. We all burst out laughing as my tummy growls again. Jordan says, "Looks like our mummy-to-be is hungry?"

Mum's head pops up and she questioningly asks, "Mummy-to-be??"

"Surprise, we're pregnant," I say with a smile, looking at Mum. "With twins."

Skye yells, "Fuck me dead, said Foreskin Fred."

Mum smacks Skye in the arm, and scolds her, "Language, Skye."

I laugh.

Looking over at her, I say, "Skye, you need to stop hanging around Mike."

"Ohh, honey." Mum says as she envelopes me in another hug and through what I hope are happy tears blubbers, "Mac, I'm so happy for you." She reaches over towards Jordan and grabs his hand, giving it a squeeze. She draws back and grabs my cheeks, pulls me in and kisses my forehead. "You gave me such a fright, baby girl."

"I'm sorry Mum, I'm never planning on doing that again. Besides now that he's dead there's no one else to hurt me."

Mum looks up shocked. "What do you mean he's dead?"

Looking towards Jordan confused, I say, "You didn't tell her?"

Mum interrupts, "Tell me what?"

Taking a deep breath, I proceed to tell her what happened. We both have tears falling down our cheeks by time I've finished retelling what happened. I look to my lap and whisper, "Mum, I killed someone." Shyly I look up at her. "How do I live with that?"

Mum tilts my head towards her, wiping away my tears. "Now you listen to me, Mackenzie Merlot. He made his own bed and he now has to lie in it forever. You did what you needed to do to survive and to save those babies. If anyone thinks differently, then they will have me to deal with."

Staring at Mum in shock, I know she's right, if I hadn't done what I did, it would be me in the morgue instead of him. It's a hard to describe my feelings right at this moment. On one hand, I have relief. I'm relieved that I'm finally safe, but I also feel remorse. I'm remorseful, for killing someone, but I also feel sadness. I'm sad that someone is dead, even if he was a psychotic asshole douchehole.

We are all sitting in silence when there is a knock on the door. Officer Kincaid and Officer Hamilton come in. I take a deep breath as I think they are here to arrest me for killing Clint.

Officer Hamilton is the first to speak, "How are you feeling, Kenzie?"

Hesitantly, I reply, "Okay, I think. Relieved that he's dead and can't hurt me anymore. Scared that you're going to arrest me for killing him."

Officer Hamilton takes a seat. "I can assure you that we are not here to arrest you, but I do need to get your side of what happened, before we can officially rule his death as self-defense."

She sets up a tape recorder on the bed trolley and presses record to take my statement. Taking a deep breath, I recount everything that I remember. When I'm finished, they both look at each other, and I think to myself, "Ohh shit, I'm going to jail. My babies are going to be born in jail." I don't realise that someone is speaking to me until I hear my name being called; I shake my head. "Sorry, I missed what you said."

Officer Kincaid looks pissed that he has to repeat himself. "As I was saying, from what you have told us and the report from the coroner; the injury that Mr. MacNicholson received was not intentional. You pushed him away in self-defense and I might add; you have a mighty good left hook. The wound to the side of his head was pretty impressive." He smirks. "But you didn't hear that from me."

Officer Hamilton says, "Once you are released, we will need you to come down to the station to sign your statement. I'll type up what you've told us today, and then this matter will be finalised. Mr. MacNicholson doesn't have any family, except for a cousin that we are trying to track down. I doubt she'll contest any of this. The evidence is all there, and add in the previous history, there's no lawyer who would touch it. Rest up, Kenzie, and we'll see you in a few days."

Just after they leave, the doctor comes in. He wants to keep me in for another night, my blood pressure is still a little high and they want to ensure everything is okay.

Later that afternoon, Jordan and I lie in each other's arms, his palm gently resting on my belly. I look up into his eyes and for the first time in a long time I'm calm and relaxed. We are finally free...or so we thought.

Mum and Skye left this morning. I told them I'm fine and between Jordan, Mike, and occasionally Sarah hovering around me, I have someone with me at all times. It's quite overbearing to tell you the truth. I know they mean well, but I really want some alone time.

They have just pulled away when Jordan gets a call from one of the staff at Malt Me and he needs to head over there ASAP to sort an issue out. I'm secretly happy, finally I'll get alone time.

I grab my Kindle and head to the kitchen. Pouring a jug of soda water and lime, I grab a glass and head outside. I'm lying on the lounger when he comes downstairs. "I'll be back as soon as I can."

"There's no rush, babe. I have my Kindle and the babies and I are fine. Plus I know you, either Mike or Sarah have been summoned and will be here soon."

He leans down and places a gentle kiss on my lips and pulls back to rest his forehead on mine. "Maybe, I'll be back as soon as I can"

"I'm fine, babe, trust me."

"I'll be back as soon as I can. Text or call me if you need anything." He opens the side gate and heads to his Jeep.

Finally I'm alone, I lie back and instead of reading, I start playing Candy Crush. Hearing someone come down the driveway, I'm putting my money on Mike, but I'm surprised at who I see walk through the gate.

55

TRAITOR

I can't believe Clint is gone. He and I have always been there for each other, until he met her that is. Then his life became all about her. Mackenzie this. Sweetcheeks that. Fuck her!

When it comes down to it, I'm the only one who's ever been there for him, just like he was there for me when I needed him. Family always comes first, and that's why I have to end her, to get revenge for Clint.

Arriving at her place, I wait for Jordan to leave. I broke into the brewery last night and made a few little modifications, so he'd have no choice but to go.

Kenz is all alone now.

Getting out of my car, I make my way over to their house and I walk down the driveway. Reaching over, I open the gate and slam it shut; with the force of the slam, it pops open again.

She jumps when the gate bangs, looking up, she seems shocked that I am here. "Shit, De-Niece, you scared me,"

"Yeah, well, you get that," I spit. The dumb bitch looks at me confused, *fuck she is stupid*. With my hands on my hips, I stand there and stare at her. "You are one fucking stupid mole. You have everyone wrapped around your little finger, well not me. They'll drop everything to help you, when really you are just a stupid bitch. I mean, you let my cousin kidnap you; twice."

The look of shock on her face with that revelation is priceless. "And I'm here today to get payback for you taking him away from me. All he did was fall in love with you, and you killed him. As one final favour to him, you will not see tomorrow, your babies, or your precious Jor ever again."

Mackenzie stands up. "Yo…You're his cousin?"

"Oh My God, bitch, catch up. Yes, Clint's my cousin, but if you really cared about him you would know that."

She's just standing there, staring at me, so I take my chance and lunge for her. I knock her onto the lounger before we roll off with a thud onto the pavers. I manage to roll her onto her back and I straddle her chest. I start swinging, punching, and hitting any part of her body that I can. She lies there screaming. I spit, "This is for my cousin, you heartless fucking bitch." I swing my arm back for one final blow but my arm it is yanked back and I fly through the air. Crashing through the French doors, falling to the floor inside with a thud, in a shower of glass and splintered wood. There's an excruciating pain in my left side; I look down to see a splinter of wood and glass sticking out of my abdomen, blood pooling beneath me.

Everything starts to go fuzzy. Everything is dwindling away. A cold numbing sensation rushes over my body, the pain subsiding. Rolling to my side I groan in agony and grunt, "See you all in hell," before everything goes black.

56

MIKE

It's my day off and I just kissed De-Niece goodbye as she races off to work. After making another coffee, I head to the lounge room. I sit in my brown leather recliner and relax to enjoy *Bold and the Beautiful*. It's my guilty pleasure, but I'll never admit it to anyone. It's just finished when I get a text.

JORDAN – *Hey asshat, any chance you can head over and check on Kenz? I've had to go to the brewery urgently*

ME – *Sure can, I'll grab her a dozen cheeseburgers and head over*

JORDAN – *Thanks man*

I finish my coffee, turn off the TV, place my coffee mug in the sink. From the bench, I grab my wallet and keys and head over to hang with Kenzie.

When I pull up, I see De-Niece's car there, seeing her here makes me smile. I'm glad she's making an effort. I know she doesn't particularly like Kenz for some reason, which is weird cause everyone loves Kenz.

Getting out of my car I hear yelling coming from the backyard; it sounds like De-Niece is screaming at Kenz. Running down the driveway, I get to the gate and I see De-Niece straddling Kenz. She's screeching and my heart drops. I hear her yell, "This is for my cousin, you heartless fucking bitch."

She swings her arm back to lay into her again. I drop the food, run over and yank her back, pulling her off Kenz. She falls backwards, hurtling through the French doors with a crash.

Looking over, I see Kenz is barely breathing I grab my phone out of my pocket and dial triple zero. Cradling Kenz in my arms, as we wait for the ambulance, I rock us back and forth, mumbling, "No, no, no, I'm so sorry Kenz."

The ambos come down the driveway and they head towards De-Niece, I shout, "Not her, she's the one who did this. Help Kenz, please, she's pregnant, please help her." Stepping back, I let them attend to Kenz.

Looking up, I see Officer Hamilton and Officer Kincaid walk through the gate. Hamilton looks at everything with wide eyes and shock. Kincaid goes over and talks to the paramedics. Officer Hamilton comes over to me. "What the hell happened here?"

I'm staring at her, but it isn't until she touches my arm that I register she's talking to me. "Huh?"

"What happened here?"

I proceed to tell her what I walked in on, and then I look towards De-Niece just as the paramedic places a white sheet over her body. Stumbling backwards, I realise, she's dead.

My phone starts to play Jordan's tone, *Wash It All Away* by Five Finger Death Punch. I grab it from my pocket and answer, "Hey dude. You need to get here now."

"What the fuck?" he shouts through the phone.

"Ummm, De-Niece is dead and Kenz is in pretty bad shape." I manage to say before I drop my phone and vomit.

I collapse to my knees and proceed empty my stomach onto the lawn. Once I'm finished, I ease back onto my heels and I stare up at the sky. Shaking my head in disbelief at what I just walked in on.

Hearing Kenz moan shocks me back to reality, and I race over to her and grab her hand, squeezing it tightly. She looks towards me; her eyes well up with tears and she starts to sob. With my free hand, I push the hair on her face away. "It's okay, Kenz, Jordan is on his way. I'm so sorry. I had no idea."

She has a death grip on my hand, and just as I turn back towards her, Jordan barges through the gate. He freezes when he sees the sheet, but as soon as he sees Kenz on the stretcher, he races over to her. "Ohh, baby, I'm so sorry I wasn't here."

They've just taken Kenz away. I'm sitting on the garden edging when I hear one of the officers say that it's okay to remove the body. It's when he says body that shock sets in.

Holy shit, I killed someone.

Holy shit, my girlfriend was working with the enemy.

57

JORDAN

As soon as I hang up from Mike, I race out to my Jeep and speed home. Luck must be on my side today as every light is green and traffic is light. Pulling onto our street, I see there are police cars and an ambulance outside our place.

Climbing out of my Jeep, I race down the driveway, and I immediately see a white sheet covering a body. My heart sinks, and then I hear Kenz groan. Racing over to her, I see the left side of her face is swollen and turning purple. Mike is holding her hand and throwing up. She sees me and starts to sob.

The ambo interrupts us, "Sorry, guys, but we really need to get Mrs. McRoberts to the hospital. You can ride with us or we can meet you there."

"Kenz, I'm coming with you. I'm just going to check on Mike, and I'll meet you in the ambulance." She nods her head.

Walking over to Mike, who is now sitting on the garden bed edge, I see that his face is green. He doesn't look too good. Reaching out, I squeeze his shoulder, "Dude, are you okay? What the fuck happened?"

He just sits there staring into space. I don't think he even realises I'm speaking to him. Shaking him, I shout, "Dude!" He finally looks up at me. "Are you okay, man?"

He shakes his head. "Dude, I killed De-Niece."

Now it's my turn to stare in shock, before I can say anything Mike says, "I got here and she was on top of Kenz, hitting and punching her. I grabbed her off Kenz, and she went through the French doors. I'm so sorry, Jordan, this is entirely my fault. I didn't know she was his cousin. I swear, I didn't know"

The ambo leans over the fence and says, "Mr. McRoberts we have to go now."

"Okay, I'll be right there." Crouching down, placing my hands on Mike's shoulder, I look into his eyes. "Dude, I have to go with Kenz. Are you going to be okay?"

He nods his head. "Yeah, yep, yeah. I'm okay. I have to wait here to give my statement. Go be with Kenz."

As I walk away, I worry about Mike.

58

KENZIE

I'M ADMITTED STRAIGHT AWAY AND IT'S NURSE TARA ON DUTY. SHE WALKS over to my bed and smiles at me. "Well, well, well, we meet again, Mrs. McRoberts. If I remember correctly, you said we wouldn't be seeing each other until the birth of your lil' ones." She looks around the room. "And I don't see any little ones in this room so I'm guessing you told me a big fat porky." I can't help laughing but I cringe as my face hurts like a bitch when I do anything at the moment. She finishes my obs and leaves.

A few minutes' later, Jordan walks in, our eyes meet across the room. "Fuck me, Kenz...your face. Your arms. Are you okay?"

"Depends on your definition of okay," I laugh, "But apart from feeling like I was beaten up, I'm doing pretty well. I asked Tara to make an appointment with Jeannie. Dr. Greene is here delivering a baby, and she'll check in before she leaves."

Jordan sits on the bed holding my hand, gently stroking the back like he does to calm me down. Looking into his eyes, I see worry, and that scares me. Lifting my hand to his cheek, he leans into it. "Jor, I promise I'm okay. Things could be a lot worse. If Mike hadn't turned up when he did, who knows what would have happened? I guess we now know who Clint's missing cousin is. How did we not know? I just don't understand."

Jordan looks into my eyes. "I don't think we will ever know. Mike's pretty shaken up; he looked so broken when I left. He was waiting to make his statement, but the coroner turned up so the officers had to speak with her first."

I look at him confused, "Coroner, why is the coroner there?"

"When Mike pulled her off you, she went through the French doors. A piece glass and wood splintered off and went into her guts. She bled out and died."

"Holy fuck, are you serious? Oh My God! How's Mike?"

"Not sure, I haven't spoken to him since I arrived here."

"Babe, leave me and go and see Mike. He needs you now. I'm fine and the babies are fine, I'm just sleepy." To emphasize what I just said I lie back, close my eyes, and pretend snore. I smile when I hear Jordan laugh; it's that deep throaty one I love. "Okay, Faker McFakerson, I'll go and check on Mike, BUT if you need anything call me. I'll be back first thing tomorrow, and I'll bring a change of clothes."

"Sounds good to me. Now go check on Mike, he needs you now. I promise, I'm fine."

Jordan leans down and kisses my cheek. "Rest up, Kenz." Then he bends down to my belly and kisses it twice. "And you two lil' ones, be nice to Mummy. She's been through a lot, and even though she's a fighter, she needs her rest too." He kisses my belly again, twice, before leaving, closing the door quietly behind him.

A few moments later, the door swings opens, I presume Jordan has come back, but in walks Sarah with coffee and muffins. *God, I love this girl.* She smiles at me, as she kicks the door shut with her foot. "Seriously, girl, we need to stop hanging out here."

"But the beds are so comfortable." We both burst out laughing.

Sarah places the coffee and muffin on the bed trolley. I fill her in on all that went down this afternoon. When I finish, I look up at Sarah. Her mouth is hanging open and she has a shocked look on her face, "Fuck me dead, said Foreskin Fred."

"Seriously, Mike is rubbing off on everyone, but I agree. How did we not know?"

"I'm speechless. Umm, how's Mike doing? He must be devastated."

"Jordan is heading to be with him now." I sigh, "He saved me Sarah." A lone tear escapes my eye.

Sarah leans over and hugs me gently. "Poor Mike, I'm guessing that's where Jordan was off too? I passed him on my way in, he seemed happy that I was here."

"Yeah, he doesn't like leaving me alone at the moment. It's frustrating, I just want 'me' time, but there's always someone around. At least you've been giving me space."

Sarah looks agitated when I mention that she hasn't been around much, but I can't query her any further as Dr. Greene enters my room.

Sarah says goodbye and says she will pop round tomorrow when I'm released. Leaning over, she gives me another hug and leaves. Once she closes the door, Dr. Greene starts up the ultrasound machine; thankfully everything is fine with our munchkins.

Nurse Tara comes in and gives me an endone for the pain, which should help me sleep. Taking the tablet from Nurse Tara, I swallow it down. I'm so exhausted that I fall into a deep sleep and don't wake until just before sunrise the next morning. I'm stiff and sore, but I'm feeling good mentally, but not physically. Physically, I hurt all over.

My breakfast tray has just been cleared and in walks Jordan and Mike. Without thinking, I jump out of bed. I wince in pain because I did it too fast, but I need to hug Mike. "Thank you, Mike. If you hadn't got there when you did, I would not be here today. I'm sorry that I have caused all of this."

He kisses my cheek and hugs me back. "Kenz, this is not your fault. I'm just glad I got there when I did. Seeing her on top of you will be etched in my mind forever."

We end our hug and Mike helps me back to bed. "Besides Jordan has agreed that I get free beer for life. I mean that's the mandatory payment for saving you, and Mac and Cheese."

"Did you just call my babies, Mac and Cheese?"

"Yep, Mac and Cheese." He bends downs and whispers. "Hey Mac and Cheese, Unky Mike will also buy you beer when you're bigger. Well I'll get it free from your dad; he does own a brewery and all that other shit." He looks up at me and we all start to laugh.

59

KENZIE

...6 months later

TODAY IS THE DAY THAT WE GET TO BRING OUR BABIES HOME FROM hospital. Rory and Indi were prematurely born at thirty-two weeks. My blood pressure spiked and Dr. Green wasn't taking any chances. The girls were born via C-section later that day. And today, as a family, we get to head home together, for the first time.

The last two months have been hectic. We've been juggling our time between the hospital, the brewery, and being at home occasionally to sleep. Jordan has been my rock through everything, as usual.

Our girls are beautiful; they both have dazzling blue eyes. Rory has golden blonde locks like me, while Indi has curly sandy blonde hair like her dad; we still don't know where the curls come from though.

We sold the house we renovated, as it held too many uncomfortable memories. We bought a brand new brick home closer to the brewery. It has four bedrooms, ours with an ensuite and a humongous walk-in-robe, which rivals Carrie's from the *Sex and the City* movie. It has an office with a full wall of book shelves, that I may have filled, a guest room, media room, and an open plan kitchen/dining/living room, which leads out to a spectacular timber patio area that overlooks the most amazing pool area. It still has a beer shed for Jordan to experiment at home.

Jordan even built a cubby house for the girls, not that they'll be able to use it for a few years yet, but there was no stopping him. He would do anything for his girls, me included.

Smiling, I fondly remember a time when I was five months pregnant. Jordan and I were closing up at the brewery one Saturday night, everyone had just left and I was horny; I was a total nymphomaniac while I was pregnant. I couldn't get enough. I never thought I'd see the day that Jordan would tell me to back off, but that happened on quite a few occasions. I'd finally treated myself and bought some maternity lingerie from Hot Mumma and it had arrived.

Leaving Jordan out at the bar, I went into our office to tally the books for the night when I started to get that tingly feeling down below. I also realised that we had yet to officially christen the office; that thought only turned me on even more. That morning I decided to wear my new lingerie, and Jordan had yet to see it, so I stripped off. I was wearing my new navy and vivid blue microfiber bra and matching undies. Lying down on the office couch, I waited for Jordan to come and find me.

My heart was racing as I was hoping that he wouldn't reject me, again. I knew it had been a bit much but I couldn't help it, those hormones were making me crazy. While waiting, I fell asleep, but I was pleasantly awoken to the feeling of Jordan running his fingers over the fabric of my undies. I moaned in pleasure as I rolled onto my back. Opening my eyes, I found Jordan standing next to me in only his boxer briefs. His eyes were full of lust and hunger. Sitting up, I kissed along his chin towards his delectable lips; I licked his lower lip before taking it into my mouth and sucking. I coaxed his mouth open, before plunging my tongue into his, moaning as he sucked it like a lollypop. I the connection and whispered, "Make love to me, Jordan."

He stood up and pulled his boxer briefs down, his cock sprang free. I flicked my tongue out over the tip as I grabbed onto his shaft and started stroking from base to tip. I took his cock deeper into my mouth, hollowing my cheeks to take him completely. His cock hit the back of my throat, I scraped my teeth along his shaft before sucking him back into my mouth. He ran his fingers through my hair as I was sucking. Before long, I felt the first spurt of hot salty cum hit the back of my throat. Sucking him dry before releasing him, he lowered his head and kissed me. He carefully lowered me, so I was lying down to the couch.

He kissed down my neck, sucking my breast through my bra before lowering the cup and biting my nipple. With his other hand he massaged my other breast and I moaned. Since becoming pregnant, I have loved having my breasts sucked and massaged, even more so than before. He reached around and unclasped my bra, lowering the straps before flinging it aside. He attacked my nipples and breasts with such vigor that my orgasm ripped through me without warning. I was still wriggling in ecstasy when he ran his hand down my body and rubbed my pussy through my now soaking, wet undies. He pushed the material to the side and ran his finger up my slit, before slipping it in. He was still sucking on my nipple, he added another finger, and I let out pleasurable moan.

Jordan pulled back, removing his fingers, and I cried out, but he grabbed the top of my undies and quickly removed them. Then he buried his face in my pussy. He nibbled and sucked on my clit. "Ohh, Jordan," I moaned, he then used his thumb and started massaging my clit. I could feel my orgasm building as he plunged his finger in, before sucking on my clit again. He slipped in another finger, causing my orgasm to peak. I crashed and tumbled over the edge.

Once my tremors stopped, he kissed his way up my body; paying attention extra to my sensitive breasts. Finally, he kissed me on the mouth, it was hot and heavy. The taste of my juices still on his lips. I felt his cock at my entrance and I lifted my hips as he penetrated me in one thrust. Due to my growing belly it was uncomfortable so he pulled out. He helped me up and then sat down, I lowered myself onto his rock hard cock. Lifting up onto my knees and I rode his cock like I was a jockey in the Melbourne Cup, impaling my self deeper and deeper each time. He grabbed my nipple and rolled it between his thumb and forefinger, leaning forward and sucking occasionally. I threw my head back and moaned. My orgasm erupted like a volcano, moments later, Jordan released his seed deep inside of me.

I eased myself off his lap and sat on the couch next to him. I looked over to him and ran my hand down the side of his face. "I love you, Jordan McRoberts."

Smiling he looked over to me and leaned into my palm, turning his head to place soft kiss there, "And I love you, Kenzie Louise McRoberts nee Merlot." He placed his hand on my belly and gently rubbed. "Mac and Cheese, I love you guys, too."

Yes, Mike's weird and wonderful name had stuck for the twins; even Dr. Green was using that name.

We've just arrived home from the hospital, and for the first time, it's just the four of us. Finally as a family, we are under the same roof. I'm standing in the doorway to the nursery staring at our beautiful girls, who are sound asleep in their cots, and I could not be happier.

Even though the road to this point was rough and definitely bumpy, I wouldn't change a thing. I am, whom I am today, due to what has happened to me. Its taken me a while to accept that, but there is no point in worrying about things that I cannot change, or the past.

I'm Kenzie Louise McRoberts nee Merlot.

I am strong,

I am a survivor.

EPILOGUE

...2 months later

IT'S BEEN EIGHT MONTHS SINCE CLINT AND DE-NIECE TRIED TO RUIN OUR lives for the last time, but for me it's been eight months of growth. I've been through so much when it comes to Clint, but with the help of my family and friends, I'm a much stronger person.

There are no more pity stares, people treat me like the Kenzie from before any of this ever happened. In addition, I now have two adorable little girls to dote on. People finally see me for the that I am strong.

Everyone is over for a new tasting session. Everyone is laughing and having fun, but I look over to Mike and I notice that he's here, but not here. As much as he won't admit it, I know he is having a difficult time accepting what happened.

I really wish he'd let someone in. I see it in his eyes, I've been there before. He's struggling to move forward. To an extent, I think he blames himself, but there only two people to blame: Clint and De-Niece, and neither of them can hurt us anymore.

Mike used to talk to me about it, but he's closed himself off again. I worry about him and want my friend from before back.

Taking someone's life has an adverse effect on you and how you see the future. I know it did for me. Without the support of Jordan,

Mike, Sarah, and Jeannie, I wouldn't be coping as well as I am. Mike helped to save me, now it's my turn to help save him.

THE END!!!

MALT ME PLAYLIST

Israel's Son – Silverchair
Barbie Girl – Aqua
...Baby One More Time – Brittany Spears
Nothing Else Matters – Metallica
Dream On – Aerosmith
Lanterns – Birds of Tokyo
Runaway – The Corrs
This Life – Curtis Stigers
Ruby – Kaiser Chiefs
Stronger – Brittney Spears
Crazy – Seal
Chasing Cars – Snow Patrol
I Don't Want to Be – Gavin DeGraw
Wash it All Away – Five Finger Death Punch
Light My Fire – The Doors
Romeo And Juliet – Dire Straits
Until We Burn In the Sun (This Kids Just Want A Love Song) – Bedouin
Soundclash
Come Fly With Me – Frank Sinatra
Shut Your Mouth – Garbage
Addicted To You – Avicii
Walls Fall Down – Bedouin Soundclash

Lose Your Way – Sophie B. Hawkins
Never Tear Us Apart – INXS
Take Me To Church – Hozier
Halo – Beyoncé'
Love Shack – The B-52's
Pachelbel: Canon in D Major – Johan Pachelbel
(Everything I Do) I Do It For You – Bryan Adams

This playlist can be found on Spotify.

THE
Liquor Cabinet
SERIES
Tequila
HEALING
WITH HER THERE WILL BE no regrets
DL GALLIE

With her there will be no regrets.

I had been fooled once. Misled and lied to. There was no going back from that. The fact I was so easily tricked and betrayed gnawed at my bones, and it was causing me to self-destruct.

I've put up walls around me the size of Texas, and no one will break them down—not even the pretty waitress with doe eyes, and a warm smile.

Sav is there whenever I decide to wallow in regret, a bottle and a glass my only company. And even though I'm determined to not let anyone in, Sav somehow worms her way into my life without even trying.

Every time I look into her eyes, I can see there's something different about her. She's an enigma, her life a mystery I want to solve.

It's only when the devil from her past comes knocking that I realise how much danger she's really in. Her life is threatened, and it's up to me to protect her.

If that means I have to walk through hell twice, then that's what I'll do.

For my mum,
Thank you for everything, you are the best mum that anyone could ask for. If I
am half as fantabolous of a mum as you are, then I'm going a goodly job.
Love you long-time, mumsie XoXoX

PROLOGUE

IT'S MY STUPID DICK'S FAULT. I'M ALWAYS THINKING WITH MY DICK, AND AS a result, Kenz and Jordan nearly lost everything, including Mac and Cheese. All because of me, my dick, and a hot blonde piece of ass named Ho Bag Slutface, also known as De-Niece.

Never will I fall for another woman, too much happened last time, I can't risk it happening again.

My self-imposed dick purgatory; except for random pussy but that doesn't count, was going well until Savannah Blac got a job at my local bar, The Black Dungeon. I can't stop thinking about her. The curve of her tight ass, the way it swishes side to side as she walks, or the slight bounce of her perfect tits as she passes drinks across the bar.

Every time I close my eyes, I see her. I imagine her wavy, golden blonde locks wrapped around my fists, tugging her towards me as I sink myself balls deep into her tight pink pussy from behind. Her sapphire blue eyes sparkling under the dim bar light as I slam into her over and over, and she screams my name while I give her the best orgasm of her life. Before I take her back to my place and wake up next to her in my king-sized bed, our arms and limbs wrapped around each other, her eyes dazzling in the morning sunlight.

Shaking my head to clear those dirty sweet thoughts, I concentrate on what Jordan is saying and the tequila shooter in front of me. When I look up, I see Sav walking behind the bar after her break, and I can't help but smile. She has wormed her way into my heart, and I don't know how I feel about that.

Fuck, she's gorgeous; my dick is so hard right now. I really need to find another bar to drink at, but just the thought of not seeing her crushes my heart. Picking up the shot in front of me, I say a silent "cheers" to the world for bringing her into my life. With the next shot, I say a silent "fuck you" to the world for bring her into my life...why does the universe keep doing this to me?

Welcoming the burn of the tequila as it slides down my throat, I pick up the third shot, look to Jordan, and say, "Bottoms up!" After sinking the third shot, I signal Sav for more tequila and sambuca shots and two more beers for Jordan and me.

Seeing her smile makes me grin, but then I remember that chicks are nothing but trouble and cause nothing but strife, especially the super fucking hot ones.

Remembering that I promised myself I'll never go there again, I start to think about a naked grandma, with flabby wrinkly skin, and sagging boobs. Yeah, that works for about five seconds because Sav turns around and smiles at me; she fucking smiles and it's mesmerising. It brings back memories of our one time together. *I'm screwed*, I think to myself as I keep watching her.

Shaking my head, I again consider finding another bar to drink at, but just the thought of not seeing her crushes me; I can't do it, I'm a sucker for punishment. No, I deserve this punishment for all that has happened, this is my penance to pay.

Looking over at Jordan, I think, *how can he still be friends with me, after what's happened?* I start to think of Malt Me. I could always drink there, but everyone there knows...they know I'm partly to blame for De-Niece and all the shit that went down. They stare at me with their judgey eyes; I don't need them to add to my guilt. I already feel remorse, regret, and like shit, and any number of other words to describe feeling like an asshole fuckwit.

Looking over, I see Sav smiling and I find myself also grinning back. I realise that I only ever smile when I see her. Closing my eyes, I take a deep breath to try and shake those thoughts from entering my mind, but I can't. Savannah Blac is the most beautiful woman in the world. There's nowhere else I would rather drink, the pain from seeing her is my punishment, even though I deserve much more. Besides, I love this bar; it's my happy place.

It's simple; I just have to stop thinking about Savannah Blac, no matter how perfect she is. *Nope, nah uh, not going there...again with her, even though that night was amazing.*

Everything changed when I found the gorgeous, feisty woman broken and crying in the ally behind the bar. All bets were off, she needed me and I was more than willing to step up to the plate.

Looking down at her, I saw that she was frightened, broken, and fragile; my heart broke for her. Hearing me walk towards her, she looked up at me, with tears pouring down her cheeks. Taking a deep breath, with sad eyes, she whispered, "Please. Help me."

1

MIKE

...8 months earlier

How did I not know? I'm speechless, literally speechless. My girlfriend is a monster, was a monster. I was in love, with a complete and utter psychopath. How did I not see that she was just using me, helping the enemy? How could I have been so blind? How could I not have picked up on it?

I'm such a fucking fool.

Looking back towards the house, I see them cover her body with a white sheet. Immediately, a red patch develops where her wound is, it's in the moment that I realise; I just killed De-Niece.

Holy shit, I killed someone.

Holy shit, my girlfriend was working with the enemy.

Holy shit, I killed someone.

They have just taken her body away. Officer Hamilton finishes up talking with the coroner before coming over to me, I'm still sitting in the same spot; I haven't moved a muscle. I'm in complete and utter shock, with all of the discoveries and events from today.

How did I not know? I keeping asking myself the same question over and over, and each time I have the same answer; I don't know. Our relationship keeps playing over and over in my head, trying to see if I missed the signs, but nothing pops out. Even our first meeting seems random, but I guess in hindsight, it wasn't random after all.

...I've just finished my twenty minute warm up on the treadmill and smile when **"Numb" by Linken Park** *blasts through my headphones. Carefully, I hop off the treadmill to head over to the bench press. Just as I turn around, I bump into this blonde chick, quickly reaching out, I grab her arm to stop her from tumbling onto the navy carpet. I've seen her here the last few days; well I noticed her tight, pert ass and I couldn't help but smile. Ripping my ear buds out I say, "Shit, I didn't see you there."*

She looks up and smiles at me. "It's fine. I probably shouldn't have been walking so close to the treadmills anyways."

Her smile goes straight to my dick; I haven't felt like this since last week when I hooked up with what's her face from the bank. Shaking my head, I think to myself that I don't want her to leave, her smile is beautiful, it lights up her face. "Well, actually I should be apologising to you. After all, I am the one who bumped into you. I'm Mike."

"I'm De-Niece." She reaches out her hand to shake mine, and she smiles at me again. I take her hand, it's silky soft, and I imagine her wrapping her delicate fingers around my cock, stroking it up and down, before she leans forward and sucks.

She tries to pull her hand back and that's when I realise that I'm still holding onto her, I quickly let go. "It was nice to meet you, Mike, I might see you around." She steps around me, turning back and winking at me before she heads towards the locker rooms.

De-Niece and I run into each other at the gym several times, over the next few weeks, before she finally asks me out. I'd decided that I wasn't going to go there because I really like this gym, and I didn't want to fuck up...for a change. But when she asked me out, I thought why not, she is smoking hot after all...if only I knew.

Officer Hamilton taps my shoulder and brings me back to the present. "Are you okay, Mike?"

"I...I...I don't know." Shaking my head, still staring at the house, I mumble, "I just killed someone." I look up at her. "I guess you're here to haul my ass to jail?"

"Yes, Mike, I am."

Snapping my head towards her in shock, I counter. "Fuck me, seriously?" Shaking my head as I stand up, she takes my wrists and hand-cuffs me.

"You are under arrest in relation to the death of De-Niece Carmichael. You're not obliged to say or do anything, unless you wish to do so, but whatever you say or do may be used in evidence. Do you understand?"

Nodding my head, dejectedly, I respond, "Yeah, I understand."

Officer Hamilton leads me up the driveway and places me in the back of the car. When she closes the car door, I start to realise that I'm in some seriously deep shit.

I can't believe this is what my life has become.

When we arrive at the station: I'm fingerprinted, photographed, and placed into a room to be formally interviewed. Sitting in the room, I look around and it hits me again that I took someone's life. I make it to the bin in the corner just before I throw up, again.

Wiping my mouth with my handcuffed hands, I turn around to sit back down, just as Officer Hamilton and another officer enter.

Officer Hamilton offers to get me a glass of water, while the other officer waits, sitting down. I notice him eyeing me suspiciously before looking back at the papers in front of me. She returns with my glass of water and hands it to me, before taking a seat next to the other officer.

Eventually, he looks up and I know that I'm in serious trouble; there is no expression on his face at all. I'm scared as to what he is about to tell me. "I'm Officer Ferguson, this conversation will be recorded and handed to Department of Prosecutions. They will decide if you will be formally charged. In your own words, please tell us what happened this morning at the residence of Jordan and Mackenzie McRoberts?"

I'm nodding at what he is saying, it's all so surreal, and I can't quite believe that this is happening. Taking a deep breath, I close my eyes and recount all the events from today. "Umm, Jordan texted me to go over and be with Kenz, as he had to go into Malt Me 'cause of some issue. He hates her being alone at the moment. When I got there, I noticed my girlfriend's car, and when I was walking down the driveway I heard shouting. I raced down the driveway and when I got to the fence, I saw that De-Niece was on top of Kenz and…" Pausing, I have a drink of water before I continue, "I was stunned to see her punching and hitting Kenz. I dropped the food bags and ran towards them. I pulled her off Kenz and she went through the French doors. I didn't really pay attention to her; I was focused on Kenz. She groaned and I ran over to her, to make sure she was okay. I didn't even hear the doors smash, I was focused on Kenz, it wasn't until I heard her whisper 'see you in hell' that I realised she went through the doors. Kenz moaned again; I'll never forget that sound. I quickly called an ambulance as Kenz was in a bad way, and Jordan had told me she was pregnant. While I waited for the ambulance, I held Kenz in my arms and called Jordan. You guys and he got there and now we're here." Snapping my head to Officer Hamilton, I hesitantly ask, "Do you know if Kenz is all right?"

I zone out, thinking of Kenz, *fuck, she is okay?*

I vaguely remember Officer Douche writing notes as I spoke, but I was on autopilot and didn't really take heed of what was happening around me. I'm brought back to reality when Officer Hamilton reaches over and touches my arm.

"Mike, we don't have any information on Mrs. McRoberts at this time." She pauses, I can see that she's worried and that scares me. "From here, we will print up your statement, and once you have signed it, you will be free to go. The Department of Prosecutions will let us know if manslaughter charges will be laid against you. We will be in touch, either way."

"Fuck me," I say out loud. Then I whisper, "I can't fucking believe this." As I rest my head on the table.

Officer Ferguson adds, "Look, from what you have told us and the previous history regarding Mrs. McRoberts, the deceased, and her recently deceased cousin, I highly doubt that you will be charged, but don't hold me to that." He stands. "I'll go get this typed up for you to sign, and then we will take you home."

"Thanks."

He leaves but Officer Hamilton stays. She looks over at me. "Are you sure you're okay, Mike?"

"Honestly, I have no idea. I killed someone, who turns out wasn't whom I thought they were, and now there's a chance I'm going to jail for it."

"Mike, I agree with Ferguson, I highly doubt you will be charged. Just think of the positive, Kenzie is safe because you saved her."

"We don't know she's safe, no one can tell me and that's killing me."

"Mike, listen to me. She was alive when she left in the ambulance, and that's because of you. You, Mike. Regardless, that you didn't know who Ms. Carmichael was, you saved someone today."

"I guess so, but how do I live with the fact that A: I killed someone. And B: my girlfriend was a fucking psycho bitch, working with the enemy, and C: I fucking killed someone." Pausing, I rest my head on the table. "How the fuck, did I not know?" Slamming my fist on the table, I lift my head up, shaking it from side to side. "How did I now know? I feel like such a chump."

"Don't beat yourself up, Mike. From what I know of these two cases, no one knew."

Officer Ferguson walks back in. "Mike, please read over your state-ment, and if you agree with it, sign at the bottom. Then you are free to go. But I do need to remind you, that you are not to leave the state or country until the matter is finalised."

Nodding in agreement I take the statement from him and read it over. It's exactly what I said, so I grab the pen, sign at the bottom where is marked, and hand it back to him. "So what happens now?"

"Thanks, the Department of Prosecutions will be in touch to let you know what's going to happen. So as of now, you are free to go, Mike."

"Mmhmm." I manage to say as he undoes my cuffs. I'm lead out of the interview room and escorted to the car park, where Officer Hamilton drives me back to my place.

The car trip is silent but not awkward. There are so many scenarios going through my mind at the moment, I don't know up from down. I'm broken and lost. When we get back to my place, I thank her for dropping me home and then I head inside.

As I'm unlocking the front door, I realise that my car is at Jordan's place. *Fuuuuck*, I think to myself. Once the door opens, I make a beeline for the kitchen and I grab a bottle of tequila from the kitchen. Jose and I sit on the couch together. I plan to get rip-roaring drunk, but first, I text Jordan for an update.

Mike – *Hope all is OK with Kenz and the munchkins*
Jordan – *Yep, all good, asshat. I'm on my way over. Be there in 10*

Ten minutes later, Jordan walks in the front door, and I've already finished a quarter of the tequila. I'm starting to feel numb, and for the first time today, relaxed but empty. Jordan sits down next to me, concern all over his face. "You okay, dude?" Without looking, he grabs the bottle and takes a swig…I wait for it. "Fuck, tequila, uck."

Laughing, I say, "Yep, I needed it after the afternoon I've had. I've just gotten back to the police station."

"What the fuck, dude?" he says, as he goes to the fridge to get two beers.

Taking another mouthful, I laugh and sigh. "Yep," letting the 'p' pop. "I have officially been charged in relation to the death of De-Niece, and I may or may not be fucking charged with manslaughter. Everything has been sent to prosecutions and they will let me know."

"Fucking hell, Mike, are you shitting me?"

"I shit you not, Jordan." Nodding towards the tequila, I add, "Hence, tequila, straight from the bottle." Raising the bottle, I nod towards him and say, "Bottoms up!" I lift the bottle to my mouth and take a drink; I savor flavour as it hits the back of my throat, warmth coursing through me as I swallow. Looking towards Jordan, I ask, "How are Kenz, Mac, and Cheese?"

"Really, Mac and Cheese?"

"Really, really. Now tell me, are they oaky?"

"Yeah, they're all okay. Kenz is pretty banged up, but she's tough, just like my lil' munchkins. As soon as she found out about you, she sent me here to make sure you were okay. She's worried, Mike. To be honest, I'm worried about you. Are you all right?"

"Dude, I have no fucking clue how I feel right now. I killed some-one, my girlfriend was a fucking psycho working with the fucking enemy, and my family has been put through the ringer in the last seventy-two hours. I feel like a chump, a fucking chump. Seriously, dude, I'm so, so sorry."

"What are you sorry for? If it wasn't for you, who knows what would have happened today? I owe you."

"You're not pissed that I was fucking the enemy?"

"Fuck no! You didn't know, dude, hell, none of us knew. How is that your fault?"

"I just feel bad, how the fuck could I not know she was a fucking fruit loop, related to a fuckwit? I'm never going there again, no girl-friend, no relationship…ever."

"Dude, look at me!" I look towards Jordan, after taking another swig of tequila, "This is in no fucking way your fault. Nobody knew, NOBODY." He emphasises nobody.

Putting my hand up, I try to interrupt him, but he ignores me, *asshole*. "We were all clueless when to came to fuckface douche canoe and bitch face mole. This is no one's fault but theirs, Mike. You saved Kenz today, and for that I will be forever in your debt."

I have nothing to say because I don't feel any of that, right at this minute; I doubt I will ever feel any of that. In order to throw him off track, I do the only thing I can, I raise the tequila bottle, before taking another mouthful. "Dude, my car is still at your place. Can you swing by tomorrow so I can get it?"

"Sure, we can go see Kenz, too. She's really worried about you. Fingers crossed she can come home too, and then we can hang at our place, just like old times."

"Sounds like a plan. Again, I'm so sorry, Jor."

"Stop apologising, Mike, you have nothing to me sorry about."

Jordan and I chat for a while, and I continue to drink my bottle of tequila, but really I just want to be alone. He must sense I want to be alone as he says, "Dude, get a good night's sleep and I'll be back in the morning."

"Yes, Dad." I say like a smart-ass. "Thanks for coming over, it means a lot."

"Anytime, Son, anytime," he says, slapping my leg in a dad-like way.

Standing up, I sway as I'm on my way to pissdom and escort Jordan out. He does the manly one arm hug, back slap, and it feels just like old times, but things will never be the same again; not for me anyway.

After he leaves, I head back inside and shut the front door, sitting back down on the sofa. I finish the bottle of tequila before passing out.

2

SAV

Sitting, alone in the lounge room, I sadly look around. I used to love being in this room. It was full of happy memories; Dad sitting in his brown leather recliner, reading, Mum sitting on the caramel sofa, doing her Sudoku puzzles, and Jace and me, sitting on the floor by the bay window playing a game. We were your typical Aussie family but that all changed, in an instant.

Now, this room feels empty, void of any emotions except fear, sadness, and loathing.

Uncle Kelvin comes barging in, shouting, "Where is it? It's mine!" He's drunk, again and his short muscular body sways from side to side as he moves from room to room, searching for something he believes is his. He makes me stay where I am until he has finished searching; not that I want to follow him. I've no idea what he's looking for. Just like every night, when he doesn't find whatever it is, he storms out of here in a mood, slamming the front door behind him.

I cringe when I hear him start his car; he's in no state to drive with the amount of alcohol coursing through him. As soon as I hear his car back out of the driveway and drive off, I race to the front door and lock it, sliding down until I hit the floor, I cry, the tears pouring out like Niagara Falls.

This has been my life for the past six weeks; and will be for the foreseeable future.

The following night is the same; Uncle Kelvin barges in, searches, and as usual, comes up empty-handed. If only he'd tell me what he's looking for, I could then help him find it, then he would leave me alone and I could get on with my life.

Tonight is a particularly tough night; it would have been Mum's birthday, which was always such a happy occasion. Dad used to spoil her on her birthday every year, thinking about them makes me smile. Then the reality of them being gone hits me and I get upset.

From the library I hear him thrashing around and I start to cry. My eyes well with tears and I'm consumed by grief. Why did he have to come tonight of all nights?

I cry for them.

I cry for me.

I cry for what Uncle Kelvin has become.

I cry for what will never be.

They would be so disappointed right now. Not at me, but at Uncle Kelvin, how could he do this to me? To us? To their memory? We are meant to be family, family doesn't do this to each other.

All this shit started after the reading of the will, everything was left to me, everything: the house, the money, the business, and every single Blac property. Uncle Kelvin was pissed, beyond pissed, he could not comprehend how his sister wouldn't leave him anything. I would gladly hand everything to him, if it meant that they would still be alive. The only thing stopping me is Mum and Dad's final wishes, I want to uphold their memory as best as I can and make them proud.

Every night I ask what he is looking for, so I can help find it and get rid of him, and every night he won't tell me. He just tells me I'm spiteful like them and I'd lie about it.

I wish I knew what he was looking for.

Pulling my knees closer to my chest, I sit on the sofa in Mum's spot, rocking back and forth, hoping and praying he will leave soon. Hearing something smash, I realise that I need to get out of here. This isn't what Mum and Dad would want for me.

Once again, Uncle Kelvin has stormed out of here, empty-handed. It's so hard, I wish they were here, I miss them everyday, it's getting harder and harder to go on.

Laughing to myself, I thought the hardest thing I have ever done was burying my parents and brother; that was nothing compared to reading the letter they left.

...Seven weeks earlier

After leaving the lawyer's office, I came straight home; I flew up the stairs and ran into Mum and Dad's bedroom. I could still smell them, and as soon as their scent hits my nose, the tears started flowing; tears and snot pouring down my face, my body shuddering from the sobs. Jumping onto their bed, I snuggled into their pillows and I cried. Once I had calmed down, I pulled the letter from leather jacket pocket. Holding it in my hands, I stared at Mum's writing for ages before getting the courage to open the beige envelope in my hands.

My eyes welled with tears again, but I gave myself an internal pep talk and finally opened it. Taking a deep breath, I read the final message from my parents. I guess they didn't expect one of us to die alongside them, as the letter is addressed to both, Jace and me; this caused the tears to start again. Finally composing myself, I took a deep breath I read the letter.

To our dearest children, Jace and Savannah,
If you are reading this, then both your father and I are no longer with you. For that I apologise, but please know we love you so very much and we are very proud of you both.
The lawyer would have explained that we have left everything to you both. You will be comfortable for the rest of your lives, you know how to run the company, so we know it will be left in good hands. Knowing that you will be looked after will give both your father and me comfort.
There is a safe in the library with the stocks, some extra cash, and my jewelry. Savannah, the jewelry is yours, please do not let anyone else in the family take this. They can have anything else in the house, but the jewelry is yours and yours only. The code for the safe is your birth date and time; please keep this code and the safe hidden.
There is also a safe deposit box at the bank. Please keep this safe; it is imperative that this remains protected. Do not let anyone know about this. Its contents are extremely important to your father and me, as well as, your grandparents. Please, please, keep this safe and secure; at all costs.
We hope you live full and happy lives. Tell any future grandchildren that even though we have never met them, we love them very much. If you are ever lonely or afraid, look up into the sky, and we will be looking down on you, giving you the strength to carry on.

With all our love,
Mum and Dad XoXoX

Lying in their bed, I read the letter over and over. It was after reading it for the third time that I decided to take action. With their words, they gave me the encouragement I needed; even from the grave they were still looking over this. It was that night, I decided to plan my escape from this living hell.

3

KELVIN

WHAT THE EVER-LOVING FUCK? MY BITCH OF A SISTER AND HER WANKER husband didn't leave me anything, not a fucking cent. They left everything to her, Savannah. "What do you mean I get nothing?"

"I'm sorry, Kelvin, everything has been left to Savannah, and in most cases, that's what happens. Any living descendants inherit directly from their parents."

"Well, this is bullshit!" I shout. Shoving my chair back, I storm out of the lawyer's office, slamming the door behind me. Leaving the solicitor shocked and open-mouthed, and Savannah crying; like the sissy ass bitch that she is. Hearing him console her only makes me even more pissed off. She is now the sole owner of Blac Family Jewelers, and once again, I'm shafted.

Making my way to the Grand, I take a seat at the bar and order a beer and double bourbon. Slamming back the bourbon, the burn on the way down feels good, but I'm still pissed off. Ordering another two shots, I down them one after the other, and now that I'm a little pissy the anger is subsiding.

I can't fucking believe that they didn't leave me anything; it feels just like when Ma and Pa died and they left everything to my sister. Granted she was fifteen years older then me when they passed, and I was still in high school but still, I'm their son. As always, Kelvin misses out and this time, I didn't even get a mention, that's what pisses me off the most. Even from the grave my sister is still messing with me.

Guess now I will just have to have some fun with my dear old niece. She's a push over, so I should be able to find what's mine. It will be just like in high school. She was a few years below me, and with the aid of the basketball team, we used to pick on her. That was until Jace finally hit puberty, man, did he give me as ass-kicking that day...but that lil' fucker ain't here now to protect her. Oh, this is going to be fun.

4

MIKE

It's been four weeks since I took another person's life.

It's been four weeks of torture.

It's been four weeks of replaying that moment over and over.

It's been four weeks of hell.

I'm so lost.

Whenever I close my eyes, I see the same thing: De-Niece on top of Kenz, pulling her arm back, unleashing her fury, and saying the nastiest of things. I'm slowly getting better, I think. I no longer throw up when the memories return, so that's a win...I guess. I've had the same dream each and every night for the past four weeks, and each night I wake up in a cold sweat.

It constantly haunts me that my girlfriend, the person I loved with all my heart, the person who I was just about to propose to, did this to my family. How did I not know she was a psychopath working with a psychopath? Related to a psychopath?

I don't trust anyone anymore; well except for Kenz and Jordan.

One thing I do know, I will never, ever, have another girlfriend. Women only lead to heartache and pain. Random pussy yes, but never a girlfriend.

What hurts the most is that I now hate being around Kenz and Jordan, I let them down. I feel like I should have known. I should have done more. Were the signs there and I missed them? Or am I just weak and stupid? I've gone over our relationship so many times, and I can't believe I didn't know. Seriously, how do you not know your girlfriend is a fucking psycho bitch? I don't know anything anymore.

The silver lining to all of this, I now have a great friend, Officer Hamilton. She and I have struck up a surprising friendship. She is the best wingman ever, she shits all over Jordan. She hates that I always refer to her as Officer Hamilton, but it's too weird calling her Kelly.

Tequila is another newly acquainted friend and my way of coping with the dreams. Drinking myself into a stupor so my mind and body are numb, it works most nights, but there is nothing to erase those memories; they will haunt me for all eternity.

A new pub, The Black Dungeon, has just opened up near my house, so I can drink and stagger home. I don't have to worry about driving. I am responsible and shit like that…occasionally.

It's a pretty awesome pub that I hope to bring Jordan to for a friendly drink, one of these days, if I can get over the guilt and stand to be around him. It's soooo hard to be near him and Kenz; I imagine it would be a lot worse had it been Kenz to die, but thank fuck that didn't happen.

To combat the loss of Jordan, I have a new nonjudgmental non-back chatting bestie: Jose Curevo. Jose and I have become the bestest of friends. He's awesome and best of all, he makes me forget, and forgetting is good.

Another new hobby I've discovered is pussy, random pussy. I fucking love losing myself balls deep inside someone for a few hours. No talking just fucking, it's an awesome way to forget.

My life has become a rotation of booze and pussy, sometimes both at the same time. Being sober makes me remember that girlfriends are nothing but trouble, but pussy is fun.

The other night, to mix things up, I decided head into town rather than going to the Dungeon. Walking from bar to bar, I eventually ended up at Club Deux, where I met up with this hot redhead and her blonde friend. What I thought was going to be a quiet night with Jose turned into a night that I will not ever forget.

Don't ask me their names, I have no fucking idea, and to be honest, I don't fucking care. What I can tell you, though, is that I had the most erotic threesome that I have ever had the pleasure to be a part of. There was no judgment or anger, just primal, hot, out of this world fucking. Now I've ventured into threesome territory before, and I'm definitely a fan, but this night is one that I will go down in the history books.

It all started when Red caught my eye as I walked into the club, my cock immediately twitching when she smiled at me. Her hazel eyes were full of lust, and she was eye-fucking me as I sauntered over to her. Just as I sat down, her blonde friend appeared on the other side of me. Making me the meat in the center of a pussy sandwich, my cock was rock hard and we hadn't even spoken a word yet.

After ordering us a round of drinks, which included several shots, a beer for me and some fruity shit for them, we made small talk. Red threw her drink back before grabbing my hand and leading us to the dance floor. She proceeded to bump and grind her pussy all over me. My hands roamed all around her hot little body. My cock was starting to ache at this point, it was as hard as steel.

Pulling her closer, I sank my tongue into her mouth; she tasted like pineapple. Our mouths moved steadily to the beat of the music while our tongues danced together. Grabbing my hand, she placed it at the apex of her thighs, nudging her dress up, giving me access to her crotch.

Stretching my fingers higher, I discovered she wasn't wearing any undies. In the middle of the dance floor, I rubbed her bare, naked pussy, which was extremely wet from her arousal. Reaching up further, I cupped her pussy and rubbed my palm down her slit; she ground herself against me, moaning into my mouth as she pulled me closer to her body.

Ever so slowly, I ran my finger up and down her slit before plunging inside her tight warm passage, and slipping another finger inside her. I finger-fucked her on the dance floor, while our tongues continued to wrestle for supremacy. She came gloriously over my fingers, throwing her head back and moaning, the entire dance floor oblivious to what we were doing.

Once her orgasm had finished, she pulled my hand out from

between her legs and proceeded to suck all her juices off my fingers, while staring deeply into my eyes; holy fucking hotness.

We were about the leave the dance floor when Blondie joined us; she grabbed Red's cheeks and shoved her tongue into her mouth before whispering something. Red looked over at me, smiled seductively before leaning over and kissing me. She tasted like pussy, pineapple, and sex. Breaking our kiss, she winked at me, before turning back towards the bar, leaving Blondie and me alone together in the middle of the dance floor.

Blondie leaned towards me, wrapped her arms around my neck, and smashed her lips against mine, I could taste Red and tequila on her lips as she pulled me closer to her tight sexy body; I groaned into her mouth as our kiss deepened. She started running her hands all over my chest and back, before wrapping her leg around mine and grinding herself on me.

I was lost in our kiss when all of a sudden; I felt a hand reaching around us and it started to grope my cock through my jeans. Opening my eyes, I saw Red behind Blondie, rubbing her pussy on Blondie's ass and nibbling on her earlobe.

My cock got even harder at the sight before me. Reaching over I pulled Red closer to us and shoved my tongue into her mouth, again tasting tequila. Pulling away, I turned my attention back to Blondie, kissing her deeply while gripping Red's ass, squishing Blondie between us.

While I was kissing Blondie, Red leaned over, nibbled on my ear, and whispered, "Let's get out of here." *You don't have to ask me twice*, I thought to myself as I grabbed both of their hands and tugged them towards to bar. Before leaving, we did another round of tequila shots and then headed back to my place.

There was a cab waiting out front, so we all jumped in, again I'm sandwiched between them both. Giving the cabbie my address, I sat back and got comfy as the girls began rubbing my cock, while I alternated between kissing them.

Reaching up, I started to massage Blondie's tits through the thin fabric of her little black dress. From the corner of my eye, I saw her hand slip below the hem of her dress, her legs inching open, inviting me in. Snaking my hand down her tight stomach, I slid my hand under her dress and joined my fingers with hers. Gently parting her pussy lips, we slipped our entwined fingers in an out of her warm wet pussy.

She started riding our fingers, when Red's fingers joined us. The three of us finger-fucked Blondie while the two of them rubbed my cock; closing my eyes, I leaned back and enjoyed the ride.

I'm bought back to reality when I heard the cabbie clear his throat, "Umm, we're here." Opening me eyes, I realised that we'd arrived at my place. Looking at him through the rearview mirror, I smirked and threw the fare at him. We exited the cab and headed inside for a night of unforgettable pleasure.

Unlocking the door, we headed inside. Being a gentleman, I offered them a drink; they saw the tequila on the counter from before I went out and wiggled their eyes towards it. I poured three shots and we toasted, and I said, "Bottoms up!" and they giggled.

Red said, "Cheers!"

Blondie looked at me and seductively said, "Here's to a night we will never forget." Watching her do that shot was sexy as hell, my cock started throbbing, and I knew tonight was going to be sexually wild. We had a few more shots before the fun began.

I'd just placed the tequila bottle on the bench when Red grabbed my hand, pulling me into the lounge room. Spinning me around, she pushed me down onto my couch; straddled my lap and attacked my face. Our lips crashed together as she started to ride me, grinding herself over my hardening cock. My cock was ready to explode, it was stiff as a board; I could cut steel with it, it was becoming painful, straining behind my pants.

Blondie must have had a sixth sense because she ran her hands up Red's back, pulling her off me. Together they poured tequila into each other's mouth before kissing each other. The sight before me was so sexual; I'd never been that turned on in my life.

They each climbed onto the couch, on either side of me. Leaning over me, Red poured tequila into Blondie's mouth, who bent down and kissed me, transferring the tequila into my mouth before leaning up and kissing Red deeply. Blondie took the bottle from Red and did the same thing. *Now this is the way to drink tequila*, I thought to myself and smiled, as I felt the burn of the liquid sliding down my throat.

Turning around, she placed the bottle on the coffee table, lowered to her knees and popped open the button on my jeans, unzipping my pants with her teeth. Reaching her hand inside my boxer briefs, she cupped my throbbing cock and lightly squeezed. Lifting up slightly, she edged my pants and boxer briefs down, and finally my aching cock sprang free. Gasping at the size of my cock, she wrapped her tiny hand around me, and stroked up and down.

Red got down onto her knees and the two of them kissed over the tip of my cock, giving me a double head job. Kissing and sucking over the head of my cock, I moaned. Having two mouths on my cock was the best feeling ever, their tongues flicking out, fighting each other for control over my cock.

One of them took my cock into her mouth and sucked while the other stoked and sucked my balls before they kissed each other over the head once again, repeating the process over and over. That was the hottest head job I have ever had. It wasn't long before I exploded, without warning. My milky cum spurted free, their tongues fighting to get a taste.

When I finally came back to earth after my shattering climax, I noticed that they are both naked. Red pushed Blondie back onto the couch, and spread her legs while she dove in; nipping, licking, and sucking her dripping wet pussy.

Grabbing a franga from the coffee table drawer, I sheathed my cock and knelt behind Red; spreading her ass cheeks before slamming myself balls deep inside her. Her pussy felt like heaven, her moans increased when she screamed, "Fuck me harder!" I picked up the pace and continue to slam in and out of her.

Before either of us came, she crawled up Blondie so their pussies were now rubbing each other. Pulling out of Red, I started to rub my cock up and down Blondie's pussy, plunging deep inside of her. She moaned in pleasure as I slid in and out of her tight passage.

Blondie arched her back and I felt her pussy muscles tighten around my cock. It was enough to push me over the edge, together our orgasms ripped through our bodies.

Red kissed her way up Blondie's chest, her tongue slamming into her mouth; the sight in front of me mesmerized me. Reaching up, Blondie grabbed my hand and together we finger-fucked Red. Our fingers sliding in and out, her breaths became shallow; I knew she was close. Slipping my fingers out of her pussy, I inched around and slipped a finger into her ass. That sent her skyrocketing and she screamed, "Fuuuuck!" Riding Blondie's fingers in her pussy and my finger in her ass, she tumbled over the edge into the abyss of unadulterated pleasure.

The three of us lay here on the couch, catching out breaths as our bodies returned from heaven.

For the rest of the night, we proceeded to fuck in every position possible –*Mr. Kama Sutra would be proud*- and in every possible combination: the three of us together, just Red and I, Red and Blondie sixty-nining each other while I watched, me fucking Blondie while Red fingered herself watching, Blondie sucking and fingering Red whilst Red deep throated my cock, tweaking her and Red's nipples before reaching a hand down to massage her clit as I spilled down her throat.

It was unbelievably fucking hot, but without a doubt, there was no greater pleasure than having someone ride your pulsating dick while another's bare, slick pussy rode your face, and they tongue wrestled together above you, massaging each others breasts and rubbing their own swollen clits. Nirvana came to mind as I released my load once again.

The crème-del-a-crème of the evening, the final double head job of the night from the Bobbsey twins, but this time I tongue fucked one and finger-fucked the other. I was drowning in pussy pleasure; I could have died in this position, and I would have been a very happy man.

Just before dawn they both get dressed and went home. I was left, lying on the lounge room floor, with the biggest smile on my face.

Best. Night. Ever.

5

SAV

A week after what would have been Mum's birthday, I started to relax; I was feeling like me again. The stores were doing well and I hadn't seen Uncle Kelvin in a few days. *Maybe he has given up on his quest,* I thought to myself that night when I was in the shower.

After my shower, I climbed into my bed but I couldn't sleep. I lay there staring at the ceiling, a million different scenarios through my head. *What the fuck am I going to do?*

Just before 9:00 p.m. there is a knock at the front door. I sit bolt upright in bed when the knock comes again. Getting up, I walk down the stairs and yell, "Coming!" All of a sudden, a feeling of dread washes over me and I slow my pace.

Reaching the foyer, I swing the door open without checking the peephole; my heart stops, my breathing stills. Standing on the other side of the door is a man in a ski mask. He comes barging in, shoving me into the wall while three other masked men push past into the house. He tightly wraps his hand around my throat, growling, "Where is it, bitch?"

"Where's what?" I manage to squeak out, the pressure on my throat becoming unbearable.

Just as the stars start to appear in my vision, another masked man comes through the door, shoving the person holding me and snarls, "Enough, we need her coherent."

It's a woman, I think to myself as I clutch my neck and slide down the wall, gasping for breath, tears pouring down my face. The first guy steps away from me and the bitch crouches down. "Sorry for my colleagues, they have no manners when it comes to a pretty girl. Now, tell me where it is."

Through my tears, I manage to say, "Where's what?"

She laughs and slaps my face. "You want to play games, little dove, fine by me but know this, I always get what I want." Standing up, she turns and says, "Search the place, intel says it's here somewhere."

Bending back down to eye level she threatens, "Things will be much easier, little dove, if you just tell me where it is. Simply tell me and we leave."

"I...I...don't know what you are after, tell me what it is, and if I know, I'll tell you, I promise."

WHACK

WHACK

WHACK

"Do I look stupid to you?"

WHACK

"You know what I'm after."

WHACK

"Now tell me and I'll leave you to get back to your measly little life, unharmed."

WHACK

"Lie to me, and I cannot guarantee your safety."

WHACK

Standing up, she leans against the front door, starting intently at me. "I'm waiting," she spits.

"Honestly, I have no idea what you are talking about or what you are looking for."

"Tsk tsk tsk, I don't like liars, Ms. Blac." Stalking towards me, she bends down and grabs me by my shoulders, slapping me hard across the face. Roughly grabbing my upper arms, she shoves me up and marches us into the library.

Looking around, I see majority of the books have been pulled off the shelves. I'm shoved onto the couch and the guy who pushed me against the wall straddles my waist, my heart drops as I think he's going to rape me. He grabs my face, leans down and snarls, "Last chance, bitch, tell us. Where is it?"

The tears are now pouring down my cheeks, taking a deep breath and in a soft voice I stutter, "I...I...I don't know, I don't know." I take a deep breath. "Please just let me go. Please. Please. Please."

He jumps off me and cackles, "He said you were a sooky bitch who'd play dumb. I guess for once a client was right." Shaking his head he walks around the library. "Last chance, bitch, where is it?"

All of a sudden, I get this rush of adrenaline. I stand up, glare at them, and growl through clenched teeth, "I have no fucking idea what you are after, now get the fuck out of my house."

This pisses them off; they look at each other and the lady nods at him. Before I know it, I'm on my back and he is punching and slapping me. "You have a death wish, little grasshopper, tell me where it is and all this will stop." He keeps punching and hitting me. Standing up, he starts kicking me. I can hear them talking, but everything is going fuzzy and it's getting harder and harder to breathe. "The bastard is not gonna be happy." Is the last thing I hear before it all goes black.

When I come to, I'm not sure where I am and I start to panic. Blinking a few times to bring my vision back to normal, I look around and realise that I'm in a hospital bed, thankfully I'm alone. Tears well in my eyes and I start to cough. Taking a breath, I wince in pain, it hurts like a bitch. My whole body is aching. Everything hurts.

The door to my room opens and a nurse enters. "Hi, sweetie. I'm Doreen. Do you know where you are?"

"I'm...I'm in hospital." Pausing, I ask, "What happened?"

"You were badly beaten and unconscious when you were brought in. You're a bit banged up, but you are in safe hands now."

"Who...how did I get here?"

"Kelvin, I believe he's your uncle, bought you here."

As soon as she mentions Uncle Kelvin, I start to panic. My heart rate increases, it becomes hard to breathe. I can hear waves whooshing in my head, mixed with the beeping sound of the monitors in my room going off.

Doreen gently rubs my arms, and in a soothing voice tells me to breathe and calm down; it reminds me of Mum and I start to hyper-ventilate again. *I miss my mum.* I'm struggling to breathe now, the pain increasing, the panic coursing through my veins in overdrive. Doreen reaches over and pushes a button on the wall behind me. Within minutes, the room is filled with people. Even though I'm in the room; I can't hear or process what they are saying, everything is muffled.

My breaths are now coming in short, fast bursts; it's excruciatingly hard to breathe right now. I'm starting to see black spots; I'm in a full-blown panic attack right now.

All of a sudden, I feel calm, a wave of warmness rushes around my body. I hear Doreen say, "Shhhh, Savannah, let it relax you." She soothingly rubs the hair along my hairline when I start to feel my body relaxing as the sedative makes its way through my system. My breathing evens out, and I start to feel calm, my eyes are heavy and I fall into darkness.

When I wake again a few hours later, Uncle Kelvin is sitting at the end of my bed. Quickly I close my eyes again, I don't want to face him. "I know you're awake," he sneers.

Taking a deep breath, I open my eyes and stare at the window. Before we get a chance to say anything to each other, the nurse comes in. "You're awake, honey, how do you feel?"

Glaring at Uncle Kelvin, I say, "I feel like I've been beaten within an inch of my life and I have no idea why."

"Stop it, child, you're over reacting, as usual," Uncle Kelvin says.

"Excuse me, sir, if you speak to my patient like that again I will ask you to leave. I don't care that you are family."

I whisper to myself, "He's not my family."

Doreen turns back to me and finishes my obs. She smiles at me and I'm pretty sure she heard what I whispered. "Honey, do you remember what happened?"

"It's all pretty fuzzy right now."

"That's understandable, honey. You were unconscious when your uncle bought you in, you were badly beaten." Looking over her shoulder towards Uncle Kelvin she says, "The police want to speak to you when you have a moment." Looking back at me she adds, "Let me know when you are up to it, and I'll arrange it for you."

Uncle Kelvin jumps up. "You need to have an attorney present when you speak to them. You can't trust them."

I lean up on my elbows, the pain radiates through my body, but I stare directly at him and between clenched teeth I growl, "Get the fuck out of my room. I will talk to whom ever I want, when I want. You have no control over me."

Laughing, he shakes his head as he moves to the door, with his hand on the door handle; he looks back at me. "I should've fucking left you there to die...alone." Turning, he opens the door and slams it shut on his way out.

Before the door has slammed, the tears are pouring down my face, crying hurts but I can't help it. The chasm has opened and there is no stopping the tears. Doreen stops what she is doing and envelops me in a hug. It reminds me of a mum hug and that just makes the tears come quicker. Eventually, I calm down and compose myself, Doreen pulls back, and she looks caringly at me. "Are you okay, honey?"

Shaking my head from side to side, I chuckle; I have no fucking clue about anything now. "I've no idea how I feel right now. All I know is that I hurt all over." My eyes well with tears, I quietly murmur, "I miss my family. I'm all alone." I start to cry again, and again, Doreen wraps her arms around me until I'm all cried out and have calmed down.

I'm kept in hospital for five days, when I'm finally released I'm happy and sad: happy to be out, sad to be going home to an empty quiet house. The first few days at home were tough, I ached from head to toe, and it hurt like a bitch to move. My store manager, Sierra, popped by daily to check on me. Bringing me coffee and cakes most days, just like when I'm at the store with her. I'm so lucky to have great staff to assist me. I've been a bit aloof since I lost Mum and Dad but Sierra really has made things much easier. She has been my rock since I lost everyone, along with my best friend but he is busy setting up a new venture; I'm so proud of him.

Taking the doctors advice, I rest up and do what the hospital physio recommends. I am soon healed, but the bubbly Sav is gone. All that remains is a shell of my former self.

Thankfully, Uncle Kelvin has stayed away; I haven't seen him since the day I woke up in the hospital. The police have been by twice to interview me, but I'm not much help. The events of that night are still a blur, but deep down, I know who arranged it.

I'm too scared to tell the truth. I wish I were stronger to tell them what I know, but I'm afraid. Hoping that if I play dumb, it will all go away, and I can get on with my life and figure out what he is after. I'm now determined, more than ever, to find out what he is after and keep it safe from his grubby mitts.

I will do whatever it takes to keep what is rightfully mine and uphold Mum and Dad's wishes…whatever it takes.

6

MIKE

THIS WEEK HAS BEEN PRETTY SHITTY, WELL SHITTIER THAN USUAL. YOU'D think I would be on cloud nine as I have officially been cleared in relation to De-Niece's death. Even though legally I'm not responsible, mentally is another story; the guilt is still eating at me.

After getting home from work on Thursday, I throw together a bag, grab my swag, swing via the bottle-o and stock up on beer and tequila, and I head to my property. It's about fifty minutes out of the city. I have ten spectacular acres, it's my happy place and exactly where I need to be right now.

Whenever I'm feeling like shit, or I just want to get away, I head out for a few days and clear my head. The place was covered in tress when I bought it; I had a small patch cleared so I could easily camp. Recently I had a little self-contained cabin built and got the water, electricity, and plumbing services all sorted.

There was a little shed there when I bought the place so I gave it a little refurb while the builder were there. Shelving was added for all my tools and shit, and I now have a secure place to leave my quad bike and all the gear.

Just my luck, traffic is really, really shit today, and it takes me nearly two hours to get there. By time I arrive, it's just on dusk and I decide that a night under the stars is called for. Rather than staying in the cabin, I unroll my swag, start a fire, set up my camp chair, and settle in.

Cracking open my first beer, I sit back and stare up at the evening sky. The twilight sky is turning black and is filled with dark, ominous clouds; much like how I feel at the moment. My first beer goes down a treat, and I know that this is just what I needed.

Why did I not do this sooner?

Later that night, when I'm well on my way to pisseddom, my guilt starts to eat away at me again, and the questions begin floating around.

How could I not know that my girlfriend was a fucking fruit loop?

Why did I think with my dick?

How did I miss the signs?

What could I have done differently?

Why oh why, did I meet a skank named De-Niece Carmichael?

The next morning, I'm woken to the sun glaring in my face, with a stiff neck and sore body from passing out in my chair. After restoking the fire, I take a piss and call work. I tell my boss that I need a personal day today; thankfully she is great and tells me it's okay. Not that I really give a shit, I wasn't coming in no matter what she said.

I'm starting to get hungry, so I get up and head into the cabin; unpacking the food and stuff that I bought from home. Switching on the kettle, I make myself a coffee and cook myself scrambled eggs and bacon for breakky. When I've finished and cleaned up, I grab a shower and decide to spend the morning quad biking. Once I have on my safety gear, I head off. This was just what the doctor ordered. I spend the next few hours cruising around the property and forgetting about all my worries. *Fuck, I love this place*, I think to myself as I watch a family of kangaroos graze on the grass.

Later that morning, my phone starts to play, *Wash it All Away* by Five Finger Death Punch, and I groan. I'm not in the mood to deal with Jordan right now, so I ignore it. Not five minutes later, it rings again. This time I decline the call and send it straight to voicemail. I've never done that to Jordan before. It pretty much rings again straight away. Again, I decline it but this time, I put it on silent as well. I don't want to deal with anyone at the moment. I just need Mike time…beer…Chicken Twisties…and tequila.

After taking a walk around my property, I grab another beer and decide I need some tunes. Getting my Bose mini player from the car, I set it up. Picking up my phone to connect it, I see that I have fifteen missed calls and five texts from Jordan. I start to feel guilty for ignoring him. Shaking my head, I say, "Fuck it." I just can't deal with him, or anyone, at the moment.

Once again, that day keeps playing over and over in my head; I'm just glad it ended the way it did and that I got there in time. There is no fucking way I could live with myself if anything had happened to Kenz...or Mac and Cheese, I decide to numb the pain with more beer and tequila.

Grabbing another beer and my bottle of tequila, I take up residence next to the fire. The afternoon is spent sitting by the fire, drinking beer, shooting tequila, and getting absolutely hammered. I think to myself that a batch of Kenzie's famous brownies would be awesome right about now.

Sexual Healing by Marvin Gaye comes on and I change up the words to Tequila Healing instead, I think it's pretty awesome, so I put the song on repeat.

Get up, get up, get up, get up!
Wake up, wake up, wake up, wake up!
Oh, tequila let's get down tonight
Ooh tequila, I'm hot just like an oven
I need some lovin'
And tequila, I can't hold it much longer
The bottle's getting lower and lower
And when I get that feeling
I want tequila healing
Tequila healing, makes me feel so fine
Helps me to forget that she was a fuckin psycho
Tequila healing, baby, is good for me
Tequila healing is something that's good for me

I'm pretty hammered and that song has been sung quite a few times. I'm feeling pretty good right now, and by good I mean, numb. The best thing about being hammered, I forget all of my worries and my shitty fucked up life.

Just before midnight, I stoke the fire up, climb into my swag, and stare up at the night sky. There are millions of tiny little stars, twinkling on a midnight black background; it's an amazing how many stars there are out here without the city lights obscuring them. Sighing, I start to wish that I were a million miles away, living a happy carefree life on one of those twinkly little stars.

A few days later, just after lunch, I hear a car coming up the driveway. Looking over, I see Jordan's Jeep stirring up dust as he eases to a stop near the shed. *Shit, I'm in trouble as both McRoberts are here.* Kenz is the first to get out and she looks pissed, Jordan is next and he looks just as pissed.

Stalking over to me, Kenz unleashes her wrath. "Mike Mustange, you have had us all worried." Poking me in the chest. "You take off for five days and don't tell anyone where you are going. You ignore Jordan's calls and mine. You have some explaining to do, mister." She's right up in my face at the moment, she's fuming by now. Her hands are on her hips, her big, beautiful, pregnant belly is right at eye level, her eyes are full of fury, but I also see relief in them as she stares at me, waiting for my reply.

"Well, hello to you too, Kenz. I'm fine; thanks for asking." Leaning forward, I place my hands on her belly, and in that weird voice that people use around kids and babies, I say, "And how are my two favourite munchkins? Giving Mummy grief, I hope." Winking up at Kenz, I say this.

"Not funny, Mike, you've had us all worried. You've been gone for five days, five fucking days, Mike."

"What do you mean five days? I only just got here."

Jordan whacks me up the side of the head. "Dude, it's Monday. You've been MIA since Thursday. I'm guessing by the size of Mount Canmore and Tequilaville over there, that you've drunk yourself into a stupor and the days have all blended into one." Pulling up a chair, he sits next to me. "Mike, dude, talk to us. What's going on? And don't say nothing. You've not been the same since the shit with douche face and De-Niece went down. You're pulling away from us, drinking waaaaay too much; you're not yourself, dude. Kenz and I are worried about you."

"Holy fuck, five days, really? It seriously feels like I only got here yesterday. I'm sorry, guys, I just needed to get away."

Kenz comes back to join us and hands us all a coffee, I didn't even realise that she disappeared. Fuck, I really am off the rails. Taking the coffee from Kenz, I take a sip. "Thanks, Kenz. I'm sorry to have worried you guys. I'm just not in a good place at the moment." Looking over at Kenz, I put my coffee down, taking a deep breath. "I feel guilty, so fucking guilty."

Kenz leans back and rests her hands on her belly. "Why do you feel guilty? What did you do, Mike?"

"I fell in love with a monster and that monster nearly killed you, Mac, and Cheese." I lower my head in defeat.

"Mike Mustange, you look at me and you listen. It was not your fault that she was a psycho fucking bitch, psycho runs in the family I'm guessing…"

"But…" I interrupt.

"Shut the fuck up, Mike, and let me finish."

"Wow, feisty, Kenz, is in the house."

"Seriously, Mike, you did nothing wrong. None of us knew. None of us." Kenz waves her fingers in a circle between the three of us and emphasises none of us the second time.

"Yeah, but…"

"No, Mike. There are not buts in this scenario. YOU DID NOT FUCKING KNOW. No one did, PLUS if it weren't for you, I wouldn't be here. You saved me and the munchkins, Mike, YOU!" She puts an emphasis on you.

Jordan pipes in. "Dude, she's right, as usual." He blows a kiss to Kenz after saying this. "This is no one's fault, except for Clint and De-Niece. They both paid the price for their actions and that is not on you."

"I know all of this, but how did I not know? That's what I cannot get past. I feel like a chump."

Kenz gets up and squats down in front of me, "Mike, listen, we were all chumps. If anyone is to blame, it's me. I'm the one who let Clint into our lives, but my therapist made me realise that it's not our fault, we cannot control other people's actions. Maybe you need to go and see her, she really is awesome, and I think it will do you the world of good."

"I'll think about it, Kenz." She glares at me. "Fine, text me her number and I'll give her a call." Looking over at Jordan, I add, "Dude, is she hot?"

We all laugh, Kenz says through giggles, "I think you'll be just fine, Mike." Kenz smiles and winks at me. She tries to get up but with her big, pregnant belly she is kind of stuck. I can see her mind ticking over as to how she's going to get up.

"Need a hand there, fatso?"

Glaring at me she snarls, "Did you just call me fat?"

"Yep, now do you want a hand? Or do you want to squat there all day?"

"Just help me up, asshole."

Laughing, I get up and help Kenz stand. I wrap my arms around her and pull her in for a big squeezy hug. She wraps her arms around me tightly; we stay that way for a few moments. Pulling back, she smiles at me, and for the first time since it all happened, I think that I will be okay. "Thanks, Kenz. I really appreciate your kind words, even if I don't agree with them."

The three of us spend the rest of the day sitting by the fire, catching up, just like old times, it felt amazing to be Mike again. Just before dark, Kenz and I load a shitfaced Jordan into the Jeep. He's had a few too many beers and is gibbering about loving us both so much, and how he cannot wait to be a daddy. This makes both Kenz and I smile; drunk Jordan is fun relaxed doesn't-have-a-care-in-the-world Jordan, non-drunk Jordan is serious and straight laced and great to be around, but not as entertaining as drunk Jordan. Kenz gets into the driver's seat and winds down the window. "Are you sure you'll be okay, Mike?"

"Yeah, Kenz, I will. I just needed to get away, clear the noggin. I promise I'll head back to reality tomorrow."

"Glad to hear it. Why don't you come over for dinner?"

"Sounds good, Kenz. Thank you. You know I love you, right?"

"Yeah, I do and I love you, too, Mike. See you tomorrow at our place for dinner, that way I know you will be home and safe."

"Night, Kenz. Promise to be there for dinner." Standing there, I wave and watch her drive off, not quite believing that I will be okay, but I do know that I need to change how I'm living my life. I want to be me again.

After waving them off, I grab another beer, a packet of Chicken Twisties and sit by the fire to once again drown my sorrows. My last thought, before I pass out, is that my life will never be the same...never.

7

SAV

It's a sunny Tuesday afternoon, three weeks after being released from hospital; I'm sitting in the library with a cup of coffee, reading *Fractured Affections* by Elizabeth Wills on my iPad. It's a heartbreakingly beautiful story, and I have a total crush on the lead dude. I'm currently hoping someone like him will come to life and rescue me from this living hell. As I'm gazing out the window towards the garden, I realise that I haven't seen Uncle Kelvin for over a week now. It makes me smile and I start to relax; maybe this is all over.

Later that afternoon, I grab a glass of wine and head back to the library, which has become my new favourite room. Snuggling down on the brown suede lounge, I stare into the fire. The cracking of the burning timber and the flickering flames relaxing me, there is nothing more soothing than a glass of wine while sitting by the fire. Gazing into the fire, I realise that I'm smiling and finally, I feel like me again, and dare I say it, happy.

No sooner had I finished that thought and Uncle Kelvin comes barging through the front door. *I really need to get the locks changed,* I think to myself. Tonight, he can hardly stand up; he's pissed as a fart. The smell of whisky permeates the air and I can smell it from where I'm sitting. *This isn't going to be good,* I think, as he stumbles into the room. He doesn't say a thing, the quietness is disturbing. He plonks himself down on Dad's recliner, it creaks under his weight and roughness and I cringe. He glares at me, and sneers, "Where is it, you little bitch?"

I've had enough of this and tonight I'm feeling brave. "I have no idea what you are looking for, asshole, tell me and maybe, just maybe. I can help you."

"You're just like your mother, a lying vindictive little whore. What she had is just as much mine as it was hers, and now you're hiding it from me."

"I...." but I don't get to finish my sentence as he lunges towards me, slamming his hands on my thighs, the sting of the slap tingling as he gets up in my face and snarls, "Where is it, bitch?"

My heart is racing, my happy feeling of moments ago evaporating, being replaced by unyielding fear. I stutter, "I...I honestly don't know what you are looking for."

He raises is left hand and it collides with my cheek, it stings like a bitch. "Fucking little liar." He turns around and storms out of the house, slamming the front door behind him with such force that the windows and paintings on the walls rattle.

Pulling my legs up, I hug them and cry. Resting my forehead on my knees, I continue to cry, and before I know it, it's pitch black outside, the only light coming from the fire. Standing up, I head upstairs to shower and hopefully wash away the horrible memories of today.

When I'm in the shower, I decide that for my safety and sanity, I need to leave and get away from Uncle Kelvin and any other thugs that he may send after me.

It's time to take my life back, and it starts now.

8

MIKE

MY LIFE HAS BECOME A CYCLE OF GOING TO WORK, DRINKING MYSELF stupid, enjoying myself in random pussy, and occasionally sleeping. The guilt still eats away at me, I wish I could turn it off and be me again, but life's a bitch, just like my ex.

It's a bright and sunny Sunday morning, and it's been three weeks since Kenz and Jordan intervention at the property. My head is still all over the place and I still feel like shit. No matter how many times I'm told it's not my fault, I still feel responsible; I really wish I would let it go and be me again.

I was fucking the devil herself, how is one meant to get over that?

I'm in the laundry shoving my sheets into the dryer when I get a text. Digging my phone out of my pocket, I see it's Officer Hamilton.

Officer Hamilton: *Hey Mike! Wanna meet up for a beer?*
Me: *Sounds good. Name the time and place*
Officer Hamilton: *Malt Me at 3pm*
Me: *Sunday arv sesh sounds good to me, c u then*

Not really keen on the location, but the company and beers will be great, I still feel like everyone there gives me the evil eye due to what went down, but maybe it's all in my head.

I took Kenzie's advice and I have been seeing her therapist, Jeannie.

She is helping, but I think it will be a long road. Maybe facing everyone at Malt Me is what I need to do, rather than hiding away like the pussy I've become. The old Mike would face it head on and that's exactly what I'm going to do. "Bring it, assholes," I say, as I'm getting out of the shower.

I'm getting out of my cab when another pulls up and Officer Hamilton gets out. She sees smiles, waves. "Hey, Mike."

"Hey! Officer Hamilton."

"Seriously, call me Kelly. I'm not on duty."

"Yeah, but it's so cool saying Officer Hamilton. If it makes you feel better, just call me 'Hot Dude.'"

"Yeah, that's not gonna happen, 'Mr. Not Hot Dude.'" She air quotes my non-nickname, "Let's get our drink on."

"Yeah, nah, that name's not gonna happen, Officer Hamilton, but yes, let's get our drink on." Throwing my arm over her shoulders, we walk into Malt Me for an afternoon of beer, fun, and shenanigans.

Being a Sunday arvo, the place is packed, as usual. Looking around I can't help but smile. I'm so happy for Kenz and Jordan, their dream has come true. They have managed to turn Malt Me into something awesome. After all the shit that went down, they really deserve all the happiness and success in the world. Looking over at Officer Hamilton, I say, "I'm so proud of all that Kenz and Jordan have achieved with this place."

"Yeah, it is pretty amazing. The guys at the station love it here, especially when they have the live band here playing." Pushing me towards the bar, she says, "I'll get us a table, you get the beers. And a serve of wings too, please, I'm starving."

With a mock salute, I say, "Sir, yes, Sir," and I march towards the bar. I'm leaning on the timber bar, when a head pops up and it's Jordan. "Hey, asshat, didn't realise you were working today."

"Amy and Heather both called in sick, so I'm here helping out. It's actually been fun being behind the bar again. I think I need to do it more often. What brings you here today? Got a hot date?"

"Get fucked, no dating for me. Just here with Officer Hamilton for a catch up." I point over my shoulder towards where she is sitting

"You hit that yet?" Jordan says, nodding in head in her direction.

"Nope, and not going to. I don't like her like that. She's just a mate, a good mate. She's the female version of you."

"So she's awesome then?"

"If you say so, asshat." I quickly change the subject because my love life is and always will be non-existent. "Where's our sexy mumma-to-be?"

"In the office. She wants to get all the paperwork and stuff sorted before Mac and Cheese arrive." He places two beer mugs and a jug of Grid Mesh Larger on the bar for me, I don't even have to ask, he knows exactly what I like.

Smiling, I raise my eyebrows. "Duuuude, you called them Mac and Cheese."

He chuckles, "Yeah, we all are, well except Kenz. Even Dr. Green is calling them Mac and Cheese."

"My work here is done then." Laughing, I grab the beer mugs and jug. "Hey, if you get a break, come join us." Looking around I add, "It's pretty packed today, I'm so happy for you guys."

"Yeah, it is pretty bloody awesome." Pausing, after looking around, he adds, "Dude, I own a fucking brewery. I still find it amazing that my drunken idea at the Oktoberfest has come to fruition."

"Wow, look at you using big words." He gives me the finger. "Okay, I'm off to get my drink on. See you when you pop over."

Walking across the bar, I smile when I realise that she grabbed a table near the glass wall that looks into the brewery; this table has unofficially become mine. She looks up and smiles. "Took your time, I'm dying of thirst here, dude."

"Ohh, poor baby." I place the jug and mugs on the high top and take a seat. She goes to pour us each a beer when she realises that they are already full.

"Shit, I forgot your wings."

Slapping the table she says, "Totally knew you would, so I flagged down a waitress and already ordered some."

Faking hurt, I cross my hands over my heart and look at her with sad, puppy dog eyes. She laughs, shaking her head. "Suck it up, princess," Picking up her beer, she raises it and toasts, "Cheers, to a beertabolous afternoon."

Clinking our glasses, I add, "To a beertabolous afternoon," before taking a sip. "Man that's a good drop, my man Jordan sure knows how to brew wickedly awesome beer."

"He sure does."

Jordan and Kenz join us before they leave. Kenz is huge at the moment and has the cutest little waddle when she walks. I mentioned it to her once and got a tongue-lashing. I didn't mean to offend her, but I guess when it's weight related, chicks will take it the wrong way, no matter how innocent it was meant.

Officer Hamilton and I have a great afternoon and for the first time in weeks, I don't think of what happened, or that it's my fault. But most of all, I don't feel like the staff here is judging me. Maybe things are going to be okay after all.

9

SAV

EVERYTHING IS SET, THIS TIME NEXT WEEK; I'LL BE FREE. I WILL LEAVE MY home, my friends, my life, and never have to see Uncle Kelvin again…I hope. As much as it bugs me to know what he is looking for, getting away is my only chance for survival and happiness. There is still quite a lot to do before I sneak away, but for the first time since losing everyone, I'm excited for the future.

Tonight, I was given a reprieve; Uncle Kelvin didn't come over. Since I made the decision to leave, he's been here every night, sometimes twice. This is the first night in weeks that he hasn't been by, I take that as a good sign and that me leaving is the right thing to do.

Next on the leaving list is to go to the bank and get the items in the safety deposit box; I'll set up another when I get settled. If the lawyer hadn't mentioned it to me the day of the will reading, I wouldn't have even known about it.

Before heading to the bank, I grab two coffees and I head to the store to meet with Sierra and go over my plan. She is the only one who knows I'm leaving for good, but she doesn't know why and to be on the safe side, she doesn't know where I am going.

Sierra is all up to date with everything and I have said good-bye to all the staff. They think I'm just getting away for a bit to clear my head, and they all wish me well. We get to the door and I embrace Sierra tightly. "Thank you for everything, Sierra, I would be lost without you."

"It's my pleasure, Savvy. You are like family to me and I'm happy to help." Pausing she whispers, "Your secret is safe with me, I promise not to let anyone know that I know."

Pulling back from our hug, she takes my hand and squeezes it tightly as I walk out the door. Turning around, I wave and head towards the bank.

After going through all the security checks at the bank, I'm led into the safety box deposit room. Taking a deep breath, I unlock the box and open it. As soon as I lift the lid and see what's inside, I know this was what Uncle Kelvin has been looking for.

Taking another deep breath, I remove everything from the box and place it into my backpack. I relock the box; sign the forms to close it, and I quickly get out of here. As I'm walking out, I start to giggle, *You'll never get it now, asshole*, I think to myself with a wickedly happy smile on my face.

Exiting the bank, my eyes keep darting everywhere. I'm scared of running into my uncle, I'm not sure I could lie to him if he asks what I'm doing or what's in the bag. Once I'm outside, I inhale deeply, hold my breath, and quickly make a run for it. Climbing into my car, I sigh and let out the breath that I was holding. Thankfully, I never saw Uncle Kelvin or anyone, I'm sure I had some help from Mum and Dad today. Again I take this as another sign that I am doing the right thing.

Tomorrow is the first day of my new life.

10

KELVIN

IT'S SO FRUSTRATING, FIRST THE LITTLE BITCH DIDN'T DIE WITH THE REST OF them, and now she won't tell me where it is. As soon as she hands it over, I will leave her alone...maybe. Her innocent act is starting to grate on my nerves. She's a lot tougher than I gave her credit for, even those goons couldn't find it, or get it out of her. The beating she took was brutal; I'm impressed she didn't cave. *I'm going to have to up my game if I'm to get what is rightfully mine.*

I'm currently at the Grand and not in the mood to deal with her whinging, whiny, woe-is-me crap, so I decide to stay here and get acquainted with Jack. *I might stop by the brothel on my way home,* I think to myself as I throw back another shot of Jack. Having a few days break will be great, I fucking love seeing the look on her face when I barge in.

Today has really dragged on and my last meeting really pissed me off. *A night of terrorising the little bitch will be fun,* I think as I'm driving down the street.

Pulling up at the house, I see a 'For Sale' sign out the front and my blood starts to boil. "What the fuck is she up to now?" I ask out loud, just as I see Cheryl, the real estate agent coming out.

She comes over to my car. "Good evening, Kelvin, I didn't think you'd be by tonight. I was just finalising the listing photos for Savannah. The town won't be the same without her."

"What?" I spit.

"She left town."

"What do you mean she left?"

"She told me it was too much living in the house, so she's decided to sell and leave town."

"What the fuck?"

Cheryl looks shocked at my outburst. "I thought you knew, you are family after all."

"Hmm, yeah, well the little bitch didn't tell me. What did she do with all the stuff?"

"The movers were here today. They left about an hour ago." Cheryl looks at her watch. "I have to run to another appointment, Kelvin. It was nice seeing you again." She waves as she turns and walks to her car.

Standing on the pavement, I look up at the house. As soon as Cheryl is gone, I race up the driveway, head around the back, and use my key to get inside. Maybe with the house empty I will find what I'm after. I put my key in the lock but it won't turn, "Son of a fucking whorebag bitch!" I shout when my key won't budge. I mumble, "The little ho changed the locks on me, I knew she had what I was after. Well, looks like I will just have to hunt the lil' cunt down."

As I walk back to my car, I dial my guy and ask him to find her. She won't get far and when I find her, she's going to pay.

11

MIKE

...Present day

As usual, I'm sitting at the bar at the Dungeon, trying to drown my sorrows and forget about all the shit that has happened and how crappy my life is at the moment. Maybe tomorrow I will wake up and realise that it was all a dream, and I never met De-Niece, and she didn't ruin my life.

From time to time, I go and visit Kenz and Jor but they have it tough at the moment. Kenz delivered Mac and Cheese eight weeks early, and they had to stay in hospital, but today is the day that they get to come home. I don't know how they do it. I'm not as strong as them and I still feel guilty for everything. I know they have said that they don't blame me, and that I need to move on, but it's pretty hard not to feel like a chump.

Sav, the hot new bartender has just placed my beer in front of me when my phone lights up, it's still on silent from being at work. Jordan is calling me, but I'm not in the mood to talk, so I let it go to voicemail. As usual, he doesn't leave a voicemail; he immediately sends a text.

Jordan – *Yo asshat, we just got home with Mac and Cheese, would love to catch up*

For the first time in a few weeks I smile, those two little munchkins have me wrapped around their little chubby fingers. The thought of seeing Mac and Cheese makes me happy.

Looking up, I see Sav staring at me. She quickly looks away, but my smile only gets bigger when I realise that she was checking me out. *No, Mike, don't go there,* I tell myself, as I ask Sav to settle the bill. Looks like I'm going to Jordan and Kenzie's place tonight.

Mike – *Sounds good to me, be there soon*
Jordan – *Great. Can you pick up dinner on your way. Thanks. Your choice*

His reply is totally something that I would do, and I can't help but laugh, garnering a few strange looks from those sitting at the bar nearby. Bringing food is the least that I can do, it's been a rough few weeks for them.

After settling the bill, I finish off my beer, wave bye to Sav and head off to go see my lil' munchkins, ohh and Kenzie and Jordan. As I'm walking to my truck, I let him know I'm on my way.

Mike – *No worries asshat. Chinese and I are on our way*

Kung Fu Palace is the best Chinese place in town, even though it's out of the way, I don't mind. I order way too much food for three people: two lots of spring rolls, three lots of steamed dumplings, large special fried rice, snow pea and cashew chicken, sweet and sour pork, sizzling beef, honey chicken and Mongolian lamb.

While waiting, I head to the bottle-o next door; a celebration is called for because Mac and Cheese finally came home today, so I decide to splurge. I buy a case of GH Mumm and a bottle of Jack Daniels single barrel, so we can finally wet these babies' heads; *I love this tradition.*

Parking my car in my usual spot on the front lawn, I walk in the front door. I no longer knock, but after what I just saw when I walked in, from now on I will knock and wait for the door to be opened. Kenz is sitting on the couch, tits out, which are massive by the way, and she's feeding Mac...or Cheese, not sure which one. "Fuck, Kenz, put those titties away or at least put a sign up on the front door."

"Mike, watch your language and you can knock, that's what polite people do."

"Pfft, A. I'm not polite and B. Not a chance in hell if I get to see those babies every time." I look towards Jordan and give him a nod and wink; Kenzie's tits look amazing all milk filled. I think to myself, *Wonder what her milk tastes like, wonder if she'd let me try it.* Kenz just shakes her head as she does up her top and smiles at me. *Damn keep those babies out for a little longer,* I wish to myself.

Jordan walks over to me to help with the food and drinks. He smacks me up the side of the head before grabbing the Jack Daniels and bubbly. "Mike, I know what you are thinking and no ducking way."

How the fuck does he know what I'm thinking? That's when I realise that I am still staring at Kenz, standing in the doorway. "Come on, dude, you don't know what goes on in my mind."

From the lounge Kenz laughs, "Yeah, not much at all goes on up there." She winks at me like I just did to Jordan.

"Lucky I love you, baby girl." I place the bags on the table and I walk over to Kenz, placing a quick kiss on her forehead. Looking down I see Mac and Cheese are lying on the couch. They have gotten so much bigger since I saw them last. *I really need to come over more often.*

Kenz and Jordan put the kids down while I set up the feast; I totally ordered way too much food. We all sit down to eat, my eyes keep glancing at Kenzie's chest, and each time Jordan kicks me under the table. It feels just like old times, and for the first time when I'm around them, I don't feel guilty or think about De-Niece and all the shit that has happened.

As I'm driving home later that night, I smile and think that maybe life isn't so bad after all and that everything will work out fine.

12

SAV

It's been just over six months since I made my escape, and I finally feel content and happy. No longer am I constantly looking over my shoulder in fear that he will have found me, he's not that smart...I hope.

Some days are harder that others but generally speaking it's all good. I miss home, but mostly I miss my friends. I feel bad skipping out like that but I had no choice, I needed a clean getaway. I certainly do not miss my uncle, that's for sure. I so wish that I could have been there to see the look on his face when he got to the house to find it for sale and then to discover that the locks were changed; it would have been priceless.

Sierra called me the day after I left and said that Kelvin came barging in, just as the store was opening. He was fuming that I had taken off and was spewing obscenities; it wasn't until she threatened him with calling the police that he left.

Deciding to sell the house was tough, but I needed a new start, and I know that Mum and Dad would have been proud of me for making that decision. Deep down, I know that they would have been happy that I wasn't letting my uncle win.

The house sold immediately, which I knew it would, it's a lovely house. It selling quickly only confirmed that I had made the right decision; I know that the new family will love the house as much as we did.

The local store was and still is operating well; thanks for Sierra and the amazing staff working for us, well me now, which is a bonus. All the stores are currently doing well, and in this economic climate, it amazes me. Profits were through the roof when I left, and from the recent reports, they are still going up. Sierra and I chat at least once a month, unless there is an issue that I need to tend to.

When I went in to tell them that I was leaving, it's was really difficult. I didn't elaborate as to where, or how long I'd be gone, but I informed them that Sierra knows how to reach me if I'm needed. I did stress that I didn't want Uncle Kelvin to know where I was, and they were only too happy to oblige. He's not very well liked in town. I'm so lucky that the staff are happy to look after the store for me. I trust them, just like Mum and Dad did.

As soon as I arrived, I opened another safety deposit box and placed everything from Mum and Dad's into this one. Keeping it safe, just like they wanted.

Things are finally getting back to normal. I left my old life behind and I'm getting on with my new life, tending bar at the local tavern, The Black Dungeon, something completely different for me. Hopefully it will make it harder for my uncle to find me, if he is even looking for me, that is. Working at the Dungeon is great, the staff is fun and the customers are awesome; it makes work exciting. I've become quite close to one of my colleagues, Jodi. She's awesome, loves a wine or five, is obsessed with milk bottle lollies, and has a beautiful soul. We hit it off immediately and are heading out this weekend for a night of dancing and wine, shockingly we are both off on Friday night. I can't wait to let loose. I can't remember the last time I went out and had fun. I'm pretty excited for my night with Jodi.

There's this one guy who comes in all the time, Mike Somethinstang, he is one fine specimen, and I can't stop thinking about him. Closing my eyes, I remember the first time we laid eyes on each other: I was behind the bar and when I stood up, right before me was Mike, my heart skipped a beat, and my undies immediately became wet. His blue eyes were staring back at me, and I became jelly and all giddy. I've never felt like this around a guy before. I'm pretty sure that I made a complete fool of myself in that moment, but it doesn't matter, I don't need anyone in my heart, or life.

He broke our staring contest and ordered a beer with a tequila shooter; a man after my own heart. After I pulled his beer and poured his shot, he turned looked around for somewhere to sit, before turning back to the bar and taking a seat there, my section for the night.

All night long, I kept sneaking glances at him. He's smoking hot, kind of like Jason Statham—six plus foot tall, broad shoulders, and muscular tattooed arms. His crystal blue eyes were boring into me at one point, my cheeks heated with excitement and my undies became wet; again.

There was something intriguing about him and I couldn't help but smile back. My eyes roamed over his face, taking in his chiseled jaw, hidden by a scruffy yet well-groomed goatee. His bald head shining in the overhead light and a smile that lit up when I smiled back at him. And the kicker, he was a beer with a tequila chaser guy; my exact choice of poison.

Over time, I've tried a few times to flirt with him, which is totally against my rules, he flirts back...I think, but it never advances further than flirting. When I got this job, I told myself that I would never date a customer, but I'm really attracted to Mike, and I know he is attracted to me, too.

When we chat, it feels like we are the only two people around, everything around us fades away and it's just us. We are two atoms drawn together, but there is an invisible force holding each of us back. Some days I let my guard down and try to push through the invisible fence, but it's strong and unbreakable. It's probably for the best, since I'm running and trying to protect what's mine.

Some nights, he looks broken, alone, and sad when he comes in. When I see him like this, all I want to do is jump over the bar and wrap him in a hug. Then I'd kiss away his worries, and we'd have hot, dirty, kinky, mind-blowing, out-of-this-world sex on the pool table.

Other nights, he is so happy and carefree, these are the nights that he flirts up a storm but he never acts upon it. I've casually asked Jodi and the others about him, but none of them know much about him either.

The nights he doesn't come in I feel sad and empty, I can't explain the feelings that he brings out in me. I wish I knew if he felt the same way about me, it would then help me decide if I should take a chance or not. However, if he approached me, I'd say yes before he even gets to finish the sentence.

Lately, I find that when I'm alone, my thoughts immediately wander to him. Whenever I close my eyes, his face pops into my mind and I immediately smile; my heart rate increases and pulsating sensations build between my thighs. This vision is a nightly visitor when alone in bed. At the rate I'm going, I'll need to replace B.O.B. soon, but Mike is totally worth it.

It's Friday afternoon and Jodi will be here soon for pre-going out drinks. The tunes are cranked, and I'm adding the finishing touches to my make-up, when there's a knock at the door. I quickly finish putting on my lippy and as I'm walking down the hallway, I yell, "Coming!"

Opening the door, I say, "Hey, Mole." Jodi is standing on my doorstep with a bottle of sambuca in one hand, bubbly in the other, and a huge smile on her face. Her chocolate brown hair has been straightened and her make-up is flawless. As I hug her hello, I add, "Holy smokes, woman, you look hot."

Stepping aside, I let her into my duplex. She places the bottles on my coffee table and excitedly replies, "I know, right? But Mole, you look hawt. That top makes your eyes pop and holy shit; your ass in those jeans is out of the world hot. Wish my ass looked like that."

"Whatevs, Jodi, I wish I had your legs. They look like they go all the way to heaven." Winking, I say, "Let's get this party started."

"They sure do go to heaven," she says, with a smug look on her face before grabbing the sambuca, taking the cap off, and taking a swig. Shaking my head at her, I laugh and know that we are going to have the best time tonight.

I head to the kitchen to grab two champagne glasses, but when I get back to the lounge room, Jodi is chugging from the bottle. She smirks and shrugs her shoulders when she sees me. We both start laughing as she places the bubbly back on the coffee table.

"I love your place, Sav, it could do with a new paint job, though."

"Yeah, I asked the landlord and he's happy for me to repaint. He's even going to supply the stuff."

"Wow, that's awesome. I'm still waiting for my outside light to be repaired. It shocks me every time I switch it on."

"Holy shit, that sucks." Grabbing the bottle I take a sip and cough, sambuca isn't my drink of choice. "Sorry, not really a sambuca fan, tequila is my poison." Jodi digs into her bag and produces a bottle and hands it to me with a big smile. "You are awesome, woman."

"Again, I know. I couldn't resist seeing you have a drink before I gave this to you. I remember you saying, one night to a customer drinking tequila, that it was your all-time fav."

Smiling as she says this, because I know the customer whom she is talking about is Mike. "I say a lot of shit to customers, but that was one time I was telling the truth."

Twisting the cap off the bottle, I look to Jodi and say, "Cheers, Mole!" We clink our bottles together and take a drink. I love the warmth that spreads through my body as the tequila slides down my throat. I close my eyes and savor the flavour until I hear Jodi clear her throat. "Fuck me, woman, that was erotic, watching you drink that. You really do love tequila."

Nonchalantly, I just shrug my shoulders, I mean, what am I to say to that? I take another sip and emphaise my enjoyment. We both start laughing as I place the tequila bottle onto the coffee table. "So, where are we doing dinner?"

"Eating is cheating, Sav."

"I need to eat if you want me to last the night."

"I hadn't really thought of dinner, sorry, Sav."

"It's all good, Jodi. Why don't we try that new wine and tapas bar in the city? I can get a feed, and we can start the night with cocktails, before we head somewhere to dance."

"Sounds like a good plan to me. I'll call a cab. You don't mind if I crash here, do you?"

"Nah, that's fine," I say, as I'm zipping up my boots.

While we are waiting for the cab, we have a few more shots…this is going to be one messy amazeballs night.

Jodi and I got back to my place just as the sun was coming up. It's midafternoon when I wake up and I feel like death warmed up. My head is pounding, my legs ache from dancing for hours on end, and I feel like I could vomit for Australia and take home the gold. Jodi is one wild child; I have not had that much fun in a longtime.

After going to the bathroom, I head to the lounge room to check on Jodi, but she is nowhere to be found. I head to the kitchen for a much needed glass of water and a huge coffee. I have just turned on my coffee machine when I get a text.

Jodi – *Thanks for a great night, mole. I haven't danced like that in sooooo long. We have to do it again. See you at work tonight*
Me – *With how I feel right now not sure I will make it to work tonight. Definitely have to do it again*
Jodi – *Bitch, you better be there*
Me – *Yes, Mum. See you tonight*

After my coffee, water, and Advil, I head back to bed for more sleep; hopefully I'll feel human when I wake up. I set my alarm so I'm not late for work. I fall into a deep sleep where a certain baldheaded hottie makes an appearance.

I walk into work and the first person I see is Jodi. She looks fresh as a daisy, and I wonder how she does it. I still feel and look like shite. She looks up, and when she sees me, she starts laughing. I give her the finger as I head out back and sign in.

The night flies by as it is super busy, due to a big footy game in town tonight. I'm thankful it went fast. I knock off just after midnight, and as I'm leaving, I find myself sad that Mike didn't come in tonight.

13

MIKE

It's Saturday afternoon and I'm over at Kenzie and Jordan's for a new tasting session. Normally, I'm all over these sessions. but my heart just isn't in it today, plus I still get judgey eyes from a few of the Malt Me employees. Obviously some still hold me responsible for De-Niece, and I really can't blame them. I still blame me, too.

Don't get me wrong, I'm happy to spend time one-on-one with Kenz, Jordan, and the twins but not in a group like this, it's still too soon. Thankfully the baby monitor goes off.

"I swear, my girls have perfect timing, I'll be right back," Kenz says, as she puts her drink on the table. She stands up and kisses Jordan on the cheek before heading inside. Seeing them, for a fleeting moment, I wish I had something like them, but then I remember that chicks are nothing but trouble and the feeling passes.

"Let me help you, Kenz, besides I haven't had Mac and Cheese cuddles for days. I'm sure they are missing their Unky Mike." Yes, I would rather deal with a shitty baby nappy than have everyone judge me.

"Seriously, stop calling them Mac and Cheese."

"Nope, nah, uh, not gonna happen. My lil' angles will always be Mac and Cheese to me, and until they tell me otherwise, the nickname stays." Kenz glares at me. "What are you gonna do, woman?"

"I'll...I'll cut off your beer supply."

"You wound me, Kenz." I push past her. "Come on and let's go see my girls."

We are just inside the patio doors when I slap Kenz on the ass for fun, and she squeals. I hear Jordan yell, "Keep your hands off my wife!"

We are both laughing. "Nope, not a chance, asshat." I quickly slam the patio door before he can whip my ass.

"Lucky I like you, Mike."

"Pfft, you love me, Kenz."

"Nope, pretty sure I love Jordan."

"You keep telling yourself that, Kenz baby, you're still in denial." I turn and face her, seductively rubbing my hands over my chest, swinging my hips as I sing, "You love me, you wanna kiss me."

"Yes, Mike, that must be it," she sarcastically replies, as she side steps me and heads towards the twins' bedroom.

We quietly poke our heads in, just in case they went back to sleep, but when we open the door, both of them are lying in their cots, playing with their toes. My face immediately lights up when I see them, these two totally have me wrapped around their little fingers, and I don't care that it makes me a total pussy.

Smiling, I look towards Kenz as she picks up Rory, and I head over to Indi's cot. "Kenz, you and Jordan sure make cute kids."

"Yeah, we do, don't we?"

"Modest much?" I say, as I bend down and pick up Indi. "Hey, Indi girl." And I give her a gentle kiss on her head. She looks up at me and goos, as she pulls on my goatee. Again, I can't help but smile. I'm lost in the cuteness that is Indi and don't realise that Kenz has changed Rory.

"Earth to Uncle Mike, you going to change her or just stare?"

In a goo-goo baby voice, I say, "Unky Mike can do it, can't he, Indi?" She blows a raspberry at me. "I'll take that as a yes." Turning towards the change table, I gently lay Indi down, as I'm pulling down the nappy cover thingy, she does the biggest fart, "On second thought, I'll have Rory cuddles. I don't do shit."

"You're such a pansy, Mike." Kenz hands me Rory and she changes Indi. Once they are both changed, we head to the kitchen to get their bottles. I'm a little upset that I don't get to see Kenzie's cans but I'll get to feed Rory, so I still win. Kenz and I head to the family room and we each feed the girls.

These two sweethearts are the apples of my eye; I can't wait until I have kids of my own. I get upset at this thought because I will never get that chance. I'm never having a girlfriend again. Kenz must sense my despair as when I glance up, she's looking intently at me. I know that a Kenzie lecture is not far away. No sooner have I finished that thought she starts.

"How you doing, Mike? And before you say fine, I know that's complete and utter horse shite."

"I'm...I really don't know how I'm doing, Kenz."

She gets up and comes to sit next to me. After she settles Indi back into her feed, she looks at me. "Spill, Mike Mustange, what's going on in that bald head of yours?"

"I'm just coasting along, Kenz. Nothing excites me anymore, I'm not even excited to be here today." Her head snaps up at that, "See, I'm in a funk." Pausing, I let out a sigh, "At times I still feel guilty. I know that you don't think it's my fault but, Kenz, I was literally fucking the enemy. How much of a chump was I to not know who she really was?"

"Mike, I have said this to you a million times. None of us knew; we were all clueless."

"I guess I just question my judge of character now." Reaching over I squeeze her hand. "Kenz, I will never forgive myself for what happened with De-Niece, but I'm just glad that I got there in time. I no longer feel guilty for killing her." Pausing, "I...I feel guilty for letting you and Jordan down."

"Mike, you didn't let us down. As you said, if it wasn't for you, who knows what would have happened? Now look at me, Mike."

I raise my head and look at Kenz, she has her *don't fuck with me* look on her face. "Now, I don't want to you dwell on that. I'm fine, Mac and Cheese are fine, Jordan is fine, and those fuckers are rotting in hell."

"You called them Mac and Cheese and you swore."

"Focus, Mike. Everyone who matters is fine, well, you're not fine, but I'll get you there. There is no point in dwelling on what we can't change. All we can do is focus on the future AND that future will include you finding a lovely lady that I will allow around my munchkins."

"I hope you're right, Kenz."

"Of course I'm right, Mike. I'm always right."

"You're ohh so modest, too."

"And that's why you love me." She shrugs. "Now, let's get outside and join in the beer tasting."

We both stand and I one arm hug Kenz. "Thanks, Kenz. I appreciate the pep talk."

"Anytime, Mike, anytime. Now, let's go get our beer on."

Shaking my head and laughing, I say as we head back outside to join everyone, "Shit, you've been hanging around Jor too much. You even talk like him now."

Jordan walks over to us and grabs Rory out of my arms. "Well, when you crash into your soul mate, literally, it's bound to happen." He places a kiss on Kenz's temple and she smiles lovingly up at him.

"Fuck, you two make me sick. If love means that I have to hand in my man card, I'll happily stay single."

The rest of the afternoon flies by, and I actually enjoy myself once I let go of the guilt. As usual, Jordan has created some smashing beers. I cannot wait to have a Sunday arvo sesh and enjoy them at Malt Me.

14

KELVIN

THERE IS NO WAY IN HELL I AM LETTING THAT LITTLE BITCH GET AWAY WITH this. It's been six months since she took off, and I'm no closer to finding her. I need to call in reinforcements. When I get my hands on her, and what's rightfully mine, I will not be held accountable for what happens.

Picking up my phone, I search Google and get the number that I need. Grabbing a bourbon, I dial the number, and get a voicemail asking me to leave my details. I leave a message and pour myself another drink.

No sooner have I sat down and my phone rings. "Yeah?"

"Well, you're a rude fucker, aren't you? I'm looking for Kelvin Jones"

"Yep, that's me."

"I understand you need me to find someone?"

"Yeah, I'm looking for my niece."

"Why not go to the cops if she's family?"

"Because I don't want the little bitch to know or hear that I'm looking for her, it has to be a surprise when I find her. Your ad says you are discreet."

"That's right, she won't even know I'm there."

"That's perfect then. You're hired."

"I never said I'd do it."

"What?"

"You seem like a pompous asshole. I'm not sure I want to work for someone like you. Besides, how do I know you can afford me?"

"Do you think I would call you if I couldn't afford it? I'm not stupid."

"You're lucky that I need the money so I'll take the job. My fee is five hundred per day, plus accommodation. Now, give me as much information as you can about your niece."

"Fuck, that's steep."

"It is what it is, now do you want me or not?"

"Fine, but I'm pretty sure you are ripping me off. The bitch's name is Savannah 'Sav' Blac. Family owns the Blac Family Jewelers chain. She recently sold a house in Wentworthville. That's all I know."

"Age and description would also help."

"She's twenty-something, fucked if I'd know. She has amazing blue eyes like my late sister, blonde hair, legs that go on forever."

"Enough, send me through a photo. As soon as I receive a four-day advance and her photo, I'll get started. I'll give you a daily update."

"You better find her, it's important."

"They all say it's important. I'll be in touch."

Hanging up, I sigh. *Fuck this is going to cost me a fortune,* I think to myself as I scroll through my phone to send him a photo of Sav. After making the payment, I text him her photo and proof of sending the money.

Kelvin – *Proof of payment and photo*
James – *Thanks. I'll send an update when I have something*
Kelvin – *Don't waste my time, asshole*

Sitting down after pouring another drink, I sigh. *Why the fuck is this happening to me?* Can't believe this is what my life has become, things were much easier before.

Sipping my drink, I think how much better life will be when I get my hands on the jackpot. It should have been mine in the first place, but no, Miss I'm Daddy's Princess had to fuck it all up. Well, who's laughing now? Me, that's who, and when I finally get what's mine, there will be no stopping me.

15

MIKE

THERE'S A NEW BAR WENCH AT THE DUNGEON AND SHE IS FUCKING stunning. I can't get her off my mind. Savannah Blac, what the fuck are you doing to me? She's my last thought at night when I go to sleep. She's the first thing I think about when I wake up. When I'm making coffee at work, she's on my mind. She has totally consumed my life, and apart from me asking for a beer or tequila shot or how's the weather, we haven't had a real conversation.

Her voodoo pussy has overtaken my mind and I'm fucked. I swore I would never go there again after the De-Niece debacle, but there is something about this girl. My force field is waning and I'm not sure how much longer I can deny myself. I need to get to know Savannah 'Sav' Blac and have her in my life.

I remember one Saturday afternoon when I walked in; I immediately spotted her behind the bar. She was squatting down, and when she stood up, I was lost in her sky blue eyes. When she turned around to get the tequila I asked for, I nearly came in my pants; her ass was heaven. Her black work pants accentuated the curves, highlighting the prefect roundness. She must do a million squats a day to get that amazing curve. What I wouldn't give to squeeze her ass as she wraps herself around me and then sink my cock balls deep inside her. But I don't see that happening anytime soon. We outrageously flirted with each other, but she seemed hesitant to take it any further.

I need to stop thinking about the goddess named Savannah Blac!

I've agreed to meet Kenz at the Dungeon today for an afternoon sesh. Pretty sure she wants to meet up to give me another, "It's not your fault, pull your head out of your ass speech." Deep down I know it's not my fault, but I still feel like a piece of shit for not knowing that my girlfriend was a psycho, ho bag, bitch face, working with the douche canoe fuckface.

As I'm getting ready to meet Kenz, I ask myself the million dollar question: *How did I not know that I was fucking a fruitcake?* It's beyond me how I didn't know, and eight months later, I still feel like a fucking chump. Some how, Kenz and Jordan don't blame me but I don't care what they say. I'm partly to blame.

Looking up at my reflection in the mirror, I have an 'ahh ha' moment. It's time to get on with my life; I can't let the past, or that bitch, hinder my future. After all, I'm Mike Fucking Mustange and I'm fucking awesome.

Bending down, I put my boots on and think that maybe Sav is the girl for me. We get along well, we both like tequila, I'm hot, she's smokin' hot. She makes me smile and laugh, her ass is amazing, and she is the sexiest woman I've ever met. Nodding to myself, I decide that I really want to get to know this girl better, but first, I need to get Kenz off my back.

While I'm waiting for the cab, I decide that I will keep my Sav feelings a secret from Kenz. I'm still not one-hundred-percent sure that I want to go there yet, and if she finds out, she'll meddle like she always does. I can see it now, 'Operation Get Sav and Mike Together' will be put in motion, and I'm not quite ready to make that leap yet…or at all. Jeannie will be happy that I'm at least open to the subject now, that's a step forward in the right direction.

I'm running late, as usual, and I know she's going to be pissed. I won't have Jordan to defend me, as he is on daddy duty. It will just be Kenz and me, and to tell you the truth, I'm really looking forward to some one-on-one Kenz time. She and I haven't been out for drinks together in a long time, too long, in fact. I'm really looking forward to a messy tequila filled afternoon/night.

Finally, the cab turns up, and as I get in; I decide that tonight is the night, no more Mike woe-is-me Mustange. It's time for the return of Mike I'm-fucking-awesome Mustange.

16

KENZIE

THIS HAS GONE ON LONG ENOUGH; MIKE NEEDS TO STOP BLAMING HIMSELF. I thought after our chat at the tasting, he was on the mend, but he's still blaming himself. Today is the day that it stops. *I'm on a mission.* Jordan is going to watch the girls and I'm meeting Mike at The Black Dungeon. We will eat wings, drink beer, sink tequila shots, and I will finally get him to lose the guilt over what happened. *'Mission Save Mike' is a go.* Jordan agrees with me, so it was pretty easy to convince him. He wants to see Mike happy and himself again, just as much as I do.

As usual, Mike is late, but I strike up a conversation with this awesome bartender. Her name is Sav; she's newish to town. We hit it off immediately, and I think that now that Sarah is preoccupied, she could be my new partner in crime. Thinking of Sarah I start to feel sad, something is up with her, and once I have Mike back on track, she will be next on my fix list.

I've just ordered another beer, thinking about what's going on with Sarah, when Mike finally walks in. I must say, he is looking mighty fine this afternoon, actually he generally does. Today he is wearing his Wrangler jeans and black button-down shirt; and just for me, he's wearing his black Johnny Reb ankle boots. If I weren't happily married to Jordan, I'd totally do him.

"Looking good, Mr. Mustange," I say, jumping up to give him a hug and kiss on the cheek. As I'm releasing Mike, I notice that the bar chick is seething at our hug, and I notice Mike checking her out too. This totally changes the path of 'Mission Save Mike.' I cannot wait to put it into action.

"Mrs. McRoberts, as usual, you look stunning. Why could it not have been me you smashed into, all those years ago?" He slaps me on the ass, before taking a seat next to me at the bar; we both start laughing. He nod's towards Sav to bring him a beer and I notice that she seems pissed...towards me all of a sudden. She and I were getting along so well when I first got here. *Interesting*, I think to myself when I notice that she's flirting with Mike, and he's flirting back.

"You couldn't handle me, dude." Taking a swig of my beer before adding, "Besides, I prefer dudes with hair on their head, and not their chin." Reaching over, I tug on his goatee as I say this.

We are both laughing as Sav places a beer in front of Mike, and I say, "Sav, can you please bring me another beer and four shots of Jose, please? My buddy, Mike, here, needs a swift mummy talk and Jose is needed for this conversation." Raising my eyebrows, I wink at Mike.

Sav turns to get our drinks and I yell, "Can you also add a portion of hot wings and sliders, please?"

Noticing her demeanor change when I mention that Mike is a friend, *I'm so onto something*, I think to myself. Mike and I start talking about Jordan and the girls. When she comes back, she happily hands me my beer, and effortlessly pours six shots and replies, "Can do, Kenz, and since you're stuck with this guy." She points and wiggles, her finger at Mike. "Here's an additional two...on me."

Smiling, I swiftly reply, "Fuck, I love you. We so need to hang out, remind me to give you my details before I leave tonight." Sav nods, before turning and serving the others at the bar.

From the corner of my eye, I notice Mike inwardly groan and cringe at my encounter with Sav, and I totally know that I'm onto something here. There's definite chemistry between them, AND they have both been, not so discreetly, checking each other out.

'Mission Save Mike' just keeps getting better and better.

17

MIKE

Walking in, I immediately see Sav is working. My heart rate increases, I feel happy, and my cock starts to twitch at her beauty. I see her hand Kenz a beer, *that's my girl*, I think to myself as I walk up to her. "Mrs. McRoberts, as usual you look stunning. Why could it not have been me you smashed into, all those years ago?" Winking at her, I slap her ass as I sit down at the bar next to her. Waving my arm, I grab Sav's attention and order a beer, and another for Kenz; she's a guzzler.

Kenz snort-laughs when I smack her ass and I can't help but smile a real smile, I haven't had a real smile on my face in a long time. Kenz really brings out the best in me, and after all these years, her snort-laugh still sets me off. Taking a sip of my beer, I look over to Kenz, who is also smiling. She winks at me, and I know that we are going to have a great, but messy, evening together. *Bring it on!*

It's almost closing time and Kenz and I are plastered, like shitfaced, can hardly stand plastered. Together we have had up-deen-dozen shots, a gazillion beers, four million wings and a fantabolous time.

I've noticed Sav giving me weird looks tonight. I don't know what's up, and every time I go to ask Sav, Kenz grabs my attention and I get sidetracked. *I hope I haven't pissed her off and ruined my chance before I've even got it.*

Sav calls last drinks, and Kenz and I grab another round of shots and one final beer chaser. She's going to be feeling this tomorrow, but it was so much fun, we need to do this again. We've just finished our drinks and stand up to leave. Kenz wobbles around the bar and whispers something to Sav. Walking back to me, she links our arms and as we are leaving, turns to Sav and says, "See you next Wednesday."

After standing around outside, for what feels like forever, a cab finally pulls up. Jumping in with Kenz, I get the cabbie to drop Kenz off first and then me; I'm not waiting another billion minutes. We get to Kenz and Jordan's place, and I see her to the door. Jordan meets us and just shakes his head at me and smart-assly says, "Thanks for looking after my wife, I told you, no shots."

Bursting out laughing, I reply, "You've met your wife, try telling her no, or 'you've had enough'. Besides, she was a few beers in by time I arrived. But seriously, dude, thanks for letting me have her tonight. It was just what I needed." I see Jordan smile in appreciation, just as Kenz vomits on the front verandah. "And, on that note, I'm out of here. See you Wednesday for Origin."

Jordan shouts, "Thanks, asshole, see you Wednesday!"

Waving, I turn and race back to the cab. Before I know it, we are pulling into my driveway. I pay the cabbie and I head inside, stripping off before collapsing onto my bed and falling into a deep and drunken slumber.

For the first time in months, I easily fall to sleep and don't dream. My chat with Kenz this evening was just what I needed and only cemented my new outlook on what happened and life in general. Finally, I agree that I'm not to blame, but I still feel like a chump. I'm just as much of a victim as she and Jordan. When I wake the next morning, I decide that I'm taking my life back; Mike Mustange is back, people.

18

SAV

WHO THE FUCK IS THIS CHICK ALL OVER MIKE? BUT MORE SO, WHY THE fuck do I care? He's just a baldheaded, uber hottie who comes in here, he has a heart of gold, and he's fun to be around. From the bits he has said, I can tell he's going through something rough, and that's enough for me to keep my distance. I don't need more drama, I left to get away from it and I don't need that here...but I can't get Mike Mustange off my mind.

Looking up, I see him smiling and that, in turn, makes me smile; he has this voodoo effect on my pussy. Hence why, at the moment, he is the main attraction of my nighttime fantasies; poor Buzz. *Buzz is going to die at the rate I'm using him at the moment.*

I know I'm meant to be lying low until I'm sure Uncle Kelvin given up his quest to get what is supposedly his, but there is something about this guy that has me hooked. The nights he doesn't come in, I find myself sad, but as soon as I see him walk in, my face lights up and my body reacts to the sight of him in a way that I have never felt before. I imagine what it would be like to be under him as he pounds into me, my legs wrapped tightly around him, holding him closer, so he can get in deeper.

My night gets better when I realise that his friend, is actually is just, his friend. Kenz and I chat throughout the night and I really like her. We hit it off immediately and swap numbers to catch up again.

When Mike ducked to the loo, she asked me to their annual Origin party next week. Immediately, I said that I'd love to go but I'm not sure I should, since I'm a New South Wales supporter and we are in Queensland. But Kenz seems awesome and I'm lonely. I'd love to make another friend, and as an added bonus, I get to see Mike outside of work. Is it bad that I'm more excited about that than I am about gaining a friend?

It's finally starting to feel like home here. Don't get me wrong, I miss my friends from Wentworthville, and I feel bad that I haven't kept in touch, but I had to get away from Uncle Kelvin. Even all these months later, I'm not sure I'm strong enough face him again.

Most of all, it's nice to just blend in and not have anyone know my history. I couldn't stand the sad pitying looks anymore, but here I have a clean slate and no one knows about my tragically sad past. Here I'm Sav Blac, new girl in town. Where as back home, I was Sav Blac, poor orphan girl.

Another person to make me happy is Mike Mustange. Fuck, he's hot, like panty-melting hot, but he looks sad and lost; kind of like me. There is something about him that I'm drawn to; he's an enigma that I want to crack open. Even though I don't really know him, he makes me smile; he makes me happy and not sad. This happiness only occurs when he is around but his sadness scares me.

I'm finally in a good place and I don't want him to ruin this. I don't want anything to ruin my happiness. But there is something about him that I'm drawn to. I'm like a moth to a flame when it comes to Mike Mustange. I want to throw caution to the wind and just go for it, but I'm a total chicken and can't.

I'll just keep admiring his ohh-so-fucking-fine form from a distance—sigh. What I wouldn't give to have those muscular tattooed arms wrapped around me as I hold him close to my body. My breasts pushed up against his chest as I stare into his sky blue eyes...ohh well, looks like I'll just be imagining it's him when I give B.O.B. a work out...again.

After such a long shite period, things are finally looking up for me.

19

KELVIN

IT'S BEEN ALMOST TWO WEEKS AND JAMES IS NO CLOSER TO FINDING SAV. It's really pissing me off. I'm already down five G's and there is no end in sight. This asshole better come up with something other than, "I'm working on a lead," or "I'm close." Maybe I need to pull him and get someone else to do it.

Walking into The Grand Hotel for a pub feed and beer, I take a seat at the bar and start to calm down. The ice-cold beer is just what I need, I can feel the yeasty goodness starting to relax me. Smiling, I order another beer when my phone rings. I don't feel like talking but when I see it's James, I answer.

"Hello, James."

"Kelvin, I have good news."

"I'll be the judge of that."

"You're such an asshole" Pausing for effect, he continues, "Maybe I'll just keep my find to myself then."

Standing up, I head outside, as I don't want anyone hearing this conversation. "Like fuck you will, I'm paying you here, asshole, now stop fucking around and tell me."

"I found her."

Silence, I'm stunned that he actually came through for me. "Come again?"

"I found your niece, Sav Blac is working bar in Brisbane, Queensland."

"Well fuck a duck, you actually found the little bitch. I started to think you were leading me up the garden path."

"Listen here, you little weasel. I always come through, you go bad-mouthing me, and we will see who's the whiney little bitch. Now, I expect the balance to be in my account within the next twenty minutes. As soon as I have confirmation of the deposit, I will call you back with her address and place of employment, AND then I want you to lose this number. I never want to hear form you again."

"Fine by me."

Hanging up, I log into my banking and send the asshole his final payment, screen shot it, and text him. A few seconds later, my phone rings and he gives me the details on Sav. I pocket my phone, and smiling, I walk back inside, order another beer, and a Parma. This night cannot get any better.

While I'm waiting for my meal, I whip out my iPad and Google her location. After I have what I need, I look up where she works. "What a fucking dump," I mumble, "No surprises she'd work in a shithole." Now that I know where she is, I need to come up with a plan. It would be too easy to just contact her; I'm going to have some fun.

By the end of the night, I have it all worked out. Looks like I'm heading to Brisvegas…time for the fun to begin.

20

MIKE

THIS IS THE WEEK FROM HELL AND IT'S DRAGGING EVER SO SLOWLY. ALL I can think about is Origin on Wednesday night and hanging with the gang. It feels like forever since we've all hung out together, and for once, I'm not feeling guilty. An added bonus is that I will get baby cuddles. Who knew I, Mike Mustange, would fawn over two teeny tiny adorable little munchkins, but when they are as cute as Mac and Cheese, it's not hard to.

Finally, it's Wednesday and I'm super excited for Origin tonight. The boss must have gotten laid last night, as he is in a really great mood and he let's us all leave early. Not giving him a chance to change his mind, I pack up and get out of there.

After leaving the office, I head to the gym for a workout before heading home to get organised for tonight. My workout lasted longer than I expected, so when I get home, I quickly grab a shower and get changed into my Queensland jersey, *Go Queensland*, I think as I pull it over my head, my well-worn R.M Williams jeans, and broken in black chucks. Once I'm dressed, I call a cab and head outside to wait for it.

Ten minutes later, it arrives and I give him Kenzie and Jordan's address; I also get him to stop in at the bottle-o since I didn't have time. Racing inside, I grab a carton of beer and a bottle on Pinot for Kenz. As usual, I'm running late and it's just after 7:00 p.m. before I arrive.

Opening the front door, while balancing the carton and wine, the first person I see when I look up is Sav. *What the fuck is she doing here?* Before my brain clicks in, I blurt out, "What the fuck are you doing here?" I immediately think, *Dickhead Mike*, so I quickly add, "And in a Blues shirt." *Nice save*, I think to myself.

Kenz walks over, punches me in the arm and says, "Don't be rude, Mike. I invited her so be nice. Besides, it's not her fault she goes for the wrong team." She winks at Sav before grabbing the wine and heading into the kitchen.

Walking inside, I place the carton on the island bench and walk over to Sav, who by this point is looking really uncomfortable, and I feel like an ass for making her feel like that. "Hey, Sav. Sorry about that, I just wasn't expecting you to be here."

She hesitantly looks at me and replies, "I can go, if you'd prefer?"

"No, please stay." I panic at the thought of her leaving and I really want her to stay. Leaning over I whisper, "Besides if you leave, Kenz will ride my ass, and she's dangerous when she's pissed off."

WHACK

Rubbing my arm; I turn around to see Kenz there, holding a beer for me and glass of wine for Sav.

"I heard that, asshole, no brownies for you later." She hands us our drinks, and adds, "Sav, please ignore this asshat. He doesn't know when, or how, to behave."

Jordan comes over and hands Kenz her wine/ "Hey, Mike, I see you are in fine form this evening."

"What is it, pick on Mike night?"

In unison, Kenz and Jordan reply, "Yep!"

Sav laughs, and says, "I'd love to stay." Pausing she looks intently at me and adds, "Plus I can't wait to see New South Wales kick your ass."

Kenz, Jordan, and I all burst out laughing. I look over at Sav and in between laughs I declare. "Keep dreamin', babe, keep dreamin'."

Sav smirks, takes a sip of wine, points at me. "Okay, Mr. Queensland, let's make a bet. If New South Wales wins, you have to do anything that I suggest."

"...And when Queensland wins? What do I get?"

"Whatever you decide, but we need to decide here and now, so it's all on the table."

"Okay, when Queensland wins, you have to go on a date with me."

Where the fuck did that suggestion come from? I look over and notice Sav's cheeks have flushed, and she looks towards the floor with a smile on her face.

Looking back up at me shyly, she asks, "You want a date with me? Really?"

"Yeah, why not?"

Sav pushes her hand out. "Deal."

I spit in my hand and shake her outstretched one. Her skin is silky smooth, and I immediately picture her hand wrapped around my cock, squeezing tight as she strokes up and down. Shaking my head, and discreetly adjusting my cock, I say, "Deal."

"Eeww, did you seriously just spit and shake my hand?"

"Ah, yeah, sorry about that. I'm used to doing deals with Jordan, and we've been spitting on it since we were ten years old." I walk over to the TV cabinet and grab a tissue, turning around; I grab her hand and gently wipe off my spit. Her hand feels so good in mine and my touch lingers longer than it should.

Looking up, I see Sav smiling and it makes me smile. She pulls her hand back and I long to have her hand in mine once again. "Thanks, Mike, I've got it."

"No worries, Sav. Again, sorry bout that. Promise on our next bet that I won't spit." She smiles at me again and a rush of happiness courses through me, smiling back I ask, "So, what do I have to do for you when you don't win?"

"Well, when I win, you have to help me paint my duplex."

"Okay, I can handle that, but it's not gonna happen, so don't get too excited. Queensland has it in the bag."

"We'll see," she cheekily replies, before taking a sip of her wine. "This wine is divine, what is it?"

"Huh, that rhymes. Umm, it's a New Zealand one that I can't pronounce from the Marlborough region." Again, I find myself smiling, looking over I notice a sad looking Kenz walking back down the hallway. Walking over to her, I pull her in tight for a sideways hug. "What's up, baby girl?"

"That was Sarah, she's stuck at work and can't make it, but I know it's a lie. She's holding back on me."

"What makes you say that?"

"Her voice gets high-pitched when she lies and her pitch was opera worthy just then. She also quickly hung up on me. When have you ever known her to not want to talk? Even if she was at work."

"Maybe she's having an off night, is Josh not coming too then?"

"We never mentioned Josh, but I think they are having trouble. I haven't seen him in forever."

"Ohh well, more wings for me then. The four of us can still have a footytabolous evening, though." Everyone laughs and we settle in the media room just as the game begins.

The four of us have a great night and for the first time in forever, New South Wales fucking wins, and I'm now going to be at Sav's mercy. She has an evil glint in her eye; I'm scared.

Getting up to get another round of drinks, I hesitantly ask, "So, Sav, when does my punishment happen?"

"Wouldn't you like to know?"

"Seriously, when do you want me?"

"I don't want you, I just want your body." I'm left standing there open-mouthed at what she said. She quickly adds, "I want your body for painting. Ummm, be at my place at 10:00 a.m. Saturday, does that work for you?"

"Sounds good to me, Sav. Do you need me to bring anything?"

"Nah, just yourself. Actually you better bring a change of clothes, too." She heads over to Kenz and they open another bottle of wine. I'm left standing there, kind of stunned…and totally horny. Why do I need a change of clothes? Hmm, this could be interesting.

21

SAV

I'M SUCH AN EVIL COW, USING MIKE LIKE THIS, BUT THE WAY HE REACTED when he arrived really pissed me off. If I'm being totally honest, it cut me deep, real deep, and that surprised me.

Mike and I agreed to meet at 10:00 a.m. to get the duplex painted, I failed to mention that it is only the lounge room that we are painting, so he should be happy. I'm really happy that my landlord said it was okay to repaint, this place will finally feel like home after I do that.

She totally blew me away when she offered to pay for it; her only stipulation was no shitty colours. To appease her, I agreed to meet at the paint shop so she could help choose. Earlier in the week, we met up at the paint place and agreed on a colour. She paid for everything and I left with all that I needed to get the job done.

It's just before 10:00 a.m. when Mike arrives, and I can't help but smile. He has a tray of coffees and a huge box with him. I take the coffees from him and he follows me into the kitchen. He places the box on the kitchen bench and I take a peek inside, there is every kind of cake in there. My mouth immediately waters. Looking up, I see Mike staring at me, and my cheeks heat when he grins at me. As usual when I'm around him, I find myself smiling. I've noticed that I always am when Mike is around.

"What's all this?"

"Food," he smartly replies.

"No shit, Sherlock, are we expecting the Queensland team to come and help? There's enough food here for the entire squad."

"Ha, no just us. Painting works up an appetite so I thought I'd come prepared, plus I wasn't sure what your cake of choice was."

He passes me a coffee, our fingers grazing as he hands it to me. The world around us ceases to exist; it's just Mike and me. The spark from our fingers touching, jolts right through me, the electric zap that occurs would be enough to light a small country town for weeks. My insides clench and my cheeks turn pink as my mind runs wild with dirty thoughts. I'm brought back to reality when I Mike says, "Your skinny salted caramel latte, with two sugars."

My smile widens, when I realise that he brought me my coffee, exactly how I like it. "Why thank you, but don't think you will be getting out of painting just because you bought coffee and a sugar coma with you."

"A guy's gotta try." He winks before adding, "At least we're only painting the lounge room, I was dreading doing the whole place and with that huge front window, it's just three walls. It will be easy as. We should have the under coast and first coat done today and be finished tomorrow."

"How did you know it was just the lounge room?"

"Kenz let it slip."

"Well, no more free tequila for her when she comes into work."

"What about free tequila for me?"

"Depends on how good of a painter you are," I cheekily reply.

"For free tequila, I'll smash this painting out and you'll be amazed. Just you wait and see."

"Mmhmm, we'll see." I bring my cup up to my lips and I take a sip of my coffee; I close my eyes and enjoy this liquid gold as it hits my taste buds. "Man, Mike, this coffee is to die for. I need to know where you got it from."

"A coffee shop." Winking at me, as he also takes a sip.

"No shit, Sherlock, which coffee shop?"

"Java Lava."

"Is that the one next to Stratton College?"

"Yeah, that's the one, it's totally out of the way from anywhere, but ever since college, I always get my coffee from there."

"Looks like I have a new coffee shop. What are their brownies like?"

"They are pretty good, not as good as Kenzie's though. She makes a killer brownie."

"I know, those ones on Wednesday were to die for."

We take our coffees to the front verandah and chat. It's so comfortable and feels like we have known each other for years. There are no awkward silences and we have even finished each other's sentences on a few occasions. I don't know if it's wishful thinking, but I think Mike is flirting with me, and I really like it when he does.

Just as we are finishing our coffees, I get the feeling someone is watching me. I discretely look around but don't see anything out of the ordinary. Once inside, I place the coffee cups into the bin and we get into the painting.

Mike was right, we get the under coat and first coat done by midafternoon, and we decide to call it a day. He agrees to meet back here at the same time tomorrow.

Walking Mike to the door, we say goodbye, and I give him a kiss on the cheek. Pulling back, I look up at Mike and see lust in his eyes. Before it goes any further, I take a step back. "Thanks for your help today, Mike, I don't think I would have got this done by myself."

"Happy to help, Sav. Besides, a bet's a bet." He turns, opens the front door, and looks over his should as he walks out saying, "Night, lovely lady, see you tomorrow morning."

"Bye, Mike." I close and lock the screen. I feel sad and lonely now that he's gone. As I walk to the bathroom, I realise that once again after being around Mike, I'm smiling and happy.

Deciding to have a bath and chillax, I grab a bottle of wine and begin filling the bathtub when I get a text. It's from an unknown number.

Unknown – *I'll see you soon*

Without thinking, I delete it; it must be a wrong number. Just as I put the phone down another text comes through.

Mike – *I had fun today*

My heart flutters as I read his text, and a wave of euphoric happiness washes over my body. *I had fun today, too,* I think to myself; actually it's the most fun I've had in a longtime.

Sav – *I had fun too. Thanks for all your help. See you tomorrow*

Placing my phone back on the counter, I grab a wine glass and head into the bathroom. Lighting a few candles, I climb into the tub, immerse myself in the jasmine-scented bubbles, and relax.

Once the water turns cold, I climb out, put on my navy satin, knee-length nightie, turn on *Netflix*, and get absorbed watching the Winchester boys fight demons on *Supernatural*. It's just before midnight when I climb into bed; my last thoughts before I fall into slumber are of Mike.

The next morning, just after 10:00 a.m., Mike arrives and before we get stuck into the painting, we again have coffee on the verandah. Just like yesterday, he stopped at Java Lava on his way over, and this time he got a brownie for me and banana bread for him. The conversation flows, it is comfortable and nice and I find myself smiling and deliriously happy.

Looking up, I see Mike staring at me. "What?" Wiping my mouth before I add, "Do I have something on my face?"

Mike laughs at me, "Nope, nothing on your face. It's just nice to see your real smile and not the fake one."

"I do not have a fake smile."

He scrunches up the paper bag his banana bread came in and throws it at me. "Yeah, you do." My reflexes aren't the best and it collects the side of my head. I sit there, shake my head in shock. I look over at Mike and we both burst out laughing.

"Wow, you were right when you said you were unco."

"I'm not unco, I'm just not all that coordinated."

"Yes, the definition of unco."

He takes a sip of his coffee and I watch him swallow, his Adam's apple moving ever so seductively as the coffee makes its way down. All of a sudden there's a pulsating sensation between my legs, and I'm pretty sure my cheeks heat as well.

Quickly I stand up and head inside, I'd hate for Mike to know what I'm thinking. "I'm heading inside to get started, you finish your coffee and come in when you're done."

As I'm squeezing past, Mike suddenly stands up, we bump each other and he reaches his hand out to steady me. We stand there staring into each other's eyes; the heat radiating from his touch is scorching. Time stands still as the rest of the world fades away. Taking a deep breath, my tongue darts out and I lick my lip before biting on it. I realise that Mike is still holding my arm and we continue to stare intently at each other. There's an electric current fusing us together, neither of us wanting to break the connection.

Reaching up, he pushes a lock of hair behind my ear; the movement causes me to come to my senses. Pulling away, I quietly say, "Sorry, I guess I am unco."

Turning, I quickly race inside with my heart beating faster than I have ever felt it before. As I open the door, I think to myself, *What the fuck was that?*

22

MIKE

I'M STANDING ON SAV'S FRONT PATIO AND I'M STARING AT HER AS SHE races inside. *What the hell just happened?* One minute we are chatting, the next was like a scene from a movie.

Time stood still.

The only noise was the erratic beating of our hearts.

And in the blink of an eye, she's running off.

I'm at a loss as to what I should do. Do I go inside and demand we talk about it? Or do I just play dumb and leave it be? *God, where's Kenz when I need advice?*

As I walk inside, I'm thinking about the moment we just had. I know she felt what I felt and I guess that's why she ran off quickly. Looking at her, I decide that I don't want to spook her, so I play it safe and go with her; it never happened. *I must have imagined it.*

This is tough, I've sworn black and blue I will never have another girlfriend, but right at this moment, I want something with Sav. I want everything with Sav. If she pushes me away, or doesn't want this, I'll be devastated. Pulling up my big boy pants, I take a deep breath and continue inside.

When I get inside, Sav is nowhere to be seen. My heart sinks, until I see her walk down the hallway. She pauses midstep when she sees me, but her eyes also light up at the same time. It gives me hope until her sweet angelic voice says, "Let's get this finished."

My heart sinks; I guess she isn't feeling what I'm feeling, after all. With a fake smile I mumble, "Yep, ah, sure, no worries."

We get straight into painting. Sav turns up the music, and I get the hint that this conversation is over…before it even began.

In no time at all, we have finished painting and the place looks amazing, Sav and I make a great team. Thankfully, our little encounter from this morning hasn't had an impact on our relationship…or whatever this is.

We have just cleaned up the last of the paint supplies, and I start moving Sav's furniture back into place. I've just positioned the couch, when Sav walks in and I pause, she looks stunning the in afternoon light. The rays of sunshine on her golden locks create a halo effect, turning her into an angel: *my angel,* I think to myself.

My cock hardens at her beauty and before I can say anything, she turns and heads into the kitchen. To hide my growing cock, I take a seat on her couch and adjust myself. Sighing as I sink into the lounge, it feels good to finally sit down. Closing my eyes, I lean back and relax, I also think of Grandma naked, to get my cock to go down.

Sav is taking a while, and I start to think that maybe she wants me to leave when I hear her clear her throat. Opening my eyes, I see her standing next to the coffee table with a jug of beer and two ice-cold beer mugs.

Smiling, I curiously ask. "What's all this?"

She takes a seat next to me and I grab the jug, pouring us each a glass of beer. Handing her a beer, she says, "Well, I wanted to say thanks for helping with the painting, so I asked Jordan for a mini keg of your fav Malt Me beer. I've also ordered Chinese from Kung Fu Palace and there's salted caramel Tim Tams in the fridge for dessert."

"You seriously did all of this…" pausing, I can't believe she has done all of this, "…for me?"

"Yep. I really appreciate your help, Mike. If you hadn't help me, I would still be painting." Taking a sip of beer, she adds, "I really appreciate it."

She places her beer back on the coffee table and a lone tear cascades down her cheek, lowering her head she looks towards her lap.

Without thinking I reach over, lift her chin up, and I wipe away the tear with the pad of my thumb. Cupping her face with my palm, I run my thumb gently along her jaw line; she leans into my open palm and exhales. "Why are you crying, Sav?"

"I'm just…I'm just really thankful for your help. Not since…never mind, let's have a beer to celebrate my newly decorated lounge room."

"I'm down with having a beer, on the proviso that you tell me why you were crying and are now clearly upset."

Sav leans forward, grabs her beer, and chugs it back in one mouthful. She pours herself another and looks towards me. She smiles sadly and takes a deep breath. "My parents and brother were killed in a car accident earlier this year."

"Holy fucking shit, I'm so sorry, Sav."

"Don't be. I hate the pity I get from people when they find out, which is why I haven't told anyone here. I got overwhelmed just now, because if Jace were still alive, he and I would have done this together." She wipes away a stray tear and smiles. "Actually, he probably, no definitely, would have been my roommate. Mike, he wasn't just my brother, he was my best friend." She takes a breath; the tears are now steadily flowing down her cheeks. "I miss them so much, Mike. Some days, I wish I was with them, too. It hurts so fucking much."

Reaching over, I wrap my arms around her and console her. She snuggles into me as the sobs overtake her. I tighten my arms around her and rub her back in circles, like I've seen Jordan do with Kenzie when she's really upset.

We stay sitting like this for a while, her sobs have subsided but she's still emotional. I realise that I like this, having Sav in my arms. It feels right, not awkward, like she was made for me. We fit together perfectly, like two pieces of an intricate puzzle.

She pulls away from me and immediately I'm sad at the loss of her in my arms, but she smiles and it takes my breath away. No longer is it a sad smile, but it's a genuine Sav smile, and as usual when I'm around her, I find myself genuinely smiling too.

"Thanks, Mike."

"No need to thank me, Sav. I'm here anytime, day or night."

"You are too good to be true. Good-looking, nice, funny, and you love tequila. I'm glad to have met you, Mike Mustange."

"You think I'm good-looking?" I tease.

Her cheeks turn a pretty shade of pink; she's flustered as she replies, "I…I never said you were good-looking."

"Yeah, you did. And I quote 'Good-looking, nice, funny' and then something about tequila but I was hooked on the good-looking part. Care to elaborate further?"

"You, sir, are delusional. I said you were a good guy an..." Before she can finish there is a knock at the door. "That will be dinner." She eagerly says as she jumps up.

I mumble to myself, *"Fucking delivery guy."*

"Just 'cause dinner is here, doesn't mean this conversation is over."

"Whatevs. And yes, this conversation is over: done, dusted, kaput, the end, credits rolling. Moving on."

Sav answers the door and the heavenly scent of Kung Fu Palace permeates the air, I smile and groan. She pays the delivery guy and brings the food over. While she unpacks it, I head to the kitchen to get sporks and top up our jug.

As I'm refilling the jug, I smile. I'm blown away that she did all this...no one has ever done anything like this for me before. It makes me happy knowing she went out of her way arranging this. I know I'm going to sound like a girl, or Jordan, but I feel giddy and my heart is racing. Maybe, just maybe, I can explore what happened this morning further, but I'm not going to push her.

She was pretty upset when she was telling me about her family; I can't imagine what she's gone through. I'm not that close to Mum and Dad, but I still think it would suck. I guess I do know what she's going through, in a way. With all the shit that happened with Kenz and Jordan, I'd be lost without them.

"Dude, you better not be eating the Tim Tams, or worse, drinking all the beer."

Laughing, I close the fridge and head back into the lounge room. "Holy shit, are you feeding an army? You do realise there are only two of us, right?"

"Yeah, I did kinda go overboard but Fung Fu Palace is the bomb, and there's always leftovers."

"Pfft, leftovers. Woman, watch a learn."

We settle in, stuff our faces with food, and have a great night together. Sav shares a little more about her family but I get the feeling she's still holding back. I guess I don't blame her; it's hard opening up, and to a relative stranger, it would be even harder.

We have just cleaned up our mammoth meal, and I proved to Sav that Kung Fu Palace is no challenge for me. I'm actually impressed with all that I've eaten. I won't tell her that I kind of feel sick but that's my secret to keep.

She has poured us another beer and we are chatting about anything and everything. I've really gotten to know Sav tonight, and the more I know, the more I really like her. I'm tempted to break my no girlfriend rule when she stands up suddenly. I think that she is going to ask me to leave, as it's getting late. Instead she skips to the kitchen, returning with a bottle of tequila, two shot glasses, and my promised Tim Tams.

"Oh My God! Sav, you are the best. Marry me now."

My comment causes her to trip, the tequila slides across the chaise of the couch, and she falls onto my lap. Giggling, she looks up into my eyes, and before I have a chance to see if she's okay, her mouth is plastered to mine. Her tongue pushing for access and I hear her quietly moan.

Willingly, I open my mouth and our tongues wrestle. I pull her so she is straddling my hips, my hands grabbing her perfect ass, pulling her closer to me. She grinds herself on my cock and it immediately hardens. She's rocking back and forth as my hands work their way up her back.

Gently caressing her neck and shoulders, I pull her tighter to me and deepen the kiss. We both moan at the same time, Sav pulls back and rests her forehead against mine. I see indecision in her eyes, but before I can say anything, she pulls her singlet over her head. She's not wearing a bra, and at eye level are her perfectly pert, pink hard nipples, the sight before me is heavenly.

Leaning forward, I take her pink nub into my mouth and suck; she throws her head back in ecstasy as I suckle harder. With one hand, I massage her other breast. It fits perfectly in the palm of my hand. I squeeze her nipple before I suck on it, and I start to massage that one I had previously been sucking.

Sav continues to grind herself on my cock, and if she doesn't stop, I'm going to come in my pants. I wrap my arms around her and stand up, I place her onto the chaise and I squat between her open legs. Ever so slowly, I run my hands up her calf and thigh, before skimming my palm over her mound. I grip the top of her shorts and undies before stripping her naked.

I groan when I see her bare pussy glistening with her arousal. I lazily run my finger around her navel before sliding it down to her clit. I give it a flick before running my finger up and down, spreading her wetness. Slipping my finger inside, she exhales the breath she had been holding; her pussy is warm and inviting.

Watching Sav writhe in pleasure as she rides my hand is so hot. I insert another finger, plunging them in and out of her tight pussy; her moans getting louder and louder, her thrusts faster and faster. Leaning forward, I nibble on her bottom lip before sliding my tongue into her mouth. Her pussy walls tighten around my fingers, and I know she's going to come soon. I continue to kiss her as I insert a third finger. I feel her body shudder around my fingers, as she sucks the life out of my tongue. Never have I been so turned on watching another person come.

Removing my fingers, I sit up and I lick them clean. "Fuck, Sav, you taste amazing." Sav is still laying there, her breaths still labored and she looks stunning. Her pussy begging for more, I lower my head and suck her clit into my mouth before licking down her slit. "Oh my God! Your pussy is divine."

My tongue continues to dart in and out of her entrance, before I suck and nibble on her clit. She arches her back, and she starts to tweak her nipples, shoving my face further into her pussy. I suck on her swollen nub, before inserting a finger into her wet folds. Slipping my hand under her ass, I spread her juices over her tight hole, before I insert the tip of my pinkie into her ass.

Sav moans in pleasure as I push my finger further into her ass, when I insert my thumb into her pussy she screams, "Ohh, Mike!" as her second orgasm of the night rips through her body. Her body shudders as the pleasure courses from head to toe.

Gazing up, I see Sav looking down at me. Her cheeks flushed from two successive orgasms and the biggest smile I have ever seen on her face. Even though I haven't come yet, I have never felt such happiness before, and I smile back at her.

All of a sudden Sav tries to cover herself. I grab her hands, entwining our fingers, still sitting between her legs. "What do you think you're doing?"

"Well, umm, I'm naked. I kind of feel exposed."

"Well, I like you exposed." I wink before adding, "You are so fucking beautiful, Sav."

Sitting back on my heels, I pull her to the edge and kiss her. Our lips are gently caressing each other; I'm lost in the emotion of this kiss. When I pull back, I rest my forehead against hers and gaze at her and smile.

My lips are tingling, actually my whole body is prickling; I'm dizzy with lust. *I love kissing Savannah Blac,* I think to myself, before I lower my lips to her once again.

She deepens our kiss and wraps her legs around my waist, grinding herself on my growing erection. Wrapping my arms around Sav, I stand up and walk us down the hallway to her room.

Lowering her on the to bed, I stand up and quickly remove my clothing. Settling myself between her legs before kissing her again. She drapes her arms over my shoulders, pulling me in closer; the feel of her tits pressed against me is amazing.

She pushes me away and I think that she doesn't want this anymore, but she reaches into the top draw of her side table and grabs a condom. I pull back, take it from her, and quickly sheath my cock before I line it up with her entrance. Ever so slowly, I inch my dick into her pussy. Both of us growling at the sensation, never has a pussy felt so good wrapped around my cock.

Our pace quickens, the thrusts becoming stronger and deeper, our kisses frenzied as we lose ourselves in each other. Before I know it, I feel Sav's walls tighten around my cock and it sets me off. We both detonate in unison, shouting each other's name as we ride out our orgasm together.

I ease out of Sav and lay next to her, we both roll onto our sides and gaze at each other, panting. No words are said but our eyes say it all, we are both falling for each other.

Sav and I fall asleep, wrapped in each other's arms. My last thought before I drift off is that this feeling is nice and I don't ever want it to end.

For the first time in a long time, I feel happy and content, nothing could ruin this feeling right now…or so I thought.

23

SAV

WHEN I WAKE THE NEXT MORNING, I ACHE FROM HEAD TO TOE, AND I have never felt more alive. I don't think I have ever had that many orgasms in one night, and we're not talking ish ones; these were mind-blowing, body-shuddering, out of this world orgasms. Rolling over, I see Mike, snoring softly and my heart flutters. My eyes roam over his muscular back, but then I start to panic. This wasn't meant to happen; I'm supposed to be lying low, not getting laid. I can't bring Mike, or anyone, into my life until I know that Uncle Kelvin is gone for good. It's too dangerous for Mike to be in my life right now. *Fuck, fuck, fuck-ity, fuck, what have I done?*

Mike must know I'm awake because he reaches over and begins to massage my breast. Closing my eyes, I let out a moan; his hands on my body feel amazing. Quickly, I push his hand away, jump out of bed, and head into my ensuite; slamming the door behind me. *No, No, No, I can't let this happen, even though I really, really want to,* I think to myself, as I lean on the vanity. Hanging my head towards the floor, I let the tears fall down my cheeks.

The feelings and emotions coursing through me at the moment are out of control. I love what Mike and I experienced last night, If I was in another situation, I would happily explore a relationship with Mike, but I can't. I'm petrified that he'll become collateral damage if Uncle Kelvin ever finds me.

I can't do that to him.

I won't do that to him.

I just can't.

This needs to end before it goes any further. But in doing so, I know that I'm going to break Mike's heart because I know it will break mine too. Breaking his heart is the last thing that I want to do, but it has to be this way.

Mike knocks on the door. "Are you okay, Sav?" I panic that he is going to open it and come in, but he's a gentleman and doesn't open it. I'm frozen, staring at myself in the mirror; I don't know what to say or do. Closing my eyes, I take a deep breath and quietly yell. "Yeah, I'm all good. I'll be out in a minute."

"Okay," he hesitantly replies.

I splash some water on my face, before gabbing my pink, waffle dressing gown. Slipping it on, I take a deep breath and head back into my bedroom to face Mike.

When I open the door, Mike is sitting on the edge of my bed, still naked with the sheet across his lap, I force a smile since he is looking at me. He looks worried and I feel like shit. After what we experienced last night, we should be ecstatically happy, but instead he's dejected and sad. I'm a total chicken and don't ask how he is. I say, "Morning," and offer up a fake smile.

"Morning, babe. You sleep goodly?"

"Like a baby, I was completely worn out."

Smirking, he replies, "Me, too, I haven't slept like that in months."

Reaching his hand out towards me, I step closer to him, but I don't grab his hand, instead I take a seat next to him. Glancing towards him, the sheet has moved and reveals more of his nakedness. I notice that his morning wood has popped out to say hello. Seeing that makes me start to cry...I'll never have his glorious cock inside of me again.

Snapping his head towards me when I start to cry, he whispers, "Sav," as he wraps his arm around me and pulls me into my shoulder. This causes me to cry harder, and I feel like a bitch. He's so sweet and I'm about to break his heart. Glancing up at him, I murmur, "You need to leave, Mike."

"What? Why?"

"I...I...I'm, I just can't do this, Mike," I mumble. "It's not safe." I mustn't mumble the last part quietly enough because Mike lifts my chin so I'm looking directly at him.

"What's not safe, Sav?"

"It's nothing, it's just not safe to be with me. Let's place last night into the 'last-night-was-fucking-amazing-but-can't-happen-again' basket and go back to being friends."

"I don't want that, Sav. I felt something last night, babe, and I know you did, too." He runs his hands over his head, looking back at me. "Where's all this coming from?"

"I'm sorry, Mike, I just can't do this. Last night was beyond amazing but we just can't. I...I just can't." The tears are pouring down my cheeks.

"I call bullshit, Sav, but I'll go and give you space...for now, but don't think I'm giving up on this. I know what I felt last night and I'm not going to let this slide." He stands up, quickly dresses, and before he leaves, he bends down and kisses me on the forehead.

When I hear the front door close, I fall back onto the bed and I cry. My whole body shudders, as the sobs break free. Last night with Mike was out of this world amazing. What I wouldn't give for it to happen again, but I can't. I don't want Mike to get hurt if Uncle Kelvin finds me.

The following week is agony. I can't eat. I can't sleep, and work just drags. Mike comes into work every night but I can't look at him. It breaks my heart seeing him; he looks just as sad as I do. As soon as I see him walk in, I find any excuse to be out the back. The stockroom has never been so clean, the boss is impressed and really happy with me; at least that's a positive to come from this.

Jodi notices me take off on Friday night, when Mike comes in, and she corners me out the back, as I'm shoving a handful of Allen's Milk Bottles into my mouth. "Sav, what's going on with you and the hot hulk?"

Giggling at her comment, I say through my mouthful, "Hot hulk I like that and nothing, absolutely nothing is going on with said hulk."

"Yeah, right, Mole, I'm not stupid. You and he used to flirt up a storm, and I've noticed this week that every time you see him, you come back here. This storeroom has never been this clean or organised, so I know you're hiding from him. Plus he looks like someone ran over his kitty cat."

"Mike hates cats." I pause before quietly adding, "I made a mistake sleeping with him last weekend."

"You slept with him? Fuck, I owe Jude twenty bucks. He said that's what happened. So do I need to kick his ass for breaking your heart?"

"You bet on me?"

"Yeah, but do I need to kick his ass?" She grabs a handful of Milk Bottles from our secret stash.

"No, you'd need to kick mine."

"What the fuck? Why would you turn him away? He's hotter than hot. Are you crazy?"

"I'm crazy for letting it happen in the first place. Jodi, that night was the best of my life, and now it will never have it again. I'm such a fool." I start to cry again.

Jodi wraps her arms around me. "Shhhh, it's going to be all right, Mole, but why the fuck are you turning him away? The sexual attraction between you two is hotter than Channing Tatum's abs. Blind Freddy can see it, hell even Jude picked it."

"I just can't. There's a part of my life that I don't want to catch up with me, and if it does, I don't want anyone to get caught in the crossfire. If I hook up with Mike, there's a chance that he'll get hurt. I can't, and most of all, I won't let that happen."

"Shit, what are you running from?"

"It's best you don't know. Please, please don't say anything to anyone. Promise me, Jodi?"

"All right, I promise, but I don't think you should push him away. There is a real spark between you two, and I'd hate for you to miss out on happiness for a what-if."

"Thanks, Jodi, but it's better this way. Let's get back out there before we get in trouble."

We each grab another handful of Milk Bottles and head back out to the bar. Mike is still sitting there and looks up. When he sees me coming towards him, his face lights up; it melts me and only makes this harder. Jodi offers to serve him but I tell her it's fine.

As I'm walking over to Mike, I'm giving myself an internal pep talk. When I reach him, I fake a smile and say, "What can I get you?"

"Hello to you too, Sav. I'll take my usual and another night with you; please."

"Your usual I can do." I pass him his beer and turn to get the tequila. "As for me, sorry that will never happen again." I say this as I slide his tequila across to him, offering a weak smile as he picks it up and sinks his shot.

"Why? Please, at least tell me that?"

"I already told you Mike, I just can't. Please drop it." A tear escapes as I say this, and I quickly wipe it away.

"That's bullshit and you know it, Sav. I'll be here when you're ready to talk."

"You'll be waiting for a long time, Mike."

"I'll wait forever, Sav."

"Mike, no, please don't. Just move on and forget all about me."

"Sav, babe, there is no way in hell I'll be forgetting you, or the other night, anytime soon." He leans over the bar and whispers, "I've tasted your pussy and it's the most delectable pussy I've ever had the pleasure of devouring, and I want more. Your pussy is like crack and I'm addicted. I. Need. More. And, babe, I'm not going anywhere."

Gasping at what he just said, I'm left speechless as he sits back down. He picks up his beer, takes a sip, and smiles at me as if he just said the sky is blue. I stare at him in shock, but I immediately start to remember what his magnificent tongue can do; my undies dampen and I start to smile.

Something by the door catches my eye and my heart immediately stops. Shaking my head, I quickly run over to the door and race outside, but there's no one in sight. Turning around, I walk back inside, this Mike situation is fucking with my head, making me see things. As I'm heading back to the bar, Mike grabs my arm and I jump in fright. "Sav, are you okay? You're as white as a ghost."

"I'm fine, Mike, I just needed some fresh air."

"Yeah right, please talk to me. Maybe I can help?"

Snapping, I yell, "Mike, I'm fine! Just drop it. Please?"

"Fine, but know I'm here for you."

Why the fuck did I sleep with Mike Mustange?

24

KELVIN

Look how happy she is, fucking bitch. With all that is hers, she should be living it up somewhere amazing, not living in a shitbox like this. For a fleeting moment, I think that maybe she doesn't know about anything in regards to what I want, but if she doesn't know, why did she run?

I'm camped outside her place, and a baldheaded guy walks up to her door. She seems very happy to see him. Looks like the little slut has a new boyfriend as well. I'm not sure who this guy is, but he stays all day and when he leaves he looks happy…*not for long*, I think to myself, as I head back to the motel.

When I get back to the motel, a wickedly evil plan forms. I laugh out loud; messing with her is going to be ohh so fun. Phase One, texting.

Unknown – *I'll see you soon*

The next morning, I head back to her duplex and surprise, surprise loverboy is there again; sitting here will be waste of time today, so I head to a local bar to bide my time.

It's just on dusk when I pull up at her place, and I see that dinner has been delivered. From the looks of things, loverboy is still there too. "Damn it!" I shout into the empty car. I was hoping to make a surprise visit tonight, but I don't want any witnesses. I'll wait here until he leaves, then I'll pop in and say good night to my dear old niece.

I've been sitting in my car for over four hours now, and there doesn't seem to be any movement inside, but all the lights are still on. Sneaking over, I quietly climb the front stairs and hear moans and groans coming from her place. That confirms my suspicion that the baldheaded fuck is her boyfriend.

This could be interesting, I think to myself as I'm driving back to the motel. This will change my original plan but it will work out in my favour. As I enter my room, I decide to watch them both for a few days before I make my move.

The next morning, I'm back watching her place bright and early, eventually loverboy leaves. Slamming the door on his way out, I notice that he's really pissed off; naw, shucks, looks like they had a fight. I hope the bitch is miserable.

Taking the chance, I follow him back to his place, so I know where he lives. I'll head back to the little bitch's place later in the morning. It's just before lunchtime when I pull up but she's leaving for work. A night sitting in a bar sounds great to me, I quickly take off and head towards the Black Dungeon. Getting to the pub before her, I head into the corner booth that I have been in for the last week, watching her.

Thanking my lucky stars that she only ever serves from behind the bar, the brunette hottie she works with is extra nice, though. Maybe I can have some fun with her, but she seems to be uptight and won't give me any attention; Jodi is a fucking dick tease bitch; no surprises that her and Savannah would be friends—bitch attracts bitch.

I've noticed the last few nights that whenever loverboy comes in, Savannah ducks and hides out the back, but tonight she serves him at the bar. From here, I can see that there is trouble in paradise. Looks like the using the boyfriend plan is a bust. I've had enough and I'm growing impatient, so I decide to make my presence known tonight… let the games begin.

Looking towards the bar, I see she is talking to ex-loverboy this time. In order to gain her attention, I make a noise, her head snapping towards me. She looks directly at me and I smirk before quickly ducking outside and around the corner, hiding in plain sight.

From my vantage point, I see her come barreling out of the doors, looking around at the empty street. There is fear all over her face and she looks like she is struggling to catch her breath; that makes me so, so happy, I laugh with glee. When she can't see me, or anything in the vicitinty, she heads back inside.

On my way to my car, I laugh and laugh, today was perfect and this tormenting gig is fun. Climbing into my car and I head back to the motel. *Revenge is going to be sweet,* I think as I drive away.

25

MIKE

As usual, I'm at the pub so I can be near Sav. I've turned into a pussy-whipped guy; I'm fucking like Jordan. Even though she is ignoring me, it's nice to be close to her. The afternoon rush is over so I take the chance to talk to Sav. Finally, she is serving me, not hiding, giving me a glimmer of hope. We are talking when all of a sudden she freezes. Her face goes as white as a ghost, her eyes are locked on the front door. She takes off towards the door and heads outside. A feeling of dread washes over me, so I get up to go after her.

Before I reach her, she's already back inside, heading to the bar; reaching out, I grab her elbow. She is shaking like a leaf, and if possible, she is whiter than before. "Are you okay, Sav?" I ask.

"I'm...I'm fine Mike, I just needed fresh air. Just drop it. Please," she begs.

"I call bullshit, Sav. I don't believe you for one second. Please tell me what's going on, maybe I can help?" I'm still gripping her elbow when she pulls free.

Snapping, she yells, "Mike, I'm fine, just drop it!" Pausing, she lowers her voice and pleads with me, her voice wavering, "Please, Mike, *just drop it.*" She emphasises the last three words.

"I'm not happy but fine, just know I'm here for you, Sav. Any-fuck-ing-time, day or night." After watching her walk back behind the bar, I sit back down and finish my beer. Sav is avoiding me again and I'm frustrated as all shit. *Women are so confusing*, I think to myself as I finish my beer and head home.

When I get to my place, I grab a bottle of tequila, sit in my favourite easy chair, and catch up on the latest *Bold and the Beautiful* episode, but I can't concentrate. Sav is all I keep thinking about. After the best night of my life, she rejected me and became this different version of Sav: distant, vacant, and aloof.

Last weekend was beyond amazing, and now she wants nothing to do with me. I know I can be an ass at times, but I really thought Sav and I were heading somewhere.

I yell at the TV, "Fuuuuck, why are chicks so confusing?"

Grabbing the bottle of tequila, I sit back and try to come up with a plan to win over Sav, but I just keep getting pissed about the brush off that she gave me. I'm more confused than ever right now. I finish off the bottle of tequila before passing out in my chair watching *RAGE* on *ABC*.

I'm woken early Saturday morning by banging on my front door. Groaning, I slowly get up but hear two little giggles and I smile. Mac and Cheese have come to visit Uncle Mike.

Racing to the door, I open it to find all of the McRoberts clan standing there. My shitty mood instantly disappears and I smile. Reaching out, I grab Indi, *I think*, before saying, in the baby voice that you cannot help but put on when you are around kids, "Hey, gorgeous girl, how's my fav lil' munchkin?"

I head inside with Indi, *I think*, and the rest of them follow me. Kenz sees the empty bottle of tequila on the coffee table and turns to me angrily. "Mike Mustange, why is there an empty bottle of tequila on the coffee table? And now that I look at you, you're tequila hungover."

Sighing, I sit down and bounce Indi on my knee for a bit, trying to stall. "I'm waiting, Mike Mustange." Looking up I see her standing there with her hand on her hip. Jordan takes a seat next to me and mumbles, "Good luck, dude."

I can't help but laugh and this only pisses Kenz off further. Taking a deep breath I look up at her. "I've had a rough, shitty week, and yesterday after seeing Sav, I couldn't handle it anymore. When I got back here, I just needed to forget and de-stress. I thought a night with Jose was better than going out and screwing around."

"Mike, you've been down this road before, drinking is not the way to deal with things. Now, what happened with Sav?"

"Well, umm, we painted her place last weekend and we had a really nice time. It was fun and then after dinner and a few beers, we slept together."

Looking up, I see both Kenz and Jordan, open-mouthed, staring at me in shock. At the same time, they both speak.

Jordan says, "No fucking way."

While Kenz says, "What did you do to screw it up?"

"Thanks for that vote of confidence, Kenz. She is the one screwing it up. She's pushing me away. I really felt like we had a connection. Now I feel like she used me, and I feel like I'm being sucked back into the 'Mike is a chump' vortex."

"Well," she snaps. Looking at me, she sees how broken up I am, she softly adds. "Have you spoken to her, Mike?"

"I tried last night, Kenz, at the pub. She was working and we were chatting, but then the oddest thing happened and she ran off."

Jordan asks, "What happened?"

"We were talking, well I was, and then she froze, like she saw a ghost and ran outside. When she came back in, she was shaking and whiter than she was before. She told me she was fine and took off back to work. Then she did all she could to avoid me. So I left and came back here to have a party with Jose."

Kenz sits next to me, grabs my hand, and squeezes. "Mike, don't give up on her. I don't know Sav all that well, but I know she's hurting over something. Be the Mike that I know and swoop in and rescue her. You and her are meant to be, Mike, I feel it in my bones."

"I hope you're right, Kenz. I care for her deeply. When we had finished painting, we had a few beers and it felt so good to be with her. We opened up to each other, she told me some pretty personal things. To have her now act like this, I'm totally confused." Looking up at them, I confess, "I really like Sav, guys, like, like her. I haven't felt like this since before the she-devil." Pausing, I smile and add, "Actually, I've never felt like this about anyone."

Both Kenz and Jordan's mouths drop open in shock, and for the first time ever, it seems Kenz is speechless. Not wanting any more attention on Sav and me, I say, "So, what brings the McRoberts gang here today?"

They both are still looking at me in shock, and Kenz is still frozen, when Jordan says, "Well, we are taking the girls to the beach, and we thought we'd stop and see if Unky Mike wants to come, too?"

"A day at the beach sounds awesome. Kenz, you got any brownies?" I think to myself, *I would love for Sav to join us, maybe another time...I hope.*

"Not today, sorry, dude, but I did try a new choc chip peanut butter cookie recipe. Jordan has already eaten half of them, so I guess they must be okay."

Smiling, Jordan adds, "Dude, they are no brownie, but they are still pretty amazeballs. There is not much that my wonderful, hot, sexy, awesome wife can't do."

Raising my hand, I smart-assly add, "She can't walk without tripping over, but her cooking skills certainly make up for her unco-ness."

"Fuck off, Mike!" she defensively says, while giving me the finger.

Jordan scolds her, "Kenz, babe, settle down, he was only joking. What's up with your emotions at the moment?"

"I don't know." Sheepishly, she looks over at me. "Sorry, Mike. I didn't mean to snap like that."

"It's all good, babe. But can I say, that was hot seeing you get all feisty like that."

Shaking her head, smiling, she says, "You are totally weird. Now, go get changed, so we can head to the beach, before it gets too hot."

Getting up, I head down the hall and I hear Kenz say to Jordan, "I'm going to get Mike and Sav together, you didn't see them that night at the Dungeon."

Jordan whisper-shouts. "Stay out of it, Kenz."

As I'm changing into my boardies and singlet, I decide that I'm going to win Sav's heart, and I will do whatever it takes; including getting Kenz to help me if needed.

But first, I need to get to the bottom of her pulling away.

26

SAV

My life here was going so well and then stupidly, or amazingly, depending on how you look at it, I let go last night. Now it's all falling apart, why-o-why did I sleep with Mike Mustange?

I'll tell you why, he's a baldheaded, six-foot demigod, with a heart of gold. I was thinking with my vagina, rather than my head, that's why, stupid vagina. But it can't go any further, what if Uncle Kelvin finds me? I can't have him being collateral damage, I just can't.

It's moments like this that I really wish Jace was still here. He'd know exactly what to say and do. He'd tell me to pull my head out of my ass and go for it with Mike, because Mike is a good guy, and I deserve to be happy too.

What if Uncle Kelvin finds me?

What if Mike's in an accident?

I can't lose another person that I love, yes love. I am in love with Mike Mustange after one amazing night.

I just can't risk it!

While I'm sitting here contemplating what I'm going to do, there's a knock at the door. I freeze. What if it's Mike, back to confront me after this morning? When I hear them yell, "Hello, anyone home? I have a delivery for a Ms. Savannah Blac."

Sighing in relief, I get up and shout, "Coming," as I head to the door. Swinging the door open, there's a young delivery dude with a huuuuuuge bunch of lilies and ginormous box with a silver bow.

"Hi, are you Savannah?"

"Yep, that's me. Who's it from?" I ask excitedly. I've never received anything like this before.

"No idea, sorry. I'm just the delivery guy, where do you want me to put these and this?"

"Umm, on the table will be great."

He shuffles past me and puts the flowers and package on the table. Turning, he asks me to sign the clipboard that was sitting on top of the box. I sign and he leaves, closing the door behind him.

When I realise the flowers are lilies, I smile; lilies were Mum's favourite and they smell heavenly. Opening the box, I see that there is a six-pack of *Schofferhoffer* and a tub of *Skittles*. Standing there staring at the box, a strange feeling washes over me when I realise there's no card, which I find odd. *Why would I receive an anonymous package that has Mum, Dad, and Jace's fav things in it?* That strange feeling intensifies as I put the flowers in some water.

I don't need this right now; my life is confusing enough. I decide to have a bath, maybe it will relax me, and I will see things more clearly. The candles are lit, the wine is chilling, and the water is the perfect temperature. My iPod is charged and currently Everclear is singing about a heroin girl, and the bath bubbles are bubbly and smell divine. I submerge myself and try to relax, but I can't.

I can't stop thinking about Mike Mustange.

Every time I close my eyes, my mind drifts back and I see his head between my legs. Vividly, I remember the intoxicating feeling that overtook my body as his tongue lavished me and his hands massaged my breasts.

Taking a sip of wine, I close my eyes and try to relax, but once again Mike appears. With my eyes still closed, my fingers drift down my chest and over my nipples; twisting and pulling as they snake their way down to my pulsating pussy. I rub my clit in circles before slipping a finger inside. I place my wine glass on the ledge behind me and pull on my nipple with my free hand. My fingers continue to thrust in and out. I moan, "Mike!" as my orgasm hits and I slosh water all over the bathroom.

Opening my eyes, I see water splashed everywhere but I don't care. My body is still tingling from the most intense self-induced orgasm

I've ever had. *I'm so screwed*, I think to myself as I climb out of the bath. Drying off, I change into my sleep shorts and singlet before mopping up the mess that I made.

Climbing into my bed, I smile. It still smells like Mike and I drift off to sleep, once again, thinking about Mike Mustange.

This week is going extremely slow and my mind is all over the place. I keep stuffing up orders, dropping things, and turning up late or early. Mike is constantly on my mind. He has been into the Dungeon every shift, and I've tried my hardest to avoid him. For the most part, I have succeeded, but it's getting harder and harder to stay away from him. I have to remain strong.

On Wednesday, I received another bunch of lilies and once again, no note. This is really starting to freak me out, I wish I had someone to talk to, but I'm better off being alone. I don't want anyone to get hurt because of me.

It's now Saturday night and the Dungeon is packed. I'm rushed off my feet as Jodi, the bitch, called in sick. Understaffed, plus Saturday night equals bedlam at the best of times. Mike is here, again, and tonight is the night that he finally confronts me about last night. We didn't really get a chance to chance to talk properly after I thought I saw Uncle Kelvin, but thankfully, it gets busy and can again brush him and his inquisition off...for now anyway.

I'm not one-hundred-percent sure, but I'm pretty certain it was him. The uncertainty is what is freaking me out. I deduce that it wasn't him because if it were, he'd confront me; there is no way he'd hang back. He wants this more than life itself, so if he found me, I'd know about it.

On my way home after the shift from hell, I think about everything going on: mystery packages, Mike, Uncle Kelvin; what the hell am I going to do?

27

KELVIN

I'M SITTING IN MY FLEA-INFESTED MOTEL ROOM, DRINKING A CAN OF *EMU* beer, and I can't help but laugh. My surprise package should be delivered to the little bitch, right about now. It cost me a fucking fortune to send all the shit to her, but taunting her is going to be so much fun. Laughing as I get up to grab another beer, I think about her reaction. I so wish I could be there to see her face when she gets it.

It gives me ideas on sending other packages, but I don't want to waste too much money, or time, on this. This investigator already cost me a fucking fortune. *Thank fuck he came through though,* I think to myself as I grab another beer.

A few days later, I decide that I need to get out of this shithole. As I'm putting my shoes on, I decide to swing by the bitch's house and see if she got my latest surprise, but she's not home. It's late afternoon so I guess that she will be at work. My throat is a little dry, so I decide to head to the bar and see the little whore.

Seeing the shock on her face when I popped into her line of sight last week was priceless. I can't wait until I confront her face-to-face. This toying with her is so much fun, until I get what's rightfully mine, I'm going to play.

I've decide to up my game. I'm now sending daily anonymous notes to her. I've been leaving them at her duplex, on her car, and at her work; luckily she works with idiots and they are happy to take the notes whenever I drop by.

After dropping a note off at her place, I have to get out of there quickly as her friend with the kids turns up. I was hoping to see her face when she got this one, but I guess, it will have to wait for another time.

As I'm driving away, I remember how scared she was after the last attack, so I decide that another attack is in order. After I arrange it; I get a good feeling, this will be it. Soon, I will finally get what is mine.

28

SAV

I'M HIDING OUT AT HOME BECAUSE I'M TOO GUTLESS TO FACE MIKE, OR anyone, for that matter. It's fine, I have my books, tequila, and wine so all is goodly. I'm staring at the walls that Mike and I painted and become sad. I miss spending time with him, but I can't get close to him. I'd never forgive myself if Uncle Kelvin did anything to him. I'm now convinced it was him that I saw the other night, and I won't risk Mike getting hurt, he's too nice for that.

Sighing, I get up and think that it's WTF–Wine Time Finally–when there is a knock at the door. Pausing midstep, I try to pretend I'm not here but they knock again. I stay frozen on the spot, then I hear, "Open up Sav, it's Kenz. I know you're home." Pausing she adds, "I have wine."

Laughing, I turn and head towards the door. Swinging it open, I see Kenz's sparkling green eyes and a super big smile, her cheeriness and smile are infectious, and I find myself beaming back at her.

"Hey, lady, I thought it was time we hung out, it's been far too long."

"It sure has, Kenz, it sure has. Come on in."

Turning, I see a piece of paper poking out from under the front doormat. I bend down and pick it up as Kenz shuffles past me. I open the piece of paper and freeze. My hands start to shake and I gasp. Kenz spins around and looks worried.

"Are you okay, Sav?"

"Umm, yeah, it's all good, but I just remembered that I have an appointment to get to. Can we do wine another time?"

"Yeah, sure that's fine." She walks towards me and reaches out to rub my arm. "Are you sure you're okay, Sav? You're as white as a ghost."

"Yeah, nah, I'm fine. Just tired. I did close last night and didn't sleep very well when I got home."

Kenz hands me the wine. "Here, you keep this here for our catch up. By the way, the lounge room looks great. You and Mike did a really good job."

"Yeah, it came up so much better than I imagined. Mike's pretty awesome."

Smirking at what I said, Kenz says, "He sure is awesome. We will catch up soon." She squeezes my arm and heads out. Closing the door behind her, I lock it before sinking to the floor, wrapping my arms around my knees, hugging them to my chest, and I cry.

A few hours later, I'm still sitting in the same spot by the front door. My eyes are swollen from crying, my face is all mascara stained, *so much for waterproof,* and I'm stiff from not moving for a long time. All of a sudden, there is a thump at the front door; I startle with fright. As I stand to open the door, the hairs on the back of my neck prickle. I unlock the door, and I'm just about to turn the handle, when it's shoved open, and I fall back on my ass with a thud.

Looking up, I see a masked man standing over me; before I have time to move, he kicks me in the stomach. The pain is nothing like I've felt before; I curl into a ball to protect myself. He grabs my shoulders and pushes me flat, straddling my chest. Lifting his palm, he slaps me hard across the face and roughly grabs my chin. My face is tingling and I see stars from the shock and force of the slap, I begin to cry.

He gets right up in my face and spits, "This is just a warning, give him what he wants and you will never see me again. You don't want to see what I'm capable of." He slaps me again before standing up, looming over at me; he glares. "Remember my warning, bitch." He steps over me and kicks me in the hard in ribs again before walking out, slamming the door behind him.

Lying on the floor in agony, I continue to cry. My ribs are aching, it hurts to breathe, and my face is still tingling. The sobs overtake my body, and with each breath, it gets harder and harder to breathe; eventually I pass out from the pain.

It's the middle of the night when I wake up; the room is dark except for the streetlight shining through the front window. I'm still on the floor in the lounge room, but this time I'm numb; I cannot feel anything. I'm staring at the ceiling, feeling defeated when I realise I need to pee. Rolling to my side, I try to sit up, but I struggle. Every time I move, my ribs throb; at least my face has stopped tingling and it's less painful to breathe now.

Finally, I manage to stand up. The room starts to spin, so I stand on the spot, waiting for it to pass. Holding onto the door for support, I wait for the dizziness to pass. As soon as I feel okay, I slowly make my way to the bathroom. I go to the toilet and then wash my hands. Looking up, I see my reflection staring back and I don't recognise the girl I see.

She's broken.

Alone.

Ready to give up.

The tears start to fall again; I don't know what to do.

The night after my attack, someone knocking at my door wakes me; I recognise the knock as Mike's. It makes me smile but also sad at the same time. I lay here hoping that he will eventually go away, but he's a persistent bastard and keeps knocking. Groaning, I ease out of bed, cringing at my rib pain and yell, "Be there in a minute, Mike!"

He shouts back, "How did you know it was me?"

Smiling as I walk down the hallway, I hurry to the door. Opening it with a big smile on my face, I huskily say, "I know your knock. It's as unique as you, Mike Mustange." I wink and smirk, placing my hand on my hip.

He smiles back at me and then his face drops, "Holy shit! What happened to your face, Sav?"

Shit...fuck...shit, how am I going to get out of this? I think to myself. Deciding to go with a half-truth, I reply shyly, "Some asshole tried to mug me when I was coming home. He hit me, but I kicked him in the balls and he ran off."

"Fuck, Sav, why didn't you call me? I would have come and helped you."

"As you can see, Mike, I'm fine. Nothing to worry about. I was just about to make coffee, you want to come in?"

Turning to the settee on my verandah, he picks up a tray of coffee and a Java Lava paper bag. My tummy rumbles at just that moment, and we both laugh. He says, "Guess you're happy I'm here then?"

Without evening thinking, I reply. "I'm always happy to see you, Mike. Now, give me my coffee, asshole."

"Wow, you're just as much of a grump bum in the morning before coffee as Kenz is."

Laughing, he passes me a coffee as we both head inside to the couch. I wince as we sit, but I don't think Mike noticed, he and his banana bread are having a moment and I smile. "Should I leave you and your banana bread here alone?"

Midbite, he smugly replies, "If you don't mind, that'd be great."

Shaking my head, I just laugh at him. We sit here in silence and enjoy our coffees. Glancing over at him, I wish things could be different, but I now know that after last night's visit; there can never be a Mike and Sav. Mike looks up and sees me checking him out and he winks at me. Ovaries: BOOM.

Mike and I chat for about an hour, we have inched ourselves closer to each other, and he starts to rub circles on my thigh. It stirs my insides. I glance over and see him staring intently at me. Without even thinking, I lean over and kiss him.

His lips are softer than I remember, I moan as I slip my tongue into his mouth. Our tongues caressing, hands wandering over each other, he tweaks my nipples through my singlet and I run my hands over his smooth head. Wrapping my arms around his neck, I straddle his hips and deepen our kiss.

He groans as I rub myself on his growing erection. He wraps his arms around me, squeezing me tight, crushing my ribs and I flinch in pain. That's enough to bring me back to earth and I quickly jump off Mike. Looking down at him, I feel like a total bitch when I say, "I'm sorry, Mike, I...I shouldn't have done that. I...I think you need to leave."

He doesn't move a muscle; he sits there staring up at me. His eyes boring into my soul, I'm so close to saying fuck it when Mike stands up. He gets right up into my face and says, "Sav, you can keep pushing me away and I will keep pushing back. I feel something here and I know you do, too. I'm not going anywhere, babe, so you better get used to it." I go to interrupt him but he places his finger over my lips. "I'm not finished. I know you are hiding something and that something is big. But I want you to know, I'm here when you're ready to talk."

He gently brushes a tendril of my blonde hair behind my ear; his touch makes my body tingle from head to toe. He leans closer to me. I can feel his breath on my neck; it's warm and smells like coffee. Closing my eyes, I sigh when he quietly and seductively whispers in my ear, "I'm...NOT...going...anywhere, Sav." Bending down, he kisses my cheek, before turning around and leaving. He quietly closes the door behind him as he goes.

I'm left standing there, by my couch, in shock, panting and completely turned on. I really want to chase after him but I know I can't. I'm now even more confused than before...if that's possible.

The next week passes by in a blur. It's a continual cycle of work, sleep, avoid everyone; and repeat. Mike has sent me a text daily to see how I am; I reply with, "yep, all good" **inserting a smiley face or emoji**. He also sends me random funny GIFs; they always make me laugh.

Kenz has blown my phone up with texts, missed calls, and voicemails. I'm horrible and haven't replied to her, well that was until I received a text from Jordan, pleading with me to reply to Kenz. Apparently, she is driving him nuts. I messaged her, apologising about being busy and not getting back to her sooner. She seems to buy it when we make arrangements to catch up next week.

I'm dreading going into work tonight, I'm just not in the mood but I'm on with Jodi. She owes me an explanation for flaking the other week, not that I can be too mad because I have been all over the place the last few weeks. She has become a great friend and always manages to puts a smile on my face, so I'm sure it will be a good shift...if only I knew what would happen.

29

MIKE

I'm really worried about Sav, especially after her mugging. I'm so pissed she didn't call me to help her. Ever since, she hasn't been herself and it's not just because she's avoiding me. Normally she has the biggest smile on her face, and when she enters a room, the atmosphere immediately brightens. But lately, she seems so sad, broken, and despondent; not that happy Sav that we all love.

Each time I have seen her this week, I've tried to get her to open up, but she's shutting me out. She's been shutting everyone out, at least it's not just me. It seems all that she does at the moment is work and sleep. She never goes anywhere—yes, that sounds stalkerish, but I'm really worried about her.

I'm over at Kenz and Jordan's, and Kenz and I are chatting while we wait for Jordan to get home. I'm cuddling and playing with Indi and Rory - I still can't tell the munchkins apart, but they are so cute that thankfully cutie pie or munchkin works. We get onto the topic of Sav. "Mike, what's up with Sav?"

"What do you mean, Kenz?"

"Something is off, she doesn't seem herself at the moment. The other day, I went over to her place to catch up and have a wine. She picked up a note that was tucked under the doormat, and when she read it, her face went white and she made up some excuse about forgetting an appointment. She told me we would have to catch up another time. Whatever was in that note really freaked her out."

"She never mentioned anything about a note to me, but yeah; I have noticed that she's not herself. She was mugged about a week ago, so maybe she's just freaked out from that."

"Shit, that sucks ass. Why didn't she tell anyone?"

"Beats me, Kenz. We have kinda been on the outs since we slept together, and it hasn't gotten any better. But she seems different and not herself, that's for sure. " Pausing, I look over at her and add, "I really like her, Kenz. I know I said after De-Niece that I wasn't going there again, but I can't stop thinking about her. Her pushing me away has really fucked with my head. Maybe it's better if I just leave it be. Kenz, what if she's like De-Niece?"

She punches me in the arm, really hard. For a little chick, she has a wicked right hook. "Mike, you're an asshat."

"Why am I an asshat?"

"Oh My God! Mike Mustange, you are a total douchcanoe asshole if you think that about her. Sav is nothing, NOTHING, like that crazy, psycho bitch Barbie." She pauses then adds, "May she burn in hell for all eternity with her equally psycho cousin."

"Tell us how you really feel, Kenz. But I get it; I'm just freaked out. I told myself I was never going there again and when I do open up, it punches me in the junk." I look over to Kenz and smile. "But there is something about Sav. I haven't been able to get her off my mind since she started at the Dungeon. I find myself there most days, and if I don't see her, I get sad. When I do see her, my heart warms and I get all tingly and shit. Fuck, I'm turning into Jordan, I'm becoming a pussy."

"No, Mike, it just means you've met someone special, maybe even 'the one.' Your reactions are normal, Mike. You've never felt this before, and it's making your man bits all giddy, and your teeny tiny little brain doesn't know how to react to that."

"My man bits don't get giddy, thank you very muchly."

"Whatevs, Mike. All I'm saying is that you really like Sav and that's why you are freaking out. And you want to know a secret?"

"It's you, Kenz, you're gonna tell me regardless of what I say. So spill."

"I think she likes you too, but she's scared for some reason."

Snapping my head up, I look at Kenz. "Then why did she fuck and chuck?"

"I don't know, Mike, but you need to find out. Now, go and see what's up with our girl. I need another girlfriend and I kinda like this one."

"But you have Sarah."

"Something is up with her. She's doing a Sav and pulling away from me. I ran into Josh the other day, apparently they broke up."

"What the fuck?"

"Tell me about it. That was the first I heard, too."

"What did Sarah say when you spoke to her?"

"She's been avoiding me, BUT I guess if she and Josh have just split, then that would be why. I know what she's like. I'll give her space until she's ready...or until I can't stand it anymore, and I'll pin her down 'til she talks."

"Okay, well let me know if she needs anything. Can I ask a fav, Kenz?"

"Of course, Mike. What do you need?"

"Do you think I could steal Jordan for a guys' night tonight?"

"Of course, but on one condition."

"I'm kinda scared right now, before I agree, what's your condition?"

"Next weekend, can you watch the girls? I wanna take my man out for a night. It's been forever since he and I have had any one-on-one time."

"Ummm, if you have them in bed, and I don't have to change a shitty ass, I can do it."

"I can help with the sleeping part but I have no control of their bowels." She sweetly smiles at me.

"Fine, I'll do it. Lucky I love you, Kenz."

The front door opens, just as I say that and Jordan walks in. "Dude, why the fuck are you loving my wife...again?" He bends down and places a kiss on Indi's head before heading over to Kenz and Rory.

"Your wonderful wife is letting you off your chain tonight, and we are going to the Dungeon, guys' night. Then I'm on daddy duty next weekend, so you and your hot mumma can get your jiggy on."

Kenz shakes her head, and says. "And by 'get our jiggy on' he means dinner and a few cocktails."

I burst our laughing, "Kenz, darlin', you and 'few' don't go together...ever." I air quote few.

"Fuck off, Mike, I do so know how to handle myself. I'm a mum now and I'm totally responsible."

Jordan and I both start laughing. "Just like you were responsible the night I let you and him loose at the Dungeon, a few weeks ago. If I remember correctly, you fertilised the front garden, the verandah, and the bed."

"I blame Mike."

"Hey, don't blame me, lady. I told you Jose wasn't a good choice. But yeah, we totally had a great night, up until I got you home that is."

"Dude, you dropped her off and took off quicker than a fat kid inhaling a bucket of KFC. I had to deal with her drunk ass and look after Indi and Rory…for the next two days."

I'm in stitches listening to this. "Fuck, I love you guys. All right, asshat, the master has given you the night off. Go get changed and we will head to the Dungeon for a night of funness."

"Who died and made you boss?"

"Dude, I've always been the boss. You just haven't realised until now. Now go, I need to get my drink on."

Jordan looks towards Kenz. "Are you sure, babe?"

"Yep, all good. Mike helped me with the girls and I'm about to put them down. Fingers crossed they sleep through like they did last night. Ever since Mike said it, I've been looking forward to a quiet night. It's gonna be me, wine, Jerry, and Striker."

I look at her confused. "What flavour Jerry? And who the fuck is Striker?"

"Duh, Choc Chip Cookie Dough, and Striker is the hero in the book I'm currently reading. It's a book that Sarah recommended. Actually, Mike, you'd really like this one."

"Sweet, send me the link and I'll one-click when I get home."

"You are such a fucking girl, Mike. Grab a beer, I'll help Kenz get the girls down and then we can go."

"And you love me and my girlyness. Hey, do you have any of the beer?"

"And which beer would that be?"

"The new one that I really like."

"Nah, not at home. It's only at Malt Me. We could go there tonight, if you want to?"

I panic when he says this because I really want to see Sav. "Nah, it's all good. You probably don't want to go back to work; we can go to the

Dungeon. They have these amazing wings at the moment. I think you'll like them."

"Yeah, we are going there for the wings and not some hot, blonde bar bitch." *Fucker*, I think to myself. "Now pass me my princess so we can get our drink on."

I hand Indi to him and whisper, "She's not a bitch," before heading to the kitchen to grab a beer. While I'm waiting, I download that book onto my phone that Kenz mentioned, and I start to read while I wait. She's right, as usual; *Fractured Affections* is great. It's different and this Striker dude is awesome, just like me, and Reagan is a total MILF.

Tonight is going to be epic; I can feel it now.

30

MIKE

JORDAN AND I ARE IN A CAB ON OUR WAY TO THE DUNGEON, AND I START to get nervous when we pull up. I'm really looking forward to seeing Sav tonight, but I'm also apprehensive at the same time. I start to panic a little when I realise that there is a chance she won't be working. We walk inside and my eyes immediately scoot around the room looking for her. Glancing towards the bar, I see a sexy ass up on a ladder; two perfect buns encased in dark denim; I recognise that ass. My eyes roam up higher, and low and behold, it's Sav.

Smiling, Jordan and I head towards the bar. I adjust my dick but it's getting harder and harder, literally, as we get near. Up close her ass is just perfect, I totally want to bite that butt and sink myself balls deep into her tight hole. She totally looks absolutely stunning tonight.

She spies Jordan and me. I'm totally caught checking her out, and she nearly falls of the ladder when I wink at her. She carefully climbs down and walks over to us, just as the other bartender comes to take our order. She reaches out and grabs his arm, I'm jealous of the hold she has on him. "I got these two, Randy. Can you swap the Heni keg over, please? It just ran out." He nods and heads out back to change the keg over.

She smiles at us. "Hey, guys, what can I get ya?"

Jordan takes a seat and I stand, my cock is still at half-mast and I need him to go down before I can sit comfortably. *Think of Grandpa and*

Grandma doing it, I keep saying to myself. "Hey, Sav. Mike and I will have his usual, thanks."

She looks at Jordan apprehensively. "Jordan, you want a beer with a tequila chaser? I thought you and tequila go together like oil and water?"

I start to laugh. "No tequila for pussy boy, he'll take a black sambuca." I slap him on the back before looking back at Sav. "Hi, by the way." I feel like a bloody teenager, I'm so nervous around her tonight. My heart is racing, my palms are sweaty, and every time I look at her, my cocks twitches.

It's pretty full at the Dungeon tonight and tables are sparse, so Jordan and I decide to hang at the bar. Not that I'm complaining because it means I'm closer to Sav.

Sitting at the bar with Jordan reminds me of our college days and of a less confusing time in my life. "Dude, this reminds me of our college days."

"Yeah, it kinda does hey. What was the name of that bar we used to go to?"

"Umm, it's right on the tip of my tongue." I pause as I try and think, "Yep, I got nothing. Total mind blank."

"Naw, is your little brain struggling to remember?"

"Fuck off, asshat, you tell me the name then, Mr. I-Can-Remember?"

"Yeah, nah, I'm drawing a blank. How about we make a wager, person to remember first wins. Loser paying for tonight's drinks?"

"You're on, dude, prepare to lose."

We both spit and shake on it, just as Sav comes over. "Oh My God, you two are bloody gross." We both just shrug our shoulders at her.

"Yep." Jordan and I say in unison.

"Ugh, just wash your hands before you touch anything." Shaking her head at us. She add, "Can I get you boys another round?"

"That would be awesome, Sav. You sure you don't want to work at Malt Me? We could do with someone like you there."

"Thanks, but I'm happy here, Jordan. I'll get your drinks and be right back."

Just as Sav is sliding the shots across the bar, I shout, "Dirty Duck!"

"Fuuuuck, I lost...again." Jordan complains.

"Dude, you should know better than to bet against me. You think you'd learn after all these years."

"Fuck off, asshole, you can drink lime and soda for the rest of the night."

"Get fucked, asshat. Don't be a sore loser."

Jordan and I are having a great night and it is just what I needed… if only I knew what was around the corner.

31

KELVIN

TONIGHT IS THE NIGHT THAT I'M GOING TO LET THE LITTLE BITCH KNOW that I've found her, and I won't be leaving until she knows that I mean business; no more Mister Nice Kelvin. The attack was a bust, I was hoping that the thug I hired this time would have scared her shitless, but she seems to have grown a backbone since moving here. She just went about her everyday life as if nothing happened; that was a waste of fucking money.

The aces I hold up my sleeve, to get her to cave, are loverboy and her mummy friend. *This could get interesting and I like it,* I think to myself as I finish off another *Fosters.*

From my research, I know that she will be working this evening so looks like I'm off to the pub for the evening; at least the bitch works at a pub and this can be extra fun. I arrive before her shift starts so that I have more of a chance to hide myself. I want my reveal to be spectacular. I don't want the little bitch to see it coming.

Her bootylicious, bar bitch friend, Jodi, is working tonight, and I flirt up a storm with her each time she comes by my booth. What I wouldn't give to pound my cock into her, but I have other things to tend to first. A night with her can be my reward once I get what's mine.

Looking towards the bar I see loverboy and his friend take a seat at there. The sexual attraction between her and him is electric, but there's tension that's as thick as my cock. You could cut through it with a knife…the tension, not my cock.

Finally, I see Savannah go towards the bathrooms and head out back; it's now or never. Getting up from the table, I head towards where she went, my heart rate increases as I realise I'm about to get what's mine. *It's show time*, I think to myself as I walk across the bar.

Sneaking up behind her, I tap her on the shoulder. She jumps before spinning around. When she realises it's me behind her; the look on her face is priceless, and she's frozen on the spot. I seriously wish I had a camera right now. "Why, hello, niece."

"Wh…what are you doing here?" she stutters.

"I've come to get what's mine and I know you know what it is. This dumb, sweet, innocent act ends tonight." Pausing, I grip her upper arm tightly and between clenched teeth I spit, "I want it now!"

Pleading, she whines, "I have no idea what you want, Uncle Kelvin."

She is pissing me off with the innocent bullshit, so I slap her hard across the face, the crack echoing down the dark hallway. "Don't fuck with me, bitch." She's holding her cheek and begins to cry. "Your tears won't work on me. The solution is simple, Savannah, give me what I want, and then I'll leave you alone."

"Fine, I'll sign the stores over to you."

I laugh, a deep belly laugh, "You really are a dumb bitch. I don't want the stores. I want what your mother, father, and grandparents kept from me. You don't want to end up with the same fate as them, do you?"

She's staring up at me in shock. I don't think what I just let slip has actually registered yet. Roughly, I bend down and squeeze her upper arms again and begin violently shaking her from side to side, her head lolling about as I shove her out the back door and into the alley. "I will give you a week to give me what's mine, Savannah, otherwise I can't guarantee the safety of loverboy." Pausing for effect, I stare directly into her eyes and I sneer, "Or your hot mummy friend and her babies."

"No, please don't hurt them, Uncle Kelvin. Please?" Her begging is quite pathetic.

Slapping her across the cheek again, I get right up in her face and I spit, "Don't fuck with me, bitch, I want what's mine. You have one week."

Spinning around, I walk back towards to door I just came through, turning before I warn, "And don't even think about contacting the police, that will just make things much more dreadful...for them, anyway."

Opening the door, I step through, before closing it, I look back at her, quivering and shaking in the alley. Laughing, I declare, "And, Savannah, don't disappoint me." With that final remark, I slam the door and leave the bar, laughing on my way out.

32

MIKE

JORDAN HAS JUST LEFT TO HEAD HOME BUT I DECIDE TO STAY ON, HOPING to chat to Sav, as I haven't spoken to her in a few days. To be honest, I'm worried about her. She seems so sad, so vulnerable, even frightened at the moment. I want the happy, always smiling, makes me laugh, sends blood rushing to my cock, Sav back. Well, she still stirs my cock; she's always sexy, just sad and aloof.

Heading out the back for some fresh air, I take a deep breath when I hear crying coming from behind the industrial bins. I cautiously make my way over and crouching down, I see it's Sav. She lifts her head up, her cheeks streaked with black from her mascara, as the tears cascade down her beautiful cheeks. She looks broken and fragile, but most of all terrified. Taking a deep breath, with sad eyes, she whispers, "Please, help me."

Racing over to her, I bend down and pull her into a hug. For the first time in weeks, she doesn't pull away; she wraps her arms around my waist and continues to cry. Her cries increase into full-blown sobs, her tears wetting my shirt but I don't care. All I care about is making Sav feel better. I hold Sav in my arms for what feels like hours, but in actual fact it's only a few minutes.

She pulls back and looks up at me and smiles; her expression melts my heart. But her smile doesn't last long, her eyes frantically dart around the alley. All I can now see in her eyes in fear. "Sav, babe, what's wrong?"

"Ummm...I'm just having a rough night."

I scoff, "Rough night my ass. When I came out here you were beside yourself and you said 'please help me' when I approached you."

"Nnn...no I didn't. I said please leave me alone."

"Sav, don't lie to me."

She hangs her head and starts to cry again. After a few moments, she lifts her head and looks up at me. "I...I can't do this again. I thought I got away. I've got to get out of here." She tries to get out of my arms but I hold her tighter.

"Let me help you, Sav."

"No, I...I have to go."

Sav manages to get free and runs off. I'm standing there in the alley watching her run back inside the bar. *She may have gotten away from me, but I will help her, whether she wants me to or not.*

33

SAV

When I finally get home after my shift, I find Mike sitting on my doorstep. I pause midstep. "What are you doing here?"

He looks up at me; I see lust and confusion in his eyes. "I just wanted to make sure you were okay."

"Well, as you can see, I'm fine. You can leave now."

"Sav, babe, I'm not going anywhere until you tell me the truth."

"Mike, I'm fine. There's nothing to tell."

"You are not fine, Sav, don't bullshit a bullshitter. Now, I'm going to ask you one more time, what's wrong?"

"I...I...I'm not fine but I don't want to drag you into my problems, Mike. They are mine and mine alone."

"Sav, I'm not going anywhere until you tell me. If you like, I can call Kenz, and we both know what she's like. She won't let it go until she knows what's going on. It's your call, me or Kenz."

My heads snaps up, I believe that he would do that and Kenz is relentless when she wants to know something. Sighing, I look up at Mike and smile shyly. "Fine, come inside. I'll tell you, but you have to promise to not tell Kenz...or anyone, for that matter."

He crosses his heart and says, "Cross my heart, hope to die. Stick a needle in my cock."

Laughing, I shake my head and give up in defeat. "Fine, come on in and I'll tell you." Walking past Mike, I unlock the door, flick on the light switch, and walk inside. "Take a seat, I'll be right back."

To stall and wrap my head around the events from tonight, I head into my bedroom and change. Sighing in relief as I take my bra off, I hate wearing that thing, before slipping on a pair of denim shorts and a black singlet. After changing, I head back out, taking a deep breath I give myself an internal pep talk. *You tell him, he freaks, he leaves and then I can plan my escape*, all good. Repeating this over and over as I head down the hall towards Mike and the lounge room.

Halfway down the hall, I decided that this conversation needs tequila, so I stop and grab a bottle of Patrón, two shot glasses, and two beers before heading toward Mike.

Pausing midstride, I see Mike sitting on my couch; he is so ruggedly sexy; *I wish things could be different*, I think to myself. My girly bits start throbbing and I imagine him pinning me to the couch as he ravishes my body...again. He looks up and smiles at me, it shoots straight to my girly bits and my undies dampen. The throbbing between my thighs increases the closer I get to Mike. I shake my head; I can't be thinking of this right now, I have much bigger things going on. "This conversation needs tequila. I know you like tequila, so I didn't think you'd mind. I grabbed some beers as well."

"Wow, I'm kind of scared of this conversation if both tequila and beer are needed." Pausing, his eyes roam over my body, stopping at my tits before he looks me I the eyes. "Sav, I'm not going anywhere until I get the truth, so take a seat and tequila me up, baby."

Laughing, I sit next to Mike and pour us each a shot; I down mine and pour another. Passing Mike his shot, our fingers touch and I feel an electric spark between us. I know he feels it, too. He's staring intently at me, his eyes ablaze with lust; a reflection of what mine currently look like.

My breathing becomes shallow as we keep staring at each other. Breaking the connection, I look towards the window, staring at the curtains. *I can't be falling for Mike.* There is too much at stake, especially now that Uncle Kelvin has found me and I finally know what he is after. I can't and won't let him hurt Mike, or Kenz and the babies...or me.

Looking back up, I see Mike starting intently at me. "I'm waiting, Sav."

"I know, I'm just trying to decide where to start."

"The beginning is usually a good place."

"Fuck you, Mike," I snap, "This isn't easy for me. I thought I'd gotten away and now...now it's all gone to shit 'cause he found me."

"Who found you?"

"My uncle."

"What do you mean he found you?"

"It's all going to start again." The tears started to flow, "I can't do this for a second time, I barely survived the first." Mike reaches over and wraps his arms around me. I relax into him, it feels so good to be in his embrace, and now I'm even more conflicted.

He pulls back and looks into my eyes. "I'm confused, Sav, which is easy I know, but I thought you said you didn't have any family left after the accident?"

"I did and I don't. He's not my family, we may share the same bloodline, but that's it. He lost the right to be called family when he had those thugs attack me."

"What the fuck?"

"I'm gonna need another shot before I start." We both have a shot and I take a sip of my beer. "As I said a few weeks back, my world came crashing down eight months ago when I lost Mum, Dad, and Jace. What I didn't tell you is that after the will reading my uncle turned nasty. He'd come over blind, rotten drunk most nights and he'd ransack the house, looking for something. He'd always rant that I was hiding it from him, just like my parents; that I was a selfish bitch and so on. He himself never hit me but the verbal abuse was just as bad. One night, four people came to the house. They ransacked the place pretty bad, looking for it and...and one of them physically assaulted me." The tears start to flow again, taking a deep breath I add, "I ended up in hospital for a few days. I know he hired them to scare me, or for them to find what he's been looking, for but I had no proof." Taking another gulp of beer, I continue, "It was while I was in hospital that I decided I was going to leave. I made arrangements to sell the house, closed up everything, and here I am."

"Fuck me, what as ass. He's your uncle. He's your family."

"You're telling me. I also lied, Mike. I wasn't mugged last week. Someone came here and attacked me." Pausing, I look over at him. "I'm pretty sure he was behind the attack, too."

"Are you fucking shitting me, Sav?" Shaking his head, he's pissed, but I can tell, he's also worried about me. "What in the hell does he want?"

"I didn't know at first but when I was packing up to leave, I discovered what he was looking for. I've safely hidden it away again, as per Mum and Dad's request."

"What was it?"

"For your safety, Mike, I can't tell you. It's not that I don't trust you, but I can't risk Uncle Kelvin hurting you. He's had me attacked twice, who knows what he is capable of?"

"Let me help you then, I can call Officer Hamilton and she'll be able to do something."

"No!" I shout. "I don't want to involve anyone, especially not the police."

"You told me."

"Not by choice, had you not found me tonight, I never would have told you. Please just forget what you heard and forget you ever met me."

"Ha, that's not going to happen. I care about you, Sav. I want to help. Not sure what I can do, since you won't let me contact anyone, but I will do whatever is needed to keep you safe. The first thing I am going to do is get us another beer, have another shot, and then we will come up with a game plan."

Before I have a chance to say anything, he's in the kitchen getting our beers. I'm floored, I can't believe he wants to help me, be my hero, even though for the last few weeks, since Uncle Kelvin turned up, I've been such a bitch to him. Yet here he is, wanting to help, and he doesn't even know what I'm protecting or why. I watch him as he walks back into the lounge room and I smile. *Maybe I do need Mike Mustange on my team.*

He hands me the beer and pours us another round of shots. He looks at me and I can feel his stare all the way down in my soul. "Sav, I know there's more to the story, and I don't expect you to tell me everything now, but I hope that one day you will. In the meantime, I will do everything in my power to protect you. I can't explain it, but I'm drawn to you. I have this deep-seated need to help and protect you. Please, let me help you. Let me be your hero, Sav."

"Mike, no, I can't ask you to do that. My uncle is deranged and psychotic. He won't stop until I give him what he wants. Tonight he was scary; I have never seen him like that before. I can't risk him hurting you. I couldn't live with myself." Looking up, sadly I add, "Mike, as much as I want an 'us' there can't be an one, I won't risk you."

"Why don't you just give whatever he is looking for to him?"

"No! I can't!" I shout, "Mum and Dad specifically asked me not to in a letter they left for me. I will do everything in my power to honour their last wish."

"You are so stubborn but I understand why you are doing this. We will just have to come up with another game plan then."

Mike and I sit on my couch, drinking beer and tequila, and it feels good to just forget everything for a few hours. After three-quarters of a bottle of tequila, and a few too many beers, I'm feeling pretty tipsy. I look over at Mike and the throb between my thighs starts up again. *Fuck he's gorgeous.*

Without even thinking, I lean over and kiss him. His lips are silky soft, yet rough at the same time, he tastes like tequila mixed with beer, uniquely Mike. I love it and I moan. Gently, I run my hands up his chest, I can feel his heart beating; it's beating in time with the throb in my pussy.

Pulling back, I realise that he wasn't kissing me back. I look towards my lap, feeling like a chump when I mumble, "Fuck it." I straddle his lap, place my hands on each of his cheeks, holding tight, and crash my lips against his. My tongue seeking entrance into his mouth and this time he opens up, our tongues mesh together in a slow exotic dance.

After one of the most intense kisses of my life, I pull back and stare deep into his eyes. "Mike, I want this, I want us. You're right. I can't let Uncle Kelvin dictate my life. I **KISS** want **KISS** you **KISS**, Mike."

"What about what you said before? And Uncle Asshat?"

"Ha, Uncle Asshat, I like that. Don't get me wrong, I'm scared shit-less, Mike, but tonight, here with you, this here, it feels right." Smiling up at him, I continue, "You make me feel special and safe. When I'm with you the world around us ceases to exist and I absolutely love that. Will you have me, Mike Mustange?"

"Fuck yes, Savannah Blac, I'll have you any way I can." My face breaks out into the biggest smile. I'm staring at the gorgeous man in front of me and I could not be happier.

He looks deep into my soul, reaching up he gently caresses my cheek. "Right now though, I want you to wrap your arms around me and I want you to kiss me. Then I'm going to go home and let you think about all of this. I will be back in the morning, and if you still feel the same way as you do now, then I, Mike Francine Mustange, am going to make all of your dreams come true. Now, kiss me, woman."

Leaning forward, I wrap my arms around his shoulders and kiss him, quickly pulling back. I laugh, "Francine? Your middle name is Francine? That's the funniest shit ever."

"Yeah, it does suck, but it's a family name passed down to the first born. If you tell anyone, especially Kenz, I will go Al Capone on your ass."

"Whaaaat? Kenz doesn't know, how is that possible?"

"I'm just awesome, now, promise me you won't tell her."

"I promise, Mike Francine Mustange, your middle name is safe with me."

"Good, now kiss me again, woman."

Our lips crash together again and I'm lost in everything that is Mike; the world around me fades away. Mike and I kiss for what feels like hours but it is only a few minutes. I've never felt like this before; I'm scared and excited, all rolled into one horny, sexually, frustrated ball.

Rolling my hips, I feel his cock coming to life beneath me. I smile and start shamelessly grinding myself against his growing erection, moaning when it brushes against me. Reaching down, I stroke it through his shorts, but he grabs my wrist, halting me.

"Not tonight, Sav, I want you to be sure about this before I make love to you. You deserve to be treated like a princess. On that note, I'm going to go home and leave to you think about all of this."

I'm sad at the thought of him leaving, but I can see why he's doing it. I've completely changed my mind in the space of three hours, but I know that I want, no need. I need Mike in my life, and if this is what I need to do to prove to him, then reluctantly I'll do it. Mike is definitely worth the wait, what's another twelve hours anyway?

Grudgingly, I hop off his lap but he pulls me back down and kisses me again. He breaks our kiss and whispers, "Sav, I'll be back tomorrow morning, and I hope that you still feel this way. I've never felt like this with anyone before. I want you, Sav, more than anything. I want you to make sure this is what you want, because I guarantee that once your mine; you will never be alone, scared, or afraid of anything again. I will always be there for you, Sav, always."

"I want you too, Mike. I know I'm a hormonal, psycho bitch at the moment, but I finally know what I want, and it's you." Wrapping my arms around his waist, I get up on my tippy toes and I place a quick kiss on his lips before turning and walking to the door and opening it. "Now, out. I want you back here sooner rather than later."

Laughing, he walks towards the door and wraps his arms around me tightly and whispers, "You, my dear, are not a hormonal, psycho bitch. You are one sexy bitch, and I can't wait to make you mine tomorrow."

He kisses me on the cheek before slapping my ass and walking out the door. He's halfway down the front stairs when he turns and says, "Sweet dreams, Sav, think of me fucking you tomorrow."

Standing in my doorway, I'm left open-mouthed, shocked, and completely turned on. It's a struggle to not chase after him and mount him right there in my front yard. I watch him drive off before heading back inside and clearing up the empties.

After cleaning my teeth, I change into my sleep shorts and singlet. Grabbing my iPad, I start reading book two in the Affections series by Elizabeth Wills, *Mended Affections*. So glad that Kenz recommended this one to me. It's so emotional, but it's beautifully written at the same time, Elizabeth has a way with words that completely sucks you in and absorbs you.

Just as I'm about to turn the light off, my phone beeps with an incoming text.

Mike – *Nite princess. Can't wait to see you tomorrow*
Me – *Night handsome. I can't wait to ride you tomorrow, guess Buzz will have to do for now*

I giggle to myself at my teasing reply.

Mike – *Like hell you will. I will BUZZ the hell out of you you tomorrow with my cock ;P*

I laugh even harder at his reply and the throbbing between my thighs intensifies. *I can't wait for tomorrow,* I think to myself as I place my phone on the side table.

There is the biggest smile on my face, as I turn off the side lamp. I realise that I'm in love with Mike Francine Mustange.

34

MIKE

THIS PAST WEEK HAS BEEN ONE OF THE BEST. IT ALL STARTED WHEN I LEFT Sav's place in the wee hours of the morning last Saturday night, or Sunday morning...I never know with that shit. It killed me to leave, but I wanted her to be one-hundred-percent sure this is what she wanted. I couldn't handle being rejected again.

Sunday morning, I was back at her place at 10:00 a.m. When she opened the front door, she took my breath away—her bed hair was sexy, her sleepy eyes popped open, and they smiled. Yes, her eyes smiled, when she saw me, and her sexy mouth lifted into the biggest smile. Actually, I think she smiled at the coffee, but whatever, Sav is the sexiest woman I've ever met.

She invited me in and we sat apart on the couch, staring at each other, drinking our coffee, but not saying anything. The air was electric, neither of us quite sure how to act after our conversation last night. I know in my heart what I want, but I have to be cautious, I don't want to spook her. *I really want to be with Sav*, I think to myself as I take a sip of coffee.

Looking up, I see Sav staring at me and her smile is gorgeous. Running my hand back and forth over my smooth head, I say, "So, how you doing?"

"Did you just 'Joey' me, Mike?"

"Huh?" I look at her confused.

"Joey, from *Friends* he used to say, 'How you doin'?' when trying to hit on someone."

Laughing I reply, "Ha, he so did. No, wasn't my intention, but if it works, then hell yes, I'm 'Joey'ing' you."

Laughing she stands up, straddles my lap, and kisses me. Pulling back, she looks into my eyes and says, "You can 'Joey' my anytime, Mike." Leaning forward she kisses me again, I close my eyes and lose myself in this kiss.

The world stands still.

Everything around us ceases to exist.

It's just Sav and me.

I could not be happier right at this moment.

She pulls away and I feel lost, but looking at Sav, I see she is smiling, really smiling. I in turn cannot help but smile. Since I have known her, I don't think I have ever seen her smile like this; there is a spark in her eyes that I haven't seen before.

My cock starts to twitch; I start to feel embarrassed, but then I feel Sav ever so lightly rubbing herself on my growing erection. She wraps her arms around my neck, pulling me in closer, and kisses me with such force that our teeth crash together. Our lips are fused in one of the most emotion-filled kisses of my life.

Grabbing the hem of her of her shirt, I lift it over her head, and throw it on the floor. Raking my eyes over her chest, a low growl escapes my lips at the gorgeous sight before me. Her tits are covered in black lace and they look amazing. She smirks at me as she reaches behind her back and unclips her bra, lowering the straps slowly down her arms, before flicking it across the room.

Her tits were gorgeous encased in lace, but in all their naked glory, fuck me, they are stunning. Leaning forward, I wrap my lips around her nipple and suck it into my mouth, while pinching and rolling the other between my thumb and forefinger.

Arching her head and body, she shoves her tits further into my mouth, moaning in pleasure as I massage her breasts. Gently she runs her fingers over my head, groaning louder as I suck harder. "Fuck me now, Mike."

"Yes, ma'am."

She grabs my cheeks and stares deep into my eyes, "Don't." **KISS** "Ever." **KISS** "Call." **KISS** "Me." **KISS** "Ma'am." **KISS** "Again." **KISS** I don't get a chance to reply because all coherent thoughts escape me right at this moment. I'm mesmerized. Sav is striping off, clothes are flying across the room. My eyes rake over her naked body.

She reaches out to remove my pants and boxer briefs; my cock hardens further when I feel her fingers brush against my heated skin. She pushes me onto my back, lowering herself between my legs, taking my hard throbbing cock deep into her mouth and sucking; her tongue dancing around the tip. "Fuck, your mouth feels so good on my cock."

Sav mumbles something but I don't understand, as her mouth is full of my cock. Reaching a hand down, she starts to fondle my balls, while simultaneously grazing her teeth up my steel shaft. My eyes are closed. I'm close to coming when all of a sudden; I feel her pinkie pushing against my asshole. Immediately, my eyes dart open and I look down to see Sav staring at me. I'm lost in her beauty until I feel her edging her finger in deeper. Before I can say anything, I'm coming down her throat, her finger pushing in deeper, as I have the most intense orgasm of my life.

Once she has sucked every last drop, she kisses her way up my chest. Nipping my nipples before straddling me and kissing me deeply.

"That was amazing, Sav. I have never come so hard in my life."

She giggles before kissing me again. Pulling back she whispers as she starts to grind my cock. "I'm going to fuck you now, Mike."

Even though I have just come, my dick immediately springs back to life. Sav lifts up, and gently lowers herself over my shaft, taking it all the way to the hilt. We fall into a rhythm that feels like nothing I have felt before.

Reaching up, I pull her to me and kiss her deeply as she continues to ride my cock. Sitting up, she starts to ride me faster, sliding up and down. Her hands go to her tits and she starts tugging on them, it's the hottest sight that I have ever seen. We play with her tits together before she guides my hand down to her clit; together we tug and pull at her swollen nub.

"I'm close, Mike," she breathlessly says.

Increasing her thrusts, together our orgasms take over our bodies and we shout out each other's names as I come for the second time this morning. Once our orgasm has subsided, she falls on top of me. I wrap my arms around her, hugging her close to my body.

When our breathing returns to normal, she climbs off me, and snuggles into my side. We don't say anything, it's not awkward; it's perfect. In this moment, I realise that I have strong feelings for Sav.

We are lying in each other's arms on her couch, still panting from another marathon sexcapade when there is a knock at the door. We both groan, we don't want to have to get up but the knocking continues. Reluctantly, I get up, pull on my shorts, and head to the door.

Opening the door, I see that no one on the porch, but there is a box sitting on the doormat with 'Savannah Blac' written on the top. Bending down, I pick it up, and bring it inside, placing it on the coffee table, just as Sav sits up and pulls her singlet over her head. I inwardly sigh as her gorgeous tits are now covered, but she's not wearing a bra, so I can still see her nipples. As I sit down next to her, I reach over and give one a pinch.

Smacking my arm, she squeals, "Ouch, what was that for?"

"Just saying 'hi' to the girls, they look lonely and sad to be covered by your top." I pause. "I know for a fact, the girls love hanging freely in the wind."

"You're a fiend, Mike Francine Mustange, but the girls thank you for the attention. If you play your cards right, they might come out for a visit again very soon." She winks at me, before looking towards the box.

Scooting towards the edge of the couch, she opens the package and gasps. Inside there are empty packets of Skittles, empty beer bottles and flowers, torn to shreds. Sav immediately bursts into tears and wraps her arms around me. I pull her closer to me, hugging her tight and rubbing circles on her back to calm her down. Her sobs have now overtaken her body and she's shaking in fear.

She eventually calms down, grabs the box, opens her front door, and heads downstairs, disposing of the package in the garbage bins. She slams the front door behind her and sits back down next to me. Taking a deep breath, she looks towards me. "That was a package from Uncle Kelvin."

"What the fuck?"

"Those three items were Mum, Dad, and Jace's fav. He sent a similar package a few weeks ago, but this time he's shredded the flowers and sent empties. I can't trust a word that he said last night, and this just confirms my decision to not give him what he wants."

"Are you sure that's wise? He seems pretty fucked up, if you ask me. Sav. I don't want anything to happen to you."

"I'm sure, Mike. I promise I'll handle this." Jumping up, she turns to me, smiles seductively, rips her shirt over her head, turns around, and heads towards the bedroom. When she passes the kitchen, she asks over her shoulder, "Are you coming?"

Jumping up, I stalk over to her, wrap my arms around her waist, pulling her tightly against my chest and whisper into her ear, "You and I will both be coming very shortly."

She turns her head back to me and I kiss her. My hand sliding and tickling its way up her tight tummy before massaging her tits, tugging and pulling on her pert pink nipples as I increase the kiss. She turns around and wraps her arms around my neck, pulling us closer together. Our lips fuse in one of the most passionate kisses of my life.

My hands find their way under her ass and I lift her up. She wraps her legs around my waist and I make my way to her bedroom. As I lower her to the bed, I growl, "We are not leaving this bed for the next twelve hours. I'm going to make love to you and worship every inch of your body."

She shimmies out of her undies before seductively saying, "Well, what are you waiting for?" She pulls on her own nipples, closing her eyes, and moaning. Seeing her play with her tits is the hottest thing I've ever seen, and each time is hotter than the last.

Quickly I strip off my pants before jumping onto the bed next to her. Leaning down, I take one of her nipples in my mouth and suck, grazing my teeth along the tip before sucking it again. Sav's back arches, she grips the sheets tightly and moans, shoving her beautiful tits further into my face. I lose myself in her tits, her moans getting louder and louder, increasing the hardness growing between my legs.

Looking down at Sav, I line my throbbing cock up at her entrance and slowly enter the tip before pulling back out again. She whimpers each time I do this; she starts to lift off the bed and then I plunge my cock deep inside her. We both moan, her pussy clenching my cock as I thrust in and out.

"Ohh, Mike," Sav moans, "I'm close."

Picking up speed, I pump harder and faster into her. Before I know it, we are both tumbling over the edge, as our orgasms erupt. I'm grunting my release and Sav is quaking under me. I collapse on top of her, both of us panting, gasping for air.

Once our breathing has evened out, I roll off of her and she snuggles into my side. I wrap my arms around her, pulling her closer to me.

I start running my hands up and down her arm. I have never felt this content and happy.

We spend the rest of Sunday naked, lazing around together, eating Kung Fu Palace, and fucking like rabbits. It was the perfect day and the best way to end the weekend.

Sav and I have decided to keep our new relationship on the down low, for the meantime, well until we can come up with a game plan for Uncle Kelvin. It will be hard to keep my hands off her when we are around others, but she thinks it's safer this way, and I want her to be happy...I'd probably agree with anything to make her happy.

Personally, I think we need to call the police but Sav is adamant that this is not to happen. She wants to deal with this herself; man she is stubborn. Maybe I can covertly speak to Office Hamilton and get some pointers. It really bugs me that this asshole is doing this to Sav, but I will do everything in my power to protect her.

35

KELVIN

THAT LOOK, I KEEP PLAYING IT OVER AND OVER IN MY HEAD: PRICELESS. IT was pure shock when she saw me, I could not be happier. Well, I could be, if the little bitch would just give me what's mine. I've given her a week.

This morning, I dropped off another package, just before lunch. This time I stuck around to see her reaction, but that bald dude picked it up and took it inside. However a few minutes later, the door flung open, and she raced down to the bin and dumped it. Watching her, my smile falters, I realised that there was no fear on her face whatsoever. "Fuck!" I shout into the car. *I need to up my game. I refuse to lose what's rightfully mine.*

I'm really pissed off that she's not caving. So I decide that everyday until I approach her again, I'm going to send her packages. Deciding to send them to both her home and work, I'm going to rattle her until she caves.

As I'm driving away after arranging this week's deliveries, the best of the best ideas pops into my head. The little whore seems to be getting chummy with that baldheaded twat. Whenever he leaves her place, he always has a super big smile on his face. If she doesn't cave after my ultimatum, I know how I can get what's mine.

I'm an evil genius, I think to myself, phase two is perfect.

36

SAV

THIS WEEK HAS BEEN BOTH UNBELIEVABLY AWESOME AND AT THE SAME time, unbelievably shitty. Uncle Kelvin seems to have upped his mind games by sending me daily packages; to both home and work. I'm trying not to let him get to me, but it's hard. Luckily I have Mike on my team.

Mike has been over every night but he hasn't stayed over. When I'm around him, I'm happy. I haven't felt happiness like this since before Mum, Dad, and Jace died. I'm sad that they won't get to know and meet Mike, but I know they would be happy for me.

I'm not going to be seeing Mike tonight as he's watching the twins for Kenz and Jordan. Not going to lie, I'm sad but I'm also looking forward to a long soak in the tub, a block of *Cadbury's Snack Chocolate* and *Orange is The New Black* on Netflix.

Just as I'm heading to the bathroom to run the bath, my phone pings with a text.

Kenz – *Hey lovely. Are you free tonight to check in on Mike as he's watching the girls…solo*
Me – *No concrete plans. Happy to check in on him*
Kenz – *Thanks. Don't tell him I sent you*
Me – *Your secret is safe with me*

I do a happy dance as I head to my bedroom. An evil and sexy idea pops into my head as I strip off and get changed.

Forty minutes later, I pull up at Kenzie and Jordan's place, just as they are walking over to Jordan's Jeep. "Hey guys," I say as I walk towards them. They both turn around; Jordan's mouth drops open and Kenzie's eye pop wide.

Jordan wolf whistles and I smile. "Woo Woo, Sav. You look smokin' hot. Do you have a hot date tonight?"

My cheeks heat a shade of pink. "Maybe," I squeak out, thinking to myself that maybe this outfit was a bad idea. I'm wearing skinny jeans and a black deep V halter-top, which really makes my girls look amazing, and black wedge sandals.

Kenzie looks at me knowingly and walks over, wraps her arms around me, and whispers, "You and I soooo need to talk, I need the Sav and Mike goss." Pulling back, I'm shaking my head as if to say 'nothing is going on' but Kenzie gives me her 'Kenzie stare,' and I can't help but smile. I mouth, "Next week" and wink.

She turns towards the car, "Come on, Jor, let's go." She turns back to me. "We were just heading out but Mike's here watching the girls. If you want to say hi. I know you want Rory cuddles and I know they'd love to see Aunty Sav." I don't miss her smug remark.

"Are you sure it's okay? I actually came to see you too, Kenz."

"Yeah, I'm sure. We can catch up for coffee next week." Winking at me, she adds, "Just behave." *Bitch*, I think to myself as turn and head towards the front door. Taking a deep breath, I slowly make my way to the house.

My heart is erratically beating.

I'm nervous.

I'm excited.

I feel like a schoolgirl as I raise my hand and knock on the door.

37

MIKE

I'VE JUST CRACKED A BEER AND PULLED UP *BOLD AND THE BEAUTIFUL* ON the *Telstra* box when there's a knock at the door. Sighing, I pause and go to the door. Opening it, I'm left stunned when I see Sav standing there…she looks fucking hot. "Hey, gorgeous, what are you doing here?"

"Well, I heard you were babysitting, and I thought that you might like some company."

"I'll take any time I can get with you." Reaching out, I wrap my arms around her waist and kiss her. Our lips crashing, tongues entwining together, she moans into my mouth, and it goes straight to my cock. Pulling back, I look deep into her eyes. "We need to stop that, otherwise I won't be held accountable for what I do next, and I don't think the neighbours will appreciate what I have in mind."

Giggling, she steps past me and starts pissing herself laughing. Looking towards the TV, I see her staring at what's paused on the screen. *Ohh shit,* I think to myself, *how am I going to explain Bold being paused on the TV?*

"What's so funny?" I decide to play dumb.

"Ummm, you watch *Bold*?"

"Yep." I let the p in yep pop.

"Are you serious?"

"Yep, I'm not ashamed to admit it, well maybe to Jordan, but yes I watch *Bold* and I love it."

"Hmmpf, I would have pegged you as more of a *Days of Our Lives* fan."

"My Nana and I used to watch this when I was in high school and she'd come to visit. I got hooked, and after she passed away, I started watching it again, it's now my secret guilty pleasure."

"That's sweet but I'm totally telling Jordan, this is too good to keep a secret."

"Like fuck you are!" I yell and I must do it a smidge too loud as one of the girls cries. "Fuck. Wait here and I'll go and settle her."

Thankfully, Indi goes straight back to sleep after a quick back rub. When I come back out, Sav is sitting on the couch, sipping on her own beer and she pats the couch next to her. "Come here, spunky, and we can watch *Bold* together. I promise not to share your dirty little secret but it's going to cost you."

Sitting down next to her, I grab my beer and she snuggles into me. "So, what's it going to cost me to keep this secret?"

She glances over at me, "I haven't decided yet but I'll be sure to let you know when I do. Now shh, I bet Brooke is about to say something very really, super duper important."

"Don't sass Brooke, Sav. Or I will have to punish you."

Sav seductively looks at me as she leans forward to grab her beer, giving me a perfect view down her top. "Maybe I want to be punished, Mike."

"Ohh, when we leave here, you will be punished…with my cock… repeatedly…all night long."

"Bring it!" she huskily says, winking at me before turning her attention back at the TV.

Sav and I have a nice, relaxing night together, hanging out and watching the girls; seriously these two munchkins are the cutest babies in the whole entire world. We eat pizza, drink beer, and chat, getting to know each other better. Everything is comfortable with Sav and we don't once mention her uncle.

We end up making out on Kenzie and Jordan's couch, and we are so wrapped up in each other that we don't hear them come home. We don't notice anything until we hear Jordan squeal like a girl, "Ouch, fuck, Kenz, what was that for?" He rubs his arm right where Kenz punched him.

"Told you they'd be doing it when we got home."

We both immediately sit up, feeling like we've been caught by our parents. We look at each other and burst out laughing. I shift Sav off my lap; while Kenz and Jordan snuggle on the chaise together. Kenz looks at us, wiggling her eyebrows. "So, how was your evening?"

In unison we say, "Great!"

"Okay, you two, cut the crap, when did you…this happen?" She's spinning her finger in circles, pointing at us.

Getting up, I head to the kitchen and come back with four beers. After handing them out, I sit next to Sav and she snuggles into my side. I lean towards her and place a gentle kiss on the side of her head. Sav quietly sighs as I do this, garnering a "Naw!" from Kenz.

Sav snuggles in closer; I tighten my hold on her. She rests her hand on my thigh, and her finger runs back and forth, her touch causing my cock to stir; I can't help but smile.

Looking up, I see Kenz and Jordan are staring intently towards us. Jordan gives me a subliminal high five and subtly toasts his beer towards me. Kenz is bubbling with excitement; she can hardly sit still. "I'm waiting, guys. Spill. Now."

Sav and I both laugh at her enthusiasm and we give the *Cliff Notes* version of the last week, leaving out all the Uncle Kelvin crap. Gauging from the super big smile on both of their faces, I'd say that they are happy for us.

We have a few more beers with them before we call it a night. Sav decides to stay at my place, but first we swing by her duplex to drop off her car and get a change of clothes…not that she'll be wearing anything.

We get to her place and she quickly races inside. Feeling like a perv, I lean against my car, watching her as she skips up the stairs, and wolf whistle at her sexy ass, those pants mold to her perfectly. I can't wait to strip her out of them. She emphasises swinging her ass from side to side as she gets near the top of the stairs, and my cock starts to stir. She turns and blows me a kiss before she ducks inside. I have to adjust myself, as it's getting uncomfortable in my jeans.

I decide it's safer for me to wait down here if we are to make it back to my place. It's better that I don't go inside, otherwise we'd never make it to Casa del Mike.

I'm staring up at the sky and I realise that I'm genuinely happy, a feeling that I haven't known in a very longtime. I haven't felt like this since for she-devil and I know it's all to do with the hottie upstairs. I'm so lost in that thought, I don't notice a person coming up behind me.

Just as I register their presence, they whack me across the back of the head, and I stumble forward. Before I have a chance to react, they hit me again, and I fall to the ground. The last thing I see, before I black out, is a menacing figure standing over me, laughing to himself.

38

SAV

WHEN I COME TO, MY VISION IS FUZZY AND MY HEAD IS THROBBING, SO I close my eyes again. I feel like I drank an entire bottle of tequila and have the hangover from hell. "Ugh!" I moan. All of a sudden, my eyes flip open and I realise; I'm tied to a chair in a room, with newspaper covering the windows. The paint is cracking and peeling and it smells musty. My eyes wander around the room and they fall upon Mike, on the floor in the corner, his arms are tied behind his back and his legs are bound; I start to panic.

"Mike!" I shout but he doesn't move. I try to get to him but I can't. "Mike!" I shout again. This time he stirs and I begin to cry. "Mike," I blubber. "Mike, can you hear me?"

"Sav?" he groans and slowly opens his eyes. When he sees me strapped to the chair, his eyes pop open wide, and he tries to sit up but winces in pain. "Fuck, my ribs."

Mike rolls onto his side and winces again; he manages to get up into a sitting position and looks around. His eyes landing on me again. I burst into tears when I see the dried blood on the side of his face.

"Mike, you're bleeding. Are you okay?"

He stammers, "I...I...I don't know. My heads hurts like a bitch and my ribs, I think one's broken." Pausing, he looks over at me. "Don't worry about me. Are you okay, Sav?"

"I think so. What happened? Where are we?"

"The last thing I remember is watching your ass as you went into your duplex and thinking that I can't wait to get you back to my place. Then there's nothing until I heard you call out for me, just now. How about you?"

"It's all fuzzy, Mike. The last thing I remember to leaving Kenzie and Jordan's, everything after that is blank." The tears stream down my face and I start to hyperventilate.

The door to the room opens with a thud and I jump in fright. Looking up, I freeze when I see who is standing there. I whisper, "Uncle Kelvin?"

"Morning, sunshine," he says, as he slams the door behind him, again I jump in fear.

"What's going on? Where are we?"

He doesn't answer me, he just manically laughs. He walks over to Mike and stands on his wrist; Mike screams out in pain. I yell and plead for him to stop, but he just continues to laugh and press his foot down harder.

"Tell me what I want and I will leave loverboy alone."

"I...I..."

"Don't tell him, Sav," Mike says through gritted teeth.

Uncle Kelvin lifts his foot off Mike's hand, turns around, swings his leg back and kicks Mike in the ribs, repeatedly. Mike grunts in pain, wincing each time the boot collides with his side. I'm begging for Uncle Kelvin to stop but he keeps kicking Mike, over and over.

"Shut your God damn mouth, boy. This is a family matter."

"Fuck you, you psychotic piece of shit. When I get out of here, you are going down. Now let Sav go."

Uncle Kelvin ignores Mike and walks over to me. He leans on the arms of the chair, gets right in my face, his breath causing me to gag, and sneers, "Tell me where it is and I'll leave you both alone, it's up to you. I've got all the time in the world."

The tears start to roll down my face again. I look over to Mike; he looks like he's struggling to breathe. Uncle Kelvin grabs my chin roughly. "This can all be over in an instant, just tell me where the fuck it is."

I'm torn right at this moment, I want to honour Mum and Dad's wishes, but at the same time, I want him to stop punishing Mike. I can't speak; the sobs have overtaken my body. It only pisses him off further. He stands up and slaps me hard across the cheek, knocking me and the chair over. I land on the ground with a thud and see stars when my head hits the floor.

"Fucking stubborn bitch," he snarls, as he turns and walks out of the room. Slamming the door behind him.

When I come to, Mike has my managed to get himself free and untie me from the chair. My head is resting on his thigh, and he is gently running his fingers through my hair.

Smiling, I stare up at him, and for a moment, I forget about the hell that we are in. Then it all comes crashing back to me. I take in a deep breath and begin to cry again.

"Shhhh, don't cry, Sav, we'll be okay. I'll get us out of here."

"How, Mike? This is my entire fault. I knew I should have stayed away from you. I'm sooo sorry, Mike, so, so sorry."

"Shhhh, it's going to be fine."

"I hope so, Mike, how are we free?"

"Uncle Douche isn't very good with knots. I managed to wriggle and twist free." Lifting up his wrist I see that it's red, inflamed, and bleeding slightly.

"Ohh, Mike, your wrist." Lifting his wrist, I place a gentle kiss just below the redness.

He smiles down at me and whispers, "All better now." His smile is calming; I lay back down in his lap, staring up at him.

We sit there quietly for a few moments. I shuffle into a sitting position when I feel something in my back pocket. I realise that I have my phone. I'm thankful that my uncle didn't find it when he took us. Just as I go to tell Mike, the door crashes open with a bang.

"Ohh look, the two lovebirds are up." He marches into the room and grabs me by my hair, wrenching me off Mike, before throwing me into the corner. I brace for the impact but it still takes the wind out of me. He storms over to me and lifts me into a sitting position, squeezing my upper arms tightly, getting in my face he demands, "Have you comes to your senses yet?"

Mike yells, "Sav, don't tell him! You're strong, think of your parents."

He turns towards Mike. "Shut the fuck up, punk."

"Punk?" Mike taunts him, "No one says punk anymore, douche. Now leave her the fuck alone."

He stalks over to Mike, bends down, and pulls out his penknife. Flicking the blade out; he stabs it into his thigh, twisting it around.

Mike screams in pain, I scream for Mike and Uncle Kelvin laughs, a manic sound that grates through me.

Looking at Mike in pain, I start to uncontrollably sob. I knew this would happen and now the person that I'm in love with is suffering because of me.

Uncle Kelvin slashes Mike's legs and arms over and over, yelling. "Just fucking tell me!" I can see Mike is in horrendous pain and my heart is breaking, but I can't speak. I'm heaving to breathe and I feel like I'm about to pass out again, but I need to stay awake. Mike is being so tough, gritting his teeth, trying to not let my uncle see how much it hurts. He finally stops torturing Mike and as he stands up, he licks the blade clean while he stares directly at me.

I'm cowering in the corner, fearful that he will start slashing me next; the tears continue to flow down my cheeks. He points the knife at me. "I'll give you one more chance, you little bitch, tell me what I want or next time the cuts won't be so gentle." Pausing, he walks over, squats down in front of me, grips my chin roughly, and says in a calm, menacing voice. "And then you will be responsible for his demise." He pokes me in the chest as he says this, before getting up and slamming the door on his way out.

Immediately, I crawl over to Mike. Ripping my shirt off, I wipe at all the cuts and then I wrap it around his leg where he dug the knife in to try and stop the blood flow. I get the improvised tourniquet tied and wrap my arms around Mike. "I'm so sorry, baby. I will fix this, I promise."

He wraps his arms around me and pulls me closer, flinching as he does. "For a short fucker, he sure is strong," Mike says. I sit cross-legged next to him when I remember the phone in my pocket. I look over my shoulder to make sure the door is closed and I slip it out.

Mike's eyes widen and he encourages me with his eyes. He whispers, "Text Kenz to contact Kelly."

Sav – *Help us Kenz. Text Kelly. We are in trouble*

Immediately my phone rings but thankfully it was on silent. I quickly answer and don't give her a chance to talk, "Kenz, I can't explain but Mike and I need help. He says Kelly will be able to track and find us, please hurry."

For the first time ever, Kenz doesn't argue or ask questions. She says okay and be safe before hanging up.

Just as I have put my phone back in my pocket, the door swings open again but he doesn't come in. He throws two bottles of water towards us and then slams the door shut again.

Mike and I sit there staring at the bottles of water. I'm beyond parched but I'm not game to eat or drink anything that he gives us. Who knows what it will be laced with?

The day continues along same path; he comes barreling in, threatens me, tortures Mike. I've almost caved so many times, but each time I go to speak, Mike steps in and stops me.

Mike looks like he is about to pass out, and I decide that the next time I'll tell him. Mum and Dad will understand; I can't let this go on. No sooner have I finished that thought, the door once again slams open, and I think, *it's now or never.*

39

KELVIN

THIS COULD NOT BE GOING ANY BETTER. I GET TO TORTURE LOVERBOY, AND I can see that I'm slowly breaking down her walls. She will be telling me exactly what I want to know, in no time at all.

This torturing gig is actually fun, tiring but fun. I was shocked at how easy it was to stab into his flesh. I thought the knife would struggle but it slid in so easy. Surprisingly, it was harder nicking his arms and legs. Her screams spurred me on, though. I'm impressed at how tough this bastard is, he never passed out once.

Deciding to play with them, I open the door and stand there. The late afternoon sunlight shining behind me, leaves me as an ominous figure in silhouette. After staring at them, I toss a couple bottles of water into the room. I don't say a word; the only sound is the bottles hitting the concrete floor. Neither of them moves, they just cower and huddle in the corner together, pussies.

She looks frightened and he doesn't look too well at all; his face is pasty and he looks like he has a fever. That makes me smile and I know it won't be long until I get what I want. Tuning my back on them, I slam the door and snicker as I walk away.

I'm sitting in the adjoining room, watching a movie, and I start to cackle to myself. If only dear old sissy could see me now, she would be rolling over in her grave; this makes my laughs increase. If she had just given me what I wanted in the beginning, none of this would have had to happen; she'd still be alive and I could be sitting on a beach in Thailand. *Soon that can happen,* I think to myself, as I laugh and laugh.

Jumping up, I decide that I've had enough of this shit, I don't want to wait any longer. I'm going to end this once and for all. I'm determined to get the location and finally I will get what is mine... nothing will stop me now.

40

MIKE

Sᴀᴠ ᴀɴᴅ I ʜᴀᴠᴇ ʙᴇᴇɴ ʜᴇʀᴇ ꜰᴏʀ ᴡʜᴀᴛ ꜰᴇᴇʟꜱ ʟɪᴋᴇ ᴅᴀʏꜱ, ʏᴇᴛ ɪᴛ'ꜱ ᴏɴʟʏ ʙᴇᴇɴ half a day. I'm hoping and praying Kenzie gets the message to Kelly; I'm not sure how much more I can withstand. All I know is that I have to be strong for Sav. We are huddling in the corner, staring at the water bottles. I really want to drink that water but I'm pretty sure he has laced it with something, and I need to stay awake and alert if I'm to protect her.

She is starting to shake from fear; I wrap my arm tighter around her, even though the cuts hurt like a bitch every time I move. I'm rubbing her arm gently, hoping to sooth her. "Hey, Sav, did you know that when I was little, I used to think that at night time, sharks would swim through the pool filter and into our pool?"

She pulls away from me, totally confused. "What?"

"When I was little, I used to think that sharks…"

"Yeah, I heard that but why in the hell are you telling me that?"

"I wanted to take your mind off this, and that's the first thing that came to mind."

Laughing, she says, "Well, when I was little I used to call my elbow an oboe."

"Well, I used to call the fire trucks, firefucks and I'd shout out at the top of my lungs 'Look, Mum, a firefuck' whenever I saw one. She was so embarrassed and would cover my mouth if we saw one."

"I bet you were a total shit of a kid." I just stare at her and smile. "I take from your nonanswer that I am correct." She pauses and adds, "I was a complete..." But she doesn't get a chance to answer because Kelvin kicks open the door and barges into the room.

Looking up at him, I see he has a gun in his hand and it's pointed directly at Sav. My heart literally stops beating, and I reach out to grab Sav's hand; she is now shaking uncontrollably.

"You ready to talk, bitch?"

I push Sav behind me to try and protect her.

"Ohh, how sweet, loverboy is trying to protect you. It won't do any good, though. As soon as I get the location and get what's mine, there's a bullet for each of you in here. Now, last chance, bitch, where the fuck are they?"

Sav is still behind me and she has completely zoned out, she looks catatonic, just staring into space, tears pouring down her face. My heart is breaking for her.

Kelvin shoves me out of the way and slaps Sav across the face, but she still just stares into space. I land with a thud and the pain in my thigh from the gouge is unbearable. Blood immediately starts pouring down my leg as the wound opens up. I manage to pull myself up onto my knees, just as Kelvin points to gun towards Sav's head. I yell, "Noooooooo!" and I charge for him, knocking him over, the two of us crashing to the floor.

The gun slides across the cement and lands just near the door. I scramble over to get it, but Kelvin jumps on my back and slams my head into the concrete a few times. I start to see stars and feel like I'm about to pass out.

He climbs off me and grabs the gun, pointing it at Sav once again. "Last time, bitch, where's my gems?"

Sav is still staring into space and this only pisses him off further. He takes a step closer when we hear a noise in the other room, and someone yelling "Police!" He looks towards the door, confused. While he is preoccupied, I take the chance and jump up; Kelvin turns and fires the gun.

BANG!

The last thing I hear as we both crash to the ground is Sav screaming my name, and then darkness takes over me.

41

SAV

It's been three days since we were rescued.

It's been three days since Uncle Kelvin was arrested.

It's been three days and Mike has yet to wake up.

When Mike charged my uncle, he pulled the trigger, and Mike was shot in the shoulder. The bullet went straight through but he lost a lot of blood, and he lost consciousness. They managed to stop the bleeding, but he won't wake up.

I've been by his bedside for the past three days, and I won't be leaving until he wakes up, and I know he's okay. Kenz and Jordan have been by daily, but it's hard for them to stay with the girls. They keep trying to get me to go home, but I'm not leaving Mike. He's here because of me. I told myself that this would happen and now he is unconscious, lying in a hospital bed...because of me.

I knew Uncle Kelvin was a psychotic dickwad but I didn't realise how psycho he really was. Turns out, he was behind the 'accident' that killed Mum, Dad, and Jace. He also admitted that he hired the thugs back home and here to scare me. He was pissed off that everything was left to me when they died. Little does he know, that even if I had died too, Mum and Dad never left him the gems anyway. All belongings were to be auctioned off and the funds donated to the Heart Foundation. Either way, he was screwed.

I get satisfaction knowing that he will be rotting in jail until his trial, and for the rest of his miserable life. He has officially been charged with the murder of Mum, Dad, and Jace, two counts of kidnapping, kidnapping causing grievous bodily harm, and for orchestrating the attacks on me.

That gives me comfort, but I will be much happier when Mike wakes up. What I wouldn't give to see his beautiful blue eyes staring back at me, followed by him saying something really inappropriate.

"Please wake up, Mike," I whisper.

Resting my head on the edge of his bed, I grab his hand and squeeze it, like I have for the past three days, and I start to cry, again. Deep down I knew this was going to happen, and now that it has, I feel terrible.

"This is all my fault, it should be me in this bed." The tears overtake my body. "Please wake up, Mike." **SOB**. "I'm so, so sorry." **SOB**. "I love you, Mike." **SOB**. "Please don't leave me." **SOB**.

"I love you too, Sav."

My head shoots up and I see his bright baby blue eyes staring at me, and I start to cry again. "Mike, you're awake. Thank God!" Jumping up, I wrap my arms around him, and I feel him wince in pain. I quickly pull away and sit back down. Grabbing his hand, I squeeze it tight, he squeezes it back and I start to cry again. "I'm so sorry this happened to you, Mike. This is all my fault."

"Shhhh, babe, don't cry. It's not your fault, but can you fill me in on what happened? The last thing I remember is dickwad pointing a gun towards you."

Before I get a chance to tell him what happened, the nurse comes into the room. She asks me to leave so she can assess Mike. I head out into the corridor just as Kenz, Jordan, and the girls arrive. I run up to Kenz. "He's awake!" I smile and shout.

"Ohh, thank God for that," Kenz says in relief as she hugs me, and Indi pokes her finger up my nose. I laugh, "Hello to you, too, gorgeous." I turn and give Jordan and Rory a hug, too. "The nurse is in with him at the moment."

We all take a seat in the corridor while we wait. It's awkward, I feel like they are judging and blaming me; I don't blame them really. It is entirely my fault.

Now that Mike is awake, I'm really nervous to be around him and his friends. I know he said he loves me too, but he's high on drugs right now. I know he hates me. This all happened because of me. The awkwardness is killing me, so I quickly jump up and tell Kenz and Jordan that I have to go. Before they can protest, I turn and run down the corridor.

By time I get to my car, the tears are pouring down my face and I'm a sobbing mess. Sliding down the side of my car, I cry uncontrollably, wrapping my arms around my knees, hugging myself. The tears finally subside and I contemplate going back inside, but I can't face them, not yet. I need time to wrap my head around everything, but most of all, I need to figure out how to say goodbye to the only man I have ever loved.

MIKE

When I wake up, Sav is resting her head on my bed crying. I hear her say she loves me; it makes me all warm and fuzzy to hear that so I whisper back, "I love you too, Sav." Her head shoots up and her face is broken, but she has a big smile on her face. She throws her arms around me and it hurts like a motherfucker, that's when I realise I'm in a hospital bed. My shoulder hurts just as badly as my leg does, but before I can get any answers the nurse walks in.

Before I know it, Sav is gone and I'm being poked and prodded. The nurse tells me that I was shot and have been unconscious for the past three days. *Three days, fuck me.* Thankfully everything seems to be healing fine and there shouldn't be any permanent damage. Just before she leaves she says that the doctor will be along soon.

As she is leaving, I ask her to send Sav back in. She quietly closes the door and I close my eyes again. When I hear the door open and I look towards the door smiling, my smile falters when I see Jordan and Kenz walk in, sans Sav.

"It's nice to see you awake, Sleeping Beauty," Jordan says, and he comes over to the bed and takes a seat.

Kenz walks around to the other side. "I'm so glad you're okay, Mike, you gave us all quite a scare."

I'm not really listening as I'm still staring at the door, waiting for Sav to come back in. "Where's Sav?"

Kenz and Jordan look between themselves warily when Kenz tells me, "Umm, she left."

"The fuck?" I realise they have the twins with them. "Sorry, munchkins, what the fire truck? Did she say if she's coming back?"

"Sorry, Mike, she didn't say anything."

I'm gutted that she left without saying goodbye, and if I know Sav, which I'm pretty sure that I do, she will be blaming herself over this. Now she's going to shut me out. *Well, I don't think so, love, I've worked too hard to get you to open up and let me in.* I know without a doubt; we are meant to be together. I will do everything in my power to prove that to Sav, I feel it in my bones. Now that Uncle Asshat is out of the picture, there's nothing stopping us. Speaking of Kelvin. "What happened to Uncle Douche?"

"Well, he shot you and he's currently rotting in jail." Pausing, Kenz adds, "It also turns out that he was responsible for the car accident that killed Sav's family, so he's being charged with that, too. Kelly and Officer Ferguson will be by later to talk to you and get your statement."

"Crikey dick. No wonder Sav is freaking out. How is she?"

"She's pretty upset up and confused right now, Mike."

Jordan adds, "I can't imagine how she's feeling right now. Knowing your uncle killed your family then he almost killed you, too. And all over a handful of rare gems."

"So, that's what he was after. Sav would never tell me, she said it was safer that way." A light bulb goes off in my head. "Is she Savannah Blac from the Blac Family Jewelers chain?"

They both nod. "Yep, that's the one dude," Jordan says.

Kenz adds, "Your girlfriend is the sole owner of the second biggest jewelry chain in Australia. Her family is jewelry royalty in this country." She looks to Jordan and then continues, "The gems that her uncle wanted are really rare and have been passed down for generations. He wanted them to sell and clear a massive gambling debt. Hence, trying to bump everyone off."

"Fuck! What a bastard. Kenz, I'm going to need your help."

"Sure, anything, Mike, you know that. What do you need?"

"I need you to help me win Sav back. I know her and she's going to pull away because she feels guilty for what happened to me. I'll bet my left nut, she feels fuckin' guilty that she survived and her family didn't. She's going to push everyone away and take off, again. I can't let her leave." I try to sit up, so I can get out of bed to go and see her, but the pain in my shoulder is unbearable. "Fuck!" I wince in pain.

"Kenz, please go to Sav. Make sure she doesn't do anything stupid and rash. See if you can get her to come and see me. I need to see her." Quietly, I add, "I love her."

Both Kenz and Jordan's mouths pop open in shock and in unison they say, "Fuck me dead said Foreskin Fred."

Kenz is still frozen in shock, when Jordan says, "I knew you liked her, but love her, wow, Mike. I thought after the she-devil you would never love another."

"I know, right? But there is something about Sav, I think I knew it from the first time she served me at the Dungeon. The first time I saw her, I knew she was it for me. She's special and I will do anything to keep her here."

…I remember the first day I saw her. It was a Tuesday night, and as usual, I was sitting at the bar throwing back tequila with a beer chaser when she walked in. The rest of the room faded away and the lights behind the bar bathed her in a beautiful glow. My God she was stunning. She looked over towards me and smiled; my heart melted. Then our eyes locked for the first time and it was magical. I could feel her stare deep within in my soul and it warmed me. She smiled at me again and I couldn't help but smile back. I'm pretty sure we both felt a magnetic pull in that moment.

I was done for, and even though I had sworn off women, I knew in that moment that I needed to get to know this angel. After that night, I found any excuse to go to the Dungeon, and if I didn't see her, I felt empty. Even if I just saw her in passing and we didn't chat, it was enough to keep me going until the next time.

I think I was in love with her from our first meeting.

"Naw, Mike's, in loooove." Hearing Kenz say that pulls me back into reality. I look over at her and she is smiling at me like the cat that caught the canary. "Told you, you'd find the one. Now, let's come up with a game plan to keep our girl here."

I knew I could count on Kenz. It's time to win over my girl!

"Please, Kenz," I plead. "I can't lose her."

43

SAV

It's been five days since shit went down with Uncle Kelvin, and it's been two days since I've seen Mike. I feel so guilty for all that happened to him so I have stayed away. I just wish that I had followed my gut instinct and kept to myself. If I had, then Mike would not be lying in a hospital bed, recovering from being tortured and shot.

Rolling over in bed, I sigh. I guess, the only positive about this is that Uncle Kelvin is behind bars...where he belongs. I was devastated to learn that he was behind the car accident that killed my family, all because he wanted the family gems. I can't believe this all happened over a handful of jewels.

Climbing out of bed, I head towards the kitchen for a much-needed cup of coffee. Entering my kitchen I sigh, coffee reminds me of Mike, and thinking of Mike reminds me that due to my family, he's currently in a hospital bed. At that thought, a lone tear falls down my cheek and I whisper, "I'm so sorry, Mike."

Wiping away the tear, I grab my mug, make my coffee, and I decide to head to my front patio to drink my steaming hot cup of goodness and bask in the morning sun; this patio was one of the reasons that I chose this duplex. Just as I sit down, my phone pings with a text.

Mike – *Morning gorgeous*

His text makes me smile but at the same time it breaks my heart. I sit here for ten minutes staring at the screen, typing and deleting, typing and deleting, before finally deciding on what to send him.

Sav – *Morning. Hope you're feeling better **insert photo of my coffee on the patio***

Smiling to myself at sending the pic because I know that Mike hates hospital coffee. *I'm such a bitch*, I giggle to myself as I sip my coffee. Immediately I get a text back.

Mike – *Hope it's scorchin hot…like you*

His reply makes me smile, genuinely smile, and for the first time since it all happened, I feel happy.

It's amazing how Mike has that effect on me, and I like it. But before I take my next breath, reality comes crashing down on me, and I realise the he is currently in hospital because of me…me. As I finish my coffee, I decide that I have to face Mike. I can't keep hiding…even though I love it here in my Sav bubble.

Quickly I shower and change into my denim shorts and white singlet, which I know that Mike likes. I jump in my car and head to the hospital. Along the way, I see Java Lava and decide to stop in to get four coffees, three brownies and one banana bread; I know that Kenz and Jordan will be there, too.

Twenty minutes later, I pull up at the hospital…next to Jordan's Jeep. Smiling to myself when I realise that I know Mike and his friends so well. *It will be hard walking away from them all.*

Grabbing the tray of goodies, I head into the hospital. I'm walking down the corridor towards Mike's room when I see Jordan. He is in the hall trying to soothe Indi. Reaching out, I touch his shoulder and he jumps in fright. Indi groans, and then snuggles back into Jordan.

"Shit, Sav, you scared the crap out of me."

"Sorry, Jordan." I pat Indi on the head and feel she has a bit of a temp, "Is she okay?"

"She's teething at the moment. Today she has a slight temp and is a little grumpy. She's a bit like the patient in there but I'm pretty sure, you are just the medicine that he needs."

Butterflies flap in my stomach when I hear Jordan say this. "How's he doing?"

"He's being a douche again, so I'd say he's back to normal. All going well, he'll be home by the weekend."

"That's awesome. About the home, not the douche part, but then if he wasn't a douche we'd think something was wrong."

"That's true, I wouldn't change him for the world, douchness and all."

We both laugh as I pass him a coffee. "There's also a brownie."

"You're awesome, Sav. Thanks. Go on in and see our patient, he will be happy to see you."

"Thanks, Jordan. See you soon."

Turning, I take a deep breath before hesitantly knocking and slowly pushing the handle down and nudging the door open. When I walk in, both Mike and Kenz look over at me.

Kenz smiles at me, stands up, and walks over to me, with Rory sound asleep in her arms. She gives me a one-armed hug. "Hey, lovely lady," she says and kisses me on the cheek. Grabbing a coffee from the tray, she quietly says, "I'm going to check on Jor, back in a sec." She winks at me as she quietly closes the door. I know she doesn't care about Jordan, well she does, but at the moment she just wants to give us some privacy.

Looking towards the bed, I see that Mike is staring at me intently, his gaze wandering over my body. Pausing at my boobs, before he looks directly into my eyes. The corner of his lips lifts into a sexy grin; his stunning blue eyes are bright and filled with desire and lust. The butterflies from before take flight again, and a slight pink tinge over-takes my cheeks.

"Hey, Mike," I shyly say as I walk over to the bed, placing the coffee and food bag on the bed trolley.

"Hey, gorgeous." Leaning forward he grabs a coffee and looks in the bag. "What do we have here?" He pulls out the brownies and banana bread and groans in delight. "Oh My God! Sav, you are the best. I've been dying, the coffee here tastes like piss and the food is total horseshit. This here, is the best thing anyone has ever bought me." Taking a sip, he moans, looks back to me, and smiles. "Thanks, you have saved my life, Sav." We both start laughing.

Suddenly I remember that he's in a hospital bed...because of me. I stop laughing and look directly at him. Seriously I say, "If it wasn't for me, you wouldn't be drinking piss flavoured coffee, eating shitty food, or be lying in a hospital bed." Tears begin pouring down my face. Through my sobs I manage to say, "It's because of me you're here." **SNIFF** "I'm so so sorry, Mike."

Climbing out of bed, he walks over and wraps his arms around me, hugging me close to his chest. He whispers quietly, "Shhhh."

Rubbing my back in circles to soothe me, he pulls back, placing a hand on each of my cheeks and directs my gaze towards him. "Sav, listen to me. I'm only going to say this once." Pausing for effect, he continues, "It's not you fault, Sav." I try to interrupt him but he shakes his head side to side and places a finger over my lips to silence me. "I do not blame you, if anything I feel like I failed you. I should have protected you better."

Hearing him say that, the floodgates open and I wrap my arms around him. He squeezes me back, and I cry into his shoulder until the door opening interrupts us. Kenz and Jordan come back in and they pause midstep at seeing me falling apart in Mike's arms.

Quickly, I pull back. I can't deal with this at the moment, as I step back from Mike, I close my eyes and say, "There's ahh, umm, brownies and banana bread in the bag. I'll catch you guys later." Turning, I look to Mike and smile. "Glad you're back on your feet, Mike," pausing, I add, "I have to go, take care."

Turning, I quickly exit his room before I make a beeline for the doors and outside. I can hear Kenzie calling after me, but I have to get out of here. I sprint through the car park, climb into my car, and I get out of there as fast as I can.

Halfway home I have to pull over, I can't see thought the tears. I'm struggling to breathe through the sobs. My heart is breaking right now. I know without a doubt that I'm hopelessly in love with Mike, but I can't let go of the guilt, it's eating away at me.

Screaming into the empty car, I thump the steering wheel in frustration. *Chasing Cars* by Snow Patrol plays and I scoff, this song is perfect for my life right at the moment.

Once I've calmed down, I head home, get changed, and head to work. On my way to work, I give Sierra a quick call to get an update; our latest marketing campaign has done amazingly well and profits are up. When I get to work, I jot down a note to give Sierra an amazing bonus. She has done so much for me and I'm so thankful to have her on my team.

Pulling on my apron, I head out and begin work, thankful for the distraction. I'm on autopilot and before I know it, my shift if over and I'm heading home again.

Once home, I change into my PJ's and climb into bed. I lie there, staring at the ceiling, crying. Every time I close my eyes, I think of Mike and how wonderful a life with him could be. Eventually, I cry myself to sleep.

For the next week, my life is one continual cycle.

Wake up, think of Mike.

Have my morning coffee, think of Mike.

Go to work, think of Mike.

Come home, think of Mike.

Climb into bed, think of Mike.

Cry in bed while thinking about Mike, before I eventually pass out from crying...and thinking about Mike.

This week has been so hard, not as hard as loosing Mum, Dad, and Jace but a close second. I'm trying my best to erase and ignore Mike from my life, but Mike Mustange is hard to forget. Everywhere I look, I'm reminded of Mike, he's fucking everywhere. Just when I think I'm doing okay, something will happen and my heart breaks all over again.

Mike has been blowing my phone up with texts and calls, but I can't face him. I delete them immediately, not reading or listening to them. Kenz and Jordan have also been texting me, but again, I ignore them, too.

Mike has been into work the past two nights, but thankfully we are doing a stock take at the moment, so I've been working out the back. Jodi has been a trooper and covers the bar for me so I can hide like the big sook that I am.

It's a Friday night, and oddly enough, I have it off; I'm pretty sure Jodi spoke to the boss on my behalf and he gave me the night off. Besides, he knows my head's not in at the moment, and there's a concert on nearby tonight, so we will be super busy. It's better if I'm not there to screw everyone else up...silently, I thank him and Jodi for my night off.

I decide to head to the bottle-o and grab a case of wine, then I decide to stop at the local gourmet deli and buy enough antipasto to feed all of Italy.

I'm sitting on the front patio with my wine and feast when Kenz pulls up. I hold my breath, hoping that she's alone and thankfully, it's just her. She climbs my front stairs and smartassly says, "Well, well, well, what do you know, she is alive after all."

Hearing her say that I start feel guilty, but I also know that I need 'Sav time' to deal with all of this. "I'm sorry, Kenz. I just needed some 'Sav' time."

"Well, that's fair enough, but you could have just texted me that. I've been worried about you, we all have, especially Mike."

She leaves that hanging and I now feel like a total shitty friend. "I'm sorry, Kenz. It's hard to explain right now, but I just feel like a piece of shit for bringing all this onto Mike. I keep thinking, what if it had been me and you the night that my uncle took us?"

"Sav, speaking from a similar but different experience, you can't live with what-ifs. When life hands you lemons, you have two choices. One, you can grab a bottle of tequila and lick, sip, suck. Or two, you squeeze it in your eye and sook in the corner. I know which option I would choose and Sav, I'm pretty sure that I know which option you will go for too. Now, let me put my bottle of wine in the fridge, I'll grab another glass, and we will get this all sorted, once and for all."

Stunned, I sit there and watch Kenz head inside. I'm shocked at what she said but she's also right. Enough wallowing, I need to get on with my life and not let my uncle bring me down. Fuck that. I'm Savannah Blac and I'm fucking awesome and I deserve to be happy!

44

MIKE

She left; she left without saying a thing, what the fuck? I'm standing there, holding my coffee staring at the door, as it swings closed. I mumble, "She left." Then I shout, "She fucking left!"

Jordan and Kenz are standing there, looking at me and they look as confused as I do. Shaking my head I turn and ask, "What the fuck just happened?"

Kenz is the first to speak, "Mike, I don't know. I can only imagine that she is struggling at the moment. Not only did she have to watch her uncle torture you, but she also found out that he was responsible for the death of her parents and brother."

Snapping my head towards her, I ask, "What the fuck are you talking about? They died in a car accident."

"Mike, her uncle was responsible for that accident, I told you the other day. Don't you remember?"

"This week has been a total blur, but yeah, now I think back, I vaguely remember hearing that. I...I need to go to her, she needs someone right now. She shouldn't be alone at the moment."

Jordan and Kenzie look at each other and smirk, Jordan teases, "Mike loves Sav." And he makes kissing sounds.

Kenz whacks him in the arm, before she starts singing, "Mike and Sav, sitting in a tree, K-I-S-S-I-N-G."

Jordan joins in now, "First comes love; then comes marriage, followed by a baby in a tequila carriage."

We all burst out laughing.

"You two are seriously meant for each other, how did you both know to say tequila carriage?"

In unison…again, they reply, "'Cause we're awesome."

"More like a pair of nutters…but a pair of nutters who were made for each other and that mean the absolute world to me." Pausing, I smile and add, "Seriously guys, I would be lost without you pair, and the past few days have proven that. Thank you for everything."

All of a sudden, I start to sway, side to side, and nearly pass out. Jordan grabs my arm and escorts me back to the bed. Kenz races out and comes back in with the nurse.

Kenz and Jordan leave the room as soon as the doctor arrives, and once again, I'm poked and prodded. They just think I did too much and have requested that I rest. Until I have twenty-four hours without an almost black out, I won't be leaving here anytime soon.

The nurse and doctor leave, so Kenz and Jordan come back in, the girls are getting restless. They say goodbye and promise to be back tomorrow. Now, I'm left alone in my hospital room with my thoughts, and there's only one person on my mind, Savannah Blac. *I need to figure out how to win her over*, I think to myself as I stare out the window.

Sav is pulling away because she feels guilty, she is just like me. If she's not careful, the guilt will eat at her until she is broken; I know, I've been there. I refuse to let that happen to her, she has been through so much already and she deserves happiness. She brought me back to life again, happy-go-lucky Mike Mustange is back. Now it's my turn to return the favour.

I now see light wherever I look, whereas before all I saw was darkness and gloom. I'm free of the guilt over what happened last year, it no longer eats at me, and it's all because of her.

Flicking the hospital room telly on and *Bold* comes on, *winning*. As I'm watching, I keep thinking about Sav. I know I need help and there is only one person who I can ask; Kenz.

Mike – *I need your help winning over Sav!*
Kenz - ***squee** for sure. Wait 'til you get home and we will chat.*
Rest up…we have a girl to win over
Kenz - ***squee** I'm soooo fucking excited*

Laughing at her reply, I snort and that only makes me laugh more. *Fuck, I've been hanging around Kenz too much,* I think to myself.

Mike – *Thanks Kenz. You are a rock star*
Kenz – *I know. Night Mike*

I wake the next morning to another text from Kenz

Kenz – *Operation Sav N Mike is a GO!! **squee***

I laugh at how excited she is, but truth be told, I'm just as excited too. I get another text.

Jordan – *I have your balls here if you want them, loverboy. Kenz told me what you two are up to. You're so whipped. I'm happy for you asshat*
Mike – *Says the whipped one*
Jordan – *Mike's in looooove*

"Bastard!" I mumble to myself out loud, with a huge smile on my face, as it's true, not that I will admit that to the prick.

The door opens, and I'm still wearing my 'pussy ass in love grin' when in walks my doctor and his lackeys, here for morning rounds; fingers crossed I can get out of this joint today.

Looking up I say, "Morning, Doc, so can I haul ass out of here today?"

"Good morning, Mike and no, you still need to be here for a few days yet."

"Doc, I'm fine."

"Mike, you might be fine but you were just tortured, shot, and unconscious for three days. Your body needs time to recover and from what I'm reading here in your chart, you nearly collapsed just from standing up."

"I wouldn't call it a collapse, I'd say I got caught in a blip in the space time continuum."

"Call it whatever you want, you're not going anywhere, today anyway. Possibly tomorrow, but I'd say the day after that."

"Why are you so mean to me, Doc?"

"You say mean, I say health care professional. Now, lift up your shirt so I can see how the wound is healing, and then I can leave you to annoy the nurses."

The doc leaves and I'm left alone with my thoughts. It's Sav I have on my mind. Grabbing my phone, I text her.

Mike – *Morning gorgeous **insert coffee emoji***

I'm waiting for her reply, but it doesn't come for a few hours. I smile when I grab my phone and see that it's from Sav.

Sav – *Afternoon Mike **insert beer emoji***
Mike – *Sending a beer pic to a dude is hospital is cruel*
Sav – ***pic of tequila bottle and shot glass***
Sav – ***pic of her doing shot***
Mike – *That's hot...and I mean you and not the shot*
Sav – *Thanks. Shots on me when you're out.*

Ohh how I would love to have shots on Sav, I think to myself as another text comes through.

Sav – *Got to get back to work :P Have a goodly nite*
Mike – *I'd love to have shots ON you*
Mike – *Later, gorgeous XO*

I sit staring at me phone; did I really just reply XO in a text? *I'm such a pussy*, I think to myself.

Four, long, painful days later, I'm finally released from the hospital. Kenz put her foot down and I'm staying with them for a few days. Even though I have lived on my own since I turned eighteen, she's worried and doesn't trust me on my own.

Actually, I'm not complaining, she has been doting all over me and I'm eating like a king. Jordan and I have beers daily out the back and most of all, I get Mac and Cheese cuddles all day long. There is only one thing missing, Sav.

Sav and I have been texting daily, but she's still holding back. I've asked her if we can meet up in person a few times, but she ignores my request; at least she's texting me. After chatting to Kenz, I've decided to give her space but I'm not letting the string go. Sav and I are meant to be together; we are just like tequila with a beer chaser, perfectly paired.

Seeing Kenz and Jordan together makes me happy and sad. I want that and I want it with Sav; I want to push her but I don't want to scare her off either. It's really hard, like my cock at the moment. I can't even wank because the fucker shot me in my right shoulder and I happen to be right-handed...just my luck.

Tomorrow I have my final check up at the hospital, and if it's all clean, then Kenz will allow to go home. As soon as I get home 'Operation Win Sav' will be put in motion.

45

SAV

MIKE MUSTANGE IS CONSTANTLY ON MY MIND, BUT THE GUILT I FEEL outweighs everything else. He keeps asking to meet up and I keep ignoring his request. It's weird, I can text him but when it comes to meeting up or talking on the phone, fear takes over and I just can't do it.

I've asked Kenz to meet me for coffee today at Java Lava, I need her help. I know I told Kenz I'd give it a go with Mike, but I just can't right now. I need to fix me first.

I'm just about to leave and meet Kenz when there is a knock at my door. It's a knock that I haven't heard in a while and it makes me smile. I race to the door; open it up, and standing on the other side is the man of my dreams.

The world around me ceases to exist and all I see is Mike, standing in front of me with a big bunch of sunflowers. "Hi, gorgeous!" He smiles and lifts up the flowers in a cute way.

I'm rooted on the spot, I can't move, my heart is beating erratically. I flick my tongue out and lick my bottom lip, Mike groans. I realise that I'm still just standing there staring. "Hey!" I manage to mumble. "I was just on my way out to meet someone, can I pop over later today?" *Fuck, why did I just say that? I'm not ready to see him yet*, I think to myself.

"I'd love for you to come over later. How about I cook us dinner? I make a wicked lasagna."

"Sounds good, I'll bring a bottle of red." *Fuck, Sav, what are you doing?*

"Awesome, I'll see you later." He leans forwards and kisses me on the cheek, just skimming the edge of my lips, the kiss lingering longer than it should. I close my eyes and savor the moment. before wrapping my arms tightly around him and hugging him close to me.

We stand there hugging each other for a few more moments, before he pulls away. "These are for you, don't forget to put them in water, Sav. I can't wait to see you later." He hands me the flowers before turning and walking down the front steps. When he gets to the bottom, he turns around and says, "By the way, Sav, you look beautiful. See you later."

Standing at the door, I watch him drive away and realise that when I saw him then, I didn't feel as guilty as I normally do. Maybe the time apart is what I needed. Heading inside, I go to the kitchen to put the flowers into a vase.

While I'm filling it with water, a wave of guilt washes over me. I nearly drop and smash the vase, maybe I'm not as okay with this as I thought.

Walking into the café, I see Kenz sitting by the window, waving I head to the counter to order. Once I have my coffee and muffin, I head over to her. "Hey, lovely lady, sorry I'm late." Pausing, I smile as I place everything down, "I...umm...I had an unexpected visitor just as I was leaving." Taking a sip of my coffee, I moan, just as her head snaps up towards me and her eyes are giving me the 'please explain' look.

"Please explain?"

"Ummm, Mike popped over just as I was heading out. He bought be a big beautiful bunch of sunflowers and asked me to go to his place for dinner tonight." Taking another sip, I look up and see Kenz has the biggest smile on her face.

Clapping her hands she excitedly says, "Squee, I'm sooooooo excited for you two. You both deserve all the happiness in the world. I know I don't know you all that well, Sav, but I'm pretty good when it comes to reading people. Well, now days anyway, but that's a whole other story. Anyway, you and Mike are meant for each other. I feel it in my bones."

Smiling, I take another sip of coffee and think about what she just said. "Kenz, I really like, actually, no, I love him." Pausing, I add, "But

I feel so guilty; he got shot because of me. How do I erase the guilt of that?"

"I can't answer that, sorry, I'm not that awesome." She winks at me before adding, "But, Mike doesn't seem to care about that and isn't that all that matters?"

"I guess you're right."

"Hell yes, I am. I'm always right, just ask Jordan." We both start laughing, Kenz starts snorting and that sets me off. "Look, Sav, I've never, ever, seen Mike this happy, and you are what makes him happy. Can't you see that?"

"He makes me happy too, deliriously happy."

"I rest my case. Don't let your fear get in the way of your happiness. Everyone deserves to be happy."

The next hour passes quickly and it is nice to just hang and chat; I'm glad that Kenz suggested coffee. We are packing up to go shopping, and find the perfect outfit for tonight, when she runs into her friend, Sarah. She asks if we can take a rain check and I say that's fine. *I'd rather shop alone for what I have in mind.*

Saying hi and bye, I leave the two of them at Java Lava and head off on my shopping expedition.

Three hours later, I'm a few hundred dollars poorer, but I have a cute hot pink halter dress, black wedge sandals, and a sexy black and hot pink *La Senza* strapless bra and undies set.

Heading home, I take a relaxing bath and get ready for my date with Mike.

Tonight is the night that I start living again.

46

MIKE

I'VE JUST LEFT SAV'S PLACE AND NOW I'M A BUNDLE OF NERVES. LIKE I DO most times when I'm nervous, or need advice; I head to Jordan's. He knows how to calm me down and he will have amazing beer, too. It's a win/win for me.

When I get there, he's out the back with the girls. They are sitting in their paddling pool, and Jordan is spraying the hose up in the air. They are giggling their cute little heads off when the water droplets hit them. Their laughter is infectious and the nerves I had immediately disappear. I smile; guess Indie and Rory have the same effect on me as Jordan does. "Unky Mike is in da house!" I shout as I scoop down and pick up Rory. *Yes, got the name right.*

"To what do we owe this visit? I'm guessing food or beer?"

"Maybe I just wanted to stop by and say hi, but if you're offering a beer, I won't say no. Can't stay for food, I have a hot date tonight." I wink at him as I put Rory back down and head to the beer fridge to pour us each a stein.

After pouring the beers, I walk over to Jordan and hand him his. He is looking quizzically at me; he takes a sip, swallows, and says, "Okay, what have you done with the sour sack named Mike? When you left here yesterday, you were all heartbroken over Sav and miserable. Now you're all chirpy and have a date."

"Fuck off, I'm not chirpy. Can't a guy just be happy?"

He's still looking at me intently and raises his eyebrows in a 'explain now or I'll kick your ass' kind of way. "If you must know, Sav is coming to my place for dinner tonight." Pausing, I smile when I think about her. "Jordan, I'm in love with her."

"No shit, Sherlock. Blind fire trucking Freddie could have seen that."

"Yeah, well, we all know I'm a tad slow. I know she said she loved me in the hospital, but I'm not sure if she still does."

"Dude, she does."

"Yeah, right. How do you know that?"

"Dude, the way she looks when your name is mentioned is all lovey-dovey." Taking a sip of beer, he adds, "Much like the pussy-whipped look you currently have on your face."

"Fire truck off, butthole." Laughing I add, "That so doesn't have the same effect as saying," lowering my voice I say, "Fuck you, asshole."

Laughing he replies, "Not wrong there, Mike, ohh, how the times have changed."

"Who would have thought your favourite show would be *Octonauts* and that we would swear in code?"

"Pfft, *Ben and Holly's Little Kingdom* is my fav and how the hell do you know what *Octonauts* is?"

"'Cause I'm an awesome uncle, that's why." Just as I say that, both girls squeal in delight. "See, they just confirmed that I'm awesome."

"Dream on, dude. As much as I'd love to hang, I need to get these two down for a nap; otherwise, Kenz will have my balls on a platter if they get overtired. You need to get home and prepare for your big date. What you cooking anyway?"

"Lasagna."

"So, the only thing that you know how to cook?"

"Pretty much. At least I can cook one thing that's edible. There's always Kung Fu Palace if I fire truck it up, but my lasagna is awesome...like me."

"You keep telling yourself that, dude."

"I tell myself that everyday and since I'm awesome, it must work. Do you want a hand to get Mac and Cheese down?"

"Nah, it's all good, Mike, I've got it. Thanks though, you head off home and go get your lovin' on. Hey, why don't the two of you stop by Malt Me tomorrow for lunch? Kenz and I will both be there."

"Sounds like a plan, but let's do a late lunch-early dinner...or even better, a Sunday arv sesh?"

"Sounds good, man, see you then." He scoops up the girls and heads inside. It still amazes me that Jordan has twins.

On the way home, I stop at the shops and get everything to make my famous lasagna. As I'm walking past the jewelers, I see a stunning *Guess* watch in the window. It screams Sav, so I stop and buy it for her.

The lasagna is in the oven cooking and it smells fucking amazeballs. I'm all showered and to calm my nerves, I catch up on the latest episode of *Bold and the Beautiful*. The episode has just finished and there is a knock at the door.

It's show time!

Getting up, I take a deep breath and I walk to the door. Closing my eyes, I take one last breath and grab the handle. When I open the door, my heart rate speeds up when I see Sav, the wind is completely knocked out of me. My eyes travel up and down her body. She's wearing the sexiest dress I have ever seen in my entire life. It's hot pink, and hugs her body perfectly. "Fucking hell, woman, you look stunning."

She smiles and her cheeks turn pink with embarrassment. "Thanks, Mike. You don't look too shabby either."

We are standing in my doorway, just staring and smiling at each other. Both of us grinning like fools. The air around us is electric and I don't want to be anywhere else. "So, can I come in?"

Shaking my head from side to side, to bring myself back to reality, I laugh and say, "Sorry, yeah, ahh, sure. Come on in." Stepping aside, I let her in and watch her ass sashay side to side into my place; my smile increases as I take her in.

She places her handbag and two bottles of wine on the kitchen bench and totally busts me staring at her ass. Smiling at me, she smugly says, "Like what you see?"

"Fuck, yes I do, Sav."

"Wait till you see what's underneath," she says, while suggestively wriggling her eyebrows at me. Turning around and heading into the kitchen, she leaves me standing there stunned and totally turned on.

I'm currently sporting a hard-on that would saw through stainless steel.

"Where are the wine glasses?"

Too stunned to talk, I point to the cupboard next to the pantry. She walks over and reaches up to get the glasses. As she reaches up, her dress lifts and gives me a fine view of her toned legs. Closing my eyes, I imagine them wrapped around me, and I can't wait for that to happen later. I walk over to her, wrap my arms around her waist, and she jumps in fright.

After placing the wine glasses down on the bench, she leans back into me and rubs her ass on my growing erection. Tightening my grip, I nibble on her ear before whispering. "I've missed you."

She turns around in my arms and kisses me. Our lips crash together: tongues caressing and exploring, hands roaming and massaging, each of us moaning and groaning as the kiss deepens. Pulling back, she rests her forehead against mine, and breathlessly whispers, "I've missed you, too, Mike."

I'm about to drag her to the bedroom when the timer on the oven goes off. "Saved by the bell," she murmurs.

"More like interrupted," I add, before softly kissing the tip of her nose and turning to check on the lasagna.

Opening the oven, I can smell that it's done, even without checking. Sav moans again and my cock twitches. I think to myself, *Fuck dinner, I just want to sink myself balls deep inside her and make love to her for the rest of my life*. I'm bought back to reality when I hear her beautiful voice. "Mike, that smells amazing."

"Wait till you taste it, not to brag, but my lasagna is to die for."

"You've got tickets on yourself buddy," she says, as she opens the bottle of wine and pours us a glass each.

Grabbing my oven mitts, I sit the lasagna on the stovetop and go to the fridge to get the salad and dressing out. Placing them on the table, I bring the lasagna over just as Sav takes a seat. She looks at everything and smiles. "This all looks amazing, Mike."

"Thanks, Sav," I say, as I place a slice of lasagna on her plate. "Now dig in."

We both serve ourselves salad and fall into comfortable and relaxed conversation. I find myself laughing and really enjoying myself. We both clear the table and she starts to wash up while I pack away the leftovers.

When we have finished, we both head to the lounge. Grabbing her present, I give it to her as I pour us each another wine. Her face lights up when she lifts the lid and she immediately puts in on, I know she's like it. "Mike, I love it, thank you so much." She kisses me on the cheek.

Bending forward, she grabs our glasses. "A toast, to us and our future."

"I'll definitely toast to that."

We clink glasses and then snuggle on the couch together; her head rests on my shoulder. Wrapping my arm around her, I pull her back into my side and rest my palm across her belly. *We fit together perfectly*, I think to myself.

"Thanks for an awesome meal, Mike. You're right; you do cook a wicked lasagna. I do have one question though?"

"Shoot, I'm on open book."

"Why no cucumber in the salad?"

Her question throws me and I start to laugh. "I read a book recently, and this freak does something with a cucumber. Now I just can't bring myself to eat them."

She starts to laugh, like really laugh. Once she has composed herself, she turns, looks me in the eyes and says. "Oh My God! You are such a freak." She leans forward and quickly kisses me. "But you're my freak."

Grabbing her, I flip her onto her back and settle myself between her legs, she squeals in shock and giggles. Pinning her to the couch, I place featherlight kisses up her stomach, across her boobs, and up her neck. I nuzzle and nip my way along her jawline, up to her lips, before kissing her deeply. Sav wraps her arms around my neck, pulling me closer and kisses me back, gently biting on her bottom lip.

Ever so lightly, I run my hands up her sides and she giggles, breaking our kiss. I continue to run my palms towards her breasts when she throws her head back and arches her back. I take the opportunity and cup her perfect tits, squeezing them. She moans my name slowly, "Miiiike!" Grinding her pussy onto my leg as I continue to massage and squeeze her tits. Looking up at me, she whimpers, "I want you, Mike."

47

SAV

RIGHT IN THIS MOMENT, I HAVE NEVER FELT SO LOVED OR BEEN SO TURNED on. I realise that I want Mike Mustange in my life: forever. Looking up at him, I whisper, "I want you, Mike."

Before I can comprehend anything, Mike has lifted me up; I wrap my legs around him. Unapologetically I grind my pussy against his zipper and growing erection, as I continue to kiss him. Carrying me down the hallway towards his room. After placing me on my feet at the end of the bed, he reaches down to grab the hem of my dress, I grab his hand and I say, "No." Stopping in his tracks, he looks hesitantly at me as I push him back onto the bed. Seductively, I whisper, "No, let me. I have a surprise for you."

Stepping back from the bed, I undo the tie on my halter dress and I let it fall down my body, pooling at my feet in a pile of pink chiffon. I'm left standing in my strapless bra and undies; I've never done anything like this before and my heart is rapidly beating. Taking a deep breath, I look at Mike and smile. There is nothing but lust in his big, beautiful blue eyes. His look comforts me and in this moment, I've never felt sexier than I do right now.

I kneel on the end of the bed and slowly shuffle up his body, my breasts rubbing over his crotch. As I straddle him, I lean forward and intensely kiss him, shamelessly grinding my throbbing pussy on his growing erection.

Pulling back, I begin to untuck his shirt. My hands are shaking as I slowly unbutton it. I only get two buttons undone when I give up and tear open his shirt, buttons flying everywhere. He looks up at me in shock. "In a hurry, sweetness? 'Cause I can tell you now, I ain't going anywhere...anytime soon."

"Sorry, I don't know what came over me. I'll buy you a new shirt."

"I don't care about the shirt, now come here and kiss me, woman."

Leaning forward, I kiss him before pulling back. "Don't ever call me 'woman' again." Leaning down, I kiss him intently.

"Yes, ma'am," he says in between kisses.

"Last chance, Mike Must..." He cuts me off by kissing me senseless.

Flipping me onto my back again, he deepens our kiss, pinning me to the bed. He begins to massage my tits, and unashamedly I grind my pussy against him.

Our kiss is so deep, so hungry, and so erotic that it brings me to orgasm; my body trembling and tingling as the pleasure courses through my veins. "Holy fucking shitballs. I've heard of a kissgasm before but I've never experienced one until now," I murmur to myself, as my body and mind come back to reality.

Opening my eyes, I see Mike staring intently at me. "Did you just come?"

Sheepishly, I say, "Yep, I just had my first kissgasm."

"Well, I'm glad I was your first, Sav. Now let's see if I can bring you 'O' number two for the evening."

Before I have a chance to reply, Mike is kissing me again, our hands roaming over each other's bodies. One-handedly, he undoes my bra and flicks it across the room before making quick work of my undies.

I'm lying completely naked on his bed, and I see that he still has his pants on. "Umm, I think you are overdressed, mister."

"I can fix that." He quickly jumps up and removes his pants and boxer briefs in one quick motion, and then jumps back on the bed. "Is that better, milady?"

"Much, now do dirty, wonderful things to my body...please?"

"With pleasure."

His lips are on mine instantaneously and his kiss almost brings me to orgasm again. Before I can get there, he kisses his way down my neck and chest. Taking one of my nipples into his mouth, he gently bites down on the tight bud before sucking it deeply into his mouth. I moan in delight, "Fuck, I love your mouth."

He replies by licking, sucking, and nipping my other breast.

His hand snakes its way down my stomach towards my core, inching closer and closer to my throbbing pussy; I'm eagerly awaiting his magic fingers. Just as he reaches the top of my slit, he snakes his hand back up my stomach and massages my breast before rolling and squeezing the nipple between his fingers.

Grabbing his hand, I guide it down my body and together we explore my wet folds. Our fingers simultaneously rubbing circles around my clit, before sliding down my slit and plunging deep inside of me; in and out, deeper and deeper. I'm so worked up that it doesn't take long until I'm once again tumbling over the edge as our fingers continue to dance together, deep inside of me.

Kissing me deeply, he pulls back and whispers, "That's two."

Falling back onto the bed, closing my eyes, I whisper, "Mmhmm!" My breathing is still returning to normal, when I feel Mike run the tip of his finger up my stomach, drawing circles around my breasts. It tickles and I laugh, swatting his hand away. "Mike, stop! That tickles."

"Is this better?" He seductively states before sucking my nipple into his mouth and gently biting down on my sensitive tip. Releasing my nipple, I sigh at the loss of contact. "You have gorgeous tits, Sav. I could suck and fuck them all day long…forever even."

Looking up at him, I smile. "Well, what are you waiting for, Mike? Fuck my tits."

"Abso-fuckin-lutely nothing."

He crushes his lips to mine in a deep sensual kiss that invokes all these feels and pulses in all the good places. Eventually, we come up for air and he straddles my stomach. Reaching out, he gently massages my tits before pushing them together. He nudges the tip of his cock between them. Mike begins thrusting between my tits, I've never done this before but it feels amazing.

The tip of his cock pokes through the top of my tits and I get an idea. On the next thrust, I lift my head and dart my tongue out to lick the tip, continuing this until I hear him say, "Suck me, Sav, I'm gonna come."

Leaning forward, he shoves his cock deep into my mouth and I suck hard while I fondle his balls. Once I have sucked him dry, I look up into his eyes and see him intently staring back at me. "That's one for you, baby."

"Well, it seems like you are slightly winning, let's see if we can increase your lead." Before I know it, his cock is lined up with my entrance and he is teasing me. Gently inching in and then pulling back out again, he does this over and over. I feel like I'm about to explode when he thrusts deep inside of me.

"Fuuuuck!" I shout out as he keeps slamming into me.

Lifting my hips, I meet him thrust for thrust. I place my feet on the bed and lift my hips; he grips me tight and continues his assault on my pussy. "I'm close, Mike."

He grunts, "Let go, Sav. Coat me with your pussy juices." That's sets me off like a rocket. My pussy clenches around him and I explode around his cock. My whole body tingles as he continues to thrust into me. The pleasure is never-ending; I never want this feeling to end. I feel his cock harden and his body tenses as his orgasm rips through him.

Falling on top of me, he nuzzles my neck before whispering, "That's three, baby."

Wrapping my arms around him, I laugh and reply. "That's two for you."

"Baby, this isn't about me. I get just as much pleasure watching you come. Actually, it's my new favourite thing to watch."

"Even better than *Bold*?"

"So fucking better, Sav."

He rolls off me and we snuggle into each other, my back to his front. Neither of us says a word but the silence says it all. Just before I fall asleep, I hear him whisper, "I'm going to marry you one day, Savannah Blac."

48

MIKE

Life could not be better. Sav and I are over the moon happy, and we have decided to move in together. We are pretty much joined at the hip and financially it makes more sense. Not that she needs to worry about money, considering she's a bazillionaire and all.

We found an amazing cottage, just out of the city, so I only have a small commute each day. Plus, it's just around the corner from the Dungeon; we wanted something near the bar as it's our place and holds a special meaning to us both. Sav quit her bartending job and now works from home, remotely running the jewelry stores so it didn't bother her too much where we lived.

"Sav, that was the realtor. The settlement cheque from the bank cleared, the cottage is officially ours."

She comes barreling down her hallway and jumps into my arms, wrapping her legs around my waist, and kissing me hard. Breaking our kiss, she pulls back and with a megawatt smile excitedly declares, "Squee, I'm so excited to be moving in with you. I love you, Mike Francine Mustange."

"Seriously, give up on the middle name thing. If Kenz ever finds out, she will hand me my balls on a silver platter with the teasing. I refuse to let that happen."

"Okay, Mike Francine Mustange, I will stop saying, Mike Francine Mustange, just as soon as you kiss me."

"I will happily kiss you anytime, Sav, and now that we will be living together, I will kiss you anytime I want."

"We just bought a cottage," she squeals with excitement.

Lowering her down onto the chaise, I cover her body with mine, and kiss her deeply. She wraps her arms around my neck and begins to grind her pussy on my leg. Lifting up, I run my hand up her skirt and rub her folds through her undies.

Closing her eyes she moans, pushing her pussy against my fingers. Her breathing becomes faster, and she lifts her shirt up and starts massaging her tits through her silky, satin, pink bra. Her moans are getting louder, and just as she's ready to explode, I pull back and stand up. Looking down at her, I smirk. "Come on, babe, we need to go meet Amanda and get our keys."

She lies there, open-mouthed, staring at me. "Are you fucking kidding me?"

I chuckle as I reach over and drag her to the edge of the chaise. Quickly, I lift her skirt, pull her undies to the side and attack her pussy. Licking, sucking, and nibbling, I dine on her delectable pussy, bringing her to climax with my tongue only. Screaming my name out in pleasure, she explodes all over my face, drowning me in my second favourite drink.

Pulling back, I wipe my chin and smile. "Now that I've had breakfast, we can go."

Sitting up, she pulls me in tight and kisses me. "I love tasting myself on you. Now, let's go get our keys so we can christen the new place."

"Fuck, I love you and your wicked, dirty mind. Now, grab the tequila in the kitchen and let's go."

Forty minutes later, after all the I's are dotted and the T's are crossed, we are officially homeowners. Amanda has just left and Sav and I are standing in our lounge room, taking it all in.

"Can you believe it, baby? This is all ours." I outstretch my arms and spin like that nun chick from *The Sound of Music*.

"Mike, I'm soo unbelievably happy right now." Smiling over at me, she grabs the hem of her shirt, and strips it off, before quickly removing her skirt, leaving her standing there in just her bra.

"Umm, where are your undies?"

"In the bathroom," she says, staring at me as she runs her fingers down her stomach towards her pussy, which is glistening wet.

Stalking over to her, I grab her wrist. "Uhh, uh, Sav. That's my pussy." Getting onto my knees, I hook her leg over my shoulder and slide my tongue up and down her slit. We both groan in delight. "Fuck, I love eating your pussy." Continuing to suck and lick her slit before adding a finger, I feel her pussy walls tighten and just before she's about to come, I pull away, and she whimpers. "Sav, the first time you come in our new house, I will be balls deep inside of you."

Quickly I remove my clothes and Sav jumps into my arms. She wraps her legs around my waist, and I thrust deep inside of her before pushing her against the TV wall; I continue to thrust into her. We are both moaning in delight and together we crash over the edge, crying out each other's names as we draw out each other's pleasure. Spinning around, I slide down the wall with Sav still in my arms.

Looking deep into her eyes, I lean forward and take her lips in a deep, sensual kiss. "Thank you, Sav."

"Why are you thanking me?"

"You made me whole again, Sav. I never thought I would be this deliriously happy, and I have you to thank for that."

Wiping a tear away, she says, "Mike, I feel exactly the same. I've never ever been this happy and it's all because of you. I love you, Mike 'I promise never to say Francine again' Mustange"

"I love you too, Savannah Blac."

A week later on Friday night, I'm on my way home from work and I decide to stop at the bottle-o to get some wine for Sav. Ss I'm walking out, there's a lady doing a tequila tasting, and I just have to stop and taste. Oh My God! I taste the smoothest tequila that I've had in a long-time. It's almost as good as the bottle the Kenz and Jordan bought back from Mexico for me, so I grab a bottle and head to the checkout... tonight is going to be amazeballs.

When I get in my car, I send off a quick text to Sav.

Mike – *On my way home...I have a surprise*

Immediatly I get a reply.

Sav – *I have a surprise too...hurry*

Mike – *Be there in 5*

I'm intrigued to see what surprise Sav has for me. Luck unfortunately isnt on my side this evening; I get every red light on the way home and to top it off, I get stuck due to an accident.

Mike – *Stuck in traffic*
Sav – *Bugger…looks like I'll just start without you*
Sav - ***picture of her shoulder, bra strap down and a hint of purple lace covering boobs***
Mike – *You don't play fair*
Sav - ***picture of bed, candles and her leg***
Sav – *But you love me anyway…hurry home Xo*
Mike – *Considering parking car and running home. Traffic starting to flow, be there soon*
Sav – *Can't wait **SMOOCHES***

Just my luck that this would happen, Sav is such a little minx…I can't wait to get home now.

Thankfully, I pass the accident quickly and by the looks, no one was seriously hurt. From this point on, I get green ligths all the way and I'm home in no time.

Sav and I moved into our cottage last weekend and there are boxes everywhere; some are unpacked, some half unpacked, but most are still taped up. Neither of us can be assed unpacking.

Parking my car, I walk inside, dump my bag by the door, and head to the kitchen to put the wine in the fridge. After putting the wine away, I search out two shot glasses, and then I will search for Sav.

I'm bent over in a box when Sav comes up behind me, wraps her arms around me, and seductivey whispers, "Evening, sexy."

Rubbing my hands over her arms, I stand up and spin around. My mouth drops open at the vision in front me me. Sav is standing there in my favourite bra and undie set; it's a deep purple satin and it pushes up her girls magnificanlty.

"Evening yourself." My eyes dart up and down her body. "Fuck, Sav, you are so sexy."

Her cheeks turn a shade of pink and she looks towards the floor all shy. Reaching out with my index finger, I lift her chin so she is looking directly at me. "Don't hide from me, gorgeous." Bending forward, I place a kiss on the tip of her nose an she smiles. "You can't hide from me, I'll find you everytime."

Turning around, I grab the tequila, turn back to Sav and wink. "So, I thought tonight we could have some tequila fun."

Sav bursts out laughing. "Did you stop at the bottle-o on Stanley Street?"

"Yeah, why?"

She turns towards the lounge and returns with the same bottle of tequila, holding it up, she smiles and says, "Great minds think alike." She winks and then walks back into the lounge.

With her back towards me, I stalk over to her, wrap my arms around her waist and lift her up; she squeals and starts laughing. Gently I lower her to the couch, flip her over, and cover her body with mine. Grabbing her cheeks in my hands, I kiss her deeply, slipping my tongue into her mouth. I close my eyes and loose myself in kissing her. Sav wraps her arms around me and pulls me closer to her.

Reluctanly, I pull away, break the kiss, and head to the kitchen. Grabbing the salt and precut limes, I head back to the lounge. Sav is still laying on the couch, her cheeks flushed and lips swollen; my cock hardens at the sight before me. "Fuck me, Sav. You are absolutely gorgeous."

Her cheeks become a shade darker and she smiles at me seductively. She runs a finger from her chin, down her neck, before circling it across the edge of her bra.

Straddling her hips, I lean forward and kiss her quickly before I lick down the path that her finger just took. I wink at her as I grab the salt and shake it along the line I just left. Ripping the cap off the tequila, I take a swig and sigh; *this shit is amazeballs*. Placing the bottle over Sav's mouth, she opens, and I pour the tequila into her mouth. A few drops spill down her chin, leaning forward I lick the tequila and salt off her before kissing her deeply again. The salt and tequila combining as our mouths mesh together. Pulling away, I grab the lime and suck, while the lime juice is still on my lips, I kiss Sav again. She sucks my bottom lip into her mouth and moans. "Man, that tequila is amazing," she lustifuly says, as she reaches for the bottle and takes another swig before handing the bottle to me. I take it from her and place it on the coffee table.

Pulling Sav into my arms, I kiss her again and undo the clasp on her bra, flicking it across the room. Pushing her back to the couch, I kiss and lick my way down her body, twirling my tongue in her navel as I kiss my way down her stomach. I kiss her mound through the satin before nudging it aside and licking her clit. Sav moans and lifts her hips, allowing me to remove her undies.

Grabbing the tequila, I pour it on her stomach and quickly lick the spills so I don't ruin our new couch, but right at this moment, I don't give a flying fuck about it. As I'm licking the spills, Sav shakes the salt on her stomach, grabs a piece of lime and places it between her lips. Licking the salt, I suck the tequila from her belly button before kissing my way up her stomach and neck; finally I suck the lime and kiss Sav. She brazenly grinds herself on me as I continue to kiss her. Pulling back, I remove the lime rind and kiss her deeply.

My cock is rock hard and Sav reaches down and rubs me through my jeans; I'm so turned on that I grab her hand. "If you keep that up, I'm going to blow in my jeans and I haven't done that since I was fifteen."

Sav looks up at me and smiles. "Fuck me, please."

She knows I can't resist her so I lean back, unbutton my jeans, and quickly remove them and my shirt. In one swift motion, I'm balls deep inside of Sav; she's so wet that I easily slide in and out of her.

Without warning, I flip us so she is on top. Reaching out, I massage her tits, and she gets up on her knees and begins to ride me. Throwing her head back in ecstasy, she slides up and down my throbbing cock. Sav entwines her fingers with mine and together we massage and rub her gorgeous breasts.

This is my favoiurite position, I can get deep inside of Sav and I love to watch her unfold in front of me. Sav continues to play with her tits as I grip her hips and meet her thurst for thrust. I feel her pussy walls tighten around my cock. She stills as her orgasm rips through her body and screams my name; her head thrown back and eyes closed as she comes back to earth. She continues to ride me until my legs tighten and I explode, tumbling over the edge, emptying myself deep inside of her.

Opening my eyes, I look up to see Sav staring down at me with a sated smile on her face. "Definitely, the best tequila ever," she says as she lies on top of me.

"Definiely a good drop," I say before wrapping my arms tightly around her. "I love you, Savannah Blac."

"I love you too, Mike Francine Mustange."

I'm too content to say anything about the use of the middle name. It's in this moment, I realise that I am the happiest I have ever been, and it's all due to the amazing woman lying in my arms.

THE END!

EPILOGUE

Mike

Looking around, I see that everyone is happy and having fun. For the first time, in a long time, I realise that I'm at a party having fun along with everyone, too. I owe my happiness to Sav. She bought me back to life and I could not be happier.

It was a rough ride to get here, and after the events of last year, I didn't think I would ever be happy, or in love again. I now know that there is a difference between what you think is love and what is deep, heartfelt, unconditional love; and that's what I have with Sav. She came along when I least expected it, but I'm happy she did. I have never been happier.

Luckily, I also have great friends who helped me pull my head in and be the happy-go-lucky me again. Without the support and guidance of Kenz and Jordan, I don't know where I would be. I know that had they not intervened after my property getaway, I wouldn't be here. I would have drank myself to death, and then I wouldn't have met Sav and taken a chance with her

Kenz was right, not that I will ever tell her that. It wasn't my fault that my crazy ex was related to her psycho ex. They had a plan, and we were the unfortunate pawns caught in the middle of their sick and twisted vendetta, Kenz more so than anyone. If she can overcome it, I can too; after all, I'm Mike Francine Mustange, and I have the most amazing woman now living with me.

Sav and I have officially moved in together and today is our housewarming. Everyone who is near and dear to Sav and me are here today to help us celebrate, and I've arranged a super surprise for her. I can't wait for it to get here.

Sav and I are always doing little things for each other. Leaving love notes in random spots, but our fav thing to do is leave miniatures of tequila lying around. Trying to explain away a miniature in your work briefcase was fun, but thankfully my boss knows how crazy Sav and I are, and it was brushed aside. After that, we set some ground rules and boundaries for our games.

A lot can occur in twelve months, but what I've come to realise is that shit happens, some shit you can control and some shit is beyond your control. It's how you deal with it that proves the person you are.

Sav and I were destined to find each other, we are polar opposites with most things, but we also bring out the best in each other. I can unequivocally say, she saved me. I love her with all my heart; she's not only the one, she's my savior. Sav gave me a reason to live and smile again. I'm one lucky son of a bitch. One of these days, I will make Sav my wife, but in the meantime, we will enjoy tequila and each other… sometimes together.

Sav

It's amazing the difference twelve months can make. Twelve months ago, I was still living at home with Mum, Dad, and Jace and plodding along. Now, I'm an orphan, living with the man of my dreams and I'm over the moon happy. I just wish that Mum, Dad and Jace could have met Mike.

Mike rescued me from an existence that was getting me down and bought me back to life. Prior to meeting Mike, I was existing, just plodding along and not living. Uncle Kelvin didn't help things, but with Mike's help, I overcame that obstacle and I'm now living life to the fullest.

I know that Mum, Dad, and Jace would be so happy for me. My heart still aches for them, but Mike has helped fill that void. Our road to happiness has been bumpy but I wouldn't change a thing; well, maybe the kidnapping. I'd give up that but everything that has happened has led me to this point...to Mike.

Looking over at Mike, I smile to myself. He is just as happy as I am, and I love him to the moon and back. Mike brings out the best in me. He is always doing little things to surprise me, but his latest gift was beyond amazing. He arranged for my best friend from home, Logan to be here. It has been so great catching up with him, I didn't realise how much I missed our friendship.

Arms wrap around my waist and tickle me, jumping in fright; I turn around and whack Logan in the arm. "Fuck, you're such an asshole. I didn't miss that."

"Naw, come on, Sav, you totally missed me."

"Maybe," I say as I sip on my wine.

"There's no maybe, baby, you were miserable until we started chatting again, and when I told you that I was here, your life was complete."

"Pfft, you keep telling yourself that. Pretty sure my happiness is standing over there doing shots, but yes, I am excited to have you back in my life again. I missed you like crazy. I can't believe you've been here all this time. By the way, I can't wait to see your new penthouse."

"You only want me for my penthouse."

"Yes. You got me. I knew at age ten that by age twenty-seven you'd have a penthouse, and that's why I ran you over with my pushie."

"See, told you." We both burst out laughing. "Seriously, Sav, it's good to see you smiling again. I was so worried about you. Before you left, you were distant and not just because you lost your family. I was hurting for you, I wanted to do more but you wouldn't reach out or let anyone in. Then you took off without warning, that gutted me, Sav."

"I'm sorry I did that, so sorry, Loge. I thought I was doing the right thing." Pausing, I take a sip and add, "You're here now, and I met Mike, so in a way it all worked out. Don't you think?"

"I'll let you have that one, but if you ever take off again like you did, it will be on like Donkey Kong."

"Promise, I'm not going anywhere."

"Except to the bar."

"Dude, when are you going to realise that I'm..."

Mike walks over, puts his arm around my shoulder, pulls me in tight and interrupts, "The sexiest woman here."

Logan laughs, "And that's my cue to leave." He turns around and pauses midstep.

***

Sarah

I'm really not in the mood for a party tonight, but I can't keep ignoring everyone. Just because my life sucks, doesn't mean I should take it out on my friends. Hanging up from Kenz, who is making sure I'm coming, for the fifth time today; I grab my car keys, take a deep breath, and head off.

When I arrive at Mike and Sav's, a pang of jealousy overtakes me at how stunning their cottage is. Seeing all this makes me miss having my own place. Don't get me wrong, I love the apartment that I'm currently in, but it's not mine. As usual, my life turns to shit just when everyone else's seems to be taking off.

Finding Mike and Sav, I offer my congrats before seeking out Kenz. Of course, she's by the bar holding a glass of wine out for me. "Well, well, well, look, Jor, it's Sarah. You remember her? My bestie who seems to have disappeared off the face of the Earth."

"Hardy har har, bitch." I hug them both. "It's good to see you guys." Turning to Kenz, I look at her with puppy dog eyes that I know will get her. "Kenz, I'm sorry I've been such a shitty friend, but I promise, I'll explain everything...soon."

"You know I can't resist your puppy dog eyes, so I'll give you a pass...for now, but you and I will be talking; soon."

"I know, I know, and I promise that I will but for tonight, I'm going to get rip-roaring drunk with my besties and have a winetabolous time." Taking the glass of wine from Kenz, I yell, "Cheers!" and clink glasses with her.

Chugging it back, I ask for another when I hear a voice that makes me tingle all over. Spinning around, I see him, standing there talking to Sav and Mike. He has his back to me, but I'd know him from a mile away.

I'm still staring when he turns around, our eyes lock across the room, he pauses midstep and smiles. A force takes over my body and I find myself walking towards to him, his pull is too strong to ignore.

He is standing directly in front, staring intently at me, he says, "Sarah?" His sexy baritone voice completely melts me.

The room is dead silent, everyone is looking at us but they all fade away. It's just Logan and me, standing there, totally absorbed in one another; the air around us is filled with lust, sexual tension, and confusion.

Finding my voice, I stammer. "LLL…Logan, what are you doing here?"

"Sav's the friend I mentioned. What are you doing here?"

Once again I'm frozen, unable to speak. Everything I have been hiding is about to unravel, and the biggest secret of all is standing right in front of me. All six foot two inches of gorgeousness. "I…I…I have to go." Turning, I race towards to front door, slamming it behind me.

Leaning against it, I stand there hyperventilating, trying to catch my breath. I can hear chatter behind the door but the only voice I focus on is his, I here him say, "That's the girl I was telling you about, Sav."

Sliding down the door, I start to cry, my world is beginning to crumble…again.

TEQUILA HEALING PLAYLIST

Sexual Healing – Marvin Gaye
Money For Nothing – Dire Straits
Stand by Me – The Drifters
Numb – Linken Park
These Days – Powderfinger
Closer – Nine Inch Nails
Hot N Cold – Katy Perry
Coming Undone – Korn
Leave Me Alone – Natalie Imbruglia
The Sound of Silence – Disturbed
So What – Metallica
Sober P!nk
Bye Bye Beautiful – Nightwish
Hey Hey, My My – Battleme
Forever Young – Audra Mae & The Forest Rangers
John the Revelator – Curtis Stigers
Slipkid – Anvil
Girl from the North Country – The Lions
Bring Me to Life – Evanescence
Hero – Enrique Iglesias
Bad Romance – Lady Gaga
Sweet Disposition – The Temper Trap

Monster – Skillet
Broken – Seether
Get Lucky – Daft Punk feat. Pharell Williams
Sex on Fire – Kings of Leon
Supermassive Black Hole – Muse
Little Lion Man – Mumford & Sons
To Be Alone – Hozier
Carry on Wayward Son – Kansas
Better – The Scream Jets
Heroin Girl – Everclear
Highway to Hell – AC/DC
You've Got Time – Regina Spektor
Chasing Cars – Snow Patrol
I Want to Know What Love Is – Foreigner

This playlist can be found on Spotify.

https://open.spotify.com/user/1254969568/
playlist/3RnjQ2EewzWfU9TyLEk1Mx

THE
Liquor Cabinet
SERIES

Wine NOT

ALL IT TOOK WAS ONE *wrong decision*

DL GALLIE

All it took was one wrong decision.

I had it all. Great friends, amazing job, perfect boyfriend. My life was just filled with rainbows and unicorns…until it wasn't.

Everything that defined my life disappeared within the blink of an eye, leaving me alone and desperate. Two things that can make a woman do stupid things.

After accepting an offer I couldn't refuse my life went from bad to worse—except the part where I met Logan.

He's strong and kind, and seems to be the only light in the darkest corners of my life. When I'm with him I no longer feel…empty.

But the decisions I've made in order to survive won't allow me to start over. Too many secrets lurk in the shadows waiting for the right moment to strike.

When it does…it will ruin us both.

To my year ten English teacher,
Mrs. Jenny Martin

You always told me if I apply myself (and shut up) that I could achieve anything, you have been a silent support to me on this journey and I thank you for all your encouragement back at school. I wish you were still here to see what I have achieved but I know that you are up there cheering me on and still telling me to shut up.

PROLOGUE

It's so good to hang out with Kenz, Jordan, and Mike again and to finally get to know Sav. I'm glad that Kenz kept pestering me to come, I think I need to spend more time with them so I don't lose myself down the rabbit hole that I'm currently stuck in. It's hard keeping it all hush-hush, but the focus is on Mike and Sav tonight so my secret will be safe...for now.

After a rough trot, things are looking up for Mike and Sav, they are extremely happy and recently bought a gorgeous cottage together, hence the housewarming party. I'm still amazed that Mike has fallen in love and with a gazillionaire. His girlfriend, Sav, is the sole owner of Blac Family Jewellers. If you had told me twelve months ago that Mike would be all domesticated and have a girlfriend, I would have told you to put down the crack pipe. Mind you, I didn't expect my life to end up the way it has either.

"So, Sarah, where have you been hiding?" Jordan asks, as he hands Kenz and me another wine.

"Ummm, work, I literally live there at the moment." *Which isn't a complete lie.* "Mmm, this wine is heaven. It's so fruity but not too sweet, really refreshing."

Kenz looks at me and smiles. "Sarah, you totally need to become a wine critic, or even better open a wine bar. I'd have a beer hubby and a wine bestie."

"You front the mullah and I'll totally do that." As I take a sip, I think of a recent conversation I had regarding this, *maybe I should take the leap*; it would get me away from 'her.' Taking another sip, I cheekily reply, "I can see it now, the bar would be broke in a week 'cause the owner's bestie drank all the stock."

"Pfft, if I haven't drunk the brewery dry yet, I doubt I could do it to your bar." Winking at me she adds, "But I'm totally up for the challenge."

"I have a better idea, me and you run the wine bar together, like we used to talk about when we were at school, and we will become wineaires."

"What the hell is a wineaire?"

"Like a billionaire, but with wine."

Kenz slings her arm over my shoulder. "And this is why I missed you so much. You take my shit and turn it into an idea that would work."

Laughing, Jordan says, "If you two ran a bar, it would be broke before the end of the first day. Nope, not gonna happen for you, Kenz." She pouts at him, so he pulls her into his side and kisses her gently head. Looking back at me, he points with his finger that's wrapped around his beer mug. "I can totally see you doing that though, Sarah."

"Naw thanks, Jordan, but I doubt anyone would give me the capital to start it." Looking at Kenz, I poke my tongue and say, "Suck it, Kenz, your husbut likes me better than you." As I take another sip of wine, my mind drifts off to my imaginary wine bar. *I would totally love to do that, but before that can happen, I need to get my life back on track,* I think to myself.

She punches me in the arm really hard. "Pfft, whatevs, Bitch."

Magically, I don't spill a drop. "Winning!" I proudly declare fist pumping the air and lifting my leg in a slight kick to the side as I do so. Both Jordan and Kenz clap when all of a sudden my skin prickles. I freeze on the spot. I feel his presence, but it can't be him. Turning around, I scan the room, and then I see him standing over near Mike and Sav, looking ever so sexy in jeans and a button-down shirt.

My heart is racing and I swallow hard just as he turns around, our eyes lock onto one another. All that I have been hiding these past few months is all about to unravel, due to the demigod standing in front of me. I'm going to be exposed; No, No, No…Oh My God, I can't believe he's here, this can't be happening.

I'm fucked...my secret is about to be exposed.

1

SARAH

...Four months earlier

STANDING UP FROM MY CUBICLE, I FOLLOW THE REST OF THE STAFF INTO the boardroom for a last minute, urgent meeting. As I'm walking down the corridor, I start to get a sinking feeling in the pit of my stomach. I'm one of the last to arrive, so I take a seat on the windowsill and wait for the meeting to start.

My colleague, Julie, walks in and I shuffle over so she can sit next to me, both of us looking at each other curiously. Glancing my eyes around the boardroom, I see that the mangers at the front don't look happy, and that sinking feeling in my stomach magnifies.

The big boss finally walks in, slamming the door behind him; I jump in surprise, as I was lost in thought trying to figure out what's happening. Brian stands at the front clears his throat, "Thank you for coming, everyone. I know this was sudden and I appreciate you dropping everything to come to this meeting." He looks really nervous; his hands are shaking. "As you are all aware, there have been quite a few changes of late and the rumor mill has been in overdrive. I can officially confirm that, as of twelve p.m. today, the company has a new owner." Everyone in the room lets out a sigh of relief. "However, they are making some cuts." He sighs, swallows deeply, and then quietly says, "Everyone, who is in this room, is being let go. I'm sorry to say that you all no longer have a job here. This will be your last day at KDM."

The room erupts to a chorus of shouts, screams, and tears. Looking towards Brian, my heartbreaks for him. He put his heart and soul into this company and everything that he worked hard for is no longer his. Closing my eyes, I let out a big breath and shake my head, I knew times were tough but I didn't realise how tough. Snapping my eyes open again, I realise that I no longer have a job.

It isn't until Brian touches my shoulder that I realise I'm the last person sitting in the boardroom. "Sarah, are you okay?"

Looking up at him, my eyes well with tears. "I'll be fine, Brian, I'm just shocked and sad. I've been here since I finished university, what do I do now?"

"I'm so sorry, Sarah. I did everything possible to keep the doors open myself, but I just couldn't do it anymore. They didn't tell me about the cuts until the deal was done and there was nothing I could do." Patting me on the shoulder he dejectedly says, "I'm so sorry, Sarah."

"I know, Brian, I know. It's just a shock, it was the last thing I expected to hear today." Reaching up I give Brian a hug. "Thank you for everything." Rising on my tippy toes, I give him a kiss on the cheek before heading back to my desk. Sitting down in my chair, I look around at my cubicle. As I place my belongings into a box, I lower my head onto my desk and I start to cry. Once it's all packed up, I grab the box and my handbag and for the very last time, I walk out of KDM.

On the train home, I try and call Josh but I can't get hold of him. I leave a message asking him to call me when he gets a chance. On the walk home from the station, my mind starts thinking about everything and I start to cry again.

Getting to our house, I see Josh's car in the driveway and I smile, knowing that he will give me a big Josh hug, and for tonight at least, he will make me forget about this shitty day. Digging out my keys, I unlock and swing open the front door to be greeted by Josh and Sam... having sex...on my couch. Josh is on all fours his eyes closed, moaning in pleasure as Sam rams into him from behind.

The sight in front of me stops me dead in my tracks and I scream, dropping my keys on the tiles. Josh's eyes pop open, Sam stops mid-thrust, and they both stare at me open-mouthed, in shock.

Before either of them gets a chance to say anything, I turn around, slamming the front door behind me, and I run off. Putting one foot in front of the other, I run and run until I'm back at the train station. There is a train for the city sitting there, so I jump on. Taking a seat, I pull my legs up, wrap my arms around them, rest my head on my knees, and I let the tears fall. The floodgates have opened and I'm sitting there sobbing my heart out. Fellow passengers stare at me in shock, but not one of them asks if I'm okay and I'm fine with that; I wouldn't know how to answer them anyway.

Getting off in the city, I walk around in a daze, the events of today running through my mind on a continual loop: loosing my job, finding Josh and Sam screwing on my couch, and repeat. Eventually, I find myself at The Dirty Duck, our old college bar, so I head inside so I can drown my sorrows.

Taking a seat at the bar I order three tequila shots, a bottle of Pinot Grigio, and a serving of wings. The bartender returns with my drinks, and I down the shots one after the other, savoring the burn. I'm starting to feel numb so I ask for three more. "Rough day, huh?" he asks, as he pours three more shots.

Laughing, I down another shot. "You could say that."

"Wanna talk about it?"

"Well, today I lost my job, and when I got home I found my boyfriend on our couch getting fucked in the ass by his colleague, Sam." Slamming back the remaining two shots, I pour myself a glass of wine and take a big gulp.

"Wow, that sure is a shitty day." He places another shot in front of me, I look at him curiously as I didn't order another shot...I don't think. "On the house, you deserve it."

For the next few hours I sit at the bar, drink my wine, eat my wings, and chat with the bartender. He and I chat about anything and everything. I discover that Dave is studying medicine at QUT, he recently married his high school sweetheart, and they are expecting their first baby later this year. His happiness and perfect life makes me feel even shittier.

I'm pretty drunk and I start to cry again. "How did I not know my boyfriend also liked boys? I'm so stupid." Dave places a glass of water in front of me, and I drink it down in one go. He refills it and tells me it's closing time.

As I'm walking out my phone rings, and my shitty day just goes from shit to complete and utter shit.

2

LOGAN

"It's over, Logan!" Lili screams at me, throwing her arms up in the air before turning her back on me. She's having another one of her temper tantrums, and to be honest, I'm over it. She stares out the window for a few moments before spinning on her heel, she glares at me, and screeches like a banshee, "I'm done, we're done. It's done!" Pausing, she takes deep breath to compose herself. "I'm outta here." Grabbing her Gucci handbag off the dining table, she storms towards the entrance, slamming the door on her way out. I'm left standing in our, well, I guess now, my lounge room, totally flabbergasted. She was cheating on me...for our whole relationship; I'm such a schmuck...but to be honest, I'm not surprised. I haven't been happy for a while now, but I was too gutless to end it with Lili.

Sighing, I stare out the window and wish that Sav was here. She'd know exactly what to say, and then she'd whip out the tequila and all would be forgotten. I miss my best friend, I really need her right now but she gone. She has disappeared and no one knows where she is; not even her uncle. Kelvin's reaction when I asked was shocking; he was so angry and pissed off. I know there is no love lost there, but I at least thought he'd care.

I've tasked a friend to find her but I know Sav, if she doesn't want to be found, she won't be. She was the best hiding-go-seek player in

Wentworthville when we were kids, and the time she disappeared when we were eleven will go down in the history books. Mr. Blac, her dad, said no to her—for the first time ever—and she took off into the woods behind the store. She hid out for two days, evading everyone, even me. The whole town was out looking for her and she was right under our noses the whole time. She got in so much trouble...I'd give anything to go back to those times. Life was so much simpler and less complicated back then...ohh how times have changed; adulting sucks.

Turning around, I head to the bar and I grab a Malt Me Checker Plate lager, *this beer is to die for*, and I head out to the back patio. Sitting down on the lounger, I stare at the sky and watch the storm roll in. The clouds darken, the winds pick up, blowing the leaves around, causing the pool furniture to tumble over, creating chaos in its wake, much like my life at the moment.

Finishing my beer, I go inside and grab another before I head back outside to continue watching the storm. How did I not know that Lili was cheating on me? Was I just blind? Or was I too focused on my development company like she said? I know I've been busy getting DeBiers Developments off the ground, but how was I to know that I was going to get a multi-million dollar contract on my first tender and open doors that I never thought possible? Something like that never happens, especially to me, and I wasn't going to let an opportunity like that pass me by; I guess my personal life was the casualty of that.

Sighing, I sit back and watch the sky darken further, the clouds twirling and mixing together. The lightning strikes brightening the night sky, it truly is wonderful watching Mother Nature. With the next crash of thunder, the sky opens up and I'm drenched. I don't care and I don't move a muscle, well except for my beer-drinking arm. Staring at the night sky, I continue to lie there and watch, there is nothing behind this rain band and it will shortly pass, and then it will be humid as hell.

Not ten minutes later, the dark ominous clouds have passed and in its wake, we are left with a stunning sunset. The sky is bursting with colour; oranges, yellows, and reds, all mixing together as the fiery orb of the sun slowly descends behind the mountains to the west.

A chill passes over me, so I get up, grab another beer, and head to my room. Stripping off my wet clothes as I walk into the master ensuite, leaning in, I turn the shower on. Letting the steam fill the bathroom, I finish my beer before jumping under the spray and warming my body up. After drying off, I put on my trackies, grab another beer, and head into the media room for a night of drinking beer and listening to music. The last thing I remember before passing out is hearing Metallica singing about giving me fuel and fire and all that I desire.

3

VICTORIA

SLAP "Get out!" I roar. "If you ever show your face around here again there will be trouble."

"But..."

"There are not buts, missy, you knew the rules and you broke them; end of story, Crissy. The rules are there to protect us all, and you know I don't tolerate misbehavior. You have thirty minutes to get your things and leave." She begins to cry and nothing pisses me off more than crying, especially when you are to blame.

"I'm sorry, Victoria," Crissy pleads.

SLAP "Save it, time is ticking." I wave my hand at her dismissively and turn my back on her. Walking over to the bar, I pour myself a brandy before taking a seat on the lounge. Sitting down, I watch my best girl, Crissy, sulk as she walks away. As much as it killed me to do that, she broke my most sacred rule and that is unacceptable.

Ten minutes later, I look up to see her standing in the doorway. She is broken and sad, that gives me a little pleasure as I stand up to escort her out.

Taking her by the arm, we walk through the foyer towards the entry doors. "Crissy, darling, it has been a pleasure having you here." Her head snaps towards me in shock at my nice tone. "Your final payment has been wired to your account, and Simon here, will take you wherever you need to go."

"Thanks for everything, Victoria, I'm sorry to have disappointed you."

"There's no one sorrier than me right now, Crissy. You not only have disappointed me, but you broke my trust and now my business will suffer. I've lost my best girl because she couldn't follow the rules. The rules you agreed to when you came to work here." Shaking my head, I look at her angrily. "This is going to cost me."

"I'm sorry," she mumbles, as a lone tear falls down her cheek.

"Enough!" I shout, causing her to pause in her tracks. "Sorry won't fix this, Crissy." Letting go of her arm, I pause and stare at her, disdain on my face. "Now, get out of my sight."

She begins to cry harder now and pleads, "I don't have anywhere to go."

"That's of no concern to me, nor is it my problem. You should have thought of that before you defied me. Goodbye, Crissy." Turning my back on her and Simon, I walk back inside the apartment, thanking my stars that this one is leaving without incident.

As the door closes behind me, I sigh in frustration, why does this keep happening? Turning around, I look out the patio doors at the darkening night sky and wonder what I will do now. Sighing, I head over to kitchen and grab my bag off the bench. Locking the door behind me, I shoot a quick text off to the cleaners to have them prepare the now vacant apartment. As I step into the lift, I start thinking of ways to increase business and keep the girls in line. When I exit the lift, I head to the bar for a much-needed drink. Sitting in my usual seat at the bar, I once again sigh in frustration. Looking up, I see that Stephen has placed a napkin under a champagne flute and is opening a bottle of *Krug Grande.* "Thank you, Stephen, at least there is someone around here who can follow rules and do their job properly."

"My pleasure, ma'am. Is there anything else I can get you?"

"For starters, you can stop calling me ma'am, it's Victoria. And secondly, you don't know anyone who needs a job do you? I need to replace Crissy and I need to do it quickly."

"Sorry, ma'a...I mean, Victoria. I can't help you there."

"I didn't expect you to, Stephen," I say dismissively. Picking up the champagne flute, I take a sip and close my eyes; this is liquid gold and just what I needed, the bubbles instantly calming me. Opening my eyes, I look around the bar and smile at all that I've achieved. I notice that it's quiet for a Tuesday night and that makes me unhappy; I need to breathe new life into this place. "Stephen, can you please bring the bottle over to my table, I have a long night ahead of me."

"Yes, Victoria. I'll bring it right over for you after I serve these people."

Walking over to my table, I wonder what I will do. If I don't replace Crissy quickly, he will not be happy, and if he's not happy then I could lose everything I have worked so hard for. That will not happen, I refuse to give up all of this; I will do whatever it takes to keep what's mine and him happy.

4

SARAH

As if things could not get any shittier in my life, Mum and Dad have lost everything, my trust included, due to a bad investment recommended by that sleaze ball investor. I never trusted him but I'm amazed that Dad made a choice like this, very out of character AND to make things worse, they were involved in a serious car accident while in Madrid. Dad broke his leg in several places and is in hospital; he won't be able to travel for a while.

Fuck. My. Life. Right. Now!!!

Seriously, did I run over a black cat? Or was I a total an utter bitch in a previous life? How can everything fall apart at precisely the same fucking time? I wish I had Kenz to talk to, but she's been through so much. She doesn't need my worries added to her already hectic life; nope, I can do this on my own…I think.

Two weeks later, and things have gone from bad to worse. Josh is being a total douche canoe asshole, and because he paid the deposit on our house, he is kicking me out. I have three days to find somewhere to live and get my stuff out. Like seriously, he cheats…with a dude, and I'm the one who gets fucked, and not in a good way.

Mum and Dad are going through too much for me to ask about

moving back home, plus there's a chance they will loose the house too. I don't need to add to their worries at the moment. I can't ask Kenz and Jordan; they've only just gotten home from the hospital with the twins, Indi and Rory, and besides that, they have been through enough; they don't need my problems added to theirs.

I'm at the Dungeon drowning my sorrows and Sav is working, she seems shy and reserved but she knows how to mix a wicked margarita. On the weekend, that was my drink of choice to numb everything and she sure helped with that. Apparently, tequila is her drink so there's no surprise that she can mix a mean margarita. Today though, I'm drinking a lovely New Zealand Sav Blanc and chowing down on wings. Taking a sip, I sigh loudly, garnering the attention of the lady sitting a few seats over from me.

"What's a pretty girl like you doing here, drinking her sorrows away on a beautiful day like this?"

Normally I would ignore someone chatting to me, but at the moment, what more do I have to lose? Looking over at her I dejectedly say, "You wouldn't believe the shit luck I've been having lately."

"Try me," she replies, as she slides over to the seat directly next to me.

"Okay, well in one day: I lost my job, found my boyfriend cheating on me, my parents were in a serious car accident overseas, and they lost everything due to a bad investment. Now said ex-boyfriend is kicking me out of our house, and I have three days to find somewhere else to live."

"So rather than house hunting, you're drowning your sorrows in wine and wings?"

"Wine Not?" I giggle, "...and he can get fucked." Taking a big gulp, I continue, "He can get fucked in the ass by Sam again, for all I care."

"Wow, that is pretty 'shit' as you so crudely put it. Why don't I buy us a bottle and we can come up with a game plan together?" She stares directly at me, stretching out her manicured hand. "I'm Victoria, by the way."

It must be the wine talking because I take her hand in mine, shake, and confidently say, "I'm Sarah and at this point, Victoria, I'll take any and all help that I can."

"It's nice to meet you, Sarah, I think you and I are going to be great friends."

If only I knew...

5

VICTORIA

A FEW DAYS AFTER THE CRISSY DEBACLE, I HAVE A MEETING WITH A possible new member; he wanted to meet at some dive bar called The Dungeon. It's not a place I would normally be seen dead in, but his financials check out and he's too good of a member to pass up.

Our meeting went very well and Jonathan is now officially a member of Elite. I'm sipping on my glass of champagne when I look up and see a sad, yet stunning, young lady sitting across the bar. She has an aurora about her, and in this moment; I know that I have found my new Crissy.

Walking around the bar, I take a seat near her and listen in to her conversation with the bar staff. Smiling at myself, as I knew I was right, she's down on her luck. Lucky for her, I'm happy to swoop in and be her fairy godmother and turn her life around; and mine.

I'm trying to work out the best approach when she sighs and that's my chance. "Rough day?" I enquire.

She looks at me but doesn't reply, so I try another approach. "What's a pretty girl like you doing here, drinking her sorrows away on a beautiful day like this?"

She is still hesitant but she finally opens up, and her life at the moment is shittier than ever. I offer to buy us a bottle of wine and suggest that together we can come up with a plan. Without hesitating, she takes up my offer and I inwardly smile. After ordering the bottle, we take our wine and glasses and head to a corner booth. Personally, I'd rather get out of this dump and go somewhere more sophisticated but I need to play this safely. I don't want to spook her.

Sarah and I fall into comfortable conversation, well, I let her do all the talking, I want to play this to remain relaxed and surprisingly, it's not awkward with her at all. She's chatting away, and in my head, I'm pairing her up with appointments from my current client list. The dollar signs are adding up and that pleases me immensely. Alexander will be very happy too, and when he's happy, life is perfect.

Glancing at her over my wine glass, I stare and subtly watch her every move. There is a graceful poise about her, and I know that she is exactly the girl I am looking for. Tonight, she will be coming with me; I refuse to leave here without Sarah…and I always get what I want.

6

LOGAN

AFTER WAKING UP WITH THE HANGOVER FROM HELL, I'VE DECIDED THAT I'm too old for hangovers and getting shitfaced is not the answer. I'm going to throw myself into work, and that actually works out perfectly; I have a tender in for another big project in Brisbane. If, no when, I get this tender, I'll move there and see the project through myself: two birds, one stone.

Later in the week, I get confirmation that I won the tender and I'll be developing the new sports stadium for the Queensland Academy of Sports. It starts in three weeks time, but I want to be there as soon as possible. I decide a road trip is in order, plus it will allow me to let loose on the highway in my new baby, my Mercedes G-Class SUV.

My assistant, Beth, books me into a hotel in the city for ten days, and hopefully in that time, I can find myself somewhere more permanent to stay.

After three fun-filled days, I have finally arrived in Brisbane and checked into my hotel. Dumping my bags in my room, I decide to head to the hotel bar, Charlie's, for dinner and a few brewskies. It's lonely eating and drinking by myself, but when you're new in town, what are you going to do?

Over the next two days, I scope out the city to get my bearings. I find a temporary office immediately. Locating the office space was easy; finding a place to live, is another story. Everything that I have seen so far is not me at all. Looks like I'll be in this hotel for a little while longer, at least it's comfortable and the bar/restaurant downstairs is fantastic.

Returning to the hotel after I finalised the lease on the office and getting the keys, I head to the bar for a celebratory drink and an early dinner. While I'm waiting for my steak, I notice a few lovely ladies enter the bar, but after Lili, I'm not sure I want to go there again so soon. I'm still shocked that she was cheating on me, how did I not realise that she was? Was I so engrossed in my business that I became a horrible boyfriend? Surprisingly, I'm not concerned that she was cheating on me, and truth be told, I'm not really that upset that we broke up. I'm more upset that she treated me like a chump.

Before I can dwell anymore, my dinner arrives and it smells magnificent. As I start eating, my thoughts leave Lili and all her bullshit, and I start thinking about the future of LDB Developments and where I can take the company next. Winning this tender was big for the company and me; the rush was exciting, and I haven't felt like this about work for quite a while now. Maybe this move it just what I needed to refresh and reboot.

After dinner, I head back up to my hotel room. Grabbing a beer, I head out to the balcony and look over the city and ponder my future. As I stare out at the sparkling city lights, I realise that getting away from Wentworthville and moving here was the right decision; personally and professionally. *Here's to a new adventure* I think to myself as I head back inside for an early night…if only I knew the adventure that was awaiting me.

7

SARAH

I'M SO GLAD THAT I DECIDED TO COME TO THE DUNGEON TODAY. I MET this really nice lady. She has offered me a job and place to stay; it's like my fairy godmother has stepped up to the plate, finally.

Victoria escorts me to her car; it's a navy blue Mustang convertible. "Holy shit, is this your car?"

She laughs, "Yes. Do you want to drive?"

"Are you shitting me?"

"Your language is atrocious, but no I'm not shitting you, as you so eloquently put it."

"I would love to but I've had too much to drink. Speaking of, are you okay to drive?"

"Darling, of course I am, besides you drank most of that bottle yourself. I was just enjoying the company of my new friend. Now, get in."

"Yes, ma'am." I mock salute her as I slide into the car. These seats are heaven; I think I actually moan. They wrap around you like a leather glove. I can hear her mumbling something as she climbs into the driver's seat, but I am loosing myself in the comfort of this car seat.

She floors it as we pull away, the thrust forces me back into my seat, and I squeal like a schoolgirl. I begin to laugh, this is the most fun I've had in over a week now, turning to Victoria, I smile. "Thank you,

Victoria, this is the happiest I've been since everything started to fall apart."

She reaches over and squeezes my hand. "It's all up from here now, darling."

That sets me off and I start to cry; everything that I have been holding in is now flowing down my cheeks. When I look up again, I see that we are in an underground garage and Victoria is opening my door. She squats down and wraps her arms around me. "Let it all out, darling, there's nothing like a good cry."

Finally the tears stop and after that outburst I feel much lighter, almost like me again. Victoria stands up and says, "Come on, let me show you up to your apartment and around. Your roommates should be home, too."

Climbing out of the car, we silently walk to the elevators; the only sound is the clicking of Victoria's Loubitons on the cement floor. "Oh My God! I fucking love your shoes."

She sighs, "Your language is deplorable, Sarah. You swear like a trucker. If you are to live and work here, you will not swear. You will act like a lady at all times, and you will follow the rules and guidelines." Pausing, she turns to me and glares. "Are we clear?"

"Umm, yeah, ahh, sure. I can do that. Sorry."

"Glad to hear it." The lift arrives and we climb in.

We make our way up to the thirty-fifth level, the doors open and we make out way over to the apartment. She opens the door, and when I step inside my new home, my chin drops to the floor. This apartment is out of this world: the foyer has marble floors, a gorgeous ornate mirror on the wall, and a foyer table with the biggest flower arrangement I have ever seen. Straight ahead is a staircase that leads up to the bedrooms, a door next to it; I presume it's a downstairs powder room. To the right is a doorway that opens into a massive lounge room, kitchen, and doors that lead out to the balcony terrace.

"Holy fucking shit, I've died and gone to heaven." I hear Victoria scoff and I look over to see disappointment on her face. "Sorry, I'm just, umm, overwhelmed. This place is stunning."

She smiles at me and I release the breath that I was holding, I was expecting another tongue-lashing. "I'll let that one pass, it is pretty stunning the first time you see this place. Now, come with me and I'll give you a quick tour."

We spend the next twenty minutes walking from room to room,

eventually ending up in what will be my room. Victoria tells me that there are two other girls who also live here, as well as our personal chef and cleaner. After leaving my bags in my room, we make our way downstairs, just as Morgan and Angel, my new roommates, arrive home.

"Ladies, this is Sarah, she has just moved in. Sarah, this is Morgan and Angel."

We all say hi and wave to each other, Victoria escorts us all into the lounge room and Angel heads to the bar. Popping open a bottle of *Veuve Clicquot*, the cork popping makes me jump. She hands me a glass and I quickly drink it to calm my nerves. Taking my glass she refills it and proceeds to pour a glass for Morgan and Angel. Once we each have a glass, we head out to the terrace. Stepping out the door, my eyes bug out; this balcony is bigger than Josh's and my apartment...*I guess it's not mine anymore*, I sadly think to myself.

I become sad when I think of Josh; Angel notices the change in my demeanor. Leading us over to the outdoor lounge, she sits next to me and smiles. "So, Sarah, tell me about yourself?"

Taking a deep breath, I think, I may as well get this over with so I tell her all my troubles of the past week. When I have finished, I look up to see her staring at me open-mouthed. I expected to see pity but all I see is empathy.

"I hear ya, sister, my ex did the same thing, except it was with my mum. Suffice to say, I no longer have a mum or boyfriend. Luckily for me, Victoria ran into me and saved me." Pausing, she smiles at Victoria before adding, "As they say, the rest is history."

"Wow, your mum, seriously?" She nods at me. "That's got to be rough. How did you cope?"

She replies with one word, "Victoria." Smiling, she add, "She came along at the right time and saved me, she's my fairy godmother with a kick-ass shoe collection, wardrobe, and liquor stash."

"Language, Angel. But yes, I do have a kick-ass collection of every-thing you mentioned and so much more. And on that note, ladies, I will leave you to it. Angel, would you be a dear and bring Sarah by the office tomorrow at ten a.m. and we can begin?"

"Begin what?" I curiously ask.

"All will be revealed tomorrow, Sarah. Enjoy your night with the girls and I'll see you in the morning." Standing up, she heads back inside, turning around, as she closes the door she says, "Night, ladies and, Sarah, I'm glad you decided to come back with me." Spinning on her heels she waves before exiting the apartment.

When the front door closes, Morgan jumps up, grabs another bottle of *Veuve* and pops it open on her way back outside. The chef, Miguel, appears and places down the most decadent antipasto platter I've ever seen. My stomach grumbles as he walks away and we all start laughing.

We are on our third, or forth, bottle of *Veuve* when I look over at Angel and Morgan. I'm pretty pissy by this point and with my emotions all over the place. I know that tonight will be 'emotional drunk Sarah' and I giggle. Smiling I say, "I think I'm going to love it here. You guys are awesome, thank you for making me feel so at home."

They both reply at the same together, "Anytime," and giggle.

Angel stands up and comes over to me; she leans down and hugs me. "I'm glad you're here too, Sarah. Tomorrow is going to be so much fun." She pulls back and says, "'Night girls," before heading upstairs to bed.

Morgan comes over and sits next to me, topping up our glasses before she leans back into the couch and takes a sip. She moans and looks over at me and smiles. A look passes over her face as she leans forward, she places her glass on the table; she takes mine and puts it next to hers. Turning towards me, she leans over and out of the blue kisses me. Her tongue seeks access to my mouth, and it must be the bubbly, because I open up and allow her in, our tongues caressing each other. When I feel her hand cup my breast, I pull back and push away and stand up. "Umm, I'm ahh, umm, I'm going to head to bed. I'll see you in the morning, Morgan."

Turning I quickly head inside and up to my room. As I'm racing through the lounge room, I hear her say, "Night night, Sarah, sweet dreams."

Opening my bedroom door, I slip inside, close it, and flick the lock. Leaning my head against the door, I close my eyes; my breath laboured from racing up the stairs…or is it laboured from that kiss?

What the hell was that?

And why the hell did it turn me on so much?

What's happening to me?

The next morning, I'm sitting in the kitchen having a coffee when Morgan walks in. She smiles at me as she grabs a coffee and sits on the stool next to me. "Morning, how did you sleep?"

"Fine, that bed is to die for. How about you?"

"Like the dead." She takes another sip of coffee, before looking back over at me. "So, about last night..."

I put my hand up to stop her. "It's fine, Morgan. I'm flattered but I'm just not that way inclined, sorry."

"No, I wanted to apologise. I don't know what came over me." Pausing, she adds, "But if you want to do it again I wouldn't say no." Morgan gets up and goes outside. As I sit there and finish my coffee, I watch her walk away from me. She takes a seat where we kissed last night and the memory of that kiss comes rushing back to me. Smiling into my coffee, I clench my legs together as the memory is invoking feelings that I've never felt before. I'm a little turned on.

A few hours later, we are on our way to the office to meet up with Victoria for my training to begin. Angel and Morgan have taken me under their wing, which gives me comfort...it feels like I have found forever friends. Staring out the car window, I start to doubt my decision to be here and myself. I'm not sure I can do this, but at this moment in time, I'm backed into a corner and have no choice.

We meet with Victoria at the office; and by office I mean a building that overlooks the river, it's decadently decorated but in a tasteful way. I'm given a brief rundown as to what it means to be one of Victoria's girls before Angel, Morgan, and I are sent to the salon for a day of pampering and a makeover.

When we arrive, we change into the softest, pale pink robes, are handed a glass of champagne, and escorted to a waiting room...then my transformation begins. I'm treated to the full works, and when I say full, I mean my whole, entire body. I don't think there is one part that hasn't been touched, poked, plucked, or pampered. First up was waxing, *OUCH!* I was waxed in spots that I never knew could be waxed. I got my first Brazilian but with a little landing strip, in the shape of a love heart, which is really cute. Being hair free down there was kind of weird to start, with but I have to say, I like the feeling, especially when I slipped my satin undies back on. I'm kind of in a perpetual state of bliss at the moment, one flick and I'll be tumbling over the orgasmic cliff, *I like it...a lot.*

After waxing the relaxing pampering began; a full-body scrub, followed by a mud wrap. Once that was washed off, I had a full-body massage and then it was off to the salon for the final stage: hair, makeup, French manicure, and a spa pedicure.

As soon as I sit down, I'm handed another glass of bubbly and I realise that for the first time in weeks, I'm relaxed and genuinely smiling. The stylist comes over and we have a fight about my hair. She wants to cut it off short but I want to keep the length. We eventually come to an agreement and I'm now rocking bangs and my hair is a rich, chocolate brown colour, which I totally love.

When we leave, looking fabulous by the way, we meet with Victoria for an early dinner at a restaurant overlooking the river. We start with cocktails before we dine on lobster, prawns, and oysters, and for the first time in my life I'm drinking *Cristal* champagne, which by the way is amazing. It was a nice relaxing night and I think I will like working for Victoria and Elite. After dinner, we say good night to Victoria, and the three of us head to Club Duex for a night of dancing and more cocktails.

The next morning I wake with the hangover from hell to banging on the front door downstairs. Stumbling down the stairs, I open to door to an irate Victoria standing there. "Morning, Vicky," I sleepily say.

SLAP "My name is Victoria, never call my anything but that. Now go get dressed. Your late for your first lesson."

Holy shit, she slapped me. My cheek is still stinging as I make my way upstairs to get changed. As I'm rounding the corner at the top, I see Morgan duck back into her room and her whisper, "fuck," as she quietly closes the door. Not wanting to piss Victoria off any further, I quickly pull on my jeans, white tank, and navy Chucks. I quickly brush my teeth, throw my hair into a ponytail, and head back downstairs to Victoria, secretly hoping she will have a coffee waiting for me, but the tingling on my cheek tells me that it probably won't happen.

When I enter the lounge room, she looks me up and down with a look of disgust on her face. "Rule number two, you will dress like a sophisticated lady at all times. This will do for now, but in the future, keep that in mind."

"I'm sorry, Victoria. Do I have time for coffee before we leave?"

"Sorry, that's all I seem to be hearing lately. Fine, but make it quick. By the looks of things, I will have my work cut out for me. Don't prove me wrong, Sarah."

Turing on her heels, she storms out the French doors, slamming it behind her. I head to the kitchen and quickly make two coffees before joining Victoria on the balcony.

Ending her call quickly, she smiles and looks at me as I place her coffee down and says, "Your first client is booked for this evening at 6:30 p.m. His file will be delivered in the next ten minutes." She takes a sip of coffee and obviously doesn't like how I made it as she has a look of disgust on her face. Staring up at me from where she is sitting, she snarls, "Sarah, I suggest you read it thoroughly and be up to speed; Mr. Akin is one of our longest serving clients. Don't screw this up, this is your one and only shot, Sarah." Without another word, she walks past me and leaves the apartment.

Grabbing my coffee, I go and sit on the lounger and mumble, "What the fuck have I done?" There's a knock at the door and I get up to answer it, but by time I get there, Angel is closing the door holding a file. She looks up at me and smiles. "Morning, Sarah. This was just delivered for you."

Reaching out, I grab the file and say, "Thanks."

Grabbing my arm, she turns around, and we walk back into the kitchen where she makes us each another coffee, and I tell her all that just went down. "No fucking way, you called her Vicky?"

Nodding my head, I quietly say, "Yep." As I take a sip of coffee I moan in delight; this tastes so much better than what I just made.

"You are game doing that."

"Well, after the slap, it won't be happening again. My cheek is still tingling." I subconsciously rub the spot.

"Well, who's your first client?"

Opening the file, I read, as I can't remember. "It's with Mr. Akin."

"Naw, I love him. He will be perfect as your first client. Do you want me to help you get ready?"

My face breaks out in a huge smile. "Oh My God! Yes, please, I'm so fucking nervous. What if I stuff this up?"

"You will be fine, Sarah. Mr. Akin is a doll, he's just a rich, lonely old man; he's harmless."

"What if he wants more? I'm not sure I can do that."

"Give it time, you will be surprised how easy it comes to you. I never thought I would, but it's quite exhilarating and exciting, to be in control like this. Just ease yourself into it and remember, you have the power, but I assure you, Mr. Akin isn't after that."

"Okay, I'm just really nervous."

"You'll be fine. Come on, go get a bikini and we will have a spa before we get you all dolled up for your first night."

"Are you sure Victoria will be okay with this?"

"Vicky will be fine with it," she smart-assly says as we both burst out laughing.

"You are evil...I like it. Come on, let's go."

As I'm getting changed I get a text from Kenz.

Kenz – *Hey bitch. Wanna meet up for coffee?*

Seeing who it's from, I start to get upset and think that maybe I should just tell her what's going on, but I don't want to admit what a screw up my life has become.

Sarah – *Flat out at work, sorry. Rain check?*

I feel bad lying, but technically I'm working, so it's not a total lie... just a huge stretch of the truth.

Kenz – *Fine but you owe me*
Sarah – *Deal. Love your face*

Throwing my phone on the bed, I quickly change into my black and orange micro bikini, and I head down to the pool area.

When I get outside, Angel and Morgan are already in the spa, sipping champagne and chatting. Angel looks up and smiles at me. "Come join us, there's a glass on the table for you."

"Thanks." I grab my glass and slip into the spa. The temperate is just right, and I moan as I slide down into the whirling, bubbly water. "This is just what I needed." Closing my eyes, I rest my head back on the edge and relax.

"So, Angel tells me you got bitch-slapped for calling Victoria, Vicky. I would have loved to have seen that, I've heard how much she hates being called that."

"Yep," I say, as I rub my cheek where her hand collided with my face.

Smiling she says, "Well, you are officially one of us now, welcome to the bitch-slap club. Getting bitch-slapped is your initiation in and you completed yours in record time."

"Thanks…I think. So, tell me what I can expect tonight?"

8

VICTORIA

I'M SO GLAD THAT I FOUND SARAH WHEN I DID; I THINK SHE WILL BE Elite's saving grace, and my instincts have never let me down. I simply cannot afford to loose another girl, with Crissy leaving, that is the third girl in a matter of weeks. At least her leaving was easy to deal with, unlike the other two girls. I hate getting my hands dirty, but I will do anything and everything to keep Elite running smoothly.

Yesterday with Sarah went brilliantly, much smoother than I anticipated, she's a feisty one, that's for sure. She didn't argue too much about the makeover, and even though I wanted her hair lopped off, I have to say the bangs and colour were a great compromise. To be honest, I was sure she was going to put up more of a fight, that girl has quite the spirit. She reminds me of me at her age, maybe I have finally found our successor.

At dinner, she really impressed me, and these days it's quite hard to do so. When we stepped into the restaurant and the girls started on cocktails, I was expecting a messy, booze-filled night but surprisingly, all three of them behaved like ladies. I was very proud to be in their company. Heads turned when they walked in and I could not have been happier in that moment, actually if I had secured another client I would have been ecstatic.

The four of us had a lovely evening together, we will need to do it again. The key to success in this business is to keep the girls happy and content; maybe that's where I went wrong with the other girls. No point dwelling on the past though, it's onwards and upwards now that I have found Sarah. I'm pretty sure that when I dropped them off, they were heading out somewhere to continue the party, but after their behaviour this evening, I was happy to let them indulge...just this once.

However, as usual, it all came crashing down the next morning when she called me Vicky. I despise being called Vicky, thanks to Mother, but that chapter of my life is done and dusted, never to be thought about again. Mother will be turning in her grave at my success; I just wish she was here so I could flaunt it in her face. Finally I have made something of myself, I'm Victoria Chalmers and no one fucks with me, no one!

9

LOGAN

THE PAST WEEK HAS FLOWN BY, AND I'M NO CLOSER TO FINDING somewhere permanent to live. For the first time since arriving in Brisbane, I start to think that this wasn't such a good idea after all. Heading to Charlie's for dinner, I decide to sit at the bar so I'm not so much of a loaner. I order a burger and a Malt Me beer.

While I wait, I look around and I notice that there are private apartments is this building, too. I shoot off a text to Beth and ask for her to arrange a meeting with the realtor. Not five minutes later, my ever on the ball assistant tells me that I have a meeting with the realtor in three days time.

My burger arrives and I order another beer. Taking a sip, I smile to myself, being able to get this stuff on tap is major perk of moving here; beer tastes so much better on tap rather than from a bottle or can. Striking up a conversation with the barman, I discover that the Malt Me brewery and restaurant is located nearby. Since tomorrow is Sunday, I decide to head there for the day and chilax, it sure beats hanging around here by myself.

After a late breakfast, I jump in my baby and take the scenic route to Malt Me. The owners have done a brilliant job, from the looks of the building I'd say it was an old factory that they have revamped, and they've done it well. They've kept the old school charm of the building, yet modernised it and the two mesh together perfectly, I'm impressed. Sitting in my car gazing at the building, I think that I need to get the details of their builder to add to my contractors database.

Climbing out of my car, I walk through the back courtyard, which reminds me of a beer garden that I visited at the Oktoberfest, well everything except for the sunflowers but they work well with the area. Opening the timber doors, I head inside. The first thing I notice is the floor-to-ceiling glass panel that separates the bar from the brewery, which is a neat concept; kudos on the design.

Walking over, I'm looking around and bump into a guy, he looks scary: baldhead, goatee, and vivid blue eyes. "Shit, sorry, dude."

"No worries, mate." He slaps me on the back, smiles, and heads towards the bar.

Phew, I think to myself, as I walk over to the glass wall to have a look inside the brewery. This place is bloody awesome. Along the side of the building, I notice the checker plate stairs winding up to a secondary bar area that overlooks everything. After looking around for a bit, I head to the bar, totally blown away with how awesome this place is.

Grabbing a stool at the bar, the bartender walks over. "Hey, what can I get ya?"

"Hey, umm, can I get a Checker Plate lager to start, please?"

"Coming right up."

Turning around, he grabs a beer mug and fills it up, with the perfect amount of head, placing it in front of me as I give him my credit card to set up a tab. "I'm impressed, not many people can pour a tap beer properly."

He laughs at me. "Well, I should be able to pour one properly, I'm the owner." He puts his hand forward to shake. "Jordan McRoberts."

Taking his hand and shaking, I reply, "Logan DeBiers. I really love this place. I tried your beers when you popped up in Sydney at Circular Quay earlier this year, and I've been obsessed ever since. When the hotel bar guy said the brewery was nearby, I had to come here. It truly is spectacular, Jordan, well done."

"Thanks, man. I'm lucky, I have a great team behind me and my wife and girls are very supportive."

"That's awesome. Look, I don't normally do this, but here's my card. I'm in developments and a chain of these breweries would be awesome."

He takes my card and looks it over, before he places it in his back pocket. "Thanks, Logan, but I'm not looking at expanding to that scale just yet, but I will definitely keep your details and be in touch if that changes."

"That's fine. In the meantime, can I get another Checker Plate and a serve of the cheeseburger sliders please?"

"Coming right up. I suggest adding the chili fries too, they go really well with the burgers."

"Okay, add that too," I say, as I finish my beer.

Sitting here, I sip on my beer and wish that Sav was here, she'd love this place; I hope my guy finds her soon. I really miss her.

I've just finished my meal, which was amazeballs. I spin around on my stool, my eyes darting around the room around and smile. I'm determined to get Jordan and Malt Me on my development schedule and to come here with Sav when I find her.

10

SARAH

WAKING EARLY THE NEXT MORNING, I GROAN AND STRETCH OUT IN THIS magnificent bed. Seriously it's like sleeping on a cloud and these sheets are to die for. *Kenzie would be so jealous, being the sheet snob that she is*, I think to myself, as I climb out and head into the ensuite.

Looking into the vanity mirror, I smile. I feel happy, content and that everything will be okay; and it's all due to meeting Victoria. To be honest, I was worried about doing all of this, but my first assignment with Mr. Akin was really easy and relaxed. I'm pretty sure that I can do this.

Turning around, I turn on the shower and let it steam up. Stripping off my satin nightie and pulling down my undies, I flick them to the side and step under the shower spay. This rainhead has just the right amount of pressure and I moan; it feels like heaven. I'm soaping up my body and I run my fingers over my now bare cleft, and I start to tingle deep inside. Closing my eyes, I gently slide my finger up and down, the water cascading over my fingers as I work myself over. Lifting my leg, I place my foot on the shower seat and I begin to rub my clit in circles, my breathing picks up, a tiny moan escapes my lips. Just as I'm at my peak, about to tumble over the edge, there's a knock on the door, scaring the shit out of me. "Yeah, what?" I manage to squeak out.

"Victoria just called, she will be here in thirty minutes and you need to be dressed and ready for a last minute assignment!" Morgan shouts.

"Okay, I'm just in the shower. Give me five minutes and I'll be down and ready."

"Cool, I'll put the coffee on," she says, closing the door behind her, thankfully I'm in the shower and she couldn't see anything...I hope.

"Thanks!" I shout back, as I lower my leg and grumble; *I was so close*. Sighing, I quickly get washed, step out, and dry myself before lathering my body in mosituriser and doing my makeup quickly, luckily I'm just a mascara and lippy girl.

Walking into the closet, I grab a navy and white Victoria Secret bra and undies set before slipping on a yellow and white spotted sundress; perfect for a Sunday lunch. Pairing it with white, strappy wedge sandals from Nine West, I smile at myself. I grab my handbag, ready and excited for my second appointment.

I'm walking down the stairs when the front door opens and in strolls Victoria; she looks up at me and pauses, she looks stunned. "Well, the morning won't be as hectic as I thought. You do know how to dress appropriately," she dismissively says, as she walks into the kitchen, not saying anything else to me.

My face breaks into a smile because I just shocked Victoria. I think that will be my new hobby, finding different ways to shock and piss off Victoria. Giggling to myself, I walk into the kitchen, both Angel and Morgan look up and whistle. Morgan says, "How the hell do you look that good at this time of the morning?"

Walking towards to coffeepot, I just shrug my shoulders and say, "Good morning, Victoria." Pouring her and myself a coffee before taking a seat next to Angel.

"You didn't make this did you?" Victoria asks.

"You're safe... for today anyway."

"Thank God for that. That drivel you served me the other day was revolting, thankfully coffee making isn't a skill that you require. Now, come along, I want to run through a few things with you at the office before your client picks you up later today."

"Yeah, sure, okay. Just let me grab my stuff."

"We really need to work on your vocabulary, Sarah. You sound so bogan and uneducated. Women like us need to speak eloquently and refined at all times."

"Yes, Victoria," I snidely say, as I skip past to grab my things that I left in the foyer.

As I'm walking away, I hear Victoria say, "Why must you girls test my patience?"

Twenty minutes later, we are pulling up at her office and just like the last time I was here, I'm amazed at the beauty of this building. We both get out of the car and make our way silently towards the lift. The silence is kind of awkward but I'm too nervous to say anything. I'm not sure if I'm nervous to be around Victoria, or for my next assignment. My first was easy but I'm pretty sure they all won't be like Mr. Akin. Seriously, who pays this much money just to spend time with someone, and not want anything? As the lift takes us up to her office, I think to myself that I'm not sure I could do that, that would make me a hooker, escort I can do but hooker, nope.

"Sarah, today you are having lunch with Xander C. He is taking you out on his yacht, depending on how the afternoon progresses, it could turn into an overnighter. This is your one chance to shine, Sarah, don't let me down."

"Overnight? Like sleeping over?" Lowering my voice, I add, "Sex?"

"Yes, Sarah, you will do whatever he requests of you, as long as it's within the law, but I suggest you keep him happy." She turns towards me and says, "Whatever. He. Wants. Sarah."

"How is whoring myself within the law?"

"Whoring yourself, as you so crudely put it, is not what we do here. We provide companionship and if that leads to a sexual encounter, that's on you and not us. I would strongly suggest, however, if anything sexual comes up that you seriously consider it, your place here could be jeopardised if our clients are not happy."

As I follow Victoria into her office, I think, *Holy fucking shit, what have I got myself into?* Taking a seat, I stare at Victoria, open-mouthed, totally shocked. "Victoria, I'm not sure I can do that. I'm happy to provide companionship, but I don't think I can just sleep with someone, I'm not a whore."

"I never said you were a whore, darling. I just said I advise you to sleep with him if the situation arises, think of it as a random hook up." Pausing she defiantly looks at me. "Especially, if you want to keep your job here at Elite."

"Umm, o...o...okay, I'll do my best to not disappoint you." Why do I care so much if I disappoint her?

"And stop stuttering and stammering, it's unbecoming of a lady."

"I'm sorry, Victoria." Swallowing hard, I ask, "Do you have any information on Xander that will help me out?"

"That's more like it. His file is in the next office; go over it, thoroughly. Xander is very dear to me and you will do whatever he wants. I'll send Simon in to collect you when it's time to go." As she talks about Xander, I notice a look wash over her face; it intrigues me.

"Yes, Victoria." Standing up, I head to the office next door and I keep repeating to myself, "*You can do this, you can do this.*"

An hour later, Simon gently knocks on the door and tells me it's time to go. Taking a deep breath, I stand up, nervously smooth down my dress, and politely say with a smile, "Let's do this." Following him out to the waiting car, he gives off a creepy vibe and I internally call him 'Sleazy Simon.'

The car trip to the marina was quick, too quick, but we pull up and I notice all the yachts and motor cruisers, it houses some of the biggest yachts I have ever seen. Walking towards us is a ruggedly handsome older man, and by older, I mean like George Clooney old. Thankfully, he's not a creepy, old, bald, greying man; he's quite attractive and that puts me at ease.

Simon opens my door, and I take his hand, as I climb out of the white limo. The marina precinct is full but no one takes notice of me or what I'm about to do. Before I know it, I'm standing in front of Xander; I'm so nervous that I stand there and stare at him like a fool.

"My God, you are even more beautiful than Victoria said. I'm Xander C., it's a pleasure to meet you, Sarah," he says in a deep gravely voice.

"Hhh…hi!" I stammer.

He takes my elbow and leads me towards the marina slips. "Don't be nervous, love, I don't bite." Pausing he looks down at me, he is at least four inches taller than me. "Unless you want me to." He winks as he says that and laughs, totally putting me at ease.

"Well, let's save the biting for another time, shall we?" I wink back at him, wondering to myself where this confidence has all of a sudden come from.

"I like you already, Sarah. Come, the yacht is all prepared and I really want to set sail."

"Lead the way, captain." I quickly step ahead of him, smiling to myself; I start swinging my hips seductively from side to side as I make my way down the walkway. I'm just about to turn around and ask which yacht is his when he wolf whistles. Spinning around, I pause, placing my hand on my hip, look up at him, and give him my megawatt happy smile, which I'm not faking by the way, "So, which of these babies is yours?"

He points towards the third yacht from the end, my eyes bug out of my head. "Holy shit, that's a Seahawk from *Perini Navi's* 60m series?"

"I'm impressed, how do you know that?"

"My dad and I attend the boat show each year, he'd kill for one of these babies, I can't wait to tell him that I've..." I stop speaking mid-sentence, as I know I can never tell Daddy about this. He would be ashamed to know that this is what I'm now doing, all the joy I felt earlier has vanished. Staring sadly at the stunning yacht in front of me, I'm startled when Xander places his hand on my shoulder. "Are you okay? Where did you go just now?"

Lying I say, "Just missing Daddy. He and Mum are in Europe at the moment and were in a car accident. Dad broke his leg so they are delayed until he can travel again."

"I'm sorry about your dad, Sarah." He reaches over and places his fingers under my chin and tilts my head up, he's grinning at me and his smile again puts me at ease. "Let's turn that frown upside down and head out. The fresh air will do you good; there's nothing more freeing than being out at sea. What do you say?"

"I say, lead the way and thank you."

"Why are you thanking me?"

"Well, you're paying me to keep you company and here you are cheering me up, that's not entirely fair to you."

"Babe, the day is still young. Now let's get going, I can't wait to get you alone."

With that one statement, my undies dampen and I'm entirely at his mercy. *I'm such a whore*, I giggle to myself as we make our way to the yacht.

"What's so funny?"

"Nothing, I'm just really happy to be here." Surprising myself with my honest answer.

"I'm happy you're here, too. I was disappointed to hear that Crissy was no longer working for Victoria, but I'm no longer upset about that." Pausing, his eyes rake over my body and I can feel his gaze burning my skin, hunger radiating from him. When his eyes land on mine, he takes my hand, squeezes, and says, "Sarah, you and I are going to have so much fun together."

Xander climbs aboard first and turns around, offering me his hand as I step up. I lose my footing and fall into his arms. Looking up into his dark chocolate eyes, I smile. He places me back on my feet and before I know it, he is kissing me deeply. Wrapping my arms around his neck, I return his kiss. Our lips are tightly pressed together, my tongue seeks access to his mouth and our kiss intensifies, until someone clearing their throat interrupts us.

Looking over, I see the deckhand, standing there awkwardly looking at us. "What is it, Davey?" Xander says, still staring intently at me.

"Umm, sir, we are all ready to set sail."

"Thanks, Davey, that will be all. I don't need you to come with us today."

"Very well, sir. When do you want me back here to clean her down?"

Dismissively he says, "I'll text you."

"Yes, sir." With that, he leaves, and a few moments later he is off the yacht and heading towards to car park.

Xander releases me from his grip, places a quick kiss on the tip of my nose, and says, "There's GH Mumm in the galley, why don't you pour yourself a glass, make yourself at home, and I'll join you shortly."

"Sounds good to me. Would you like a drink or anything?"

"I can't really drink where I want to drink from with all these people around, but as soon as it's just you and me and the open seas, I will be feasting on you. Rest up, Sarah, your in for one hell of a sail." He turns around and heads towards the cabin, leaving me standing there, open-mouthed, shocked, and dare I say, a little turned on.

I make my way to the top deck where I find the champagne and some cheese and crackers. Kicking off my shoes, I pour a glass and take a seat. Digging in my bag, I pull out my Ray Ban Aviators, slipping them on. Relaxing back into the lounge, I sigh and take in the scenery as we depart the harbour.

By time Xander comes back to join me, we are cruising the open seas and I'm totally relaxed; three glasses of bubbly and fresh sea air will do that to you.

"The open seas agree with you, Sarah, you look relaxed."

"I feel relaxed."

He smiles at me, as he grabs another flute, pours himself a glass, and tops mine up.

"Are you trying to get me drunk?"

"Maybe." He winks at me before raising his glass. "A toast, to the start of a beautiful arrangement."

His words cause my smile to fade when I remember that he is paying me. I quickly shake away the doubts and smile. "Cheers to that." We clink glasses and both take a sip. I close my eyes and moan, savoring the flavour of the bubbles as they slide down my throat, tingling as they make their way down.

"Fuck, Sarah, if you moan like that when drinking champagne, I can't wait to hear you moan when you are coming."

My cheeks turn pink and I look towards the horizon, embarrassed at what Xander just said. Wanting to change the subject, I stand up. Placing my glass on the table, I walk to the back of the deck and lean on the railing. "So, where are we off to today?"

He shrugs his shoulders at me. "No set destination, I just wanted to get away."

"Well, I'm happy to accompany you. The water is magnificent, I'd love to dive in from up top here, it's a shame I didn't bring a bikini with me," I reply, as I lean on the railing and stare out to sea.

Xander stands up and walks over to me, cocooning me in his arms he leans down and whispers into my ear, "There's no one around except me, no need for clothes." He nibbles on my ear and again I moan, it must be the fresh air mixed with the bubbly because I spin around and pull Xander towards me and kiss him.

Our tongues meshing together, you can't tell where I end and he begins. Our bodies press tightly together, our hands exploring each other's bodies. I feel his cock pressing into my stomach, without thinking, I drop to my knees and undo his cargos, freeing his engorged cock. The slit dripping with precum, I dart my tongue out and lick the tip before taking his cock deep into my throat and sucking.

"Holy shit, Sarah. Suck me harder, baby."

Xander runs his fingers through my hair, shoving my face further onto his cock. My head bobbing up and down as I suck and nip his cock in and out of my mouth. Reaching up, I begin massaging his balls and I hear him groan. His balls tighten in my hand just as I feel the first burst of cum hit the back of my throat. "Fuuuuck!" he shouts as I continue to suck him dry.

Once he has finished, I kneel back, look up at Xander, and smile, wiping the sides of my mouth before dragging my fingers across my bottom lip, slipping my finger in my mouth and sucking. Standing up, I turn around, walk over to the table, grab my bubbly, and take a sip, looking over my shoulder at Xander I seductively whisper, "Mmm-mmm, would you like a top up?"

"Fuck me, Sarah. That was unexpected and totally amazing and yes, please, top me up."

Grabbing the bottle of bubbly from the ice bucket, I walk over and fill his glass before filling mine, but I only get a few drops, as the bottle is empty. "Bugger," I say and look at Xander with sad, puppy dog eyes.

"I have more, no need to cry. I'll be right back."

He walks down the stairs and I'm left alone, again. Leaning on the railing I look out at sea, and wonder to myself where my inner porn star just came from. I have never, ever done anything like that before in my life; I'm shocked and proud of my self. Completely lost in thought, I don't here Xander come back until I feel his arms wrap around my waist. He's grinding his cock into my ass; I circle my hips and rub back. Looking over my shoulder, I grin. "Hey you." He kisses me while continuing to grind against my ass; his arm slides down my stomach, lifting the hem of my dress before pulling it over my head.

Our lips only breaking to let the material of my dress pass by. I'm standing there in my navy and white bra and undies set, extremely turned on, wrapped in the arms of a man who is paying me to be here. I start to feel bad about this, but that thought evaporates when I feel his fingers at the edge of my now soaked undies. He grips them and literally rips them off my body. Breaking our kiss I say, "Hey, they were one of my favourites."

"I'll buy you another." Before I can reply, he is kissing me again and sinking his finger deep inside of me before pulling out and thrusting two more in. Moaning, I thrust my pussy against his hand as he increases his pace, I feel my pussy walls tighten and I shout, "I'm coming. Fuck, I'm coming!" My legs giving way as my body explodes, my juices coating his fingers as I continue to ride out this pleasure explosion.

He withdraws his fingers and sucks my juices off, winking at me as he does this. Leaning forward, I place my palms on his cheeks and I crash my mouth against his and kiss him deeply, moaning, as I taste myself mixed with bubbly. "Mmmmmm," I say, as I pull back and look into his eyes. "Wow, that was, just wow."

He smiles at me before bending down to pick up my now shredded undies and dress. He hands me my dress and shoves what's left of my undies into his pocket, smiling at me before turning around and heading towards the stairs. "Guess we better head back."

I'm left standing there only in my bra, my undies now in Xander's pocket, holding my dress when it hits me; I'm a hooker, a fucking hooker. The floodgates open as I slip my dress back on. Picking up the bubbly, I drink from the bottle before pouring myself a glass and sitting down.

Staring out at the horizon, I feel used and abused but also content and happy; I'm so confused right now. I know I signed up for this, but emotionally; this is much harder than I thought.

After getting back to land, it was awkward to say that least. I thought for sure I was going to get raked over the coals when I got back, but waiting for me at the apartment was a huge bunch of pink tulips with a note from Victoria.

Congrats on a great first weekend
Welcome to the family
Regards, Victoria

The note puts me at ease but it has also garnered hostility from the girls in the apartment next door, apparently Saskia wanted to be paired with Xander now that Crissy is no longer here, but thankfully Angel and Morgan have my back. I would be lost without those two girls; I'm ever grateful that they are my roommates.

To celebrate my first weekend on the job, Angel, Morgan, and I decide to make a jug of margaritas, and spend Sunday arvo lounging by the pool, listening to music. I'm in my room, changing into my orange micro bikini when I start to feel guilty over what I did today. *Where did that come from?* It's so not me. I don't think I can sleep with people randomly. I'm not a slut. I've never been a sleep with a guy on the first date girl. Staring at myself in the mirror, I feel disappointed in myself but I really don't have any choice, do I?

My thoughts are interrupted by Morgan telling me to hurry up, I throw on my cover-up and decide that I will stay, but no more sexual encounters. Well I guess I will have to, if I get paired with Xander again, as I have already started that, but nope, no more sex for me…at least while I'm working here.

The girls and I have a fantabolous evening filled with margaritas, swimming, and takeaway Chinese from Kung Fu Palace. I'm feeling relaxed and happy with my decision to stay. Angel and Morgan both put me at ease and make me feel like I can do this. I keep my no sex decision to myself, but I'm happy with the decision I have made. I keep telling myself, Victoria said it's up to me if I do anything sexual with a client. I just won't do it again, that's just not me.

I'm feeling slightly buzzed and happy as I'm climbing into bed, I sigh when I snuggle down, it's like I'm sleeping on a cloud. Grabbing my phone, I realise that I have a missed call and voice message from Kenz. Seeing that, all the guilt and shame comes rushing back and I burst into tears. I'm hiding so much from my friends and family…I'm such a bitch.

11

LOGAN

THE HESITATION OVER MOVING HERE HAS FINALLY PASSED AND I THINK IT'S all due to my positive attitude. The hurdles I was facing with the new project have passed and all is going well; we should be finished by the completion date, if not sooner. Secondly, I managed to find an apartment and not just any apartment. Beth found me the most amazing penthouse apartment that overlooks the river and towards the bridge...right here in the hotel I have been staying at.

When I first walked in, I knew it was for me and the first person I wanted to call and tell was Sav; man I miss her. It breaks my heart that she took off like that, but I guess I can understand. It's kind of what I'm doing; I couldn't stand being in Wentworthville after what happened with Lili. I can only imagine what it would be like living in the same place where you lost your family.

I'm pretty sure that her store manager at home, Sierra, knows something but she's keeping tight-lipped. When I left, I told Sierra to contact me if Sav needed anything, her reply confirmed my suspicion, but I left it alone. I would do anything for her, she's my best friend, and she's my family. When I lost Dad, I would have fallen apart if it hadn't been for her. Luckily, Mr. and Mrs. Blac were happy to help me out from time to time. Don't get me wrong, Grandma did her best but she was too old to be looking after a teenager.

I've ordered room service for dinner tonight, and while I'm waiting, I start thinking about Mum. I haven't thought about her for years now. She ran off when I was five, with Dad's best friend, but truth be told, it was the best thing that could have happened to Dad and me.

There's a knock at the door and my dinner is here. They leave and I sit down and to enjoy my steak when my phone rings, and I see that it's Beth. "You have impeccable timing, Beth, I'm just about to hoe into a juicy steak."

"Well, give me three minutes and then you will be celebrating."

"Do tell, Bethy."

"You know I hate it when you call me Bethy. Anyway, the realtor has just faxed through everything for your penthouse sale and settlement will be in twenty-one days." Pausing she then adds, "I have also extended your stay where you are for four more weeks, the extra week is to allow you time to work and get settled in your new place."

"Beth, you are my hero. Get everything filled out, courier them to me, and I can drop them off later this week."

"Can do, boss, enjoy your steak."

"Ohh, I plan on it. Have a good night, Bethy."

I can hear her say, "Asshole," as I'm hanging up; she makes me laugh. I'd be lost without her. Finally things are looking up for me and I have a feeling things will continue to improve.

12

VICTORIA

To say I'm impressed with how Sarah has taken to being one of my girls is an understatement. When I sent her on the date with Xander, it was a little test. From the report I got back from Xander, she far exceeded any expectation that I had, and it was a total shock. She is an exceptional young lady. Sarah continues to surprise me and it's hard to surprise me; maybe I have found a new Crissy.

I'm still disappointed that she screwed me over the way she did, but the girls know the rules. I'm just glad she left with her head held high, unlike Megan. It was unfortunate the demise that came to her but as usual, my hands are clean and everything continues as normal.

Word seems to have spread that there is a new girl in town and I have been getting requests left, right, and center for my Sarah. This makes me happier than a Cartier sale. Due to her popularity, I can charge a premium and the additional income is heaven. The poor girl will be run off her feet, but the dollars she'll bring in will make things much easier. Times have been tough of late and if I lose any more girls, I won't be happy, but hopefully Sarah is my saving grace.

In between appointments on Tuesday, I call Sarah in for tea. She looks magnificent when she waltzes into my office and I inwardly smile. I can't let on that I'm happy; rule number one, always keep them on their toes.

Smiling, I stand up from my desk and walk towards her with my arms open. "Darling, you looking exquisite." Leaning forward I air kiss her cheeks, before taking her hand, and leading her out to my terrace.

"Thanks, Victoria. You look stunning, as always."

We both take a seat and I could not be more proud of how Sarah is handling herself. We sit staring at each other, I love making the girls squirm. It's a joy of mine with the newbies, but Sarah isn't squirming and that doesn't sit well with me. After a few moments of awkward silence, I ask, "Would you like some tea, Sarah?"

"Actually, I'd love a coffee. I've been so busy today that I need a caffeine hit."

Asserting my authority, I say, "Coffee is for the morning darling, tea it is." Leaning forward, I pour us both a tea but Sarah doesn't touch hers, she is quite stubborn. I need to pull her into line quickly so I get straight to the point. "How has your week been so far?"

"Umm, it's been crazy busy but I think I'm doing well." She looks over at me hesitantly. "Have I been doing well?"

"Darling, there is nothing the matter, if anything, you have far exceeded any expectation that I had for you. You have surprised me."

"T…Thank you, Victoria," she stammers.

This is the part I love, making them squirm and guess why they are here. "You really need to stop with the stuttering, Sarah, it is unlady-like." Pausing, I look down at her tea, then back at her, willing her with my eyes to drink. Leaning forward, she adds sugar to her tea and takes a sip; I give myself in inwards high five. "The reason I called you here today, was to see how you are getting on, just a catch up." Taking a sip of my tea, I stare at her. "Do you have any questions or concerns?'

"No, none at all. The girls have been really helpful and have made the transition that much easier for me. Victoria, thank you for every-thing. I was at rock bottom when I met you," Pausing, she looks at me before adding, "You really are my fairy godmother."

"No, darling, I was just in the right place at the right time. Fate has a funny way of guiding us when we least expect it."

"Tell me about it, I was starting to feel like I had no way out, and then you came along when I needed a boost. Hopefully, I'll be back on my feet in no time and I can get back to my life."

"You want to leave?"

"Not now I don't, but I can't do this forever, Victoria."

We will see about that. "Hmmm, well if that's how you feel." I don't say anything further because if I have my way, Sarah will be here for a long time to come. She is a money-spinner and I will not be letting her go so easily.

"Well, I must be going, I need to go and get changed for the fundraiser I am attending tonight. I will see you later, Victoria."

With that she stands up, comes over, kisses my cheek, and leaves me sitting on the patio, open-mouthed and shocked. *No one tells me they are leaving; I always dismiss them.*

Sarah continues to shock me, she is an enigma that I am yet to figure out, and it's unsettling to say the least.

13

SARAH

WORD SEEMS TO HAVE TRAVELLED THAT THERE'S A NEW GIRL ON THE block, and I've been an extremely busy girl this past week, seeing at least one appointment each day. Thankfully, none have been sexual, except for the one with Xander, and if I'm honest, I'm a little sad about that, which totally surprises me. I do however think that I will keep those ones to a minimum, I don't really want to whore myself out, but it was pretty exhilarating.

Today I have back-to-back appointments, which I have never done before and I'm a little nervous. I have a luncheon to attend to with Victoria and then an evening one. After our afternoon meeting the other day, I'm now super nervous to go out with her. Victoria is very intimidating at times and to be out in public with her will be quite daunting. My last appointment is with Xander; this will be the first time I have seen him since our boat encounter. I'm really nervous, yet excited to see him again, wondering if it will become sexual again.

The luncheon with Victoria was uneventful, extremely long and boring; watching paint dry would have being more exciting. It was hard to remain happy and stoic. But I was thankful that it was an easy afternoon with her, my apprehension was for nothing. At least there was yummy food and amazing cocktails.

After rushing to get ready because the afternoon luncheon with Victoria ran overtime, I'm nearly ready for my date, if you'd call it that, with Xander. I'm putting the finishing touches to my outfit and I feel like a princess. I'm wearing a knee-length, figure-hugging, backless plum dress with a modest 'V' neckline and two inch, black strappy heels. Due to the backless dress, I'm not wearing a bra and my undies are microscopic. It's pretty daring for me but I feel confident that I can do this; the old me, no way...even though I'm freaking out that one of the girls will pop out in the middle of dinner.

I've just done up the strap on my shoe when Morgan comes into my room, she stops midstep. "Holy fuck, you look hot, Sarah. Xander won't be able to keep his hands off you." My cheeks turn pink at what she says and I smile. "Give us a twirl." She spins her pointer around indicating a spin.

Smiling as I stand up, I spread out my arms and I spin around and around, like Maria in *The Sound of Music*. Due to my heels and the long dress, I lose my balance, but Morgan steps forward and catches me before I fall over; our eyes lock, she pulls me closer, and kisses me.

Closing my eyes, I open my mouth and let her tongue invade my mouth. She wraps her arms around me and I lose myself in the kiss. A throat clearing interrupts us, pulling apart I see Angel standing in the doorway, holding up a necklace for me with a smirk on her face. "I, um, thought this might go well with the dress you are wearing." Pausing, she declares, "You look fucking hot, Sarah."

Morgan pipes in, "She sure does, Xander won't know what hit him." She smacks me on the ass and says, "Have fun, don't do anything that I wouldn't do."

Angel scoffs, "There's not much that you wouldn't do, Morgan, so, Sarah, in that case you're in for a fabulous night."

"Bitch!" Morgan yells, before adding, "But yeah, you're right. Have fun, Sarah." Morgan winks at me as she heads across out of my room.

Angel walks over to me, holding up the necklace, I lift up my hair, which I straightened and left down, so she can put it on. Turning towards the full-length mirror, I look at my reflection. I don't recognise the person staring back at me. For the first time in a longtime, I see a confident girl looking back at me. My eyes well with tears, I realise that I'm happy...being a hooker.

"What's wrong, babe?" Angel asks as she rubs my arm, just like Kenz does when I'm upset and she's worried, that thought makes me start to cry harder. **SNIFF** "I miss my friend." **SNIFF** "But I can't tell her about this, or anything that's happened." **SNIFF** "I'm a whore." **SNIFF**

Angel wraps her arms around me and holds me tight, I cry onto her shoulder. "Shhhh, it's okay, Sarah. It will all be okay and you're not a whore." I don't say anything; I just hug her and continue to cry.

When I can cry no more, I look up and see that my face is all red and splotchy. "Shit, I look a mess and Xander will be here soon."

Pushing me towards the bathroom, Angel says. "Watch and learn, sweetcheeks, watch and learn."

Five minutes later, my makeup has been reapplied and you can't tell that I was blubbering mess a few moments ago. "Holy shit, you're a magician, Angel, thank you so much."

"You're welcome, Sarah. Now let's go downstairs and have a glass of bubbly before you have to go, it will help calm you."

"Best idea ever, I don't know why I'm so nervous tonight. I've been out with Xander before, it should be a walk in the park." Angel just shrugs at me, takes my arm, and leads us out.

We are halfway down the stairs when there is a knock at the door; Angel jumps down the remaining few steps and swings it open. Xander is standing there looking drop-dead gorgeous. He's wearing black slacks, a charcoal grey, long-sleeved, dress shirt with the top three buttons undone, and a black sports coat hangs loosely off his shoulders. My pussy begins to throb and my undies dampen at the sight of the man standing before me. Clenching my thighs together, I make my way down the remaining stairs and over to him, placing a kiss on his cheek before saying, "Hi, you're early." Stepping aside, I usher him inside the apartment.

"Fuck me, Sarah. You are stunning."

My cheeks turn pink and I look to the floor bashfully, he lifts my chin so I'm looking directly into his eyes. "Don't be shy, I'm just saying it how I see things."

"Thank you, Xander," I shyly say. "Should we get going or would you like a drink before we head out?"

"If we stay here, we won't be leaving your room and I want to show you off. You will be the hottest chick at the restaurant."

"Okay then, let me just grab my purse." Turning on my heel, I walk into the lounge room to grab my purse, the only sound is my heels clicking across the marble floor.

Bending down, I grab my purse when I feel someone standing directly behind me. Standing up, I turn around and I'm now face-to-face with Morgan. Before I have a chance to say anything, she kisses me on the lips, but this time I don't kiss her back. I'm too stunned because out of the corner of my eye I see Xander and Angel watching us.

"You ready, babe?" Xander says, in a deep gravelly voice that sends shockwaves through me.

"Yep, I'm coming."

"You will be soon." I hear Morgan murmur as I step around her and make my way back towards the foyer.

Putting my hand around Xander's bicep, I pull him towards the door and say, "Let's go." Over my shoulder, I say, "Later, ladies." As I close the door behind us, I hear a chorus of "Bye" and "Have fun."

Once, we are in the lift, Xander turns to me and says, "That was fucking hot, I think I'm going to need to arrange another date." I start to feel dejected when he adds, "Would you be up for a threesome?"

My head snaps towards him, "I...um...ah, I've never considered it before. Up until last week I had never kissed a girl."

"Then I would love to be your first threesome. Let's discuss it some more over dinner."

"Okay," I hesitantly reply, as we make our way through the foyer to the waiting limo out the front. *Tonight certainly has taken an unexpected turn*, I think to myself as I climb into the limo.

Xander wines and dines me, and I realise when we are in the limo on our way home that again I had a great night with him. Looking over at Xander, the streetlights flashing by reflecting on his face, he is deep in though as I rub my hand up his thigh, "Thank you for a lovely night, Xander." Licking my lips, I lean forward and kiss him.

He kisses me back, pushing me back into the seat as his body crushes me. His hands skimming over my breasts, I moan when he squeezes them, he deepens our kiss before nipping and sucking his way down my body, as his other hand pushes my dress up slowly. Lifting my ass, he shoves my dress to my waist and groans when all he feels is bare flesh. "Fuck, you're not wearing any undies."

"I slipped them into my purse before we left the restaurant," I pant, my heart beating erratically in my chest.

"You dirty fucking girl." Before I can register what's happening, he grabs the hem of my dress and lifts it over my head. I'm sitting in the back on a limo in nothing but black strappy heels...and I have never felt sexier. Xander's eyes heat with lust when I start to skim the tip of my finger over my chest, squeezing my nipples before tracing a path down to my pussy. Running my finger down my slit, I look at Xander and whisper, "Like what you see?"

"Fuck yes," he replies. Leaning forward, he sucks on my clit before slipping a finger deep inside of me, hooking it around and flicking that magic button deep within.

"Yes, that's the spot," I moan. He continues to suck my clit and flick his fingers until I'm tumbling over the edge; my whole body shudders as my orgasm rips through me like a tidal wave. "I'm coming," I breathlessly shout as I ride his fingers until my body tremors stop.

He looks up at me through hooded eyes and growls, "I need to fuck you now and it's going to be hard and fast. You okay with that?"

I'm still blissed out from my previous orgasm that I just nod, in one swift motion, he flicks open his button, shoves his pants down to free his cock, and thrusts into me until he is balls deep inside. His cock fills my pussy perfectly, and I clench around his length as he continues to assault my pussy.

He wasn't wrong when he said hard and fast. He pounds into me over and over, grunting with each thrust; my teeth shuddering together each time he slams into me. A few thrusts later, I feel his cock harden and he explodes, just as another orgasm ruptures through me, wave after wave rippling over me. We both cry out in ecstasy as our bodies thrum with pleasure.

He climbs off, and sits back next to me; we are both breathless, panting as if we have just run the Gold Coast Marathon. Feeling self-conscious, I lean forward and grab my dress, pulling it over my head and shimmy it down over my hips.

The air smells like sex but it is also really awkward, it's similar to what happened on the yacht the other day after we got busy on the deck. I couldn't say slept together because there was no sex that time.

Looking over at Xander, I'm hesitant to say anything, I'm just about to say something and I realise that we are back at the apartment. He quickly pulls his pants back up, tucking away his now flaccid cock when the driver opens my door. It doesn't seem like he is going to move, so I lean over kiss him on the cheek and murmur, "Thanks for a lovely night, Xander." Turning around, I take the driver's hand and climb out.

Before the limo has pulled away, the tears are flowing down my face. Slipping off my heels, I run inside and wait for the lift. The doors finally open after what feels like eternity, and I push the button for our floor. Sliding down the wall, I sit on the floor and cry, sobs rack through my body. The lift doors open but I don't get out; I just sit there, crying like a baby.

I'm still sitting in the lift, sobbing, when I hear an apartment door open. I'm too upset to look up, but before I know it, Angel is wrapping her arms around me. "Shhhh, it will be okay, Sarah. I know exactly what you feel. Xander can be an ass, don't take it to heart."

"I thought he really liked me."

"I know, it's hard to separate your feelings in this job but I promise, it does get easier. Just try have fun, eat and drink things that you have never heard of before and have fan-fucking-tabolous sex when the opportunity arises."

"I'm doing things I never thought I would, ugh, what am I becoming? I feel like a whore."

"Everclear?"

"Not in this instance, I mean literally." **SNIFF** "I just got paid for out of this world sex." **SNIFF** "I'm a hooker, a prostitute, a skanky ho slutbag. This isn't what my life was meant to be."

"None of us want this life, but sometimes you have to do what's needed to survive. Sarah, you are none of those things, you are a survivor. Albeit surviving in a non-traditional way but YOU are still getting on with your life. So it's taken a little detour, big fucking whoop." Emphasising the word 'you.' "You have food and shelter, a new kick-ass wardrobe and might I add, new kick-ass friends." She smirks as she says the last bit.

"I guess you're right. I just never expected to end up here."

"Neither did I, neither did I. Now, let's get inside, put on trackies, and break out the Hagen-Daas and Netflix."

"Do we have any Ben and Jerry's?"

"Since you moved in we do, so come on. Let's go inside."

Standing up, I wrap my arms around her in a tight embrace. "Thank you, Angel, I'm so glad I ended up in your apartment and not with Saskia."

"I'm glad too, Sarah. No one deserves to live with that psycho bitch."

Just as we are exiting the lift, she devil herself, Saskia, saunters out of her apartment dressed to the nines. She's obviously been called for a late night hook up. She looks at me in tears and snickers as she enters the lift. "I knew you couldn't handle him, just pack up and go home."

Angel bites back, "Fuck off, Saskia, you're just jealous that he didn't choose you but I don't blame him, your nothing bu..."

"Stop!" I interrupt, "She's not worth it." Turning around I stare her in the eye add, "Jealousy really doesn't suit you, Sass, besides, Xander isn't into washed up, two-bit whores. He has class and his class is currently dripping down my leg. Now if you excuse us, go fuck yourself."

As the lift doors are closing, Saskia is standing there open-mouthed and fuming. Angel is pissing herself laughing as we walk through the door; Morgan comes into the foyer. "What's so funny?"

"Sarah here just tore Sass a new one."

"You called her, Sass? She hates that as much, if not more, than Victoria being called Vicky. Man, I wish I could have seen that."

"Oh it gets better, our girl here said, and I quote 'Xander isn't into washed up, two-bit whores. He has class and his class is currently dripping down my leg. Now if you excuse us, go fuck yourself'"

"No fucking way?"

"Yes, fucking way," I say. "Now, I'm going to clean up and then we can Netflix it up."

Angel and Morgan head into the lounge, talking about my Saskawhore takedown, and I head upstairs. When I enter my room, I strip off my dress and quickly have a shower, washing away the filthiness of tonight. Slipping on my trackies and a singlet, I head downstairs to find Angel and Morgan on the couch eating ice cream, and I notice a bottle of tequila on the coffee table. "You two read my mind, so what shit are we going to watch?"

Jumping onto the couch in between them, we settle in and have a night of eating ice cream, drinking tequila, and watching *The Ranch*. Ashton Kutcher is so hot, just what the doctor ordered. Tonight reminds me of Kenz and me, I miss her so I decide that tomorrow I'll give her a call.

The sun is shining and I'm up way too early, especially considering today is my day off. I've been flat out this week and I'm looking forward to a day lounging by the pool, drinking wine, and chillaxing. After my mini breakdown last night, I'm feeling refreshed and this morning I feel like I could conquer the world. Chillaxing today is the perfect way to celebrate my newfound happiness.

Heading to the kitchen, I turn the coffee maker on and while I'm waiting, I text Kenz.

Sarah – *Hey bitch. Just saying hi. Work is crazy busy. Hope you and my lil princesses are fabulous. Catch up soon Xo*

Placing my phone back on the bench, I reach up and grab a mug. My phone starts playing *Bad Things* by Jace Everett and I smile, Kenz is calling me. Putting my mug down and I answer straight away.

"Morning, bitch. What are you doing up so early?"

"Um, kids, more to the point, why are you up so early?"

"Couldn't sleep. How have you been? It's been forever since I have seen you." Feeling a tad guilty when I say this because the not seeing one another is because of me. How do you tell your best friend that you are hiding because you're an escort, living it up in an apartment, because your ex-boyfriend kicked you out? Ohh and by the way, he's gay.

"I'm tired but good. The girls keep my busy and Malt Me is doing really well. Speaking of, we are having a tasting this weekend. Do you think you can make it?"

"That sounds awesome, I'll check my schedule and let you know. We are a few peeps down at the moment so I've been flat out." *Technically not lying, just not working where I used to.*

"Okay, keep me posted. How's Josh?"

Fuck, but luckily there is a knock at the door and I'm literally saved by the bell. "Hey, Kenz, there's someone at the door. I'll hopefully see you this weekend."

"You better, bitch, love your face."

"Love you face too, bitch."

Hanging up, I place my phone back on the bench and lovingly look at the coffee pot, when there is another knock at the door. Sighing, I walk to the door, yelling, "Coming."

Swinging open the door, I'm greeted by a fuming Victoria. "Good morning, Victoria." She pushes past me and heads towards the kitchen, without saying a word.

Following her back into the kitchen, I grab another coffee mug; she glares at me as I pour two coffees. "There is nothing good about this morning, Sarah. Saskia is no longer with us and the schedule is now in a shambles. You have a last minute appointment and then tonight you're also working. I need you to bring in a new client, numbers are dwindling and this is unacceptable; both client and staff wise."

So much for a quiet day I think, then it hits me, she said Saskia is gone. "What do you mean Saskia is gone? I saw her heading out last night. But more so, how do I bring in new clients? That's not what I'm here for."

"Never mind where the little tramp is, she's gone. End of story. As for bringing in new clients, you will do as I say or you can join Saskia."

I'm shocked by what I'm hearing and also little intimidated. How am I going to bring in new clients? A last minute appointment, this must be paying a fortune, especially if Victoria is here this early in the morning arranging it. "So what and whom am I seeing on such short notice today?"

"Thank you, I was sure that you were going to fight me on this since it's your day off. It's with Xander, last night must have gone extremely well if he's requesting you again so soon and wanting this on such short notice, too."

Fuck, Xander, Mr. Mindfuck himself. Plastering on a fake smile, I say, "Sure, that's fine. Are we going out on his boat again?"

"No, to his house. The driver will be here to pick you up at 11:30 a.m. and then I'll be by tonight to pick you up at 8:00 p.m. and I will take you to the local hotel, where we seem to be having luck acquiring new clients."

"That's fine, Victoria." Taking a sip of my coffee I add, "Will I be back in time to get ready to meet you, my visits with Xander generally run late."

"Yes, there will be plenty of time. He is aware of your schedule for this evening and has promised to have you back in plenty of time. Don't frown, it's not good for your face." She looks at her watch and states, "I have to get going. I have a whole schedule to rearrange due to Saskia's departure. I'll see you tonight. And, Sarah, don't disappoint me, I'm not in the mood to be let down again."

With that she turns on her heels and storms off, slamming the front door behind her. I'm left sitting there stunned. *She really needs to get laid,* I think to myself as I drink my coffee. Taking a seat at the breakfast bar, I lose myself in my morning coffee, swinging myself side to side and I sigh, Xander, really? I'm not sure I want to see him again. Hearing feet shuffling through the lounge room, I look up and see Morgan, looking like shite.

"Morning, lovely, you look like shite."

"I feel like shite but I got a call from Bitchtoria. Looks like you and I have an appointment together today."

"What? She never mentioned that when she was here."

"So that's who was slamming doors this early. I thought it might have been next-door trying to piss us off since you gave her a tongue-lashing, and not the good kind, last night, and she was still pissy about it. So wish I could have seen that."

"Ha, well, apparently, she's no longer with us."

Morgan's head snaps up and she's wide-awake now. "What do you mean no longer with us?" she says, as she pours a coffee for herself, sitting on the stool next to me.

"That's all I know, hence why Bitchtoria is in a pissy mood at the ass crack of dawn. She has to redo the appointments. Isn't she like the forth girl to leave in the last two weeks?"

"Five, no six, there were a few girls just before you got here. Wow, wonder what's happening?"

"Beats me. But tonight, I'm on scouting duty with Victoria."

"Fuck me, times are hard if she's using us to get newbies."

"Huh?"

"Well, it's normally a let them approach us system, but times must be tough if we are bringing them in. It's going to get crazy busy in that case."

"Great, like I'm not already shattered."

"Welcome to the glamorous life that is working for Victoria Chalmers. Anyways, what's up with the double appointment?"

Looking over at Morgan, I bite my lip. "Umm, Xander saw our kiss last night before he and I left." Pausing, I quickly add, "And he wants to have a threesome with us."

"Okay, cool."

Just like that, she's okay with this. I'm in shock but also turned on by the thought of a threesome. "Really, just like that you're okay with it?"

"Yep, it's the nature of the job, darl." Looking over at me, she enquires, "Have you ever had a threesome?"

Shaking my head from side to side, I bite on my lip and whisper, "Nope. I'm kinda nervous."

She slides up beside me and squeezes my hand. "Did you like kissing me?" Shyly, I nod my head up and down as I look towards Morgan and smile. She grins back at me and somehow it relaxes me. "Then just follow my lead and prepare to be mind blown." She leans over, grabs my cheeks, and kisses me, the stool spins towards her and I spread my legs to let her in. Sliding my arms around her waist, I deepen the kiss and moan into her mouth. My heart rate increases, I've never been kissed like this before. She gently cups my breast and massages, that tingly feeling deep in my belly starts fluttering when Angel entering the kitchen interrupts us. "Don't stop on my account, ladies."

Morgan pulls away and winks at me, before turning to Angel. "Guess what?"

"It's too early to play guessing games."

"You'll love this." Morgan pauses for effect. "Saskawhore is no longer with us and our newbie here is about to have her first three-some...with Xander and me."

Angel closes her eyes and sighs. "I remember my first ménage with you." She takes sip of my coffee before spitting it out. "What the what? Saskawhore's gone, what? How? Why? Spill."

Morgan and I both laugh, and I say, "Yep, Vicky popped by this morning and told me."

"Come on, spill?"

"That's all I know. She told me 'End. Of. Story' in her snotty voice and then stormed off. A few minutes later, Morgan came down to tell me about today's new adventure."

"No fucking way, that totally blows me away. I thought for sure Saskawhore would be here till her vagina was old, wrinkly, and about to fall off. Man she was a whore, so glad she's not here anymore, morale will definitely improve next-door then."

Morgan pipes in, "Yeah but now, the rest of us have to deal with the freaky fucked up appointments that she used to keep to herself."

Angel shudders. "Damn, didn't think of that. So how did today's ménage à trois come about?"

"Xander saw Morgan kiss me last night and mentioned that he'd want that with us, I didn't think he'd be serious...or arrange it so quickly."

"Sarah, he's a male. He would have been thinking about that all night long, even when he was balls deep inside of you. Wonder if we can entice him to make it a foursome?"

"Umm, let me try this first and then we can go from there."

"Seriously?" she eagerly asks.

"I guess so, why the hell not?" They both nod at me as I say this. I think I shocked them with my reply, especially after last night's meltdown.

Finishing my coffee, I say, "And on that note, ladies, I need to go get ready." Turning towards Morgan, I shyly ask, "Umm, Morgan, what do I wear?"

She finishes her coffee, places our mugs in the sink, throws her arm over my shoulder, and we head up stairs together to get ready. "You're in good hands, babe, leave it to me. Today will be a day that you will never forget."

...And it sure is one that will go down in the history books.

14

VICTORIA

Finally, someone who just says, "Yes, Victoria," without complaining or wanting anything in return. I knew I could count on Sarah to help me out. At least this clusterfuck has so far been easy to repair, but something is going on and I don't like it. Another girl has screwed me over, and that is unacceptable. This one makes four in the last two weeks and seven in recent times. What shocks me most is that it is was Saskia this time, I didn't want to forcibly remove her but the situation required it. At lease Crissy went peacefully and I didn't need to get my hands dirty, but Saskia, she was a wild one, not surprising really. In the beginning that's what I liked about her, but I gave her too much free rein, I've learned my lesson, it's time for a change.

It's time to bring the girls inline and reiterate to them that no one fucks with me, no one. An intervention with the girls is needed, and it needs to happen soon, I can't afford to lose another girl. Thankfully, I found Sarah when I did, never thought I would thank a client but him wanting to meet in that dump led me to her.

She is a diamond in the rough, that's for sure. Her language is appalling but she has this aurora that sucks you in. She's taken to the job like a pro. With a bit more refining, she will be the best girl that has ever worked for Elite. With the guidance from Morgan, Angel, and myself, I can turn her in a cash cow, even bigger than Crissy was.

Pouring myself a brandy, I sit on my leather couch. I keep thinking about what's happening with the girls at the moment. This situation is really grating on me, why all of a sudden is this happening? Is someone trying to sabotage me? I hope not, after all, I'm Victoria Chalmers; no one fucks with me!

15

SARAH

IF YOU HAD TOLD ME FIVE WEEKS AGO THAT THIS WAS GOING TO BE MY LIFE, I would have laughed in your face and told you to take another toke because you were smoking crack. It's amazing how in the blink of an eye everything can change, and then when you are at rock bottom, an opportunity of a lifetime comes along and completely turns your life around. Without Victoria and Elite, I would have been alone, jobless, and homeless. This isn't what I envisioned my life would be, but surprisingly I'm really enjoying this, and to be honest, trying to snag a new client seems exciting.

A few hours later, Morgan and I arrive at Xander's. His house was over the top, exactly what I pictured for him. He opened the door and I was sure I was going to pass out, a rush of endorphins ran through my body as I realised I was about to partake in my first threesome. He invited us in and led us out to the patio. He went back inside and returned with three mojitos: alcohol, just what I needed to calm my nerves.

As I suspected there was very little small talk, the air was thick with lust, confusion, and excitement. Before I knew it, Xander was leading us upstairs towards the bedroom. Xander and Morgan ran the show, and for the most part, I was just a bystander, and truth be told, I was fine with that, not that I knew what I was doing anyway.

I have to say it was quite arousing watching two people go at it in person; it's way different to watching porn. When they both turned their attention to me, holy shitballs, Batman. I'd never experienced pleasure like that before; I didn't know where to concentrate. Four hands roaming my body, two mouths sucking and nibbling simultaneously, it was mind-blowing.

In typical Xander style, once it was over, he left, without a word, leaving Morgan and I lying in his bed. Looking to Morgan, I noticed that she didn't seem fazed. She just stood up, grabbed my hand, and led me into the ensuite to shower and get freshened up. Leaning in, she turned the shower on, and once the water was warm, pulled me into the most heavenly shower I have ever had. The shower stall was big enough to fit several people, there were eight wall jets and an overhead rainwater tap thingy; it was pure bliss. The water temperature was perfect and just what my body needed.

Morgan and I showered in silence before she started to wash and soap up my body. I had never had a girl touch me like that before, but after what we had just done together, a shower was nothing. We soaped each other up, kissing and indulging in a little more fun before hopping out—I quite enjoyed the girl on girl action. I think because girls know what they like, they know how to evoke the pleasure just right. Once we were dressed, we headed downstairs to the waiting limo. When we got home, Morgan and I didn't have time to chat, as I had to get ready to go out with Victoria.

I'm lying in the tub, relaxing my body, as it's sore from earlier. I never knew that a threesome could be so physically draining. Closing my eyes, I remember the events from earlier today and I can't help but smile, it was exciting and so not what I thought it would be. The books make them look so sexy and erotic, don't get me wrong, I had fun, but I can't say I'll be rushing out to have another one. I'm more a twosome type of girl; sorry Angel there will be no foursome either.

Stepping out of the bath, I dry off and lather my body with moisturiser and spritz on my perfume. Walking into the closet naked, I put on a fire engine red strapless bra and undies set. Turning to the dresses hanging up, I can't choose between the red knee-length strapless or the midnight blue, floor-length, one shoulder dress. I'm standing there staring at both when Morgan comes in and whistles at me. Laughing, I smile and turn around. "Hey, which should I wear?" Lifting up each dress to show her.

"Umm, the blue. It will make your eyes pop. Save the red for the first date with whomever you snag."

"Thanks. Did you need me for anything?"

"I just wanted to check and see how you were doing, you were pretty quiet when we got back from Xander's earlier."

"I'm fine, Morgan, just tired and worn out. The soak in the bath reinvigorated me and now I'm ready to go." Slipping the dress over my head, I do a spin. The material feels amazing against my body and when I look in the mirror, I feel and look like a princess. Turning towards Morgan I ask, "What do you think?"

"Whomever you choose tonight, will be eating our of your hands. You are fucking gorgeous, Sarah, I'm a little envious of you."

"Envious of me, please."

"Seriously, Sarah. You have taken to this job like a duck to water, no wonder you are the fav."

"Pfft, I'm not the fav."

"Yeah, you are, but you know what? You deserve it. You've been to hell and back and now the sky is the limit. I'm so happy for you, Sarah. You are a pro at this, and not in the hooker for sex slash blowjob kind of way. You are gorgeous, fun, bubbly, free-spirited, and sexually adventurous; the perfect mix for this job."

"I don't know about all of that."

"I do, I've been doing this for a few years now and everyone loves you, everyone. Listen, I've been involved in my fair share of ménages, but Sarah, I've never enjoyed myself as much as I did with you today. If you ever want another, I would happily oblige."

"Umm, I don't know, Morgan. Don't get me wrong, I enjoyed it, and this, but I can't see myself doing this forever."

"Victoria will have something to say in that, you are her cash cow at the moment, Sarah. There is no way in hell that she will be letting you go anytime soon." With that she turns on her heel and exits the wardrobe; leaving me to ponder what she said…am I really going to be stuck here forever?

I'm finally ready and as I'm heading downstairs my phone pings with a text.

Kenz – *yo, bitch! What time you getting here for Origin 2nite?*

Fuck, fuck, fuck, I think to myself. Turning around, I head back to my room. If I don't call, Kenz is going to call me, so I quickly dial her number and she picks up in the second ring.

"Yo, bitch, how far away are you?"

"Umm, that's why I'm calling. I can't make it tonight. I have to work."

"Noooo, it's Origin, Sarah. You have to be here."

"I know but something at work has come up. I have to go, we will catch up soon."

"Yeah, sure, okay. If you get off before the game ends, pop over."

"I'll see what I can do. Love you, bitch."

"Love you too, laters."

Phew, I think to myself as I slip my phone into my bag and head off to meet Victoria. As I climb into the limo, I realise that I'm still smiling, and dare I say it, glowing; guess that happens when you have a three-some with multiple orgasms.

Half an hour later, we've picked up Victoria and I'm sitting next to her in the limo; all of a sudden, I'm nervous as all hell. My palms are sweating and my heart rate is accelerating the closer we get to the bar. I'm more anxious about tonight, and bringing in a new client, than I was this morning when I was faced with a threesome with Xander and Morgan. My nerves kick up a notch as the limo approaches the bar and before we climb out, she turns to me and gives me her intimidating stare. "Sarah, tonight is very important. Don't screw it up; a lot is riding on this. Failure is not an option."

No pressure, I think to myself as I climb out of the limo.

Victoria leads me to a table near the front windows. She orders a bottle of *Krug* and we scope out the bar. It's still early so the place is pretty empty; Victoria takes this time to educate me on how to pick up a man and the dos and don'ts of procurement. I'm not really paying attention as I see a drop-dead gorgeous guy walk in, and I know he's the one. I'm half-heartedly listening to her, my eyes and mind keep wandering to the guy sitting at the bar. Finally, she tells me to go explore; there's no exploring needed, I know exactly whom I want to chat to.

Finishing off my glass of champagne, I look to Victoria and say, "Wish me luck."

Surprising me, she replies, "Go get 'em, tiger."

To make it not so obvious, I wander the long way to the bar, casu-ally glancing around. After a few moments, I decided it's now or never and I make a beeline for the guy from earlier. He's sitting at the bar all alone, and I think this is a sign, taking a deep breath I strut over to him repeating to myself, "You can do this, you can do this." *I seem to be saying that a lot lately.*

Taking a seat next to the gentleman, I turn towards him, notice no ring, and smile…here goes nothing.

16

LOGAN

It's Origin day but after a long day of meetings and number crunching for a new tender, I'm shattered. I head to the hotel bar for a burger and beer; my standard dinner at the moment. I've just ordered when someone takes the stool next to me, glancing over I see an attractive brunette sitting there. I smile to be polite and she takes this as an opening to engage in conversation. "Hi, I'm Sarah, Sarah Bryant."

"Hi, Logan DeBiers. Nice to meet you."

She leans in closer, flashing her cleavage in my face, and I get a good look down her dress. She notices me staring at her chest and she smiles seductively at me. "Would you like to join me for dinner, Logan DeBiers?"

"Umm, not tonight, I've just finished the day from hell and tomorrow, I'm heading out of town for a business meeting. As soon as I finish my burger, I'll be heading back to my room 'cause I'm shattered."

She looks dejected but smiles, "Okay, have a great night then, Logan DeBiers." She leans over, gently kisses my cheek, and slides a card next to my hand. When she removes her lips, I swear my cheek tingled and I was sad at the loss of contact. She turns around and walks away from me, swishing her ass from side to side as she exits the bar. I'm mesmerised as I watch the material of her dress hug her curves, she turns and blows a kiss towards me before she leaves. I can't help but smile as I watch her saunter away.

The bartender returns with my burger, I order another beer and forget all about Sarah. It isn't until I'm about to leave that I notice the card she left me, picking it up I shove it in my pocket and head up to my room. Once inside, I throw everything on the kitchen bench and head to the bedroom. Stripping off, I change into my navy basketball shorts, grab another beer, and watch some television before crawling into bed and turning out the light.

Just as I'm about to fall asleep, an image of Sarah appears, her eyes boring into me, hiding behind her bangs before she smiles, and I smile. As I'm remembering her beauty, the card she gave me pops into my mind. Rolling to my side, I try to get to sleep but it starts to bug me. Turning on the light, I head to the other room and pick it up. It's an ivory thick card, with just a number on it in heavy gold block writing; on the backside of it is an embossed gold dove. "That's weird," I say, chucking it back on the bench, I head back to bed but I can't sleep. I lay there staring at the ceiling and I can't stop thinking about Sarah or that card; it's intriguing.

My curiosity gets the better of me so I hop up again, grab the card, and dial the number; it goes straight to an answering service. I leave my details and jump back into bed. The last thing I remember before falling to sleep is Sarah's beaming smile and hypnotic eyes.

The next morning, I have a final meeting with my realtor about the penthouse to sign all the documents, officially making it mine before I head to the airport. I've just left the office when Beth calls to say the meeting later today has been postponed, and she has rebooked my flights for next week. *Beth is a gem,* I think to myself as I realise that I have a free afternoon and I'm pretty excited. Deciding to grab a coffee, I head to the Java Lava café. I've just placed my order and while I'm waiting, my phone rings, I don't recognise the number. "Hello."

"Is this Logan DeBiers?"

"Yes, who is this?"

"Yes, sorry, my name is Victoria, you met one of my girls last night and left a message. Is this a good time to chat?"

"Huh? One of your girls, no I met a Sarah in a bar."

"Yes, she's one of my girls. I much prefer to do business face–to–face, Mr. DeBiers, are you free for lunch?"

"Umm, yeah, business, what I'm confused?" My coffee order is called; grabbing my coffee I head to the nearest table and take a seat.

"All in good time, Mr. DeBiers. Now what do you say we meet at *Cha Cha Cha* at 1:00 p.m. and I can give you all the information?"

Now the old Logan would have said no immediately but I'm trying to be spontaneous and different, prove she-bitch wrong, so I decided why not? I need to eat anyway. "Okay, Victoria, that sounds great. I will see you then."

"Excellent, Mr. DeBiers, I look forward to meeting you later today."

After hanging up from Victoria, I drink my coffee and wonder to myself what in the hell I have gotten myself into.

After getting lost, I finally find the restaurant, I'm ten minutes late and I hate being late. Walking inside, I ask the maitre'd for Victoria, thankfully they know whom I'm referring to as I didn't get her last name. I'm escorted over to her table in the back of the restaurant and she stands to greet me. "Mr. DeBiers, it's nice to meet you; I'm Victoria Chalmers."

"Mrs. Chalmers, it's lovely to meet you. I apologise for being late but I got lost, my sense of direction is shocking and I'm new to town."

"It's Ms., Mr. DeBiers but please, call me Victoria."

"Okay, I'll call you Victoria if you call me Logan."

"It's a deal, Logan." She winks as she says this and takes her seat.

Our waiter comes to the table. "Can I get you a drink, sir?"

"Yes please, can I get a beer, whatever you have on tap will be fine."

"Certainly, sir." Turning to Victoria, he asks, "Can I get you another glass, Ms. Chalmers?"

"Thank you, Toby, that would be wonderful." Turning her attention back to me, she leans her elbows on the table and gets right down to business. "So, Mr. DeBiers, you're interested in my Sarah?"

17

VICTORIA

"So, Mr. DeBiers, you're interested in my Sarah?" Looking over, I see confusion on his face.

"What do you mean 'my Sarah'?" He air quotes 'my Sarah.'

"Well, Mr. DeBiers. Sarah is one of my girls and from the chemistry I saw between the two of you last night, and your subsequent phone call, I put two and two together."

"I...I don't understand. I met a girl at a bar and called her, but instead of speaking to her I'm speaking to you. Is she a hooker?" He leans forward and whispers the last part, pulling back when Toby returns with our drinks.

"Thank you, Toby."

"Are you ready to order?" he replies.

"Can we please have a few more moments? I'm not sure I will be staying," Logan replies. Toby nods his head and returns to the bar.

"Mr. DeBiers, what's not to understand?"

"What and who are you?" He looks completely confused.

"My name is Victoria Chalmers, owner and proprietor of Elite. Sarah is one of my girls, and if you'd like to see her again, I can arrange that."

"What exactly does that mean?"

"Sarah works at Elite. We are the best agency in town. She would be available to attend functions, spend time with you..."

"She's a hooker?"

This gets me laughing every time I meet up with a new client, and I can't help but cackle. "Mr. DeBiers, no I do not employ hookers. I supply and employ escorts, which according to the Oxford dictionary means 'A person who may be hired to accompany someone to a social event.' Not a hooker by definition. Should said social encounter fall into a sexual nature that is between you and her." Letting him digest that, I then add, "The price will vary depending on the social activity, duration, and notice given."

"I...umm...I...I don't know what to say. I've never done this before."

Laughing, I say, "There's a first time for everything, Mr. DeBiers. Why not give it a go, what do you have to lose?"

"Well, apart from money, my dignity, and my reputation. What if this gets out?"

"I assure you, at Elite everything is confidential and discreet. You'd be surprised whom I have on my books. I'm not here to judge, I'm here to provide companionship and a good time. Nothing more, nothing less."

"I'm just not sure." Pausing, he then mumbles to himself, "I've never done anything like this."

"Mr. DeBiers, we only live once. Why not give it a go and then see where it leads from there?"

"I'm still not sure, it just doesn't feel right."

"Stop, you're beating around the bush, I don't have time for what ifs and it doesn't feel right. I will give you some time to think about it." Handing another card to him, I state, "This is my card, it has my direct number on it. When you have made up your mind, give me a call. I don't have all day."

"Umm, Okay, thanks."

"Your welcome. Now, I must run, I have another meeting across town to get to. I hope to hear from you soon, Mr. DeBiers."

Before he has a chance to respond, I'm heading out the door...*he'll call, they always do*, I think to myself as I head towards my waiting car.

18

LOGAN

VICTORIA HAS JUST LEFT AND I'M SITTING HERE STUNNED. HIRING AN escort, can I really do this? The old me would not have even called in the first place, the new me is actually considering this, because Sarah is stunning and I'm intrigued by her. Silky chocolate brown hair, beautiful eyes that suck you in, and a body with curves in all the right places; she's every man's dream girl. As I sit here and stare into my beer, I seriously start considering doing this. There is something about Sarah and I want to get to know her. We may have only said ten words to each other last night, but I'm drawn to her...I need to have her in my life.

Fuck, where are you, Sav?? *I really need you right now,* I think to myself as I sit here, staring out the window at the river, contemplating all of this. I'm playing out every different scenario in my head, but it all comes back to Sarah, what harm could it do? *It's just talking, I'm not paying for sex, and it will be okay...right?*

The staff here are looking at me curiously as I'm mumbling to myself, when I notice the looks I decide it's time to leave. After settling the bill, I decide to walk along the riverfront, the long way to the hotel, soon to be my home; I'm still amazed that I got the penthouse.

Before heading to my room, I head to the bar, have a Malt Me beer, and pick up my phone. My nerves kick up when it starts to ring, it's Beth letting me know that some time-sensitive documents have been delivered, and I need to sign them immediately. I tell her I will sign tonight and post them off tomorrow morning for her. After hanging up, I make my decision and dial Victoria's direct line. I'm ready to hang up but the call connects; I pause and don't say anything.

"Mr. DeBiers, I was expecting your call."

"Good evening, Victoria."

"Have you come to a decision, Mr. DeBiers?"

"I have, yes." Pausing, I swallow hard and then quickly say, "I'd like to meet with Sarah."

"Marvelous, I knew you would. When you would you like to arrange the first meeting?"

"Umm, I hadn't really thought about that."

"Typical man," she scoffs. "Well, let me help you out. Sarah is available any evening this week, but if you'd prefer a daytime visit, I'm sure I can shuffle things around for you."

"No, no, don't disrupt her schedule. How about tomorrow night?"

"That will work. The first meeting will be at my bar, Equinox. What time would best suit you?"

"I should be done by 7:00 p.m., will that work?"

"Perfect, Mr. DeBiers. I will see you tomorrow night at 7:00 p.m. and Sarah will join you at 7:30 p.m., once we have everything finalised and you've wired the first payment to me. Welcome to Elite, Mr. DeBiers," she says in a chipper tone, which is disturbing to say the least.

"Thank you, Victoria, and please, call me Logan."

"Goodnight, Logan."

As I disconnect the call, I start to regret my decision, but then I close my eyes and a vision of Sarah appears. Any qualms I had disappear; I cannot wait to get to know this woman.

19

VICTORIA

MY LUNCH WITH MR. DEBIERS WENT EXTREMELY WELL…EVENTUALLY. FOR a moment there, I feared I was going to lose him, but thankfully luck was on my side. After storming off and leaving him sitting there, he called me back later that evening, and he is now the latest member of Elite.

He is very interested in Sarah and they will be meeting tomorrow night here at our bar. I want to watch over her and see how she does; I've yet to see her in action. She has not yet let me down and I hope it continues; I've had enough to deal with of late. The girls really need to fall into line, or I will be forced to intervene…again…like I did, with Saskia recently.

I'm not happy when I need to specifically get involved, but no one, and I mean no one, messes with me…or there are consequences to be paid.

Today has been hectic and I'm just packing up for the evening when Simon walks in with an envelope for me. He places it on my desk and says he will be back after dropping Sarah and Logan off to dinner, and when he returns, he will wait in the bar until I'm ready to head home for the evening. Nonchalantly I wave him off. *You don't tell me what the plan is,* I think to myself as I reach for the envelope.

Reaching into my desk draw, I grab my letter opener and slide it along the envelope edge. Replacing it and closing the draw, I turn my attention back to the envelope in my hands. As I'm pulling the letter out, a feeling of unease washes over me. Reading the letter I gasp, there in block letters is my greatest fear...someone knows.

Staring back at me are five words, five words that I never wanted to see.

I Know What You Did

My heart is racing, if this gets out we'll be ruined, but if it does, I refuse to go down alone. I'll take him with me and anyone else who gets in my way.

Picking up my phone, I make the phone call that I hoped I never would have to make. They pick up on the first ring.

"Yes," they curtly reply.

Swallowing hard, I quickly say, "Someone knows."

"Fix it." That's all they say before hanging up.

As if my night could not get any worse, Simon walks back in. "Sorry to bother you but we've lost another."

"What do you mean, we've lost another?"

"Ma'am, Angel is no longer with us. As I was leaving to get the girls, I ran into her outside. She handed in her apartment key, business credit card, and phone and left."

My blood starts to boil, this cannot be happening. I'm losing girls left, right, and center and now the threat. "Thank you, Simon, place her things on the lounge, I'll deal with them later. Looks like I'll be here for a while."

"As you wish." He turns, placing the items on the lounge and leaves me alone in my office. Pondering what step to take next, a genius idea starts to develop. It's not going to be a pretty one...not for her anyway.

20

SARAH

I'M LAZING IN BED, STILL OVERWHELMED WITH THE HAPPENINGS OF THE past few days. They are a few days that I will never forget: I had my first threesome and I tried to secure my first client. Both were equally exciting but in completely different ways, but as soon as my eyes locked on whom I now know as Logan, all nerves I had vanished and a sense of calm euphoria washed over me.

We only spoke for a few moments, but I must have left just as much of an impression on him as he did with me. He immediately joined Elite and now tomorrow night I'll be having dinner and drinks with him.

Waking the next morning refreshed, which I haven't done in week now, I'm excited for the day ahead of me. Thankfully, my luncheon was cancelled last minute; therefore I now have the afternoon to pamper myself. I'm so nervous about tonight, I haven't had butterflies like this since my first date with Josh. Just as I'm about to jump into the shower, my phone beeps with a text from the asshat himself.

Josh – *Why does Kenz think we are still dating?*
Sarah – *Haven't told her*
Josh – *Well I did. Come get you shit*
Sarah – *Soon*
Josh – *Now. Or I chuck it*

Sarah – *Busy at work now. I'll get when I can*

After that final text, I shut off my phone, I refuse to let him ruin tonight for me. It only seems fitting that the asshole that caused all this, makes contact when I'm finally starting to feel happy again. Guess that's the world letting me know that Sarah Bryant doesn't deserve happiness.

After a long hot shower, I'm starting to feel like me again, when there is a knock at my door. Before I can shout 'come in,' it opens and both Morgan and Angel enter.

"Why, please come in, girls?" I say like a smart-ass with a smirk and a smile.

"Well, I guess us and the bubbly will turn back around then." Pausing, Morgan lifts the bubbly. "Please can we stay, pretty sure you want some bubbles," Morgan replies cheekily.

"Come on, Morgan, we can take this to the patio, she obviously doesn't want any bubbly," Angel says, smirking at me but her eyes don't light up as usual. She pops open the bubbly and pours three glasses, handing one to Morgan, holding mine hostage.

"You two are so funny. Now, Angel, please pass me my bubbles, I'm really nervous about tonight."

Morgan laughs, "If you're nervous about dinner and drinks, I wonder how nervous you were the other day before our threesome?"

"Hardy har har, but surprisingly, I'm more nervous about tonight. You guys, this Logan dude is beyond fucking hot. I'm getting wet just thinking about him."

"Oh My God! You've got it bad for this guy. Don't let Vicky get wind of this. She will pull you off his list quicker than Saskawhore can suck a cock." Angel clicks her fingers as she says the last part.

We all laugh. "Believe it or not, I miss Saskawhore and just talking about her cock sucking skills has put me at ease. Who would have thought that was possible?"

Morgan goes to grab my bubbly. "No more bubbles for you, clearly you are drunk, you're thanking Saskawhore."

Before she can grab my glass, I chug it back and hand her the empty. "Why yes, I would love another glass to calm my nerves."

"Lucky I love your face." Morgan takes my glass and tops it up.

We spend the rest of the afternoon giving each other makeovers and laughing, but Angel isn't herself. When I asked if she was okay, she snapped at me. Apart from Angel's outburst, this afternoon reminded me of my college days when Kenz and I used to do this, a pang of sadness washes over me, but then an image of Logan appears and mood instantly brightens.

It's just on 7:30 p.m. when the limo pulls up at the office, as I'm walking up the stairs, my nerves kick up a notch. When I walk into Equinox, my eyes find Logan sitting at the bar, all traces of my nerves vanish, and I'm flooded with butterflies and excitement.

Logan must feel my presence because he turns around and gazes directly at me, our eyes meet across the bar. It's like a scene from the movies, everything around us fades away except for Frank playing in the background, it's just the two of us, it's magical.

Standing up, he walks towards me, leaning forward, he snakes his arm around my waist, pulling me in close before placing the softest of kisses on my cheek. When he removes his lips, I can still feel the heat from where they touched my cheek, I miss the connection. Looking up, I see him staring intently at me, I can feel his stare deep within my soul; I've never felt someone's eyes bore into me like that before. "Good evening, Ms. Bryant. You look absolutely ravishing tonight." I completely melt at what he says. My cheeks heat with embarrassment and I can't help but grin back at him.

"Mr. DeBiers, you look pretty goodly yourself." I manage to stutter in reply.

"You do realise that goodly means of large size?"

Giggling, I push my hair behind my ear, "Yes, I'm aware but I think it works much better this way. In Sarahland, it means better than good, amazing, just wow, fantabolous."

"That's quite a definition. Well, I'm happy to be goodly in your eyes. Would you like to have a drink at the bar before we head out to dinner? I made 8:30 p.m. reservations at *Moo Moo*."

"Wow, I've always wanted to eat there. And yes, a drink would be lovely."

"I picked goodly then," he cheekily says, winking at me, before ushering me towards to bar and an awaiting Victoria, I hadn't even noticed her sitting there. She is beaming her fake smile at us and I find it hard to not roll my eyes at her.

"Good evening, Victoria," I say, as I lean forward and we air kiss.

"Good evening, Sarah. You look lovely tonight."

"She looks amazing," Logan says, snapping my attention away from Victoria and back towards him.

"Well, I'll leave you two to your evening. Welcome to Elite, Mr. DeBiers." She out stretches her hand to him; he shakes it before turning his attention back to me. "Sarah, I'll see you tomorrow morning at the weekly meeting."

"I'll see you tomorrow, Victoria." Turning my attention back to Logan, completely dismissing Victoria, I'm sure I will hear about doing that tomorrow but at the moment, Logan is all that I care about and can concentrate on.

"Good night, have fun," Victoria says and she stands up to leave.

In unison, Logan and I say, "Bye, Victoria." He and I burst out laughing, garnering attention from other patrons. Victoria shakes her head as she heads towards her office.

Our drinks are delivered, I hadn't even realised that a round of drinks had been ordered. Picking up my glass, I look towards Logan. "A toast, to a night we will never forget."

Raising his glass, he replies, "I'll certainly drink to that."

Before we both take a sip, we clink our glasses together before. Over the top of my champagne flute, I take Logan in; he is absolutely gorgeous, his dark hair is neatly styled, his chiseled jaw is clean-shaven, and his eyes are dark and dangerous. To be honest, I'm a little intimidated in his presence but most of all, excited for what lies ahead for us.

We fall into comfortable conversation, it feels like we have known each other for years, before I know it, it's time to head to the restaurant for dinner. Any intimidation that I felt earlier has evaporated and it's replaced with excitement and wonder.

As we are making our way to the waiting limo, I think to myself that this is a great first date. When I see 'Sleazy Simon' I shudder and it hits me that this isn't a date, Logan has paid to be with me. As I climb in into the car ahead of Logan, all my prior happiness evaporates when I remember that I'm an escort, and this will never go anywhere...or could it?

21

LOGAN

Watching Sarah's ass as we walk to the awaiting limo, I can't help but smile, my cock agrees too, he's been twitching ever since she walked into Equinox earlier. This evening has been amazing so far, Sarah and I get along like a house on fire; it feels like we have known each other for years. For the first time since Lili, I find myself genuinely smiling.

Sitting next to Sarah, I look over and notice that her demeanor has changed in the time it took us to walk from the bar to the car. Reaching over, I grab her hand and entwine our fingers, rubbing the back of her hand with my thumb. "You really are beautiful, Sarah, inside and out. I know we have only just met, but I'm drawn to you. I can't explain it and after only being with you for an hour, I know that I want to explore this further."

"Logan, I feel all of that too, but..." Pausing, she then dejectedly adds, while shaking her head, "Nothing, it's nothing."

"No, don't stop, tell me what you are thinking. Don't be afraid to be honest with me."

She looks over at me with sad eyes. "Logan, I'm an escort, you've paid to go out with me."

"So, I'll stop paying then, I'll do anything to be able to see you. Sarah, I want to be with you and I will do it any way that I can. If it means paying, then I'll pay."

"Logan, no, I can't let you do that."

"Sarah, be honest." Grabbing her hand and squeezing tightly, I gaze into her eyes. "Do you feel what I'm feeling?"

She doesn't say anything for what feel like light-years, but very quietly I hear her say, "I am," as she nods her head slightly.

Reaching my hand up, I gently lift her chin so she is looking at me. "Sarah, we will work it out."

The conversation comes to an end as we have arrived at the restaurant. I get out first and turn around to help Sarah out; when she places her hand in mine I feel a zing. I know in this moment that I will do everything in my power to keep Sarah in my life.

We have an amazing dinner together, and just like at the bar, conversation flowed like we were lifelong friends catching up after an extended absence. After I've settled the bill, I don't want to evening to end, so I ask Sarah if she'd like to come back to my place for a nightcap. There is no hesitation whatsoever and she immediately says yes.

We grab a cab and ten minutes later, we are back at my place. The air in the elevator to the top floor is electric, it's taking everything in my power to not press her against the lift wall and kiss her senseless. The elevator dings and I thank the interruption because my will around this girl is fading...and fast.

Unlocking the front door, I step aside to allow Sarah in first, and to check out her ass again. She pauses midstep and I bump into her. "Holy fucking shit, you seriously live here?" She turns around to look at me and her face is lit up like a Christmas tree. She quickly says, "Sorry, that wasn't very ladylike."

Laughing, I say, "It's fine, I'm pretty sure that is what I said that first time I walked in here, too. The view alone pretty much sold me on this place."

Walking further into the penthouse, I'm mesermised watching Sarah take it all in. Eventually she turns towards me. "Logan, this place is stunning."

"Thanks, but I'm pretty sure the view I have right now is much better." The sparkling city lights behind Sarah only magnify her beauty.

She walks over to the French doors and puts her hand on the handle, looking at me over her shoulder she asks, "Do you mind if I go outside?"

"That's fine. I'll get us some drinks, is bourbon okay with you?"

"Are we talking Jim or Jack?"

"Neither, Mark." She looks at me with a confused expression. "Maker's Mark," I clarify.

"Never had it before but I'm game." Winking at me, she turns back to the doors and heads outside.

I'm left standing there, completely enthralled with this woman. I pour us each a drink, and I'm excited to see where this leads, but I'm also worried that if it gets out that I met Sarah through an escort agency what it could do to my reputation. Looking out the doors, I see Sarah and I find myself smiling and happy. As I'm walking out to the balcony, Doe Zantama's quote, *"Don't let the fear of what could happen make nothing happen,"* pops into my mind, and in this moment I decide to go for it, consequences be damned.

Sarah turns when she hears me approaching and smiles. "Logan, the view from out here is even more amazing than from inside. I can see why you fell in love with this place."

"Yeah, it is pretty amazing. I was lucky to get this place. Here you go." Handing her the tumbler of amber liquid, she smiles at me. Our fingers graze in the handover, that same spark from before zaps us again.

She looks up at me and I know that she felt it too.

She raises her tumbler and says, "Cheers." Bringing it to her lips she breathes in the rich, fruity, spiced honey aroma and then takes a sip. I watch as she closes her eyes and savours the flavour, my eyes locked on her slim, gorgeous neck as she swallows. A slight moan releases from her mouth as she opens her eyes. Holy shit, I have never been turned on watching someone drink Maker's Mark before.

"And…" I enquire.

"Holy shit, that's so smooth and it doesn't have the burn that Jim and Jack have."

"Yeah, that's 'cause it's made with red winter wheat rather than rye. It's the rye that causes the burning sensation."

"Hmmpf, well I learned something new today and I think I have a new fav drink." Pausing, she looks directly at me. "And a new friend, too."

Hearing her add that last bit brightens my smile. Raising my tumbler, I say, "I'll drink to that." Clinking our tumblers, we both stare intently at each other as we sip our nightcap. Reaching over, I grab her glass and place it on the railing. Turning back to Sarah I pull her closer, wrapping my arms around her waist; our eyes lock on each other. Huskily, I say, "Sarah, I really want to kiss you right now."

Swallowing hard, she faintly says, "I really want you to kiss me right now."

That's all the invitation I need, I lift one hand and cup the back of her neck; with the other still around her waist, I tug her closer. Slowly, I bend down and gently place my lips on hers, applying a slight amount of pressure. She wraps her arms around my lower back, pulling me in tight. She opens her mouth, inviting me in. Licking across her lips, I gently slip my tongue into her mouth. Our lips caress, our tongues dance, our hands explore. The taste of Maker's Mark mixed with Sarah is exquisite; *my new favourite flavour.*

This is one heck of a first kiss.

Pulling back, I rest my forehead on hers. Both of us panting; out of breath; hearts erratically beating. "Wow," we both say in unison before our lips crash together again, this kiss is ferocious and full of passion.

Lifting Sarah up, she wraps her legs around me as I make my way over to the outdoor lounge. Sitting down, Sarah straddles me as we continue to kiss. Kissing Sarah has been bumped up to my new favourite thing to do.

Just before midnight, I escort Sarah downstairs to the waiting limo to take her home. "Sarah, I had an amazing time tonight."

Shyly, she looks up at me, her eyes sparkling in the moonlight. "I had a great night, too." Biting her lips she asks, "Umm, I'd love to see you again?"

"I'd like that, too," I eagerly reply. "I guess, I'll call Victoria and arrange it."

She looks kind of sad when I mention Victoria. "Um, yeah, that would be great." She steps closer to me and gently places a kiss on my cheek, just skimming my lips. "Good night, Logan." Turning her back on me, she climbs into the limo and I close the door, giving her a smile before I do.

Standing on the sidewalk, I watch the limo drive away. Once it has turned the corner, I make my way back inside and up to my penthouse; feeling happy and overwhelmed with how quickly I'm falling for Sarah.

When I get back to the penthouse, I pour myself another Maker's Mark; smiling as I do so when I remember Sarah taking her first sip. I get hard just thinking about her. Grabbing my phone, I head outside before texting Sarah.

Logan – *Thank you for an amazing nite. I look forward to see you again soon*

Immediately a reply comes through.

Sarah – I *did too, thank you. I can still taste the Maker's Mark and you on my lips. Sweet dreams*

Her reply is exactly what I was hoping for. My cock hardens and throbs as I remember all of the details of tonight. Placing my tumbler on the arm of the chair, I unzip my fly, lower my boxer briefs and take out my cock. Closing my eyes, I grip it tight and stroke, imagining that it's Sarah's delicate fingers wrapped tightly around me. My strokes get faster and faster, my breathing and heart rate accelerate, and it doesn't take long before I'm coming all over my hand and dress shirt.

Using my shirt, which is already a mess, as a cloth, I wipe up and head inside. Jumping into the shower, I clean up and climb into bed. Closing my eyes, I'm met with visions of Sarah and I happily together. With a smile on my face, I drift off to sleep and dream of a happy life with Sarah.

22

SARAH

WHEN I WAKE UP THE NEXT MORNING, THE FIRST PERSON I THINK OF IS Logan. I find myself grinning from ear to ear, giving the Luna Park clown a run for its money in the smile department. Sliding my slippers and silk robe on, I skip happily across the hall to Angel's room to tell her all about my night. When I open her door, I find that her room is empty. All of her belongings are gone, the sheets and doona are neatly folded and sitting on the end of her bed. Turning on my heel, I cross the hall to see Morgan.

Knocking gently, I wait and eventually I hear. "Come in." Opening her door I enter her room.

"Umm, where's Angel?"

"I guess she would be sleeping. After all it is..." Grabbing her phone she looks at the time. "8:00 a.m. in the God damn morning."

"Nope, she's not and her room is empty."

"Maybe she went out for a run."

"No, empty, empty. All her things are gone and the sheets and bed crap are neatly folded on the end."

She sits bolt up right in bed. "Did you say folded and neat on the end of the bed?"

"Yep, why?"

"That means she's gone. Like gone gone, Saskawhore gone."

"What? How? What?" I ask all confused.

"Beats me. Last night after you left, she went out, I presumed she was meeting up with friends and didn't think anything of it. I was just excited to have a night alone."

"Give her a call, I can't believe she'd take off like that without saying goodbye, especially to you."

Morgan grabs her phone and dials Angel and puts it on speaker. It goes straight to a recorded message. "The call could not be connected, please check and number and try again."

"What the hell?" we both say in unison.

Before we can talk further, there's a knock at the door. "I'll get it, but we need to discuss this further and find Angel."

"Agreed," she says, as I head downstairs to answer the door.

Opening the door, there's a delivery guy standing there with the biggest bunch of tulips I have ever seen. "Morning, I have a delivery for Sarah Bryant?"

"That's me." He hands me the flowers and leaves. "Thanks," I say, as I close the door and head into the kitchen to find a vase.

Morgan skips into the kitchen and as she turns on the coffee maker she notices the flowers and says, "Holy shitballs, that's a beautiful bunch of tulips. Who are they from?"

"Umm, I haven't looked at the card yet."

Before I can grab the card, Morgan snatches it up and opens it.

"Sarah, thanks for a lovely evening," she says. "It's not signed, who did you go out with last night?"

"The guy I brought in the other night, Logan."

"Well, someone is smitten..." Before she can continue the front door opens and Victoria waltzes in.

"Thankfully, one of my girls can do their job without issues. Angel is no longer with us. Morgan you will take on her clients and Sarah will help out when she can, but her schedule is booked solid for the next two weeks. Between Logan, Xander, Chow, and Mr. Akin she will have very little time." Pausing, she looks at the flowers. "Tulips, how boring. Ohh, and Xander has requested the two of you again today, guess he's besotted with the two of you but Sarah, you're not going. Morgan, you will see Xander by yourself, he won't be happy but pay..." She pauses before quickly saying, "Logan is new and we need to keep the newbies appeased."

Before either of us can reply, she is heading back out again, slamming the door behind her.

Morgan looks at me, "Angel wouldn't just leave like that, something's not right."

"When are things ever right with Vicky, and why does Xander get special treatment all the time?"

"He's always had special treatment but since you started here, he says jump and Vicky says 'how high?' Which totally isn't like her, maybe he has compromising pictures of Vicky, like in trackies, Uggs, and a singlet or depraved sexual ones."

"Who cares about her and him? I'm worried about Angel. She wouldn't just leave like that."

"I know, but what can we do?" Morgan asks.

"Nothing right now, seems we both have dates on our day off. Will you be able to handle Xander when he realises that I'm not there?"

"I'll be fine, he doesn't scare me," she says, as she pours us a coffee each. Sitting at the island bench, we each drink our coffee in silence. My mind is all over the place; I can't stop thinking about Angel and Logan. Just thinking of Logan, I get butterflies and my skin prickles with excitement. I'm really excited to see him again.

Over the next two weeks Logan and I see each other just about everyday; sometimes he books through Victoria but most of the time not. I manage to see him in between Elite clients. If we don't see each other, we chat on the phone or text one other.

I'm really starting to fall for Logan DeBiers.

It's hard hiding this from Victoria and Morgan, but I'm drawn to Logan like a moth to a flame; I can't stay away from him. I know deep within my soul that Logan is my soul mate, I know it's crazy, considering we've only known each other a few weeks, but my mum and dad met and married within three months; maybe I'm destined for the same.

I'm dying for a decent coffee, but I also need a run, so to kill two birds with one stone; I put on my running gear and joggers, slip a twenty into my sports bra and off I go. Running in the middle of the day probably isn't the best idea I've ever had, but the weather outside is gorgeous today and not too hot. Taking the scenic route, I run through the botanic gardens, along the river, and past the train station. By time I get to Java Lava, sweat is dripping off me, but I'm feeling goodly...nothing is better than getting those endorphins pumping.

Grabbing the door handle, I swing it open and enter when I come face to face with Kenz and Mike's new girlfriend. "Ohh, hey, Kenz."

"Hey, bitch, how are you? Haven't seen or heard from you in a while."

"Yeah, umm, I've been busy." *Fuck I hate lying to her but I just can't tell her, not yet anyway.*

Kenz turns to her friend. "Sav, can we take a shopping rain check?"

"Yeah, sure, that's fine. You two have fun. Catch ya's later." Sav turns and heads out the door, leaving Kenz and me standing in the doorway. For the first time in our relationship, the silence is awkward. She grabs my arm and leads us to the counter to order our coffees.

Once we have our coffees, we head to the table that is unofficially ours and we sit down. At the same time, we both say, "So, what's up?" We both burst out laughing and just like that, we fall back into the Kenzie and Sarah rhythm.

"So, what's been happening with you? We missed you at Origin the other week and our latest tasting."

"Umm, yeah, sorry about that, work has been crazy busy." *Sorry, but I was getting paid to have sex with a guy who owns a yacht, but I'm not a hooker. It's just companionship and if it leads to sex so be it,* I think to myself. "Speaking of, what a series?"

"Don't try and change the subject, what's going on, Sarah?"

"Josh and I broke up." *Yeah, I'll go with that, she will know I'm upset over that.*

"Yeah, I know and what hurts is that I heard it from him and not you. What happened?"

"I came home from work early one day and I found him and Sam on the couch together."

"Isn't Sam a dude?"

"Mmhmm," I reply, nodding my head. "Yep, Josh is gay."

Kenz spits out her coffee. "Holy fucking shit, I so did not see that coming."

"You and me both. And to top it off, he kicked me out, claiming that he paid the deposit and all that shit so it's rightfully his."

"Are you serious?"

"Yep." Taking a sip of my coffee I moan. "I miss this place, we should catch up here more often."

"Hold up a minute, where are you living then?"

Fuck, shit, fuck, I didn't mean to let that slip. "Umm, some girls from work had a spare room so I moved in with them." *Not entirely a lie.*

"Why didn't you tell me, Sarah?"

"I was ashamed, Kenz. How did I now know that my boyfriend was gay? We'd been together for so long. I...I just, ugh. I've missed you, Kenz."

"I've missed you, too."

Thankfully the limelight gets taken off of me and we chat about Kenz, the girls, Malt Me, and the recent drama with Mike, Sav, and her crazy uncle. I'm so happy for her, last year was pretty full on for all of us, especially Kenz. To see my friend sitting across from me stronger than ever, it gives me hope that I can get through all of this, too. Kenz is telling me a story about a number three-poop explosion when I get a text, thankful for the distraction because that shit is just wrong, literally.

Grabbing my phone, I see that I have a text from Logan.

Logan – *Hey gorgeous. You free this evening?*

Smiling as I read his message, I quickly reply.

Sarah – *Just catching up with Kenz. Wanna meet up for a late lunch? I'm working tonight*
Logan – *It's a date. I'll text you where when I book*
Sarah – *Awesome. Can't wait*

After placing my phone back in my bag I notice Kenz staring at me with a ridiculously goofy grin on her face, "What?" I enquire.

"Who was that? And don't say no one 'cause I know you, Sarah. That's your 'I'm in love' grin."

"Pfft, I'm not in love but I have met someone."

She leans forward in her chair. "Do tell and give me all the juicy, kinky details."

"Kenz, he's wonderful. New to town, in development and he's a total gentleman."

"So, where did you meet?"

Shit, shit shit, I start to panic. "Umm, at a bar. I was meeting up with someone from work and I met him. The rest is history, but it's all new so I don't want to jinx anything." *Phew, that was a good cover, kinda the truth but a little was left out...like the fact that he pays to spend time with me.* "Sorry to cut this short, but I have to get going. How about we arrange to catch up soon?"

"Sounds good. Why don't you come for dinner one night and you can see Jor and the girls, too. Bring Mr. Sarah too, so I can give him the Kenzie seal of approval. And I'll make sure my gaydar is on, too."

"Oh, you're so not funny, bitch, but dinner with you guys sounds great. Not sure about Logan yet. I kinda want to keep him to myself for now...if you know what I mean."

"Fine, you big spoilsport. But it was great to catch up with you, I've missed you."

"Me too, Kenz. Sorry for being a shitty friend."

"Your not a shitty friend, I'm a shitty friend."

"How so?"

"Well, I didn't reach out to you when I knew about you and Josh breaking up, I should've reached out. Hell, I didn't even know you had moved."

"I'm sorry, Kenz, it all happened so quickly and I was embarrassed. I know I have nothing to be embarrassed about with you, but this one was tough to take."

"Fair enough but no more hiding stuff, deal?"

"Deal." *Even though I'm hiding a doozy of a secret.*

Standing up, we both head outside and say our goodbyes. I walk Kenz to her car. After waving her off, I head back towards the river to finish my run. Twenty minutes later, I decide that's enough and I head home.

As I'm entering the building, Victoria is huffing out. "Morning, Vicky...toria. How are you?" Leaning in for our customary air kisses and fake hug.

"Ugh, you're all sweaty." She pushes me away. "I'm glad I caught you, Kristy is no longer with us so I need to you take her 3:00 p.m. appointment today with Mr. Chow, so I've cancelled your evening appointment as this thing with Chow could run late."

"Umm, I have plans with Logan this afternoon."

"I don't have it down on the books."

"Umm, he texted me this morning."

Grabbing me roughly by the arm she drags me to the side of the foyer and pushes me up against the pole. "All appointments are to go through me, Sarah. You of all people know this."

"This isn't an appointment, it's just friends."

"No!" she shouts, "All meetings with clients are appointments, they must be paid for."

"But..."

"No buts, Sarah. This is unacceptable behavior." She rubs her temples "I don't have time for this. You will be ready for Mr. Chow at 3:00 p.m., no arguments."

"Fine," I huff, and turn away from her to go upstairs and get ready for a boring afternoon looking at dumb paintings. I'm only a few steps away from Victoria when she forcefully grabs my arm, spins me around, slapping me hard across the face, the crack echoing through the foyer; garnering us a few looks from the people nearby. Rubbing my cheek, I stand there in shock, staring at her in disbelief.

"You will not speak to me like that and walk away, remember who I am, Sarah. I can make all of this disappear in an instant." She waves her hand around and snapping her fingers. "Don't push me, Sarah. You don't know what I'm capable of." She turns on her heel and climbs into her waiting limo.

Standing there in shock, staring as the limo pulls into traffic, I grab my phone and call Logan. It goes to voicemail. "Hey, Logan, it's Sarah. I have to cancel lunch; I have a last minute work thing at some gallery this arvo. I'll text you tomorrow and maybe we can catch up then. Bye." I hang up just as the lift doors open and I head upstairs to get ready for my appointment, upset that I won't be seeing Logan this afternoon.

I'm just getting out of the shower when Morgan comes running in, tears pouring down her face. Racing over to her, I wrap my arms around her tightly. "Morgan, what's wrong?"

"It's...It's..." She's so upset that she can't speak. Leading her to the window seat, we sit, and I wait for her to calm down. She looks up at me and I know what she's about to tell me isn't going to be good. "She's dead."

I'm stunned, "Who's dead?"

"Angel."

My mouth drops open, I'm in shock. "Whaaaat?" I manage to ask, as the tears well in my eyes.

"She was on the news just now, a breaking bulletin. Her body was found this morning." Pausing, she looks at me. "She was murdered, Sarah."

I'm speechless.

"Sarah, she's dead," Morgan whispers, before she bursts into tears again.

Hearing that for a second time is enough to set me off too, and I start sobbing. We sit there holding each other when there is a knock at the door downstairs. Neither of us moves; we just sit there, holding each other as the tears continue to fall.

The knocking gets louder and quicker, they obviously aren't giving up. Letting go of Morgan, I quickly pull off my towel and slip on my robe and head downstairs. Opening the door, I find Simon standing there; he looks me up and down and with disdain in his voice to says. "Umm, you are meant to be ready to meet Mr. Chow."

"Ohh, Simon," I say, as I wrap my arms around him. Pulling back when I realise I'm hugging 'Sleazy Simon' I tearfully say, "Umm, Angel is dead, she was murdered. Morgan just saw it on the telly."

"Fuck. I better call Victoria and give her a heads up. Please go and get ready."

"Simon, I can't work. Did you hear what I said? Angel was murdered."

He doesn't say anything; he pushes past me into the lounge room, his phone to his ear. Heading back upstairs, I find that Morgan has moved from the window seat to the bed, she has finally stopped crying but she's clearly upset. Before I can comfort her, my phone rings and it's the alarm sound, Victoria's tone. Picking it up, I answer, "Hi, Victoria."

"Simon tells me you're not ready. You have ten minutes to get organised and downstairs."

"Victoria, Angel was murdered. I can't work this afternoon."

"You can and you will. It's of no concern to us that she was murdered. These things happen."

"Victoria, that's a tad harsh."

"Call it what you will. She left, she obviously had issues that we knew nothing about. Now, forget her. You have nine minutes now, Sarah." Pausing, she sighs before adding, "Don't disappoint me, young lady." And she hangs up on me.

Throwing my phone back on the side table, I take a seat and rub

Morgan's arm. "Morgan, sweetie, are you going to be okay?" She just stares vacantly at me. "That was Vicky, I still have to work this afternoon and I don't want to piss her off. She's already in a shitty mood and I don't want to anger the beast within." Morgan smirks at this. "It's just a gallery thing with Chow, I'll be back by six. Will you be okay until then?"

"Yeah, I'll be fine. It was just a shock. She left so suddenly and then now this. Something isn't right, Sarah. I can feel it in my bones."

"I know what you mean." Standing up, I reluctantly start getting ready. "Listen, you and I will chat tonight. We will get to the bottom of this, we owe Angel that much."

"Okay, you better go before the beast, as you called her, comes here. I can't deal with her in person right now. Thank God I'm not working today or tonight, I can't, I just can't."

Stepping out of the closet, I look to Morgan. "Do I look okay?"

Morgan's face breaks out in the biggest smile. This is the first time I've seen her show any emotion that's not sadness since she entered my room. "Yes, you are fucking stunning, Sarah. Wish I could get ready that quickly."

We hear Simon yelling from below to hurry up. "Coming!" I yell, leaning down, I kiss Morgan on the forehead. "Back as soon as I can."

Turning, I grab my bag and shoes and head out the door, as I'm closing it, I hear Morgan quietly say, "Have fun." There is no emotion in her voice at all; she is broken at the moment.

Skipping down the stairs, I sit on the bottom step and slip on my ballet flats. Just as I stand up, Simon walks into the foyer. I smile at him, "Let's go."

If only I knew what was going to happen this afternoon.

23

LOGAN

I'VE JUST STEPPED OUT OF THE SHOWER WHEN I HEAR MY PHONE BEEP, indicating a voice message. Picking up my phone, I see that I have a missed call from Sarah; I dial my message bank and listen to her message. I'm sad that she had to cancel our lunch date, but I'm also kind of relieved, I was going to have to call and cancel on her. Beth slipped a last minute, afternoon cocktail thingy into my calendar and had the reminder not gone off, I would have missed it. One of my contractors scored an invite and apparently it's a who's who gallery function, and as I'm new in town, he thought it would be a good way to network. Networking I'm all for, but art I don't give a flying fuck about it.

I'm in the lift heading to the waiting limo when my phone rings. Digging it out of my pocket, I notice it's Victoria. I'm not in the mood for her right now so I silence the call and let it go to voicemail.

The car pulls up in front of a gallery in the Valley and I climb out. Looking up, I see that this is a pretty big affair; they've gone all out with this gallery opening. Walking along the green carpet, I make my way to the door. Giving my name to the doorman, I'm ushered inside. When I enter I'm greeted by the owner and handed a glass of bubbly and given a rundown of the artist and her works. I totally tune out, it's all abstract art that reminds of art that Sav and I used to do when we were younger, not art at all in my eyes.

Excusing myself, I walk around, deciding that I'll do one lap and then find the bar. Rounding a corner near the back, I stop dead in my tracks and stare. Standing in front of me, looking absolutely stunning in black slacks and a purple, silky button-up blouse is Sarah. She is chatting with five other ladies but none of them compare to her beauty. She must sense my presence as she looks up and finds my eyes locked on her. Her eyes bug out of her head in shock when she notices me, she gives me a slight smile, but I immediately notice that she's upset, faking her happiness with the group.

She excuses herself and walks over to me, I'm mesmerised by her beauty. The rest of the room fades away and when all of a sudden; she's standing in front of me. "Mr. DeBiers, this is a nice surprise." Leaning forward, she kisses me on the cheek and whispers, "I'm so glad you're here, meet me by the restrooms in five minutes."

"Ms. Bryant, lovely to see you again but I must be going." Nodding at her, I walk away towards the bar. Grabbing two champagnes, I head towards the restrooms, in a roundabout way. There's a half decent painting on the wall near the restrooms, so I pretend to be interested in it.

As I'm looking at the painting, a tingling sensation runs from head to toe and I know she's nearby. Looking to my left, I see Sarah standing next to me. Grabbing my elbow, she leads me to the foyer of the restrooms. There are couches off to the side before the hall leads to the unisex bathrooms; Sarah and I take a seat on the corner lounge. Placing the bubbly on the coffee table, I look over and see tears welling in her eyes. "Sarah, what's wrong?"

"Ohh, Logan," she says, before bursting into tears.

Lifting her onto my lap, I wrap my arms around her and she snuggles into my shoulder and continues to cry. Rubbing her back gently, I let her cry, whispering, "Shh...It will be okay," repeatedly to her.

She pulls back, looks at me, and gives me a slight smile, she is so upset, and grief is all over her face. Lifting my hand, with the pad of my thumb I gently wipe away the wetness from under her eyes, even all red-rimmed from crying her eyes are still spectacular. She is still the most gorgeous girl in the world. "Sarah, what's wrong?" I gently ask when her tears have subsided. Before she can reply, a Chinese man walks in and heads straight to the restrooms, not noticing us sitting here, but Sarah notices him and she quickly jumps up.

"Logan, I'm working. I'll...I'll, call you later."

I'm about to reply when she walks away quickly and heads back to into the gallery. I'm left sitting there stunned, all I want to do is run out into the gallery, wrap my arms around her, and whisk her away from here and comfort her; she is clearly upset over something. Grabbing my phone, I text her.

Logan – *Call me as soon as you get home. I'm worried about you.*

Immediately the three little dots appearing, indicating she is tying a reply. Finally my phone vibrates and as her reply comes through.

Sarah – *Promise XO*

Smiling at her reply, I pocket my phone and head back into the gallery. After one more lap, I decide that I've been here long enough, finding the owner, I buy the painting by the bathrooms for the penthouse, say my goodbyes, and head home. It's nice being able to say home again and I'm actually excited to hang my new artwork; Beth and Sav will flip when I tell them I bought a painting.

The car service drops me off and Charlie's is calling my name; this having a great bar where I live is awesome. Stopping in, I grab a quick beer when my phone rings. Looking down, I smile it's Sav. My PI managed to find her when she and boyfriend, Mike, were involved in an altercation with Kelvin. I never trusted that smug bastard and I'm so happy that he is currently rotting in jail. It's so good to have her back in my life and in the same town. Amazingly, we are both in Brisbane. Swiping the screen I answer, "Savannah, run away lately?"

"You're never going to let me forget that, are you, Loges?"

"Not anytime soon, Savvy, not anytime soon. To what do I owe the pleasure of this call?"

"Well, I'm calling to invite you to our housewarming party next weekend. Mike and I picked up our keys today."

"Okay, maybe that will make me forgive you. You sound so happy again, almost like before..." Drifting off, I don't finish that sentence. It's still raw finding out the Kelvin was behind the accident that killed the rest of her family.

"I'm happy, Loges. Extremely happy and it's all to do with Mike. Maybe you can bring the new lady friend that you mentioned."

"I'll see if she's free but it's all still pretty new, meeting the friends is a big step."

"Logan, if this mess has taught me anything, it's that, you need to jump head first into life. Life is too short. To quote a wise man 'I'm here for a goodtime, not a longtime.'"

In the background I hear Mike yell, "More like fucking awesome man." We both laugh and I realise that I do want Sarah to come with me and meet Sav and Mike.

Still laughing I say, "Tell Mike hi and yes, I'll be there next weekend, possibly with Sar..."

But I'm cut off to hear giggles and Mike yelling, "Laters, Logan." Followed by more giggling, which in turn makes me laugh. *Mike is perfect for Sav*, I think to myself as I finish my beer and head upstairs.

The lift doors open and in the foyer, sitting by my door, is Sarah. She looks up and when she sees me, she jumps up, throws herself into my arms, and starts to cry. Within seconds, I wrap my arms around her, lifting her up; I cradle her in my arms and unlock the front door.

24

SARAH

AFTER I LEAVE THE GALLERY, I GET SIMON TO DROP ME BACK AT THE apartment but rather than going inside, I aimlessly walk around the city. Eventually, I find myself at Logan's place so I head inside. The lift takes me up to his floor, my hands become clammy, butterflies appear in my tummy and I'm nervous, really nervous. I haven't ever felt like this about anyone, not even Josh. Today when my eyes found him at the gallery, I was so excited. All I wanted to do was run and jump into his arms, but unfortunately that's not possible…for now.

The lift reaches the top floor, the doors open, and I head over to this door. Knocking, I wait but there's no answer. My feet are rooted to the floor; I don't want to leave. I need to see Logan, like I need my next breath. Sliding down the timber door, I rest my forehead on my knees and get comfortable.

A few moments later, I hear the ding of the lift. Looking up, I see Logan stepping out; the sight of him instantly calms me. He's absolutely stunning in his jeans and black dress shirt. He notices me sitting there and smiles, immediately I jump up and throw my arms around him and break down in tears. I cry for Angel, I cry for what my life has become, I cry for not being able to freely be with him. I cry to let it all out.

Carrying me inside, we end up in the lounge room. With me still in his arms, he sits down on the couch and continues to embrace me tightly as my sobs increase. Looking up at him, through my tears I whisper, "She's gone, Logan."

"Who's gone?"

"Angel, they found her body this morning. She...she was murdered. That explains why I haven't been able to reach her since she left."

"Ohh, Sarah, I'm so sorry."

We both fall silent but it's not uncomfortable. Sitting here in Logan's arms feels right; it's where I'm meant to be. He breaks the silence, "Sarah, have you had dinner yet?"

"No, I'm not hungry."

"Well, that's too bad. I'm going to order Chinese and we will head out on the patio, eat so much Chinese that we will turn Chinese, and drink beer until we can't stand up. I'm going to give you the Logan treatment."

For the first time since I heard the new this morning, I smile. "I will only eat Chinese if it comes from Kung Fu Palace, but you can drink beer and I'll drink wine."

"After my friend took me to Kung Fu Palace last week, there is nowhere else I would get it from. As for wine, I actually have your fav in my wine fridge, I might even join you on the wine."

"You have my wine?"

"Yep, I was hoping we could do this one night and it looks today is my lucky day. I'll call the Palace while you get our drinks. Meet you on the patio in five minutes."

Standing up, I head towards to kitchen but I turn on my heel and wrap my arms around Logan. "Thank you," I whisper. "This is just what I needed."

"It's my pleasure, Sarah, now wine me up, baby."

I giggle at his reply. "You did not just say that did you?"

"Wine yes I did."

By now we are both pissing ourselves laughing. "Dude, you are so corny."

"Don't you mean corky?"

Again, I burst out laughing and this time a Kenzie snort breaks free and my giggle increase. "Oh My God! Stop, I'm going to pee my pants."

"Okay, Okay, I'll stop. Five minutes, Sarah."

"Yes, boss," I say, as I head towards the kitchen.

Reaching into the wine chiller, I grab the bottle of Tulloch Verdelho and place it on the island bench. Turning, I grab the stemless wine glasses and wine bucket out of the cabinet. Picking up the bucket, I place a few ice cubes in before opening the wine saying to myself, "Viva Verdelho" from their advertising campaign last year before, gently resting it in the bucket.

Heading out to the patio, I balance the two glasses in one hand, the bucket in the other, and I somehow manage to open the door without dropping anything. Sitting the bucket on the high-top table, I reach for the bottle and pour us each a glass.

Taking a sip as I walk to the railing, I place Logan's and my glass down and look out at the sky. It's just on dusk and there seems to be a storm in the west that is slowly making its way towards the city. The black clouds mix with the setting sun, and even though the clouds are gloomy, the vividness of the sunset makes the night sky magical.

I'm lost in the night sky and don't hear Logan come out. He wraps his arms around my waist and pulls me close, my back to his front; it's perfect. Resting my glass on the railing, I wrap my arms around his; closing my eyes, I snuggle into his neck. He places a gentle kiss on my temple, and rests his chin against my shoulder.

Spinning around, I wrap my arms around his neck and kiss him. Our lips fuse as one as we tenderly rub each other's back. His tongue seeks access to my mouth and I willingly open, letting him in. Our tongues mesh together, pulling back I suck his bottom lip into my mouth, letting it pop away. Resting my forehead against his, I close my eyes and enjoy the moment, finally feeling content. Opening my eyes, I look deep into his and smile. "Thank you," I whisper, wrapping my arms tighter around his waist, before resting my head on his shoulder.

He hugs me tighter, whispering, "I'd do anything for you Sarah, anything." The apartment buzzer interrupts the moment. "That must be dinner, I'll be right back." He kisses my forehead before heading inside to answer the door. Grabbing our glasses, I sit them on the table before heading to the kitchen to get plates and cutlery.

When I get back outside, Logan has unpacked the food and he is staring at me intently. "What?" I say, as I sit down at the table across from him.

"I just realised that I'm happy and I think it's all to do with you, Sarah. I was lonely and just plodding along, and then I met you, and now I find that when you aren't around I deflate, but as soon I'm with you, I feel happy and alive again."

"I know exactly what you mean, Logan." She leans forward and squeezes his hand and happily smiles at him. "Now let's eat, this smells amazing and I'm actually hungry now."

We each pile our plates with food and dig in. As usual the conversation flows, it's all going well until Logan asks me a question that knocks me for six. "Where do you see yourself in five years?"

His questions stuns me, I always knew that working for Victoria wasn't a lifetime gig. "Umm, I'm not sure. I mean, I don't want to work for Victoria for the rest of my life."

"Well, I knew that. You did what you had to do to survive, there's no judgments here, please don't think that. What you did took guts and I admire you for taking the risk. Think about it, what do you ultimately want to do with your life?"

Without hesitation, I reply. "I want to open a wine bar. Kenz and I used to joke about it years ago, but then both our lives took different paths."

"Why don't you do it?"

"What? Open a wine bar? In my dreams, Logan. For starters, I'm currently a hooker, have no permanent place to live, and then there's the start up capital that I'd need."

"I'd be happy to front the money, Sarah."

"Fuck me, are you seriously that loaded?"

"LDB is doing very well, Sarah. I made a few brilliant choices and now I can pretty much do what I want." Pausing, he adds, "Within reason, of course."

"Thank you for the offer, but before I take on a venture like that, I need to get my life back on track." Taking a sip of wine, followed by a deep breath, I smile and look at Logan. "Logan, I think that's what I want to do with my life, I'm going to open a wine bar. Maybe this job came along because it would allow me to save the money that I need to start it. I just have to do it for a little while longer and then I'm going to do it."

"Why not leave now, let me help you?"

"Thanks for the offer but this is something that I need to do on my own. For once in my life, I'm not mooching off Mum and Dad, not that they have anything left after Dad's last investment failure. This is all me, albeit it's not conventional but it's all me, Logan. It's kind of freeing."

"That's very honourable, Sarah. You really are a magnificent woman."

"You're not so bad yourself, Mr. DeBiers." I stare at him intently as I say this, smiling seductively at him.

We place our glasses on the table, stand up and reach for one another. Our lips crash together as we hold each other tightly for the most intense kiss of my life. Jumping up, I wrap my legs around Logan, pulling him closer.

Our kiss becomes frenzied as Logan walks over to the lounge where we had out first kiss a few weeks ago. He gently lays me down, lowering himself over me, cocooning me under him. He continues to kiss me before nipping and sucking along my chin and down my neck. Gently he bites my nipple through my top, reaching down, I grab the hem and not so sexily, I manage to get it over my head, so I'm left in my daggy white bra. *It always looks sexy in the movies*, I think to myself as I lie back down and stare at Logan.

Logan pulls back and takes in the sight of me lying there; cheeks flushed, chest heaving. "Fuck me, Sarah. You are beautiful."

"Pfft, I think you need you eyes checked. This is the daggiest bra that I own. Had I known this was going to happen, earlier I would have dressed in my sexy stuff."

"Sarah, you are sexy no matter what you wear, but right now, I want to strip you naked and devour your body."

My cheeks darken, my heart rate accelerates with excitement; licking my lips I sit up slightly and unclasp my bra, flicking it aside. Reaching down to remove my pants, I hear Logan groan. My eyes dart towards him and I see that he has taken off his shirt; I'm frozen on the spot. His chest is magnificent, I pant with lust as my eyes roam over his chest, gazing upon indent after indent. He has the most amazing eight-pack I have ever seen and then I see the Holy Grail: those side muscles that form a 'V'. Lifting my hand, I trace his abs before running my finger along his 'V' pack. "Fuck me, Logan. You're ripped."

"As are you. You're smokin' hot, Sarah." Leaning down he kisses me again. Pulling back, he says, "Naked, now."

We both get to work, stripping off our pants and underwear. Lying back down, I expect Logan to kiss me again but he squats down next to my throbbing pussy. Staring directly at me, he spreads my folds, sliding his finger up and down before squeezing my clit and rubbing circles with his thumb. Lifting my hands, I begin to massage my breasts, squeezing and rolling my nipples between my fingers. Moaning as the tingling sensation deep in my belly intensifies. My eyes are closed and I lose myself when I feel his breath on the inside of my thighs. He dips his tongue deep inside of me before sucking on my clit. Inserting another finger, with a flick of his wrist he pushes inside of me, thrusting in and out as he continues to suck and nibble my clit. My hand reaches down and I shove his head further into my pussy, grinding myself shamelessly against his face, "Ohh, Logan," I cry out. Suddenly my body erupts with pleasure and I'm tingling from head to toe as my orgasm takes over my body.

When my body shudders have stopped, he lifts his head from between my thighs and kisses his way up my stomach. Stopping to suck and fondle my breasts before kissing and licking his way up my neck. He tenderly holds my cheeks and lowers his lips to mine to kiss me. This kiss is slow and sensual; I wrap my arms around him and pull him closer. Gently he lowers himself on top of me; I can feel his hardness at my entrance, rolling my hips, inviting him in. In one swift motion, he sinks himself balls deep inside of me, just as the rain starts to gently fall. We are both so lost in the pleasure that we don't care about the rain. Logan continues to thrust in and out of me, leaning up on his elbows he stares intently at me as we rock back and forth together. Leaning down again, he kisses me as I feel the first wave of my orgasm begin to build. Moaning into his mouth, he begins to circle his hips, which rubs my clit. My legs tighten, my toes curl, and my orgasm rips through me. I groan in ecstasy as my body shudders with the most intense and amazing orgasm of my life. Opening my eyes, I see Logan tense before his own release overtakes his body.

He collapses on top of me as the heavens open, pulling back he kisses me deeply before whispering, "I think we should go inside before we catch pneumonia. We can have a shower to warm up and maybe go for round two."

"That's sounds great, Logan, but I don't think I can move. I'm spent, that was amazing."

Without warning, Logan scoops me up and we head inside. Entering his ensuite, he flicks on the lights, and the black granite sparkles in the glow. I spot a massive tub in the corner and smile. "Can we have a bath instead?" I ask, as he sits me on the vanity.

"We can do whatever you want, Sarah."

Turning his back on me, he puts the plug in and begins to fill the tub.

Pouring in some jasmine and lavender bubble bath, he swishes it around before putting his hand out towards me. Jumping off the counter, I take his hand and he helps me step into the tub before slipping in behind me. Wrapping his arms tightly around me, I relax back into him and sigh.

After soaking in the bath, I slip on one of Logan's light blue dress shirts; it's long enough to look like a t-shirt dress. My clothes are soaked from the rain, so I place them in a plastic bag. Turning to find Logan staring at me, I cheekily ask, "Like what you see?" and I lift my eyebrows at him.

"Fuck yes, I do. You look better in that shirt than I do."

"Pfft. I highly doubt that but thank you for the compliment." Pausing, I look to the floor before looking back up at Logan. He looks gorgeous in his trackies and navy Chesty Bonds singlet. "Umm, I think I better get going. I'm sure you have an early morning."

He takes two strides towards me and gently places his hands on my cheeks and looks deep into my soul; his stare burning a path deep inside of me, invoking feelings that I haven't felt in a long time. "Sarah, I'd happily be tired tomorrow if it means I get to spend extra time with you. You are more than welcome to stay, but it's entirely up to you."

Lifting my palm, I caress his hand that's holding my cheek, and lean into it. "As much as I'd love to stay, I think I should go."

Getting up on my tippy toes, I place a quick kiss on his ever so soft lips. Dropping the bag of wet clothes, I wrap my arms around his neck and deepen the kiss. Closing my eyes, I lose myself in all that is Logan. I pull back and gaze into his eyes. "I better go before things go too much further."

He laughs and looks towards his crotch, I can see his erection tenting his trackies. "Umm, I'm already there."

Giggling, I look back up at him. "Sorry, Logan, but if I fix your current situation, I won't leave and I really need to get home. We need to keep this on the down low. If Victoria finds out about us, I can loose everything. You could loose everything." Pausing, I add, "And who knows what she'll do to you. I won't risk that. Give me time to come up with a plan." Swallowing deeply, I gently run my palm over his cheek before adding, "Logan, I want a future with you."

"I want that too, Sarah. I will wait but not too long. I haven't felt this happy and content in a longtime. Besides, you are worth waiting for."

Bending down, I grab the bag of wet cloths, slip on my ballet flats and head towards to door. Logan opens it for me and places his hand on my lower back, escorting me to the elevator. "While you're in the lift, I'll call down and get them to hail a cab for you."

"I'm happy to walk, Logan."

"You are not walking at." He looks at his watch. "One in the morning...dressed like that."

"Wow, I didn't realise how late it is. Yes, a cab would be great."

"Glad you agree. Sarah, I care deeply for you. I'd hate for something to happen to you."

"Logan, I know exactly how you feel. I promise to be safe. When will I see you next?"

"I'm pretty busy with this new contract this week. Do you think you'd be able to sneak over late one night?"

"I'll do my best. Will all depend on what appointments that I have booked."

His demeanor changes when I mention possible appointments and it sucks donkey balls that I'm stuck in this situation at the moment. "Logan, I will do everything in my power to get out of this. I just need time."

"I know, Sarah, I know. I just want you all to myself...now." Pausing, he shuffles on his feet as the lift arrives. "Sarah, you're not sleeping with anyone else are you?"

"Not anymore I won't be. But I was only sleeping with one other client, the rest were all companionship, the true definition of an escort."

He smiles at me. "That makes me happy. Now get in that lift before I throw you over my shoulder and take you back inside, where I'll ravish your body from head to toe."

Swallowing deeply, I reply, "You don't play fair, Logan. I'll chat to you tomorrow. Night."

Stepping into the lift, I turn around and push the ground floor button. Before the lift closes, Logan puts his hand in to stop it and gives me a quick kiss before stepping back out. "Good night, Sarah. Sweet dreams."

The elevator doors close and the last thing I see is Logan smiling at me. Lifting my fingers to my lips, I kiss them and blow the kiss towards Logan. He lifts his hand and pretends to catch it and place it gently on his cheek. Once on the ground floor, the doors open and the concierge is there is escort me to the awaiting cab out front.

Climbing in, I give the driver the address of the apartment and I sit back in my seat. Closing my eyes, I smile to myself. I'm over the moon happy and finally things are looking up for me…or so I thought.

25

VICTORIA

SARAH IS STILL MANAGING TO ASTOUND ME; I HAVEN'T FOUND A GIRL LIKE her in a long time. Not only did she come along at the right time, but she also was Elite's saving grace and it has kept 'him' happy, very happy indeed. It's nice to know that after all of these years, I haven't lost my touch.

Everything would be perfect if the girls would stop disobeying me and it's troubling that my saving grace is starting to slip into that category; to say it's disappointing is an understatement. Why must they disobey? It's simple, follow the rules and everyone is happy. What frustrates me the most is that when they are brought to account, they beg, plead, and cry. Why won't they just leave without incident? Their heads held high? If they did, it would all be perfect.

Luckily for me, I have people on hand to help me when things don't go smoothly. I snap my fingers and they jump into action. They've been working overtime of late. Actually, it all started to go downhill just before Sarah came aboard. I'm really hoping it's all just a coincidence but I don't believe in coincidences. My gut is telling me she is somehow involved. If I find out that she has betrayed me, I will not be held responsible for my actions, and she will suffer the consequences, just like the others did.

My thoughts are interrupted when my phone rings, Simon's name flashes on my screen. He should be picking up Sarah for the gallery gala with Chow right now. "Simon!" I sharply say, as I answer the phone.

"Umm, Victoria, we have a problem."

Rubbing my temple in frustration, I snap, "Unless someone is dead, I don't want to hear about it. Just get Sarah to the gallery...now!"

"Well, someone is dead. Angel Hurley was found murdered this morning."

"What did you just say?"

"Angel is dead, her body washed up on the banks of the river this morning."

Shit, shit shit! I think to myself, "She no longer works at Elite, how is that any concern to us?"

"Both Sarah and Morgan are quite upset. Sarah is refusing to go."

"I don't think so. Put her on the phone."

"Yes, ma'am." I can hear him talking to Sarah and then there's a shuffling down the line.

"Victoria," Sarah sniffles, "Angel was murdered."

"Sarah, that is unfortunate. But she no longer works here, how is her death anything to do with us?"

"She was our friend."

"That is of no consequence to me. You have a 3:00 p.m. appointment with Mr. Chow. If you want to keep your job here at Elite, I suggest you get there in the next ten minutes." Pausing, I sternly add, "Am I understood?"

"Yes, Victoria."

"Good, now hand the phone back to Simon and go get ready."

Oh My God! How did this happen? I need to fix this immediately. I'm thinking when Simon takes the phone back.

"Victoria, I'm back. Is there anything else?"

"Simon, make sure that Sarah gets to the gallery on time. I'll call Chow and tell him she's running late. After you drop her off, get back here as quickly as possible. I think I'm going to need your help."

"Yes, Miss. I'll see you within the hour."

"Thank you, Simon."

Hanging up, I quickly dial Alexander. He answers on the first ring. "Yes."

"We have a problem?"

"We do not have a problem, you have a problem. You assured me that Angel would not be an issue, yet that situation is now splashed all over the news. Fix it."

He hangs up before I have a chance to reply.

Walking over to the office minibar, I pour myself a brandy and quickly drink it. Pouring myself another, I pick up my glass, and make my way over to my desk. *Why do these problems keep coming up?*

An hour later, Simon knocks on my office door and in that time, I have come up with a plan. "Simon, please do come in. I have a special job that needs the utmost discretion."

"Anything, what do you need?"

"I want you to follow Sarah Bryant. Things have been going off course lately and I bet my *Prada* collection that it's all to do with her, if not, I know she's hiding something."

"Yes, ma'am. I will do my best."

"I know you will, Simon, I know you will."

Simon leaves my office and I'm agitated and antsy, I'm not one for unanswered questions. To try and take my mind off everything, I decide that an afternoon at the spa is in order. When it hits me, Morgan is off and she's close to Sarah, I will invite her to the spa with me and do some of my own detective work.

Morgan reluctantly agreed to join me at the spa for the afternoon; she is really broken up over Angel, not my problem. I told her that a driver will be by to pick her up in thirty minutes and that I will meet her there.

An afternoon of pampering was just what I needed to reinvigorate the soul and recharge my batteries. Unfortunately, Morgan didn't know anything in relation to Sarah. If anything, she kept gushing about her. If she wasn't fangirling over Sarah, she was crying over Angel; it was quite annoying and not at all rejuvenating.

After dropping Morgan off at the apartment, I headed back to the office. These days I seem to be living there, trying to fix all the problems that my once great girls have caused. The business hasn't been the same since Megan, Tanya, Crissy, Saskia, Cassy, Tish, Kristy, Alyssa and Angel were relieved of their employment, willingly or otherwise. Luckily for me, I did not have to personally get involved; I hate getting my hands dirty, that's what my henchmen are for.

My thoughts are interrupted by a call from Simon. "Simon," I sternly answer.

"I have news on Sarah. I dropped her off at the apartment after the gallery thing with Chow but she didn't head inside. She aimlessly walked around the city and then ended up at Charlie's Bar; if I'm not mistaken, it's located within the building where Mr. DeBiers recently purchased a residence."

"It could be coincidence, as I know the girls like that bar, but I don't believe in coincidences." Biting my lip in frustration, I add, "Simon, stay there. The bar closes at 1:00 a.m. if she doesn't leave around then or earlier, she's with DeBiers. Thanks for the update."

"My pleasure, ma'am."

Just after 1:00 a.m. I get a text from Simon.

Simon – *She left just after 1am...alone. No sign of DeBiers.*
Victoria – *That's a relief*

Even though she wasn't seen with Mr. DeBiers, doesn't mean she wasn't with him; I'm still skeptical. My Spidey senses are on high alert and Sarah Bryant is the cause...what is she up to?

26

SARAH

THE LAST FEW DAYS HAVE BEEN WONDERFUL, AND IT'S ALL TO DO WITH A six-foot tall demigod named Logan. We have spoken on the phone every day, sometimes twice, text each other constantly and tonight, once Morgan is asleep, I'm going to sneak over to his place.

Since the passing of Angel, Morgan has become a hermit and has withdrawn into herself; even a spa afternoon with she-devil didn't pull her out of her funk, but that could have been due to the company. At the moment she only leaves the apartment for appointments, and then when she's home, she locks herself in her room. I'm worried about her. I really want to be there for her, but tonight is the only night this week that I can see Logan.

Putting on my running gear, I lace up my sneakers, say bye to Morgan, and I head out. She doesn't seem to notice but if I make it look like I'm running, it's easier to cover up if I somehow get caught.

Thirteen minutes later, I'm jogging up the stairs of Logan's building and I can't wait to see him. Pausing, I look around as I have a feeling someone is watching me, but there is no one who looks out of place on the street; I guess my mind is playing tricks on me. I've felt this way ever since we found out about Angel.

Waving to the desk clerk, I make my way to the elevators and push the call button. Luck is on my side as the door opens immediately; I press the button for Logan's floor. When the doors open, Logan is waiting for me, leaning against the wall with his left leg bent at the knee and foot resting on the wall. He's wearing dark jeans and a plain black t-shirt.

"Hey, how did you know I was here? I wanted to surprise you 'cause I'm earlier than I thought."

"Grant." I look at him dumbfounded, *Who the hell is Grant?* "The desk clerk. I slipped him a twenty to give me a heads-up when you arrived."

"Sneaky, sneaky," I say. Stepping into his space, I throw my arms around his neck and kiss him. It quickly turns heated and he grabs my bum, lifting me up. Wrapping my legs around him, he walks us inside and directly to his bedroom.

Within one minute, we are both naked and Logan sinks his throbbing cock inside of me. We fall into a steady rhythm before he flips us over so I'm straddling him, managing not to slip out in the process. Rocking back and forth, I throw my head back as the tingly sensation begins to develop deep in my belly. My hands make their way to my breasts, I begin to massage and fondle my nipples, while Logan reaches between us and begins to rub my clit in circles. His touch on my clit is the spark needed to light me on fire and I explode. I see fireworks behind my closed eyes as the tremors pass over my body. As I'm coming back to earth, I feel Logan tense underneath me. Increasing my thrusts, I clench my walls tighter and milk his orgasm until I feel his hips jolt; he erupts inside of me with a growl.

When he has finished, I fall forward and rest my head on his chest. We lay like this until our breathing returns to normal. Lifting my head, I look deep into his eyes and I realise that I'm falling in love with Logan and I smile. It's totally crazy, we've only known each other for a few weeks, but the feelings I have for and with Logan are like nothing that I have ever experienced before. He lifts his hand and pushes a strand of my hair behind my ear. "What are you smiling about?"

"Nothing in particular. I just realised that for the first time in months, I'm happy. Deliriously happy and that's all because of you." Climbing up his body, I rest on my elbows and I kiss him, this kiss feels different. There is so much emotion behind it, I don't want it to end but we are interrupted by Logan's phone ringing.

We ignore it but they immediately call back. "Guess you better answer that." Climbing off the bed I head into the bathroom, over my shoulder I huskily say, "Come join me after your call."

Smiling, he picks up his phone and the expression on his face changes as he answers. Turning on my heel, I head into the ensuite and turn on the shower. Once the water is warm, I climb in and let the hot water fall over my body—*whoever invented the rainwater head is a godsend*. I've just lathered my body with his body wash, when Logan climbs in. His shoulders are tight and he looks tense. "Is everything okay?"

"Yeah, it's fine. Nothing for you to worry about." He closes his eyes and steps under the water, ignoring me. Whoever was on the other end of the call has really upset him. I want him to relax so I pump more body wash into my hands and begin to massage his back and shoulders. He moans and immediately relaxes, slipping my hands around; I begin to soap his pecs and abs, garnering a growl this time. Sliding my hands down further, I grip his cock tightly in my fist and begin to stoke.

He flips around, pinning my hands above my head and kisses me, snaking his hand down my stomach, he begins fondling my slit. Moaning into his mouth, I pull my hand free and reach down to his and resume stroking his cock. We continue to kiss and caress each other intimately, until we both tumble over the orgasmic cliff, murmuring each other's name as the pleasure rockets through our bodies.

Untangling from each other, we silently wash ourselves before hopping out. Logan puts on satin boxers and I get back into my workout gear. We head to the lounge room and enjoy the wine and cheese that he set out for us before I arrived. After finishing the wine and chatting for hours, I get up to head back home. Lacing our fingers together as we walk to the door, I whisper, "I don't want go."

He nuzzles my ear and whispers back, "Then don't, stay."

Shaking my head, I say, "I can't, but soon you won't be able to get rid of me."

"I'll never want to get rid of you, Sarah, I think I'm falling in love with you."

My head snaps towards him in shock, my mouth open. "Logan, I feel the same way." Jumping towards him, he catches me, our lips colliding in another heat-filled kiss; I swear each kiss is hotter than the last. Breaking away, I rest my forehead on his and proclaim, "I really, really need to go or we will get caught. I'll text you tomorrow." He lowers me down and opens the door. He goes to escort me to the elevator and I put a hand against his chest. "You need to stay here, otherwise we will kiss again, and it will be another thirty minutes before I leave."

"And the problem with that is?" he smart-assly replies.

"You are a bad influence on sweet, innocent, little me."

"Sweet, yes. Innocent, hell no. But I'll happily stay here 'cause I can watch you sexy ass as you walk away."

"You're a fiend, Logan DeBiers. I'll see you soon." I place a quick kiss on his cheek and head towards the elevator. Swishing my hips from side to side, Logan wolf whistles at me and I blow a kiss over my shoulder. The lift arrives and I climb in, giving a gentle wave as the doors close. Leaning back against the railing, I sigh, I'm over the moon happy right now.

Climbing into the waiting cab, I head back to my apartment and that feeling of being watched is back, again I look around but like before, I don't see anyone. Unbeknownst to me, there is someone lurking in the night, watching my every move and reporting back to the one person who has the power to destroy everything.

SARAH

...Present day

IT'S THE WEEKEND, FINALLY AND I'M OFF...FOR THE FIRST TIME SINCE Wednesday; Victoria has booked me solid every-single-day. I've had back-to-back appointments and no downtime at all. I feel like I'm being punished for something but I have no idea what. Due to this, Logan and I haven't had any time together, he's been so busy too that he couldn't even 'book' time with me. We won't be able to see each other until tomorrow, as we both are busy catching up with friends this evening, and neither one of us wanted to let our mates down.

I'm climbing out of the shower and my phone beeps with a text... again. Wrapping my fluffy pink towel around me, I pick it up and see yet another message from Kenz, reconfirming, again, that I am coming tonight.

Kenz – *Don't forget it starts at 6*
Sarah – *For the millionth time today I WILL BE THERE*
Kenz – *Wow, you used shouty caps, I believe you now*
Kenz – *See you at 6pm*
Sarah – *Yes Mum, I'll be there*

Today is Mike and Sav's housewarming and Kenz has guilted me into coming. I'm excited to see everyone, but I would much rather spend the evening with Logan. Slipping on my deep plum halter dress and Nine West wedges, I'm ready to go.

Victoria is in a great mood and has given me Simon as a driver for the evening; he seems pissy as he opens the car door for me. Twenty minutes later, we will pull up to the party. He drops me off and I'm only ten minutes late. I hate being late but traffic was a bitch. As I walk up the driveway of Mike and Sav's cottage, I feel sad. They have this gorgeous house and I'm living in an apartment and working as an escort. *I really need to quit so I can have all of this*, I think to myself as I head inside behind another couple.

Once inside, I find Mike and Sav to offer my congratulations and say how awesome the house is. Just as I'm walking up to Mike, he's deep in conversation with Sav and Jordan when he says, "If you fart and no ones around, did you really fart?"

"What?" Sav asks with a confused look on her face.

"You know, like that tree forest thingy, but with farts?"

"Dude, you need to stop smoking crack." Jordan pauses, "Hey, Sarah." Mike and Sav turn and grin at me as Jordan hugs me. He leaves me with the hosts and goes off to find Kenz.

"Dude, she'll be at the bar." The three of them laugh at my statement as Jordan heads towards the makeshift bar and his beautiful wife. Turning my attention back to them, I say, "Mike, this place is awesome. Hi, Sav. I'm Sarah, it's nice to officially meet you." I stretch out my hand.

"Nice to meet you officially, too." She shakes mine and smiles, making me feel at ease and that I can do this, and have fun; while keeping my secret safe in the process. I chat with Mike and Sav for a bit when I hear Kenz laugh, turning around, I see her with Jordan. No surprises, near the bar, I tell Mike and Sav that I'll catch up with them later, and I make my way towards my bestie and her hubby.

Walking over to Kenz and Jordan, Kenz smiles when she sees me and smacks Jordan in the chest. "Well, well, well, look, Jor, it's Sarah. You remember her? My bestie, who seems to have disappeared off the face of the earth."

Hugging Jordan again, I say, "Hardy har har, bitch." Before embracing Kenz tightly, *It's good to see her again*, I think to myself. Pulling back, but still gripping her tightly, I give my best puppy dog eyes. "It's good to see you guys and, Kenz, I know I've been such a shitty friend, but I promise, I'll explain everything...soon."

"You know I can't resist your puppy dog eyes, so I'll give you a pass...for now, but you and I will be talking; soon."

"I know, I know, and I promise that I will but for tonight, I'm going to get rip-roaring drunk with my besties and have a winetabolous time." Taking the glass of wine from Kenz, I yell, "Cheers bitches!" and clink glasses with her, followed by Jordan.

From over where I just was, we hear Mike yell. "Back at ya, lady!"

Kenz, Jordan, and I fall into easy conversation; just like old times. About an hour later a chill comes over me and then I hear him. His voice is embedded in my brain and when I turn I around, I see him standing on the other side of the room. He has his back to me and is chatting to Mike and Sav, all my fears and secrets are standing not five meters away from me. I'm scared but at the same time, so happy that he's here...but how?

Suddenly, he turns around and pauses midstep when his eyes lock on me. He stares at me open-mouthed, my face mirroring his. A force takes over my body and I find myself walking towards to him, his pull is too strong to ignore. Before I know it, I'm standing directly in front of him. He reaches out and grabs my hand, squeezing it gently. "Sarah?" His sexy baritone voice completely melts me. "What are you doing here?"

The room is dead silent; all eyes are focused on Logan and me. I'm frozen, staring at him, my face pales and I feel like I'm going to throw up. Not quite believing that he is standing in front in me, in the middle of Mike and Sav's living room. The music playing fades away and all I see is Logan, he and I are the only ones there. We are absorbed in one another; the air around us is filled with lust, sexual tension, and confusion.

I'm snapped back to reality when I hear Logan say my name again and he gently rubs my arm. Shaking my head, I stammer. "LLL... Logan, what are you doing here?"

"The friend that has just come back into my life is Sav. What are you doing here?"

I'm shocked, all words leave my brain; I'm stunned to see Logan standing in front of me. Looking around, I see everyone staring intently at us. Everything I have been hiding is about to unravel, and the biggest secret of all is standing right in front of me. All six foot two inches of gorgeousness. "I...I...I have to go."

Turning away from Logan and my friends, I race towards to front entrance. Vaguely I hear Kenz and Jordan calling out to me, but I put one foot in front of the other and I get out of there. Once outside, I slam the door behind me, struggling to breathe as a panic attack sets in. Leaning against it, I stand there hyperventilating, trying to catch my breath. I'm brought back to reality when I hear Logan say, "That's the girl I was telling you about, Sav."

Sav shouts back, "Sarah is your hooker?"

Hearing that, my breathing stops and I slide down the door and begin to cry, I hear Jordan and Kenz say in unison. "What?"

28

LOGAN

I'M CHATTING TO SAV AND MIKE, WHEN THE HAIRS ON THE BACK OF MY neck stand up and a feeling of excitement and calm washes over me. Shaking it off, I say, "I'll get us a round of drinks, be right back." Turning around, I see Sarah in all her beauty standing by the bar, staring intently at me. I completely zone out, not believing she's here and before I know it, she's standing right in front of me. All eyes are on us and the room goes deathly quiet. She asks me what I'm doing here, and I explain that Sav is my friend that I mentioned. I ask her what she's doing here, but before I get an answer or a kiss, she spins away from me and runs off. Leaving me standing alone in the middle of Mike and Sav's lounge room with everyone staring at me.

I'm shocked frozen and I just stand there and watch Sarah run off, tears welling in her eyes. I hear her friends by the bar yelling after her, but she slams the door on her way out. I'm so confused at her sudden departure. Sav walks over to me, nudges my arm and asks. "How do you know Sarah, Logan?"

"She's the girl I was telling you about." I know the moment it clicks for Sav and then she shouts, "Sarah is your hooker?" Immediately covering her mouth when she realises that she said that out loud...for everyone to hear.

I'm shell-shocked, all of Sarah's fears have just been revealed and

I'm still standing here, stunned and all alone. My brain clicks into gear and I race outside to go after her but she's gone.

I'm walking back up the driveway when Mike, Sav, Kenzie, and her husband all come outside, confusion etched on their faces. Kenzie is the first to speak, "What the hell is going on?"

Sav and I look at each other but before we can reply, Kenzie demands, "Someone please explain why Sav thinks Sarah is a hook…" She trails off her eyes open wide, "Oh My God! You're her Logan, aren't you?" She pause and then mumbles to herself, "She mentioned you at coffee but she was very hush-hush about it all."

Looking at Kenzie, I quietly say, "Yeah, I am."

Hesitantly Kenzie asks, "H…How did you and Sarah meet?"

"In a bar."

"Don't fuck with me, Logan," she vehemently spits.

"Kenz, settle down," Jordan interjects and calmly rubs her arm.

"No, Sarah is my best friend, I knew something was up and now I want the truth." Pausing, she looks directly at me before shouting in her mum, don't fuck with me voice, "Now, Logan

Not wanting to betray Sarah, but not really have any other choice. I tell them how we met and give them the Cliff's Notes version of Sarah's life for the last few months.

"Fuck me dead, said Foreskin Fred," Mike, Kenzie, and Jordan all say in unison.

Before any of them can say anything, I add, "She was embarrassed and ashamed to tell you guys. She didn't want to add to your problems. She mentioned you had all had it tough, in one way or another, so she did it all on her own."

By this point, there are tears sliding down Kenzie's cheeks. "Ohh, Sarah, you stupid girl." She turns to Jordan and he wraps his arms around her. Mike rubs her back caringly, as Sav turns to me.

"Logan, I'm so sorry. I didn't mean to out you guys like that. You need to go find Sarah and make sure she's okay."

Kenz turns from Jordan and says, "No. I'll go. I'm her best friend and I know what she needs."

Mike says, "Wine and Jerry's?"

Logan says, "She's lucky to have you guys. She's told me all about you and I was looking forward to meeting you all. I just wish it was under nicer circumstances."

Kenz smiles and says, "Well, if Sarah and Sav both like you, you must be alright." She stretches out her hand. "I'm Kenzie and this is my husband, Jordan." She points to him over her shoulder and I shake her hand.

"As you know, I'm Logan," I say, as I shake Jordan's hand.

Turning we see Sav and Mike whispering over by the door, they both look up and Sav says, "I'll get the ice cream and you can take a bottle of wine from here." Turning she reaches for the door handle and then looks back at me, quietly adding, "Please tell Sarah I'm really, really sorry." She opens the door and slips inside.

Mike rubs the back of his neck and says, "Sav feels really bad that she outed Sarah like that, it was just a shock."

"Tell me about it," Kenz says, as she wraps an arm around Jordan's tighter.

Sav emerges with a bag and it's rattling. "God, Sav, what are you trying to do? Get Kenz and Sarah drunk?"

"Yep, after what was exposed tonight, because of me, she needs and deserves it."

Kenz and Jordan head off to find Sarah, it kills me not to go after her, but Kenz assures me that she'll look after her. Sav, Mike, and I head back to the party. As soon as we walk inside, all chatter stops and all eyes are on us; it's awkward as all hell. Thankfully, Mike creates a distraction by shouting, "It's tequila and toast time, baby!"

He strides over to the bar, grabs a bottle of Patron and the plastic shot glasses, then proceeds to pour and hand them out, threatening anyone who tries to drink or sook out. He finally gets to Sav and me; he drapes his arm over Sav's shoulder, gives her a kiss then looks to everyone. "Sav and I want to thank you all for coming here tonight to celebrate our new cottage. Sav, you are the love of my life and I'm looking forward to our adventure together. In true us style, even our housewarming is entertaining." He winks at me. "So, a toast. To love, life, happiness, and fucking awesome tequila. Cheers, bitches!" The room erupts into a chorus of 'cheers', 'fuck yeah' and a few 'ughs' as everyone takes their shot. Someone coughs and Mike whispers not so quietly to Sav, "Pussies." Sav and I both laugh. "Shit, did you hear that? I was trying to be quiet."

"From what I know of you, Mike, quiet isn't your style."

Sav bursts out laughing. "He knows you already, Mike. Man I

missed you, Loges." Pulling away from Mike she gives me a big hug and whispers, "I'm so sorry, Logan. I didn't mean to out you both like that, I feel like a big turd right now. It was such a shock that it was our Sarah that you are in love with."

"I'm not in love with her."

"Pfft. You're not fooling anyone, you totally are."

"Let's just see how she feels tomorrow before we start getting too excited." I notice that Sav sinks into herself. "Shit, Sav, I didn't mean it like that."

"No, I know. I just feel bad for Sarah, I can't imagine what she has been through and to do it all by herself." She smiles at me. "I'm glad she had you though."

"It's not your fault. It's not anyone's fault." Pausing, I add, "Look, I think I'm going to head home. I'm not really in a party mood anymore, and I want to be home in case Sarah stops by."

"I understand. Thanks for coming, Loges, and again, sorry."

"It's all good, baby girl. Want to do lunch one day this week?"

"Sounds good. Text me when you are free."

"Will do. Thanks for a great night, guys." Hugging Sav goodbye, I shake hands with Mike, before heading outside to wait for the cab that I ordered.

Thirty minutes later, I'm climbing into bed but I can't sleep; I can't stop thinking about Sarah. I'm worried about her. Knowing Sarah, she won't answer if I call, so I send her a text.

Logan – *Hope you are okay. Thinking about you*

Immediately I get a reply.

Sarah – *I'm fine. Kenz is here. Chat tomorrow*
Sarah – *Nite nite Logan Xo*

I write and delete love you on the end of my next text several times before deciding the first time I say it will not be via text so I don't type it.

Logan – *Nite Sarah. Sweet dream gorgeous Xo*

After chatting with Sarah via text, albeit briefly, I feel confident that we will be okay. I fall into a deep sleep where I dream that Sarah and I live together and we get our happily ever after...if only it was as simple as that.

29

SARAH

BEFORE I KNOW IT, THERE'S BANGING ON MY FRONT DOOR AND I JUST KNOW it's Kenzie; I guess Logan told her where I live. "Sarah Bryant, you open this door right now, otherwise I'll just set up a picnic out here and drink the wine and eat the ice cream by myself...I would much rather sit on a couch and do it with you. Your choice?"

Kenz always makes me laugh, so reluctantly I get up and unlock the door. She places the bags at her feet and envelopes in me a Kenz hug; just what I need. This causes the waterworks to start and I break down in her arms. We stand in my doorway hugging until I have no more tears to cry. Sniffing, I pull away, look at Kenz and whisper, "I'm sorry I kept things from you, Kenz."

"I'm sooo mad at you right now, Sarah. But I understand AND I have wine and ice cream, so you will tell me everything from the beginning, and then we will call it even...but don't you ever keep a secret like this from me again." She looks me dead in the eyes. "Deal?" Choking back a sob, I just nod my head. She bends down, picks up the bags and walks inside. "Fuck me dead, this is where you live? Wow, Sarah, you hit the jackpot."

She walks into the kitchen while I close the door and whisper to myself, "Yeah, but I sold myself to the devil in order to get it."

"What was that?" she says.

"Nothing, just muttering to myself." Pausing, I take a deep breath. "So, ice cream or wine first?"

We both look at each other and together we say, "Wine!" Before we burst out laughing, just like we always did…in three minutes Kenz has out me at ease, and I know that she'll help me get back on track. Joining Kenz in the kitchen, she puts Jerry in the freezer and I grab two wine glasses from the cupboard. Placing them on the counter as she opens the bottle. "I really miss uncorking a wine, twisting a metal cap just isn't as exciting."

"I know, right?" I reply, smiling. Even though the biggest secret of my life was just exposed, Kenz and I are still the same. It gives me hope that this will all work out.

Over the next few hours, I fill Kenzie in on everything and I mean everything. This time I don't omit anything, like I did when we had coffee the other week.

"Holy shit, you're just like Julia Roberts except you had a threesome and work for the devil. At least you landed the hot dude." Pausing, she takes and sip before adding, "WOW, Sarah, just WOW."

"I'm not a hooker." Kenz glares at me. "Well, okay, I guess technically I am, but I can't do it anymore." Taking a sip of wine I add, "Kenz, I really like Logan."

"No shit, Sherlock, the chemistry between you two was electric back at the party. Hell, the whole place came to a standstill watching."

"How was it after I left? I bet the rumors are flying. I heard Sav say I'm the hooker."

"Umm, yeah, there was talk, but we all went outside so no one could hear our conversation. Mike said he'd fix it, so I bet he'll get riproaring drunk, bring out classic Mike, and your revelation will be forgotten. The focus will be on Mike and his crazy drunk antics."

"God, I hope so. Fuck, how did my life get to this point?"

"Well, your bf…"

Smacking her in the arm, I interrupt, "Hardy har har, bitch. I don't need a reminder of what a clusterfuck my life has become. Why is it always everyone is happy and I'm on a downward, out of control spiral?"

"You're not out of control, Sarah. You are just off the beaten path and now you are back on track. First things first, you need to leave the Julia job."

"But if I do that, where will I go? What will I do?"

We are both silent thinking about what's next for me. Kenz tops ours glasses before asking, "Forgive me if I'm wrong, but don't people like you make lots of money?"

"Kenz, you can say hooker, it's fine."

"Okay, fine, don't hookers make lots of money? You should have a heap put away...unless you have secret sniff sniff habit."

"Yeah. It pays pretty well and no, no sniff sniff habit."

"Well, there you go, find somewhere to live, move out of this place, and then go from there. Hell, come and live with Jordan and me."

"I couldn't do that to you, Kenz, you guys have the girls. The last thing you need is an ex-hooker living with you."

"Sarah, you are family, and family helps each other in tough times. Hell, if you had just told me months ago, you could have moved in with us when all this happened."

"Yeah, but then I wouldn't have met Logan."

"Yes, you would have."

"How? Huh, tell me how?"

"Where were we tonight when you saw him? Mike and Sav's. You two would have eventually crossed paths and fallen hopelessly in love."

"You are ever the romantic, Kenz. I hope I get my happily ever after."

***

"You will, I feel it in my bones."

The next morning I wake up still on the couch, with a blanket over me and no Kenz. My head in pounding from the hangover from hell and the sunlight shining in is blinding. Grabbing my phone from the coffee table, I see three text messages.

> **Kenz –** *Morning bitch. Headed home early, miss my girls & Jor. Call me when you are alive. Love your hooker face*
> **Logan –** *Morning gorgeous. Wanna meet for coffee?*
> **Victoria –** *Call me when you wake up. It's important*

Reading my messages, my emotions go from laughing, to happily smiling, to sighing. Heading downstairs, I head to the kitchen to put on coffee. While I'm waiting for the machine to brew my heavenly morning drink, my phone rings and the sound pierces through my brain. *UGH, why did I drink so much?*

"Good morning, Victoria."

"About time you answered. I need to see you immediately. Simon is on his way, you have five minutes."

Before I have a chance to argue, she hangs up. "Well fuck you, too," I say to the room. Picking up my mug, I place it back in the cupboard and I grab my travel mug; coffee on the go this morning it is.

Filling my mug to the brim, I screw on the lid and quickly head upstairs to get changed. Forgoing a shower, I decide to spray extra perfume and quickly redo my makeup. Slipping on a white tank and my denim overalls, I grab my Chucks and head downstairs. As I hit the bottom step, there's a knock at the door; looking at my watch I mutter, "Fuck, Simon's early."

Opening the door, I find a smiling Logan standing there with two Java Lava coffee cups. Smiling back at him, I usher him in, stepping aside. "Morning, please tell me one of them is for me?"

"Morning to you too and no, they are both mine."

My mouth drops open in shock, before I pout and push out my bottom lip, looking sweetly at him. Sitting on the bottom step, I slip on my Chucks as I continue to play the poor I 'need coffee girl.'

"Well, when you look at me like that, how can I resist?"

"You can't," I reply as I stand up and grab a coffee from him. Taking a sip, I close my eyes and enjoy the goodness that is currently dancing around on my taste buds. Placing the cup of liquid gold on the entry table next to my travel mug, I turn to Logan and wrap my arms around him. Resting my head on his chest, I lose myself in all that is Logan, the beating of his heart instantly calming me. "Sorry, I took off last night." Pausing, I look up at him. "It was just a shock seeing you there. Thanks for sending Kenzie here, it was just what I needed."

"I was just as shocked to see you too, and I'm glad that Kenz was here for you. It killed me to stay away."

"But you're here now." Wrapping my arms around his neck, I pull him down towards me and I kiss him.

He breaks our kiss and says in his deep husky voice that sends my insides crazy. "I was so worried about you, Sarah, but I'm glad to see that you're ish okay."

"Ish oaky, I like that." We wrap our arms around each other and hold each other tightly; the only sound is the beating of our hearts and the music coming from the other room. Our moment is interrupted by a knock at the door. "Shit, shit, shit," I whisper. "That's Simon, I have to go see Victoria. You can't be seen here. Hide in there." I point towards to coat cupboard. "Wait five minutes before you leave. I'll call you when I'm done."

He kisses me again before slipping into the cupboard as Simon knocks again. "Coming!" I yell.

Grabbing my coffee, I open the door to an irritated looking Simon. "Morning, Simon. Let's go." Quickly I close the door behind me, grabbing his arm, I lead us towards the elevators. He jerks his arm free as if being touched by me is horrible. The air is thick with animosity and it's really uncomfortable as we make our way to the waiting car below.

Ten minutes later, we pull up at the office. Not waiting for Simon, I open the door myself and head inside. Simon is hot on my heels, which is unusual, and he knocks on Victoria's office door and stands to the side like a bodyguard. *That's weird,* I think to myself as Victoria opens the door.

"Ohh, Sarah, what are you wearing? You look so unrefined." She shakes her head as she turns on her heel and heads behind her desk. Smirking at her disapproval, I follow her into the office. I expect Simon to follow, but he waits outside like a little lap dog.

"Sarah, I know."

Looking at her confused, I ask. "Know what?"

"I know everything about last night."

"Look, I'm sorry I got drunk with my friend but I haven't seen her in ages. It shouldn't be an issue who I associate with when I'm not at work."

"I'm not talking about her, I'm talking about Mr. DeBiers."

Oh, fuck, I'm in trouble now. "What about him?" I ask, trying to hide the fear that is currently racing though my body.

"You went to an event with him that wasn't on the books. Simon informed me."

"Mike and Sav's housewarming?" *Fucking, Simon, that traitorous bastard.* "Hang on, I went alone. Simon dropped me off and I ran into him there. He's friends with my friend's girlfriend. I haven't seen any of them since I started here, so I wasn't aware of the connection until last night."

"So, you haven't been seeing him outside of work?"

"No, I have not, last night was the first time I had seen him since he and I attended the event last week." *Oh My God! I'm totally going to get busted here.* "Victoria, that's one of your rules, I wouldn't disobey you like that. I need this job, you know that."

"But..." Before she can probe me further, her booking line rings. As always, any meeting is put on hold when that line rings. She answers in her snotty, holier than thou voice, and it grates on my nerves. Zoning out, I don't pay attention until I hear her say, "Mr. DeBiers, she will be ready at 3:00 p.m."

This piques my interest and I sit up in my seat. *Remain calm, Sarah,* I tell myself as I take a sip of coffee. Sitting there I wait for her to finish the call. "Um, Victoria, I'm off this weekend. Remember?"

"Well, Mr. DeBiers is off to the Hunter Valley on business and he needs a companion. You fly out this afternoon and will be back midweek."

"Ahhh, okay. But from memory I'm booked with Xander on Monday," I shudder as I say his name, " and also Tuesday for the hospital gala."

"I can attend in your place. Mr. DeBiers is paying a premium for this, so he trumps any bookings that you have." Pausing, she looks me up and now, shaking her head. "Now, head back to the apartment to pack. And please, dress like the lady I know you are. You and your dress sense will be the death of me."

"Yes, Victoria." Inwardly I smirk because I love getting under her skin and to be honest, I chose this outfit with this in mind.

Getting up, I bid her farewell in the posh, fake way that gives her a lady boner and skip outside to find Simon waiting for me. "Home, Simon," I say in a hoity-toity voice. He rolls his eyes at me as he walk towards the car.

Grabbing my phone, I text Logan.

Sarah – *You are a genius.*
Logan – *Yes, yes I am. See you soon*

As I climb into the car, I find myself smiling and excited for the next few days. After what happened last night, I was petrified that Logan and I would be over before we even began...if only I knew what would happen while we were away.

30

LOGAN

SARAH IS CONSTANTLY ON MY MIND.

She's my last thought before I go to sleep.

She's my first thought when I wake in the morning.

I've never clicked with someone like I have with her, but I'm scared that our sneaking around is going to have serious consequences for her, deadly consequences for her. Thankfully, when her friends found out last night, the fallout wasn't anything like she or I expected, but now I'm even more determined to get her away from Victoria and Elite.

The sudden death of her friend and roommate didn't sit right with me, so I've hired someone to look into Victoria and Elite. What he has found so far is clean, too clean for my liking. What surprised me the most is that Victoria is not the only principle, there's a mystery party, why the secrecy? Trying to dig up information on him or her is proving difficult, and this revelation and lack of information is extremely concerning. For Sarah's safety, and my sanity, I need to get her out of there, and soon.

I've just finished going over the weekly report that Beth sent me when I decide that Sarah and I need to get away, just the two of us where no one knows us, and we can be us. Picking up my phone, I call Elite's booking line. Making up a bullshit last minute business meeting in the Hunter Valley, I say that I need Sarah to accompany me to and decide to tack on a few extra days just for us. Not surprising, Victoria jumped at the chance and charged me a premium, but if it means I get to spend time with Sarah, then so be it—she's worth every cent and more.

I'm just finalising everything when I get a text.

Sarah – *Can't wait for spend a few uninterrupted days away with you*

Smiling, I immediately reply.

Logan – *Me neither. No need to pack clothes **WINK***
Sarah – *You'll love what I have packed*
Sarah – *....or haven't packed **WINK***
Logan – *Can't wait. See you soon gorgeous*

Quickly finishing up, I send Beth this week's action list and leave her a voice message about my impromptu leave of absence—her reaction at my spur of the moment decision will be shock and awe. I have never done anything like this since starting LDB. Leaving the office, I race back to my penthouse, pack a bag, and head over and pick Sarah up for our getaway.

The car pulls up at her place and she's waiting on the sidewalk. My cock twitches when my eyes land on her. She's wearing a black and white, Aztec print, boob tube dress with black ballet flats. Her hair is loose and blowing in the wind, she is a vision. Stepping out of the car, I lift her into my arms and spin her around before kissing her. Pulling back, I look at her as she lifts her sunglasses onto her head and her eyes sparkle in the afternoon sunlight. "My God, Sarah, you look fucking gorgeous. I can't wait to get you alone."

She giggles, "Well, you will have to wait, not sure our fellow passengers would appreciate an X-rated show on the flight."

"What passengers? I charted a flight for us."

"What?"

"It's just you, me, the pilot, and steward. As soon as we reach altitude, you and I are initiating ourselves into the Mile High Club."

She stares at me opened-mouthed, lifting her hand, she cups my cheeks before seductively saying, "Who says I'm not already a member?" Kissing me on the lips before quickly climbing into the car, I'm now the one left standing there open-mouthed and in shock.

Turning around, I go to grab her bag but the driver has already placed it in the boot. As I climb into the car, I'm grinning from ear to ear and I'm really looking forward to the next few days.

The flight is too turbulent for us to join the Mile High Club together but we do make out like teenagers the whole way. By time we land in Newcastle, my cock is rock hard and I cannot wait to get to the accommodation and check in.

An hour later, we pull up to *Casa La Vina Villas* and check into our villa. Watching Sarah as she takes it all in is mesmerising, her face lights up as she checks the room out. When she discovers the private patio with an outdoor Jacuzzi and BBQ she squeals in excitement, I can't contain myself. Striding over to her, I wrap my arms around her and nuzzle her ear. "You are fucking gorgeous, Sarah." She grinds her sexy ass against me, my cock stiffening. "You are a minx."

"Mmhmm," she whispers as she begins to circle her hips. Spinning around she kisses me deeply, wrapping her arms around my neck, rubbing her pussy against my leg. Stepping back, she unzips the side zip of her dress, the black and white material fanning at her feet. She's left standing there in a matching pale pink strapless bra and G-string. Reaching behind her back, she unclips her bra, hooks her fingers in the side of her G, and ever so slowly removes them. Standing back up, she winks before turning around and racing out to the Jacuzzi. It's bubbling away as she climbs in and sits on the edge, facing me. Her fingers trail down her neck, circling her nipples and pinching, she closes her eyes and moans. Before lightly tracing over her stomach and sliding down her slit, inserting a finger. Opening her eyes, she looks at me and through a moans whispers, "Are you coming?" Pulling her finger out she slides it slowly up and rubs her clit in circles.

My eyes are locked on her hand between her thighs as I quickly undress and join her in the Jacuzzi. Spinning her around, I lower myself between her thighs and nudge her fingers out of the way. Darting my tongue out, I lick her mound. Taking her clit into my mouth, I gently bite down and suck, her fingers run through my hair and she moans. Slipping a finger into her and hooking it around, I find her magic spot and wiggle. "Logan," she groans. Inserting another finger, I continue to lick and finger her until I feel her walls clench around my fingers. "I'm coming," she whisper-shouts. Her body shudders as her orgasm rips through her body. She falls into the water limply and wraps her arms around my neck, nuzzling her way up to my lips and kissing me. We kiss for a few moments until she pulls back, pushing me to sit down. She straddles my hips and impales herself on my rock hard cock. We stare intently at each other as she continues to ride me. Before long, we are both shouting each other's names as we each succumb to the intense orgasms rocking through our bodies.

Sarah climbs off me and lowers herself into the water, moaning. Even though I have just come, hearing her moan like that stirs my cock once again. Linking my fingers with hers, I settle in next to her and we stare up at the twilight sky. The silence is peaceful and in this moment, I'm happier than I have ever been. Turning my head, I look towards Sarah and smile. She looks to me, smiles, and whispers, "Thank you."

"What are you thanking me for?"

"Being you." Pausing, she swallows and sits up. "Logan, I've never felt like this with anyone before. We connect on every level. You're always on my mind. I...I think I'm falling in love with you."

Sitting up, I turn and face her, grabbing her hands I squeeze tightly. "Sarah, I know exactly what you mean. You bring out the best in me and I've never been this happy before."

She jumps out of the water and crashes her lips to mine, knocking us back under the water. We kiss underwater, only breaking the surface to breathe; kneeling together our lips are locked in the most romantic, emotion-filled kiss. Placing my hands under her ass and lifting, she wraps her legs around me, and I slowly enter the tip of my cock into her. She pulls back and slams down onto my cock. We use the buoyancy of the water to thrust back and forth, the friction building into the most intense orgasm of my life. Our bodies become one as we rock back and forth, our lips fused. Feeling her pussy walls clench around my cock, she screams as her orgasm explodes and I follow soon after.

Standing up with Sarah still wrapped around me, I carefully climb out and head inside our villa to the shower. Sitting Sarah on the vanity, I turn the shower on, and once the water is hot enough, we hop in. Soaping each other up, our hands massaging and caressing each other, it turns sexual and I take her up against the shower wall.

We separately get washed and climb into bed naked and cuddle, we both lie here content in each other's arms.

Just as Sarah falls asleep, I hear her whisper, "I love you, Logan."

Kissing her gently on the head, I whisper, "I love you, too." With a smile on my face, I drift off to sleep looking forward to the next few days.

The next few days in the Hunter Valley with Sarah are magical. We visit wineries; take a horse-drawn carriage ride, and a hot air balloon tour at sunrise, with a champagne breakfast when we land. The more time I spend with Sarah only cements my love for her. Neither of us has said it to each other directly, but each night as we drift off in each other's arms we quietly whisper it.

I'm awakened on our last day with Sarah between my legs and my cock down her throat. I have to say, that is the best way to be woken up. After she has sucked me dry, she straddles my legs, leans forward and whispers, "Morning, sexy."

Smiling up at her, I grab her by the waist and flip her onto her back. "Morning, gorgeous," I say before crashing my lips to hers, the little minx lifts her hips and rubs her pussy against my cock, bringing him back to life.

Spreading her legs wider, I nudge the tip against her pussy lips before pulling back. I do this a few times before thrusting my hips forward and impaling myself to the hilt. Her pussy is warm and inviting as I keep thrusting, each thrust becoming harder and faster. Sarah digs her nails into my back and screams my name as her body shudders beneath me.

She nudges me and I know that she wants to go on top so we roll together; she gets up on her knees and rides me. Closing her eyes, she massages and squeezes her breasts as I rub her clit. I'm just about to come when I hear her moan and she squeeze her legs against mine, together we orgasm.

Falling on top of me, she sighs. We lay there, both panting, trying to catch our breath after our morning workout. Eventually she rolls off me and we lay in each other's arms, drifting back to sleep.

After waking up, we decide to head back to our favourite winery, *Tulloch* for another tasting and then head to *Tempus Two* for lunch. The day is perfect and the best way to end our getaway together.

We had just cleaned up dinner and were soaking in the Jacuzzi together when I asked Sarah about leaving Elite…that was when it all went downhill.

"Sarah, when we get back, I want to you quit Elite."

"Logan, I told you I would but I can't right now. I'm still not back on my feet. I know it's not ideal but I have no other options."

"Let me look after you, Sarah, you're better than this."

"I'm not," she pleads

"Sarah, you are. This job isn't you, you're not a hook..." I pause; I didn't mean to say that.

She sits up and splashes water, staring at me open-mouthed and shocked. "Go on, Logan, finish that sentence. I'm a hooker, a fucking whore, a prostitute. You think that's all I do at Elite, don't you? Well, guess what, asshole..." She pauses for emphasis. "You are sleeping with a hooker. " Taking a deep breath she shouts with tears pouring down her cheeks, "You are fucking a hooker, Logan, you're just as bad as me!"

Climbing out of the Jacuzzi, she storms off, slamming her wine glass down on the table as she heads inside. I feel like a real asshole and just sit there replaying the words I just said to the woman that I love. Hating myself right now, I decide to give her a few moments to collect herself before I go apologise, but I don't get a chance to because I hear the villa front door slamming. The slam causes the patio door and windows to rock from the force of the impact. *Fuck, I've really hurt her*, I think to myself as I climb out.

Heading inside, I take a quick shower and slip into my boxers for the first time since arriving. Walking back into the living room, I see that Sarah hasn't returned so pour myself a scotch and throw it back. It burns on the way down but with the way I just spoke to Sarah, I deserve it...and more. In one conversation, I managed to ruin what has been a fantastic getaway and crush the woman who means everything to me.

A few hours later, Sarah returns but she doesn't look at me or say a word. She heads into the bedroom, slips on her nightie and climbs into bed. From the lounge room I can hear her crying and I feel like a bastard, but I'm too gutless to face her. So I stay where I am and spend the night on the sofa...not the way I wanted to end our romantic getaway.

The trip back to Brisbane was awkward to say the least. Sarah never said one word to me, she's still really angry with me and to be honest, I don't blame her. What I said to her was harsh, but I want her to be safe...and with me.

The car pulls up to her apartment and she goes climbs out without saying anything. I know I fucked up but this silent treatment is killing me. Reaching out, I grab her wrist. "Sarah, please, I'm sorry."

She whispers, "Sorry won't cut it, you really hurt me, Logan. I...I thought you cared about me, but obviously I was wrong." With that statement she pulls her wrist free and climbs out, slamming the door in my face. Normally she would wait on the sidewalk until I was around the corner, but tonight she marched inside without looking back.

That night when I'm lying in bed and missing Sarah, I decide that if she won't do anything about it, I will. I need to take things into my own hands if I'm going to get her back.

31

VICTORIA

SARAH AND LOGAN RETURN EARLY FROM HIS EXTENDED APPOINTMENT AND her demeanor has changed. My senses, which have never let me down, are now on high alert; especially when he calls to request a face-to-face meeting.

The meeting with Mr. DeBiers went exactly as I thought; he wants me to let go of Sarah because he's in love with her. As I reminded him, he signed a contract to spend time with my girls, not to fall in love; this isn't *Tinder*. He tried to argue with me but I put him in his place, no one tells me what to do and as of 10:51 a.m. today, Mr. DeBiers is no longer a client at Elite.

My next meeting is with Sarah. To throw her off the scent, I treat her to an afternoon at the spa, followed by a champagne high tea. Looking over at Sarah, I see that she is relaxed and that's when I strike. "So, when did you fall in love with Mr. DeBiers?" My question takes her by surprise as she spits her champagne out in shock.

Wiping her chin, she looks at me shocked and replies, "I'm not in love with him."

"Don't lie to me, Sarah. You know I don't tolerate liars."

"Victoria, I'm not lying. I care for him but I'm not in love with him."

"He tells a different story." That stops her in her tracks, *lying little bitch*, I think to myself as I sip on my bubbly and stare at her.

"I…I…don't know how I feel about him, Victoria."

"Well, you don't have to worry. He is no longer a client at Elite. No one tells me what to do, he came in this morning demanding that you be released."

"He did what?" Her reply shocks me, I thought that they has conspired together, maybe there is hope for me to keep her yet.

"He requested that I let you go as you are both in love. I told him my contract with you is none of his business." Testing her I add, "He offered me a lot of money to buy you out."

She looks over at me but doesn't say anything, her jaw drops open in shock, eventually she asks. "What did you say?"

"I told him that I'm not in the game of selling women, well not in that way. He wasn't happy, especially when I told him he was no longer welcome here at Elite."

"Okay, but you do know that this isn't my dream. One day I will leave, and I think it will be sooner, rather than later. Now that my friends know, I need to move on." She looks down to her lap and then looks back at me. "Victoria, I think I want to leave."

Her statement shocks me. "Well, that will not be happening anytime soon, Sarah. You are my moneymaker and I refuse to let you leave."

"You can't do that, you don't own me."

"Sarah, darling, I have owned you since the night I met you at Dirty Duck. You are mine for the foreseeable future."

"I beg your pardon?"

"Enough!" I shout, "You do not speak to me like that. Sarah, I saved your pathetic ass and that ass is mine." Pausing for emphasis, I take a sip of my bubbly before adding, "Sarah, if you leave, I will ruin everything and everyone who is dear to you."

"You wouldn't." I see hesitation in her eyes.

"Just try me, Sarah. If you leave, I will drag Logan's name so far through the mud that he will never come back from it."

"But…"

"There are no buts here Sarah. You. Are. Mine. Now go get ready, you have an appointment tonight."

"Since when?"

"Since now and must I remind you not to talk back to me."

"Fine, I will stay but you have to guarantee me that Logan and everyone else will be safe."

"You have my word." I see her relax at this. "But you fuck with me in the slightest and just see what I'm capable of. You have forty minutes to be ready. Simon will pick you up and deliver you to Cyril Barnstead. You're in for quite a night."

Her head snaps towards me when she realises she is in for a rough night. She is conflicted about staying but I can see it in her eyes, she will do anything to keep Logan and his reputation safe. If she does this tonight, I know that she will do anything and everything that I say from now on.

I now know without a doubt that she loves him and now she is mine. She will not let me take Logan down, and that's fine, because this will work to my advantage. I always win, always. However, if she screws me over, she will pay…just like the others.

32

LOGAN

My meeting with Victoria went as I had planned and now I'm worried for Sarah's safety. I have a sick feeling that I have just made her life a living hell. I've tried to call her but she's either ignoring me or busy, I'm hoping she's just ignoring me. Victoria's warning on the way out scared me.

"Mr. DeBiers, I'll warn you now, no one messes with me and lives to tell the tale. Take this warning seriously; otherwise I can make life extremely difficult for Sarah. You wouldn't want that now, would you? You are no longer welcome here or a member of Elite; now get off my property and out of my sight. Ohh, and don't think about contacting, Sarah to say goodbye, I'll pass on your regards."

Now I'm even more determined to get Sarah out of there, sooner rather than later. My PI is still looking into Victoria and Elite but so far nothing, hopefully he can help me, otherwise, I'm at a loss what to do to save the woman I love.

My thoughts are interrupted when Sav waltzes into my office. "Dude, where have you been? We had a lunch date booked and when I got here the place was locked up tighter than Fort Knox." She sits down and looks at me but her expressions changes immediately when she sees my face. I hate that she can read me like a book. "Okay, what's wrong? Or more to the point, what did you do? Your worry line is prominent."

"I don't have a worry line."

"You do, now spill?"

"I think I fucked up with Sarah. I may have called her a hooker to her face, and then I met with her boss to let her go, and I think I made things worse."

"Shit, Logan, you're a fuckwit. You majorly have fucked up."

"Thanks for the pep talk, it really helped."

"What? It's the truth, but the question is, what are we going to do to fix it?"

"You don't happen to have a time machine so I can go back and not rip Sarah to shreds."

"That I can't help with but together we will come up with a plan and get your girl back. Did all of this happen due to the party fallout?"

"Yes, no, I don't know." Looking up at her, I sadly add, "Sav, I love her so fucking much. I think I screwed up the best thing to happen to me since you hit me with your bike all those years ago."

"Well, let's fix this then. Why don't you come over tonight? I'll make Mexican and we can come up with a game plan to win her back."

"Not sure I'll be good company."

"How's that different to every other time we catch up?"

"Hardy har har, bitch." I look over at her and hesitantly ask, "Do you really think I can win her back?"

"Loges, the chemistry between you two is off this charts electric, and that's from me only seeing you two together for like four seconds. Trust me, we'll get her back. Now come on, let's go."

"Ummm, unlike you, I have work to do. I'll be over just after six. I'll bring the wine."

"Dude, we are having Mexican, it's either beer or tequila."

In unison we both say, "Or both." Immediately laughing our asses off, just like we used to, and then it all comes crashing back to me. I haven't laughed like that since Sarah and I were in the Hunter. It only makes me miss her more.

"Dude, you were thinking about her again. Weren't you?"

"Yeah, I can't stop thinking about her."

"Wow, you've got it bad." She stands up. "Okay, I'm off to start on our feast, see you just after six."

"It's a date, Sav. Have I told you how glad I am to have you back in my life?"

"Only all the time, but I am pretty kick-ass, so it's understandable." With that she walks out of my office, leaving me sitting there smiling and appreciating my best friend, but at the same time, missing the person I love with all my heart.

The afternoon drags and come 5:00 p.m., I decide to call it quits and head home. I grab a quick shower, call a cab, and head over to Sav and Mike's cottage. We all have a great night; I end up getting absolutely shitfaced on red wine and tequila. No brainstorming to win Sarah back occurred, but it was nice to let loose and get to know Mike. He's a great guy and I can see why Sav is so happy. He is perfect for her...just like Sarah is perfect for me.

33

SARAH

My fight and breakup with Logan is still weighing heavily on my mind. Actually, it's all I have been able to think about for the last ten days, five hours and thirty-four minutes—yes, I know how long it has been. Trying to forget Logan DeBiers is hard but he really hurt me with what he said, even though most if it was true. Maybe I should look at finding a way to leave; I always said I wasn't going to do it forever. Perhaps now is the time to move on. But first, I need to find a way to do so without she-devil fucking over everyone that I care about *Ohh, I don't know*, I think to myself as I climb into the shower.

Drying off after my shower, I head into my closet to get read for another appointment with Xander and Morgan; I'm not excited at all. Victoria is punishing me at the moment. She is giving me back-to-back appointments every day. I haven't had a day off since I returned from my disastrous trip with Logan; thankfully she was joking and it was cuddly, old man Cyril and not Saskawhore's freaky Cryil.

On Tuesday, she sent me on one of the more kinky appointments that Saskawhore would have loved. She knows I don't do those ones but I'm being punished, I just know it. The bitch had an evil glint in her eye when she told me about it…I'm definitely being reprimanded; at least I will have Morgan with me today. Her and I click really well and we always have fun together, even if we have to endure Xander.

Looking at my reflection in the mirror, I close my eyes and sigh deeply. *I can't do this anymore*, I think to myself as I finish putting on my mascara. Walking back into my wardrobe, I see the dress that I wore the first night I met Logan and sadly smile. I say to the room, "I miss you, Logan." Picking up the dress, I hold it tightly to my chest and I start to cry. As I slip the dress over my head, I realise that for the first time since starting at Elite, I feel like a whore; damn you Everclear for making me sing that to myself. Logan's words keep flying around my head and he's right, I am better than this.

Pursing my lips together in frustration, I remember that I forgot to put lipstick on; I head back to the bathroom and put my lippy on. As I'm blotting, I decide that tonight will be my last night at Elite. I just hope everyone doesn't hate me if Victoria goes after them. I'm ending this and Sarah 3.0 will begin. I don't care that I will be jobless or homeless because Kenz is right. I've saved enough money to get my own place, and I have a little nest egg set aside that I can use until I find my feet again. I'm Sarah Bryant and it's time to take MY life back.

I'm sitting on the end of my bed, putting my shoes on, when Morgan walks in. Her hair is piled in a messy bun on the top of her head and she's wearying a charcoal jumpsuit. Smiling at her I whistle and she does a little spin before plonking down next to me. "Ready for a fun night?" she says, but not with the usual enthusiasm she has. Ever since Angel was murdered Morgan has been quiet and reserved.

"Ready as I'll ever be," I reply, standing up I walk over to my dresser and grab my clutch. Turning back to Morgan, I stretch out my hand and she links her arm with mine, and we make our way down stairs to the waiting limo.

Morgan climbs in first and as I stare into the afternoon sky, I really wish the car was taking me to Logan, instead of to Xander. Hopefully after tonight, the next time I am in one, it will be taking me to him.

Sitting next to Morgan, the limo pulls away. She grabs the bottle of bubbly and pours two glasses as I pull out my phone and text Victoria.

Sarah – *I need to speak with you*
Sarah – *Urgently*

Her reply is immediate.

Victoria – *Tomorrow, 10am*

I shake my head at the abruptness of her reply, but really. it doesn't surprise me at all. Victoria has been off lately, nothing anyone does seems to be good enough, and the appointments seems to be getting desperate and degrading, like she's taking anybody to just bring in money. We are bordering on being whores and not the escorts that we used to be. We hardly ever attend galas and mingle with high society or celebrities at gallery openings, it's always a restaurant followed by a room in a seedy hotel. Thankfully I've become a pro, pun intended, at getting the seedy guys drunk and they pass out before anything happens. This change only cements by decision to leave.

The limo pulls up to the hotel and the concierge opens the car door for us. I nod my thanks and wait for Morgan. Linking arms again, we head inside and make our way up to Xander's suite. He opens the door after I knock and from his demeanor, and the strong smell of bourbon, I know that tonight is not going to be smooth sailing.

Morgan walks in first, kissing Xander on the cheek on her way past. Taking a deep breath, I walk into the suite and sweetly say as I quickly shuffle past him, foregoing the customary kiss, "Hey, Handsome, are you ready to go for dinner?"

He grips my wrist, pulls me towards him and plants a wet, rough kiss on my lips, before slapping me on the ass, hard, and pushing me into the suite. My pulse quickens as I make my way to the couch and take a seat next to Morgan. She's leaning forward popping open the bubbly that was in the wine bucket; *guess we aren't going out this afternoon.*

Taking a glass from Morgan, I walk over to windows and gaze at the river and traffic below. The view out the window and drink helps to calm my nerves, a little, until Xander invades my space and stands next to me. An eerie feeling envelopes the room, and all the nerves that had just disappeared return with a vengeance. He glances over at me and the look in his eyes, at this moment, tell me that this afternoon will not be pleasurable.

A wave of unease washes over my body and fear begins to build within me. Not knowing what to do, I awkwardly smile at him and wait. The silence is deafening. After a few moments, he looks between Morgan and me before snarling. "It's show time, bitches!"

He roughly squeezes my arm, pulling me closer to him, sliding his hand up my leg as he roughly bites my neck. Grabbing his wrist and squeezing with all my might, I look at him confused, "Time for what?"

I say as I push away from him. Looking towards Morgan for help, I see that she has zoned out and is just sitting there sipping her bubbly, oblivious to the scene unfolding right next to her.

He ignores my question and demands, "Bed. Now, Sarah." He begins to untuck his shirt and undo his belt; he looks at me with menacing eyes and shouts. "Now!"

"No, Xander. Not like this, please?" I plead with him, his eyes are glassy due to the bourbon, but beneath the haze, I see rage simmering deep within. From the corner of my eye, I see Xander raise his hand, but before I can get out of the way he slaps me hard across the cheek. "What do you mean, no?" he sneers, his eyes darken as his shoulders tense with anger before he hits me hard across the other cheek.

Clutching my cheek, I squeak, "I said no, Xander. I'm not sleeping with you tonight...or anymore for that matter and neither is Morgan. I'm done."

"No one tells me no, especially not a hooker. Now, get your clothes off, get on the bed and spread your legs. You are done when I say you are done."

A surge of adrenaline pumps through my veins and I face him, between clenched teeth I snarl "I. Said. No." Pausing between each word, taking a deep breath I add, "We're leaving."

Turning on my heel, I make my way to the door of the hotel room, just as I'm reaching out for the door handle, my shoulder is grabbed and I'm spun around. **SLAP** "I say when you leave and you're not going anywhere, bitch." **SLAP** "Victoria said this would happen, but I told her that you weren't silly enough to fall for twat boy but looks like for the first time ever, I was wrong. I'll let you go, but not before I get what I want." **SLAP** "Now, as I said before, clothes off and on the bed."

Standing there, I'm staring at him speechless, frozen, and not able to move. Gone is the sweet and seductive Xander, standing before me is a wild beast. I'm beyond scared but I can't do this anymore. It's in this moment that I realise I want a life with Logan, and that I love him deeply; I have to get out of here, and now.

Taking another deep breath, I say. "No, I...I can't, Xander. I won't. I just can't. I'm so sorry."

"Wrong answer, Sarah." He lunges for me and punches me in the face, grabbing me roughly; he pushes me towards Morgan. I trip on the end of the couch and my head catches the coffee table corner on my way down. Lying on my side, my vision blurs and before I pass out, I see him dragging a struggling Morgan into the bedroom.

When I come to I can hear him with Morgan in the other room. He's grunting, flesh is hitting flesh and Morgan is crying. Using the coffee table, I lift myself up and I race into the bedroom, trying to pull him off her. Grabbing his shoulder, I pull with all my might.

He stands next to the bed, his face red from exertion and he stares menacingly at me. "So, you decided to join the party, did you?" He reaches out and grabs at my dress. Quickly I step back, but I'm not fast enough. He grips the neckline and pulls, tearing my dress off, leaving me standing there in my bra and undies. A surge of adrenaline races through me body and I step forward, shoving him in the chest.

"You bitch," he spits. Pulling his arm back, he punches me in the face again before propelling me viciously into the wall. My head hits with a thud and I fall to the carpet, passing out.

I'm awakened to Morgan shaking me. Opening my eyes I see that she is naked, covered in bruises and bite marks. There is blood between her thighs and her eyes are swelling shut. "Ohh, Morgan," I manage to say before wrapping my arms around her. She winces in pain but curls into me, quietly crying.

We sit together, huddled on the floor, not saying a word to each other. When I look up next, it's dark outside and Morgan is asleep in my lap, by now her body is purple and her eye sockets are as black as the ace of spades. Gently I lift her head, and I make my way into the other room, thanking the universe that Xander is no longer here.

Picking my purse up from the floor by the door, I grab my phone and I call the one person I know who will help me without judgment. Dialing I put the phone to my ear and wait for the call to connect, they pick up on the second ring.

"Hey, bitch, I was just thinking of you."

"Help me, Kenz." I start to cry.

"Sarah, what's wrong? Where are you?"

"Morgan and I need you, Kenz, please?"

Frantically she replies, "I'm on my way. Where are you?"

Through my tears, I manage to tell her where we are. She tells me she's on her way.

Grabbing a robe, I slip it on and go back to Morgan after calling the front desk and arranging a key for Kenz. Morgan is still curled into herself, but she's awake now, as soon as she sees me she swallows deeply and then bursts into tears. Racing over to her, I gently ease her up and wrap my arms around her, whispering, "Shhhh."

"Sarah, he was a monster. I've never seen him like that before."

"I'm sorry, sooooo sorry, Morgan." Swallowing the lump building in my throat because I need to be strong for her I ask, "What happened?"

Leaning against the wall, she closes her eyes and says, "After you hit your head, he turned towards me but I couldn't move. I was frozen with fear. I...I just left you there and I sat on the couch staring at you laying there, not moving. Before I had time to process what was happening, Xander grabbed me by the wrist, squeezing tight, really tight." Morgan begins to rub her wrist absentmindedly. "He then dragged me towards the bedroom, he turned around an threw me over this shoulder and stalked into the bedroom. I started kicking and screaming, tears pouring down my cheeks, I kept pleading with him. *'Please, Xander, don't do this; this isn't you. Please, Xander, please.'* But he ignored me; he was in his own world. His eyes glazed over and I knew in that moment that there would be no reasoning with him. When we reached the bedroom, he threw me violently face down onto the bed before straddling my hips. Roughly grinding himself on my ass, I could barley breathe or move. I began crying, he shoved me harder into the mattress, the tears wouldn't stop, Sarah. I've never been so scared in my life. With a force I have never seen before on any man, he tore my jumpsuit off me and flipped me over. I closed my eyes 'cause I couldn't look at him. I remember him growling for me to open my eyes but I wouldn't. He hit or punched me in the face so hard I felt like I was going to pass out. I opened my eyes and realised that I was only in my bra and undies, but not for long. He reached out and ripped them off my body. Leaning down, he...he bit my breasts and twisted my nipples, again I screamed out in pain. No one came, no one. I wriggled and wriggled to get free, my hands hitting at his head and body, but he just didn't stop. He kept biting and sucking my tits. Eventually he lifted his head up and he looked directly at me. I've never seen a face full of anger like that before. He slapped my face repeatedly, Sarah, I just lay there and took it. I did nothing to stop him. My head thrashed to the side, I started to see stars and everything around me faded in and out. I've never been hit that hard before in my life. Eventually, I passed out."

"Ohh, Morgan, I'm so sorry."

"That's not the end of it, Sarah."

"Fucking hell, he's a monster."

"I came to and I felt him sitting between my thighs. I heard the jiggle of his belt and the lowering of his zipper, I began to panic again when I saw his dick pop free. It was rock hard and the tip throbbing and deep purple in colour, without warning he thrust deep inside of me. The burn was unbearable. I screamed out in agony but before I could scream again; he punched me before wrapping his fingers around my throat. I couldn't breathe. Between the not breathing and the stabbing burning feeling between my legs, I passed out from the pain. When I woke up again, you were here. Sarah, he raped me." Morgan begins to cry again.

"Shhhh," I whisper. "It will be alright, I've got you now."

The door to the suite opens and Morgan freaks out; she races into the bathroom and slams the door. I'm still sitting on the carpet when I hear Kenz. "Sar, I'm here, babes, where are you?"

Hearing her voice opens the floodgates again and I begin sob. "I'm in here," I manage to say, but I'm not sure if she heard me as it came out as a jumbled mess. Looking up, I see her walking in and the look on her face confirms that I look as bad as I feel. "Ohh, Sarah, what happened?"

Hearing her makes me sob even harder, I lean my head on my knees and continue to cry. Kenz walks over to me and carefully wraps her arms around me. I shuffle and wrap my arms around her waist, pulling her closer to me, gripping her tight. I sit there, holding tightly onto my best friend and I cry; I cry like I have never cried before, I let it all out.

Movement by the door startles me and I look up into the worried eyes of Logan. "What are you doing here?"

He shuffles on his feet before leaning on the doorframe, "Kenz called me and said you were in trouble so I told her I'd meet her here."

"Well you can leave, after all, I'm nothing but a whore who deserves all that I get. Well, I guess you got your wish. Besides, I'm fine."

Leaning back against the wall, I close my eyes and whisper, "Kenz, please make him leave."

With my eyes, still closed, I feel her stand up and they move into the main room. Their voices are quiet and I can't hear what is being said, but a few moments later I hear the click of the door closing and feet shuffling back. Looking up, I see it's Logan still here and Kenz left. *Bitch*, I think to myself.

Taking a deep breath, I swallow and confidently say, "I don't want you here, Logan, I'm fine, I'm just a hook..." but I can't finish the words as I start to cry again. Logan is in front of me crouching down, he hesitantly reaches out and brushes a strand of matted hair behind my ear, and he looks deep into my eyes. "Sarah, I'm so sorry for what I said. You are none of those things, you are a fighter and I took my frustrations out on you. If I wasn't such as ass..."

I don't let him finish; I wrap my arms around him and hug him tight. His embrace calms me and is just what I need right now. No other words are needed in this moment, for now there is nothing more to be said...we can broach that elephant at another time.

34

LOGAN

WHEN I GOT THE CALL FROM KENZ TO SAY THAT SARAH WAS IN TROUBLE, I didn't hesitate to help. Even though I said some horrible things to her last week, I still care deeply for her. She didn't deserve any of them, I could have handled it a hell of a lot better, but as usual, I approach things with the usual Logan DeBiers stubbornness. I just hope that I haven't lost the best person to ever come into my life.

Getting the address from Kenz, I haul ass to the hotel and I end up pacing in the foyer waiting her; the wait is nerve-racking. Hearing my name, my head snaps up and Kenz is running towards me.

"Hey, what's going on?" I ask, as she races past me towards the check-in desk.

"No idea, but after I get this key we will know." She steps to the counter and is bouncing on her feet, she looks just as agitated and worried as I am. Finally the clerk looks up.

"Can I help you?"

Kenz quickly says, "Umm, my friend is here. She said there would be a key for me. She's in room 2207."

"You must me Mackenzie, can I please see some ID before I give you the key?"

"Yep, sure." She digs in her monstrosity of a handbag and finally passes over her license.

"Thanks for that, here you go. The lifts are to your left."

She snatches the key from the clerk and we race towards the eleva-tors. Repeatedly I punch the button, willing it to come quicker. Finally the doors open and we both race in. We reach the floor and make our way to the door, as we are standing there I start to panic that she won't want me here. I replay in my mind the horrible things that I said to her when I hear the click of the door opening.

I let Kenzie go in first, following her in, she yells out and we hear a muffled sound coming from the bedroom. Hanging back, I look around, it's a pretty nice suite, I hear Kenzie's shocked reaction from the main room and I make my way there. The bed sheets are all messed up and it looks like there is blood on them, turning towards them at the end of the bed, my heartbreaks at what I see.

Sarah is a crumbled mess, clinging to Kenzie for dear life. She is sobbing and there is nothing I can do. She looks up at me and her reac-tion is shock, which is quickly replaced with anger when she demands to know why I'm here. I explain and she glares at Kenzie; I feel for Kenzie in this moment. Sarah is not happy that I'm here, and asks Kenzie to make me leave.

Kenzie and I move into the main room, before she has a chance to speak I say, "I'm not leaving, Kenz. I need to be here for her. I need to show her that I care and that I'm not the asshole I was the other day."

"Look, I don't know what happened and had I known I would not have brought you here…" I go to interrupt her but she gives me a look that says 'shut the fuck up and let me finish' so I let her continue. "But I know Sarah, deep down she wants, no, needs you here. I'm going to go but I swear, Logan, if you fuck this up you will have me to deal with. Now, go back in there and look after my best friend."

"I promise, I won't let anything happen to her, but first, we need to get her out of this room. Can you go downstairs and book another room for us, we can't stay in this one."

"Sure, no worries." She puts her hand out, and shakes her fingers, indicating she needs money. Grabbing my wallet, I give her my credit card, and before I can say anything, she is out the door.

Turning around, I head back into the bedroom. Sarah's head pops up when she hears me approaching and her face is void of any emotion. She starts talking and telling me that she doesn't want me here but I ignore her. I crouch down to her level and carefully I push a stand of hair behind her ear, cup her cheek in my hand, and I grovel. I'm only halfway through my apology when she wraps her arms around me and starts to cry again. "Thanks for coming," she sniffles into my shoulder.

The bathroom door clicks open and Sarah freezes in my arms and grips me tighter, when she sees Morgan standing there she releases her hold on me and races over to her. "Morgan, Logan and Kenz are here to help."

"I...I just want to get out of here, Sarah. I want to go home."

Before I get a chance to reply, Kenz comes into the bedroom, I didn't even hear the main door open. "Okay, I managed to get another room. I also asked them to call the police, they will direct them to the new room."

Sarah and Morgan's heads snaps up, Morgan shrieks, "Police? Why would you do that?"

Sarah turns to her and gently say, "Morgan, you've been raped and beaten, and I was attacked, we have to report this."

"No, I can't. I'm a hooker, I deserve what happens to me."

In unison, we all yell, "No!"

"Morgan, look at me, I know you don't know me, but you have to report this, regardless if you are a hooker or not." Morgan looks up to Kenz, not believing what she's saying when Sarah butts in.

"Morgan, who gives a shit what we are? You and I have been beaten black and blue that in itself deserves punishment."

Kenz interrupts me, "I know what you are going through and as much as this will be tough, you need to do this. Sarah and I will be here with you. Whoever did this, cannot not get away with this."

"I can't," she pleads, before burying her face in her hands and crying.

"Look, let's get into the new room and we can talk about this later," I say.

Standing up, I reach out for Sarah but she flinches away from me, hugging Morgan to her side and walking ahead of me. Her flinching like that was a kick in the guts, especially after the hug we just had, but I guess I can understand. Kenzie helps them towards the door but Morgan is exhausted and collapses onto Kenz. Taking a step forward, I lift her into my arms, Sarah smiles at me and it warms my heart to see her smiling again, I find myself grinning back at her. Morgan wraps her arms around my neck, but my smile falters when I feel her body shake from the sobs rippling through her body.

We head towards to lifts together, and the four of us make our way up to the new room. Settling Morgan in the bed, I head back to the lounge room, where Kenz is ordering coffee and Sarah is sitting on the lounge staring into space. "You know her well," I say to Kenz as I meet her in the kitchen.

"Yep, Sarah always says coffee or wine can fix anything. I don't think she needs wine at the moment, but I know her, that will come later. For now we drink coffee." Pausing, she looks up at me. "Thank you, Logan."

"Don't mention it. Look, I know I was a complete asshole and said some horrible things to her, but I still care deeply about her. Hopefully now, she will leave Elite and let me take care of her."

"Before she does that, we need to get her and Morgan to speak to the police. I know it's going to be tough, but I know they can both do it. They are both strong."

"I agree with you there. I'll call reception and tell them to send them up here and to not touch the other room." Pausing, I look to Kenz. "You realise she will hate us for this."

"Yeah, I do, but I don't care. Whoever did this needs to be punished, Sarah is lucky she wasn't raped, too."

From the other room, we hear the shower turn on. "Bitch," Kenzie and Sarah say in unison. Looking at one another they smile and race into the ensuite. "Are you stupid, Morgan? You're washing the evidence away. The police will need swabs and all that." I can hear Kenz yelling at Morgan.

"Kenz, don't speak to her like that. She's in shock," Sarah vehemently spits back.

"Sorry, but she's washing all the evidence away."

"I told you, I'm not talking to them," Morgan stubbornly replies.

"Well, that's too bad, they are on their way." There's a knock at the door. "Looks like they are here. Sarah, you stay here and help her. I'll go out there and you both come join us when you're ready."

Kenzie enters the room and I introduce her to the officers. We tell them that Sarah and Morgan, who are in the other room, have been beaten and we think that Morgan has also been raped. We also tell them that Morgan doesn't want to speak to them, and Sarah is also hesitant.

After ten minutes, they are both still in the other room, I excuse myself and head in there. Standing outside the bedroom door, I can hear crying and Sarah whispering to Morgan. My heart is breaking for them both right now and I don't even know this girl. I raise my hand and gently knock on the door, I hesitantly ask, "Sarah, Morgan, can I come in?"

"Yeah," they both quietly say.

Opening the door, I find them in the hotel's robes sitting on the floor, facing each other; Morgan is hugging her knees. Her hair is still damp after her shower and even though her face is swollen and purple, I can tell that she is broken. Looking towards Sarah, I smile and she smiles back at me. Even though her eye is swollen shut and her face is fifty shades of purple, she's still the most beautiful woman I have ever seen. "Sarah, is everything okay here?"

She shakes her head. "No, yes, I don't know. Logan, this mess is all my fault."

"No, sweetheart, it's not. It's my fault; I shouldn't have said the things that I did. I should have protected you."

"Can I have a hug?" she quietly asks.

"Of course you can. Can you stand or do you want me to come over there?"

"I can stand. I think." She carefully gets up, wincing in pain as she does. She takes three careful steps towards me and wraps her arms around me waist, resting her head on my chest. Gently, I wrap mine around her and rub the base of her neck with one hand and hold her close to me with the other; her shoulders begin to shake as she starts to cry again. "Shhhh," I whisper, "I've got you now."

She composes herself and looks up at me. "Logan, I really don't want to speak to the police. Please just let this go. Morgan and I were chatting and we just want to forget that any of this has happened."

"I'm sorry, Sarah. I can't. You both need to report this." Spinning her around, I hold her upper arms and rub them while I whisper, "Look at yourself, Sarah." She keeps staring at the floor so I gently place a finger under her chin and lift her head slightly; our eyes lock in the mirror. She refuses to look at herself. "Sarah, look at yourself. This needs to be dealt with, if I ever find him, he is going to look a lot worse than this."

"Logan, I can't. Please just drop it."

"Well, you tell them then." Turning my back on them I storm out of the room, kicking the bed on my way past in frustration. When I enter the lounge again, the two officers and Kenz turn to me and stop talking. "She's so stubborn. She's now refusing to talk to you or even press charges, she feels like it's all her fault."

The female officer, whose name I forget, says, "That's not uncommon in situations like this. We are happy to hang around for a bit, in case she changes her mind but while we wait, we'd like to talk to you both and get a bit more information if we can."

From the doorway we hear Sarah, "That's not necessary, I'll tell you what I can, but Morgan doesn't want to."

35

SARAH

STARING AT MYSELF ON THE MIRROR AFTER LOGAN STORMED OUT, I DON'T recognise the girl reflected back at me. Aside for the swelling and bruising, I'm a shell of my former self and I realise he's right; I need to do something but I'm scared.

Looking to Morgan, who is still sitting on the floor, staring into space, I decide that I will do this for us both. Walking over to her, I crouch down and gently place my hand on her knees. "Morgan, honey, I need to talk to them. I'm not going to force you to, but I really think you should."

Morgan just stares at me, shaking her head from side to side. "No, I can't. I'm sorry, Sarah." She starts to cry again.

"Hey, it's fine. No apologies necessary. You wait here and I'll hurry this along, okay?" She just nods at me before turning her head and staring out at the night sky.

Taking a deep breath, I head out to the main room. The four of them are deep in conversation about giving me time and don't hear me enter. From the doorway I say, "That's not necessary, I'll tell you what I can."

Walking slowly over to the couch, I take a seat, wincing in pain as I sit down. Four sets of eyes watch my every move. Closing my eyes, I take a deep breath. "I can't tell you much. All I know is we were here to meet him, we were going to dinner and then I'm not sure; probably back here for...umm, you know. But when we got here, he decided otherwise." Pausing, I swallow hard. "That's all I can tell you."

Logan stands up and shouts, "That's fucking bullshit, Sarah, that's not all there is!"

Kenzie grabs Logan's arm and pulls him into the kitchen, I can hear her ripping into him and it makes me smile. Officer Jones comes and sits on the coffee table. "Look, Sarah. I know this is scary, but you need to tell us a name at least."

"Xander, that's all I know. I honestly don't know his last name." Hanging my head in shame at not knowing that information.

"Thanks, Sarah. We will leave you be. We have your details and if your friend changes her mind, give us a call or if you remember anything else please call me. Here's my card." She passes me her card and I spin it in my fingers, staring into space after I say goodbye to them.

The front door clicks and I look around the room, Kenz and Logan are in the kitchen whispering to each other. All of a sudden, I smell coffee and smile.

While the three of us are in the lounge room chatting, Morgan sneaks out of the hotel room. How we didn't hear her leave still amazes me. I've tried calling her but her phone goes straight to voicemail. I'm really worried about her.

After Xander attacked Morgan and me, I left the apartment and moved in with Logan. Even though he said some horrible things to me, they were all true and my feelings for him are much too strong to ignore. Plus he came running when I was in trouble.

I held my ground and refused to go back the police, I just want this to be over and bringing them in will only prolong that. Kenz and Logan didn't agree with me, but eventually they stopped asking me to.

Logan has been working from the penthouse and Kenz has stopped by every day to visit. I'm thankful for their support and friendship but I just want some me time.

Ten days after the attack, I'm finally starting to feel like me again. I still have not been able to reach Morgan, and that worries me. After lunch today, Logan has to head into the office, and finally, for the first time since the incident; I'm alone. It's so peaceful being here by myself, so I curl up on the patio with a coffee and read the next book in the *Storm* series. This book is forking awesome and the craziness that has become Lexi's life is a great escape.

My peace is disturbed when my phone rings, picking it up I see that it's Victoria. Against my better judgment, I answer the phone. Walking over to the edge, I look out at the river, hoping the water will have a calming effect on me as I take this call. "Hello, Victoria."

"So you are alive."

"No thanks to Xander."

"I'm sure you're exaggerating, besides that's all in the past, dear, now when are you returning?"

"I'm not. Victoria, I'm done."

"You will be done when I say you are done. Sarah, your have twenty-four hours to get back to the apartment."

A surge of confidence flies through my body and I quickly reply, "No, Victoria. I'm not coming back and you can't make me."

"Is that really what you think?"

"I don't think, I know."

She laughs in her fake hoity-toity laugh, "You will return to the apartment. End. Of. Story." Pausing for a few moments, she adds, "You wouldn't want anything to happen to Mackenzie, Rory, Indy, or Morgan now, would you? And you definitely don't want it to get out that up and coming businessman, Logan DeBiers, uses an escort agency. Would you now, dear?"

"You wouldn't."

"Just try me, Sarah. You have twenty-three hours and fifty-seven minutes to get back to the apartment. After that time, I guarantee you that I will follow through on my previous threats. Mr. DeBiers will be splashed all over the front page of every newspaper in Australia and around the world."

Before I can reply, she hangs up on me. Dropping my phone, I slide down the wall and sit on the patio floor, my heart hammering in my chest. Hugging my knees so I'm squishing my boobs, I start to cry. The tears cascade down my cheeks, leaving mascara track marks in their wake. I thought it was too easy to get away.

My heart is breaking once again but this time I'm choosing, well, being forced, to walk away because I refuse to bring Logan down, and I will not compromise the safety of Kenz, Mac and Cheese, or Morgan. Unless I heed to Victoria's demands, she will destroy those that I care about the most and I cannot let that happen. I refuse to let them suffer due to my stupid decision.

Things were starting look up again after the attack. Moving in with Logan was perfect, all my worries were lifted and I was smiling again; really genuinely smiling. But in typical Sarah style, it's all fucked up again. Now, all because of me; his life and business are being threatened by the devil herself; unless I do this. I have to do this. To save Logan, I have to walk away, but I don't know if I'm strong enough to stay away this time.

Taking a deep breath, I stand up, head into the bedroom, and pack what few things that I have with me. Once packed, I head into the kitchen, placing my bag on the black leather breakfast barstool. Through my tears, I write a goodbye note to Logan, struggling to breathe as my heart breaks into a million tiny shards.

Logan,
I'm sorry. I can't do this with you right now. I need to find myself and I refuse to bring you down with me while I do that.
You will always be in my heart and thoughts.
Love always and forever,
Sarah

With tears pouring down my cheeks, I place the note on the island bench, next to my access card, before grabbing my bag off the stool. Turning around with my shoulders held high, I walk out the door towards the lifts and push the call button. I know this is the right thing to do, even if I'm dying on the inside. With a ding, the lift doors open and for the last time I leave the one place that I was truly happy.

The last week has been agony. I'm missing Logan with all my heart and Victoria is running me ragged. She keeps sending me out to social gatherings and galas with Xander. He's such a smarmy bastard, I can't stand to be around him, but thankfully he hasn't tried to sleep with me again. What I wouldn't give to attend a boring art gallery with Chow. The other clients are all just handsy and slimey, thankfully no hanky-panky; not even from Xander and that's frightening.

Bitchtoria is trying to break me but I refuse to let her win. I'm going to find a way out of this, and in the meantime, I'll cozy up to the devil herself until I can make my move and trust me; I will take her down.

The hardest part of all of this is missing Logan, I've been ignoring all of his calls and I've pretended not to be home when he has stopped by, but it's getting harder and harder to ignore him. There is a magnetic pull between Logan and me and it's strong, but I have to do this...for him...for us...for everyone, even if I'm miserable in the process. One of these days, I will give in and answer his call and when I do, I know I'll crumble, but I have to be strong...for now at least.

Logan was my saving grace. He came along when I was at my lowest. He made me feel happy and safe; I started smiling again, the old me was resurfacing. Soon, I'll be able to be with him again, but first I need to finish this. I need to find a way to end this and get my life back.

36

VICTORIA

THAT FEELING OF BEING WATCHED IS BACK, IT HAS BEEN, ON AND OFF, FOR the last few weeks now. I'm sure I'm being paranoid but with all that is going on anything is possible. Since Xander lost his shit with Sarah and Morgan, I keep waiting for a visit from the police but so far nothing; and that's just as frightening, if not more so.

No one has seen Morgan since the incident, but ever since Angel was found, she hasn't been herself. To be honest, for once a girl leaving has been for the best.

Business is booming again, and the cliental has returned to those worthy of being an Elite client. Sarah is booked solid for the next few days, which gives me pleasure. Since her return, she has been sad and dejected, she's become a 'yes' bot and this has pleased me immensely. I keep giving her the more hands-on appointments, waiting for her to crack; I will break her yet...just you wait. I've even sent her to galas with Xander and he has ramped up his obsession with her, similar to when she first started. She has to realise that no one tells me they are leaving. I make the rules and everyone will abide by them; regardless of whom they are.

Sarah broke not one, but two cardinal rules, don't fall in love and don't fuck with me. When that trust is broken, it's hard to win back said trust. Even though she is exceeding my expectations at the moment, I don't trust her one iota, and trust is key in any successful business.

I've just hung up from Mr. DeBiers again; he's still trying to get me to let go of Sarah. He is relentless, I will give him that but she's my moneymaker, and I will not be letting go of her anytime soon. I didn't want to go there, well, yeah, I did, this time I threatened her safety. Not that I would ever do anything to harm her, well not personally, but he doesn't need to know that. I can guarantee that nothing per se will happen to her, but accidents do happen.

I'm still confused to everyone's fascination with her, but after twenty years in this business, nothing surprises me. When she first started, she reminded me of when I became an escort, working for Esteban. I was hoping to mold her into me, possibly even passing the reins over to her one day, but now that will not happen.

Esteban, I haven't thought of him in a very long time and I can't help but smile. He was the father that I never had and he molded me into the sophisticated lady that I am today. It was a shame he passed in the manner that he did, but Alexander and I didn't need him anymore.

Simon calls to tell me he is running late, so I'm decide to wait in the bar, and I'm glad that I did. I feel his presence before I see him, looking around the bar I see him and smile. He starts making his way over to me and I start to grin, watching all the women swoon over him when he's mine, all mine. "Good evening."

"Good evening, Sir. Care to join me?"

"Why thank you." Before he sits down he kisses me deeply and I become a puddle of mud. He is the only person who makes me weak at the knees. Breaking our kiss, he winks before taking the seat next to me. Stephen comes over with a tumbler of scotch and a glass of champagne for me.

Looking over at him, I smile. "So I guess you and I have a date."

"Yes, Vicky, you and I have a date, but I'd much rather be in your office ravishing you."

"After what you recently pulled, what makes you think I want that?"

"You know you want me," he arrogantly replies but he knows me too well. "Just like every other woman in this room, you want me between your thighs."

"Don't be so crass."

"You love it when I speak dirty to you, Vicky. You want my cock buried balls deep inside that sweet cunt of yours as I pound into you, biting your tits as I choke you, summoning all sorts of pleasure."

His words cause me to clench my thighs together, my pussy throbbing with want and need. I swallow hard; he smirks smugly at me before he throws back his drink. Standing up, he puts his hand out to me. Accepting his outstretched hand, I stand up. He tugs me closer to him and smashes his lips against mine in a searing kiss. Pulling back, he looks into my eyes and he knows he has me hooked. "The office, five minutes. You know what I like."

He shoves me towards the exit and I nearly trip on my heels, but I regain my composure and head towards the door. On my way out, I notice a man standing by the bar talking to Simon. He looks familiar but all I can currently think about is what's about to happen and the throb in my pussy.

When I get to my office, I quickly unlock the door and head over to the seating area. I'm feeling particularly naughty this evening so I defy him; I remove my undies and my undies only. I go and sit on the coffee table. Inching my skirt up, I run my finger up and down my slit, making myself wet, the need for him to ravish me increasing. Perching myself on the edge, I spread my legs wide and continue to pleasure myself, so when he enters he can see my bare, wet pussy. Leaning back on my arm, I wait.

A few moments later, the door slams open and Morgan is thrust into the room, she falls to her knees and scurries towards my desk. She is crying when he storms into the office, furiously slamming the door behind him. Quickly, I remove my finger, close my legs and jump up, thankful that I defied him tonight. "What's going on?"

"Seems we have a problem, a massive fucking problem," he snarls, before stalking over and kicking Morgan in the face, knocking her out cold. He turns to me, fuming. "I thought you took care of our problem."

"I did, I assure you that I did. She has been cooperating and being the model employee, just like in the beginning."

"Well, obviously she's been deceiving you because someone has been snooping in our affairs, Victoria, and they know everything. They know every-fucking-thing, Vicky."

37

LOGAN

Once again, Sarah is ignoring my calls. It has been seven, painfully long days with out her. I'm going out of my mind here, I need her in my life and at this point, I would do just about anything to have her safely beside me.

My PI and I are currently playing phone tag and that is pissing me off too. Earlier today, I yelled at Beth for something that I fucked up, and now I feel like a douche for doing that. Everything is falling apart at the moment, it's like I stepped on a crack, killed a black cat, and smashed a billion mirrors.

Finally, my PI and I speak. "Justin, please tell me you have something. I'm going out of my mind here."

"Logan, it's good to chat to you as well. I'm fine; thanks for asking."

"Yeah, yeah. Just tell me what you have…please?"

"WOW, you really love this girl don't you?"

"With all my heart, I need something so I can get her out of there."

"Well, today will be your lucky day. I hit the jackpot with what I've found, but before I tell you, please don't do anything stupid. These two are batshit crazy."

"What do you mean two? I thought…I don't know what I thought."

"Well, you thought wrong. She runs it with her husband, and from what I've discovered, they take anyone out who is threatening their empire or gets in their way. That girl you mentioned, Angel, she was killed by them. My guys have proof that their driver, a umm, Simon Jameson, killed and dumped her body. It looks like they have killed many more ex-employees, too. The number listed as missing is staggering. They also have a subsidiary that deals in drugs and the sex trade. Logan, you need to get your girl out of there and quick smart."

"Holy fucking shit." *What have you gotten yourself into, Sarah*? I think to myself. "I promise I'll be safe, Justin. I'm going to get my girl out of there, you can hand what you've found over to the police. I want these assholes taken down and I want them to stay down."

"Can do. Now go get your girl."

"Will do. Thanks again, Justin. I really appreciate all your help."

"Anytime, Logan, anytime."

Hanging up from Justin, I sit in my office chair and let out the breath that I didn't realise that I was holding. "Fuck, fuck, fuck," I say to myself before I grab my phone again. Dialing Sarah's number, I hope and pray that she will answer me this time. Thankfully she finally picks up on the second ring. "Hi," she shyly says. "I'm so sorr…"

Interrupting her, I forcefully ask, "Sarah, where are you?" I feel bad for being abrupt but my main concern right now is Sarah and her safety. After what Justin told me about Victoria and her husband; I'm scared shitless.

"I'm at the apartment, Logan. I'm about to head outside and finish that *Storm* series that you recommended. I'm addicted and that Anthony dude is one crazy fucker."

"Sarah, listen to me…you need to get out of there; we have real life crazy fuckers to deal with."

"Why? What are you talking about? You're kind of scaring me, Logan."

I'm trying to get Sarah to listen to me, but I'm so worked up that I'm not explaining myself very well. She doesn't understand the danger that she is currently in. While I'm still on the phone, unsuccessfully trying to explain myself, I race down to the underground car park, jump into my car, and race over to her place, but a feeling of dread washes over me.

38

SARAH

"Sarah, you need to leave, now!" Logan shouts through the phone.

"Why? What's going on, Logan? You're kind of scaring me right now."

"You need to get out of there, Sarah. I'll be there to pick you up in five minutes."

"Logan, you're scaring me. What's going on?"

"I'm not trying to scare you, Sarah, but please, get out of there and wait downstairs for me. It's not safe for you there. Please," I beg.

"Okay, fine, I'll be downstairs in ten minutes."

"Five minutes, Sarah."

Hanging up from Logan, I race upstairs and quickly pack a bag, our conversation playing over and over in my head, but I can't really make sense of anything. All I know is that he is scared for me and wants me to leave. I trust him so, for once; I'm following his instructions. Zipping up the bag, I swing it over my shoulder; grab my handbag off the dresser and head back down the stairs. Swinging open the apartment door, I'm met with an enraged Victoria. With all her might, she pushes me back into the apartment, and in behind her walks Xander, with a frightened Morgan in his grasp. Her cheeks are stained with tears and her left eye is swollen shut and a deep shade of purple.

"Morgan!" I shout and try to get to her, but Xander shoves me hard in the chest.

"Shut the fuck up, bitch," Xander snarls before throwing Morgan towards the lounge room. Turning his attention to me, he roughly grabs me by my upper arm and drags me behind him into the room, throwing me onto the couch. His eyes are dark with rage, and in this moment, he gives me the creeps. Fear is coursing through my veins and I'm petrified.

Morgan groans in pain. Immediately I drop to the floor and crawl over to her, she's in the fetal position rocking back and forth, mumbling to herself. She flinches when I lightly touch her arm, but when she sees it's me, through her one good eye, she lifts herself up wincing in pain, wrapping her arms tightly around my neck. She starts to cry harder and I whisper, "Shhhh," as I rub her back gently.

"Ohh, how nice, slut two caring for slut one. It's such a shame that it has to end like this because you two are phenomenal together... maybe I'll get one more in before it all has to end."

From the bar, Victoria scoffs as she pops the cork on a bottle of bubbly. *How can she be drinking at a time like this?* I think to myself as she pours two glasses, handing one to Xander before placing the bottle on the coffee table next to Morgan and me. She returns to the bar, grabs her flute and raises it. "A toast. To good times and the end of Sarah Bryant."

"What?" I say.

Xander replies, "Cheers to that." They both silently salute each other before each taking a sip.

I'm sitting there stunned; I have no idea what is going on. Morgan is in a catatonic state, so I can't use her to help me get out of this. "I...I don't understand. What's this all about? I broke up with Logan, what more do you want?"

Victoria cackles as she stalks over to me, taking a seat on the coffee table edge she stares intently at me. "Well, my dear, it seems your ex-boyfriend." Air quoting ex-boyfriend, she continues, "Has been digging into Elite and me. Somehow he has discovered everything that Alexander and I have been up to, and now, you will suffer for his digging. We need to teach him a lesson." Pausing she takes a sip as Morgan moans. "Morgan here, was simply in the wrong place at the wrong time, just like Saskia, but since the demise of Angel, she has not been performing to her full potential. So it's a win/win for Elite and me to get rid of you both. We've worked too hard for it to all come crashing down now."

"Oh My God, you killed them, didn't you?" Victoria just smirks at me before taking another drink. "You killed them all," I whisper. Tears well in my eyes and I quietly ask, "Why?"

"Because we are Victoria and Alexander Chalmers. No one fucks with us, especially a little slut like you."

Morgan sits up and we both sit there open-mouthed and stunned at that revelation. Everything starts falling into place; to say I'm shocked is an understatement. "Oh My God! That explains why Xander always got special treatment from us girls, and why nothing was done when I told you that he beat the shit out of me and raped Morgan."

From behind me, Xander starts clapping, Morgan scurries towards the bar as he stands up and looks directly at me. "Ding! Ding! Ding! We have a winner. Luckily you're a better fuck than you are smart. It will be a shame that you won't be around anymore, but I can always find another cunt to fill the void. I refuse to be taken down by a slut and sloppy work." He turns around and shoots Morgan in the head, right between the eyes. She falls to the carpet, her lifeless eyes stare at me as blood pours down her face, pooling on the carpet beneath her.

A scream slips from my lips but stops when I hear another gunshot ring through the apartment. Turning my head, I see Victoria falling to the floor, landing on top of Morgan with a thud. "Bye bye, wifey, you got too cocky and this is all your fault." Staring at the dead bodies in front of me, I start screaming again. Xander lunges towards me and slaps me hard across the cheek, the butt of the gun catching my cheek-bone. "Shut the fuck up, bitch." Dropping the gun next to the couch, he slaps me again and again before storming to the bar and pouring himself a scotch. Drinking it back before pouring another, he looks at me at says, "You and I have an empire to rebuild, Sarah. You and I will rule this city."

"You're a fucking crazy monster. I will never be by your side."

He doesn't say anything, he just stares and at me laughs; pouring drink after drink down his throat, muttering incoherently to himself.

Pulling my legs to my chest, I hug them tightly as I stare at Morgan and Victoria's lifeless bodies. My heart is beating so fast in my chest that it feels like it will burst through. I'm snapped back to reality when Xander crouches down in front of me and starts clicking his fingers in front of my face, I didn't even see him walk back over to me. "Hello, Earth to Sarah!" he shouts.

Shock is taking a hold of me, I start shaking my head from side to side, the tears cascading down my cheeks. "You...you killed them. Th...they're dead."

"Well, thanks for stating the obvious there. Now, if you don't want to join them with a bullet in that pretty little head of yours, I suggest you think carefully about what I said earlier. While your thinking about our future, pucker up and start sucking my cock...or better yet, bend over the back of the couch and let me fuck you. Sarah, it's our time to reign and it all begins now, just like it did with Vicky and me all those years ago when we took out Esteban."

I'm beyond frightened at the moment, I can hear Xander speaking but nothing is registering, it's all muffled. I'm snapped back to realty when my phone starts to ring. The damn Bluetooth on the *Bose* mini system connects and announces to the room, "Logan calling."

"Well, well, well, isn't that nice. Your non-boyfriend is calling my little whore. Go on; answer it. Tell him you are fine." He bends down and squeezes my cheeks roughly. "And don't fucking mention a thing about any of this...understood?"

Before I have a chance to answer, it's stops ringing and I breathe out a sigh of relief. Only for it to start ringing again. "Answer it, bitch, and put it on speaker." He looks at me before yelling, "NOW!"

Picking up my phone, I answer. "Hey, Logan."

"Sarah, where are you?"

"I'm...I'm with Morgan." As I say her name I look down at her body and my eyes well with tears. "She's turned up just after you called. She's not doing too well at the moment and she needs me. I can't leave her like this, Logan." Taking a deep breath, I add, "I'll call you when she's okay and I have her settled. Umm, Logan, I...I love you."

Xander grabs up my phone and throws it against the bar, smashing it into a million pieces. "You fucking little whore. I didn't believe Vicky when she told me that you were in love with the fucker. I just thought he was enamored with your hot little ass, like all of us are." He winks at me and I shudder. "Speaking of ass, bend over the couch now, I want to pop your ass cherry."

I'm frozen on the spot, I don't move a muscle; I'm in complete and utter shock. He wants to screw...my ass...with two dead bodies in the room, one of them being his wife. A surge of adrenaline courses through my body, I stand up and glare at him. "I'm not fucking you with your dead wife and my friend in the room. Actually, I'm never screwing again, you psychotic piece of shit."

"Like they care," he scoffs. "Now, strip off your clothes and bend over the couch." He starts stroking his cock through his pants and licking his lips, staring intently at me. "Now, bitch!" he bellows.

Swallowing hard, I look around the room for something to use as a weapon, but I'm pulled back to reality, literally, when Xander grabs me by my ponytail and throws me over the coffee table onto the couch, landing with a thud on my back. I shuffle back, trying to get away from him, but he's too strong for me. Pulling his arm back, he punches me in the stomach, knocking the wind out of me. "Ugh!" I moan as I curl into a ball to protect myself. Rolling me onto my stomach, he straddles my legs and shoves my skirt roughly up my hips, tearing my undies from my body. He frees his cock from his pants before pressing his body to mine. He whispers, "I'm go to fuck you one last time, and then I'm going to fuck you as I choke the life out of you." He licks my ear before sitting back up, I can feel his cock slide down my ass crack and it's in this moment I realise that he is going to rape me. My body tenses; fear taking me over. Closing my eyes, images of Mum, Dad, Kenz, Jordan, the girls, and Logan flash before me. I sadly smile; knowing that they will all be safe once I'm gone.

Tears pour down my face when a surge of adrenaline courses through my veins. With all my might, I wriggle and try to buck him off me. As he pushes me further into the couch, my arm drops off the side of the couch and my hand lands on his gun. My eyes fly open and I grin, gripping the butt of the gun tightly in my hand, I flick off the safety, and with all my might, I roll over and pull the trigger. The last thing I remember before passing out is the deafening sound of a gunshot.

39

LOGAN

When the line with Sarah goes dead, I jump out of my car, not caring that I'm double-parked, and I race inside the building. Repeatedly, I punch the lift call button and eventually it opens. Racing in, I hit the button for her floor. The thirty second lift ride is excruciatingly slow. The elevator finally slows at her floor and when the doors open I hear a gunshot.

"Sarah!" I shout as I race towards the door.

It's locked! I take a step back and with all my might, I kick it down. The frame splinters and the door crashes into the apartment, smashing when it hits the foyer floor. Stepping over it, I race into the apartment but come to a halt when I enter the lounge room. The first person I see is Victoria slumped over a body, both of them lying in a pool of deep red blood. My heart stops, until I realise the person she's on top of has red hair, *"Thank God it's not Sarah,"* I think to myself, but then my heart breaks when I realise it's Morgan.

Looking around the room, I see a man slumped on top of a brunette, and I know that it's Sarah. Racing over to the couch, I pull him off her and I sigh in relief. I shout her name but she doesn't stir, she's covered in blood and I start to panic. Squatting down next to her, I check her body for wounds but I can't find any. Picking up her wrist, I check for a pulse and thankfully I find one. Gently I left her up and sit on the floor with her in my arms, crying in relief that she's alive.

Pulling my phone from my jacket pocket, I call triple-O and tell them we need the police and an ambulance.

I've just hung up when Sarah stirs in my arms; she opens her eyes and blinks a few times. She stares up at me for a few moments before the waterworks erupt. "L...Logan," she sobs, before pushing herself up and wrapping her arms around me.

"Shhhh," I whisper, kissing her head. "I've got you now."

About twenty minutes later, I hear from the foyer. "Police"

"In here," I whisper-yell, as Sarah has passed out in my arms.

Looking up, I see two officers enter the room, followed by two ambo officers. They all pause midstep, open-mouthed and take in the scene.

"Who are you?"

"I'm Logan DeBiers and this is my girlfriend, Sarah Bryant. She needs medical attention, she keeps losing consciousness."

The ambos enter the room and one comes over to me. I lay her on the couch so he can assess her. The other ambo assesses Victoria, Morgan, and Xander, but he confirms that they are all dead.

"I'm Detective Ferguson, can you shed some light as to what happened here?"

Walking over to him, I give him as much as I know about what happened. I also tell him what my PI had discovered. They both look shocked but not completely taken by surprise. "You don't seem so shocked by what I've just said."

"I'm not. Victoria and Alexander Chalmers have been on our radar since the disappearance of Megan Hill six months ago and the recent murder of Angel Hurley piqued our interest."

"Holy shit. So Sarah is pretty lucky to be alive right now?"

"Yes, your girlfriend is extremely lucky, Mr. DeBiers. The Chalmers have been operating some very dangerous and shady endeavours but we have never been unable to nab them for anything. With the help of your PI, who I will need the details for, we should be able to close these two outstanding cases."

Before we can talk any further, the ambos are wheeling Sarah out, but she is still unconscious. "Excuse me, I need to go with her." Reaching into my pocket I hand over my business card. "Here are my details, feel free to call me anytime, but I'm sure I will see you at the hospital shortly."

"Thank you, we will see you when Sarah is up to chatting with us."

Sarah is admitted to hospital, but thankfully she has no major injuries, we just need to wait for her to wake up. The doctors advised that from all the excitement, if you'd call it that, her body has shutdown and needs time to recover. They said it's up to her as to when she wakes up.

After the doctors have left, I step out of her room and make a few calls. First, I call Beth and ask her to cancel everything for the rest of the week for me. Then I call Kenzie to let her know what happened, not looking forward to that call, she picks up after several rings.

"Hey, LDB, how are ya?"

"I've been better. Umm, Kenz, Sarah is in the hospital."

"What?" she bellows down the phone, deafening me. "Which hospital? I'm coming."

"She's at the Royal…"

Interrupting me she quickly says, "Be there soon," and hangs up on me.

Walking back in Sarah's room, I drag the recliner chair closer to her bed and take her tiny hand between mine. Lifting it to my lips, I place a kiss on her palm before gently placing it back on the bed and holding it tightly. "Please, Sarah, come back to me."

40

SARAH

MY BODY FEELS HEAVY AND I'M STRUGGLING TO OPEN MY EYES. THERE'S A loud noise ringing in my ears and a weight is crushing me. Suddenly the weight is gone and I can hear Logan. I manage to open my eyes. "L...Logan," I whisper as I start to cry. He wraps me in my arms and I feel safe, the heaviness takes over and once again everything goes black.

My body jolts and it feels like I'm floating. We come to a stop and I hear doors opening, metal clanking, and voices. I don't recognise any voices and I can't open my eyes. Logan, I feel and hear him but I can't open my eyes to see. Again, darkness takes over.

The next time I wake, I feel lighter than I did before and there's a constant beeping and voices. This time I hear Kenz and Logan, I try to talk but nothing comes out. I'm so tired; I drift back into blackness.

Finally my eyes open, after blinking a few times, my vision adjusts to the brightness and I glance around the room, I realise that I'm in a hospital and my body is aching. Someone next to me moves, they are holding my hand tightly and I hear them whisper, "Sarah, please come back to me."

Logan, I think to myself. "Hey," I manage to whisper; a lone tear falls down my cheek. "I'm sooooo sorry, Logan." Tears begin pouring down my face and my vision blurs. He stands up and carefully slides onto the bed and pulls me close to him. Wrapping my arm around his abdomen, I snuggle into him and cry. I must fall asleep because when I wake again the sun is just starting to rise outside and Logan is sound asleep next to me.

Looking over at him, I smile and he whispers, "Are you watching me sleep?"

"Maybe." Snuggling into his side, I breathe in his scent and it instantly calms me. Looking up at him, I hesitantly ask, "Logan, what happened?"

Before he can answer, a nurse walks into the room and asks Logan to leave so she can assess me and get me showered. He kisses me on the forehead and says he'll go get coffee and be back.

Forty minutes later, I'm freshly showered and sitting in the unflattering, itchy hospital gown when the door to my room opens. I'm hit with the amazing smell of coffee and Logan. My tummy rumbles really loud and Logan stops midstep, looking at me, and he laughs. "Well, hello to you, too."

"Hey," I manage to say, trying to pull the blanket up because I look like a mess.

"Are you cold? Let me help you." He places the coffee and bag on the bed table and helps me pull the blanket up.

"Not really but I look like shit, I don't want you to see me like this."

Looking at me, he smiles, pushes a strand of hair behind my ear, and kisses me forehead lovingly. "Sarah, you are absolutely beautiful. Black eye and all."

"I think you need your eyes tested." My tummy rumbles again.

"Well, let's get you fed and caffeinated and then we can get you out of here. I ran into the nurse, and she said you will be discharged later this morning."

My face drops when he tells me this, I don't want to go back to the apartment. Logan notices the change in my demeanor, as he places my coffee on the table he enquires. "What's wrong, Sarah? You're as white as a ghost. Do you need me to get the nurse?"

"No, I'm fine." Twirling the coffee cup in circles on the bed trolley, I look up at him and quietly whisper, "I don't want to go back to the apartment."

"Sarah, you're coming home with me. Your place is officially a crime scene." My head snaps up, tears welling in my eyes once again. "She's really gone, isn't she?"

Pushing the trolley to the end of my bed, Logan sits on the edge and pulls me into his arms. "Yes, Sarah, she's gone." He holds me tightly as I cry for both Morgan and Angel. Once I've composed myself, he fills me on in everything that the detective told him yesterday as I sip on my coffee and nibble on my carrot and walnut muffin. When we have finished our coffee and muffins, Logan climbs into bed with me and I drift off to sleep in his arms.

I awake to the sound of giggling, Logan is entertaining Indi and Rory in their pram and Kenz is staring at me. "Morning, Sleeping Beauty. How you doing?"

"Did you just Joey me?"

"Normally I would be, but at this specific moment I'm just asking how you are."

"I…I don't really know, to tell you the truth." A lump forms in my throat as I say this.

"Yep, I know that feeling, but trust me when I say, you will be fine. You are strong and you have wonderful friends to help and support you."

Kenzie's words open the floodgates and once again, I'm crying. She climbs into bed next to me and wraps me in her arms. Pulling away, I shuffle around and rest my head in her lap; she rubs my hair and lets me cry. Kenz doesn't say anything but she says everything with her actions, she's my person and I'd be lost without her.

Opening my eyes, I look up to see that I'm still lying in Kenzie's lap, she has my iPad and is reading. She notices me stirring and says, "This book is amazeballs, Sarah. This M Stratton is forking awesome, I'm totally swooning over Noah and Lexi is totally kick-ass."

"Don't let Jordan hear you say that, you know he gets jealous when you gush over fictional characters."

"Pfft, he'll get over it." Putting the iPad on the bed trolley she shuffles around, I realise her legs must be dead from me laying on them. "Sorry, your legs must be killing you from my fat head sleeping on them, but if it's any consolation, I feel much better now."

The door to the room opens and Logan walks in. "Glad to hear that you feel better." Leaning down he kisses my forehead before nodding at Kenz. He places a tray of coffees on the bed table and takes a seat on the recliner.

"Logan, you are a gem. I've been dying for a coffee but Sleeping Beauty here had me pinned to the bed." Grabbing a coffee, she moans, "God, I love coffee."

Logan and I both laugh; it feels good to laugh again. Looking between Kenz and Logan, I realise that I'm lucky to have such great people in my life. There's a knock on the door and it edges open, peeking around is Mum. She smiles at me, and when I see her, I jump off the bed and race over to her. "Mum," I say through tears as I wrap my arms around her, hugging her tightly. I feel a hand rub my back and I look up to see Dad standing there. "Daddy," I say before wrapping an arm around him, I'm enveloped on a Bryant family hug. The three of us stand there hugging, Mum and I crying, and for the first time in months, I know that everything will be fine. Mum and Dad are back in Australia, Victoria and Xander are no longer a threat, I have my best friend back, and I hope, that Logan and I can get back on track, too.

The moment is interrupted when a detective and Officer Hamilton enter my room. They ask everyone to leave so I can give my statement; I ask if Kenz can stay, I don't think I can do it by myself. Mum, Dad, and Logan exit my room, as the door is closing, I hear Logan introducing himself to Mum and Dad, and once again I find myself smiling.

After the door closes, Officer Hamilton is the first to speak, "Kenzie, it's nice to see you again, and for once, I'm not here to speak to you."

"Shocking I know. We missed you at Mike's housewarming the other week."

"Yeah, I was on night duty. I heard it...." A throat clearing interrupts our conversation. "Sorry, this here is Detective Ferguson, he is the lead on this case. He has been following Victoria and Alexander "Xander" Chalmers for quite a while now. Sarah, he has a few questions for you, are you up for answering them?"

Nodding my head. "Umm, yeah, I think so."

For the next forty minutes I recall everything from the moment I met Victoria at The Dirty Duck up until yesterday. I omitted the names of clients because I don't want to get any of the nice ones in trouble, but I'm pretty sure they will have the names from the books. No surprises that 'Sleazy Simon' rolled over and spilled his guts about all the dirty work that he did for the Chalmers over the years that he worked for them.

After the detective and officer leave, Mum, Dad, and Logan come back in and they are all laughing. Seeing them together like that gives me a warm and tingly feeling inside. Josh never had that kind of relationship with my parents and here's Logan joking around, and he's only known them for less than an hour.

Kenz nudges me and winks; I swear that girl knows exactly what I'm thinking. She and I are grinning and giggling at each other, just like we used to when we were thirteen when Mum says, "What are you two giggling like schoolgirls over?"

"Nothing," we both say at the same time and this cracks us up. While we are still laughing the nurse comes in, and says that morning visiting hours are over, and that they can came back for this evening's hours. They take turns hugging me bye and they all leave, Logan hangs back and sits on the edge of my bed. Leaning forward he rests his forehead against mine and whispers, "I'm so glad that you are safe. When I heard that gunshot, my heart literally stopped beating, and then when I saw all the blood and you not moving, I thought I'd lost you. Sarah, you mean the world to me, and when you are released from here you are moving in with me, no questions, no objections, it's just happening."

"Okay," I whisper.

"Sarah, I mean it you are mov…hang on, did you just say yes?"

"Yes, Logan, yes…"

Kenz comes back into the room and squeals. "Oh My God, you two are getting married?"

Both our heads snap towards her, Logan's face pales, and I quickly say, "Fuck no." Logan looks at me, "Sorry, but no, not getting married; just moving in together."

Logan whispers, "Yet!" I hear it and butterflies appear in my stomach at that thought, and I can't help but grin. This year has been rough but finally I'm on my way to getting my happily ever after.

41

SARAH

...7 months later

SITTING ON THE PLANE, I STILL HAVE ON THE EYE MASK THAT LOGAN HAS made me wear since we left home earlier this morning. Home: I love that Logan and I have a home together. There was a time when I thought I'd lost him forever, but fate was on our side, and we are now together, I'm over the moon happy...wearing a blindfold on a plane; never thought I'd say that in a sentence. I'm sure that I got some weird looks as we walked together through the airport, but to be honest, as much as I'm complaining and being obnoxious, the not knowing where we are going is really exciting.

All of a sudden, I feel Logan fiddling with the blindfold and he slips it off, blinking a few times, my eyes adjust to the light. I look over to see Logan staring at me with a huge grin on his face. "Hi," I manage to squeak.

"Hi yourself." He winks at me, before handing me a glass of bubbly. "A toast," he says, raising his glass. "To us and our happily ever after." He winks at me again, as our glasses gently touch and we each take a sip.

"So, why are we finally getting out happily ever after, again? You know, I got mine when you and I moved in together."

"Happily ever afters are forever, Sarah, and our forever is just beginning. Therefore there will be many, many special occasions to add to our happily ever after, and I'm pretty sure that this one will top moving in together." He palms my cheeks and rubs my jawline with his thumb as he says this. Closing my eyes, I lean into his hand, enjoying the moment. Gently, Logan turns my head towards the window and then I see it...sparkling azure blue water and white sandy beaches below.

Snapping my head towards him, I excitedly ask, "Are we?" Turning my head back towards the window, I lean forward. " Seriously, are we heading to Bora Bora?"

"Surprise," he says.

Turning to face him, I undo my seatbelt and jump into his lap, smashing my lips to his as I throw my arms around his neck. He wraps his arms around my waist and everything around us fades away; I'm lost in this kiss and Logan. We are brought back to reality by the airhostess clearing her throat. "Excuse me, the captain has turned the seatbelt sign back on as we are about to land. Can I get you to hop back into your seat and buckle up please?"

"Yeah. Umm, sorry. Sure," I say, as my cheeks turn fifty shades of pink and I hop back into my seat. Logan just sits there laughing at my embarrassment and me. "Shut up, butthead."

"Butthead, wow, bringing out the big guns there, pinky."

"Shut up, or you won't get any sex tonight."

"Pfft, like you could not want a piece of this?" He sits there with an unsexy smug look on his face, roaming his finger up and down his body.

I can't help it and I burst out laughing. "Dream on, buddy, dream on."

"Okay, let's make a deal. You will be begging me for sex later this evening and when you do, you have to do ANYTHING that I say."

"And when I don't beg for sex?"

"Whatever you want."

"Ummm, you and me, spa day, the works."

Without hesitating, not missing a beat, he stretches out his hand and confidently says, "Deal." I'm kind of scared with how easy he agreed to this but I'm so winning this bet.

"Deal. My vag is closed for the next twenty-four hours."

"We'll see."

I'm scared....I'm excited...I'm so going to win this...I hope...

42

LOGAN

I'm so winning this bet, and by the end of the day, Sarah will be beneath me screaming my name in pleasure. This will be the easiest bet I have ever won...but I do hold an ace up my sleeve that is a kind of an unfair advantage, but all's fair in love and war.

Keeping this secret and surprise from Sarah has been killing me, we don't have secrets—well, except this one and one other, but really it's not a secret, it's just an omission of something. Thankfully, I now only have one omission that I'm hiding, and it's even better than the Bora Bora surprise...less than twelve hours to go.

Once we have cleared customs, someone from *St. Regis Bora Bora* meets us and we have a short private boat ride to the resort. The look on Sarah's face is priceless, she is so excited and happy; she's beaming. Her hair is blowing in the wind on the transfer; she has never looked more beautiful. She must sense me staring at her because she looks towards me. "What?" she asks.

"Nothing, you just look absolutely fucking gorgeous right now, Sarah."

Her cheeks tinge pink and the corner of her lips lift up in a smirk, she gives me an emphatic cheesy smile. "You don't look too bad your-self, Mr. DeBiers. Play you cards right and you might get lucky." She lifts her eyebrows in a seductive way before realising her mistake, quickly adding, "In twenty-four hours you'll get lucky."

"We'll see," I say before pulling her closer to me and holding her tightly as the boat glides across the crystal clear water. Just the feel of her in my arms has my cock twitching...*It's going to be a long twenty-four hours if she holds up her end of the bargain*, I think to myself, but I'll have her begging for me before that time, mark my word.

"Fuck me, this is stunning, Logan. I've always wanted to come here but this, this is, magical...I'm speechless."

"That'd be a first." That comments garners me a smack in the ribs and a scowl. I wink and Sarah can't contain her smile and the corner of her lips lifts slightly. I'm mesmerised by her beauty and it's in this moment that I know, Sarah is the one for me and this trip will be perfect.

We disembark the boat and make our way to check in. Lacing my fingers with Sarah's, we head inside reception; she lightly squeezes my hand. Tugging her closer, I place my arm over her shoulder and she wraps her arm around my waist; we fit together perfectly. As we approach the reception desk we are warmly welcomed. "Mr. and Mrs. DeBiers, welcome to the St. Regis Bora Bora."

"Ohh, we're not married," Sarah quickly says, my heart deflates at how quickly she shut him down, but inside I'm saying, *yet.*

"My apologies, ma'am." A laugh erupts from me because I know how much Sarah despises being called ma'am.

"Please don't call me ma'am either, Sarah will be fine."

"Duly noted, Sarah. I hope you had an uneventful journey here?"

"It was smooth sailing. It's absolutely gorgeous here, I can't wait to explore."

"Yes, we are very lucky, but I'm afraid your exploring will have to wait, Sarah. We have you booked into *Miri Miri* for a pampering package."

Sarah inquisitively looks towards me. "Surprise." I say, with a smile.

"Logan, what have you done?"

"Nothing, I just wanted you to have a little pampering so you'd be relaxed for our holiday." She jumps towards me, wrapping her arms around my neck and plastering a kiss on my lips. Gripping her tightly, I kiss her back, coaxing her lips open as I slip my tongue into her mouth. *What I would give to sink myself balls deep inside of her right now*, I think to myself. Lowering her down, I lean my forehead against hers and whisper, "Sarah, I love you and if you keep kissing me like that

I'm going to explode in my pants. Now, go to the spa and I'll meet up with you later this afternoon."

"But what will you do?"

"Sarah, we are in paradise, I'm pretty sure I can find something to keep me out of trouble. To be honest, I just want to relax so I think I'll laze at our villa and read that Stratton lady's book you keep raving about."

"The *Storm* series? Or *Fade to Black*?"

"The Black one, I finished the Storm one on the plane. She writes seriously messed up characters but it's like crack, I'm addicted."

"Told you, You'll love *Fade to Black* and Devon **SIGH**." Pausing, she winks at me. "Okay, well I'll meet up with you later?"

"It's a date."

Sarah kisses me on the cheek and then heads off with the lady from the spa, who appeared while we were chatting. Turning towards the desk, the clerk, Jonathan says, "Mr. DeBiers, I hope we didn't ruin your surprise."

"No, Jonathan, it's fine, she still doesn't know anything, just the way it's meant to be. Is everything set for this evening?"

"Yes, Mr. DeBiers everything is ready for 7:00 p.m. this evening and the others are all here, too."

"Great. Perfect. It's all falling into place and please, call me Logan."

In a little over five hours there will be no more secrets and Sarah will be getting the surprise of her life. I always thought I'd be nervous when I came to this point in my life but there are no nerves whatsoever, I'm excited for tonight and this next adventure.

The room attendant has just left and the villa phone rings. "Hello."

"Hey, everyone is here and we are all settled into our McMansion, seriously, Logan, this place is amazeballs."

"I'm glad, she still has no idea."

"She is either going to be pissed, or too shocked to say anything."

Together we both say, "And then pissed."

"Logan, you are perfect for her, and I'm so glad to be here and help you arrange all of this."

"Thanks, I appreciate it. Now, go chillax in your McMansion and I'll see you later this arvo."

"Sounds good to me. Later, dude."

After hanging up, I grab an ice-cold beer, my iPad, and head out to the deck, hoping to relax but I'm so nervous and excited that I can't concentrate. Grabbing another beer, I sit down on one of the outdoor lounges and look out at the view. It is magical here and the perfect place to make Sarah my wife.

43

SARAH

OH MY GOD, I HAVE NEVER BEEN SO RELAXED IN MY ENTIRE LIFE. I thought the spa that she-devil took us to was amazing, but the ladies here at *Miri Miri* are angels sent from heaven, with magical hands that know what they are doing. For a brief moment, I become sad at the loss of Angel and Morgan, but I tell myself that they are now happy and free.

I'm enjoying myself in the private wellness area, relaxing back in the spa, enjoying the tranquility, and a sneaky glass of bubbly when one of the staff comes out with an envelope for me. He places it on the sun lounger. "No rush, but this was waiting for you. Can I get you anything else, Ms. Bryant?"

"I'm fine, thank you. What time do I have to be leaving?"

"This area has been reserved for you for the rest of the afternoon. Please don't hesitate to ask if you need anything." He smiles before turning around and heading back inside the spa.

Resting my head back, I close my eyes to relax, but the note is eating at me so I climb out, wrap one of the fluffy white towels around me, and sit down. Picking up the card, I flick it open and I immediately recognise the handwriting. I smile as I begin to read.

My dearest Sarah,

You are the light of my life and I hope, as you are reading this, that you are relaxed and glowing. Please do me the honour of joining me this evening at 6:30 p.m. for a night that I hope you will never forget. When you are ready, head inside where your hair and makeup will be done and a dress is waiting for you.

I can't wait to see you

L

Holding the card to my chest, my smile deepens; I'm so excited to see what Logan has planned for me this evening. Looking at the time, I decide that I have enough time for one more dip before I have to head inside. Just as I've immersed myself in the water, another attendant comes back out with another glass of bubbly and a fruit platter. She places it next to me, not saying anything but her face is beaming; like I'm missing something but before I can ask she heads back inside.

I've finished the bubbly and fruit so I decide to head inside and get ready. When I walk in, the room goes silent, everyone is looking at me smiling; it's really weird. Someone claps their hands and then it's all go go go. I'm shuffled into the bathroom to have a shower; the *Clarins* products used here are divine. Stepping out of the shower, I dry off and lather my body in moisturiser before slipping on my robe once again. Walking out, I see a gorgeous, Grecian-style, ivory dress with gold embellishments hanging up and a purple and silver box sitting on the table next to it. Heading over, I lift the lid and inside is a pair of gold sandals, which match the dress perfectly, and an exquisite black and nude *Victoria Secret* bra and matching undies set. Reaching out, I run my fingers over the ultra soft material, a lone tear falls down my cheek; I never thought I would be this happy. The last seven months I have been happier than I have ever been and that's all because of meeting Logan.

Wiping the tear away, I carefully grab the bra and undies and slip into them. Pulling the robe back on, I head back out into the adjoining room and set up is a hair and makeup stand. "Please take a seat and we will begin," the lady says to me, gesturing towards the chair.

Smiling, I skip over to the chair and sit down. Another glass of bubbly is handed to me and as I sit here staring at myself in the mirror the ladies get to work; first my hair is done into a loose half up-half down style and curled, a crown of baby's breath is pinned in place. *I look like a Grecian godess*, I think to myself. Then it's time for my makeup, the lady either has been warned I'm not really a makeup kind of girl, or she is just good at her job. She doesn't do a lot, but somehow my eyes pop; using a mixture of greys and pinks she gives me a smokey, sultry look that doesn't look over the top. My blush is light and my lips look amazing, the colour is perfect and looks like it's one of mine from home. Logan obviously had this delivered to them while I was being pampered. Once they are finished, I sit there staring at myself in the mirror, I haven't felt like this happy, relaxed version of Sarah in a long time. Looking towards the makeup artist, I say. "Thank you, I wish I could do my makeup like this."

"Your welcome. Now let's get you dressed, I hear there is a man waiting for you."

When she mentions Logan butterflies appear in my stomach, much like the first night met him, and I smile like the cat that got the canary. Even though Logan and I met unconventionally, I'm glad to have him in my life. Standing up, I walk over to the dress, and with the help of the spa staff, we slip it over my head and it fits like a glove. Finally, I slip on the gold sandals, completing my ensemble. Straightening up, all of the spa ladies are grinning and murmuring. Spinning around, I look in the mirror and my mouth drops open in shock. "I...I look like a bride."

"You look stunning, Sarah." Spinning around, I see Logan standing in the doorway with his hands in his pockets. He's wearing charcoal slacks, a white linen shirt, with the top buttons undone, and a suit jacket hugs his shoulders. "Logan!" I breathlessly say. I'm lost for words right in this moment. Looking around, I realise that everyone has left and it's just Logan and me, the heat radiating between us would be enough to melt steel. "You're early."

"I couldn't wait any longer to see you." He strides over to me, placing a gentle kiss on my cheek, sparking something deep inside of me. I feel lost when he pulls away but my cheek is tingling from where his lips just were. Reaching out, he grabs each of my hands, holding them tightly to his chest. "Sarah, you came into my life when I least expected it. We've been on an amazing journey together already, and I can't wait for our next adventure together." He lifts our clasped hands and kisses them, letting go, he bends down on one knee and I gasp. "Sarah Bryant, will you do me the honour of becoming my wife tonight?"

I'm frozen, my heart rapidly beating in my chest. Inside my head I'm screaming *YES! YES! YES!* but nothing is coming out. Logan squeezes my hands and I realise that he's talking to me. "Sarah, Sarah, are you okay?"

Shaking my head, I finally manage to say, 'Yes, yes, yes." Squatting down, I place my palms gently on his cheeks and kiss him. He breaks our kiss and slips on a white gold, princess cut diamond onto my finger. Staring at it, my mouth drops open at the ring. "Logan, this is, wow. It's simple yet stunning." Wrapping my arms around his neck, I kiss him again; this one is more passionate than the last. Pulling my head back, I ask, "Tonight?"

He laughs, "Surprise." Logan runs his palms softly up and down my arms. "Tonight, Sarah, I want you to become my wife tonight."

Open-mouthed I just stare at him, and without an ounce of hesitation, I quickly reply. "Okay, let's do it. Logan, I love you with all my heart, and I would be honoured to become Mrs. Logan tonight, but you have to promise me one thing?"

"Sarah, I would do just about anything for you to become Mrs. Logan, as you put it, tonight."

"We have to have another ceremony when we get home so our family and friends can be there."

"Anything for you. Now, let's go get married."

Standing up, I wrap my arms around his neck and kiss him again. "Let's do this." Grabbing his hand, I lead us to the doorway; opening it we walk down the hall into the waiting area of the spa. When we enter the staff all start clapping and whistling. Logan pulls me into his side, and I wrap my arm around his waist, and once again I'm beaming.

A man, in a chauffer's uniform, steps forward. "Mr. DeBiers, Ms. Bryant, your chariot awaits."

Logan and I link fingers as we walk out to the waiting golf buggy; the driver whisks us away, towards my happily ever after. We stop suddenly and Logan turns towards me, lifting the blindfold from the plane out of his pocket, he's smirking at me again. "Seriously?"

"Seriously. Now turn around so I can place this over your eyes."

"Fine," I huff. "Don't mess my hair or you die," I add with a smile, spinning around, but deep down I'm excited to see the next surprise. Logan ties the blindfold in place and then we are off again. Once again, the buggy stops, I feel Logan climb out and I'm left sitting here blindfolded. I can hear the waves gently crashing ashore. I smile, when I feel

Logan grab my hand and escort me off the buggy. The ground sinks beneath my feet and I realise that we are on the beach. He pulls on my hand, halting me in my tracks, leaning forward he whispers, "Surprise." Lifting off the blindfold, I blink at the light and take in the view before me.

My mouth drops open in shock. "Fuck me," I declare, covering my mouth with my hand at my faux pas. Before me are my family and all our friends. Turning towards Logan, my eyes well with tears. "Logan," I manage to squeak out as the first tear falls.

"You like?" he hesitantly asks.

"More like, love." Shaking my head, my eyes continue to scan the scene before me. To the left is a large round table, set with candles and light pink roses, obviously for the reception. Down by the water is a timber arbor with white chiffon flapping in the wind and decorated with light pink flowers and greenery. "This is stunning, Logan." Turning to face him, I grab his hand and squeeze it. "I'm speechless."

Amanda, the celebrant from Kenzie and Jordan's interrupts us. "Are you ready?" she asks.

"Absolutely," I quickly reply. Logan leans over and kisses my cheek before walking down to the arbor by the water, leaving me standing there with Amanda. Kenzie and Dad appear, I can't hold back at tears anymore and the floodgates open. Kenz races over to me and wraps her arms around me. "Shhhh." Rubbing my back, she adds, "Surprise."

Laughing at her, I pull back. "You are a bitch, a totally big bitch, but you're my bitch sista and I love you for this." Dad steps towards us and he smiles at me. "Daddy," I manage to say before I start crying again. He envelopes me in a dad hug and it calms me immediately.

"Hey, munchkin," he says. "You've got a good one there." He nods his head towards Logan, and I look to where he nodded and smile.

"I sure do."

"Let's get this show on the road," Kenz says.

Amanda and I have a quick chat so I know what's going on. I nod to everything that she is saying but I'm not really listening. I'm staring at Logan...my fiancé...my soon-to-be husband "I'm ready." Looking towards the sky I shout at the top of my lungs in excitement "I'm getting married." Everyone laughs. Logan smiles and winks at me, I know this is meant to be and it couldn't be more perfect.

Amanda heads towards Logan, Sav takes her spot next to Logan as his best man, and I have Kenz by my side, just like I was beside her on her special day. *A Thousand Years* by Christina Perri begins to play and that's Kenzie's cue. She heads down the aisle and Dad links his arm with mine. "You look beautiful and your mum and I are so proud of you."

"Thanks, Daddy," I choke out. Taking a deep breath Dad and I head down the aisle. My eyes are locked on Logan, my face is beaming, my eyes blurry with tears, and I realise that I am about to marry the man of my dreams in paradise.

Dad and I stop before Logan; he kisses me on the cheek, hands me over to Logan, does the manly handshake, one-arm hug thing and then he takes a seat next to Mum. Her face is streaked with mascara but she's smiling, she blows me a kiss before burrowing into Dad's side. Handing my bouquet to Kenz, I then turn and face Logan. Amanda begins to speak and I wink at Logan, everything around me fades away. As usual, I'm lost in everything that is Logan. I'm snapped back to reality when Logan squeezes my hands and clears his throat. "Sarah, you came into my life when I thought I had everything, but the more time I spent with you, I realised that I wasn't truly happy until I met you. We've been through so much together already, but I wouldn't change a thing because it led to this point in time. Sarah, I promise to always have wine and Jerry whenever you need it, but most of all, I'll always be here when you need me. Sarah, I love you with all my heart and soul."

Swallowing the lump that formed in my throat, I clear it and take a deep breath. "Logan, this is hard 'cause I've literally have twenty minutes to wrap my head around being engaged and now getting married." Looking out at everyone, I sternly say, "And you all are on my shit list for keeping this from me, but that can wait." Looking back to Logan, I wink. "Okay, sorry, here goes. Logan, you are everything that I dreamed and hoped for when I was a little girl and this is perfect." Flicking my hand around at everything, I wipe a tear before gripping Logan's hands again. "I never wanted this big 'look at me wedding' and this, this is beyond my wildest dreams. Logan, you are not only my partner but you are also my friend. You give me the strength and courage to go after my dreams, and when we get back, not only will we be starting a life as Mr. and Mrs. Logan; we will be starting a whole new chapter together. I can't wait for the next phase in our life. I love you, Logan."

Stepping forward, he dips me back and kisses me deeply. Everyone cheers and Amanda says, "Not yet, Logan."

"Oops, I just couldn't wait."

"Two minutes, I promise," Amanda says. "Logan and Sarah, you have chosen today to become one, and with these rings that you are about to exchange, they symbolise your love and life together. Logan, please repeat after me. With this ring, I marry you and bind my life to yours. It is a symbol of my eternal love, my everlasting friendship, and the promise of all my tomorrows."

Logan slips on a white gold band onto my fingers and repeats the vows; rubbing my finger after slipping the ring on, I begin to cry. It's now my turn, I slip the ring on his finger and through my tears I repeat the vows.

"Logan and Sarah, today you have joined your hearts and love with not only each but also your family and friends. It is with great pleasure that I officially declare you husband and wife. Logan, again, you can kiss your bride."

Logan lifts his hands, encases my cheeks, and kisses me. My eyes close, my leg lifts and I quietly moan into our first official kiss. We rest our foreheads together as everyone around us cheers. "Wife, moan like that again and I won't be held responsible for what I do in front of our guests."

"Husband, don't make promises you can't keep." Before he can reply, I crash my lips against his and he dips me back, our lips not separating; everyone around us cheers and hollers again. Flipping me back up, Kenz hands me my bouquet. Logan takes my hand, our fingers entwine and I throw my arm up in the air in celebration of our nuptials and smile. Millions of bubbles appear around us, Indi and Rory giggle excitedly and chase the bubbles down the aisle. Jordan apologises and chases after them, scooping them up in his arms, so they can reach the higher bubbles.

Logan and I make our way down the aisle and over to Amanda. A table has been set up in the middle of a love heart made out of different shades of pink rose petals, and we sign the registry and pose for a few photos. The rest of the guests make their way to the table and Logan and I head down the beach for a few more photos.

We are walking along the beach, hand in hand as the sun begins to set; the orange orb of the sun is encased in purples, oranges, reds, and pinks—it's magnificent. Logan pauses and wraps his arms around me, "I love you, Mrs. DeBiers."

"I love you too, Mr. DeBiers." Dipping me down again, he kisses me deeply just as the sun dips below the horizon, leaving in its wake millions of tiny stars shimmering in the midnight black sky. "We better get to our reception, I need to yell at a few people."

"Save the yelling for tomorrow, wife. For today, let's just enjoy it."

"Fine, but how the fuck did you pull this off?"

"I'm awesome," he says with a cocky grin on his face.

"Yes, you are awesome, husband. Now let's get to our reception so I can take you back to our room and lose our bet." I pull on his hand and start walking back to everyone.

"I like the way you think, wife." Winking at me, he adds, "My wedding present to you is a null and void on said bet."

"My hero, but I'm still getting sex, right?" I say, he stops suddenly and laughs, he pulls me into him and kisses me again.

"Sarah, I will be by your side for the rest of your life, anytime day or night that you need me; I will be there." My eyes light up at this, hand in hand, we silently continue the walk towards our wedding reception.

Jordan notices us first, clears his throat and declares, "Welcome Mr. and Mrs. Logan DeBiers." Everyone turns towards us and they start clapping and cheering. Indy and Rory toddle over to me and I drop to my knees to cuddle them. "Don't you two look lovely in your sauce covered dresses." They giggle before poking Logan's leg and running towards the water, Jordan chasing after them yelling for them to stop.

Standing up, I turn around and laugh at seeing Jordan trying to stop the girls from going for a swim. Kenz taps my arm and whisper-shouts, "That will be you soon, missus," before running down to the waterline and helping Jordan. I stand there watching the four of them splash around; I'm so happy that Kenz finally got her happily ever after.

Logan comes over and hands me a glass of champagne. "Here's to you wife."

"Why thank you, husband." Raising my glass, I look towards my husband. *I love saying that.* "To us."

He clinks his beer mug against my glass. "To us." He hooks his arm around me as we watch the McRoberts family splash around.

The rest of the night is spent mingling with our family and friends. I don't think I've stopped smiling, this is the happiest I have ever been, and it's all to do with my now husband. Sometimes life throws you a curve ball, but what I've learned is, it's how you swing and deal with it that makes you the person you are. I'm pretty sure that I've hit the home run.

EPILOGUE

ONCE AGAIN I HAVE A GODDAM BLINDFOLD ON. "SERIOUSLY, LOGAN, THIS blindfolding thing is getting old."

"I promise this will be the last time...in public anyway, in the bedroom, it stays."

My panties dampen when I think about the blindfold and what Logan and I did in paradise on our wedding night. "Fine, it can stay in the bedroom ONLY after this." Putting a lot of emphasis on the word 'only,' but truth be told, I'd go and do anything with Logan, blindfold and all.

He opens a door and carefully ushers me inside, taking a few steps forward, he tugs on my hand to stop me. He lifts up the blindfold and I'm standing at the entrance of an empty brick room, but on the wall is a sign. "What's this, Logan?"

"This is yours, Sarah."

"Are you shitting me?"

"No, I'm not shitting you. This is your bar, Sarah. This is my wedding gift to you."

"You bought me a fucking bar, seriously?"

"Seriously. A few months ago you mentioned that you wanted to open a wine bar one day, and one day is now."

"Fuck me dead, said Foreskin Fred, did you seriously buy me a bar?"

"Look at me, Sarah." Turning toward him, my breath catches. My husband is gorgeous and he just bought me a bar, a fucking bar. "Sarah, this is all yours, well ours, but yours. I want you to be happy and I know that this." Waving his hand around the room. "This has been your dream, and as your husband, it's my responsibility to make your dreams come true."

Throwing myself into him, he catches me and I wrap my legs around him, placing quick kisses all over him. "Thank you, thank you, thank you. You are the best husband ever, and when we get home tonight, you can do anything you want to me."

Pulling his head back so he can look directly into my eyes, "Any-thing?" he asks.

Leaning forward, I whisper in his ear. "Any-fucking-thing that you want. Now, husband, take me home so you can have you way with me and then I have a wine bar to open."

"Well, when you put it like that, let's go."

With myself still wrapped around him, Logan heads outside and hails a cab, directing him back to our penthouse. We could have walked because it's only a few blocks away but we have more pressing matters to attend to. The cab pulls up a few minutes later, Logan throws a twenty at the cabbie, pulls me out, and drags me inside.

Before the lift doors have closed, Logan is pushing me towards the sidewall. His hands explore my body, squeezing and kneading my breasts through my shirt. A moan escapes my lips, closing my eyes, my head lolls back; Logan takes the opportunity and kisses his way up my neck. Our lips crashing together, he plunges his tongue deep into my mouth before nipping on my bottom lip. The lift doors open, he grabs my ass and lifts me up, I wrap my legs around him, my skirt bunching up around my waist. Not breaking contact, our lips are fused together as we make our way to the penthouse door. Without dropping me, he manages to get the door unlocked and open, striding inside; he kicks it shut with his foot.

Once inside, I rip my shirt off, pearl buttons flying everywhere, tinkering across the floor. Logan spins around and slams me up against the front door; his dick is already hard and is rubbing against my clit through my satin purple undies, invoking all sorts of pleasure and moans from me. "Logan," I whisper as he pulls back, lowering his zipper and shoving his pants and boxer briefs down. His cock springs free and the tip is glistening with precum. I lick my lips and my eyes heat with carnal hunger. He grips the side of my undies and tears them off me, sliding his finger through my wetness, up my slit and circling around on my clit. "Fuck me now," I whisper. With a thrust of his hips, his cock is deep inside of me. We both grunt as he continues to pound into me, my head banging on the door, but I don't care. The pleasure coursing through my veins in this moment is all-consuming. My orgasm begins to build, and when Logan slips a hand between us and begins to rub my clit, I detonate like a rocket; I launch off into ecstasy and scream his name, riding out this pleasure explosion. As I'm coming back to earth, I feel his cock harden and his body shudders as he releases his seed.

We stay locked in each other's arms, me still pinned to the front door, our breathing laboured, hearts erratically beating. Our foreheads resting together, opening my eyes, I see Logan staring at me. "Wow," is all I manage to say. Kissing Logan on the top of his nose, he smiles at me as he lowers me down, my legs still jelly like after such as intense orgasm. He pulls up his pants before grabbing my hand; he pulls me into our room and head towards the shower. Leaning in, I turn the shower on before spinning towards him. I look up at him and silently unbutton his shirt. As I push it off his shoulders, I lean forward and place tender kisses over his chest and up his neck. Once his shirt is off, I push his pants and boxer briefs down; he steps out, kicking them to the side. Stepping back, I remove my skirt and heels. Turning around I step into the shower, Logan follows me in. We begin to soap each other up, staring at each other, still not speaking.

Once we are all washed, I wrap my arms around him. "Thank you, husband."

"You are most welcome, wife. Now let me take you to bed and show you, slowly this time, just how much I love you."

"That's perfectly alright with me." Kissing him on the cheek, I turn off the water. We climb out of the shower and quickly dry off, before falling into bed together.

For the rest of the night, we show each other repeatedly how much we love one another. In the early hours of the morning, we fall asleep in each other's arms and it's the most relaxing sleep I've ever had.

...Six weeks later

I'm currently standing in the middle of my recently finished and fully stocked wine bar, and I could not be happier. Today is the grand opening of Wine Not. The last month has been bedlam trying to get the bar up and running, but when your husband, *I still love saying that*, owns a development company, things get done quickly, very quickly. Considering how fast he got it all done, I think he's been planning this for a while.

Sensing him before I see him, I turn around to see him walking towards me. He's dressed in dark denim jeans and an olive green button-up shirt; he's looking just as sexy as the first night I met him and I smile. "How you doing, wifey?"

"I'm nervous as all hell. What if no one turns up?" Biting my lip as my nerves continue to build.

"Sarah, have you looked outside? There's a line down the block waiting to get in and the reservation book is full for the next week. This is going to be the hottest place in town."

Taking a deep breath, I smile, kiss Logan quickly, take another deep breath, and say. "Let's do this."

Walking towards to front doors, I open them to a round of applause. I smile in embarrassment but deep inside I'm ecstatic with the reaction I just received. First in line is Kenz, no surprises there, with Jordan, Mike, and Sav next to her. Just behind them is Mum and Dad, having the six of them here, seven if you include Logan, makes me so over the moon happy that I don't have to hide what I do for a living anymore.

"Welcome, everyone. Wine Not is officially open!" I excitedly shout.

Another round of applause and cheers erupts from the crowd. I step aside to let everyone in, hugging and kissing my family and friends on their way past. The staff quickly jumps into action and assign people to their tables or the bar.

Opening night goes by in a blur, I think it went well but I'm currently floating on cloud nine—I have my own wine bar, thanks to my husband and I'm finally living the dream. For a while there I was lost, alone, and heading down a dangerous path, but under not so conventional circumstance, I met a wonderful man who put me back together. He made me whole again, and now Sarah DeBiers nee Bryant is going to have a winetabolous life with the man of my dreams and a plus one…shhhh!

2ND EPILOGUE

Wine Not has been open for three weeks now, and we are just as busy now as we were in opening week; Logan was right, this place is the hottest new bar to open. It's a Sunday afternoon and everyone is here for a catch up. After we all reunited, we agreed to a monthly catch up and it rotates as to which couple hosts. This month I'm excited to host because it will be my first one at Wine Not.

Mike and Sav are the first to arrive; he has his arm draped around her shoulders and she snuggles in close to him. They are deliriously happy, smiling and laughing—no doubt Mike said something really inappropriate that is somehow funny. In all the years I've known Mike, I don't think I have ever seen him this happy, and who would have thought his happiness would come in the form of my husband's childhood best friend, Sav—it's such a small world.

Next to arrive is the McRoberts clan. Indy and Rory come racing in with a frazzled looking Jordan and Kenz close behind. I hear Jordan telling Kenz that they are getting faster and faster and they need those backpack lead thingies and Kenz snaps, "We are not putting our girls on leads, that's just wrong." And they head towards Mike and Sav, who are sitting at the bar. From where I'm standing, I giggle to myself and think that will be Logan and I soon; I can't help but smile and I subconsciously rub my tummy.

Walking over to the twins, I squat down and they both jump into my arms and hug me at the same time, knocking me on my butt and they fall on top of me. The three of us giggle, and then I panic that I may have hurt the baby, so I sit up and place them between my legs, and we start to play with the dollies that they bought with them.

My skin prickles and I look towards to door, and in walks my sexy as sin husband. He's dressed in his denim jeans that hug his ass perfectly and my favourite charcoal, short-sleeved, button-up shirt. He sees me on the floor with the girls, winks and heads towards to bar and everyone else.

After a few moments, I stand up and head over to join everyone. Kenz hugs me hello and I turn and snuggle into Logan's side, He places a gentle kiss on my forehead and I melt into him. Kenz passes Sav a glass of wine and then hands me one, *SHIT*, I think to myself. She grabs another glass and hands it to me. "Umm, not for me, thanks."

"Pfft, when have you ever turned down a wine?" Pausing, her mouth drops open. "Fuck, you're up the duff!" she exclaims, "Aren't you?"

I've never been one to lie or hide anything—well except for before but that was different, so my face begins to burn and turn red. I look up towards Logan and quietly say, "Surprise." Logan immediately wraps his arms around me and spins us around, pressing his lips against mine and kissing me. When he places me down, he looks me in the eyes. "Really?"

"Really, Really."

From the bar, I hear Mike say, "Did they just quote *Shrek* to each other?"

In unison Sav and Kenz say, "Shut up, Mike." Jordan laughs and Kenz smacks him in the stomach.

"I'm nine weeks along." Watching Logan, I can see his mind ticking and then it clicks. Nodding I say, "Yep, the night that you gave me the keys to this place is when peanut here was conceived."

"I love you, Sarah DeBiers. You are going to be the best mum."

"I love you, Logan DeBiers. You are going to be the best dad."

Logan pulls me in close and kisses me deeply. I forget where we are and I kiss him back. It isn't until we hear hollering and whistles that we turn towards the bar and to the beaming faces of our friends. We pull apart and walk over to them, the girls envelop me in hugs and the boys do their manly shake/hug thing.

Mike clears his throat. "Well, while we are celebrating, umm, Sav and I are getting married. I asked her to be my ball and chain forever." Sav whacks him in the stomach and he grunts. "I mean lovely wife," he says through clenched teeth.

Kenz says, "Looks like it's a double celebration then."

"Nothing you want to celebrate, Kenz?" I ask.

"How about we celebrate friendship, family, and love."

Everyone grabs their drinks and we all toast to friendship, family, and love. Our glasses all chink together and we all fall into easy conversation: drinking, eating, and enjoying each other's company. The six of us have a winetabolous night together and it feels so good.

Finally, I'm content and happy in life. I'm married to a wonderful man, we both have successful businesses, we are expecting out first baby, and all of our nearest and dearest are living life to the fullest. Life could not be any better; we all got our happily ever after.

THE END !!!

THE FINAL SHOT PLAYLIST

FML – Godsmack
Red Red Wine – UB40
Sunsets – Powderfinger
Pony – Ginuwine
Beautiful – Christina Aguilera
Just A Girl – No Doubt
Unconditionally – Katy Perry
Dancing in the Dark – Amy Macdonald
Faded – Alan Walker
Poker Face – Lady Gaga
You Make me Feel Like a Whore – Everclear
Just Dance – Lady Gaga
Sweet Dreams (Are Made of This) – Eurhythmics
Primadona Girl - Martina & The Band
Fuel – Metallica
Bleeding Love – Leona Lewis
Come Fly With Me – Frank Sinatra
Bad Things – Jace Everett
Down Under – Men at Work
I Don't Wanna Live Forever – ZAYN feat, Taylor Swift
Bad Intentions – Digital Daggers
Wannabe – Spice Girls

Untouchable – Garbage
Down in Flames – Daughter Jack
I'm Gonna Be (500 miles) – The Proclaimers
Fly Me to the Moon – Frank Sinatra
What a Wonderful World – Louis Armstrong
Dream a Little Dream of Me – Ella Fitzgerald
Just the Way You Are – Bruno Mars
It's Not Over – Daughtry
Need You Now – Lady Antebellum
Oh, Pretty Woman – Roy Orbison
Make War – From First to Last
Crawling – Linkin Park
Rolling in the Deep – Adele
You're the One that I Want – Film Musical Orchestra (Grease)
A Girl Like You - Edwyn Collins
Bitch – Meredith Brooks
Question Everything – Five Finger Death Punch
A Thousand Years – Christina Perri
Nothing Else Matters (Instrumental version) – Apocalyptica
Tomorrow – Silverchair

This playlist can be found on Spotify.

THE *Final* SHOT

FINDING A *happily after* IS THE EASY PART

DL GALLIE

Finding a happily after is the easy part.

Finding a happily ever after is the easy part. Keeping the ever after happy...now that's the tricky part.

Take Mike and Sav – it's their wedding day, and it's supposed to be the happiest day of their lives. But Mike is faced with one complication after another while all he wants is to get to the part where they can finally say, 'I do.'

Then there's Sarah. She is over the moon happy with Logan, and expecting their first bundle of joy. But as usual, things never go smoothly for Sarah.

And let's not forget Kenzie. No matter what she does nothing ever goes according to plan. But she's determined to step in and help her friends find their happily ever afters...no matter what.

To my lil munchkins; **Piper** and **Kade**.
You two mean the world to me.
Love you long-time.

1

KENZIE

FOR THE FIRST TIME IN WHAT FEELS LIKE FOREVER, I'M AWAKE BEFORE THE girls. With a smile on my face, I quickly strip off my PJ pants, undies, and singlet and cozy up to Jordan. He's facing away from me, so I press my breasts against his back and drape my arm over him, snaking my palm down to his cock. I grip it tight and gently begin to stroke him, as I nuzzle along his neck and up to his ear. His body stirs and he effortlessly rolls onto his back. He gropes my ass and lifts me so I'm straddling him. Gripping my cheeks, he pulls me down and secures his mouth against mine. Circling my hips, I begin to grind myself on his now stiff cock. Wrapping his arms around me tightly, we continue to kiss. Lifting up, I position his rock hard cock at my entrance and lower myself down, his length filling me completely. I moan into his mouth as we begin to thrust together. Sitting up and resting on my knees, I continue to ride him as he plays with my breasts. "I'm close," I whisper as I continue to slide up and down his cock. He lowers his hand and squeezes my clit, the pressure sets me off and instantly my insides explode. My orgasm ripples through my body. As I'm coming back to Earth, I feel Jordan tense beneath me. Knowing he's close, I begin to ride him faster, my pussy walls tightening around him. "Ennfff. Ahhhh!" Jordan groans, as his orgasm releases inside of me.

When his body stills, I roll off him and we both lie their panting.

Our breathing returns to normal when we roll onto our sides to face each other. "Morning," I whisper.

"Good morning, indeed," Jordan says with a smile. "That is by far the second best way to wake up."

Smiling, I ask, "And what's the first?"

"Your lips wrapped around my cock."

Smirking at him, I cheekily reply, "Duly noted for next time."

Before I can reply, he leans towards me, runs his fingers through my hair, cups my head, and brings his lips towards mine. We kiss passionately and just as I'm ready to mount him again, the girls giggling on the baby monitor interrupts us. Jordan breaks our kiss and whispers, "Man, they have impeccable timing."

"Mmhmm," is all I say, as I flop back on the bed and grin. After listening to the girls for a few moments, I look towards my husband and smile. "I'll get them if you start breakfast." Looking at the alarm clock on the bedside table, I add, "We will need to leave here by 8:15, at the latest."

"I can't believe Mike is getting married today. Who would have thought?"

"I always knew he'd get his happily ever after. If anyone deserves it, it's Mike. He's found the yin to his yang with Sav."

"I could insert a really inappropriate Mike joke here, but I'm a responsible dad and all that shit, so I will just lie here and do this." He leans over and takes my nipple into his mouth and gently bites down and sucks before letting it pop out of his mouth. He winks at me as he does the same to my other breast.

"Fuck it," I say, I push Jordan back onto the bed and straddle him before I impale myself on his cock. He sits us up and wraps his arms tightly around me as we rock back and forth vigorously. My lips crash against his and before we know it, we are both tumbling over the orgasmic cliff, screaming our release into each other's mouth.

Pulling back, I look deep into my husband eyes and huskily whisper, "I love you, Jordan McRoberts."

"I love you too, Kenzie McRoberts."

Reluctantly I climb off Jordan; I would love nothing more than to stay in bed with him all day, but today is a special day, one that will go down in history.

2

MIKE

"Fuck, fuck, fuck. I can't do this. I feel like I'm going to throw up," I whined, my face fifty shades of green.

Jordan laughs as he passes me a shot of tequila. He slaps me on the back and says, "Here, drink this and calm the fuck down, dude."

Grabbing the shot that Jordan puts in front of me, I slam it back, without flinching. The burn instantly calms me. "Another," I growl, I know I'm being a douchehole but I'm so fucking nervous, it's not funny.

My eyes watch Jordan like a hawk, I watch him grab the tequila bottle and fill up the glass again. Reaching out to grab the shot, the asshole smirks at me before he slams it back himself, and instead hands me a bottle of water; fucking water. "Nope, no more tequila for you. Sav...and Kenz would have my balls on a platter if you turn up shitfaced to your own wedding."

Sav...at the mention of my woman, I instantly calm down and smile. I look towards Jordan and with the biggest smile on my face I proudly say, "Fuck, dude, I'm getting married today."

"That tends to happen when you give the love of your life a sparkly ring and say those four magical words..."

A knock at the door interrupts Jordan, and before either of us can say come in, the door swings open and Kenzie waltzes in, with Indie and Rory toddling beside her. She's wearing a stunning red wine-coloured bridesmaid dress and her hair is piled messily on her head; she looks stunning, as always. And my lil' munchkins, they look adorable in their white and yellow flower girl dresses. Kenzie smiles at me and says, "Heya, Mike, how you doing?"

"Kenz, I'm getting married today, you can't be hitting on me like that anymore." I wink at her, before I add, "AND in the presence of your douche…I mean husband."

"Hardy har har, asshat." I follow her eyes and she notices the open tequila bottle. "Now, I know what you are so calm. It will, umm, ahh, ease what I'm about to tell you."

My head snaps up from watching Mac and Cheese and my stomach starts to roll. "Ooooookay, tell me."

"Ummm…"

"Don't fire truck with me, Mrs. McRoberts, not today. Now spit it out."

"Sarah just went into labour. So her and Logan can't make it and Sav is currently having a mega meltdown now that her Best Brides-dude can't make it."

"Shit, shit, shit," I whisper. Looking up at Kenz, I eye her suspiciously. "Is that all?" I anxiously add.

"Yeah," she hesitantly replies.

"Okay, well, let me talk to Sav, I'll calm her down and then we can get hitched."

"Yeah, nah, that's not gonna happen. She doesn't want to see you. She thinks you seeing her before the ceremony will jinx things. And now that Logan can't be here, she thinks she cursed and it's a sign telling her this is a mistake."

"Fuck that shit, " I declare as I look down to Mac and Cheese and whisper, "Sorry, munchkins, but fire truck just didn't cut it at this moment."

Indie looks up at me and grins. *Man, she's cute,* I think to myself but before I can finish that thought, she giggles, "Fuck that." While at the same time Rory says, "Shit, shit, shit."

I can't help it; I burst out laughing. Looking over I see Jordan grinning and Kenz is open-mouthed in shock. I bend down and scoop Indie up into my arms, kiss her forehead and say, "Thanks, gorgeous girl, that was just what Uncle Mike needed right now. Love you, munchkin." I put her down next to Rory and look over to Kenz, who surprisingly isn't pissed about the cuss incident. "Sorry about the swears BUT today is my wedding day and come hell or high water, it's happening. Now lead me to my wife-to-be and I'll talk her down through the door." Taking a deep breath, I add, "Today Savannah Blac WILL become Mrs. Savannah "Sav" Mustange. Now lead the way before I hulk out and lose my shite."

"Well, okay then." Kenz smirks at me. "Let's go." She turns towards Jordan and warns, "I'll be back as soon as I can. Enjoy daddy time but no ice cream."

"Pfft, I'll give my girls ice cream if I want to." Kenz death glares at him. "Okay, no ice cream. Now go and get this wedding back on track."

Kenz steps up to Jordan and kisses him quickly and I can't help but smile. I had always admired Kenz and Jordan's relationship and now I have the same with Sav, but only better...it is me, after all. After kissing the girls on their heads, she turns towards me and smiles a megawatt Kenz smile. "Let's go calm down your wife-to-be."

3

SAV

"FUCK, FUCK, FUCK, THIS CANNOT BE HAPPENING," I SAY AS I HANG UP THE phone. I've just thrown my mobile on the couch when Kenz walks in, by the look on her face she has just spoken to Sarah. "Kenz, what the fuck am I going to do? I need Logan here. I can't do this without him. This cannot be happening. What the fuck am I going to do, Kenz?" I know sound like a whiney bitch right now, but I need him here.

Kenz walks over to me and places her hands on my shoulders, "Calm down, Sav. It will all be fine." She hands me my glass of wine and I chug it back.

"More," I demand, shoving the glass back at her. Kenz must sense my unease, as without saying a word, she grabs the bottle and tops up my glass. Again, I take a big gulp and apprehensively look towards Kenz.

"Better?"

"Are Logan and Sarah here?" I snap.

"Ummm..."

"Kenz, I'm sorry for bringing out bitchy Sav. I'm just freaking the fuck out right now."

"I can understand. Let me go get Mike and we can get this all sorted."

"NO!" I screech like a banshee. "He cannot see me before the cere-mony, it's bad luck and all that shit. We are already jinxed enough as it is. I don't have my Best Bridesdude and I'm down a bridesmaid too. And I really really want a milk bottle right now and I don't have any."

"Well, I can help with one item." Kenz walks over to the mystery box of tricks she brought with her and pulls out the biggest bag of milk bottles that I have ever seen. "Tada," she proudly declares.

"You are a fucking lifesaver, Kenz. Gimme, gimme, gimme." I snatch the bag from her hands, rip it open, grab a handful, and shove them into my mouth. I moan in delight. With my mouth full I mumble, "Fuck, I love you, Kenz," as I shove another three milk bottles into my mouth. Kenz goes to grab the bag from me. "Nah, uh, these are mine, back off, bitch."

"Okay. How about I leave you and your milk bottles alone, and I'll go chat to Mike and see if we can get this sorted."

"Mmhmm," I mumble through a milk bottle mouthful.

I plonk down on the couch and start to panic again. *What if this is a sign that I'm not meant to get married?* I think to myself as I shove another handful into my mouth, washing it down with a sip of wine.

4

SARAH

"FUCK, SHIT, FUCK." I SAY, AS I BEND OVER AND CLUTCH MY BASKETBALL-sized stomach. "Looooogan!" I shout from the ensuite just as a trickle, and when I say trickle I mean Niagara Falls flood, of water gushes out of me. "Loooogaaaaaan!" I scream again.

"What's up, babe?" I hear him casually say as he walks into the room. "Fuck, shit, fuck." He runs his fingers through his hair like he does and it instantly calms me, and all of a sudden I want to jump his bones...fucking pregnancy hormones. I'm snapped back to reality when I hear him chanting to himself. "Okay, I can do this. We can do this."

Bending over and resting on the vanity, I take a deep breath, the pressure in my stomach is getting tighter and tighter. Looking back up, I see Logan's face has turned white and he is freaking out. Mr. Cool-Calm-And-Collected is freaking the fuck out, and that in turn, freaks me the fuck out. "Honey..." I don't get to finish that sentence because another contraction slams into me and I scream out in pain. The pain subsides and I look up to see Logan's eyes closed and he's falling to the ground...the fucker just passed out on me.

Somehow, I manage to make my way over to him and shake my head as I crouch down next to him. Raising my hand, I slap his face to wake him up, but the fucking asshole is out cold. "Fuck you, asshole," I say to the room. "I'm the one in labour here and you pass out." I sit back on my heels and rub my tummy. "Fuck, shit, fuck," I say once again as I take a deep breath. *You can do this, Sarah, you survived Bitchtoria and Xander, you can handle this too*, I tell myself.

Spying my phone on the counter, I grab it and call an ambulance, as there is no way my dear husband will be driving me. After calling and telling them I'm in labour and my husband has passed out, I stand up, leave Logan on the ensuite floor, and head into the walk-in wardrobe to get my hospital bag. Thankfully, I'm organised because my due date isn't for another two weeks.

Just as the ambos arrive, Logan stirs. I can tell that he is embarrassed beyond belief and I cannot wait to tell Sav all about this. At the thought of Sav I gasp out loud. This garners Logan's attention, and he jumps up and walks over to me. "Are you okay, babe? I'm so sorry I passed out."

"Yeah, nah, I'm all good but..." tears start to pour down my face, "...it's Sav and Mike's wedding today. I've ruined their special day."

"Naw, babe, you haven't ruined anything."

We are cut off by the ambulance officer, "Sorry to interrupt, but we really need to get Mrs. DeBiers to the hospital. Your blood pressure is higher than I'd like." He must sense my unease because he adds, "Bub seems fine, but let's get you to hospital so we can get you and the baby settled. Which hospital are you booked into?"

My mind is totally blank, I can't think. "I...I...Ummm." Thankfully, Logan comes to the rescue.

"It's the Royal and Dr. Green is our OB."

"Thanks. I will radio ahead and let them know we are on our way..." Before he can finish, I double over again as another contraction rips through me.

"I hate you. You fucking asshat dweebface!" I scream at Logan through the pain.

"Love you too, babe."

"Fuck you, asshole," I screech as the contraction begins to take hold. "Dude, I'm sorry," I cry. "I need to get this thing out of me, NOW!" I growl.

"Okay, let's get you to the hospital," the ambo says. Logan grabs my bag as the ambo gets me to lie on the gurney. Once I'm strapped in safely, we head to the hospital to meet our baby.

5

LOGAN

TODAY IS THE DAY THAT MY BEST FRIEND MARRIES HER SOUL MATE AND I could not be happier for Sav, or Mike. They are perfect for each other and I'm so glad their paths crossed. Life hasn't been easy for her, but she's finally on the road to her happily ever after, just like me. If you had told me twelve months ago that I would be married with a kid ready to arrive any day now, I would have told you to put down the crack pipe. But here I am, happily married to Sarah; we both have thriving businesses, and baby DeBiers is due to arrive in two weeks time.

Just as I'm unpacking the last of the dishes from the dishwasher, I hear Sarah scream for me from the bedroom ensuite. "Loooooogan!" Thinking it's just another, house-sized—insert sarcasm—spider, I slowly head towards our room. She screams my name again, but this time the scream is laced with something I've never heard before. Picking up the pace, I race in and ask casually, "What's up?" I walk in to find Sarah hunched over, clutching her tummy and standing in a puddle of water.

My eyes bug out of my head. "Fuck, shit, fuck," I murmur out loud, mostly to myself. At this point, my heart is speedily beating away within my chest, my hands are clammy, and I kind of feel like I want to throw up. I run my fingers through my hair and massage my temples to calm myself down, but it's not working, I'm totally fucking freaking out. *We still have two weeks*, I tell myself as I continue to stand on the spot and stare at Sarah. Internally I slap myself. "Okay, I can do this. We can do this."

Sarah leans on the vanity as another contraction rips through her and that's the final straw. My vision blurs and down I go, blackness envelops me and I'm out for the count.

I blink my eyes open and my cheek is tingling, I'm disorientated until I remember what happened. I sit bolt upright when I hear Sarah gasp. Looking over, I see her sitting on the end of our bed with tears pouring down her face. Racing over to her, I take her hands in mine and try to reassure her that all will be okay. She mumbles about ruining Mike and Sav's day; I try to calm her down but nothing is working. I sit next to her, wrap my arms around her, and let her get it all out. We are interrupted by the ambo, and we give him the hospital details. Once Sarah is safely strapped to the gurney, we leave the penthouse and head to the hospital.

While we are in the ambulance, we both make calls. Sarah calls Kenz and I call Sav. She picks up on the third ring. "Dude, you're late," she snarls down the phone.

"Well hello to you too, Sav, I see bridezilla is with us today."

"Fuck off, asshat, now where are you? I need my Bridesdude," Pausing, she then adds, "You've lost the best part 'cause you're late."

"Umm, yeah, about that…"

"Don't fuck with me, Logan, not today."

"For once Sav, I'm not. Sarah just went into labour. We are in an ambulance on our way to the hospital." I'm met with silence and that scares me more than anything. Pulling the phone from my ear, I look to see if we have been cut off but it's still connected. "Sav, you still there?"

"Logan, please tell me this is all a joke and you are really on your way?"

Shaking my head I confirm, "'Fraid not, Savvy. I'm gonna be a dad very soon."

The call is interrupted with Sarah moaning through another contraction. I drop my phone and grab her hand and calmly say, "Breathe, just breather, babe."

"Fucking don't tell me to breathe. I'm not stupid. I'm just trying to push a fucking basketball out my vagina, you fucking asshole." I don't say anything else to Sarah; I just squeeze her hand and smile reassuringly at her.

The contraction has passed and she squeezes my hand. "I'm so sorry, baby."

"It's okay. We will get through this together."

Vaguely I can hear Sav yelling at me, and then I remember that I was on the phone with her. "Sav, sorry, yes I'm here. Now calm down."

"Don't tell me to calm down. My bridesdude isn't here and bridesmaid number two is in labour. That's half my wedding party. Logan, I need you here. I can't to this without you."

"Sav. Stop. You can do this. You love Mike, just think of Mike and becoming Mrs. Sav Mustange."

"Yeah, okay," she says. But I know Sav; she's just saying that to appease me. I bet she's currently freaking the fuck out, and I wish I could be there for her, but I'm about to become a dad...holy fuck. "I'm about to become a dad," I say.

"Yeah, you are," she replies, I can hear happiness in her voice.

"Okay, Sav, let's make a deal. I go become a dad and you go become Mrs. Mustange. Deal?"

"Umm, yeah, sure. Okay. Good luck, Loges, I'm so happy for you."

"Ditto, Savvy. Now, go get married, and I'll call you when master or miss DeBiers enters the world."

"Yes, Dad," she cheekily replies.

"That's the spirit. Now, go get married."

Hanging up from Sav, I pocket my phone just as Sarah is hanging up from Kenz. Looks like her call went much smoother than mine. We are pulling up to the hospital, and as the back doors of the ambulance are opened, it hits me again that I'm about to become a dad...fuck!!!!!

6
—————

KENZIE

WALKING BACK FROM COLLECTING MIKE, I CANNOT HELP BUT LAUGH. THIS morning I said today would go down in history, but I mainly meant that Mike was getting married. Now we will be having a wedding and a baby but we will only have the wedding if I, well Mike, can calm Sav down. Her call with Logan completely freaked her out, now I'm on Mission   'Get-Sav-and-Mike-married-so-I-can-go-to-the-hospital-to-become-Aunty-Kenz.' Wow, that was a mouthful.

Looking towards Mike I ask, "So....how are you going to calm down bridezilla?"

Mike's head snaps towards me. "She's not that bad...is she?"

"Let's just say, before I came to get you, she was chugging wine and stuffing her face with milk bottles."

"Ohh, fuck."

"Yep."

"Any suggestions?"

"Nope, nada. Getting you was my idea. You're up now."

"Thanks."

We walk the rest of the way in silence. When we get to the room, I turn to Mike. "Okay, let me go in, and I'll tell her you are here but that you will not look at her."

"Yep, okay." He pauses. "Thanks, Kenz. Can you give her a hug and kiss for me...feel free to slip the tongue in and film it for me."

Shaking my head, I punch him playfully in the arm. "You wish." As I slide the room key in the lock, I look over my shoulder at him and say, "You should have seen us on the hens' night." I raise my eyes suggestively and wink as I close the door on an open-mouthed and shocked Mike.

I'm giggling as I walk into the room. Sav has taken off her wedding dress and is sitting on the floor, in her wedding lingerie, the bag of milk bottles is long gone, and she's now drinking wine straight from the bottle. She has mascara streaks down her face; my heart breaks for her. "Sav, honey, it's all going to be fine."

"How, Kenz? Logan isn't here. Sarah isn't here." She pauses and looks up at me sadly. "M-m-mum and D-d-dad and J-j-jace aren't here." With those last three names she bursts into tears. Racing over to her, I envelop her in a hug and let her cry, I rub her back in the Sarah soothing way. She pulls back and sadly adds, "Today is meant to be happy, and I'm sitting here in my bra and undies, crying and drinking wine from the bottle. Sooo not how I imagined myself on my wedding day. It's not normal."

"Who says this isn't normal? In the scheme of things, this is Mike and Sav normal. And might I add, how smokin' you look in said underwear, Mike will flip when he sees you."

"Yeah, I guess." She take another drink from the wine bottle and sniff-snorts deeply, "How's my man holding up?"

"You can ask him yourself." Her head snaps up, confusions etched all over it. "He's outside."

"Nope, nah, uh, I cannot see him. It's bad luck."

Holding up my hands in defense, I say, "Sav, he's not coming in. He just wants to talk to you through the door."

"You promise?" she sadly asks.

"I promise. Come on, talk to your husband-to-be." Putting my hand out, I help her up and we make our way over to the door. "Mike, you there?" I yell through the door.

"Yeah, Kenz. I'm here. How's my girl doing?"

"Mike?" Sav asks.

"I'm here, baby. I wish you'd let me in so I could hold you in my arms."

"Mike, we can't. It's bad luck. It's tradition."

"Sav, honey, we bucked tradition when you had a Best Bridesdude."

I can't help but laugh at that, which garners me a glare from Sav.

"I know but...but it's different. Don't..."

"Hey, baby, it's fine. Let's just talk then."

Grabbing the bottle of wine, I perch on the coffee table, drink, and watch Mike calm Sav down. Seeing how she relaxes just hearing his voice, I know that everything will be fine...with the wedding anyway.

7

SAV

KENZ HAS JUST LEFT ME TO GO AND SEE MIKE, AND AS SOON AS THE DOOR closes I completely lose it. Falling to my knees, I put my head in my hands and cry. The tears cascade down my cheeks and I notice a teardrop fall on my dress, and my heart stops. Quickly I stand up, and lower the side zip on my strapless gown and step out. Carefully, I drape it over the end of the bed. Walking over to the minibar, I grab the wine that Kenzie brought with her and I twist it open; first time ever I have been happy to have a twist top wine. Lifting the bottle to my lips, I chug and chug. The fruity elixir tingles on my taste buds and I can feel the cold liquid flow down my throat. Closing my eyes, I instantly relax and take another sip; in my head I sing, *It's my wedding day and I can drink if I want to*. Taking a deep breath, I grab my milk bottles and sit in the middle of the room...all alone...on my wedding day, and I begin to cry...again.

Vaguely I hear the beeping of the door, but I'm so lost in my own head that nothing really registers, until I feel arms wrap around me. I hug the person back; not knowing whom it is at this point. Eventually we break free and it's Kenzie. She tells me that Mike is outside. I begin to panic again and freak out, but she assures me that Mike will stay outside and that we will only chat through the door.

We make our way over to the door and as soon as I hear his voice asking about me, I feel okay, like a weight has been lifted. Even though it's through a door, he calms me as if he's right beside me.

"Mike, what are we going to do?" I hesitantly ask.

"Sav, babe, I want nothing more than to marry you, but if you want to wait so Loges and Sarah can be here, then I will do that." He pauses. "Babe, I only want you to be happy. You are my number one priority, wife or not."

Tears well again in my eyes. "Mike, I love you so much. I don't know what to do. I want to marry you, like so much, but I also want Logan to be here, too. I'm so confused." A sob breaks free and I fall to my knees, my hand rests on the door.

"Sav, let me hold you?"

"Mike, no, we can't see each other."

"No, just your hand. I promise I won't look, and unlike that time at the beach when you changed, I really won't look."

The memory of that day causes me to laugh. "Okay," I manage to say though my laughter. Reaching up, I pull the handle, the door immediately pushes open, but thankfully I'm behind it, so I can put my weight into it so that he doesn't come in. All of a sudden, I see his hand and fingers wriggling. Reaching up, I grasp his hand in mine and pull it to my face, snuggling into it.

We don't say anything; we just sit there, the door between us as I hold his hand. The moment is so romantically perfect that I know, everything will be okay.

8

MIKE

HEARING SAV CRYING THROUGH THE DOOR IS HEARTBREAKING. I WANT nothing more than to be inside that room with her, but she's as stubborn as a mule. So here I am…sitting in a hotel hallway, with my arm through the gap, and my fiancée is holding my hand with a death grip. The longer we sit here; I can feel the tension easing out of her. "Sav, babe?" I ask after a while.

"Yeah?" she quietly asks.

"Do you think you can pass me a beer? I'm thirsty."

She giggles and when I hear that laugh; I know that all will be okay with today and us. Sav lets go of my hand and shoves my arm back through the gap and slams the door on me. A few moments later, the door cracks open and a beer is passed to me in the hallway, and then she says, "Hand," wriggling her fingers like I did to her moments ago.

Taking a sip of beer, I slide my arm back through the door, and this time, she laces her fingers with mine. "Mike?" she sadly asks.

"Yeah, babe."

With a quiver she whispers, "What are we going to do?"

"I want nothing more than to marry you today, Sav, but I know you, and I know that you want Logan to be with you on our special day." It's weird to admit, but I know they she is currently smiling. "I will do whatever you want."

"I don't know," she says on a sob and she begins to cry again.

"Sav, baby, please let me in. You need a hug."

"No, I have Kenzie for that right now, plus I don't want to jinx it in case we do get married today."

"Man, you are stubborn," I say shaking my head, "BUT it's one of the many things that I love about you." Pausing, I run my hand over my smooth head. "Okay, here's what we will do. You will stay here and drink wine with Kenzie, but don't get plastered, 'cause well, it's your wedding day and I kinda sorta want you coherent. I will fix this." Taking a deep breath, I add with a huge smile on my face. "Savannah Blac, we WILL be getting married today, and I will get your brother from another mother here." Quietly I add, "Somehow...I hope." Spinning around, I bring her hand to my lips, and kiss the top of her hand. "Love you, babe."

Without waiting for an answer, I jump up and take off down the hallway, just as I'm at the corner I hear Sav yell, "I fucking love you, Mike Fr...Mustange, and I cannot wait to be your wife."

Shaking my head, I yell back, "Love you too Soon-to-be Mrs. Mustange," as I turn the corner. Digging my phone out of my pocket, I call Logan but it goes to voicemail, I don't leave a message, I send him a text.

Mike – *Logan, call me when you can. Savs freaking out. We have a wedding to rearrange*
Mike – *Ps. Congrats on the bub but he/she could have waited a few more hours **joke***

Slipping my phone back into my pocket, I race back to my room and when I push open the door I shout, "Yo, asshat, we have a wedding to rearrange!"

9

SARAH

"Oh My Fucking God, what have I done? This pain is out of this world, I can't do this, Logan, I can't do this," I screech, with a death grip on Logan's hand. After his earlier pass out, he is now cool, calm, and collected, me on the other hand...I'm freaking the fuck out.

"Babe, just breathe and calm down. You can do this. I will be right by your side, every step of the way."

"What if you sook out again?"

"Sarah, that's not gonna happen." But from the look on his face, he's as sure as I am that it won't happen again—meaning not sure at all.

Another contraction hits and this one is really sharp and painful. I manage to breathe through it, with Logan holding my hand and giving me all the support that I need. It passes and I blubber, "I can't do this, Logan, I'm not going to be a goodly mum. I'm going to suck, I'm not Kenzie."

He grabs the wet cloth and pats my forehead, brushing my hair back; he kisses my forehead and looks deep into my eyes. "Sarah, you will be an amazing mother. You give your all to everything and..." he rubs my tummy, "this lil' one is so lucky to have you as his/or her mum."

"Her," I whisper.

"I'm thinking girl too, and therefore she will be fierce, strong, and kickass, just like her mum."

His words cause me to choke up and the tears begin to flow. "I love you, Logan."

"Love you too, Sarah." He leans in and side hugs me when I feel the vibration of his phone. "Do you need to get that?"

"Nope, they can wait. My girls need me."

He climbs onto the bed and snuggles into me. His phone vibrates once again. "You better check that. We have time…for now."

He shuffles up and digs his phone out; he smirks and turns it around to show me. Thirteen missed calls from Sav, one from Mike and a text. I watch my sexy husband intently as he reads his message and he begins to laugh.

"What's so funny?"

"Mike texted me, apparently Sav is having a freak out, because you and I aren't there, and we have a wedding to rearrange."

"I've ruined their special day," I sadly say.

"No, you haven't, you've made it even more special." He kisses my forehead and when his lips press against my skin, all fear that I had evaporates, Logan is really my person. I smile up at him and soak him in…until another contraction hits.

"I need to push," I shout.

Logan jumps off the bed and races to get a nurse. They both return just as the contraction passes. The nurse assesses me and says she's off to call the doctor as baby DeBiers will be arriving very soon.

Fuck, I'm about to become a mum.

10

LOGAN

I'VE NEVER BEEN SO SCARED, YET SO BLOODY EXCITED AT THE SAME TIME, IN all my life. I'm about to become a dad, fuck me. And I've never felt so helpless, all I can do is step back and watch the love of my life writhe in pain. That last one was rough, and when the nurse and I returned, she told us that our lil' girl is about to enter the world.

Quickly, I set up the *Bose* with the music that Sarah wanted for the birth. I've just hit play when another contraction rips through Sarah and again she's screaming, I squeeze her hand...well, she vice grips my hand and I do everything in my power not to sook out again; I still cannot believe I passed out earlier. I'm snapped back to reality when Sarah yells, "Turn this fucking, sissy ass music off...I need hardcore, rar-rar-rar music."

I laugh when I realise that Enya is playing, I walk over and skip to our metal playlist and Five Finger Death Punch blares through the speakers. "Much better," she says, as she flops back onto the bed.

"How you doing, babe?"

"Just dandy," she smartassly replies. "I'm currently trying to push a watermelon out of the eye of a needle, and it fucking hurts like a mofo bitch." She looks at me with a murderous glare, "You?" she snarls.

"Umm, yeah..." Thankfully I'm interrupted when Dr. Greene walks in and I say a silent prayer to the big guy upstairs.

"Ready to meet your lil' one, Sarah?"

"If it means all this will be over, then yes. I am never, ever, doing this again."

Dr. Greene laughs as she situates herself between Sarah's legs and takes a look. She pops her head up. "Okay, Sarah, on the next contraction I want you to push and stop when I tell you to."

Just as she finishes, another one hits. Sarah grips my hand, and with all her might she pushes and yells, until the doctor says stop and that she can see the head. She fiddles around again and says on the next one to push with everything that she has. The next one happens much quicker than the last, and my awesome, amazeballs wife pushes and pushes, when all of a sudden the room is filled with a teeny, tiny little cry. My eyes well with tears at that sound, I thought the BADUNK BADUNK of the heartbeat at the ultrasound was the best sound in the world but this by far trumps that.

"Congrats Mum and Dad, you have a boy."

Sarah and I snap our heads to one another in shock; we were both so sure he was a girl. Leaning down, I rest my forehead against hers and we both whisper at the same time, "Love you." We are interrupted when the doctor asks me if I want to cut the cord. A force takes over my body and I walk to the end of the bed. I take the scissors that she hands me and I snip where the nurse points. Then I look at our son, he is the most handsome baby I have ever seen. The nurse whisks him away to check him out and I stand there staring, totally stunned.

I'm tapped on the arm. "Would you like to hold your son?" the nurse asks me but I'm totally speechless: I'm a father.

"Ummm, sure, yeah, okay."

The nurse carefully places him in my arms and I look down at my son, tears welling in my eyes. "Hey, buddy, I'm your daddy." In an instant I'm in love; I used to think people were full of shit when they'd say that, but fuck me, I'm in love. "Should we go meet Mummy?" He goos and wriggles in my arms. "I'll take that as a yes."

Turning around, I walk over to Sarah. She looks absolutely shattered, but when she sees the blue bundle in my arms, her face breaks into the biggest smile; it's one that I will never forget. "Buddy, this is your mummy. She's the most amazing woman in the world, and I love her and you to the ends of the Earth and back." Gently I hand our son over to Sarah, and I place a kiss on her forehead and whisper, "You did goodly, Mummy."

Sarah's eyes are glued to the baby. Gently, I shuffle onto the bed next to them and the three of us sit there as a family. I've never been happier in my entire life.

11

KENZIE

"It's a boy," I shout to the room, well to Sav and I, as we are the only ones here. Logan just texted to say Sarah had the baby, and I could not be happier for my bitch sista.

Sav's head snaps up and she smiles. "Does that mean they are coming now?" Her voice laced with anxiety and hope.

Sadly, I look to Sav. "No, darl," I say as I rub her arm, she's still sitting by the door in just her bra and undies, drinking wine and eating another bag of milk bottles—luckily, I stocked up. Earlier, I managed to get her to drink some water and eat a bowl of wedges. Sitting down next to her, I grab the bottle and take a swig when it hits me. "Yes," I scoff as I jump up. "Sav, I have a plan. Give me thirty minutes, maybe an hour to get it sorted and," I look at my watch, "come 5:30pm, you and Mike will be getting married."

"How?" Sav asks.

"Just trust me." Bending down, I place a kiss on her forehead and race out of the room, heading towards Mike, Jordan, and the girls. Running through the corridors like a mad woman, I get to the room and bang on the door. "Mike, let me in. I know how to fix this!" I yell as Mike swings open the door. Pushing past Mike, I plop down on the sofa, next to the girls, who are currently watching TV. Turning towards the guys, I fill them in on my bloody awesome plan, which they both agree, will be perfect.

Jumping up, I kiss Jordan, hug Mike, and race away to get this wedding back on track—there WILL be a wedding today.

12

SARAH

I'M SO IN LOVE WITH MY SON, OUR SON. I'VE BEEN STARING AT HIM EVER since Logan put him in my arms. Reluctantly, I drag my eyes from him and look up at Logan. "We did goodly, Daddy."

"We sure did. I'm so in love with him."

"Me too," I gush. "Soo, umm, name? I'd only been thinking of girls names."

"Me too...I have no bloody clue."

We both laugh. The moment is interrupted when the nurse comes in and asks if I want to try feeding him. I'm frozen with fear, she must sense my nervousness because she goes into awesome nurse mode and eases me into it. He latches on naturally and I feed our son for the first time. "And what's this lil' one's name?" she asks.

Again we both freeze. "Umm, baby," I laugh. "I was sure he was a girl so I had been thinking of girl names only."

She laughs, "You'd be surprised how often that happens. Well, when you think of it, just let us know. At the moment he's Master DeBiers. Okay, well, I'll leave you to feed. Just buzz if you need anything else." She turns and walks out of the room.

Logan sits in the chair next to bed and we both think about a name for our lil' man. My mind runs over the names I was considering when one from my list jumps out at me and I whisper, "Morgan." Looking over to Logan, I say, "Morgan, I want to name him Morgan." Pausing I add, "Morgan DeBiers." Looking back down, I say in that quiet soothing mum voice, "Hi, Morgan. Your mummy and daddy love you very muchly."

There's a knock at the door and in pops Kenz. "Hey," she whispers as she walks over to the bed, she's dressed in her bridesmaid dress—bet she got a few weird looks when she walked in.

"Hey. Nice dress," I quietly say back. "Aunty Kenz, I want you to meet Morgan, our son."

Her head snaps up. "Told you it was a boy." She snickers as she runs her finger gently down Morgan's cheek and he gurgles. "He likes me already. You did goodly, Sarah." A clearing voice gains my attention. "You did good too, Logan." She stands up. "Okay, as much as we want to gush over the cutest lil' boy in the world, we have a wedding to get to."

Both Logan and I look questioningly at her. "Huh?" I ask.

"Well, today is Mike and Sav's wedding day and they WILL be getting married today. Logan will still be her Best Bridesdude, standing at her side, and you will be there, too. You, and now Morgan, will be attending via Skype."

I shake my head at her. "Kenz, you amaze me."

"Nope, I'm not leaving my wife and son, hours after he was born," Logan declares.

In unison, both Kenz and I shout, "Yesss!" We both laugh but I cut her off. "Logan, we will be fine for an hour or two. Let Sav and Mike have their special day, they deserve it."

Logan walks over to the bed and sits next to me, "No, I'm not leaving you."

"Yes, you are," Kenz interrupts. Logan glares at her and I giggle, he has never seen this side of Kenz before.

"Are you sure?" he asks.

"Really, really." I nod.

"Seriously, with the Shrek thing again?"

"Yep, really, really." I wink and smile at him, "Now, go be there for Sav and Mike. You can skip the reception and come hang with your baby mumma and son."

Kenz jumps up and down on the spot. From all the crap she brought with her, she thrusts a suit bag at Logan and points to the bathroom. "You, change. Now."

"Don't argue with her, dude, just do as she says. The quicker you go, the quicker you can get back to Morgan and me."

Logan reluctantly shuffles into the bathroom and grumbles as he goes; I laugh as Kenz turns, grabs her laptop bag, and sets it up on the bed trolley.

Looks like a wedding is happening today after all.

13

SAV

IT ALL HAPPENED SO QUICKLY. ONE MINUTE I WAS SITTING WITH KENZ, wondering if I would actually be getting married today. Then I was excited to hear Logan and Sarah had a baby boy, and then I was all alone. Grabbing the wine, I chug and try to process what just went down, when there's a knock at the door, a knock that I know and love with all my heart.

"Hey, baby," I say though the door, I rest my palm against the door like they do in the movies, and I imagine that Mike is on the other side doing the same.

"Hey, wife," he replies.

"I'm not yet your wife," I say on a sob.

"You will be soon, baby. Kenz is putting a plan into motion as we speak. I want you to finish your wine, get up, put some clothes on 'cause I know that you will be sitting there in your bra and undies only —as much as it pains me to say that," I can't help but grin at how he knows me so well. "You are going to slip on your dress and become the most beautiful bride in the world, and before you know it, you will be Mrs. Mike Francine Mustange."

"Your middle name is Francine?" I hear Kenzie ask, and I burst into laughter, tears are pouring down my face; happy tears this time. When I hear Mike whisper, "Fuck, fuck, fuck." I laugh even harder. Without thinking, I open the door and throw my arms around Mike's neck. My lips crash against his and I kiss him with everything that I have. I jump up and wrap my legs around him as we continue to kiss. Pulling back I look deep into his eyes and say, "I love you so much, Mike, and I cannot wait to marry you. Now go, and let me get all pretty."

"Sav, babe, you are already the sexiest woman alive." His eyes rake over my body and I swear that I can feel his gaze searing my skin. "Fuck, Sav, do we really have to get married? I'd much rather go into that room there and fuck you until you can't remember your name... and then we can get married." He slams his lips against mine for another intense kiss.

Our kiss is interrupted, "Dude, get a room."

My head snaps to the left and I see Logan, standing next to Kenz in his suit. "Loges," I squeal in excitement. I unwrap myself from Mike and I race over and wrap my arms around him. "You're here," I cry.

"Yep, I'm here and, Sav, you're practically naked...in a hotel hallway...on your wedding day." He looks over my shoulder at Mike, points and says, "Mustange, get out of here so we can get you two married, and I can get back to my wife and son."

"You don't have to ask me twice." Mike walks over to me, squeezes my ass and whispers into my ear, "I can't wait to fuck you, Mrs. Mustange."

My cheeks darken and my girly bits tingle with anticipation. "Me neither," I reply. I kiss his cheek and skip back into the room, over my shoulder I shout, "You coming, Kenz?"

"Gimme a minute," she says.

I can barely make out her and Mike chatting when I hear him say, "Fuuuuck."

Two seconds later, Kenz is in the doorway and says, "Let's do this."

14

MIKE

Fuuuuck! I THINK TO MYSELF WHEN I HEAR KENZ, BUT AT THIS POINT IN time, I really don't care because I have a half-naked Sav in my arms and she is about to become my wife.

I few moments later, I stare and watch an excited Sav skip back into the room, Logan following behind her. Kenz stays next to me and I brace for it, I can't believe after all these years, she finally knows my middle name. With a sly smile she says, "Hey MFM!"

"Mackenzie, do you need something?" I nochantly, with a smidge of smartass, reply, using her first name.

"Nope, I'm better than I have ever been before. My best friend just had a healthy baby boy, my brother from another mother is about to marry the girl of him dreams, AND I finally know your middle name. This is the best day EVER!!!!!" She places emphasis on the last word, before adding, "Francine".

"Fuuuuck!" I growl, but before I can say anything else, she's inside the room, slamming the door in my face. Shrugging my shoulders, I turn on my heel and head back to my room to get ready to marry the girl of my dreams. "I'm about to get married!" I shout as I race towards my room.

Twenty minutes later, I'm in the courtyard, with Jordan at my side. Our celebrant, Amanda, is in the middle, and proudly sitting on a table is Kenzie's laptop with a smiling Sarah and baby, Morgan, watching on from the hospital.

Jordan slaps me on the shoulder and says, "It's now or never, asshat."

"I'm right where I'm meant to be." Just as I say that, "Hallelujah" by Rufus Wainwright starts to play. Indy and Rory come toddling down the aisle, giggling and looking absolutely gorgeous. They get to the front; I bend down, hug and kiss each of them, before Mrs. McRoberts comes and escorts the girls to the front row. Looking up, I see Kenz walking down the aisle, her eyes are glued to her husband's and I cannot help but smile. I used to admire and envy their relationship, and now I have my own...only better.

The music changes to Pachelbel's Canon and I look up again to see the most beautiful bride I have ever seen. Sav and Logan walk towards me, and everyone murmurs about how stunning Sav is. It's all white noise to me, I am mesmerised by the angel walking towards me. Without thinking, I walk towards her; I place my palms on her cheeks and kiss her. She pulls back and smiles. "Ummm, that bit comes later," she breathlessly whispers.

"I know, but Sav, fuck me, you are stunning."

Her cheeks darken in embarrassment. "Mike, get back up there so we can get married and then," she lowers her voice so only I can hear, "you can fuck me for the rest of our lives."

Logan clears his throat and winks at us, oops; I think she may have said that a little louder than intended. With a smirk, I look towards him, shrug my shoulders and lift my eyes brows in a bom-chicka-wow-wow way. He shakes his head and we all laugh. I turn and head back to take my spot next to Jordan, while Logan and Sav continue down the aisle. He places her hand in mine and kisses her cheek; he then looks to the laptop, winks, and goes to help Mrs. McRoberts with the girls.

The ceremony passes by in a blur, I speak when asked to and somehow I recite my vows from memory, when all of a sudden, Amanda declares, "I now pronounce you husband and wife, Mike, you may kiss your bride...again."

I step towards Sav, grip her cheeks and for the first time, we kiss as husband and wife. Everyone cheers and hollers, and millions and millions, okay, maybe not millions, but a heaps of bubbles engulf us, just like I imagined—yes, I imagined this for my wedding day. The noise startles baby Morgan and he starts to cry, Sarah makes her apologies and disconnects. When the screen goes blank, I see pain etched on Logan's face. I grab my wife's ass; I love saying that, and whisper into her ear, "Let's get this wrapped up so Loges can get back to the hospital."

"Your wish is my command, husband." I wink at her and I almost say to hell with it all, I want to drag my wife back to our room and make love to her. With a smile, I gaze at her and wink; her cheeks darken in a way that suggests she was just thinking the same thing.

Thirty minutes later, we are all done and dusted. Logan has just left and is on the way back to the hospital. Kenz and Jordan are heading back to the room to get the girls settled before bed; they will meet up with us and everyone else later for an informal reception...that Sav and I don't make it back to for an hour...or two.

15

SAV

Mike and I stop off at our room—Kenz and Sarah rented us a suite for the night and as soon as the door clicks shut behind me, I know that we will not be leaving this room again for the foreseeable future. The air is electric and just from my husband's presence my whole body is alight. My tingles heighten when I feel him step behind me. He doesn't touch me for what feels like eternity, and then it happens, ever so gently he runs his fingertips up and down my arms. A shiver runs through me at his touch, my insides clench, and I moan, knowing what's about to happen. Leaning back, I grind my ass against Mike. Turning my head, I look over my shoulder and look directly into Mike's eyes and whisper, "Fuck me now, husband."

Mike grins back at me and before I know it, he spins me around and slams me up against the door. His lips crash against mine in a heat-filled, no hold barred kiss. Gripping my wrists, he places my arms above my head, pinning them to the door. Ever so slowly, he kisses along my jaw, down my neck, and across my collarbone. His kisses set my skin on fire, I moan and arch my back. With his free hand, he gently cups my breast and squeezes, another moan slips from my lips. "Please, Mike," I whisper, as Mike lowers the side zip, pulling his hand away, my dress falls to my feet in a pool of chiffon and satin.

"Fuck me," Mike growls, as he takes in the sight of me in my undies and strapless bra. Before I can reply, his lips are on mine; I wrap my arms around his neck, pulling him in closer, needing to feel his body against mine. Lifting my leg, I hook it around his thigh and grind myself on him. The friction of my lace undies and his leg is enough to set me off, and I tumble over the edge, moaning into Mike's mouth as the pleasure courses through me. He breaks the kiss and with a smile on his face murmurs, "That's one."

"I better even things up then," I hungrily reply. Dropping to my knees, I make quick work of his belt, fly, and pants, I reach into his boxer briefs, grab his cock, and begin to stroke. As soon as it's free, my tongue darts out and licks the bead of precum on the tip. Giving it a few more strokes, I stare up at Mike as I take the tip in my mouth and suck. His cock hits the back of my throat, and I moan around him as I continue to bob up and down. His cock hardens in my mouth and I know he's close, so I quicken my pace and before long he erupts into my mouth, growling as I suck him dry.

His cock falls out of my mouth with a pop and I look up at him. "That's one." I wink.

"Come here, you minx," he says. Reaching out, he lifts me to my feet and places his hands under my ass, lifting me up. Wrapping my legs around him, I lean forward and kiss him as he undoes the clasp on my bra and flicks it to the side.

Pulling back, I rest my forehead against his; never have I felt so content and happy in my life. "I love you, wife," he whispers.

"I love you too, husband, now take me to bed and make love to me."

"As you wish," he says.

He quickly steps out of his pants, kicking them out of the way. He walks us over to the bed and gently lowers me down. Shuffling up the mattress, he crawls up my body like a predator, his eyes never leaving mine. Gripping the side of my undies, he pulls them down my legs and discards them. Kissing his way back up my legs, he settles himself between them and kisses my mound. My back arches when his breath hits my clit and I moan. His tongue darts out and he licks up and down my slit before sucking and nibbling my clit. My body ignites, my breath hitches in my throat, I've never felt ecstasy like this before, until he inserts a finger inside me and hooks it around, hitting that magic spot. Out of nowhere, my orgasm erupts and I scream as I ride the wave.

My body stills and I collapse back into the bed, Mike crawls up my body, and I think he's going to pay the girls some attention, but he bypasses them and kisses me deeply. Breaking our kiss he whispers, "That's two."

A giggle escapes my lips, I look up at him staring down at me and I smile. Mike is looking intently at me, his eyes penetrating deep into my soul; I have never felt more loved with that one stare. Wrapping my arms around him, I pull him down and hug him tightly. A lone tear escapes my eye ,but my eagle-eyed husband notices. "Sav, babe, what's wrong?"

"Nothing, it's silly. I'm just sooo goddam happy right now and I want you to make love to me."

"I'm over the moon fucking happy, Sav, and I would love nothing more than to make love to my wife on our wedding day."

He leans down and kisses me passionately; he shuffles around, lines his cock up with my entrance and ever so slowly, he sinks himself into me. Together, we fall into an erotic rhythm, staring at one another. We thrust back and forth, our bodies in sync with each other. Gripping his ass, I hold him close to me as I erupt for the third time, this one more powerful and intense than the previous two combined. The last wave of pleasure is simmering down when I feel Mike's body tense, and he erupts inside of me with a grunt. He collapses on top of me, the two of us breathing heavily and completely content.

Subconsciously, I run my hands up and down his muscular back and he shivers under my touch. "So, umm, should we get dressed and attend our reception?" I ask.

"I want to say no and stay here naked with you, but I think we need to put our clothes back on and be a proper responsible bride and groom."

"Never thought I'd hear you tell me to put clothes back on…twice in one day but, I agree."

We both reluctantly get redressed and we make our way to the reception, only an hour late, but it's our day, so fuck 'em. We have a great night celebrating our nuptials and the early arrival of Morgan… with plans to have another get together when the DeBiers clan can join us.

EPILOGUE

Kenzie

EVEN THOROUGH THE UPS AND DOWNS, THE SIX OF US HAVE MANAGED TO stay firm friends...no, we are more than friends, we are family—the family that we have chosen and I could not be happier. My life was complete the day that I bumped in Jordan at college. Fate was a bitch and didn't let us get our happily ever after immediately, but I think the journey made us stronger, I know it did for me. I now have a loving husband, we have a super successful brewery, and two adorable little munchkins...my life is complete.

Jordan

Life has a funny way of working out, sure it may not always be smooth, but in the end if you persevere; you will get your happily ever after. Mine came crashing into my life at college and I would not change a thing, well almost. Whatever happens, I know that I will always have Kenz by my side; she's my biggest cheerleader, but if I'm totally honest, I'd be lost with out her. She's my everything, without her I'd wouldn't be a dad to the two most amazing little girls in the world, and I wouldn't have the extended family that I have…NOW we can finally live, hoppily ever after.

Mike

If you had told me that I would be married and ecstatically happy, I would have told you to put down the tequila. After 'the incident,' I swore I would never settle down, but fate is a bitch, a bitch that I kinda like because she led me to Sav. My life would not be what it is without her in it, she completes me. But as corny as that sounds, it's true. I know without a doubt that she and I were meant to meet, and hopefully one day, we will have kids and then everything will be perfect in my life.

Sav

Life can be a bitch at times, but I'm pretty sure that everything happens for a reason. Sometimes that reason is soul destroying and you want to give up, but that little voice cheers you on, and then the most amazing thing happens and that sadness slowly but surely disappears. You meet that one person who pulls you from the darkness into the light. Together you heal and become one; Mike is that person for me. He and I are now married and I have never been happier. Sometimes I feel guilty for being this happy, knowing that Mum, Dad, and Jace aren't here, but I know that they'd want me happy, and I know that they'd approve of Mike and love him just as much as I do. Together, we will live happily ever after.

Sarah

Everyone thought that because I came from money, I had it easy; that was far from the truth. Mum and Dad made me work for everything that I ever received. It was their strictness that helped me though one of the toughest times in my life, but there was also something else that got me through, Logan. With all my heart, I believe that everything happened so that Logan and I could meet. I know we probably would have eventually met through Sav, but I don't think we would have had the connection that we do. Logan and I are two peas in a pod, and now we are three peas in our pod. I thought I was happy before Morgan arrived, but I was wrong, he was the final piece to the puzzle. Now I'm finally living my happily ever after.

Logan

They say things happen for a reason, I believe that I was meant to be in that bar the night Sarah and I met. It's corny to say, but I think I was in love with her the moment our eyes connected when she strutted up to me. I would do anything for her, as she would for me, we are stronger together, and now that we have Morgan, the three of us will be a force to be reckoned with. Add our friends to the mix and we are unstoppable. Without out them in our life, there would be a gaping hole. Everyone needs love and friendship in their life, and I'm the luckiest son of a bitch in the world because I have both and I wouldn't change one fucking thing.

We all had our final shot at happiness, and like a fine liquor, it was rough along the way but once it settled, it was absolutely perfect…just like our lives now.

THE END!!!!

THE FINAL SHOT PLAYLIST

White Wedding – Billy Idol
Hallelujah – Rufus Wainright
Hakuna Matata (from The Lion King) – Nathan Lane
Craxy – Seal
Crazy in Love – Beyonce, JAY Z
Someone Like You – Adele
Hit Me With Your Best Shot – Pat Benetar
Can't Take My Eyes Off You – Frankie Valli
We're All In This Together – Ben Lee
I'll Be There For You – The Rembrants
Unchained Melody – The Righteous Brother
The Unforgiven – Metallica
The Unforgiven II – Metallica
The Unforgiven III – Metallica
In The End – Linkin Park
Coming Undone – Korn
Push It – Static-X
All Of Me – John Legend

This playlist can be found on Spotify.

ALSO BY DL GALLIE

STAND ALONES

Out of Nowhere

Antecedent

Doc Steel

Oops

Off the Books

Fractured:A driven world novel - coming 12 August

Deck...the Balls - coming 30 November

Seven Nights

Seven Kisses - coming 28 December

In the Dark of Night anthology**

Secrets anthology**

***only available in paperback direct from me*

FALLING NOVELS

Falling for Dr. Kelly

Falling for Dr. Knight

Falling for Agent Cox

Falling for Agent Cruz

Falling:The Complete Collection

THE UNEXPECTED SERIES

When it comes to love, expect the unexpected

The Unexpected Gift

The Unexpected Letter

The Unexpected Package

The Unexpected Connection

The Unexpected series: The Complete Collection

THE CASTAWAY GROVE COLLECTION

Love has arrived in the Grove

Oasis

Unequivocal Love

Five Words

Broken Rules

...and a few more to come.

The Castaway Grove Collection, Vol 1

THE LIQUOR CABINET SERIES

Liquor has never been so disturbingly saucy

Malt Me (Book 1)

Tequila Healing (Book 2)

Wine Not (Book 3)

The Final Shot (Book 4)

The Liquor Cabinet: Series boxset

ACKNOWLEDGMENTS

There are soo many people I need to thank for helping me on this journey and writing these things never gets easier and I always miss someone so, *thank you everyone.*

My *family; Troy, Piper* and **Kade**. You three are my rock. My everything. I wouldn't be doing this if it wasn't without your support and encouragement. I love you guys to the moon and back.

Karen, my editor. You started as juts my editor and now, 20 plus books later you are also a friend and I will forever be grateful for **THAT!**

Tash, the uber awesome cover designer for the series and boxset. You put up with my million and one chnages without whining and we end up with an amazing cover. Thank you from the bottom of my heart for all that you do. I also need to thank *Murphy Rae*, the original series and boxset designer. You made me such beautiful covers and it was a hard decision to update them but they will always sit with pride as the 'OG' on my shelf and in my heart.

There are too many fellow authors to mention but to everyone I have crossed paths with, thank you for believing me in. Your support. Your guidance and the wines when we get to catch up.

And finally, *you, the reader.* The messages I receive from you always seem to come through at the right moment.

Cheers,
Dana Xo

ABOUT THE AUTHOR

DL Gallie is from Queensland, Australia, but she's lived in many different places all over the world, including the UK and Canada. She currently resides in Central Queensland with her husband and two munchkins. She and her husband have been together since she was sixteen, and although they drive each other crazy at times, she couldn't imagine her life without him.

Shortly after her son was born, DL began reading again. With encouragement from her husband, she picked up the pen and started writing, and now the voices in her head won't shut up.

DL enjoys listening to music, drinking white wine in the summer, red wine in the winter, and beer all year round. She's also never been known to turn down a cocktail, especially a margarita.